The Special

J E Pendleton

The author, J.E. (Jim) would enjoy hearing from you and is interested in where your interests lie. You may drop him a line at the locations listed below, or simply visit his website to stay current on future projects.

jependleton.com
jim@jependleton.com
Twitter: @jependleton

This book is a work of fiction. While the primary character is based on my uncle Billy (William Wade Pendleton), other characters are either a product of my imagination or used fictitiously. Any resemblance to actual persons, living or dead is entirely coincidental. While some overall events contained in this work of fiction are historical fact, the relationship between my characters and historical events is simply a result of my own imagination.

ISBN 978-1-939351-00-5

WOODWIND PRESS

Printed in United States of America

The SPECIAL

The story of a car, a romance, and a war.

J.E. PENDLETON

Chapter 1

I walked in to hear my least favorite words, "hold on, he just walked in" my wife was saying. After forty years at the phone company I knew any call for me was trouble. What I didn't realize was that my life was about to change forever.

After a fifteen minute conversation with a total stranger I hung up the phone and without another word headed to the bar; I needed a drink.

"What was that all about?" Nancy asked.

"You won't believe me if I tell you," I said, as I poured a pair of drinks.

"Try me." She said.

"That was a guy from California and he claims to have a car my uncle Billy built."

"But your uncle Billy died in World War II."

"I know, 1944 to be exact."

"But this guy is in California? How could he have anything that belonged to your uncle?"

"I know Billy hitchhiked to San Diego after he graduated from high school to work for Consolidated Aircraft."

"Did he "build" a car, what does that mean?"

"I don't know, but what I do know is I have to get to San Diego as quickly as I can." I emptied my glass and poured another.

I couldn't sleep that night. My mind raced with the possibilities from Bob Mercer's call, I was excited and anxious to call his father, Frank. I waited as long as I could stand it and called at 11 AM Central time, reasoning to myself that surely anyone in a rest home was up and around by 9 AM.

The phone rang twice and then was answered by a strong male voice. I asked if this was Frank Mercer and the voice replied it was. I introduced myself and told him about Bob's call the night before.

"Yes, Bob has already called me. I was expecting your call," he said.

"Mr. Mercer," I replied, "I'm calling to find out about my Uncle Billy's car."

"Your Uncle Billy and my dad, they built that car together. Your uncle, he was one of the best mechanics I ever knew, and I've known a few. They were partners in the car, you know. I'm old and I don't know how much longer I'll be around. I made a promise to myself that I would keep my dad's word to your uncle that the car would be there when he came back. And besides all that, Sally wanted it that way. It was the least I could do for all the people that had a hand in building the Special, it's like a member of my family that car. Bob, my son, hell he just wants it gone so he can sell the land. Money in his pocket is all he gives a shit about."

"You knew my uncle then?"

"Hell yes I knew him, knew him well, he was the closest thing to a big brother I ever had. He lived in my dad's house with us you know."

"Did he live there long?"

"Whole time he was in California, far as I know."

"Who was Sally?" I asked.

"Sally was," there was a long pause, I was beginning to think our connection had been broken, then, "oh, hell I talk too much!" he said in a voice suddenly husky with emotion.

"Can you tell me anything about the car? I was thinking of coming out there to get it, if that's okay with you. I would be happy to buy your half."

"Hell son, it don't belong to me. It was my dad's and your uncle's. Ain't no one in my family cares one hoot about that car 'cept me. They just want it gone. I'd be proud for you to have it, but I got to tell you, it's in pretty bad shape. See, I've been in this home since my wife passed back in '89. Had me a stroke and hell I can't do anything. The damn roof leaked on that shed and Bob, hell he don't care. He let it go till the roof fell in. It's a wonder really, that he didn't just set it on fire or have a bulldozer cover it up. Son, if you want that car, you just come on out and get it, but you have to listen to the story first."

"When can I come out?" I asked, thinking this might be an easier conversation to have in person.

"Come now if you want to. I wouldn't wait too long. Bob, he's anxious to sell that property and pocket the money. My dad got that land back about 1930 to settle a debt. No tellin' what it's worth now and Bob's got that money spent ten times over."

"I'll be out as soon as I can, today or tomorrow, this week for sure. I would like to come by and meet you and maybe visit for a while. I'd like to hear about my uncle and the car if you don't mind." I said, hoping to have the chance to learn all I could about my uncle, the car and about Sally.

"Son, you come on. I already told you that you have to listen to the story first anyway. Besides that, only time anybody comes visitin' is when they want somethin' or it's Christmas and they get to feelin' guilty."

"Frank, one last thing. What kind of car is it?"

"Well hell, son, it's a race car, didn't Bob tell you nuthin'?" Mercer asked with surprise in his voice.

"Yes, he did, but what kind of race car?"

"It's a streamliner. They ran it up at Rosamund one time."

My heart was pounding, I couldn't believe what I was hearing! My Uncle Billy raced on the dry lakes! How could it be possible that I didn't know anything about this? How could it be? Who was Sally? Was she Frank's wife? There were a thousand questions ricocheting in my head.

I had some phone calls to make. I found a trailer and was off for California, known as the land of milk and honey during the thirties. As I drove, my mind raced thinking about the events of the last couple of days and what was waiting in California. You know the way your mind works, I had visions of the California my uncle knew sixty years before. I could see his car pristine and beautiful. Then I would picture the stereotypical urban sprawl as seen on TV and the car as an unrecognizable lump of rusty iron covered in graffiti. I followed this up with every possible scenario I could imagine, my mind hard at work trying to predict an impossible future.

I followed a route similar to the one that Billy traveled 60 years before only I was driving a modern SUV on an interstate expressway. Billy had hitchhiked.

Once on the road I called Frank again – he sounded excited that I was on the way. I settled in for the long drive.

That night I stayed in Arizona. The next morning drove straight to San Diego and the retirement villa; such a funny name for the old folk's home. I was anxious to hear the history of the car and how it came to be. I had no idea what I was in for.

Thirteen hundred miles from home and extremely nervous, I turned the black Suburban into the parking lot of a retirement home. The enormity of what I had just done descended on me. I felt nearly crushed by the weight of it. Then a thought suddenly exploded inside my head. Had I been duped? Was this whole thing an enormous prank and I, its more than willing victim? My fear of that was almost overwhelming as I parked at the back of the lot, the length of the Suburban and the empty car trailer requiring the remote parking spot.

I took a few deep breaths trying to control the jitters as I thought back on the strange course of events that brought me half way across the continent. I had to correct myself, there wasn't really a "course of events"; just a five minute phone call from someone I never heard of before. Now, two days and over thirteen hundred miles later I was sitting in a sun drenched parking lot in southern California trying to calm my anxiety.

The call had supposedly been placed from the very building I stared at across the parking lot. The building was nondescript, single story, painted in earth tones; it could have just as easily been in Omaha, Tampa, or even Fort Worth, my home town. But it was here in California and that part of the story made some sense. I tried to reassure myself that if this was a hoax, the perpetrator was at least knowledgeable, so maybe it wasn't a hoax after all. I screwed up my courage a notch and got out of the car.

Chapter 2

I walked into a spacious lobby where there were several elderly people, some in wheelchairs. As I walked through the door the conversation stopped and all eyes turned toward me. Most of the faces smiled, a few of the folks waved. I had the distinct feeling that I was expected and scouts, or maybe vultures, had been stationed at the entrance to await my arrival. This possibility did nothing to calm my nerves.

In the center of the room was a kiosk with a sign warning all visitors to "Sign in". A very attractive lady about my age sat behind the sign and as I approached she greeted me with a bright smile and said, "You must be Jim." Before I could answer, her console buzzed and she said, "Excuse me" and lifted the handset.

"Hello Babe", she said in a very resigned voice the bright smile turning to irritation, "Yes he's here, he just walked in, I haven't even had time to introduce myself." A short pause, "Well, if you would quit calling me every five seconds to see if he's here I would have already! We'll be there in just a minute!" She laughed as she hung up the handset. She looked up at me "Sometimes I could wring that man's neck! He's been calling me all morning wanting to know if you're here yet. He's as bad as a kid on Christmas Eve. I'm Shirley, by the way. We're all glad you're here, we haven't heard anything else out of Babe for the past two days!"

I replied that I was indeed Jim and that I was glad to meet her, but I was there to see Frank Mercer, not someone named "Babe". She said she knew the whole story, but if we didn't hurry up and get to Babe's room "all hell will break loose!" With that she was up and leading the way down one of the wide hallways that opened onto the lobby.

As we walked past two silver haired ladies they both smiled at me and one of them said, "Hi Jim, we're so happy you're here. Maybe Babe will settle down now." I was shocked at the welcome I had received. Was Frank "Babe"? I felt that every person there knew all about me and I knew no one. The feeling was comforting and disturbing at the same time.

"Who's Babe?" I asked totally confused.

Shirley chuckled, "Oh, you're about to find out," and led me down another wide hall. It was very bright from sunshine cascading through windows along one wall and reflecting off the white paint. I wished I hadn't left my sunglasses in the car. I noticed handrails down both walls, a reminder of the people that inhabited this place.

We stopped at a door that bore a sign reading MERCER. Shirley knocked once on the door and opened it without waiting and went in motioning me to follow. I noticed out of the corner of my eye that the two gray haired ladies had followed us and were watching. They both still had big smiles on their faces.

We entered an apartment typical of most retirement centers. The entry had a small kitchen off to the side and opened onto a larger sitting area that was the main room. A short hallway led to the rest of the apartment.

A man with a full head of silver hair and sitting in a wheel chair greeted us. His eyes were the brightest blue I had ever seen. When he smiled only the left side of his face moved. The right side remained frozen in almost a grimace. He raised his left hand to me and said "Jim, it's so good to meet you. I'm Frank, but everyone calls me Babe, you can too."

I took his hand and was a little surprised at the firmness of his shake. "Frank, it's an honor to meet you. It was wonderful of you to search me out and start all of this."

His eyes flashed. "I told you to call me Babe." It was a command delivered by someone who was used to giving orders.

"Yes, sir," I said, vowing not to make that mistake again.

The eyes softened, the twinkle returned and he smiled. "Your uncle gave me that name, you know." I was immediately enthralled.

He waved me to a chair close by his side. His eyes never left me, nor did his lopsided grin relax. I could tell he was thrilled I was there. Through all of this he never even acknowledged Shirley. I glanced up at her and she just smiled at me and said "You're welcome Babe, I'll see you two later," as she turned and left.

"How was your trip?"

"It was fine Babe. I didn't have any problems. The weather was great. I enjoy driving, so it was fun actually."

"That's great, that's great. Did you bring a trailer?"

I told Babe that I had borrowed one from my friend Rick, but that I was by myself. "I tried to get my son to come, his name's Jim also by the way, but he had commitments at work. I thought I might need help getting the car out of the building and loaded."

Babe said "Too bad your boy couldn't come, but I think we can find someone to help if we need to."

Babe asked about my family and we exchanged the normal small talk, but I could tell he was anxious to get on to something else and so was I.

"That damn stroke left me in this chair. I've been this way for years. At first I was bitter and wondered 'why me?' but I eventually got over that. My dad died of the same thing younger than me even. Guess I was lucky. Lucky to be in a damned old wheelchair, ha, but at least I'm on the right side of the grass. From what I see on the Discovery channel, we must suffer from a screwed up gene."

"How old was your dad when he passed away?" I asked.

"Forty four."

"That's young. What year was that?"

"1944, the same year your uncle died. Yeah, he was young, too young to die." I could see the tears begin to well up in his eyes. For the second time since I arrived his smile faded just a bit. "I still miss him you know. He was a helluva man even if he was my own father. He was cursed with that same damn defective gene just like

I am. They say it causes defects in the walls of your veins and arteries and shit. Course, he smoked most of his life just like they all did back in those days. I never did smoke, just couldn't see the sense in it. No one knew that much about what was bad for you back then, but smoking just didn't appeal to me. Hell son, even the athletes smoked in those days. Babe Ruth and Lou Gehrig, after them so did Mickey Mantle, Roger Maris and all of 'em, they smoked their whole lives. Most of 'em, they paid the price. Me, I just never did smoke," he trailed off and he was looking out the window, his eyes fixed on some distant object, his mind somewhere else. I knew he had left me. I gazed out the window for a while myself, my mind playing over what he said and thinking of my own losses. We all have them; they're part of life just like the living.

My spell broke first. "So, tell me about this car and how you knew my uncle," I said.

His gaze left the window and turned to me. The lopsided smile came back and those startling blue eyes found their twinkle once more.

"Yeah, let's talk about the happy things in life. Do you like cars?"

"Babe, I'm crazy about them, especially hot rods. This really seems weird, but I especially like those built before World War II. I'm also interested in many of the racecars from that era. Like the Millers, have you ever heard of them, they were built here in California you know?"

Babe laughed. He laughed until he cried. He laughed until I thought he was going to choke. I couldn't help it, I started to laugh myself. I didn't know why Babe was laughing so hard, but it's a human reaction to join in.

Finally his laughter subsided into a chuckle. He used his one good arm to pull a tissue from the box on the table beside his chair and wiped the tears from his eyes.

"Son, you are in for a treat. This is going to be quite a story. Hell yes, I've heard of Harry Miller. My dad knew him well. I'm glad you're sitting down, because believe it or not, one of his motors was in 'the Special'."

Babe continued to talk, but I have no idea what he said after that. I was stunned. 'The Special' had a Miller engine in it? What was 'the special'? Was that Billy's car? Miller engines and cars were the crème de la crème of American classics. They even surpassed the mighty Duesenbergs. Average people didn't own Millers. Only the elite few, those blessed with lots of money or talent had owned a Miller in their heyday. Only a lucky few owned them today.

Finally my brain came back to the present. I interrupted the Babe.

"Babe, stop, stop. Did you say the car had a Miller engine in it? And what do you mean by 'the Special'?" I asked impatiently.

Babe glared at me, angry to be interrupted.

6

"Hell, yes it had a Miller engine in it and when my father and your uncle built the car, they thought about naming it the Miller LaSalle Special, but hell, no one ever called it that. It was always just the Special."

"What does the Special look like?" I interrupted him again. The glare intensified.

"If you'll let me get a damned word in edgewise, I'll tell you!" he barked at me.

"Yes sir, sorry," I said determined to keep my mouth shut. He glared at me for another moment then continued.

"Well they patterned it after my dad's best friend's car. That car was called the Stutz Black Hawk Special, you ever hear of it?"

"Yes sir, I've heard of it. That was Frank Lockhart's car. He was killed in that car trying to set a new World's Land Speed Record in 1928. Your dad and Lockhart were friends?" I asked.

"Hell yes they were friends! Best friends! They grew up together, lived right next door to each other. How do you think I got to be Frank? I'm Frank L. Mercer, the L stands for Lockhart!"

This was too much. How could all of this have happened and I knew nothing about it? I wondered once more if all this was some elaborate hoax, if not it had to be a dream. My family was somehow involved with the giants of a bygone era? I was sitting in a nursing home in California with a man I didn't even know existed a week ago and he was telling me my uncle did things and knew people sixty years ago that I had dreamed about my entire life.

"Babe," I said, "you better start at the beginning. And by the way, are you sure you've got your name right, because I'm almost positive you're Santa Claus and it must be Christmas!"

Frank roared with laughter over that one. He rocked back and forth in his chair and his face was a huge lopsided grin. Tears streamed down his cheeks. I thought for a minute he might choke. He finally regained control of himself. Then he started to talk, or maybe recite is a better description as the words poured forth.

"Okay," he said, "I'll start at the beginning. I guess it all started the first time I ever saw your uncle. It was the summer of 1941. I know it was summer because school had just let out the week before. I was ten years old and like all kids I was on cloud nine because my summer vacation had just started. It was a Sunday afternoon. My dad was home, no work on Sunday you know, and we were in the backyard and I was helping him tend his garden, he always had a garden, 'Frank why buy food at the store when it'll grow in your yard for free?' he'd tell me. The depression was just over, but money was still in short supply in those days. We lived in a big, old, red brick house in San Diego. It was just the two of us, my mom died when I was born." He said with a hint of sadness.

"I'm sorry, Babe."

"Thanks son, I am too but I never knew her, just my dad and he always worked hard to be both mother and father to me.

7

Anyway, we were working in the garden. I was helping him stake the tomato plants, you have to keep 'em standing up or your tomatoes don't get red all around and my dad, he never did like his tomatoes to be green on one side. The sun doesn't get to 'em unless they're standing up, you know. When around the corner of the house walked the tallest man I had ever seen. He was wearing a brown fedora with the brim turned up in front and carrying an old pasteboard suitcase." He said with a smile.

Chapter 3

"Hello. My name is Billy Pendleton and I saw your sign around front for the room to rent. I'm looking for a place."

Carl stood up from the tomato vine and dusted his hands off on his overalls. He stepped out of the garden extending his hand to the stranger. "My name's Carl Mercer and my helper here is my son Frank. Say hello to Mr. Pendleton, Frank."

"Hello sir," young Frank had also stepped out of the garden and was standing beside his father. Billy stooped and shook his hand.

"Frank you have the bluest eyes I believe I've ever seen. Just like your dad's."

"Yeah, I don't think I can deny he's mine," Carl chuckled. "So you're interested in the room? Where're you from?"

Billy replied "Mr. Mercer, I'm from Texas. Came out here to get a job with Consolidated and build airplanes, and yes sir, I need a place to stay."

"Well let's get one thing straight right from the start. You can call me Carl, we're not formal around here, are we Frank?" he said smiling at his son.

"No sir, we're not," young Frank said.

Billy and Carl both laughed at this and Frank wondered what he said that had been so funny.

"Let's walk around front and I'll show you the room," Carl led the way around the side of the house walking on the driveway where Billy still stood. The drive was a pair of cracked concrete ribbons extending from the street down one side of the house and ending at the doors of what appeared to be an old carriage house. On the driveway sat a sleek black coupe. Its paint glistened in the sun.

As they walked past the car, Billy admired it. "This is quite a car, Carl. I think it's one of the most beautiful I've ever seen."

"Thanks Billy. It's a '39 LaSalle. I'm the shop foreman over at Don Lee Cadillac and they like for us to drive what we sell." He said proudly.

"It sure is a beauty. Has a V-8 engine in it too doesn't it?"

"Yes it does. You interested in cars?" he asked.

"Yes sir, I love 'em. Had a '32 Ford roadster back home, not the V-8 though, it's a Model B, sold it to my kid brother when I left home to come out here. He drove me to the edge of town in it, but it sure isn't anything like this." Billy replied, still mesmerized by the LaSalle.

"Drove you to the edge of town? How did you get here Billy?"

"I hitchhiked."

"Well, that certainly shows initiative. Now back to cars, nothing wrong with a Ford. Ol' Henry, he builds 'em worth the money, and you know you can make one of those Model B 4 barrels run. Out run a V-8 any day."

"Gee, you can? How do you do that?" Billy's eyes lit up with keen interest.

"The guys out here do it all the time. A lot of those 4 barrels run a hundred or better."

"You mean a hundred miles an hour?" Billy was astonished. His old Ford certainly wasn't anywhere near that fast. It might run 80, and it was bored out! To think about running a hundred miles an hour in a Ford Model B, that would be something all right.

"Tell me how they do it. I want to hear all about it."

"Let's go look at the room first," Carl chuckled. "We'll have plenty of time to talk after." Carl said as they went in the front door.

Billy had already made up his mind. Unless the place was a complete dump or was simply too expensive, he was renting the room. He had to find out how to make a 4 cylinder Ford run 100 miles an hour. Why, that was as fast or faster than cars costing ten times as much!

"Well, that's the room, and the bathroom is just down the hall here," Carl gestured down the hall. Billy thought it was a great room, and just like his room at home it was on the front of the house. There were windows facing out the front overlooking the wide covered porch and out to the side over the driveway. Billy could look out his windows and admire the beautiful black coupe anytime he wanted.

"I'll take it," and with that he pitched his old suitcase on the bed. "I'm all moved in, now tell me more about those hundred-mile-an-hour Fords."

They both laughed . Little Frank had had enough of this. He already knew about gow jobs; that was what all the kids called hotrods back then. He had ridden in several as a matter of fact. "Dad is it okay if I go over to Lester's and play a little ball?"

"Sure son, just be home by supper time okay?"

"You bet!" and with that, Frank was out the door like a shot pausing only long enough to get his mitt off the porch banister. He grabbed his bike where it lay on its side in the front yard and running down the sidewalk as fast as he could and bounded onto the saddle. He disappeared down the tree lined street, the bicycle swaying from side to side as Frank's legs pumped up and down urging all possible speed from his mount.

"Let's get us a couple of Coca-Colas, I've got some in the icebox and we can talk about cars as long as you like if you'll help me get those tomato vines staked up. It seems I've lost my helper."

The two men got their drinks and headed back to the garden. They were comfortable with each other immediately. Each of them sensed a kindred spirit in the other. "Sure Carl, and when we finish with those tomatoes, I'd like to take a closer look at the coupe."

"You're on." And with that they proceeded to finish the interrupted project.

"You can take her for a spin if you like, but I'm sure you'll need to move the seat back some. How tall are you anyway?" Carl asked.

"I'm six foot six. Played a little basketball in school, but what really interests me is building things, especially cars."

"What kind of things do you like to build?" Carl asked with renewed interest

"Oh, all kinds of things. I built a lot of furniture for Mom in shop class at school. You know, a rocking chair, cedar chest, end table, that sort of thing. I also built a crystal radio set. I picked up Chicago every once in a while. Worked on my car some too, but really the only place I had to work on it was under the tree in our backyard. Looks like you've got a pretty nice place here yourself" Billy said, indicating the carriage house.

"Yes I do, thank you. Let me show it to you. It's an old carriage house that I've converted into a garage and workshop. I sort of thought Frank and I might work in it together, but it seems his passion runs more to baseball. Don't get me wrong, Frank spends time with me in the shop and he does pretty good too, but I think his heart really is on the ball diamond."

Carl swung one side of the double wooden door open and they walked in. Billy had expected it to be dark inside compared with the bright sunshine of the yard, but he was surprised at the amount of light that came in from a row of small multi-pane windows that ran around the top of the side and rear walls. The floor was wood. Like many old carriage houses, the floor had been formed by driving a series of wooden posts in the ground. They were tightly packed with only their upper ends exposed forming the floor. This technique had been very durable and was easy on the horses' hooves, the original inhabitants.

The place smelled of oil, metal, and old wood. As Billy looked around, it was a large rectangular space, easily capable of holding three cars he thought. There was the open space where the coupe was parked at night and then off to the left of that area was the shop. It was very well equipped. There was a small metal lathe, a drill press, band saw, and a large bench grinder. In addition to this equipment, the area held several sturdy work benches, two of which were equipped with vices, one large and one small. Plywood was nailed to the walls over the benches. The outlines of tools were painted on the varnished surface in red paint. The appropriate tool hung from a nail or hook over its painted outline. In addition to the light streaming in from the high mounted windows, light fixtures were spaced throughout the area. An aura of order hung over the place.

"Wow! What a swell shop! Are you sure this isn't your place of business? This place is better equipped than the shop at school," Billy said.

"Thank you," Carl beamed. "I like tools and making things myself. I had hopes that Frank and I would spend all our evenings out here, but he likes to play ball when he can, so till it gets dark, he's usually with his friends. Still this keeps me occupied. I can pretty much handle anything I want to do and what I can't do here, I can do at work," Carl replied.

"You said you're the shop foreman for a Cadillac dealer?" Billy asked rhetorically.

"Yes, Don Lee Cadillac. I've worked for them for years. I started with them in Los Angeles, but moved down here ten years ago. There were just too many memories in LA after my wife died, and they needed someone to run the operation in San Diego, so I took it. They've been very good to me."

"I would say so! This place is terrific! Anytime you need some help out here, you just let me know. I would be thrilled to hang out with you anytime."

"You're on. Now let's get inside and see if we can get some dinner together. Frank will be home before long and that boy can eat a horse. Besides, after hitchhiking two thousand miles I bet you're hungry yourself."

Carl pulled the coupe into the garage and they closed the doors after Billy admired it another time. Carl opened the hood so Billy could take a look at the big V-8. As Billy expected, the engine compartment glistened every bit as much as the black hood and fenders gleamed.

They shut the doors and went into the house. Billy congratulated himself on his good fortune in noticing the room to rent sign. On a whim when he saw the sign he decided to forego his original plan of staying at the YMCA. It looked like it was shaping up to be a great stroke of good fortune. He had no idea.

Chapter 4

The next morning they ate breakfast together. Frank was always up early to begin his adventures doing what boys do on summer vacation. Going fishing, visiting the docks and watching the ships load and unload, riding by the Marine Corps Recruit Center to watch the new recruits drill, but most of all for Frank, playing baseball.

Carl offered to drop Billy at Consolidated on his way to work. Billy jumped at the chance; after all it was a good excuse to get a ride in the coupe.

Billy was hired on the spot as a metal fabricator on the B-24 Liberator bomber project. He was told to report the next day ready for work. That afternoon he caught a bus and spent the rest of the day riding around San Diego playing tourist. Of course, he had seen pictures and read about the city and his father was stationed there before going to France during the war, so he had some firsthand information on the city, but none of it really prepared him for the beauty of the area.

That night Billy told Carl and Frank about his experiences. They congratulated him on his new job and discussed various sites in the city that he might visit; Point Loma and the Army installations there, the bay and the Naval and Marine facilities. Carl told him about a couple of restaurants and theaters where kids his age hung out.

Carl offered to give him a ride to work the next morning then asked, "Do you have any plans to buy a car?"

Billy said that he would like to. He had some money saved plus the money Jimmie, his younger brother, had paid him for the roadster. He planned to hold that in reserve in case he needed it to get settled, but now it looked like he might not need it for that purpose after all.

"Carl, I would like to get something to get me back and forth to work. Something pretty cheap, but good. Do you know of anything?" Billy asked.

Carl replied, "I'll look around. Maybe we can find something. There's always someone with something for sale at work. The used car man owes me a favor or two. I'll check with him. By the way, some of the boys in the shop are running in the time trials on Sunday morning. I was thinking about going; you want to tag along?"

Before Billy could even open his mouth, Frank chimed in, "I want to go!"

The two older men both laughed and Frank once more wondered why the adults were laughing as he looked first at one then the other.

"Sure son, you can go. Billy?"

"I'd love to go Carl. Thanks for asking, but what exactly is a time trial?"

"The local car club called the Road Rumblers puts it on. It's where they run their cars on a piece of deserted highway out at

Kearney Mesa. They have some timing equipment that a guy named Otto Crocker, over at the University designed that can time them down to the hundredth of a second. They run the cars through the time traps one at a time. The cars are divided into classes like stock roadster, modified, or streamliner. The fastest car in each class wins. We might even see one or two of those hundred-mile-an-hour Fords. I hear some of the boys from LA are coming down, including my boss."

"That's for me! I can't wait to go. I'll look forward to it all week. Do the police give them any trouble?" Billy asked.

"Not where they've been running lately. It's a pretty deserted piece of road. The few people that live out that way are usually in church that time of morning. It'll be over by noon."

Billy spent his first week at Consolidated. He loved the work. He was assigned to the department that built the huge Davis wing, so-called after its designer. His first job was a part of a two-man team riveting panels together that formed the massive structure. As the apprentice, Billy's job was to "buck" the rivet. He held a heavy steel bar against the small end of the rivet while his more experienced partner used an air driven hammer known as a "gun" to pound the rivet. The pounding caused Billy's 'bucking bar' to bounce or "buck" and when combined with the hammer's rapid blows, it mushroomed the small end of the rivet and produced a strong tight clamp to hold the pieces together. At the end of the first day, he understood why all the people in his department had cotton stuffed in their ears. The noise of all the rivet guns was deafening, but it was a fascinating place for a young man interested in creating things. He had never experienced anything like it before. On his lunch breaks he would explore the plant. Some days he watched the huge machines turn enormous pieces of steel or aluminum into finished airplane parts. Other days he visited the final assembly area where the big planes received their finishing touches before they were rolled out the door and sent to the flight line.

The aircraft were an impressive sight. They were the largest bombers in the American inventory. Four huge Pratt & Whitney engines sprouted from polished aluminum wings. Machine gun blisters were on all sides of the giant planes. Billy thought of them as flying battleships and they were held together by thousands upon thousands of the very rivets he was helping drive each day. It was a fascinating place to be for Billy and thousands of others like him.

As exciting as his new job was, Billy found that his thoughts kept turning to the time trials on Sunday. He had never attended anything like that. Carl said the cars ran down the road one at a time. The only races Billy had ever seen were dirt track races at Arlington Downs back home in Texas. There, a whole pack of cars raced around the same mile long dirt oval that the horses raced on, throwing up tremendous rooster tails of dirt as their tires searched for traction. Billy had enjoyed his visits to those races,

14

but the cars were expensive purpose-built racecars far beyond his means, even one or two of the much lauded Millers occasionally showed up, all driven by professional drivers. Carl said Sunday's racers were just average guys, guys just like him that would be racing cars they had built themselves in their own garages. Billy tried to control his impatience and focus on the job at hand. His lead man said he would be using the pneumatic rivet gun himself soon.

Chapter 5

Billy awoke to a knock on his door Sunday morning. Carl called to him to get up and get ready. Billy was already out of bed and pulling on his trousers before Carl had finished telling him to get up. It was still pitch dark outside and Billy could smell the aroma of fresh coffee and bacon cooking.

He walked into the kitchen just as Carl was cracking the eggs. Carl turned as Billy walked in. "Billy, if you'll load the ice chest in the trunk of the coupe, I'll finish this and see if I can get Frank out of bed."

As Billy came in the back door it was just in time to see Frank walk in rubbing the sleep from his eyes. His hair looked like a pile of hay, clumps pointing in every direction. His shirt was only tucked in on one side and he wasn't talking. Billy rubbed the top of his head as he went by and said "What's wrong Babe, didn't you get your nap out?" The reference to Frank's idol, Babe Ruth, brought a grin as Frank continued to rub his eyes.

As soon as breakfast was over they hopped in the coupe and started on their journey northeast out of town. The coupe had no trouble climbing the grades as they left the lights of the city. The first glow of dawn was breaking over the steep hills as the close-mounted headlights shone cones of light onto the still dark roadway. While rounding one switchback they caught just a glimpse of a deer bounding across the road. The sight of the deer had finally brought Frank fully awake, "Wow! Did you see that? Think we'll see any more?"

"I don't know Babe, but this is sure the right time of day to see 'em," Billy replied.

Carl was happy to see that Billy and Frank had struck it off so well. Even in the few days Billy had been there, he already seemed part of the family. He ate his meals with them and jumped in to handle chores around the house without being asked. Carl had found him playing pitch with Frank a couple of afternoons as well.

"Tell us about your family, Billy", Carl said. Frank abandoned his search for more deer to look up at his new friend.

"My dad is a painter and paper hanger. He works for himself and also subcontracts work. He's a real craftsman," Billy said with obvious pride. "He loves to fish. In fact we went to the Gulf Coast a couple of times fishing. Dad had a new Ford pickup and all four of us loaded up and went down there. We caught a lot of fish and had a swell time. My dad was stationed here in San Diego before he shipped out to France during the war. He was stationed out on Point Loma in the Coastal Artillery. He really loved it here. He told me I would like it." Billy said.

"My mom, well, my mom is just great. She's the best mom a guy could ever have. No offense Carl, but she can sure cook! I don't think I've ever had biscuits as good as hers."

Carl and Frank both laughed at this. While Carl was a great mechanic and could fix nearly anything, he wasn't that adept with a spatula and a saucepan. His biscuits especially, weren't known for their light flaky texture. Frank brought tears to Billy's eyes when he discovered him using a sack of Carl's biscuits as baseballs while practicing his batting one day. Billy watched more than one of them fly over the roof of the garage after leaving the end of Frank's bat with a solid crack.

"Then there's my brother Jimmie. He's a couple of years younger than me. Now don't be getting any ideas Babe, but he is totally fearless. We live at the bottom of the hill on Broadus Street back home. I've seen him come down that hill on his Schwinn going lickety-split, standing up on the seat holding his arms straight out like he was flying. Another time, he hitched a ride across town with one of my buddies by holding onto the back fender of a motorcycle while being towed along on his bicycle. Red, that's my buddy, said he got that motor up to 60MPH going down Hemphill Street and Jimmie never turned loose. My dad found out about it and he was so mad I thought he was going to kill them both! Jimmie's a great brother, besides being a daredevil, he's the kind of brother that would never let a guy down in a pinch."

"Does he play baseball?" Babe asked.

"Sure does Babe, but not as good as you." This cheered Frank up; he was almost getting jealous of his new friend's brother. "He plays basketball and runs track too. He helps Dad on some of his jobs sometimes. Jimmie had enough money saved up to buy my roadster when I came out here."

The world around them had turned into the soft light of early morning and they were now on a strip of level ground for the first time since leaving the house. The road stretched straight ahead into the distance. Carl reached to turn off the headlights.

"Speaking of roadsters, look at this," and pointed to the road ahead. Both boys in the seat beside him sat up and peered out the windshield. A roadster was hurtling toward them in the other lane. It had no fenders or windshield. Its driver could barely be seen over the edge of the cowl. As it flashed by with a terrific roar, both boys' heads snapped around to see it retreat through the back window. "Wow!" came from both throats simultaneously.

"Carl, was that one of those hundred-mile-an-hour roadsters?" Billy asked still staring out the back window.

"Might have been; probably one of the boys doing a little test and tune before the trials start. Look ahead of us."

As both boys turned to look out the front they saw cars off both sides of the road and people milling about, a lot of people. Most of the people they saw were young, around Billy's age or a little older. Most were boys, but there were some pretty girls. These were girlfriends brought along to watch their beaus show their prowess on the asphalt and there were lots of spectators too. Sprinkled across the throngs were a fair number of older men about Carl's age. Many of the men and boys were bent over hoods of cars or busy stripping fenders and mufflers from their mounts. Carl continued driving down the road, slower now so as not to run over all the people walking back and forth in front of him until he came to a sort of tower on the left hand shoulder. Here he pulled off the road and parked. Billy realized the "tower" was really a trailer with some sort of elevated platform built on it. Three men were seated on the platform, their heads bent over a sort of bench sorting papers and setting up some sort of equipment that from a distance resembled the shortwave radio in Billy's shop class. "That's the timing tower," Carl said. "It's where the timers measure the speed of the cars. They also control the road from there and tell the starter when it's safe to flag off the next car."

"How far do the cars run?" Billy asked as he continued to look at the various cars and the crowds.

"They get ¾ mile to accelerate up to speed, then they time them through a ¼ mile, after that they have a mile to stop. Two miles total," Carl replied.

"How do they know when a car is off the road at the far end? Can they see that far?" Billy asked.

"They have a sort of telephone that some of the guys built. They run the cable for the phone and the timers down to the far end of the track. Guy named Otto Crocker designed it, a really smart guy. His equipment can time a car down to one thousandth of a second. They also have some binoculars and a system of colored flags to tell when the course is clear in case the phone goes out." Carl explained.

There were quite a few people there that were obviously spectators, but also many that were involved with the cars, either as drivers, crew or to supervise the racing. Billy was surprised to see a concession stand built as a trailer, selling hot coffee and donuts. It seemed to be doing a good business with several guys standing in line.

The nearest racecar to where they parked was a black Model A roadster with 82 painted on the door in white shoe polish. It was similar to the one that had flown past them on the road. Billy was immediately drawn to it and Carl followed. Frank tagged along, pitching a much used baseball up and catching it in his mitt, a ball cap perched on his head.

The Model A had been stripped of its fenders, windshield, and headlights. All those items were stacked in a pile alongside the car. The hood of the car was propped open and two young men were squatted beside the engine working on one of the two carburetors. As Billy and Carl walked up, one of the young men turned and looked up, "Hi," he said with a smile.

Billy and Carl returned the greeting. Billy said, "I sure like your car. What have you done to the engine?"

"It's a Model B engine. It's bored out, got a Winfield cam and these V8 carburetors. Stan here, made the exhaust pipes for it."

"How fast will it go?" Billy asked with keen interest.

"Fastest we've ever been is 103."

18

Billy whistled and the proud owner rewarded him with an even bigger grin. "Got a bigger set of tires on back this time on these 16 inchers. That should let us run a little faster if we can ever get this damn carb fixed. The piece of shit just runs gas out the vent and all over the place. Guess we've got some trash stuck in the needle & seat or somethin.'"

"Good luck to you, hope you get it fixed. We'll be looking for you later," Billy said as they walked off.

"That's quite a car," Billy said to Carl as they walked past the timing tower. Billy looked up as they walked by. The three men on the top platform were in a serious discussion over the equipment used to time the cars. Billy noticed the tower had a couple of loudspeakers attached to its sides. "Why are they using bigger tires on the back of that Model A? I've noticed lots of the cars have bigger tires on back."

"The larger diameter allows them to run faster given the same RPM from the engine. A larger tire will go further for each revolution. The real trick is, does the engine have enough power to turn the same RPM while driving the taller tires? The faster you go, the more power it takes. The wind resistance gets stronger the faster you go. That's why they remove the fenders and windshields. It's a temporary effort to better streamline their cars." Carl replied.

"You seem to know a lot about this. Have you been racing yourself?" Billy asked.

"Yeah, I used to be involved in racing some. Never was a driver, just worked on the cars. Let's head over toward that blue car." Carl pointed across the road toward a tiny open wheeled car. Billy had never seen anything quite like it.

They crossed the road and approached the blue car. Billy was totally focused on the car. He had no idea what it was. It was beautifully proportioned and had an almost jewel-like quality. The wheels were most striking. They were large diameter with broad flat spokes and appeared to be cast from aluminum. The body tapered to a graceful point, commonly called a boat-tail, behind the small open cockpit. The robin's egg blue body panels were held on by hundreds of screws. Each screw head had a hole drilled through it and long pieces of shiny thin wire crisscrossed through the holes securing them all together. Up close it gave a strange spider web effect to the car.

"Well, look who's here!" For the first time Billy noticed a very well dressed man about Carl's age standing by the car. He came forward with a big grin to take Carl's hand and embrace him. He was obviously happy to see Carl.

"Hello Boss" Carl said returning the embrace. "How have you been?"

"Can't complain Carl, can't complain. You sure provided us a beautiful morning for this and I tell you, I like running on the asphalt a lot better than all that dust at the lakes. But I see there are a few problems," he said as both men turned to watch a Model T Ford truck clatter past, barely making five miles per hour, its bed

19

filled with baskets of vegetables. The driver was wearing faded overalls and a straw hat. He stared at the goings on, eyes wide with amazement. Both men laughed.

"Yeah, it does have its limitations doesn't it?" Carl chuckled. "Tommy let me introduce my friend Billy Pendleton. Billy just moved out from Texas to go to work for Consolidated. He's staying at the house with Frank and me. Billy, meet Tommy Lee."

The well-dressed man Billy now knew as Tommy Lee offered his hand. "Pleased to meet you sir" Billy said.

"Same here young man, although the people you associate with doesn't speak very well for you." Tommy Lee replied. All three men laughed at this. "Speaking of young Frank, where is the lad?"

"You know Frank; he's already found a couple of kids to play catch with. They're over there across the road. If there's a baseball around, you know where Frank will be. Billy has taken to calling him Babe. I think he likes it to tell you the truth. You know how he worships at the Altar of Ruth." Carl said smiling, happy that his son had found his own passion.

"Don't I know it? You know the last time I saw him; it was last Christmas when you came up for the holidays; he asked me when the station was going to start transmitting Yankee baseball games. That boy has an imagination! Can you believe he thinks we can televise a baseball game, and all the way from the East Coast no less!" Tommy Lee said.

"That's Frank for you, or maybe I should say 'That's the Babe for you!" And everyone laughed again.

"Billy, Tommy is my boss. He owns Don Lee Cadillac and one of the many things he's involved in is television. Have you ever heard of that?"

"Yes sir. I read an article about it in Popular Science once. That's really something, sending pictures through the air." Billy replied.

"Yeah, my dad started that. Earle Anthony, the Packard dealer and my dad's best friend, had the first station. Dad was afraid he would get ahead of us and everyone would be buying Packards, so he set up our station to compete. We broadcast one hour a day. I can't see that it helps business all that much, but it's fun and Willet tells me it's an investment in the future. Frank, excuse me, 'The Babe', might have something. If we could broadcast the Yankee's games, we might get a few people to watch, and even sell a few more cars." Tommy Lee said thoughtfully.

"Yes sir, I would say so." Billy was a bit in awe of the company he was in. He was still staring at the car. It was an amazing machine. The hood was open to reveal the most beautiful engine he had ever seen. Everything was cast aluminum and all surfaces were finished in a swirling pattern. For someone who had been raised with and around Ford cars, the view was staggering. Every component was built to conserve weight and all were as finely finished as the inner workings of an expensive watch. He walked around to the front of the car. The radiator was barrel shaped and sort of rounded on top. The red oval emblem on the radiator shell said Bugatti.

"To me, you look like a basketball man more than baseball," Tommy was saying.

"Uh, oh, yes sir, I am. I was always better at basketball, I guess because I'm tall." Billy sort of trailed off, his attention still commanded by the wondrous machine. "This is the most beautiful car I have ever seen. What is it?" he asked.

"It's a Bugatti. Made in France. It was their Grand Prix car from a few years ago. Type 35. Not as fast as the new stuff, but still fun. I thought I'd bring it and the speedster down and see which one was fastest. What do you think Carl?" Tommy said while carefully wiping off a speck of dust.

"I'd say it should be a close race. I know the speedster has the more powerful engine, but the Bugatti isn't pushing as much wind. I would be curious myself. What does the speedster do on the lakes?"

"When we ran it this spring, with the fenders off, it managed about 130, into a strong head wind though. I think it ought to do better than that. It never has run like I thought it would. The engine is rough and noisy around town, goes pretty good from a red light, it's like each cylinder firing drives you forward ten feet, but as you gain speed it just gets rougher and rougher. It's nowhere near as smooth as a V-8, let alone a twelve or a sixteen. And it doesn't run all that fast on the lakes either. I guess Harry was right when he told me it was just too big to be a four. Tremendous power down low, but nothing on top." Tommy said.

"Harry always has favored lots of little cylinders, and even if he can't run the financial side of things, he sure can build engines. What does Fred say about it?" Carl asked.

"He agrees with Harry. Says I should have been content with a 220. He said a good 220 would run off and hide from that 318 and is smoother to boot. So I asked him, then why the hell did you build it and sell it to me? And you know what he told me? He told me 'Goddamnit Tommy, that's what you told me you wanted and I haven't' ever made a penny arguing with you about what you want! You can have anything in the whole wide world and you told me yourself that you wanted the goddamned biggest Offenhauser on the planet so we built you the damned thing and now it's yours.' And Carl, he didn't even smile when he said it either." Both men laughed and Carl just shook his head. "Hell Carl, I couldn't even argue with him. That's exactly what I told him when I ordered it."

"Boss, you can be a bit demanding at times." Carl said. "Maybe you should have bought Frank's beach car engine when you had the chance. You could probably still get it, but you might have to buy the whole car." Carl was referencing the V-16 engine out of Frank Lockhart's Stutz Black Hawk Special, a car he had built to break the World Land Speed Record back in 1928. Lockhart was killed during the attempt. Carl and Lockhart had grown up together.

"That is one hell of an engine at that," Tommy said. "You know Swanson finished 6th at Indy this year with that engine."

"I know, and it's de-tuned from when Frank was running it." Carl said. "It was making 570 horsepower back in '28."

"Yeah, I know, but I've been thinking, Mercedes has a new Grand Prix car out. Prettiest thing you ever saw next to this gorgeous creature," Tommy said.

A striking woman walked up and Tommy greeted her by putting his arm around her and kissing her on the offered cheek. "Sally, this is Billy Pendleton, he's from Texas." Tommy said proudly.

Billy reluctantly tore his gaze away from the Bugatti and turned toward the newcomer. Sally was the most beautiful woman he had ever seen. Billy was dumbfounded, all thoughts of the car completely forgotten. She was dressed in tan slacks and a white short-sleeved sweater. The sweater clung to her body and accentuated the soft curves of her breasts. Her waist was tiny, her hair dark blond, held back from her face by a wide white band. As she turned to face Billy and Carl she flashed a dazzling smile showing perfect white teeth, and eyes just as startling blue as Carl's or the Babe's. Was she related he wondered? She was a few years Billy's senior. He was envious of the way she seemed to melt against Tommy's side. "Hello," she said in a husky voice that sent a tingle down Billy's stomach. Their eyes met and for the briefest instant Billy thought she was inside his head reading his thoughts. It was a very unsettling feeling and one he had never experienced before. He blushed as those beautiful blue eyes felt like they pierced his soul.

"Hello. I'm pleased to meet you, ma'am." Billy felt suddenly awkward, embarrassed even. His face was flushed, felling like it could burst into flames at any moment, but he wasn't sure why.

"Hello Uncle Carl," she said and gave Carl a hug. That explained the eyes, she was Carl's niece.

"I'm going to look at the other cars" Billy said. It was a very awkward attempt to escape his embarrassment and regain some measure of his usual self confidence.

Still a little confused by what had just happened, Billy looked around beyond the Bugatti for the first time. There sat what had to be the speedster. It was a gleaming dark blue, much darker than the light blue Bugatti. The nose of the car reminded him of a Cord, maybe it was a Cord? Though he didn't know it at the time, the speedster had been shorn of its fenders and windshield just like the Model A he had looked at. He walked around to the passenger side and saw four chrome exhaust pipes coming out of the hood side. He then noticed mounting holes in the sides that he correctly assumed mounted the missing fenders. He looked around for them, but they were nowhere in sight. The tail of the car ended in a boat tail and the car had front opening, so called "suicide" doors, because if they accidentally opened at speed, the slipstream would rip them off.

Although quite narrow, it was a two-seat car. The seats were covered in dark leather. The dash was filled with gauges. There was a large speedometer and tachometer set in a panel of aluminum fins. The steering wheel was of the style commonly referred to as banjo because the spokes were formed by a series of five small rods resembling the strings of a banjo.

"It's not very comfortable." Billy almost jumped as he was so startled. It was Sally and she was standing right beside him. He had no idea how she had gotten there without him noticing. He could smell her. She smelled like fresh soap and flowers. He once more found himself with that unsettled feeling, almost confused. He was certain he could feel the heat from her body radiating across the small distance between them, almost like the heat coming off a hot stove. Normally confident and self-assured, he struggled now for a proper response. "You've ridden in this ma'am?" He awkwardly inquired.

"You can drop the ma'am; I'm not your mother you know. Makes me feel old. Yeah, I've ridden in it. Tommy loves to drive it around and he likes to have a pretty young lady as a passenger. It helps him maintain his image, and image is very important to Tommy. Where did Tommy say you were from, Texas?" she asked, smiling warmly at him.

"I'm from Fort Worth, Texas ma'am, er excuse me, ma'am, I mean Sally!" Billy could feel his face, but especially his ears were flushed. He didn't need a mirror to know he was beet red. What was wrong with him anyway? Why did this girl, woman, make him so confused? He was certain he was about to die from embarrassment.

Sally laughed. It was a most pleasant sound and gave him that tingly feeling again. The laughter and the tingling only added to his confusion.

"I can tell your mother raised a very well-mannered son, but please, call me Sally. Do all women have this effect on you or is it just me?"

"It's just you," Billy blurted without thinking, his words only adding to his overwhelming feeling of embarrassment.

"Interesting," Sally paused and looked at him with those amazing eyes. "What brings you to California, Billy?"

"I came out here to work for Consolidated. I've always wanted to build airplanes, so California is the place to be. Are you Tommy's girlfriend?" Why in the hell did you ask that he wondered. What on earth had prompted him to ask such a thing? And of a complete stranger at that? "I'm sorry; I don't know why I said that. It's none of my business."

Sally didn't say anything in return; instead she just turned to look at him again with those startling blue eyes. Once again they seemed to flash, but they weren't accusing as he expected, the look on her face was more one of curiosity, but still she said nothing.

Billy couldn't remember ever feeling so awkward. There was another moment of embarrassed silence while Billy tried to think of something to say. Finally, "Did ya'll drive this down from Los Angeles?" he managed to utter.

The intensity of the moment finally broken. "Heavens no! I said Tommy likes to drive it around, but I meant around the city. Tommy also likes his comfort." 'Ya'll' rode down in that.' Billy blushed at the reference to 'ya'll' as she pointed to a new Cadillac V-16 formal Sedan parked nearby. "Tommy travels with an entourage. There must have been at least 20 of us that made the trip. Let me introduce you to some of the others. Come on." And with that she took a step, then paused to be sure Billy followed.

As they rounded the big Cadillac sedan, Billy saw the rest of the Los Angeles contingent. The nearest car was absolutely tiny. Billy recognized the grille as a '39 LaSalle, just like Carl's coupe, but it was only the top two thirds of one. The rest of the car was obviously hand formed. It was extremely narrow, so much so that the heads of the Mercury V-8 engine, which wasn't that wide, protruded from the open hood sides. The cockpit was just large enough to hold a very small driver. Billy knew he would never fit in it. There was no bodywork at all behind the seat, only a flat vertical panel that formed the back of the seat and mounted the small fuel tank. Dual chrome exhaust pipes ran down each side and ended at the back of the tiny car just beside the gas tank. This car also had heavily constructed 16-inch wire wheels and larger diameter rear tires. Two angle cut stacks attached to the twin carburetors protruded from holes in the top of the hood. A young man was bent over at the waist on the far side of the car with his torso in the cockpit. As Sally and Billy approached he straightened up.

Sally turned slightly toward Billy, "Billy, this is Danny Sakai, Danny this is Billy Pendleton from Texas. Billy this is Danny's car, he works at Don Lee Cadillac in LA." Danny was the first oriental Billy had ever met and was as short as Billy was tall. He and Sally both towered over the man. Billy thought Danny would make the perfect driver for this tiny car. He knew it had to be fast, after all, it was little more than a big engine and four wheels.

"Danny I love your car. Is it as fast as it looks?" Billy asked.

"It's gone over 124 at Muroc." Danny replied with pride.

Billy said, "I thought it would have been faster than Tommy's speedster."

"It *is* faster than Tommy's car" Danny said.

"But Tommy said the speedster went 130?"

Danny and Sally both laughed and rolled their eyes.

"Billy, I told you image is very important to Tommy, and he's not above lying to promote it either," Sally said.

"Billy, I've never seen that speedster top 115," Danny added with a grin.

"Oh" was all Billy could think of to say. He was used to believing the things he was told. Where he came from, telling the truth was an accepted fact of life. He had never been exposed to anyone who bent the truth to suit themselves. This was almost as big a shock as meeting Sally had been.

"Did you build this yourself Danny?" Billy asked.

"Sure did. Mal built the engine for me, that's Mal Ord, he's a genius with engines. It's a Merc V-8 bored a quarter. It's been relieved and polished." Billy wondered what that meant. Danny went on, "uses heads and intake that Mal designed himself and had cast. The rest of the running gear is Ford. It's a T frame with an A front axle. The transmission and rear axle came off a '35 Ford and the wheels are Packard."

"Where did the body come from?" Billy asked.

"Me and a couple of buddies built it out of sheet metal, a couple of old signs actually. The hardest part was the grille shell and what I call the chin fairing. See, that's the piece that sticks out and covers the axle and the spring in front. The same guy that built the body on Tommy's speedster, guy named Frank Kurtis, used to work at the dealership; he showed us how to do it. I got that grille at the body shop. They threw it away because the bottom was broken off when some old man bumped into a curb or something. I think it looks good on the car, don't you? Makes it look streamlined." Danny explained, always happy to find someone who shared his interest in the details of a great ride.

"It does, I think it looks terrific! Don't you Sally?"

"I suppose." Sally looked rather uninterested in things mechanical. "I know Tommy doesn't like it because it's faster than both his cars. He just keeps Danny around because he's crazy and funny. Danny makes him laugh. At least that's what he says. Facts are, Danny is part of the 'inner circle' and everyone needs friends, even Tommy. Not to mention he's a good employee."

"How many cars came down from Los Angeles?" Billy asked.

"Of course we brought two of Tommy's cars. Ernie, that's Ernie McAfee who works at the dealership, brought his car, Bunny Phillips, one of Tommy's high roller friends brought his Bugatti, and Bill Warth brought his streamliner. They're all nice cars; Bill's has a beautiful body. If you like Tommy's speedster, you'll love Bill's car. It has a really neat boat-tail just like the speedster." Danny replied.

"See what I told you? Tommy travels with his own entourage. Ernie keeps Tommy's cars running and Danny provides a joke or two. Let's go see Bill. He drove down with us, but he's not part of Tommy's group really, he's a very nice man. See you later Danny" Sally said, and led the way down the road through a maze of cars in various stages of readiness for their chance to run through the speed traps. As they walked, Billy noticed most eyes followed them, correction, followed Sally actually. He felt a touch of jealousy. Billy forced himself to concentrate on the cars, anything to get his mind off Sally.

It was a staggering sight. There were at least a hundred cars there to race, possibly more. Some of them were not modified in any way or at least they appeared that way, but most were to some extent. Many of them were heavily modified. The modifications were to engines for more power, but the most obvious changes were to the bodies of the cars. Almost all of them were stripped of all parts that did not make them faster. Hardly any of the cars still wore their fenders or windshields. Other items such as spare tires and even seats were removed. Quite a few of the cars had more extensive changes. Some were very narrow, only wide enough for the driver. This had been done in various ways. Most cars he saw had Model T Ford or similar bodies that apparently had been sawed in half down the middle lengthwise, a section removed, then welded back together making them very narrow. Many of the cars modified in this manner had no body work at all behind the driver's seat, just a small gas tank mounted above the exposed rear axle, just like Danny's racer. It gave them a bob-tailed stubby look. Still others were every bit as narrow as the bob-tails, but they had gracefully tapered tails behind the driver. These were the boat-tails Danny mentioned. Billy was familiar with the term because several of the faster production cars of the thirties were also boat-tailed such as the Auburn speedster. Some of the cars were very shoddy and ramshackle in appearance. Others were nicely finished and painted with close attention to detail. What impressed Billy most and what came as such a shock, was that this was a formal event for guys just like him to compete with their cars which in most cases were their normal daily driven vehicles. The very few organized races Billy ever saw were for pure racing cars driven by professional or at least semi-professional drivers. The cars had been purpose built racecars and were never driven on public roads. This event was just the opposite. In fact, it was actually being conducted on a public road!

There was a bewildering array of colors and sounds. Most of the cars had open exhaust and at times the noise was deafening. Cars were constantly in motion driving past on their way to line up for their speed runs or returning after completing a run. The loudspeakers were calling cars to the starting line in groups of five by car number and were also giving the speed of each run. Billy was surprised that most of the runs announced were over 100 miles per hour, a speed he had long considered attainable only by the most expensive automobiles, such as Packards or Duesenbergs. To add to his confusion, walking by his side, as his personal guide through this melee was the most beautiful girl, no woman, he had ever seen. He was afraid to look at her because he was sure she could read his mind and would know in an instant how enthralled he was with her presence, but at the same time he wanted to do nothing more than stare at her. Billy resolved to focus on the cars with all his might and to do his best to appear normal. He concentrated on staring straight ahead. A sharp elbow in the ribs suddenly broke his concentration. "Wake up!" Sally said with a chuckle. She actually touched me he thought! And she didn't melt!

In fact, that elbow really hurt! He almost missed what she was saying.

"That's Bill's car over there," Sally pointed to a black racer driving in their direction on its' way to the starting line. Extremely narrow and very streamlined, it had a chrome grille and a graceful boat-tail. All that could be seen of the driver was his head encased in a white cloth aviator's helmet and goggles. Chromed exhaust pipes exited the side of the hood and even at the sedate speed of the pit area, the exhaust note boomed. As the car drove past the driver managed to get one hand above the edge of the cockpit to wave at Sally, a big grin on his face, "Hi Sally," he yelled as he went past.

"Good luck Bill!" Sally called in return and the car was gone, its exhaust note still lingering in the air. Billy was sure it had to be the fastest car at the trials. To his eye, it was easily as streamlined as any Army pursuit plane. In fact it looked a great deal like an airplane minus the wings. He was anxious to see what speed the car recorded and to get a closer look at it.

"Can we go watch Bill make his run?" Billy asked.

"Love to," Sally replied as she put her am around his and leaned into his side steering him toward the starting line. Billy tried to keep his arm as still as possible, not wanting to do anything that would cause Sally to release her grip. A warm sensation flooded through his body as if someone had poured warm oil on him. He was acutely aware of the way she felt against his side, the delicate scent of her. While he was reserved and quiet, she was warm and outgoing, seemingly in constant motion, almost electric. Billy fought hard to regain his composure and to concentrate on the cars and the events taking place around him. Had it not been for Sally's presence at his side, he would have been sure that this place, with all the cars and activity was heaven on earth. Sally pushed him into sensory overload. The cars paled in comparison to her.

They arrived at the starting line. A group of five cars was in line waiting for their turn to begin their run down the road. Members of the Road Rumblers, their matching club shirts very much in evidence, staffed the starting line. All of them wore white butcher's caps, in fact Billy realized, most of the club members he saw had similar headgear. He wondered if this was part of the club attire.

"There's Bill!" Sally yelled above the din of revving motors. Bill did not see them; his eyes were fixed on the club member that sent the cars on their run down the road with the wave of a green flag. Bill was gunning his engine, he and his mount impatient for their turn to fly down the course. The starter waved his flag and Bill was away, leaving burned rubber smoking in his wake, his engine at full bellow. He up shifted to second gear and his tires chirped, and then finally into high as the car raced away becoming only a black blur far down the road.

The next car, one of the bob-tails with a four barrel engine, pulled up to where Bill had been just a few seconds before. It's driver, impatient to be on his way, blipped his throttle repeatedly making them strain to hear the results of Bill's run above the din.

The loudspeakers crackled and then a tinny voice said "Car 17, Bill Warth, Pacesetters club, 131.47 miles per hour! Fastest time of the day so far, folks!" Billy yelled despite himself. Several others whistled and yelled. Most everyone applauded even though it couldn't be heard over the sound of revving engines. Sally squeezed his arm even harder as she jumped and squealed with joy. Billy was intensely aware of her breast rubbing his arm as she jumped. He wondered if she noticed, but just as quickly convinced himself it had been purely accidental.

Normal conversation was all but impossible. There was just too much noise as the bob-tail started its run with a roar and another car moved up to take its place at the starting line. The loudspeaker continued to boom, reporting speeds and calling more cars to the staging area. Spectators and drivers alike added their yells and screams, it was deafening, the air full of energy. Billy bent down so that Sally could hear him and in her glee she grabbed his other arm with her free hand pulling him even closer and kissed him on the cheek. It was the single greatest event in Billy's life to that point. "Didn't Bill do great?!! That was a super speed! Tommy will be beside himself," she giggled.

After a few seconds to recover from the shock, Billy said "Let's go back to Bill's pit! I want to get a closer look at his car."

They turned and left the pandemonium of the starting line. As they wound their way through the people and cars, the noise subsided to a more tolerable level although there were still engines revving all around. "That was some run! 131 miles per hour, Wow!" Billy said. He was rewarded with another arm squeeze and giggle. The feel of her against his arm was incredible. They stopped and Billy bought them both an ice cold Coca-Cola pulled from a metal tub. It tasted wonderful, the bottles still dripping ice water. They continued on their way back to Bill's pit.

"That's Bill's car and trailer over there," Billy saw a 1937 Buick sedan with a small single-axle trailer attached to the back bumper. The trailer wasn't much more than an axle and two metal runners long enough to accommodate Bill's sleek black racer. They walked over to the Buick and sat down on the edge of the trailer. Much to Billy's disappointment, Sally released her hold on his arm as they sat.

"So Billy, how did you wind up in San Diego?" Sally asked.

Billy took a moment to compose his thoughts. He was not the kind of person to answer questions with superficial answers and certainly not to someone like Sally. He was completely enthralled. He would have been content to spend the rest of his life sitting right there looking into those beautiful blue eyes.

"Working on aircraft is something I've always wanted to do. I enjoy making things, building things; technical things fascinate me the most. Back in Texas there simply wasn't the opportunity to get into aircraft right away. Consolidated is building a bomber plant there, but the building won't be finished for well over a year. I thought if I came out here, I could get a head start. Maybe after the plant is built back home, I could transfer back. Something like that." He didn't add that after meeting Sally he was already rethinking the plan to move back to Texas.

"Another thing is that my father was stationed here at Fort Rosecrans before he went to France in the war. He is always telling stories about how beautiful it is and what perfect weather they have here. Back home this time of year it's at least 100 degrees and here, well, it's just perfect." Billy said, thinking to himself 'in more ways than one'.

Neither of them said anything for a few minutes, they just watched the activity around them. Billy tried not to look at her, doing his best to focus on the racers coming and going. A couple of times he stole a quick sideways glance. Once he was startled to see her staring at him with open curiosity.

"So do you live in Los Angeles?" Billy asked, trying to think of something halfway intelligent to say and at the same time hide his embarrassment from her. It seemed every time she looked at him, she looked directly into his brain.

"Yes I do," she paused for a second. "I was born there. The weather is nice, but not quite as nice as it is here in San Diego." She smiled.

"What do you do there?"

"I work at the Packard dealership"

"I bet Tommy doesn't like that!" Billy laughed.

"Oh, Tommy doesn't care," she chuckled. "In fact, I think he derives a certain amount of enjoyment from it."

"Why is that?" Billy asked.

"Trust me, it's a long story and here comes Bill, we'll talk about that some other time." She said while getting up to head toward Bill's car.

Billy only hoped the 'some other time' part was true. He wanted nothing more than to see her again.

Bill pulled up, cut off his ignition and coasted to a stop beside the trailer. There was a piece of paper taped to the side of the cowl right in front of the cockpit. Bill flashed them a tremendous grin as he began to squirm out of the tight confines of the car, having to turn sideways to get his shoulders out of the narrow cockpit.

"Bill, you had a wonderful run! Congratulations!" Sally said.

"Congratulations Mr. Warth!" Billy added.

Bill finally managed to climb out of the car. He accepted a congratulatory hug from Sally. Billy felt another tingle of jealousy. He wished he were the object of one of those hugs. Bill was a dark haired slightly built man, a little older than most of the other racers. He pulled his aviator cap and goggles off and extended his hand to Billy. "Hi. I'm Bill Warth."

Billy introduced himself. "He's from Texas" Sally added. Bill asked, "How tall are you?"

Billy blushed a bit, "Six six," he replied. He noticed Sally glanced up at him when he said that, a grin on her pretty face. Billy forced himself to focus on Bill's racer. He looked at the paper taped to the cowl. It was rubber stamped with a form bearing the Road Rumbler's name. On the form there were blanks for time through the quarter mile trap, location Kearney Mesa, date June 14, 1941, name Bill Warth, club Pacesetters, speed 131.84.

"Wow! You have the fastest time of the day," Billy said. "What kind of motor do you have?"

"Billy, it's a Model B Ford. It's got a Winfield Super Red head, twin Winfield carburetors, and a Winfield cam." Bill replied.

"Sure sounds like you're sold on Winfield." Billy said.

"He's a genius. He knows what makes motors run and he knows what makes speed. There are quite a few overhead valve engines here today, but I have the top speed with a flathead. There's a bunch of V-8s here too, but this old 4-banger runs pretty good." Bill smiled.

"I should say." Billy added. "Did you make the body?"

"Yeah, me and a friend. It's aluminum, expensive to buy, but it's pretty easy to form and it's light. My friend worked in the body shop at Lee Cadillac building custom bodies for movie stars. He showed me how to do it and then helped build it. I think the shape of the body is as important as the engine when it comes to speed. I used to have this same engine in my Model B roadster and it would barely pull the ton." Bill said.

"Pull the ton, what does that mean?" Billy asked.

"Oh shit, sorry. That means run a hundred miles per hour."

"I had a Model B back home and it wouldn't run over 85." Billy said with surprise.

"Bet you didn't have $150 in the engine either, did you?" Bill asked.

"Hell no. I didn't have half that in the whole damn car!" They both chuckled. Sally was starting to look bored again.

"I don't see any radius rods. How do you keep your axles straight?" Billy asked.

"Don't have any springs. The axles are welded solid to the frame rails. Used the rails off the Model B. Those '32 frames are pretty stout. Took the cross member out, lined up the axles, set the rails right on top, of course the whole thing is narrowed to the width of the engine and welded it all solid. Works great on the lakes. The road here is a little bumpier than the lakes, but it's a lot cleaner too, isn't it Sally?" Bill said, realizing how bored Sally was looking.

Sally rolled her eyes. "I should say so. It's 10:00 in the morning and I'm still not covered in dust."

"I read an article about the dry lakes in Popular Science a couple of years ago. Are you telling me those lake beds are smoother than this road?" Billy asked.

"Oh hell yeah. Lot's smoother, at least for the early runs. As the day wears on and more cars run, it gets rougher. Of course, then we just move the course over to a new piece of the lakebed. Works great, but it's sure as shittin' dirty!" Bill said laughing.

Billy could have spent hours looking over Bill's racer but he could tell Sally had lost interest in the technical details. "It's been nice meeting you Bill. You have a beautiful racer. I hope I get to see you run again and congratulations on your fastest time of the day. That's really super!" Billy said and they took their leave.

As they walked through the pits Sally asked, "How did you get out here, Billy?"

"I hitchhiked."

Sally was stunned. She came to a dead stop and looked at him. Every time she did that it made him squirm. "You hitchhiked? You mean to tell me you hitchhiked, what is it, 1500 miles from Texas to San Diego? Were you by yourself?"

"Yeah, I hitchhiked and I was by myself. It wasn't like I swam the ocean or anything." Billy replied.

"How long did it take?" Sally was staring at Billy with a look of awe on her face.

"Oh it took me most of a week. It wasn't a bad trip at all."

"Where did you sleep? How did you eat? How many rides did you have? How does a person do something like that?" she asked in amazement.

"I slept in cars and trucks mostly. I spent a day and night in a little town in Arizona. Man offered me a good day's wage plus a room for the night and meals to help him frame in a storeroom for his service station. Pretty easy work, heck we even got the roof decking down. He gave me $5.00 extra. It was really a good break from the travel." Billy said.

"So, you decided to come to California and you just put out your thumb and here you are?" Sally was still amazed that anyone could do such a thing.

"Sure. How would you have done it?" Billy asked. He didn't understand why she was so amazed at something he took for granted.

"I would have taken a train with a Pullman car. Probably the Pacific coast Flyer or the Sunset Special." Sally said.

"I don't have that kind of money, Sally. I'm just a working man," Billy replied.

"Oh, I think you're something more than that, Billy Pendleton." Sally said as she gave his arm a squeeze. "We better find our way back. Carl probably thinks I kidnapped you by now."

Billy silently wished she would. It had been a wonderful day so far. He had seen racing done by guys just like him. He saw one incredible car after another; cars that rivaled or surpassed any car in the world for speed, but that had been built of mostly cast off pieces from the junkyard with a little ingenuity and sweat by their young owners. Here were common guys like Danny Sakai and Bill Warth out running the custom, built-to-order sports cars of a man as rich and powerful as Tommy Lee. Billy was hooked. This was for him. This was a place where he could show his talent and his creativity and have fun with the end result. Besides, maybe he would bump into Sally again. He liked the sound of that. He resolved to build a car of his own, he was sure that would offer the best chance of seeing Sally again. He wasn't sure how he would do it, but he was certain it would happen. For the first time since meeting her he felt his confidence returning. He gave Sally's arm a squeeze of his own. She shot a quick look up at him, but he just continued to smile and look straight ahead as they walked back to Tommy's pit. It was Sally's turn to have a slightly unsettled feeling. She smiled too, sort of, and shot another sideways glance at him.

Tommy was just climbing out of the speedster as they walked up. Carl was there and so was Babe. Billy noticed the paper tag taped to the cowl. He glanced at it and saw a speed of 113.87 MPH. So Danny had been telling the truth! Tommy was grumbling about his carburetors being out of adjustment as he slammed the speedster's door. He ripped the tag from the cowl, crumpled it into a ball, and threw it as hard as he could.

"Tommy, have you tried getting Ernie to rejet your carbs? The altitude is a lot different here than it is on the Lakes." Carl asked.

"Hell yes, I've had Ernie tune the damn thing! I've had every mechanic in the shop look at it! It just won't run. That asshole Fred Offenhauser screwed me again dammit!" Tommy protested.

Billy was a little embarrassed and offended that anyone would use such language in front of a lady. He was drawing a breath to tell Tommy so when Sally squeezed his arm really hard and kept the pressure on. He turned to look at her and she gave the briefest of shakes to her head and looked straight in his eyes. It was obvious she didn't want him to say anything, and besides, the swell of her breast pressed against his arm was commanding all of his attention.

Tommy stalked off throwing his helmet and goggles at the front wheel of the speedster.

Carl took it all in stride. He turned his attention to the young couple and said "So where have you two been off to?" His eyes smiled at them. He hadn't missed the arm in arm stance. Billy blushed again like he had been caught, not doing a bad thing, but caught doing something he would have preferred no one noticed.

"Oh, I took Billy for a stroll through the pits. We saw Danny and Bill. Bill set the fastest time of the day. How fast was it Billy?" She looked up at him as she asked.

"131.84" Billy replied.

Carl whistled. "He sure has that thing humming doesn't he? That's a Model B too isn't it?" Carl asked.

"Sure is. He has a Winfield Super Red head on it," Billy replied, proud of his newfound knowledge.

Carl thought, this kid sure learns quickly. His first day at the races and before noon he's met the fastest guys at the meet, knows all about their cars and has been given a personally guided, arm in arm tour by the most beautiful girl in attendance. He wondered if Billy did everything to that level. Somehow he was sure he did. His size matched his ability. Billy reminded him of his old friend Frank, not in appearance, Billy was a giant compared to Frank, but in every other way they were very much alike.

Babe came running up. "Hi, Aunt Sally!" he yelled as he threw himself into her arms. "Billy, want to go play some pitch?" Babe asked, giggling as Sally hugged and kissed him. Billy was very envious, wishing he could trade places with Babe.

Before Billy could form a reply, Carl said, "Frank, excuse me, Babe, you can play pitch at home. This is Billy's first time at the races, he wants to see the cars and meet the people. Go find those boys again and play with them."

Babe hung his head, "okay," he said, "but Billy plays better than any of those guys!"

They all laughed. Billy was secretly relieved. He really enjoyed spending time with Babe, but he didn't want to waste any of this day on things as simple as playing pitch, not with Sally on his arm. He would make it up to Babe when they returned home.

"Babe?" Sally asked

"That's Frank's new nickname. Billy's been calling him that and I think he likes it." Carl answered.

"How do you happen to know Frank, I mean Babe, so well Billy?" she asked.

"He's renting our spare room, Sally," Carl answered.

"Oh really," she said once more freezing Billy with those blue eyes one eyebrow arching up above the other.

"Let's go look around," Carl said and the three of them went walking through the pits. Sally walked between the men all three arm in arm. Both men thought silently what an excellent arrangement that was and it would probably have come as a surprise to both of them that Sally enjoyed it as much as they did.

They walked from one interesting car to the next, stopping at each to discuss its finer details. Billy asked question after question. Carl answered all the while impressed with the depth of understanding the questions exhibited. It was obvious that Billy had more than just a passing interest in the racers and how they were built. Billy in his turn was equally as impressed that Carl knew so many of the people and so much about their cars. Sally just enjoyed the day. She was surprised by how much she enjoyed the tall Texan's company. They really had nothing in common and she was several years his senior, but he had a way about him, oh yes he did! Even though she didn't really care if a Winfield was faster than a Riley or if a V-8 could be made to turn 6000 RPM, she was at ease and at peace in the company of the two men. She had always been more at ease with Carl than her own father. And Billy, well she wasn't sure what to make of Billy just yet. One thing she was oddly aware of, was that things would never be the same. It was one of the most enjoyable days she could remember.

By early afternoon all the speed runs were over. Bill Warth's time had stood up as the fastest of the day. He made two more runs over 130 MPH, but neither as fast as the first one Sally and Billy had witnessed. All of the racers were preparing for the trip home. Most of them were bolting fenders and windshields back on their cars. A few, like Danny and Bill were loading cars on trailers or attaching tow bars to cars that weren't street legal.

When they made it back to Tommy's pit they found Ernie and some other Don Lee employees finishing loading up. The speedster and the Bugatti were on tow bars behind Cadillac V-16 sedans.

"Where's Tommy?" Carl asked.

"Hell, he's already gone," Ernie replied. "He was so pissed after that 113 MPH run that all he said was 'Screw this!' and he left." Ernie chuckled and Carl just shook his head.

Babe came running up. "Is it time to leave yet?"

"Yes son, I guess it is," Carl said.

Goodbyes were exchanged all around.

Billy and Sally walked a few steps away. Billy asked "Are you going to be okay, what with Tommy leaving and all? How are you getting home?"

"I'll be fine." She said. "I'll ride back with Ernie. That's how I got here. I don't care what Tommy does, the ride back will be more pleasant without him. And one more thing, no I am not Tommy Lee's girlfriend. Does that answer your question?"

Billy didn't know what to say. He was blushing again, remembering the embarrassment he felt after asking the question.

"You take care of yourself Billy Pendleton. I'll be seeing you." And with that she reached up pulling his head down while she stood on tip toes and kissed him, on the lips this time. It really wasn't that much of a kiss, just a quick brushing of lips, but he thought his heart might explode it was beating so hard. Then she gave him a quick smile and ran to the Caddy sedan and jumped in the back door. Before Billy could follow, Carl and Babe yelled at him to get his attention then Carl said, "Time for us to go big guy. You ready?"

All Billy could manage was "I guess so." As they walked away Billy looked back to see the pair of Caddies pulling out with their exotic cargo in tow. He caught a glimpse of Sally through the rear window of the lead car. She was staring back at him and waved. She wasn't smiling any more, then they were gone accelerating up the road on their trip back north. They watched each other out of sight. Her face never left the rear window and his eyes never left her.

Chapter 6

They sat three abreast in the LaSalle on the drive home. For a while no one said anything. Babe was tired out from all the running and he dozed off, his head on Billy's arm.

"So how did you like the trials?" Carl asked.

"I thought they were swell. I don't know when I've had so much fun. How often do they have them?" Billy inquired. Carl thought he seemed a bit subdued to have had so much fun. He was beginning to think Billy had liked more than the cars.

Carl chuckled. "They usually have at least four per year. This was the second one this year. The first one was back in April."

"I'd like to build a car," Billy said.

"Kind of thought you might. You seemed awfully interested for your first trip. Do you have any ideas yet?" Carl asked.

"I was thinking of a single seater. Something like a cross between Bill Warth's racer and Tommy's speedster. I'm too big for a car like Bill's. I wouldn't ever fit in it, and if I built a two-seater, it wouldn't be that fast. Bill told me one of his secrets is the streamlining of the body. He said it was just as important as the power of the engine." Billy said, the excitement evident in his voice.

"He's right. What kind of engine would you use?" Carl asked.

"I don't know. I like the 4 bangers, but with a bigger car and the same engine as Bill runs, of course that says a lot – that I could even equal his motor, but if I could, I'd still have a slower car. My other thought is that I'd like to be able to drive it on the street. Maybe even take a trip or two in it, like go up to Los Angeles or something." Carl glanced over at him at this last comment. Billy was looking out the side and didn't notice. "I wonder why he wants to visit LA?" Carl thought already knowing the answer.

They continued on a while, the big V-8 engine of the LaSalle pulling the hills effortlessly. "Seemed like you and Sally got along well." Carl said casually

"Yeah, she's really something isn't she? All day I thought she was Tommy's girlfriend." Billy said.

Carl laughed out loud startling Babe so that he grunted and moved around in the seat burying his head deeper in Billy's arm.

"Tommy wishes she was his girlfriend I'm sure, but she's much too good for Tommy. Tommy goes through women like a normal man changes socks. He has no real interest in them only in what they can give him and he likes to be seen with beautiful women. Sally is too smart for that. She toys with him the way he toys with other women. She's smarter than he is. I think Sally just does it for sport and maybe to pay him back for all the misery he has dealt other women." Carl suggested.

They rode on; neither said anything for a while. "Sally sure seemed to like you." Carl turned to look at Billy, but Billy was gazing out the side window again. He didn't reply.

They finished their drive into town. Carl suggested they stop for a hamburger on the way home. He didn't want to cook or clean up after. Billy thought this was a great idea. Babe finally woke up as the carhop was delivering their order and putting the tray on the driver's side glass.

"Oh boy, hamburgers! Did you get me a vanilla shake?" Then he saw it and his eyes went wide. "Oh boy!" was all he could say.

"I didn't know Sally was your niece," Billy said.

"She's not actually. Her mother and I grew up together. Sally's always called me uncle." Carl replied.

"But those eyes..." Billy thought, but didn't say anything.

They munched on their burgers, for a while, then Carl asked, "How much thought have you given to what your car will look like?"

"I'm not sure. I want it to be pretty and to look fast sitting still, but I don't know for sure. I liked Danny's car, and Bill's and Tommy's too; maybe kinda like all of them mixed together." Billy was thinking aloud.

"When I was a boy my next door neighbor and best friend was a kid named Frank Lockhart. Ever hear of him?" Carl asked.

"The name sounds familiar; didn't he win the 500 mile race?" Billy asked.

"He sure did and on his first visit. He went to that first race as a spectator in 1926. Some of the guys from California knew Frank and they knew he raced that old Model T he built himself and did pretty good with it too. We built the engine in the floor of his mom's kitchen, but anyway, they let him take a few laps in Benny Hill's front wheel drive Miller. Just to show the kid what a real racecar was like, you know. Benny Hill was the Miller factory driver at the time. The best of the best. Frank, hell, Frank had never driven any car but that old Model T and he had never raced anywhere but on ½ mile and mile dirt tracks. Well, Frank takes that brand new Miller out on that 2 ½ mile brick track and on the second lap he goes faster than Benny had ever gone. That got some folks to talking. Old Benny was sorry he ever let Frank in that car. Old man Miller, well he was totally impressed." Carl said.

"Wow! Sounds like Frank was quite a driver."

"That's not the half of it. So the story goes, one of the other Miller drivers got sick the day of the race and they put Frank in his car as a substitute driver. I've never believed that story. I've always thought those guys knew Frank was faster than any driver they had ever seen and they made a place for him on race day. So we have Frank on his first visit to Indy, having never raced on a paved track in his life, in a strange car, with absolutely no practice starting the race." Carl described the scene with enthusiasm.

"How old was Frank at the time? How did he do?" Billy asked, finding it hard to contain his interest.

"He put on a show that day. He was 23 years old. They had to call the race at 400 miles because of rain. Frank was over four miles ahead of the nearest car. He had lapped the entire field and was about to lap the second place car for the second time. No one ever saw anything like it and they still haven't to this day. That was back in '26."

"My God, that's incredible! Where is Frank now?" Billy asked.

"That's the rest of the story. Frank took his winnings from the Indy race and he bought the Miller car he was driving plus a spare. Old man Miller offered him Benny Hill's place driving the works Miller, but Frank turned him down. Miller wasn't used to being turned down and I think it pissed him off, but he was smart enough to know that Frank was the real deal. He was a phenomenal driver like the world had never seen, so he did what he could to keep Frank happy and in the seat of a Miller, of course. As you can imagine, Frank set the world on fire with those cars. Up to that time, I had been helping out on Frank's car, the old Model T racer. Hell, we'd lived next door to each other since the time we were both six years old. Frank was a genius when it came to cars. He was my best friend, but I'm not just saying that, he had a gift to drive, but also to design and build. He just *knew* what was going on with every piece of the car. He could take one look at something and tell you more than the person that designed it. He was a natural. I've worked my whole life with the best. That's all Don Lee would ever hire, only the best, but there's never been another Frank and I doubt there ever will be, but I have to say Billy, you remind me of him a bit. You seem to understand what it takes to make a racer go more than most of those guys that have been doing it for years." Carl said thoughtfully.

"Thanks Carl, but I'm no genius. Whatever became of Frank?"

"He went racing with those Millers. He set track records everywhere he went. Those were the days of the board tracks you know. They were big banked oval tracks built out of lumber. There was one in LA and another here in San Diego. They packed the people in for those races. Most of the spectators drove Model T Fords to the races and a Model T will go what, 40 maybe 50 MPH if it's downhill with a tail wind? They would go to the boards and see racers lapping those tracks at 120 MPH, lap after lap. Frank set a lap record on the boards at 144 MPH. That's the fastest lap ever driven on a closed track!" Carl paused for a minute to finish off his hamburger and the last of his Coca-Cola.

"Those Miller cars were the best in the world at the time. Every place they went they won, and that includes Europe. They were so good they didn't need a Frank Lockhart driving to win, but when you put the two together it was pure magic.

Frank could never let anything alone. The Millers were good, but when Frank looked at them, all he saw were ways to improve both the cars and the engines. Old man Miller didn't like that. He built the best in the world and he knew it, he sure didn't need some punk kid improving on his masterpieces. That caused friction between them.

Miller really did build masterpieces. They were way ahead of their time, still are I guess. Miller championed the straight 8 engine. He built lots of other configurations, but his best ever was the straight 8 and the 91 cubic inch was the best of those. That's what Frank's cars were." Carl said.

"You mean that Frank set that lap record of 144 miles per hour with a 91 cubic inch engine?" Billy asked.

"Oh yeah. That's all it was, 91 cubic inches. Those Millers were works of art. Old man Miller spent as much time and effort making everything that came out of his shop look good as he did on making them run good. That 91 was a little jewel. All the castings were gorgeous. Every piece had to look just right as well as work right. There were times that I thought Miller made decisions more on appearance than on function, but no one can argue with his results."

"But what made old man Miller so mad, was that Frank took his creations, his masterpieces, and just made them better. I wish I could say that I played a part in it, but I was just married and we were trying to get settled and start a family. I couldn't be traipsing from one racetrack to the next all over the country. I had to make a living. I needed to be home nights rather than in Frank's race shop working on the cars. Frank was a slave driver. There was no higher purpose than making those cars run better and faster. If everyone had to work night and day to do it, well that's just the way it was. Frank had a one track mind when it came to being the best on the track and nothing else mattered." Carl said.

"I can see where that would make family life a little difficult." Billy said.

"Hell it made it impossible, so I told Frank I just couldn't do it anymore. If it had been anyone else leaving the team, he would have called them a traitor and never spoken to them again. That's the way Frank was, he wasn't an easy man to be around. But, Frank and I grew up together. We were more like brothers than he was with his real life brother. He knew I was only leaving because I had to, so we remained close. I went to work for Don Lee and Frank kept racing." Carl said.

They had all finished eating and Babe dozed off again. The carhop picked up their tray and Carl started the car and pulled out of the drive-in.

"Let me tell you some of the things Frank did. Those Miller 91's were supercharged. They had a great big centrifugal supercharger mounted on the end of one of the camshafts. That thing was as big as a wheel. That was the secret to the power they made. Anyway, Frank had an old Buick touring car that he drove back and forth to the shop. He designed a power take off on the transmission of that Buick to power one of those superchargers. His idea was to test modifications to the supercharger and he used the Buick to do it. He had a kid from UCLA, an engineering student that worked with him and was his draftsman. They mounted that supercharger to the transmission and off they went driving down the street, the faster they went, the more that supercharger howled. They had rigged up some test gear to determine how much pressure; it's called 'boost', that the supercharger put out at a given RPM. Those superchargers were driven at 40,000RPM." Carl said with admiration.

Billy whistled.

"They're driving down the street with this thing blowing air into the car and the first thing they notice is that as soon as it gets up to speed, the air is like out of a blowtorch it's so hot. If you got your hand anywhere near it, it would burn you.

By the end of the day, they had designed a new inlet manifold for the supercharger that cooled the air before it went into the cylinders. Today we call them intercoolers. It was made out of aluminum and had fins all over it. Thing was almost as big as the engine itself. They had it arranged so the slipstream of the car passed over the fins and cooled the air inside of it. They calculated it should add eight miles an hour to their top speed and sure enough, it did!" Carl explained.

"They cast up those intercoolers and put them on Frank's race cars. They kept the hoods closed at all times so no one could see what they had done. A little piece of it could be seen below the frame rail, but they told everyone it was an oil cooler. They kept that secret for over a year.

Frank took one of the cars to Muroc dry lake and set a new world's speed record for engines of that size. Over 171 MPH. That record still stands."

"171 MPH! There wasn't anything today that was even close to that! And every car there had an engine bigger than Frank's!" Billy was amazed.

"Oh every car there had an engine well over twice as big as Frank's, but that's what he did and it was his undoing at the same time. When he went 171 the absolute world's land speed record was just 175. It was held by John Parry-Davis with an engine over 20 times the size of Frank's. That got Frank to thinking. He figured if he could get that close to the absolute record with his normal racecar, he could easily set a new record with a purpose built car. It became his single focus. Oh, he still raced the boards and Indy, but he had a new mission in life. He wanted to become the fastest man on earth."

"What a story! Did he make it?" Billy asked.

"Almost. You know Frank wasn't born in California. He was born in Dayton, Ohio. His father ran off when Frank was just a baby. His mom tried to raise those kids by herself. Frank had an older brother you know." Carl said.

Billy didn't, but he was fascinated with the story. Carl continued.

"The next door neighbor was named Wright. The man was a church Bishop. He was Wilbur and Orville Wright's father."

"Oh man! Frank's next door neighbors were the Wright brothers? He actually grew up next door to the Wrights?" Billy exclaimed.

"He sure did. You know I've always had a suspicion there was more to it than that."

"What do you mean, 'more to it'," asked Billy.

"Don't you think it strange that one mechanical genius lives next door to a pair of mechanical geniuses?" Carl asked.

"What are you trying to tell me, that there was something in the water there?"

"It just seems too much of a coincidence to me. You never knew Frank, but he truly was something special. He had abilities that far exceed anything I've ever seen before. I never knew the Wrights, but from what I've read, they had those same abilities. Frank was a single-minded guy. He fixated on a goal and no power on earth would deter him from achieving it. The Wrights were the same way. Frank was not an easy person to get along with. I think that was because Frank was totally consumed by his mission, he just didn't have time to do all the little things that people do to get along. Frank just didn't have time for that. Neither did the Wrights from all I know about them. Frank and the Wright brothers were just alike, cut from the same cloth maybe?" Carl said.

"Are you telling me that Frank and the Wrights were related?" Billy asked, sounding a bit perplexed.

"Yes I am, at least that's what I think anyway. I don't have any proof and I'll never be able to prove it, but that's what I think. Everything you read about the Wright brothers is that they were true mechanical geniuses and so was Frank. They were single minded in their efforts to achieve powered flight and so was Frank in the things he wanted to do. The Wrights designed and built their airplane themselves. They solved all the problems; they even built tools and test equipment to do it just the way Frank did. The Wrights were extremely secretive about their work. They were constantly in fear someone would steal their ideas and so was Frank. Maybe it was the water, or maybe it was the air above those two houses in Dayton, Ohio, but I think it was more than that. I think Frank's real father was named Wright. I think that's why his dad ran off when Frank was a baby. I think he discovered his wife was having an affair with the neighbor and had a child by the neighbor and so he left her." Carl stated with confidence.

"Oh man! It fits, but I don't know." Billy said.

"I don't either, but I think I'm right. I also think that's why Frank's mother eventually pulled up stakes and moved the family to California. That was after it became apparent that all it would ever be was an affair. They didn't have time for her or to raise a family and so she eventually gave up and moved as far away as possible. Tried to start over, but Frank was just like his father. She struggled trying to raise Frank. Even when he was just a kid, Frank ran that house. He gave all the orders and his mother and brother had no choice but to obey. It's just the way Frank was.

Frank decided he was going to be the fastest man on earth and he set out like only Frank could, to do just that." Carl said in a matter of fact tone.

"Wait a minute, who do you think was Frank's father? Was it Orville or Wilbur?" Billy asked.

"Of course I don't really know and never will, but I think Wilbur Wright was Frank's father. From all I've read, he was the most technical of the two, the hardest to get along with and extremely secretive about his work. Those are all traits that Frank shared. Wilbur died in 1912 I think, considering Frank's later success if Wilbur really was his father he would have made contact with him, but of course he couldn't because he was already dead." Carl continued with his theory.

" Okay. Go on with the part about setting the speed record." Billy was amazed. His life had certainly changed in the past month. Just that long ago he had graduated high school and here he was hearing insider gossip about some of the most famous men of the century!

"Frank set about designing a car. He had been doing this his entire life anyway. He used to draw pictures of streamlined cars during class in school. I remember the teacher caught him drawing one day. He couldn't have been over nine or ten. She took his drawing away from him and showed it to the class asking what it was. She made fun of it when he told her it was a car. It certainly didn't look like any car she was familiar with. That's because Frank was way ahead of his time even at that early age. He proceeded to tell her that the reason it didn't look like a car to her is that she didn't understand it. You would have thought there was a graduate engineer in the room giving a lecture. He explained the design and why it looked how it did. How the air flowed over it and how the shape minimized the aerodynamic drag on the car. The teacher was totally taken aback. Frank completely intimidated her. She never questioned him again. Several years later, Frank was offered a full scholarship to MIT. He didn't take it of course, he didn't have time to waste in school.

He called it the beach car. You see, in those days most of the land speed records were set on beaches. If you find the right one, they're long and straight and with the right kind of sand, they pack hard and smooth. The most famous of all was Daytona in Florida. Several records were set there as far back as 1900 or so. Malcolm Campbell set his records there. Besides, Frank understood the publicity achieving such a record would give him. The newspapers of the world were used to going to Daytona Beach to cover such things. He realized that if he could become the fastest man on earth, it would bring him unlimited fame and fortune. He grew up dirt poor so he understood how important money was to continuing the projects he wanted to pursue. That's why he chose Daytona over one of the dry lakes. Also, back in those days, Bonneville Salt Flats was relatively unknown. Besides he couldn't have gotten the news coverage he craved at some unknown place out in the middle of the desert. Reporters would much rather go to a resort and stay at a fancy hotel than camp out in the middle of nowhere.

The car he built was called the Stutz Black Hawk Special. It didn't have anything Stutz on it, but Muscovic, the president of Stutz, put up $100,000 for Frank to build the car and call it a Stutz. He also offered Frank full use of the Stutz factory in Indianapolis to build the car. Frank couldn't turn that down." Carl said with a grin.

"It was called the most technically advanced automobile in the world when it was built. Muscovic saw to it that the press covered every aspect of the car. Newspaper articles covered the build in installments. Frank only showed them what he wanted them to see of course, but he welcomed the publicity. The news coverage brought more sponsors and money to the project.

All the cars before and since that have held the record were huge machines. Most have been powered by aircraft engines, many of them had multiple engines. I think Campbell's Bluebird is around 23 liters, that's over 1360 cubic inches! The car itself is huge. Frank took the opposite approach. He already knew his standard race car nearly broke the record. What the others had achieved with sheer force and tremendous size, he proposed to do with efficiency and advanced design." Carl explained

"The Blackhawk had an engine of Frank's own design. He took two Miller 91 cubic inch straight 8's and put them on a common crank case. He retained their separate crankshafts and had each crank drive a common idler gear mounted between them. This gear drove the flywheel and transferred power to the transmission. He kept everything as compact as possible. The entire theme of the car was to punch as small a hole in the air as possible. Even though he had what was in essence a V-16 engine, it was only 21 inches wide and it displaced only 182 cubic inches. It had twin superchargers, one for each bank of cylinders and two of Frank's intercoolers actually formed the outer surface of the hood. They streamlined the car and cooled the intake mixture at the same time. When he dynoed the engine, it produced 570 horsepower, and this was in 1927."

"Wow!" was all Billy could say.

"The car itself was tiny. The body was just wide enough for Frank to get in it. The only thing sticking out of the car was his head and it was streamlined by a fairing just like an airplane. There was no grille opening. Frank understood that any air that came in the grille to cool the engine produced drag, so he mounted an 80 gallon tank filled with ice to cool the engine in the tail of the car. All four wheels had fairings on them just like airplane wheel pants."

"It sure sounds fast!" Billy exclaimed.

"It was. It had a long tapering boat tail and streamlined axles. Frank actually got the Air Corps at Wright Field in Dayton to test the body in their wind tunnel. How do you think he managed that? His old contacts with the Wrights, of course. After all, the place was named for them! When they tested that car and factored in the horsepower the engine produced, they calculated its top speed at 370+ MPH. This was when the record stood at 200 MPH. That car was over a hundred miles an hour faster than any airplane the Army had at that time." Carl said.

"Did he set the record?" Billy was totally captured by this story. He had heard of Frank Lockhart, but he had never heard all of this.

"No, not really. Oh he took the car to Daytona all right. On the first visit, something happened and the car crashed into the ocean. Frank wasn't really hurt , but he almost drowned before they got to him and pulled him out of the cockpit. The car wasn't damaged as much as you might think so they loaded it up and took it back to the Stutz factory in Indianapolis. That was in February of '28. While they were back in Indy, the record was raised to 207 MPH. Frank was in a bind for money. Everything he raised, plus all the prize money he won was already in that car. Like I told you, he had total focus.

He had always raced on Firestone tires, but some guy there in the Midwest was trying to get a new tire company started. He offered Frank $10,000 to set the record using his tires. Frank had to have the money to finish the repairs and get the car back to Daytona, so he agreed. I begged him not to do it, but his mind was made up. He got the car back together and went back to the beach on unproven tires. Jean Marcenac was his mechanic at the time and he was so scared of those tires he quit. He refused to go with Frank and 'see him kill his foolself' as he told me later." Carl said.

"When they arrived at Daytona the season was almost over. Several cars were at the beach attempting to set a new record including Campbell. It was almost a circus atmosphere. Frank made several runs on the beach, but each time the car got up to 200 MPH and refused to go any faster. Finally Frank figured out that the air was flowing over the carburetor inlets so fast it was actually starving the engine for air. He made some small scoops, deflectors really, that allowed the carbs to draw in all the air they needed. On his next run, the car really started to pull hard. His plan was not simply to smash the record as he surely could have done, but to break it by a substantial amount but well below what the Blackhawk was capable of. That way, anytime someone bested his speed, he could come back and recapture the record. That was common practice in those days.

"They say he was going well over 225 MPH when the car flipped end over end out of control. Frank was thrown clear of the wreckage, but he was dead on impact. His body landed almost at the feed of his young wife. He was only 25 years old." Carl said sadly.

"What happened?"

"The AAA did a thorough investigation. What they discovered was that when Frank turned around, his rear tire ran over a sharp seashell. They think that sliced the tire, they could tell that because the track left by one of the rear tires in the sand was wider than the other. The tire disintegrated and at over 200 MPH that was all it took."

"I'm sorry, Carl," Billy said. "I had heard of Frank Lockhart, but I never knew the whole story."

"For some reason, it hasn't been common knowledge. When Frank was racing he was almost a national hero. He was the all American story. You know, poor boy works hard and wins it all. He was almost there. Then the crash and that same year Wall Street crashed. I think Frank's story kind of got lost there. I think his death, plus the Wall Street crash also put Stutz out of business. One day they were riding high, and the next day they were gone. I've often wondered if Frank's death didn't have something to do with all that came later. American racecars were the best in the world, but after Frank's death and the stock market crash it all came to an end. Harry Miller went bankrupt and his business went under. His shop foreman, Fred Offenhauser, managed to scrape up enough to get it going again. Fred is not the dreamer the old man was though. Fred builds good engines that win races, but he pretty well specializes in proven designs and just builds 4 cylinder engines. The old man was always trying new things. Front wheel drive, boats, airplanes, you name it. For over a decade American cars were the best and fastest. Genius did that, Miller, Lockhart and all the rest. And as quickly as they had come, they were all gone. Frank's death was the end of an era."

They were just pulling into the driveway at home. Billy unloaded the car while Carl got Babe awake and in the house to bed. As he put things away, Billy reflected on the day's events. He had seen his first time trial. He met some of the best drivers at the event and discussed the details of their cars with them. He met Tommy Lee, certainly one of the richest and most powerful men of this rich and powerful state. He heard the story of Frank Lockhart from his best friend, and lastly, he met Sally. Oh Sally. Even with all of Carl's stories, on the way home most of Billy's thoughts had been about Sally. He just couldn't get her out of his mind, not that he wanted to. His lips still burned from her kiss.

When he came in the back door with the last load, Carl was sitting down at the kitchen table with an old frayed shoe box and a couple of beers.

"How about a beer?" Carl offered him one.

"Sure, I could use one right about now," Billy replied.

"I thought you might like to see a few pictures of the beach car." Carl said.

Billy looked at the pictures as Carl spread them on the table. It was a beautiful car. Long and slender with streamlined covers over each of the wheels.

"You said you were interested in building a car. When you said a single seater big enough for you to fit in, this is the thought that flashed through my head. What do you think? Would something similar to this work?" Carl asked.

"Boy would it! This would be super! We could add a grille and maybe some vents on the hood sides to cool the engine. Add some lights and of course some kind of exhaust." The exhaust on the beach car was simply stubbed out the sides of the hood. Eight pipes on each side.

Carl was gratified that Billy liked the idea. He was already forming a bond with the lanky Texan. "What do you have in mind for an engine?" Carl asked.

"I don't have an idea for that yet. With that long hood an inline engine would certainly work, but I don't know what kind. Probably whatever I can find cheap. Maybe a Buick, or Hudson." Billy replied. "Can I use your shop to build the car?"

"Only if you let me help," Carl said.

"I wouldn't have it any other way," Billy replied.

"I've got an idea or two for an engine. Let me look around a bit. What do you say we call it a night?" They both headed off to their rooms. It had been a busy day for both of them and many more would follow.

Chapter 7

The next evening true to his word, Carl announced, "Billy, I've got an idea for an engine."

Billy was excited, "What did you find?"

"This is a little exotic, but I think it would really do the job. It's an inline 6, well sort of at least." Billy looked puzzled at that.

"It's an engine that Don Lee, Tommy's father, had built years ago. When the V-12 and V-16 Cadillacs came out back in 1930, Don was certain all the movie stars would want one. Heck, it was one fine looking engine. Don supported all kinds of racing. He was always looking for ways to promote Cadillac and La Salle; after all, he was the distributor for the entire state of California. Hell, he even owned most of the dealerships in the state. How about a beer?" They got a couple of beers and sat down at the kitchen table again.

"Tommy talked his dad into letting him run the project to build a race car around the new V-12 engine. Tommy came to me because he knew I had been racing with Lockhart. There was no way I would consider building a racecar. It wasn't that long since Frank was killed and my wife died. My heart just wasn't in it, after all, I had a baby to raise by myself. I told Tommy as much. He understood, to have been raised with a silver spoon in his mouth, Tommy's not a half-bad guy. He told me he would find someone else to do it and asked for my recommendation. There was a new guy in the shop just then. His name was Frank Kurtis, I recommended him. I've got a lot of Frank's in my life don't I?"

"You sure do." Billy laughed.

Carl continued, "Tommy also asked me if I had any suggestions on the motor. I told him that V-12 was too big and heavy to put in a racecar. He was wanting to race on the dirt tracks and at Indianapolis. I think the board tracks scared him a little. They were so fast, you know. Besides most had already burned down or rotted away. I also told him that engine wouldn't be legal under AAA rules. It had too much displacement. Besides there was no way it could compete with a Miller. It was a huge engine built to be smooth in a passenger car, not burn up a race track.

Well sir, as soon as I said it couldn't compete with a Miller, I saw his eyes light up. He said thanks and was out of the shop in a flash. What I found out later is that as soon as he finished talking to me he was on the way over to talk to Harry Miller.

Harry told him the same damn thing, that the engine was just too big. It weighed too much, was too slow to rev, you know, it was a luxury car engine not a race motor. Tommy was determined to use that engine. He convinced his father that it would be good advertising for the dealership to have a Cadillac on the track. After all, look what racing did for Duesenberg!"

Carl took another swallow of beer, "Harry Miller was no man's fool. He knew Tommy and more importantly he knew Tommy's dad and he knew they could pay for any work he did. So he sat down with Leo Goosen, his draftsman, and they designed Tommy an engine based on that V-12. The very first thing they did was to cut one bank of cylinders off it. Then they designed a new lighter weight crankshaft. Finally they designed a new aluminum head with double overhead cams. Even with all this rework they knew it would never be competitive with a real race engine, but it would be more than fast enough for Tommy. He kind of fancied himself a race driver in those days.

This was during the time that Harry was enjoying his fame and success a little too much and spending money like it was water. He never was one to finish a project before he started the next anyway, and his business was starting to slip. Business was slow, no one had any money and he saw this as an opportunity to score off a fat cat." Carl said.

"The engine got built, but it wasn't delivered until 1935! Fred Offenhauser finally finished it to get it out of the shop. It was a pretty thing too. They built it to fit in the three liter, that's 183 cubic inch class, but by the time it was finished, the formula had changed to the 'junk' formula and it was no longer legal. It took so long since the project began that Tommy lost interest anyway. He bought one of the Miller Ford Indy cars and then the Bugatti. Scared himself silly at Ascot and decided he really wasn't cut out to be a race driver after all. Kurtis never got the car built, hell he never had an engine to build it around. How do you build a car when you don't know anything about the engine? He finally got cross ways with Tommy and quit. It was the best thing that ever happened to him. He's building midgets as fast as he can put them together. Has a regular factory going building race cars in LA." Carl said, pleased with himself.

"Like I said, the engine finally got finished and delivered to the LA dealership. They called it a LaSalle. Hell, I guess it's a Miller-LaSalle. I called my buddy up there today. He says it's stuck back in the corner of the storeroom covered up with a tarp still in the original wooden crate. Says it's just in the way. Been like that for five or six years, wants to know if I want it. Said he would put it on the next parts delivery truck headed this way. You interested?" Carl asked.

"Hell yes, I'm interested! How much horsepower does it have? Can we run it on the street? Wow! Dual overhead cams, Wow!" Billy was thrilled; once again, this was more than he had ever dreamed would be possible.

"I'm glad you're interested. I already told him to ship it. I don't know how much horsepower. I figure it's probably got 170-180 though. That ought to push your little car along real well don't you think?" Carl asked with a grin.

"I sure do! Carl, I don't know how to thank you. Knowing you has opened all kinds of doors in my life. One of the best things that ever happened to me was your 'for rent' sign." Billy said. "When do you think the engine will get here?"

"Early next week; the truck usually comes down on Tuesdays."

"I can hardly wait." Billy said with excitement.

That night Billy went to sleep with visions of the new car running through his head. He had to decide what kind of running gear he would use. What would he build the frame out of? Someone had mentioned Essex frame rails to him. Maybe that was the way to go. Most of the racers used Ford axles and brakes. He guessed correctly because they were plentiful, cheap and the right mix between strength and weight. He secretly wished they had gone to LA to pick up the engine. He might have seen Sally! His best chance to see Sally again was to get a racecar together as quickly as possible.

The next issue was how to drag all those parts home when he found them. Heck, he didn't even own a car yet. All problems and questions without answers, but they were the kind of problems he loved to have. He fell asleep that night dreaming of showing Sally his finished car. He hoped he would see her at one of the races sometime.

The next day while on his lunch break at Consolidated, he was telling one of his co-workers about the project. Tommy Jackson, his lead man, mentioned that he had the remains of a '35 Ford pickup sitting in his backyard. He bought it at a salvage sale at the Navy base because he wanted the engine to go in his work truck. It had burned when the fuel pump sprung a leak and sprayed gasoline on the hot engine block. Since getting it home he had removed the engine and transmission and sold the cab and fenders to another friend. Tommy said all that was left was the frame, axles and wheels. His wife was on him to get rid of it and if Billy wanted it, he could have it just to haul it off.

He had the beginning of a frame!

Another co-worker, John Overton, told him that the last time he visited Apex Auto Salvage, he saw several old Essex cars on the back row. Billy vowed he would check them out that weekend. He could hardly wait to tell Carl what he had found. It certainly paid to let people know what kind of things you were looking for.

Things were going well at Consolidated. Billy worked with a good bunch of guys and he found the work fascinating. A lot of his co-workers moved to California in the past 10 to 15 years and a good many of them were from Oklahoma and Texas. They took Billy under their wing to "show him the ropes" and to be sure he knew all the right people at the factory. These weren't the managers and executives, but rather the blue-collar guys that could provide the specialized help that everyone needed from time to time. This kind of knowledge was extremely valuable as it usually came only with years of experience. Coupling his natural ability and a keen desire to learn with his new found web of contacts put Billy substantially ahead of the normal new hire. One of the things he discovered was that Consolidated had a surplus store where they sold all manner of surplus equipment and materials. John told him that the store might be an interesting place to visit considering his new project.

While none of his immediate co-workers was involved in local car clubs or modifying their cars, Billy discovered they knew other people that worked in the plant that were involved. Several assured Billy they would introduce him at the first opportunity.

That evening, Billy took the bus home as he usually did. While he normally caught a ride to work with Carl in the mornings, Carl's job was such that he didn't get off in time to pick Billy up. This wasn't a problem since the nearest bus stop was only a block away from the house.

When he arrived home, he found Babe in the kitchen. Babe's eyes lit up when Billy walked in "So when is your car going to be finished?" were the first words out of his mouth followed by "Can I help? Will you show me how to build a car? I promise I'll work hard and I won't get in the way!"

"Whoa, whoa! Of course you can help, but I have no idea how long it will take to finish it. I haven't ever built a car, so we can learn together. I hoped your dad could show me a few things and get me started in the right direction." Billy replied.

"Sure Dad will show you. He knows everything! We'll probably have it built in a week or two." Babe said with confidence.

Billy couldn't help but laugh. "I think it may take us a little longer than that. We haven't even started yet. How about a little pitch?"

They were playing pitch in the backyard when they heard a car pulling in the driveway. The black LaSalle coupe appeared around the corner of the house. As soon as the door opened, Babe sent the baseball zinging toward his dad who must have been used to it, as he made an amazing catch with his left hand while closing the door with his right.

"We've got us a volunteer to help build a car. He tells me we'll be driving it in a couple of weeks." Billy laughed and Babe blushed a bit. Carl stepped into the backyard and they began a little three cornered game of pitch. Since Carl had no glove, both of the others took it a little easy on him.

"I think it might take a little longer than that, Frank." Carl never called Frank 'Babe' although all of Frank's friends had already started the practice. Frank reveled in the name, as Babe Ruth had always been his idol. Even though the Great Bambino was in the twilight of his career, to many including young Frank, he would always be the greatest ball player to ever live.

Billy told Carl about the Ford pickup frame and parts Tommy Jackson had given him. Carl agreed that the axles and possibly a few other items would be usable on the new car. Plans were made to go pick it up on the weekend.

Babe soon tired of all the car talk even if they were playing three corner. Besides he enjoyed playing a little "pepper" meaning really burning the ball in there and he was having to take it easy on his dad since he was without a glove.

"I think I'm going to run over to Charlie's house and play some flies and skinners. Okay?" Babe said already mounting his bicycle.

"Don't be late for supper," Carl reminded him as he rounded the corner of the house and pedaled down the driveway at breakneck speed.

"Let's take a look in the shop and plan out how we're going to do this," Carl suggested.

They went into the old carriage house and surveyed the area. Of course, Carl was familiar with the lay out, but to Billy it was all still new.

There were two sets of double doors into the old building. One set was being used to bring the LaSalle in and out of the "garage" part of the building. These doors were near the end of the building and opened onto the driveway. The other set of doors were identical but were spaced more toward the middle of the building.

Inside the building, on the same wall that contained the doors, sturdy wooden work benches lined the wall from the second set of doors to the corner. There was a large iron vice on the corner of the bench nearest the middle set of doors. Even though the building was old enough to have once stabled horses, the benches were a relatively new addition.

"These are really nice work benches, Carl. Did you build them?" Billy asked.

"Yeah, I did. When we first moved here it was soon after I lost my wife. I needed something to occupy my time, so in the evenings I would bring Frank out here and we would work on fixing this place up. He was just a toddler at the time, but he seemed to enjoy it and it helped me not dwell on my loss. When I was cleaning all the accumulated junk out of this place, I came across an old baseball. I gave it to Frank to play with and as you can see, he's hardly put one down since!" Both men chuckled. Billy had already formed an attachment to Babe. Babe's constant flow of energy reminded him of his own little brother, Jimmie, back in Texas.

Several pieces of heavy equipment were in the shop. There was a large drill press and band saw, both with heavy cast iron frames. They looked older than any Billy was familiar with using. "This is a really nice drill press and band saw. They look old." Billy observed.

"Yeah, they've been around a while. There used to be a blacksmith's shop down the street from the dealership. Almost every day as I drove past, I'd see the old man that ran it sitting in the door of the shop. He never seemed to have much business. I guess the demand for a blacksmith in the middle of town wasn't what it once was. One day I was leaving work and I noticed a sign on the door of the shop that said 'going out of business sale'. I'd always been curious about the place so I stopped and went in. It was a fascinating place, I was really sorry I hadn't stopped before. There was a large forge built out of bricks on one wall. It had a huge wood and leather bellows attached. The floor of the shop was solid clinkers out of the forge. The drill press and band saw were there along with lots of old, well-used blacksmithing tools. He'd been in business in that building for 50 years. He had apprenticed under the man that built the shop. At one time they did horse shoeing and other such work for the city and the Army. I asked about the drill press and band saw. He told me they were in the shop when he started 50 years before! Originally, they were driven by a small steam engine through a series of pulleys and belts. That's how old they are. The old man told me he converted them to electricity probably 40 years ago. I bought them from him and had them hauled here. They've been used almost continuously for 60 years, but they're still good machines. I cleaned them up some, but other than that, they're just the way I bought them. That old man's name was Turner. He must've been 65 years old at least, but his arms and chest were huge. He had a grip like iron. He helped me load them in the shop truck and let me tell you that old man was strong as an ox. He made me feel puny." Carl said.

In another corner was a small lathe. It too was old, but appeared to be in good condition. Its steel surface blued from years of use and frequent oiling. The lathe came from the dealership having been replaced years earlier with a newer, larger model.

Plywood lined the wall above the workbench. It was stained and varnished and glistened under the light. All manner of hand tools hung on small hooks screwed into its surface. The shape of each tool was painted on the shiny surface in red. Entire sets of wrenches were arranged in order of size. Hammers and screwdrivers hung at the ready.

The rafters were exposed and a steel track ran down the center of the building. It was secured to the rafters with large lag bolts. A steel trolley rolled on the track and its hook supported a small chain hoist. "Will that hoist support the weight of an engine?" Billy asked.

"Oh sure. I used it to unload the drill press and band saw and they're heavier than an engine. I don't know what it was used for, but it was here when I bought the place. It's come in handy a time or two since." Carl replied.

"I bet it does. We can use that to support the engine while we build the mounts for it. I was thinking of supporting the frame on sawhorses once we get the basic part of it built. That way we have more room to work. I still don't know how we're going to build the body. I know Danny's car was steel and Bill Warth's was aluminum. Bill said that the aluminum was a lot more expensive, but of course it's easier to form. I was thinking that since I want to drive this on the street, that steel might be more durable. I haven't ever tried making anything as complicated as a body before. Have you?" Billy asked.

"No, I haven't. We've got some guys in the body shop at work that could show us a few things I'm sure. I know a guy up in LA that could show us anything we wanted to know. I've mentioned him before. His name is Frank Kurtis. He's a wizard when it comes to shaping metal. He built the body for Tommy's speedster." Carl said.

"I remember you mentioning him. Didn't you say he was building midget race cars now?" Billy asked.

"Yeah, he sure is. He's got a shop there in LA and is turning them out as fast as he can build them. It might be worth our time to take a trip up there to visit him. Do you think you could get a day off?"

As soon as Carl mentioned LA, Billy's thoughts jumped to Sally. He realized he had no idea how to contact her. She said she'd be seeing him but he had no idea what that meant. He wondered if he would ever see her again. It took all his will power to keep from asking Carl about her. Instead he replied, "My boss is a pretty good Joe. I can talk to him and see. I don't think getting a day or two off would be a problem."

"Well, you haven't been there very long, I wouldn't want you to have a problem with Consolidated. Without your salary, we're not going to get very far." Carl warned.

"You're right there. It may be a little early to be taking time off." Billy knew Carl was right, but his heart sank at the thought he might not be able to get off to visit LA. He had no idea how he would contact Sally even if he made it to LA. He wouldn't have any time to spend with her anyway, not if he was going to visit the Kurtis shop and get instruction on how to build a body. Besides all that, he didn't think he'd be able to concentrate on a car body with hers so close by.

"Do you know how to weld?" The question snapped Billy out of his reverie of Sally, at least for a moment. He found that he thought about her most all of the time. Trying to concentrate on building the car helped. After all, he could do something on the car, take concrete constructive action, while all he could do about Sally was dream about her. He still had no idea what she really thought about him anyway. When he was honest with himself, he had to admit she probably didn't think about him at all. Better to put those thoughts out of his mind as much as possible. He knew he was setting himself up for heartbreak if he kept thinking of Sally this way.

"Yes, I can weld. They taught us how in metal shop in school." Billy noticed that Carl's shop had an oxygen-acetylene welding outfit. The welder would be extremely important in the construction of the car. "Welding is fun. I'm not as good as I would like to be, but I can get by." He said.

"That's great. We both ought to get a helluva lot of practice before we're finished." Carl laughed.

"I've been thinking about the body work. Rather than starting from scratch, what do you think about using parts off cars

52

and just cut out the shapes we need and then weld them together?" Billy asked.

"Yeah, I've thought about that too. I think that might work pretty well. You know, there's always a bunch of body parts at the bodyshop at work. A lot of our customers are wealthy people. If one of their Caddies or LaSalles gets a bump on the fender, they don't want it pounded out, they want all new parts. Most of them can afford it too. The old parts just get sold for scrap. I get along really well with the body shop foreman, I'm sure I can get whatever we need." Carl said.

"I've been designing this thing in my mind. It helps me stay focused." Billy said. Carl wondered what he meant by that. He bet he knew. He saw how Billy had looked at Sally and he'd noticed how she looked at him. Now wouldn't that be something? Sally interested in this lanky Texas kid. He knew that Tommy Lee was genuinely smitten with her. Despite Tommy's persistent efforts, Sally had never given in to him. Instead she toyed with him. Maybe that's why Tommy was so taken with her. She was certainly beautiful, but then Tommy had any number of beautiful girlfriends. Then there was the fact that she was rich, but Tommy sure as hell didn't need her money. He wondered how much Billy knew about her. He didn't see how it could be much unless Sally told him and he doubted she would have done that.

"Tell me what you've been thinking." Carl said.

Billy proceeded to tell him the ideas he had. "Like we discussed before, I think Frank's Black Hawk Special is one of the best looking cars I've ever seen. I know it was built in 1928, but it still looks modern today. To my eye, it looks as streamlined as any automobile I've ever seen. I would like to use it as the model. I don't want to try to replicate it exactly, just to use its general shape and layout."

Carl was thrilled. He too had always thought the Black Hawk Special was a very dramatic looking car. Since his best friend designed and built it, and he himself was involved in it, if only on the periphery, he was a devoted fan of the car. "I think that's a terrific idea!" He said. "Do you have any sketches or anything on paper?"

"No, so far it's all just in my head." Billy said.

Carl said, "Tell me about it."

"You told me you were getting an in-line engine, so I thought the focus should be just like Frank's car, narrow and as streamlined as we can manage. When we were at the time trials, there were several cars that really impressed me. I thought we might incorporate certain aspects of those other cars also." Billy replied.

"Which ones?" Carl asked.

"I liked Danny Sakai's car, you know the bob-tailed car with the '39 LaSalle grille?" he said.

"Yeah, I know the one you're talking about. It's one of the best looking race cars around." Carl said enthusiastically.

"Well I talked to Danny about it quite a bit. It races in a class called 'modified'. He told me that cars in the 'modified' class can't have any bodywork or streamlining behind the driver's seat. All they can have behind the seat is a gas tank. He also told me that the body must be at least 30 inches wide to be legal in the class. Those were the SCTA rules he said."

"Yeah, that's Southern California Timing Association. They sanction most of the racing on the dry lakebeds up in the Mojave. The Road Rumblers also use their rules for the trials here." Carl explained.

"Well I would like for my car to have the long tapered boat tail like Frank's car had and I'd also like to have wheel pants similar to his car, but there's a bunch of work in those parts. We could actually get the car up and running much sooner if we built it as a modified first, so I thought we should make it at least 30 inches wide so it would be legal. Besides, I think it'll take that width to make me comfortable in the car." Billy suggested.

"Yeah, we could do that. Get it going as a modified first and then add the tail and wheel pants later."

"Exactly!" Billy replied. "The other two cars that I really liked were Tommy's speedster and Bill Warth's streamliner. Both those cars have boat tails, but not as dramatic as Frank's car had. I like the long hoods on both of them. I also like the exhaust on the outside like a real race car. Both those cars have outside exhaust. I'd like to do that on ours."

"Sounds like we've got a basic design. It still wouldn't hurt to get some things on paper. We need to draw it to scale if we can. That way we can establish the basic relationship of the parts. Let's work on that this week and we'll go get that Ford pick up on Saturday if it's okay with your friend."

"That sounds swell!" Billy replied.

Every night that week, Billy and Carl sat at the kitchen table and worked on the design of the car. One of the first things they did was to set Billy in a chair and take measurements. How high he was from the seat of the chair to the top of his head. This was important because he would have to straddle the driveline. The height of the driveshaft would be determined by the height of the rear tires. Using a Ford rear axle out of the pickup, commonly known as a banjo, automatically set the driveshaft at the same height as the center of the rear wheels. Of course, they would need a limited amount of suspension travel. Adding half the height of the rear wheels to the suspension travel would give them the height of the seat bottom.

The next measurement they needed was the length of the engine. They didn't have that exact measurement, but Carl was very familiar with the Cadillac V-12 on which the engine was based. In their preliminary design, they used the length of the Caddy engine as their baseline.

They planned to use a LaSalle transmission. They were strong, hopefully one would fit the engine, and they were fairly plentiful. Carl could get the dimensions from work.

The rest of the week they played with the numbers. They would set Billy in one of the kitchen chairs and "mock-up" the engine and transmission using boxes and crates and a wastebasket to simulate the transmission. Once they were satisfied with the relationship, they recorded their measurements and added them to the sketch they were working on.

On Saturday morning they got up early and headed across town to Tommy Jackson's house. Babe went with them in his newly acquired position sitting between them on the front seat. He enjoyed the view out the windshield and he reveled in sitting between the two most important men in his life, his father on one side and his friend that nicknamed him the Babe on the other.

Carl borrowed a tow bar from work and they packed the trunk of the LaSalle with all the tools either of them could anticipate they might need. Billy had asked Tommy if there were wheels and tires on the frame and what their condition was. Tommy assured him that all four wheels were there and all four tires at least held air. Nevertheless, they carried an extra wheel and tire with the Ford bolt pattern and an air pump in the trunk, just in case.

It was a pleasant morning as most were in San Diego. The sun was out and most of the early morning fog had burned off. Babe didn't enjoy getting out of bed this early on a Saturday morning, but he did enjoy driving down the nearly deserted city streets and seeing the city come to life after its overnight slumber. They passed several milkmen that were almost finished making their rounds. Babe wondered what it must be like to be a milkman. Starting your day when everyone else was asleep. Going house to house leaving frosty bottles of milk and blocks of creamy butter and picking up empty bottles. The same thing day after day, the same route, the same houses the only thing to look forward to was a note stuck in an empty bottle asking for another pound of butter or maybe a pint of ice cream. No, playing shortstop was infinitely better than that. The more he thought about it, the more he was certain even being the junior member of the groundskeepers was better than that. At least you were awake when the rest of the world was and besides, you got into all the games for free!

Babe also saw several boys delivering their papers. Contrary to the pictures he saw of paperboys on bicycles in the Saturday Evening Post, all the ones he saw on this morning were walking, their white canvas paper bags slung over their shoulders bulging with freshly printed newspapers still warm from the printing presses. He decided right then and there that throwing papers wasn't for him either. In fact, he thought, there was only one thing he wanted to do and that was to play baseball. He would concentrate all his energy from that day forward on achieving his goal. He suddenly felt more grown up and started the process of thinking of himself as a peer to the men who sat on either side of him rather than as the child lucky to get to ride in the front seat. This was the first time such an idea had passed through his mind however fleetingly. It wasn't there to stay just yet, nor would it be for several years to come, but it had been thought of. Nothing would ever be the same again, for once a thought passes through our minds, it is forever there, it can never be removed.

Carl pulled in to a donut shop. Babe's eyes were wide as saucers and a huge grin split his face at the unexpected and very infrequent treat. "Oh boy! Donuts!" he exclaimed.

"What? You don't like my cooking?" Carl said with mock indignation.

"Oh Dad, I didn't mean that! It's just that," he paused looking for the correct response, all the grown up thoughts from just seconds before having vanished. "It's just, DONUTS!" he shouted. Both men laughed. Billy could hardly get the door open and get out quickly enough to keep Babe from climbing over him. In a flash, Babe was in the shop and directly in front of the glass case that displayed a bewildering array of deep fried delights. Babe was already seriously at work trying to decide what and how many he wanted versus how many he thought Carl would allow him to have.

The shop smelled of sugar and flour and hot grease, but fresh brewed coffee was what appealed to the men the most. While Babe continued his ordeal trying to decide what he was having, both men were already working on mugs of the steaming brew. Their morning was now officially underway.

"Come on Frank, you've got to make a decision" Carl said.

"I know, I know, but there's so many and I want all of them!" Even the gray-haired lady behind the counter laughed at this. Finally Babe made his decision. They ate at a table by the plate glass window. Nothing was said as they ate. Billy was thinking about the car and how they would build it between thoughts of Sally. Carl thought what a wonderful morning it was to be spending like this. Eating donuts with your friend and your son and on the way to get parts for your latest project. Babe just thought "I'll take a bite of the chocolate iced one, then the pink iced one, then the twist, then the milk, then start over again. Little bites will make them all last longer. And, take it really easy on the chocolate. That's my favorite and I want it to be the last one I finish." Babe mused.

When they arrived at Tommy Jackson's house they found pretty much what they expected. It was a '35 Ford pickup frame and axles. John told them that at one time it was a U.S. Navy truck. It had caught fire one day on the flight line at the Naval Air Station. Luckily, a large fire extinguisher was nearby and the blaze was put out, but not before causing extensive damage. The Navy had written the truck off and sold it for salvage. Tommy bid on it at auction and won. He had already sold the body, engine and transmission. The steering was still attached but the steering wheel was nothing more than the wire frame all rusty from the fire. The bonus was that the Ford still wore its 16 inch wire wheels and while the tires were old and thin, the wheels were in good condition. Billy thought he would use the wheels for sure. The frame on the other hand had obviously been very hot at a location approximately where the fire wall had been. Here the metal was discolored, rusty and warped while everywhere else it was straight and greasy, or at least covered by a semblance of paint.

"Tommy, I think this will work great for us. Are you sure I can't pay you something for it?" Billy asked.

"Hell no! You'd be doing me a really big favor getting it out of here. My wife's on my ass about it all the time. At one time I thought I might do something with it, but it's not worth all the shit I get from her. Hell, if you haul it off, she'll probably be nice to me for a day or two at least." Tommy said. Everyone laughed. They hooked up the tow bar and pulled it out of the yard and onto the street.

On the way home, Billy thought about the real axle ratio. "Carl, what ratio do you think that rear end is?"

"Since it's a pickup, and it belonged to the Navy, it's probably a 4.44, but it might be a 4.11. That's a little lower than what you'll want to run I'd think. Another thing is adapting it to the transmission, of course we don't have one yet, but when we do, it might take a little ingenuity to get it done, but I bet we can handle it." Carl said confidently.

When they arrived home, Babe was just itching to get out of the car and head toward his buddy's house to get in some baseball. He was on his bike and gone in a flash.

Billy and Carl decided to strip the frame of all usable components in the driveway right in front of the shop. By that evening, both axles had been removed along with the transverse leaf springs, and were stored in the shop. All the brakes were still intact, but since they were mechanical, Billy didn't want to use them. He thought the new Ford hydraulic brakes were more reliable and would be easier to adapt to the new car. "Carl, don't you think it would be a lot easier to convert to hydraulic brakes than it would be to try and modify all this mechanical linkage crap?" he asked.

"It would be a helluva lot easier. I don't like those damn mechanical brakes anyway. They work okay when they're properly adjusted, but when they get out of adjustment they're pure crap! I've had more than one of 'em scare the hell outta me."

They agreed to keep the frame for the time being. It might come in handy to use as a source of metal to make parts out of. Neither man wanted to use it as the basis for their project. The worst part of it was since it burned, they doubted its strength. Billy didn't want it because it didn't look like what he thought his project should look like anyway.

Billy mentioned the surplus store at Consolidated. They needed virtually everything and he thought it would be a good source for material such as aluminum, steel and nuts and bolts. A visit was planned for the next Saturday.

Chapter 8

The next Tuesday as Billy walked down the sidewalk to the house, instead of the black LaSalle coupe being parked in the driveway, a green GMC stake bed truck was backed into the drive right in front of the shop doors. He could see the corner of a wooden crate peeking over the side of the bed. His heart raced as he was sure this was the engine Carl had told him about. He couldn't wait to get it unloaded and take a look at it.

He found Carl in the kitchen. "Is that what I think it is out in the truck?" Billy asked.

"It sure is" Carl replied, smiling.

"Yippee!! Let's go unload it!"

Carl backed the truck into the garage area of the shop. They used the chain hoist to lift the crate and then rolled it over into the shop area and let it down. It was a sturdy wooden crate and had Miller Engineering Co. Los Angeles, California stenciled on the sides in black paint. It was obvious that the crate had been stored for some time. There were stains and marks all over it and the wood looked old. It had recently been opened and then nailed back shut. Some of the nails were still new and shiny and there were holes where the original nails had been.

Billy wasted no time prying the lid off the crate. Inside the crate were several smaller boxes and right on top was a large manila envelope with Carl Mercer printed in large block letters in grease pencil.

Carl opened the envelope. Inside was one page that read:

CARL,
        HERE IS THE ENGINE AS WE DISCUSSED. IT HAS BEEN SETTING IN THE SHOP FOR SEVERAL YEARS, I THINK SINCE '35, BUT IT COULD HAVE BEEN '36. I CAN'T REMEMBER SHIT ANYMORE.   THERE WERE SOME OTHER PARTS HERE THAT WERE FOR THE SAME PROJECT.   THEY WERE JUST IN THE WAY SO I PUT THEM INSIDE THE CRATE. HOPE YOU CAN USE THEM. IF NOT, JUST THROW THEM AWAY, NOBODY WILL EVER MISS THEM. SAME GOES FOR THE ENGINE. IT TOOK SO LONG FOR IT TO EVER GET BUILT THAT THE BOSS FORGOT ABOUT IT.   THEN WHEN IT FINALLY DID GET HERE, HE WAS ON TO GREENER PASTURES.   HE'S NEVER SAID ANOTHER WORD ABOUT IT, HE NEVER EVEN SAW THE DAMN THING! HE COULD HAVE SPLIT ALL THE MONEY HE SPENT ON IT WITH YOU AND ME, COULDN'T HE? HA! HA! LIKE HE'D EVER DO THAT! GOOD LUCK WITH YOUR PROJECT. TELL FRANK HI FOR ME AND COME SEE ME NEXT TIME YOU'RE IN TOWN.
                        YOUR FRIEND,
                        BERNIE
P.S. THERE WEREN'T ANY CARBURETORS WITH IT.

Carl had to laugh at the reference to Tommy giving the money he had spent on the engine to his employees, even if it was two of his long-time managers. Bernie was right, Tommy would never dream of doing that. He doubted that it would even enter Tommy's mind to do so. As successful as Tommy's businesses were, he rarely handed out bonus money. It wasn't that he didn't appreciate his employees, his mind just didn't work like that. On the other hand, he could be quite generous on occasion. Carl had asked him about the engine when he saw him at Kearney Mesa. Tommy told him to take and use it for as long as he liked. He hadn't exactly GIVEN it to Carl, but it was on more or less permanent loan.

"What are all these other boxes?" Billy asked lifting them out one by one. The smaller boxes totally obscured the engine.

"Stuff Bernie says we might could use. Let's open 'em and see." Carl replied.

The first box they opened was an aluminum race car steering box. It was the style used on the Indy racers, the so-called "big cars". The pitman arm was included, but was unfinished. Other than the splined hole where the pitman arm attached to the steering box, no other holes were drilled. The steering box itself was all machined and cast aluminum. It was a work of art. It was designed to mount behind the dash of the car with the end where the pitman arm mounted exiting through the cowl area of the car. Positioning the steering in that manner was common practice on race cars to relieve congestion in the engine compartments of the narrow bodied cars of the day. Henry Ford might have won the Indy 500 in 1935 had his V-8 powered entries used such steering. Ford had commissioned Harry Miller to build 10 race cars for that year's Indy 500. All were to use modified versions of the famous Ford "flathead" V-8 engine and front wheel drive. The project was done on such a tight time schedule that there wasn't time for adequate testing. As a result, all the Fords dropped out of the race because the steering box was mounted too close to the exhaust header. As the race progressed, the steering gear was literally baked until it failed, causing several of the cars to crash into the wall.

Tommy bought one of the Indy Fords, as they were known. Apparently he was familiar with the problem, or certainly someone had been and a superior steering gear was planned for the LaSalle. It had never been used for its intended purpose and Bernie sent it along with the engine.

There were some other boxes in the crate also. One of them contained several Miller emblems. There were also a couple of brass fuel tees in the box. The other box contained a large cast aluminum fuel filler like those used on Indy cars.

Finally the engine itself was uncovered. Billy thought it was by far the most beautiful engine he had ever seen. It had a pair of polished cast aluminum cam covers secured by chrome acorn nuts. The plug wires were routed in a beautiful polished aluminum loom.

There was an aluminum intake manifold with mountings for twin carburetors. The engine mounts were attached. The engine was set up such that it leaned to the passenger side. This showed its lineage to the Cadillac V-12. It appeared that the left bank of cylinders had been removed and the right bank still leaned to that side.

"I like the way the engine leans to the side. That'll let us have a lower hood line. It reduces the total height of the engine, don't you think?" Billy asked.

"Yeah, it does. Of course, they started with a V-12 engine and just removed the left bank of cylinders. They just went with what was left. You're right, it makes for a much more compact package. Besides keeping the overall height shorter, it also moves the intake toward the center of the car, so it'll all fit under a more narrow body" Carl said.

"They damn sure thought about everything didn't they?" Billy was delighted with the engine. He had been prepared to buy an engine out of a wrecked car and then work on increasing its power output. That was a difficult process in those days. Speed equipment was only available for a few engines, most notably the Ford V-8 and 4 cylinders. There was some equipment for the Chevrolet 6. Equipment for everything else either didn't exist or was extremely rare. Information was equally scarce. He realized how lucky he was to have a professionally-built racing engine drop into his lap.

"Tommy is just going to let us use this engine for free?" billy asked, his voice filled with astonishment at his good fortune.

"Yeah, he is. I think the truth is that Tommy no longer has any interest in the project. This engine was not going to be competitive the day it was finished. I think it was a harebrained idea to begin with. You know Tommy started this in '30 or '31, right after the V-12 came out. He went to Miller to do the project. I think he really wanted to use the V-16 in the beginning, but old man Miller talked him out of that, but he couldn't talk him out of the project. Besides, Miller was in financial trouble by then and he knew Tommy had the money to bankroll the work. But Harry's heart was never in the project. At least that's what I heard. I think he just used it to get all the money he could out of Tommy. Actually, I think it wasn't finished and delivered until after Miller went bankrupt and Fred Offenhauser took over. Fred is a much more practical person than Harry ever was and he wanted it out of the shop. I think Tommy eventually figured out he had been had. When the engine finally arrived, he never even looked at it. It just got shoved into a storeroom at the dealership and forgotten until Bernie and I were talking. Bernie brought it up to me and told me the story. When I saw Tommy at Kearney Mesa, I asked him about it. He said we could use it as long as we wanted to," Carl said.

"I can't thank you enough Carl. Without you, none of this would be possible. How did you know that I was even interested in building a car? I don't remember mentioning it until after we left Kearney Mesa" Billy asked.

"Billy, you're not that hard to read. The first five minutes after we met were spent looking at and talking about the coupe. Then the first week you were here, how many times did we discuss that article you had read in Popular Science? You asked me about '100MPH Fords' at least twice a day that first week. I thought you were going to hyperventilate when I asked you if you would be interested in going to Kearney Mesa. Hell son, it's obvious that you love cars and especially modified ones." Carl chuckled and Billy had to admit it must have been pretty obvious. He wondered if his feelings for Sally were as visible. The mere thought of it caused him to blush.

To cover his embarrassment he quickly said, "I'm sure glad you asked him about it. It's hard to believe that all this is sitting here in the shop. I never could have imagined all of this. This engine will make one helluva car." Billy said gratefully.

"Don't forget it'll make one helluva car after one helluva lot of work!" Carl reminded him.

"Speaking of work, let's get this thing out of the crate. Then we can see about taking some measurements and we can look at what it will take to put a transmission on it" Billy said.

"I'm sure it'll take a LaSalle transmission. The back of the block looks like it hasn't been touched."

They removed the engine from the crate using the chain hoist to lift it out, and the trolley to move it over into the shop area. They placed it in position where the car would be built, using wooden blocks to hold the engine in the approximate position it would occupy in the completed car.

"Do you think we can use the truck to go to the wrecking yard and see about a frame?" Billy asked.

"I'm sure we can. When do you think? Saturday?" Carl asked.

"Yeah, I think that would be good. We also need to go by the surplus store at Consolidated. Do you think we could do both?"

"We ought to be able to. I'll just drive it home Friday night and we can use it all weekend." Carl said.

They spent the rest of the evening mocking up the car. The engine was blocked up in position, then they rolled the front axle in on its wheels and tires. They placed it in its approximate position. Next was the rear axle. It also was rolled in using its wheels and tires and placed in position. They measured the wheelbase to get it approximately right. A wooden chair was used for the driver's seat. Billy sat in the chair and they tried to visualize how much room would be required to make him comfortable. They both agreed that being comfortable was as important as trying to make the car compact.

"Are they going to let us run that engine in the time trials?" Billy asked.

"I don't know. I've thought of that myself. I'm sure we can run it, but what class it might fit into, I'm not sure. They let Tommy run his speedster and the Bugatti all the time. Both of them have DOHC engines built strictly for racing. Neither could be considered production car based. At least ours can. We'll have to wait and see. Are you interested in running for points for the championship?" Carl asked.

The SCTA changed their rules several times on the topic of DOHC engines. Originally, they banned all DOHC engines in an effort to keep someone with more money than ability from being able to bring a Miller or other purpose built racing engine out and beating all the home-built racers. Then they changed their rules to allow DOHC engines if they were based on a production block. This was done to allow conversions for Ford 4 cylinder engines. No one had ever seen anything like the LaSalle. It would be interesting to see what they did.

"No, I really don't care that much about the points, I just want to be able to make timed runs at the meets." Billy said.

"I'm sure they'll let you do that. Hell, they'll all want to see it run themselves. Everybody likes to watch a fast car and this one sure ought to be fast." Carl said, grinning.

They both felt good about that. They were sure it would be fast. Billy was confident that Carl was right in his estimate of the engine's power output. While being down compared to the engines of the day, it would at least be on par with the owner-modified engines being raced at the time trials. He could already feel the wind in his hair and visualize himself hurtling down the road at Kearney Mesa or maybe even across one of the dry lake beds where the big SCTA meets were held. He would love to visit one of those meets, especially at the wheel of his own creation, one unlike anyone had ever seen before. He could hardly wait to get started in earnest. Maybe if he went to one of the dry lakes meets, he might see Sally again. That was a happy thought. Carl had already told him that Tommy and the other LA area racers didn't come to Kearney Mesa all that often, but if he went to the lakes, maybe he might see her again. Now that would be worth more than any amount of championship points. He would have to start talking to Carl about going to Muroc or one of the other dry lakes. Maybe he could casually mention Sally at the same time? Maybe if he were really lucky Carl would volunteer something about her.

Saturday would be another parts gathering foray. He was looking forward to it, and it would be a great opportunity to ask about a lakes trip and Sally.

Chapter 9

"Whut ken I do for you boys?" the old man asked as he squinted out of one eye then shot a stream of tobacco juice at a rusty generator lying on the ground. He was nearly bald and had several days of stubble on his floppy jowls. He wore a grimy undershirt that might once have been white and a pair of overalls that were so encrusted with old grease that Billy was certain they had never been washed. He was just as certain that it would do no good at this point. No soap he had ever seen would even begin to cut the filth and if it did, would there be anything left, he wondered.

"We're looking for an Essex frame, actually just the rails are all we're after." Billy replied.

"You boys are buildin' a racer ain't ya?" The old main asked.

"Yes, we are." Billy said.

"Thought so, I sold several of 'em to them racer boys. Yeah, I got some. Take $5.00 for 'em, but you gotta pull the shittin' thangs your own damn self, ya hear?"

He held his hand out. "That'll be $5.00 cash money."

Billy pulled his wallet out and gave the man a $5 bill. "There's a Essex back in that far corner there," the man pointed. "It's a layin' up on its side. Pulled everythin' else offen it already. Ya kin have the frame offen that 'en. It's straight as a taut string it is." The old man spit again and stuffed the bill in the front pocket of his overalls. "Got yer own tools, cause I don't loan mine." There was a rusty old bucket with a few ancient wrenches and a broken screw driver sticking out of the top sitting behind the old man. On closer examination Billy realized that most of what he thought was rust was actually dried tobacco juice. He didn't think he wanted to use the man's tools in any event.

They found the Essex, or at least what was left of it. It lay on its side like the skeleton of a long dead steer, its bones bleaching in the sun. The Essex had been stripped of all usable parts by flocks of frugal parts vultures. The drive train and axles long gone. This was great for them as it only made their job easier. All they had to do was unbolt the frame from the remains of the body and carry it out. This they accomplished in about an hour. The frame was heavy, but Carl and Billy managed to carry it out despite Babe's help.

They loaded it in the truck and tied it down. When they had passed the shack where the old man was, Billy never even saw him look up. He wondered if the man even noticed as they walked by. He suspected the old man was a lot more observant than he appeared to be. They got in the truck and left.

"Carl, do we have time to go by the surplus store at work?" Billy asked.

"Sure," was the reply.

"What's a surplus store?" Babe asked.

"It's a store at Consolidated. Consolidated is where I work."

"I know THAT!" Babe said, obviously with his feelings hurt.

"Sorry Babe, I didn't mean to imply you didn't. Anyway, the surplus store is where Consolidated sells all kinds of things that they no longer have a use for. Only employees can buy stuff at the store." Billy said.

"Dad and I aren't employees." Babe said with concern.

"I know, but you two are my guests, since you're with me and I'm an employee, it'll be okay."

"Swell," Babe replied. "Maybe I can buy an airplane."

Carl and Billy both laughed. "What's so funny?" Babe asked.

"I don't think they sell airplanes there," his dad answered.

"Babe, they just sell parts like nuts and bolts and pieces of steel and aluminum. That kind of thing." Billy added.

"Awwww, I wanted an airplane!" Babe moaned with disappointment.

The surplus store was actually a small warehouse building on the grounds at Consolidated. There were piles of surplus materials to pick through. Sheets and partial sheets of aluminum and steel were stacked in mixed piles. There were boxes of rivets and nuts and bolts. Many of the items were things that had been swept up off the floor in the aircraft assembly area. Since there were so many different sizes and materials used, it would have required a tremendous amount of time to sort it all out and restock it. Consolidated had decided to simply sell everything to its employees to save time. Consequently, everything was mixed together in bins and boxes. It was up to the buyer to sort through it.

As they searched through some sheets of steel leaning against one of the walls, they found several pieces that seemed suitable for building the bodywork of the car. Billy asked the man who ran the store what the steel was, and the man told him he thought it was 19-gauge cold rolled sheet. They eventually found six sheets that appeared to be the same. Billy bought them all.

They also found several lengths of pipe about 1 5/8" in diameter. Billy had an idea for this and purchased it as well. They bought some smaller pieces of aluminum plate and a large bag of mixed-size rivets along with a box of mixed nuts and bolts.

As he was poking around through the piles of stuff tucked back in a corner of the building, Billy found a seat. It was built out of heavy gauge steel with a low back but high side bolsters. It had springs in both the seat bottom and back with a khaki snap on seat cover that was seriously ripped and torn, the cotton wadding sticking out. He thought it would be perfect for the car. He asked the man what it came out of, but the man said he didn't know. They both agreed it looked too heavy to have been used in an airplane. The man said it had been in the store for years and if Billy wanted it, he could have it for fifty cents. Billy took it, delighted with the purchase.

They loaded all their loot in the truck and headed home. Billy bought Babe a cloth aviator's helmet, the surplus store being completely out of airplanes. Babe was wearing the helmet and all the way home he pretended he was the brave pilot fighting his way through all manner of obstacles on his flight back to base. He was Errol Flynn on the dawn patrol. His fantasies were occasionally accompanied with sound effects that made Billy and Carl chuckle. Babe enjoyed the fact that he amused them and responded with longer and louder displays. Everyone was laughing as they turned onto their street and drove the last few blocks home.

A couple of blocks away Billy realized that there was a car parked in their driveway. All three of them were laughing over the fact that Babe had just given them a blow by blow description of the intrepid pilot hitting a tree with his wing in thick fog and crashing into the commander's bedroom winding up unhurt in the commander's bed. Carl and Billy were laughing to the point they had tears in their eyes. Babe was reveling in their laughter.

The car was a new tan Packard convertible coupe. "Carl, it looks like you have company, or did you buy a new car?" Billy asked.

Carl didn't say anything, but a smile crept across his face. By this time Billy and Babe were both looking intently at the car and didn't notice the knowing look on Carl's face. They pulled into the driveway behind the Packard.

Billy and Babe got out of the truck and walked up to the Packard, their attention totally on the car. "Wow! What a pretty car." Babe exclaimed. He was looking in the passenger side window. "I wanna go for a ride with the top down!"

"Hi strangers." a female voice said. They both looked up to see Sally standing at the banister on the front porch.

"Sally!" Babe yelled and ran up the steps to give her a big hug. "Can we go for a ride Sally? Can we go for a ride with the top down?" Babe was so excited he was jumping like he had springs on his feet; the flaps of the aviator helmet were flopping up and down like a pair of bird wings. Sally was laughing at him and said, "Sure we can go for a ride, and we'll put the top down if that's the way you want it. Can I say hello to everyone else before we go?"

"Oh sure, I can wait, but not long!" Babe yelled as he continued to impatiently bounce on the porch with the helmet flaps flopping up and down.

By this time Billy was standing on the porch behind Babe. Inside he felt like jumping up and down just like the Babe, but instead he stood there in embarrassed silence, afraid that his feelings were there on his face for the world to see.

Sally stepped around the bouncing Babe to hug Billy's arm. "Hello Billy," she said as she gave him a brief kiss on the cheek and squeezed his arm. He almost recoiled from the touch. It was as if an electric jolt coursed through his body. "Hi Sally," he said and blushed. He felt his face go red and especially his ears. He hoped Sally wouldn't notice. His thoughts about Sally were still confused. He knew he adored her, but had come to the conclusion someone as wonderful and beautiful as she was could never feel that way about him. He was using all of his willpower to try and keep from crushing her in his own embrace. Instead he just stood there and kept his eyes averted.

"Hi Sally, what brings you to town?" Carl was coming up the front steps. Sally met him and gave him a hug also.

"Hi Uncle Carl, oh I needed to come down and do a little shopping in Tijuana. I heard you guys were building a new car. I couldn't come to town without saying hi, and I thought you could show me the new car," Sally said.

Carl thought, "Yeah and I'm the King of England." but he didn't say it. "Sally we're always glad to see you regardless of the reason. You know Babe would've been heartbroken if he knew you were in town and hadn't come by to see him."

"Let's go for a ride!" Babe insisted.

"Frank, calm down. Can't you see that Sally must be tired. It's quite a drive down from LA. Let's give her a few minutes to relax before she has to chauffer you around." Carl insisted.

"Oh, okay! I'm sorry Sally," Babe said, his disappointment obvious.

"We'll go for a ride in a few minutes, okay?" Sally asked, and they all went into the house. As usual, they went to the kitchen. Carl always visited with close friends in the kitchen. He reserved the living room for acquaintances and more formal occasions. In truth, no one could remember when it had last been used.

"How about some iced tea, Sally?" Carl asked.

"That would be swell," she said. Carl began making some. Everyone took seats around the kitchen table.

"How long are you staying?" Carl asked.

"Oh, I don't know, a few days I suppose," she replied.

"You're staying with us I hope?" he asked.

Billy thought he was going to hyperventilate.

"I thought I'd just check into a hotel." she replied.

Billy's spirits crashed to the floor.

"Why don't you just stay with us like usual? We've certainly got the room and you would really add a little beauty around this place." Carl suggested.

"Please stay with us Sally! Please, please, please!" Babe chimed in.

"Oh, I don't know. I don't want to impose, you've got Billy here now." Sally said.

"You're not imposing, is she Billy?" Carl asked.

Billy hadn't said a word up to this point. "Of course, she's not imposing. Stay with us Sally," totally appalled that he had suggested such a thing.

"Please, please, please!" Babe added.

Everyone laughed. "Okay, I'll stay. How could a girl turn down so many gallant proposals?" She reached across the table to either side and gave Babe's and Billy's hands a squeeze. She lingered on Billy's just a touch longer than Babe's. Billy thought he sensed reluctance as she took her hand away. His spirits soared at the thought she would be staying with them.

Carl was still standing at the sink. He was just finishing up the tea. "Good! I'm glad that's settled then, how about some tea?" He poured tea for everyone.

He asked Sally about the drive down. She had left early that morning and the trip had gone without incident. It was summer and the weather was beautiful as normal.

Billy barely heard anything that was said. Sally was even lovelier than he remembered if that were possible. He luxuriated in her presence. He absorbed her beauty like a flower absorbs the rays of the sun. She was talking to Babe and Billy was totally content just to watch her. He finally snapped out of his reverie when she turned to him and asked "Billy, do you want to come with us?" Billy had no idea where they were going, he had totally missed the conversation intent on just looking at her, but he replied, "Sure, I'd love to go."

"I'll stay here and do a few things. You kids have fun." Carl said. "I'll move the truck so you can get out."

Billy suddenly remembered all the parts in the bed of the pickup. It was loaded down. "Carl, I better stay and help you unload the truck." He said hoping against hope that Carl would turn down his offer.

Carl noticed just a trace of disappointment on Sally's face. "Don't be silly. It'll all be here when you get back. Go on, enjoy yourself. You haven't left the place since you got here except to go to work. Go on, get!"

Billy's spirits soared once more, his silent prayer answered.

Carl directed all of them to the door. "Come on, off with you. Have fun and I'll see you for supper."

Babe ran out the front door and was at the Packard by the time Billy caught the screen door and kept it from slamming. He held it open for Sally and Carl.

While Carl moved the truck, Sally and Billy put down the top. It was a beautiful car, a tan Packard convertible with red leather seats and black top. It had whitewall tires with chrome bumper guards and fog lights.

"Sally, this really is a beautiful car." he said.

"Yes, I guess so. It's just a car." Sally didn't sound interested in discussing the car. Billy had the sudden thought that he and Sally were from two different worlds. In his world, a car such as this one was such an unusual event that it would be the obvious topic of any conversation, sort of like a five ton elephant in the room. When you were in its presence, how could you talk about anything else? On the other hand, Sally seemed to be completely oblivious to the car. Such obvious signs of wealth must be common to her. It was a very unsettling thought. He realized he knew nothing about her. Was the Packard a present? From Tommy? He became jealous at the mere thought. He put it out of his mind for the time being.

Babe was already in the middle of the front seat. He still had his cloth aviator's helmet on. It had replaced the normal Yankees baseball cap. Billy briefly wondered how long that would last. Sally got in behind the wheel and Billy slid in on the other side of Babe. They all waved to Carl as they drove off down the street.

"Where to Babe?" she asked, already picking up on Frank's new nickname.

"I don't care, just drive. This is really keen!" Babe replied.

"Okay, whatever you say, Babe."

The Packard was smooth and quiet, even more so than the LaSalle. He had never ridden in a car so nice. Sally drove through town and into the hills toward Point Loma. She turned on the radio and was rewarded with Glenn Miller's orchestra playing "In the Mood".

Billy thought life didn't get much better than this. Here he was under a beautiful blue sky in this wonderful car being driven through remarkable scenery by the most amazing woman he had ever met. They climbed up the twisting turning road toward Point Loma. Billy hadn't done much sightseeing since his arrival in San Diego, his time was absorbed with work and starting the car project. The drive was every bit the treat for him it was for Babe.

They drove past the now abandoned gun emplacements where his father had served briefly before shipping out for France in the war. Billy took them all in and wondered how different they had looked when his father was here.

They finally arrived at Point Loma lookout, the end of the road. There were a couple of other cars in the parking lot. One a family sight-seeing and taking pictures, the other a carload of teenagers looking somewhat annoyed that more people had invaded their area. As Sally parked, the teenagers all got in the battered Ford sedan and sped away down the hill leaving a spray of gravel in their wake as a reminder of their annoyance.

They got out admiring the view. Off to their right was the deep blue of the Pacific Ocean. On their left was a magnificent view of the San Diego Bay. They stood on a high bluff overlooking the channel out of the bay to the ocean. In the distance you could see the naval base and beyond, the city of San Diego. It was a beautiful view. They walked along the edge of the parking area and admired the scenery. The weather was perfect, the temperature in the low 80's and a nice sea breeze blowing in off the Pacific. Babe imagined he was an airplane and ran along the edge of the bluff in front of Billy and Sally with his arms extended as imaginary wings and a full range of sound effects.

"He's having fun isn't he?" Billy asked.

"Yes he is. He's a great kid. I heard you're responsible for 'the Babe'."

"Yeah, I am, guilty as charged. It just sort of came out and once said, it stuck. I think he likes it though." Billy replied.

"Carl says he loves it. He's already got all the kids calling him Babe. I think you've made quite a hit in more ways than one." Sally said.

As they continued to amble along the edge of the parking area, Babe ran up and down the hillside as his make believe airplane. Sally pointed out the sights to Billy. You could plainly see the Navy base across the bay. A small ship was slowly moving in the distance. Billy assumed it was a Navy ship because of the gray color, but at this distance he couldn't tell for sure.

"You know a lot about San Diego. How did you learn so much about it?" Billy asked.

"I visit here a lot. I really like San Diego. I like to shop in Tijuana, it's fun to haggle over prices and the people there are so friendly. I visit Carl and Frank, excuse me, and make that the Babe, every time I come. They're like family to me. I've always thought of Carl more as an uncle than a friend. You know he and my mother have been friends for years and years. It broke all our hearts when his wife died. Then he moved down here to San Diego, I think he was looking for a new start where everything he saw wouldn't bring back memories of her." Sally said earnestly.

"I really like Carl and Babe myself. They've made me part of the family right from the first day. It's been amazing how my life has changed in such a short time." Billy said with gratitude. .

"Oh? How has your life changed so much?" she was looking at him intently, the hint of a smile on her face.

He returned her smile with one of his own. "Well, let's see. Here I am in the most beautiful place I've ever been after being driven here in the most beautiful car I've ever ridden in by the most beautiful woman I've ever known. How's that for starters?" Billy smiled, looking deeply into her eyes as he spoke.

"Oh, go on now!" she laughed and bumped him with her shoulder.

"No, everything I just said is true." Billy said honestly.

"Thank you kind sir," she said, making an exaggerated curtsey.

"Just a few weeks ago I was back home in Texas. Texas is a beautiful state, but I've never seen a view to rival this one. I come from an average family. My father paints and papers houses for a living. We got by all right, as well as anyone else, but we didn't drive new Packards. Since I've been here, I met people like Tommy Lee. I never knew anyone as rich and powerful as he is."

Sally interrupted, "Tommy may be rich and I guess a certain amount of what you call power goes with that, but mostly what that means is that most people want something from him. That's the reason he's treated the way he is. People think he'll give them something they want. He's really just another man regardless of how he acts, or even what he has tricked himself into thinking."

"I'm sure you're right, but people like me wonder what it must be like to be able to have anything you want or do whatever you want to do, whenever you want to do it," he said.

"Don't kid yourself Billy, Tommy doesn't get everything he wants, believe me. In reality there are more restrictions on Tommy than there are on 'average' people, whatever that term means." Sally replied thoughtfully.

Billy wondered if she was trying to tell him something. He still wondered about her relationship with Tommy, but he decided to let it go. It stressed how little he knew about her.

"Now, are you going to tell me where you got the Packard?" Billy asked.

"My daddy gave it to me. It's no big deal really, he sells Packards. It's just a car; it gets me where I want to go. Now a question for you, tell me about this car you're building."

"Going to build, might be a better way to put it. We really haven't even started other than to accumulate some parts."

"Do you plan on racing it when it's finished?" she asked.

"Oh sure. After seeing the time trials, I decided it was something I would like to do. I like to build things, and I want to create something that's really mine, you know, uses my design, my ideas. When I saw Tommy's speedster and then Danny's modified and Bill's streamliner, it just triggered something inside me. I'd like to combine features from all of them into one car." He was careful not to add that he had hoped racing might allow him to see her again.

"Did you hear about Danny?" Sally asked.

"No, do you mean Danny Sakai? What happened to him?"

"He was killed last week. He was riding a friend's motorcycle and got in a race with a car. He lost control of the motorcycle and hit a telephone pole. He was killed instantly." A somber expression replaced her smile.

He couldn't believe it. He'd just talked to him two weeks ago. "That's terrible. I just met him at Kearney Mesa. He was a nice guy. He went out of his way to be nice to me and answer all my questions. I was looking forward to seeing him at the next meet."

"Yeah, a lot of people are going to miss him. He was such a jokester and comic. He kept everyone around him in stitches. Danny never took himself seriously you know? Why, one time he showed up on the starting line wearing one of those kid's beanies with a propeller on top. Everyone was laughing so hard they were crying. Danny just sat there in the cockpit with his goggles on and looked around with a straight face, like what is everyone's problem? It was so funny." She laughed. Billy liked the way she laughed.

He had to smile at the thought of Danny in the beanie. He realized that he had only scraped the surface of knowing Danny, but he missed him also. You never anticipate losing a person so young. He looked across the bay toward San Diego and noticed on the slope below them that Babe was now practicing his pitching. He was going through a wind-up like he was on a pitcher's mound and then letting fly with a rock. Billy saw that he accumulated a small pile of stones each waiting their turn to be flung toward the water several hundred feet below.

"You think we ought to head back?" he asked.

"We probably should, it'll be getting dark by the time we get back to the house. We don't want Carl to get worried."

Billy called to Babe. He came running up the hillside, the flaps on his helmet flying. "We leaving?" he yelled.

"Yeah, we better get going before it gets dark." Billy said.

"Shotgun!" Babe yelled.

Billy started to protest but Sally grabbed his arm. "Okay," she yelled back at the running Babe. He was almost to their level but angling toward the car. "You drive," she said to Billy and handed him the keys. Once more he started to protest, but she squeezed his arm again. "It's just a car, remember?" she smiled.

When they got back to the Packard, Babe was already holding the passenger door open. He was taking no chances with his rights to 'shotgun'. Sally left Billy's side and walked around to the open door. "Thank you kind sir," she said doing a slight curtsy and sliding to the middle of the front seat. Babe got in beside her and shut the door. Billy got in behind the wheel. It was a real treat to drive such a fine car. He found it an even bigger treat to have Sally sitting so close. He backed out of the parking spot being extremely careful at the wheel of the expensive automobile, and drove onto the road retracing their route down the hill.

It was late afternoon and the shadows were beginning to creep across the road. They drove back past the old gun emplacements toward home. Once again Billy tried to visualize what it must have looked like when his father was stationed there.

"I really had a good time. Thanks to both you very handsome men for escorting me," Sally said with mock formality.

"You're most welcome beautiful lady," Billy said. He was rewarded with her pressing against him momentarily. It was a wonderful sensation.

"Yeah, you're welcome lady," Babe said as he bumped against her. The bump jostled her slightly closer to Billy.

"I don't know about you two, but I'm pretty tired. I've had a long day already." She covered her mouth to stifle a yawn. Then she leaned over onto Billy's shoulder. "You mind? Will this bother you?" she said as she leaned against him.

"Not in the least. Make yourself comfortable," he replied, his heart already racing from her touch. She leaned her head onto his shoulder and snuggled against his side.

Babe said "Me too," followed by an enormous yawn and then he leaned against Sally's side. By the time Billy had driven them off the point, both of his passengers were sound asleep. He was extra careful not to disturb her slumber for fear that if she awoke, she would sit up. He liked the way she felt snuggled against him.

It was a good thing he had paid attention on the drive up. This was his first time to drive in San Diego, but he had been on several rides with Carl plus the bus rides back and forth to work. He was able to find his way home without incident.

It was almost completely dark when he turned into the driveway. The truck was backed in against the doors of the shop. He could tell the bed was empty. Carl must have unloaded all their finds by himself. Billy felt a pang of guilt for not helping.

By the time he was parked and the lights off, Carl was out on the porch. He came down the steps and said "Looks like you could use some help." He walked around to the passenger door and shook Babe to wake him.

Sally was still pressed closely against his side, her head on his shoulder and chest.

"Sally, Sally, wake up, we're home." he said softly. When she didn't stir, he repeated himself and patted her knee. Carl already had Babe out and was leading him into the house.

Sally finally stirred and as she did so she hugged him and snuggled closer for an instant, her head on his chest. "Okay, if you insist," she said in a slightly husky, sleep-softened voice. "Thanks for driving us home. I'm not sure I could have made it." She kissed him very lightly on the neck. "Would you mind bringing in my things? They're in the trunk." She slowly slid out behind him and exited through the driver's door.

Billy kept an eye on her as he opened the trunk. Her head was still lowered and she was rubbing her eyes. There were two matching leather suitcases and a make-up kit in the trunk. He managed to get them all in one long arm as Sally leaned against his free side. She put one arm around his back and the other around his waist and rested her head against his chest. "I'm so tired," she said and she leaned on him into the house. Billy didn't mind a bit.

As soon as they came in the front door Billy could smell spaghetti sauce. Spaghetti was Carl's best dish. He could also smell fresh bread. Sally seemed to revive a bit. Her head came up "Ummmm. That smells good. I'm starving." Billy was able to set the luggage down as Sally headed toward the kitchen, Billy followed.

Babe was already sitting at the table, a frosty glass of milk beside his plate. He was intently watching his father take a loaf of garlic bread out of the oven. A large bowl of spaghetti and meatballs was on the table along with a bowl of salad. A gallon jug of dark red wine sat beside Carl's plate and empty water glasses were at the other plates. Sally was already sitting down beside Babe. The kitchen table was square with one place setting on each side.

"Carl, it sure smells great!" Billy said as he took his seat. "You should have waited to unload the truck. I didn't want you to do that at all, let alone by yourself."

"Don't worry about it. With the hoist it was no problem. Okay, everyone dig in." Babe didn't need to be told twice, he already had the spaghetti bowl and was transferring a huge spoonful onto his plate.

"Be sure to get some of the salad too," his father reminded him.

"Ohhhhhh!" Babe grumbled.

"Frank!" his father said.

"Oh alright" Babe said, resigned to his fate.

Carl picked up the jug "Wine?" he asked.

"I'm sleepy already" Sally replied, but Carl was already pouring. "Okay, but you might have to carry me to bed," she said.

"Billy?" Carl asked, but once again he was already pouring. Billy never had wine like this. At first he wasn't sure he liked it, but after a few sips, he seemed to be getting used to it, maybe even liking it a little.

The meal was excellent. Carl always did a good job with spaghetti, but this was even better than usual. He accepted several compliments during the meal. He suspected, and rightfully so, that besides his culinary skills, everyone's hunger also contributed to the accolades.

"That was wonderful Carl," Billy said for at least the third time as he pushed his plate away.

"I think I'm gonna pop," Babe said to chuckles all around.

"I can barely keep my eyes open." Sally was beginning to droop noticeably. "Billy, will you help me with my bags?"

"Of course," he was up in time to help her out of her chair. Once more she leaned on him for support. He couldn't imagine anything better than her warmth against him. They made it into the entry and retrieved the luggage.

The spare room, the one Sally used on her visits to the Mercers, was on the opposite side of the house from Billy's, but it too looked out across the porch and front yard towards the street. Billy helped her to the room.

"Where do you want the bags?" he asked.

"Just leave them on the floor by the closet." She responded.

"Good night, Sally," he said turning to leave, "I had a wonderful time this afternoon."

She grabbed his arm just as he reached the door, "Wait," she said.

As he turned to face her, she wrapped her arms around him and pressed hard against him, her face upturned toward his. She pulled his head down and kissed him. It was more than just a friendly kiss and for the first time, he kissed her back. It was spontaneous and unexpected, at least on Billy's part. "I had a wonderful time too." They kissed again, this one longer than the first.

"You'd better leave now," she said with a dreamy smile. She held him just a moment longer, then gently pushed on his chest and closed the door.

Billy stood in the hall. His mind raced at what had just happened. A grin began to grow across his face. He could still taste her in his mouth, almost feel her warmth against his chest. It was the most exciting moment he had ever experienced. He finally turned and headed back to the kitchen.

Carl was sill seated at the table. All the dishes had been cleared away and Babe was nowhere to be seen. Carl poured another glass of wine for both of them as Billy entered the room. He looked up as Billy sat down.

"Enjoy your drive today?" Carl asked, just the hint of a smile on his face.

"Yeah, it was great." Billy was still a little dazed. He took a big swallow of the dark red liquid.

"You want to go out and see where I put everything?" Carl asked.

"Huh?" Billy was still lost in his thoughts of Sally, "Oh, sure!" Billy replied.

Carl tossed him a towel that was lying on the table. "Well wipe your mouth off. You must've gotten some spaghetti sauce on it, and lets go." He grinned.

Billy almost panicked. He hastily wiped his mouth with the clean white towel thinking how embarrassed he was to have kissed Sally with spaghetti sauce on his mouth. He finished wiping and when he looked at the towel he saw Sally's lipstick, not spaghetti sauce. He blushed bright red. He was sure his ears would burst into flames at any second. Carl laughed long and loud as he walked out the backdoor toward the shop.

Chapter 10

Billy awoke groggy and with a headache. His mouth felt fuzzy and he was slightly sick to his stomach, he felt funny and it wasn't pleasant, shaky was the only word that came to mind. It must have been Carl's wine he thought. It was his first experience with a wine induced hangover and he didn't like it. He only had two glasses, but they were big glasses. He resolved to limit his intake in the future; that is if he survived this time!

Bright sunlight was streaming in the open windows of his room, hurting his eyes that felt dry and scratchy. He could hear birds singing outside. Billy saw by his alarm clock that it was after 8 a.m. Even though, it was Sunday morning, he decided to get up regardless of how he felt. Maybe some breakfast might make him feel better. Thoughts of last night's goodnight kiss flooded his brain temporarily erasing any discomfort he felt. He got up, pulled on some pants and headed to the bathroom, thrilled to have slept under the same roof as Sally.

Billy finished brushing his teeth, and his mouth felt better. Now for something to eat he thought. As he opened the door to leave he smelled the wonderful aromas of bacon frying and fresh coffee brewing. He headed toward the kitchen. Billy could hear the bacon sizzle and pop. His stomach growled.

When he walked into the kitchen, he found Carl sitting at the table, a cup of coffee in his hand. Sally was at the stove taking up the last of the bacon. She was wearing a thick white terrycloth robe and slippers. "Good morning glory," she said with a dazzling smile. How could she feel so good when he felt like crap he thought? Then he remembered, she only had one glass of wine last night. This was a smart lady.

"You look like something the cat drug in," Carl chimed in. "Don't tell me two glasses of Gallo's best was too much for you?" he chuckled.

"How do you like your eggs?" Sally asked.

"Fried hard please and good morning to you too; or at least I think it's a good morning. Carl, what did you put in that stuff we drank last night, Kerosene?"

Sally and Carl thought this was extremely funny. Billy poured himself a cup of coffee. "Billy, would you get the toast out of the oven, please?" Sally asked.

"Of course, anything to help, even in my near invalid state. Where's the Babe?" he asked.

"Right here," Babe replied as he walked in rubbing sleep from his eyes. Billy poured him a glass of milk as he sat down. Sally had the eggs finished and they all sat down to eat.

As he finished eating, Billy found he felt considerably better with food in his stomach. He was almost human again. He noticed how radiant Sally looked, her face framed by the collar of the robe. Even though she had no make-up on, it didn't matter, she was beautiful, maybe even more so without it. Her face glowed.

"What are your plans today Sally?" Carl asked.

"I thought I would drive on down to Tijuana and do some shopping. Want to come?" she asked.

"No, I better stay here, but Billy why don't you go?" Carl said.

"I can't leave you here alone again today." Billy responded.

"Of course you can. Have you ever been to Tijuana? We can work on the Special any time, but how often is Sally here. I'm sure she won't mind you tagging along, will you Sally?" Carl thought to himself that Sally would die if Billy didn't go. He was quite proud of himself for suggesting it in such a clever manner. He silently patted himself on the back.

"Come on Billy, go with me." Sally replied.

There was no way Billy could turn down such an offer, not that he wanted to. He pushed his willpower as far as it would go already. He was about to reply when Babe butted in, "Well don't ask me, I've got a ballgame today with the guys. After all, I already missed yesterday!" they all laughed.

"I guess you're stuck with me then," Billy said. "How long till we leave?"

"Give me 30 minutes, okay?" Sally said as she rushed toward her room.

"And Frank, you get to do the dishes," Carl told Babe.

"Oh Dad! I don't have time!" Babe complained.

"Then you better make time, son."

Billy was sitting on the front porch when Sally came out. Billy stood; he had on his only sports coat and pair of slacks. Sally thought what a handsome man he was; so tall, thick black hair, green eyes with an almost perpetual smile on his face. The smile was one of the things that attracted her to him. That and the passion he seemed to bring to everything he did. He was the most optimistic and happy person she had ever known.

"Don't you look swell!" she said with a smile. Billy did some admiring of his own. It was the first time he saw her in a skirt. She had a light sweater tied around her shoulders and as she turned around for him the hem of her skirt flared out slightly. Sally's legs were as shapely as he had known they would be. She took his arm, "You look pretty swell yourself you know," he said as they walked down the steps and across the lawn to the car.

"You drive, okay?" she asked, as she handed him the keys. He walked her to the passenger door and held it open for her to enter. He was rewarded with a dazzling smile. His heart skipped a beat.

Carl came out on the porch as they were backing out of the driveway. "You kids have fun and don't come home for supper. I have plans tonight." he called as they backed onto the street. They both waved at him as they drove away. There was a new peace in his heart as he watched the Packard disappear down the street. Billy was the best thing that could have happened to Sally. There was finally a man in her life, a decent man that would care for her and put her needs ahead of his own. Carl was a good judge of character and he knew Billy was the kind of person you could rely on. He did what he said and he would stand by you through thick and thin. These were rare qualities indeed in the world Sally had grown up in. What a stroke of luck it had been when he put out that 'Room for Rent' sign. On second thought he wondered if luck had been all that was involved.

Carl turned and walked down the drive toward the shop. He needed to take the truck back by work and retrieve his coupe. Then he planned to come back home and do a few things on the Special before cleaning up and going out for dinner. After all, even the head of the house could take an occasional night off couldn't he? Babe was spending the night with Charlie and that left Carl free for the night. A brief smile crossed his face at the thought. He started the truck and drove off down the tree-lined street.

"What do you think he meant by the 'I have plans tonight'?" Billy asked.

"I'm happy he does. When his wife died I worried that he would ever get over it. I was heartbroken when he decided to move down here to San Diego, but I think it was the best thing for him and Babe too. After a few years here and away from the daily reminders of Sarah, he started to come out of it. He's close to his old self again now. I'm glad he has plans. Carl does pretty well with the ladies you know. Lucky women have a sixth sense about men. They can tell the good ones from the bad. I really feel sorry for those that don't have it, but the smart ones; they can tell that Carl is the real deal. And don't forget those blue eyes of his. Carl can melt a heart or two." Sally said.

"You've got a set of those blue eyes yourself." Billy said. Just forming the words seemed to crystallize a thought in his mind. Her eyes were startlingly blue, just like Babe's *and* Carl's.

"Yes, I know." She said and she looked out the side of the car pretending to have her interest fixed on some imaginary point hoping this conversation would go somewhere else.

Billy sensed her unease and decided to let the issue drop. "What are we going to do in Tijuana?"

"We're going to shop of course!" Her good mood returned and she turned to face him again.

"For what?" he asked.

"It doesn't matter, it's the shopping that's important, not what you buy. Don't you know anything?" she laughed while rolling her blue eyes.

"I guess not. Don't we have to have a passport or something to go into a foreign country?"

"Not just to cross over into Tijuana. People do it every day. It's not a big deal."

"You're going to have to give me directions." He cautioned.

"It's easy, once we get to the highway, you just head south. The highway ends at the border."

They both enjoyed the drive. As was usual in San Diego, the weather was perfect. It was another bright sunny day. They had the top down. The Packard seemed to glide down the road. It was almost silent. Sally scooted over in the seat until she was beside Billy. "Do you mind?" she asked.

"Are you kidding?" he replied, and put his arm around her.

The drive was even more pleasant now. Billy had a feeling of contentment unlike any he had ever known. It was a very nice feeling and yet it was strange. It felt as if he was now whole, but until now he hadn't realized he was missing anything.

The scenery was spectacular. The blue of the Pacific Ocean contrasted with Coronado Island. The Hotel Del Coronado with its white paint and distinctive red roof stood out like a sparkling diamond. There were gray painted warships at dock, sailors in dungarees and some in white swarmed over the decks. Billy never saw a real war ship before. He was fascinated by their sleek lines and the ominous threat of big guns sprouting from their turrets. Multicolored flags fluttered at the mastheads.

Crossing the border was nothing, just as Sally had told him. He drove through narrow and cramped streets in the 'Mercado', meaning market according to Sally, section of town. All the people on the streets, and they were very crowded, turned to watch as they drove by. Billy wondered if it was the car or if they were looking at Sally. It made him a little uneasy, although many of the people smiled and a few even waved when he returned their stares. Sally seemed not to notice the stares. It was as if she had a personal relationship with everyone they passed. She waved, exchanged smiles, and even spoke to a few people in Spanish.

"Where did you learn to speak Spanish?" Billy asked.

"In school, and our housekeeper speaks Spanish."

Billy didn't know anyone who had a housekeeper, but of course he didn't know anyone that drove a new Packard convertible either, much less that would ever call it 'just a car'. He decided to let that pass. After all, did it really matter what Sally's background was, or how rich her family was as long as she was sitting beside him? He thought not, and besides there would be plenty of time for him to find out all the details if he really needed to know them.

"Let's park up ahead there on the right. You see where all those kids are in the street waving at us?" Billy indicated that he did. "Just pull in there. Domingo will watch the car for us."

It didn't take long for Billy to find out who Domingo was. As soon as they were close to the mob of kids, all of whom were motioning for them to pull into the gravel lot, one young boy ran to the passenger side of the car. As he ran alongside the Packard, he carried on a very animated conversation with Sally. Billy heard him call her 'Miss Sally' several times but the rest of the conversation was in Spanish. The boy held the door open for Sally once the car came to a stop. Billy came around the car and as he took Sally's arm she said "Gracias Domingo," and they walked away toward the street.

"Don't you think we should have at least put the top up and locked the car?" Billy asked.

"Oh no, that would be an insult to Domingo. I pay him to watch the car while we're away. No one will touch it. Domingo would protect it with his life if he had to, but no one will bother it. That's the way it works down here. They have their customs the same as we do. As long as you abide by their customs and treat them with respect, they will treat you the same way. They're a very honorable people." She said.

The street was lined on both sides with tiny shops. Their wares displayed on the sidewalk in front of each shop. At each there was at least one person more than willing to show all the items for sale and explain how theirs were the best in all of Mexico and how much they were willing to deal on the price. There was a staggering array of goods. The entire place bustled with an explosion of colors and sounds. Sally engaged in conversation with each vendor they encountered. She kept Billy up to date on the negotiations and translated the high points of what was being said.

Back home, Carl retrieved the coupe and was in the shop studying the Essex frame they purchased the day before. Many racers of the day preferred the Essex frame rails to any other. They were built of superior material and perhaps most importantly, they were long and straight and they weren't drilled full of holes. The rails themselves were stamped into a C section when viewed from the end. While this design was strong enough for the original car, Carl felt like more was needed for a high performance automobile. He and Billy discussed the frame and decided to 'box' the frame rails. This procedure involved welding a plate down the entire length of the frame on the open side. This changed the C into a rectangle or 'box'. This would make the frame much stronger. They also discussed additional strengthening, but the rails came first.

Carl began by taking measurements of the rail. He then measured and marked a piece of 1/8" steel and used the cutting torch to cut it out. The resultant piece was slightly larger than would fit into the side of the C and it was rough around the edges. He used the bench grinder to work the edges down smooth. It took a while, but was well worth the effort. The section he worked on was four feet long. He decided to make the boxing plates in shorter sections for convenience and because he didn't have any steel long enough to do otherwise. Carl constantly checked for fit as he ground on the metal. Eventually he got the plate trimmed down. He knew a perfect fit would lead to a superior weld. Once he was satisfied with the fit, he clamped the plate into place and tack welded it in. After it was tacked, he welded it continuously down each edge. He was careful to weld in short one inch sections, constantly alternating from one end to the other and side to side. He also took several breaks to allow it to cool. Carl didn't want the frame to warp from too much heat concentrated in any one spot.

As he worked he thought about Sally and Billy. He hoped they were having a good time. There had never been enough joy in Sally's life, but sometimes that's what life deals you. He hoped meeting Billy would change that. It was obvious to him the instant they met that there was a spark between them. He knew Sally and he could tell she had more than a passing interest in Billy. It was just as easy to see how taken Billy was and the more he came to know Billy, the better he liked that. The whole situation put him in a very happy mood. Good thoughts, and good work, what an enjoyable and relaxing way to spend the day. Just anticipating Billy's reaction to the work he was doing was enough to make him smile. The afternoon passed quickly.

Even as big as Billy was, he struggled under the weight of their purchases. He hoped the trunk of the Packard would hold it all. Sally also had her arms full. As they rounded the corner onto the parking lot, Domingo saw them coming. He opened the trunk and then came running to help. He relieved Sally of her load and carried it back to the car, carefully putting each item in the cavernous trunk. He then helped Billy stow all of his packages.

"Muchos Gracias Domingo," Sally said and pressed a bill into Domingo's hand. His eyes grew wide and he immediately hugged her. "Muchos Gracias Senorita!" he exclaimed, a wide grin on his face. Once again he held the door open for Sally. They exchanged more conversation in Spanish as Billy got in the car and started it.

Domingo stood away from the Packard as Billy backed up and drove away.

"What did Domingo say?" Billy asked.

"He was just telling me how much he enjoyed taking care of my car and asked me to be sure and give him my business on the next trip. He's really a good kid and quite the enterprising businessman. He also said you're the tallest gringo he's ever seen," Sally said while giggling.

Billy noticed that the car had been completely cleaned. There was not a speck of dust on it anywhere. Even the carpets had been swept. He was impressed. "He certainly cleaned up the car." Billy said, admiring the results.

"He does that every time. He takes good care of me."

"What are you going to do with all the stuff you bought?" Billy asked.

"I'll give it for gifts mostly. I just enjoy the shopping and the people. Prices are really cheap, it's just fun." Sally replied.

As they drove back to the north, they noticed that the sky was getting dark to the west.

"Looks like we may have a storm brewing," Billy said. "It hasn't rained since I've been in San Diego. Do they have bad storms here?"

"Not usually. We may get some lightning and thunder, but probably not a storm like you have in Texas." Sally said, looking at the clouds to the west.

As they left the border it was late afternoon. The shadows were getting long and there was a stiff breeze blowing in off the Pacific. The storm was brewing and the western sky was getting very dark, clouds blocked the setting sun. Night was coming on quicker than usual. You could see lightening in the storm even though it was still out to sea. There were faint rumbles of thunder as they drove north.

"Are you getting hungry?" Sally asked.

"Yeah, I am. Do you know a place?" Billy asked.

"If you like seafood, I know the best place," Sally said. She gave Billy directions to the restaurant.

The restaurant sat on a steep hillside overlooking the ocean. It was a small place, the building was wood and Billy guessed it dated to the turn of the century. There was a gravel parking lot and it was getting so dark that by the time they arrived, Billy was using the headlights to drive. The storm was much closer to shore now.

They parked the car and put up the top and rolled up the windows. Sally took Billy's arm once more and steered him inside.

As they came in the door, they were greeted by a rotund man wearing a starched white shirt and apron. He had glossy black hair slicked straight back and a pencil thin mustache graced his upper lip. His grin revealed a mouth of straight white teeth.

"Miss Anthony! So nice to see you again! It looks like you just beat the storm. Your usual table? And, who's your handsome guest?" he asked, a sly look on his face.

"Good to see you too, Tony. This is Billy Pendleton, he's new to California. I've already told him you have the best seafood in the world."

"You're too kind! We will try not to disappoint."

Tony led them through the barely lit room. The ocean side of the building was entirely wooden paned windows giving a magnificent view of the Pacific and the storm. The wind was picking up and the lightning flashes were much closer. The crack of thunder was growing louder. Only a few of the tables were occupied as was usual on Sunday evenings, especially when faced with an impending storm. The table he took them to was in the far corner with windows facing west and north. The view was spectacular. "Thank you Tony" Sally said while Tony held her chair as she sat down. "My pleasure Miss Anthony, shall I start with some wine or a drink perhaps?" he asked. Sally ordered a bottle of wine, a California vintage, as was her preference.

"I better be careful, I had a headache from drinking wine with Carl last night, remember?" Billy said, and they both laughed.

"How much wine did you drink anyway?" she asked.

"It was only two glasses, but they were big glasses!" he said just as thunder crashed and the first gigantic drops of rain hit the windows like rifle shots. The rain and the dark obscured the ocean view except for when the lightening crashed. Their corner of the room was very intimate. The only light came from the candle on their table. "So, Anthony is your last name?"

Sally laughed. "Yes it is, Sally Anthony at your service. You didn't know my name?"

Billy shook his head no as Tony returned with the wine and poured glasses for each of them. Sally ordered her favorite dish, a variety of grilled seafood for two. Tony retreated and they turned their attention to each other.

Sally lifted her glass and said, "To a wonderful day spent with a most wonderful companion," their glasses clinked together in a toast.

"To my day with the most beautiful woman I know," Billy replied. Sally looked deep into his eyes. There was a pause as she evaluated what she saw there. "Thank you," was her simple reply.

They talked, exchanging information about their lives and got to know each other. Billy discovered that Sally's daddy owned the Packard dealership in Los Angeles and was a close friend but intense rival of Tommy Lee's. He also discovered that Carl and Sally's mother were neighbors and childhood friends. They had been as close as brother and sister. Her mother had also known Frank Lockhart and the three of them were like family. The relationship became more distant when Sally's mother married Earle. He had already been a very successful car dealer and businessman and didn't consider Frank and Carl his social equals, not to mention he was many years older. This created a strain on the marriage in the early years and had also driven the three childhood friends apart.

Billy told Sally about his life and family back in Texas. He told her how his father loved to fish and about their trips to the Texas gulf coast. He told her about his mother and what a good cook she was. He told her about his kid brother, what a daredevil he was and how they were best friends. He also told her how their friends liked to visit their home and how they all seemed to consider his parents almost as their own. It seemed more an extended family than anything else, with his home as a gathering place for all of them.

Sally was enthralled listening to Billy tell his story. She could see how much he loved his family and friends. She sensed the deep emotion and the love in his heart for them. They were simple people that lived ordinary lives, but he was extremely proud of each of them. He told her stories about the kind of work his father did and what a craftsman he was. How he had served in France during the war and what a great shot his father was. How much his mother loved them all and the sacrifices she bore to give each of them all she could. And about his little brother and the adventures they had shared together. How quick tempered and fearless he was and how Billy tried to temper those strong emotions.

The light in Billy's eyes as he described those he loved was a totally enthralling experience for Sally. She wished she felt the same way about her own family. She had never formed a close bond with her father. Her older brother was clearly her father's favorite. Sally always seemed an afterthought, always a "you too Sally". Her mother tried to make up for this in the early days, but as time passed, her mother sought refuge in a bottle of scotch. Sally never wanted for any material things, but she was bankrupt of her parent's emotions. She had a much stronger relationship with Carl and Frank than she ever had with her own parents. Her bond with Carl and Frank was deep and strong and they were the main reason she visited San Diego so often, regardless of what she said about shopping. She needed to recharge herself emotionally and this was the only place she could do it. Now she had another reason to visit.

Tony brought their food. It was easily the best Billy ever had and certainly lived up to Sally's billing. Outside the rain continued to beat against the windows. Had Billy spent the time to look at his surroundings, he would have seen a small bar against the land side wall, all of its stools empty. A large mirror formed the backdrop to the bar and echoed the flashes of lightening as did the array of bottles in front of it. Only a couple of tables were occupied and with the intensity of the storm, it was doubtful any new patrons would be arriving. As Tony poured more wine another couple rose to leave.

But Billy scarcely noticed the surroundings, his attention focused totally on his companion. He loved the way the candlelight was reflected in her eyes, the way he sensed more than saw a smile on her face when she talked to him. He reveled in her total attention, the storm outside completely forgotten and unnoticed.

An especially violent bolt of lightning accompanied by an immediate thunderclap finally demanded their attention. As they looked about the restaurant, they discovered they were its only occupants, theirs the only candle still lit, their wine bottle empty.

"You think we should consider leaving so Tony can go home?" Billy asked.

Sally thought it remarkable that Billy seemed to consider other people in everything he did. She was rarely exposed to this in her world. "Yes, I think so." Billy insisted that she let him pay for dinner and he left some bills on the table. They rose to leave. Tony, ever the attentive host, appeared at the door with an umbrella to walk them to their car. The storm still raged outside.

"Tony, we'll be fine really. There's no sense in you going out in this. Then all three of us will get wet." Sally said, and they rushed out into the night.

As they ran to the car, Billy tried in vain to hold his sports coat over Sally as she ran in front of him. The storm proved to be a relentless foe. By the time they got to the car, got the door open and got in, they were both drenched to the skin and laughing uncontrollably. Billy started the Packard and as he turned on the lights to leave, the soft glow from the dash revealed Sally's white blouse plastered to her skin and almost transparent, her bra and its thin straps clearly visible. She looked at herself and then at him and they both laughed again. She leaned against him, her head on his shoulder, as she hugged his arm he could feel the soft swell of her breast. They drove away with Sally pressed tightly to his side.

84

The pair huddled together, grateful for the shared warmth of each other's body. It was difficult to say which enjoyed the drive home the most.

It was still raining when they arrived home, but the storm had spent its fury, only a sprinkle left. Carl's car was nowhere in evidence, so Billy pulled far down the drive to allow room for the coupe behind them. They ran into the house splashing through several puddles.

As they entered the front hall, Sally turned to Billy and said, "Oh! Billy I meant to get the two large boxes out of the trunk. Would you mind getting them for me?"

"Of course not! I'll be right back." Billy turned and ran back to the car. He remembered those boxes had gifts for Carl and Babe; a very nice straw fedora for Carl and a catcher's mitt and facemask for the Babe. The rain had completely stopped. There was far away lightning, the muted thunder coming long after the flash, but still bright enough to light up the night. He retrieved the boxes and headed back to the house. Billy thought about how wonderful a day it had been. He looked forward to seeing Sally one more time before the night was over. There was no longer any question about their feelings for each other. The evening erased any doubts that may have lingered. Upon reflection, he thought their bond formed the instant they met and had only grown stronger. The evening simply brought it into crystal clarity for him and for Sally too he hoped.

He mounted the steps and entered the house turning down the hall to Sally's room. The door was closed and he tapped lightly on the door. Sally opened the door and held it open as he carried the boxes in. "Would you just put them on the floor over by the closet please?" She asked as he entered. "Sure," he said. The room was dim; the only light a small lamp on the nightstand. It was furnished with heavy oak furniture that came with the house when Carl bought it. He said the furniture was from France and was quite old. There was an enormous armoire whose door framed a large mirror. The bed was an equally massive sleigh style. A row of four open windows faced out onto the front porch and another row lined the wall to the right of the bed. They too were open. You could smell the fresh rain outside. A fan ticked softly as it spun its lazy circles.

Billy squatted and set the boxes on the floor. As he started to rise, he heard the door close and the light clicked off. He stood and turned. Sally was standing facing him, her back to the door. Enough soft light entered the room from the open windows for him to see she was staring intently into his eyes, once again looking deeply inside of him. Her lips looked soft and full but they carried no trace of a smile, the moment and feelings too intense for any humor. She searched his eyes for a long moment and he hers. He would never know how long that moment lasted, it could have been seconds or hours, time had stopped. The thoughts that had been of two separate individuals vanished, replaced by those of a single being, united, newly born, learning about itself.

She was wearing her thick terry cloth robe. She opened her arms beckoning him to her. Time seemed to stand still.

They were in the big bed. Their senses filled with each other and the smell and feel of the freshly washed sheets and the smell of wet grass and fresh rain. The fan continued to tick. The flashes of the lightening brought flashes of cold blue light to their union.

After they were spent, they lay cupped together, Sally's back against Billy's front. He had her cradled in his arms, and she hugged his arms tighter around her. Sleep found them.

Chapter 11

Billy awoke to the first rays of dawn glowing through the open windows. Sally lay cupped against his body, still asleep. His face was buried in her hair, he loved the way she smelled

The most perfect feeling of contentment passed over him. He was certain that no moment in his life would ever surpass this one, the woman he loved now and forever in his arms. He lay there for a long while enjoying the sensation of her body next to his. He felt her stir, the movements slow and fluid. She was coming awake, at least in part.

"Good morning lover," she said in a soft husky voice, felt more than heard.

After a while, they once more lay in each other's arms. He knew he had to leave before the rest of the house was awake. "I love you," he said.

"I love you too, with all my heart and all my being," she replied.

"I have to go," he paused, and then added, "my life will never be the same." He stood to leave.

"Mine either, you know that don't you?" she said holding his hand, reluctant to let him leave.

"I know," he started to put on his wet clothes.

"Take my robe," she offered. He stopped and stood for a moment. She enjoyed the view. He stooped and picked up the robe. Sally was a tall woman at 5'10", but he still looked ridiculous in her robe. His long arms and legs far from covered, but still it was warm and dry, much better than his cold wet clothes, they both laughed at the sight.

"Leave it in your room and I'll get it later," she said.

He kissed her goodbye and they exchanged another caress. "Goodbye lover," she said as he softly padded out the door.

Monday at Consolidated passed especially quickly. Billy noticed that everything was more intense than usual. It seemed like all the colors were brighter, all the people nicer than ever before. He saw things more clearly, heard sounds more distinctly. All of his co-workers noticed that their normally happy friend was even happier than normal. He seemed to float through the day.

Sally stayed in bed until after Billy and Carl both left for work. Then she got up and showered. As she dressed, she thought about the night before. The memory filled her with a warm glow. It was a wondrous feeling to start the day with. She decided she had a very special shopping trip to make. She wanted to get Billy a surprise. She left a note for Babe as she left the house.

Babe,

I went shopping, I'll be back this afternoon. I left you a sandwich in the icebox. Hope you have fun today. You're very special to me.

Love you, Sally

That evening Sally had supper cooked and waiting for them all when they arrived home from work. It was a real treat. Sally was a great cook and in times past, their evening meals had been a little hit or miss.

After dinner, Babe took off on his bike to get in a little more ball before dark. Carl and Billy headed toward the shop to work on the Special. Carl was anxious to show Billy what he accomplished the day before. Sally told them to go ahead; she needed to clean up in the kitchen. Carl went out the back door, Billy lingered until he was out of sight, then he gave Sally a quick hug and kiss. Sally chuckled and said "You better run along, lover. Carl will miss you. I'll be out to see you as soon as I get finished here." With that, she gently shoved him toward the door. They were still trying to keep their relationship clandestine, but the attempt was useless, Carl already knew. It would be a while before they understood this, Sally would figure it out sooner than Billy. Special relationships between people are almost impossible to disguise.

Carl was like a proud parent when Billy walked into the shop, eager to display his handy work. He had cut and welded boxing plates into one of the Essex frame rails. It was a fine piece of work. With a minimal amount of grinding, it would be almost impossible to tell that the rail had been modified.

"This looks terrific, Carl." Billy said. Carl was proud that Billy was pleased.

"I was thinking about the frame. If we were to use quarter elliptic springs on the rear and a single transverse spring on the front, the frame rails could be straight. We wouldn't need to build any kickups on the front or the rear. What do you think?" Carl asked.

"I like that idea. We sort of laid that out before. Let's set everything in place and see how it looks."

As they were completing the mocking up of the chassis, Sally walked in. "Okay guys, I want to help. Since both of you think about nothing but this car," she noticed Billy blushed, "if I want to see either of you, I know it'll have to be in this shop. So put me to work." She commanded with humor.

"Alright, we can do that. We'll try to teach you as we go along. The first thing is that we have taken to calling it 'the Special'. That's short for 'Miller – LaSalle Special'. Since Tommy has given us the use of the engine, that's what we decided to name it." Carl said.

"Is it a LaSalle motor?" she asked.

Both men laughed. Billy replied, "Well, it is kind of. Supposedly, it started out as a LaSalle/Cadillac V-12. Harry Miller's shop rebuilt it into a 6 by cutting off 6 of the cylinders. But when we examine it, it looks like it uses mostly newly designed and built pieces. But since Tommy's father planned to run it as a modified LaSalle, we will too. It's the least we can do."

At that point, they forged ahead. At first Sally had no idea what to do, but both of her companions were thrilled that she chose to spend her time with them and they were more than willing to show and teach her all they could. To her surprise, and theirs, she enjoyed the work. She wasn't doing any of the welding or cutting, but she proved to be a very able assistant, getting tools, helping to hold pieces in place, and to everyone's surprise, she proved to be the best of them all when making patterns for new parts.

About dark, Babe rode in on his bicycle, his baseball glove hanging from the handlebars. He stayed in the shop until his bedtime. This set the pattern for many nights to come. All four of them in the shop, spending their time together and working on the Special. Billy and Carl did most of the work, but everyone made contributions.

That night they worked on finishing the 'boxing' of the frame. The frame was the foundation of the car. Sally making the patterns, Billy cutting and grinding the plates, and Carl welding them in. As they worked, they also visited with each other, telling of the day's activities or sharing plans and ideas for the Special.

They agreed to shut down about 10pm each night. Carl told Babe he could stay up until that time during summer vacation. As they were leaving the shop Sally said "Billy, would you come by my room, I have something for you."

Carl's interest was piqued, but he said nothing. After all, it really wasn't his business other than they were both family and lived in his house. He decided long before to simply let this play out as it would. He would stay out of it.

Billy was instantly excited. It had been great to have Sally with him all evening, but it was hard to keep his feelings towards her from showing too blatantly. He wanted to touch her, and hold her, and kiss her all evening, but had refrained. He wondered what she was up to.

As they entered the house, Carl told them both goodnight and he followed Babe upstairs where their bedrooms were. Billy followed Sally to her room.

As soon as the door was closed, they were in each other's arms in a long passionate embrace. When they finally came up for air, Sally had Billy sit on the side of the bed. She went to the closet and came back with a large, brightly wrapped box, and placed it on Billy's lap.

"What's this?" Billy asked.

"Open it and see," she replied.

"What's the occasion?" he asked.

"Be good to your lover day," was her response.

Billy proceeded to rip into the package. When he opened the box, he found a heavy white terry cloth robe very much like Sally's.

"Try it on!" Sally was obviously excited to give it to him.

Billy slipped it on over his clothes and was surprised that it fit quite well. If anything, it was a little large, a good thing when it came to robes he thought.

"What do you think?" she asked.

"I love it! Where on earth did you find anything to fit me?" he asked.

"I don't divulge my secrets. That way, you have a reason to keep me around," she laughed.

"Oh, I don't know, I can think of several reasons to keep you around!" and he pulled her into his embrace once more.

"I bet you tell that to all the girls," she just managed to get out before their lips met.

"I thought you needed a robe of your own. That way you'll have something to wear to your room in the morning," she said.

"You think of everything."

"I try lover, I try." She turned out the light.

It was Sally that awoke first as dawn began to filter into the room the next morning. Once again she was cradled in Billy's arms. It was the most amazing feeling for her. She never felt so safe and secure. It seemed the only person in her life that ever really cared about her was Carl. Certainly her father never showed much interest, neither had her brother. Her mother did on the rare occasions when she was sober, but those lucid periods had grown increasingly rare over the years. She snuggled more tightly against him and pulled his arms more closely around her.

Sally was going to leave to go back to LA soon. She hadn't come prepared to stay over a few days. She needed to get more of her things, plus she needed to let her mother know she was going to be staying at Carl's for a while. Her mother probably wouldn't understand, but Sally felt like she owed her that much. Sally also needed to let her father know she wouldn't be at her job at the dealership. She didn't think he would care one way or the other, but her co-workers might worry. She considered whether she should go during the week, or wait till the weekend. If she waited, maybe Billy could go with her. She would think about that today. Billy might be uncomfortable at her parent's house. She felt him stir. She had just the thing planned to say good morning to him.

That evening, Sally greeted 'her men' with dinner once again. She was spoiling them she knew, but she felt more a part of a family than ever before in her life. It was a wonderful feeling. And then there was Billy. She was almost afraid to think about him for fear he might disappear. Maybe he was only her imagination come to life. She was so at peace when she was with him. Sally vowed they would never part. Just that thought, of being together always, even if it was only in her mind, was the most wonderful to contemplate. She was totally confident in Billy and their young relationship.

After supper, as usual, Babe left to get in a little more time on the diamond. The rest of them went to the shop after cleaning up the kitchen. The men insisted they do the cleanup since she had cooked dinner. They jokingly argued the point until they all compromised on doing it together. It was short work for the three of them.

They had the frame rails laid out setting on sawhorses. The engine was resting on wooden blocks in its proposed position. The axles were also set in place. Billy had the seat he bought at the surplus store positioned in its approximate location. Their intention was to begin welding the frame together and it was very helpful to have all the pieces in place to make sure everything fit.

As they discussed how the car was to lay out, they decided what to do with the front suspension. They had the complete axle and suspension from Tommy Jackson's pick up. The thing they didn't like about using it intact was that the spring was located ahead of the axle and that would make the car sit too high. It was great for a pickup but not for a slinky race car. In order to obtain the sleek look they were after, the spring needed to mount behind the axle! After much discussion, they decided to mount it between the radius rods which would be 'split' in order to set the car lower to the ground. The Ford spring would have to be shortened to fit. Carl said he could have the spring done at work. They had an arrangement with a spring shop that would pickup and deliver to the dealership. They decided to cut the pickup rear spring in half to make the quarter elliptic springs they planned to use on the back of the car.

"You know, I've been thinking about something that Frank did to his Miller race cars," Carl said while studying the frame of the Special.

"Frank?" Sally asked.

"Oh sorry Sally, Frank Lockhart; I think you've heard your mother and I talk about him" Carl replied.

"Oh sure, but when you said Frank, my mind went to the Babe." She giggled.

"I understand, sorry to confuse you. Anyway, one thing that Frank did was he built a truss system along the bottom of his Miller's frame. It was very visible and you'll see it in some of the old photos. In fact, you can see it in the one here on the wall." Carl walked over to where a framed picture hung on the shop wall. There were also a couple of pictures of the Stutz Black Hawk Special, Lockhart's ill-fated Land Speed Record racer.

"Yeah, I've noticed that before," Billy said. "Did it add strength to the frame?"

"Yeah it did. Frank told me it made a big difference in the way the car handled. The only problem he had was with old man Miller. Harry doesn't like people to mess with his designs. As far as Harry is concerned, everything that rolls out of his shop is perfection and shouldn't be altered by mere mortals. This especially applied to a punk kid like Frank. In fact, in order to make peace with Harry, Frank eventually took them off the car. Harry was so upset with him there for a while that he wouldn't let Frank in the shop." Carl said.

"Are you thinking we ought to add them to the Special?" Billy asked.

"Yeah, I do. This isn't someone else's design, it's ours and we should make it as good as we can, don't you think?" Carl asked.

Sally was looking closely at the pictures of the Black Hawk, deep in thought. "Wasn't Frank killed driving this car?" she wondered out loud.

"Yes he was Sally." Carl replied.

"What happened?" she continued.

"A rear tire blew out at Daytona Beach where he was trying to set a new world land speed record. The AAA investigated the crash and came to the conclusion that one of the rear tires had been cut by a sharp seashell as he turned around for his return pass. They could see from the tire tracks in the beach that after running over the shell, the track left by the tire became wider indicating it was losing air." Carl explained.

"Didn't he crash the car twice? Don't I remember that?" Sally pushed the issue.

"Yes he did. The first time, it flipped into the water. Frank nearly drowned before they could pull him out of the car, but otherwise he wasn't hurt." Carl said.

"Did he stay in the car the time he was killed?" she asked.

"No, he was thrown out. In fact he landed almost at the feet of Carrie, his wife. He was dead on impact."

Sally shuddered. "I don't want that to happen to Billy," she said.

"Oh, don't worry Sally, it won't happen to me." Billy reassured her.

"Oh, and why do you say that?" she asked.

"It just won't, I'll be careful."

"Yes sir, Mr. Immortal, sir. Why don't you wear a belt like an airplane pilot that keeps you inside the car?" Sally asked.

"Then when I roll over, my head would get smashed." Billy explained.

"But what if this part of the body," she pointed at the head fairing, "was strong enough that it wouldn't collapse in a rollover?" Sally asked.

"You know, we could probably do something like that." Carl said. He had been standing back lost in thought as Billy and Sally discussed the issue.

The light bulb was turning on for Billy also. "The new Texan has a structure inside the cockpit to do just what you're talking about." He mused.

"What is the 'Texan'?" Sally asked.

"Sorry, it's a new advanced trainer for the Air Corps. It's the AT-6 Texan officially. Since it's used to train new pilots, sometimes they flip them over while taxiing or when landing. They have a sort of flat-topped pyramid structure built between the two pilots that keeps the weight of the airplane from crushing them if they flip over."

"Yeah, I'm sure we could do that. After all we need something to support the back end of the car anyway, we might as well make it strong enough to protect the driver. We could get a belt out of an airplane for you to wear." Carl said.

Sally was relieved. She was concerned about Billy driving a racer and if he was going to do it, she wanted him to be as safe as possible. She hadn't known how well they would take to her suggestion, but both men seemed to think it was a good idea. She was a bit proud of herself and was beginning to consider herself part of the team.

"Getting back to the truss system. What if we used pipe to build a truss under the frame rails? We intend to have a full belly pan on the car, so we'll need some structure to support it anyway. We could also use the same structure to mount the transmission and even the radiator." Carl suggested.

"What's a 'belly pan'?" Sally asked.

"It's the bottom part of the body. On a normal car, the body only extends down to the frame. The bottom of the car is left open, but on a racer the bottom is closed in by the body, much like the fuselage of an airplane. It makes the car more streamlined." Billy said, proud of being able to answer her question. He was rewarded with a smile.

"Yeah, Carl, I see what you mean about using pipe, but how could we bend it?" Billy asked.

"We could build a wooden pattern and fill the pipe full of sand, then heat it up and bend it around the pattern."

"Let's give it a try. Maybe we can get some of that done this week." Billy suggested enthusiastically.

"Speaking of this week, I need to go back to LA for a few days." Sally said. Billy's heart instantly sank. "I need to get more of my things, plus make arrangements to be out of town longer. Carl, is it okay if I kind of move in here for a while?" Sally asked coyly.

"Are you kidding? We'd love it. Frank will be thrilled. Billy, do you mind?" He asked, trying his best to keep a straight face.

Billy blushed, even Sally got a little pink.

"Hey, I know you two are attracted to each other. I could see it the first day you met out at Kearney Mesa. I think it's great. And seriously Sally, you are welcome here for as long as you want to stay. When are you planning to go back?" Carl asked.

"I thought this week. Would you like to come along for the ride? I mean, all of you, of course." Sally quickly added.

"How long will you be gone? I'm not sure if I can get off work or not." Billy said.

"I'm flexible. I could probably get everything done over a weekend, but it'll be a flying trip."

"I really don't like the idea of you driving that far alone." Billy replied.

"I've done it before, many times."

"I know, I'd just feel better, kind of like your idea about me rolling over."

Everyone laughed. "Billy, if you can get off, why don't just the two of you go? I know you wouldn't mind the time together." Carl suggested. "Besides, maybe you could get Sally to take you by Frank Kurtis' shop for a while. You could get some tips on forming the body for the Special. Frank and I used to work together at the dealership. He's a real nice guy and I'm sure wouldn't mind showing you a few things."

"You could come along with us and that way you could introduce me to Frank yourself." Billy suggested.

"Maybe next time. You two go by yourselves on this trip, I'll stay here and maybe I'll even get a few things done while you're gone."

"Okay, but you know you're more than welcome to come," Sally said.

That ended the night's work on the Special. Several important decisions had been made on that night. The Special was shaping up to be one of the safest and best engineered cars in the U.S. and maybe the world. This was in no small part due to Sally's contributions.

Chapter 12

Billy and Sally decided to leave for LA on Thursday evening after Billy got off work. She picked him up in the Packard and they headed north on the Pacific Coast Highway. Sally wanted to show Billy some of the most beautiful scenery in the state. She was eager to share her world with him.

Sally drove so that Billy could devote his full attention to the beautiful scenery. It was nothing like the Texas gulf coast Billy thought. In Texas the land and sea merge effortlessly. The land is flat for miles and miles, scarcely above sea level. When the two finally do meet, it is almost like a lake in places, mud flats and swampland. There are some sand beaches, true enough, but nothing to prepare Billy for the California coast line. Here the land defied the water, rising into high bluffs and huge rocks. Steep hills covered in trees close to the sea. There were the occasional seductions where the land gave way in magnificent sand beaches. Each twist and turn of the road brought a new vista more beautiful than the last.

Sally could tell Billy was enjoying the ride. He didn't say much, but then that was his nature. He would never be described as talkative, instead, he spent most of his time in thought and taking in the view. Occasionally he would utter an expletive over a particularly beautiful landscape. He would touch her thigh and tell her how beautiful it was. Any time spent with Billy was wonderful for her, but being able to share the wonders of the California coastline with him for the first time was sublime.

"How far is it to LA?" Billy asked.

"Not far Hon" was her reply. "We could make it in two to three hours if we wanted to, but I thought it would be more fun to take our time and enjoy the trip."

"I've never seen anything like this. It's just so beautiful. Everywhere I look it's like a picture postcard. Texas sure doesn't look like this."

They passed through Torrey Pines then Del Mar. Billy was interested in the track at Del Mar, the Spanish architecture giving it an exotic look in his mind. He could visualize the rich and famous arriving for a day at the races.

Coastline on their left and mountains on their right, the road twisted and turned in the space between. It was a glorious day to be on such a spectacular road, the top down, and this gorgeous perfect woman as his driver and tour guide. Billy wondered how he could have ever been so lucky.

It seemed that the entire state of California was nothing but hills and mountains. They came upon field after field of flowers. The colors were beyond description. It seemed that one surprise just led to another along this road.

"I know a small inn just up the road where we can spend the night. Is that okay?" Sally asked.

"Sure it's okay, but we have quite a bit of daylight left," implying they could make several more miles before dark.

"I thought it would be more fun to take our time. We'll get to LA in plenty of time to take care of my business. It's much nicer staying here along the coast than in the city."

"My lady, I'm totally at your disposal. Your wish is my command," Billy replied.

"I was hoping you would say that," Sally said with a radiant smile.

She braked and turned onto a dirt drive that you had to know was there to even notice. Billy was surprised and at first thought something had gone wrong with the car. Then he thought maybe it was a driveway. The drive, really more of a path, led into a wall of trees and brush and sloped downhill. They were on a bluff and from the few glimpses Billy got of the sea; he estimated they were at least 50 feet above the water.

The path ended at the edge of the bluff. Sally stopped the car and turned off the engine. The only sound was the surf down below. Billy looked back, but the highway was out of sight. Temporarily confused, Billy looked at Sally, the expression on his face enough to make her laugh. He was completely baffled by their sudden course change and stop.

"I packed us a picnic dinner. I thought it would be nice to take a swim and eat dinner on the beach. Why don't you get out and get the basket out of the trunk?" Sally said.

"I didn't think to pack a suit," Billy said.

"Neither did I," Sally gave him the most seductive look and headed down the path toward the sound of the surf.

Billy clambered out of the car, his head still spinning from the total surprise of it all. He opened the trunk to find a large picnic basket beside a couple of small suitcases. He grabbed the basket and followed the path where Sally had disappeared.

The path was steep and rocky. Billy had to watch his step to keep from tumbling head long down the trail or over the side. He was amazed that Sally had disappeared so quickly. He knew she had to have come this way, there was no place else for her to go.

The trail finally flattened out onto the sand of the beach, if it could even be called that. The sand was only a few feet wide, the surf nearly lapped over the end of the trail where Billy stood. The sand extended ahead for a short distance before ending in a jumble of rocks where part of the bluff above had collapsed into the sea. What little sand there was, was almost completely covered with piles of driftwood. He saw Sally's footprints in the sand as they disappeared around the point of the bluff back to his left.

There were only a few feet of sand here between the wall of the bluff and the surf. As Billy rounded the edge of the bluff, the beach opened up into a perfect crescent of golden sand, maybe a hundred yards long before it too ended in another jumble of rocks where the bluff had once more collapsed. Sally's footprints led around the curve of the beach.

Her footprints ended where her red blouse and khaki shorts lay in a heap. The strap of her bra and the shiny white of her panties peeked out of the pile.

He turned and looked out in the water to see her head a surprising distance beyond the surf. She was watching him as she tread water. He set the basket down and started making a pile of his own right on top of Sally's. Before the last item hit the pile he was already running into the surf.

When he reached the point where he last saw her, he stopped swimming and looked around. She was nowhere to be seen. He turned a full circle looking for her and just as he came around to face out to sea again he felt her. Her arms went around his thighs and she slid up his body until she bobbed out of the water face to face, her arms around him. She pressed close and kissed him. It was a completely arousing experience. Her arms were around his neck. He supported them both. She laughed at his surprise.

"I'm glad you're happy to see me!" and she pressed more tightly against him. "Oh dear, you are VERY happy to see me aren't you, lover?" she said with a look of mock surprise on her face as she kissed him again, giggling. Billy responded with a lopsided grin. "There's only one problem," she said, Billy's grin started to fade just a touch, "you'll never catch me!" And then she shoved away from him and swam strongly for shore, Billy in hot pursuit after only a second's hesitation.

She was right; she beat Billy to shore handily. When he finally got into the surf and could stand up, she was already standing on the beach facing him. As he came out of the water she was using both hands to slick her hair back out of her eyes. As she did so she arched her back and her hands pushed some of the water out of her hair. Billy thought he had never witnessed such perfection in his life. Her skin was perfect and almost the color of the sand.

As he walked up to her she asked, "What took you so long?"

Later they both lay on their backs side by side, the sun providing soft warmth on their skin. Sally rolled onto her side and raised up on one arm facing Billy. She slowly stroked his chest with her other arm. "I promised you a picnic, are you hungry?" She got up and disappeared from his view. The shadows were growing long as the sun, was well past its zenith, headed toward its home in the sea. Billy still lay on his back and watched the sky.

He heard her steps crunch up near him and he turned. She was setting the basket down and she wore his shirt open down the front. It was almost as large as her robe. "What's this?" he asked.

"I was getting a little chilly," she said.

"No fair. What am I going to wear?" he asked.

She fixed him with her most seductive stare. "Lover, you're perfect just the way you are and if you start to get cold, just let me know, besides this isn't covering up much is it?" as she flopped open the unbuttoned front of the shirt, holding it wide with both arms outstretched.

He had to admit that it wasn't. She opened the basket and pulled out a bottle of wine and a couple of glasses. "Vino?" she asked. Sally handed him the bottle and a corkscrew. While he worked on opening the wine, she retrieved the rest of the basket's contents. As he was pulling the cork, she pushed a grape in his mouth. He reveled in her presence, her attention, and most sublime of all, in her touch.

They lay against each other in the sand and ate grapes and cheese and bread washed down by red wine. It was the perfect meal on the perfect day. Billy's thoughts flashed back to his life in Texas for the briefest moment. This sure beat the stifling heat of a Texas summer. He marveled at the vision that wore his shirt and occasionally pushed a grape in his mouth. Was this all a dream? Could he possibly be experiencing this joy, this perfection? What price would he have to pay for this golden moment on the golden sand with such a golden nymph?

Billy discovered that dusk did not last long in this part of the world. As the sun's orb touched the crimson sea, the light would not last much longer. It was time to make their way back up the trail to the Packard. He didn't want to attempt the climb in the dark. Sally refused to surrender his shirt. Instead she pushed her pile of clothes into the picnic basket and said "you can carry those," and disappeared around the edge of the bluff toward the trail, shirt tails flapping. Billy hastily pulled on his pants and took off after her stuffing his feet in his shoes. It was a bit more difficult going back up the bluff. The path seemed even steeper and the light was beginning to fade. The shadows formed wells of inky blackness, obscuring the crooked way.

When he finally reached the top, it was almost completely dark. Sally leaned against the Packard, her legs crossed at the ankles, her hands on the front fender. She still had on Billy's shirt and it was still open down the front. And she was right Billy thought, not only did it not cover much, right now it wasn't covering anything. "I didn't think you were ever going to get here," she said. Billy put the basket down and took her in his arms.

Later, as they lay on the front seat of the Packard in each other's embrace, Billy said "Do you think we better head on to the inn? If we don't we may have to spend the night in the car!" They both laughed.

Billy cautiously turned the Packard around and they headed up the highway again, their headlights burning two holes in the night, the sound of the surf below, drowning out all other sounds. Sally leaned against him, her hand on his thigh.

The inn was not exactly what Billy had pictured. It was a collection of small bungalows on the edge of a very high bluff. In daylight he was sure it had a very picturesque view. He went in to the desk and registered them as Mr. and Mrs. W. W. Pendleton.

The hotels of the day cast a dim view on separate names on their registers. Besides, he couldn't think of anything else to do.

He came back to the car and drove them to the far bungalow. It was on the very point and highest part of the bluff. He was sure it had the best view and was the most desirable of them all. He assumed they got this one because they were the only guests. All the others were dark and there were no other cars in sight. He handed Sally the key to the door and went around to get their bags out of the trunk.

When Billy entered the bungalow, he could already hear the shower running. The only light came from the open door to the bathroom. As he set the bags down Sally appeared in the lighted doorway, "care to join me?" she asked. "I need someone to wash my back." The smile on her face was too much to ignore. Besides Billy figured he could use a shower himself.

The bed sheets were freshly laundered. The mattress was a good one. After all the events of the day, the bed and the smell of the sheets were like heaven. The windows were open and the gentle breeze carried the sound of thecrashing surf far below. Sally's warm body was pressed against his. They were both asleep within seconds.

When Billy awoke the next morning it was already light. The sound of the never ending surf was still coming in through the open windows. The bed beside him was empty. The crumpled sheets, still warm a silent reminder of Sally. He got up and pulled on his trousers. The back door of the bungalow stood open. He decided to investigate.

The door opened onto a wooden porch surrounded by a wooden railing. All that could be seen past the railing was sea and sky. It was still early morning and the day had yet to burn all the night mist away. Gulls were calling and circled by on their endless quest for food. Sally stood at the railing clad only in Billy's shirt. She had yet to button it and the sea breeze had it billowed out behind her. As before on the beach, it didn't cover much.

Billy walked up behind her and put his arms around her waist. At their touch she cooed and pulled them closer. "Don't you ever wear clothes in public?" he asked.

"The only person around is you and I rather enjoy wearing nothing with you, but I have taken to your shirt, and good morning to you too." She pulled his arms closer around her and then covered them with the flapping ends of the shirt. "See there, everything's covered up."

They stood on the porch for a while admiring the view, listening to the surf and watching the gulls cavort. Billy wished that time could just stand still. Surely there wasn't a more perfect time the time spent with Sally since she arrived in San Diego.

Sally turned to face him. "Maybe we better get dressed and be on our way," and she kissed him. This turned into more of a kiss than it started out to be. "Maybe we can get dressed in a little while," she suggested. Sally took off his shirt and handed it to him.

"Here's your shirt back," and kissed him again. Then she took his hand and led him inside.

They drove into the outskirts of Los Angeles. Sally was driving again. She knew the city and she wanted Billy to be able to look around. Besides, he thought her an excellent driver. She handled the big Packard as if it were an extension of her own body. She was a natural at it.

"Is it okay if I drop you off at Frank's shop while I go home and get my things?" she asked.

"Of course it is, dear, why would you even ask?"

"I don't want you to think that I don't want to take you home with me. If anything it's the reverse." She said cautiously.

"Darling, I'm fine with it. You know I want to see Mr. Kurtis' shop. Carl has told me so much about it"

"Well if I drop you there while I go home, we'll really have more time to spend together. Is there anything else you want to see while we're in LA?" Sally asked.

"Maybe the Offenhauser shop, and I'd kind of like to see Don Lee Cadillac." he said.

"Men!" was her one word reply, as she rolled her eyes. For an instant he was concerned, and then he saw the smile on her face.

"I guess that was a little single focused wasn't it? Show me anything you'd like, especially the things you like, okay?" he said.

"Nice recovery, but a little late don't you think?" she laughed at his moment of confusion. After all it was a woman's job to keep her man a little off balance wasn't it? And Sally would forever think of him as her man from this point forward.

Sally turned the corner onto San Pedro. "Frank's shop is just down the street," she said.

"How is it you know Frank Kurtis?" Billy asked.

"He used to work at Don Lee Cadillac. Of course, so did Carl. My mother would take me by to see Carl as far back as I can remember. They were childhood friends, remember? Mom wasn't so bad in those days. The bottle hadn't totally taken over her life at that point. Of course, Daddy never liked her going there. Don Lee was his number one competitor. On the other hand, if we ever got to see Carl, it had to be there. He wasn't welcome in our home, Daddy saw to that. In a way, I think Daddy was jealous of Carl, maybe he still is."

More pieces of the puzzle Billy thought to himself. He was certain there was more to this whole story. He wondered how much of it Sally knew, or what she might think. He was sure she would tell him someday, in her own good time.

"That's it right here." She said as she pulled up and parked at a modest brick building. The large sign across the top of the building said "Pioneer" and the windows had painted signs that read "Collision – Painting' and "Auto Tops". He was about to ask if she was sure this was the place when he noticed lettered on one of the windows in small script "Race Cars – custom bodies by Frank Kurtis".

They got out and Sally led the way into the building through the open bay door in the building's center. Billy was amazed. The shop was full of racecars. They were lined up in rows, a regular assembly line he realized. Pairs of wooden saw horses supported three almost complete midget racecar bodies and frames. The cars had front springs attached, but no axles or engines were yet fitted. There was an Indy championship car, championship cars were commonly called "big cars", at the end of the line of midgets. The Indy car was sans body but carried a DOHC 4 cylinder engine that Billy instantly recognized as one of the famous Offenhausers, even though it was the only one he had ever seen in person. The shop was a jumble of machinery. A lathe was against the front window that bore the Kurtis sign, a large drill press to one side, a mill to the other. The wall behind the midgets was bare brick. On it hung several framed pictures of race cars, a large plywood board full of tools, very reminiscent of Carl's shop, and a hand painted sign that said "all work left over 30 days sold for charges". There was another drill press, a couple of welding rigs, and a large band saw, all on the opposite wall. Behind the row of cars was a sheet metal brake and a shear. He had never been in a real race car shop before; he was like a kid in a candy store.

Across the shop he saw a tall dark haired man with a pencil mustache talking to a man in a sports coat and brown fedora. The dark haired man waved as they came in the door then went back to his discussion with the other man. "That's Frank," Sally said indicating the tall man with the mustache. Another man stopped working on one of the midgets and walked up to them wiping his hands on a rag.

"Can I help you folks?" the man asked.

"Oh, we're just here to see Frank," Sally replied.

"The name's Sid if you need anything. Just make yourself at home. Frank will be with you in a minute." Sid walked back to the midget where he and another man dressed in white coveralls appeared to be mounting an odd type of rear axle.

Billy was intently examining one of the midgets pointing out the details to Sally and didn't see the dark haired man approach.

"Hello Miss Anthony, it's nice to see you again," he said with an accent Billy couldn't identify.

"Since when did it become Miss Anthony?"

"Since you have become such a lovely young woman, of course," the man said, an easy smile on his face.

"You rogue; you always did have a way with words. Frank, this is my friend Billy Pendleton. Billy lives down in San Diego and he and Carl Mercer are in the process of building a racer, Billy this is Frank Kurtis." Sally said.

"Pleased to meet you," Frank had a firm hand. He wasn't as tall as Billy, but he was certainly taller than most. "How is Carl doing and what kind of racer are you two building?"

"Just something to run on the dry lakes. Maybe drive it some on the street too. Kind of a one man version of Tommy Lee's speedster."

"Oh yes, you know I built that car don't you? Tried every way I could think of to talk Tommy out of that big Offy, but he wouldn't listen. He doesn't listen to anyone, ever. That's why I don't work for him anymore. He still brings me things to do, but we do them on my terms, not his. That speedster would be a much nicer car with a Cadillac engine. Just imagine that car with a V-16 or even the V12, instead he spent a ton of money on that rough running Offy. Don't get me wrong, the Offy's a great engine, but it was designed to race on dirt tracks with no thought to smooth quiet operation," he sighed. There was a faraway look in his eye as he seriously considered what could have been for a moment, then the spell broke. "Please excuse me for getting carried away. Tommy brings out the passion in me, both good and bad sometimes. Forgive me, what engine are you using?"

"It's funny you should ask Mr. Kurtis" Billy smiled.

Frank interrupted, "Call me Frank, please."

"Okay Frank, it's funny, but we're using a 6 cylinder engine that Tommy Lee gave us."

"I remember that engine. That's one that Harry Miller built isn't it? Sort of half of a Cadillac V-12 wasn't it? Tommy had another of his hair brained ideas and thought it would be a world beater in the old 'junk formula' days. Might have been if it had been ready sooner. I think the formula was over by the time the engine was delivered wasn't it?" Frank asked.

"Something like that I think," Billy replied, thinking Frank sure liked to talk. The thought entered his mind unbidden that Frank could probably say yes or no in a thousand words. It took quite an effort to restrain the laugh just before it broke through.

"What brings you folks to my shop?" Frank asked.

"Carl thought you might show Billy around. Show him how you build bodies and all that stuff. I have a few errands to run and thought I could leave Billy here to visit for a while. Is that okay?" Sally asked.

"I would have been insulted if you hadn't. Billy did you know Carl Mercer helped me get my start? Bye Sally. Don't worry, I'll take good care of him." and with that Frank led Billy away to show him the finer parts of the art of building racing cars. Billy threw a glance and a wave over his shoulder as Frank led him away just beginning his lecture as if he were a professor in front of his class. Sally chuckled and walked back outside to the Packard.

Billy spent the rest of the morning listening as Frank showed him the details of his cars. He was introduced to the man that initially greeted them on their arrival. His name was Sid Cruce. Billy discovered that Sid was quite a craftsman himself. It seemed that Frank spent a large part of his day talking to customers, while Sid spent most of his days building cars. It was soon obvious that both men focused on what they did best.

The man clad in white coveralls was named Ted Halibrand. Ted wasn't nearly as talkative as the other two. While he didn't say much, Billy noticed that his eyes didn't miss anything and his work was steady with no motion wasted.

There seemed to be an almost endless stream of people coming in to discuss buying or modifying a car, or having some special piece built. Billy thought that one of the reasons Frank was so successful, besides his obvious ability of transforming thoughts into steel, was that he could communicate with people. He seemed to make everyone that walked through the door feel important.

Billy asked Sid if it was like this every day, and Sid told him it was. He said people came and went all day. Billy asked when Frank ever found time to work and Sid told him he stayed late every night. He also said that Frank was amazing in his ability to shape metal. It was the main reason Sid worked for him, he was trying to learn all he could from the master.

At lunch Billy and Sid walked down San Pedro to a nearby hamburger stand. Ted stayed behind to continue working, which Sid seemed to accept as the norm. Also as usual, Frank was tied up with a customer and told them to go ahead, he would catch up later.

In between bites of his burger, Sid asked, "Say Billy, who was that gorgeous skirt that dropped you off at the shop?"

"That was Sally Anthony," Billy replied.

"She your girl?" he asked.

"Yes, well at least I think she is," Billy replied.

"Two things for ya! If you're not sure she's your girl, why don't you introduce me to her? And I just want you to know, that if she was my girl, I wouldn't be wasting my time messing around with greasy old race cars. Billy, I'm serious, she's the most beautiful woman I've ever seen. You're one lucky stiff, and hey, she drives a swell car too!"

"Thank you, I think," Billy said and they both laughed. He could tell that Sid was trying to be complimentary of Sally in his own gruff way. "I agree with you on two counts, she is definitely the most beautiful woman I know and I am a very lucky guy. The car's not bad either!"

"Tell you what I'll do, I'll trade any race car in the shop, your choice, straight up for Sally, seeing as how you're not sure she's your girl and all." Sid offered.

Billy laughed. "She's not mine to trade, Sid, but if she were, still no deal."

"Any two cars?" Sid raised his offer.

"Nope." Billy stood firm.

"Don't blame you, I wouldn't trade her for all the cars I ever seen." Sid took another bite of his burger.

"How long have you worked for Frank?" Billy asked.

"Just a few months. Frank's only had the shop open a short while. He's kind of like a gypsy, he has to go where the work is. Frank spent most of the spring in Indianapolis for the 500 mile race. The man's a real wizard with metal, and I guess you've noticed, he really gets along with people," he chuckled. "Frank talks and Ted and I work, but then he's the boss ain't he?"

Billy nodded in agreement. "Tell me about this car you're building." Sid said. The rest of their lunch hour was taken up with discussion of the Special.

On their way back to the shop, Billy asked, "Sid, what I'm interested in the most is how to shape body panels. Can you show me anything about that?"

"Oh sure, I can show you the basics, but Frank is the master. He can do things with sheet metal that you just won't believe until you see it, and he's fast too, but yeah, I can show you how to get started. Are you using aluminum or steel?" Sid asked.

"Steel." Billy replied.

Sid whistled. "That's not the easy way to start, but the principals are the same. Steel's a little easier to weld."

"Yeah, the welding and expense were two of the reasons I decided on steel. The other is that if I do drive it on the street some, I thought steel would be more durable. I was afraid the aluminum would dent too easily."

"Yeah, you're right about that." They walked in through the big bay door and sure enough, Frank was talking to someone else. They both smiled at each other. Sid took Billy to a corner of the shop where most of the body panel shaping went on. As they walked by, Billy noticed Ted had his head down under the tail of one of the midgets. The man never quit.

The first thing Sid showed him were three-dimensional forms made out of plywood, shaped like the midget race car bodies. "These here are what we call 'bucks'," Sid said. "We use them to make our patterns and to test fit our panels. Like this." He was standing beside the buck for the tail of a midget. He took a large sheet of paper and draped it over the side of the buck. He used push pins to hold the paper in place. "See what you do is to lay the paper in place and then kind of form it to the shape of the buck. Wherever it bunches up is a place you have to shrink the metal. See you can fold the paper to take care of the bunched up places. You can also cut it and tape it if you have to. Then when you take the paper off, you have a pattern to cut your material out." He held up the paper to show Billy. "It's just like your momma making a pattern for a dress. We just use a welding torch instead of a sewing machine's all."

"How many pieces do you use to make a part?" Billy asked.

"That depends on the part, of course. I try to balance the complexity of the part to the number of pieces. Try to make your seam where the metal has a lot of 'crown'; that means where the metal makes a lot of bend. If your seam runs along a major crown, you get a lot less distortion in the metal when you weld the pieces together." Sid showed Billy what he was talking about by showing him a tail section that was in progress. "See how the weld seam runs right down the middle of the part with the most curve?" Billy saw that the seam was in the very middle of the curve and that it ran that way from one end to the other. "It's a lot easier to make your weld here. The curve makes the metal a lot stiffer so that it buckles less. Do you know how to hammer weld?" Sid asked.

Billy confessed that he did not.

"It's really pretty simple, it just takes some practice to get good at it. You'll use this a lot, especially since your body is steel. See, what you do is to be sure your panels fit together as closely as possible. The better the fit is, the better the part will be. Take as much time as necessary to get the fit as perfect as you can. You can trim close to the line with some snips or a shear and then file it down to a perfect fit."

"Once your fit is really good, then use the smallest flame possible and only add filler rod when you have to. The goal is that if the fit is really good, it almost welds itself. Tack it first. Don't get in a hurry, and move around so that one area doesn't get too hot. The hotter it gets, the more distortion there is. Leave some gaps toward the end of the panel. The welding heat will cause it to close up. Then start welding in short strips, maybe 3/4" at a time. Then lay your torch down and use a hammer and dolly to hammer the weld while it's still hot. The quicker the better. If you can get it while the steel's still red, that's perfect, aluminum don't turn no colors ya see, that's why it's harder to weld. What you're doing is stretching the metal back into shape. When you weld it, it shrinks up and when you hammer it, you're pushing it back out." Sid showed him on a couple of pieces of scrap. Billy was amazed at how nicely it worked.

"I better get back to work before Frank fires me." Sid said, "You can watch and we can talk as I work. We might even get Ted to say somethin'." Then shaking his head he laughed, "Nah, he don't ever say nuthin'!"

Billy watched as Sid checked the axle Ted had been mounting in one of the midgets. It was the strangest looking axle Billy ever saw and he asked Sid what it was.

"It's a new design. It's set up so you can change the rear axle ratio real easy like. See this cover here on the back? There's a pair of spur gears in there. The drive shaft power passes below the ring gear, see how this shaft goes down low here? This shaft has splines on the very end and the pinion, up here has matching splines. A pair of spur gears is what connects them. You can change the ratio just by pulling this cover off and replacing the spur gears. Takes about 15 minutes if you're really taking your time. It's a whole lot easier than changing out the ring gear and pinion." Sid winked at Billy. "Ted designed it hisself, didn't you Ted?" he said loud enough for Ted to hear. Ted looked up for a minute and grinned, but never said a word. When he went back to what he had been doing, they both laughed.

"Billy, is Sid taking good care of you?" Frank had walked over unnoticed.

"Yes sir, he sure is. I apologize for taking up so much of ya'll's time." Billy said

"Don't worry about it. Carl Mercer really helped me get started. He's been a good friend for years. I'm happy that I can do something to return some of the favors he's done me over the years." Frank replied

"Sid's shown me a lot. I don't know how to thank you."

"Like I said, it's our pleasure, isn't it Sid?"

"It sure is. Besides, Billy's been helping me hang this axle. Billy, is your girl coming back to pick you up?" Sid asked.

"I sure hope so. It's a long walk back to San Diego." They all three laughed.

"Just getting to see her again is payment enough for me." Sid said. Billy and Frank both laughed again.

"Sid, I'd be careful what you say about Sally. Billy here is nearly twice your size." Frank said to more laughter.

Just then Sally walked in the door. She smiled as she walked up to the laughing men. "Looks like you boys are having a good time," she said. Sally had changed into a yellow print sundress. There was no doubt she was a vision and no doubt that Sid's eyes were bugging out of his head.

"Hi honey," Billy said and was rewarded with a lingering kiss on the lips.

"I want to introduce you to my friend Sid Cruce. Sid is one of your greatest admirers. Sid, this is Sally Anthony."

Sid blushed and said, "Pleased to make your acquaintance ma'am." Billy thought better of making a bigger deal of introducing Sally. He could have had a lot of fun at Sid's expense, but decided against it.

"Sid, I'm so pleased to meet you," Sally said in a very charming voice. "And thank you for the admiration." This just made Sid blush all the more.

"And hon, that's Ted Halibrand with his head stuck in that car. Ted never stops working." They all laughed, even Ted raised his head and grinned. He nodded.

"How's Carl and little Frank?" Frank asked.

"They're doing well. We've taken to calling Frank, Babe, that was the big guy's idea here," and she poked Billy in the ribs. Billy gave a very satisfying jump and grunt. "Babe is more devoted to baseball than ever. And my king sized trouble maker here," and she punched Billy in the ribs again, "has Carl wrapped up in his project. Everyone's doing fine really." Frank and Sid were both laughing. The sight of Sally poking Billy in the ribs was a funny one made all the more hilarious by Billy's size and his good humor. He had 'bought in' to the game and gave a very satisfying jerk and jump each time.

"I didn't get a chance to talk to you about your car very much. You said it is something like Tommy's speedster didn't you?" Frank asked.

"Well yes, but the car is really sort of a combination of Danny Sakai's and Bill Warth's, with a dose of the Black Hawk Special thrown in for good measure."

A large grin spread across Frank's face. "Frank Lockhart's car! What a beautiful machine that was, but are you going to make it a single seat?"

"Yes, I think so." Billy replied.

"No room for the lovely Miss Anthony?" and Frank arched his eyebrows.

"I was hoping we could use her Packard when we're together."

"Maybe you'd better think again mister!" and Billy got another jab in the ribs.

Frank and Sid laughed even harder. Sid's ribs were beginning to hurt from laughing so much.

"They're going to use steel for the body." Sid threw in wiping away the tears. He couldn't remember laughing so hard in years.

"Steel. Well, I always had trouble with cowl shake on Tommy's car, and he's always complained that it felt flimsy. I really didn't save all that much weight using aluminum. The fenders and doors were steel anyway. Then he used that great huge Offy engine and it's just too rough for a street driven car. Especially when he steps out of a V-16 Caddy and gets in that 4 cylinder speedster. No wonder he thinks it's rough. Hell, it is!" Frank said.

Just then a man walked in the shop and Frank had to leave them to greet the newcomer. "It was certainly nice meeting you Billy, and Sally, it's always a pleasure. Come back anytime," and with that he was gone.

"Sid, thanks for your time and showing me the tricks. I know we'll use all of your techniques on the Special." Billy shook Sid's hand.

"Nice to meet you Billy, think nothing of it, I enjoyed myself. Miss Anthony, it was certainly my pleasure meeting you, and I hope you come back soon, and as much as I enjoyed his company, you can leave the big guy in San Diego next time!" Sid said and they all laughed again. Ted raised his head again and waved.

Billy and Sally left the shop. The Packard was at the curb next to a street light. "Did you get all your things attended to at home?" Billy asked.

"Oh yeah, Daddy was gone and mother was into the scotch. No one cared one way or the other. I went by the dealership and let them know I'd be gone for a while." Sally said.

"It must be nice to be able to leave anytime you want," Billy poked a little fun of his own.

"It's what comes of being the boss's daughter."

"Where are we headed now?" Billy asked as he got in on the passenger's side.

"You said you wanted to see Tommy's place. I thought we would drive by there." Sally suggested.

"Swell."

Billy wasn't prepared for the size of the building that greeted him at 7th and Bixel. Don Lee Cadillac was a massive seven-story brick building. Sally parked at the curb. She took Billy in a side entrance and on to a service elevator. They rode to the top floor and stepped out into a massive warehouse/shop space that was filled with cars. All four walls were made up of massive multi-paned windows. Most of the windows stood open because of the summer heat and a pleasant breeze circulated through the huge space. Billy's impression was that of an open airy place. The high ceiling reinforced the impression.

The first vehicle they came to was an old REO van that was an original Don Lee service vehicle. Despite its years of service and its age, it looked brand new. Billy marveled at its condition. Sally explained that the van had been completely rebuilt to like new condition by the dealership. Restored cars were not common back in those days.

There was a beautiful boat tailed LaSalle speedster. Billy stopped to admire it. "That's Willet Brown's car. He's Tommy's business manager. I think Frank Kurtis built the body for it." Sally said.

"It's gorgeous. The body is flawless and the design is really swell!" Billy said with admiration.

"Tommy was jealous of it and that's why he had Frank build him the speedster. Of course, it had to be better and faster than Willet's and I think that's where the Offenhauser motor came from. Speaking of the devil, here he is."

Billy looked up to see Tommy walking toward them. He smiled and walked up to Sally and gave her a hug and a kiss. Tommy was obviously pleased to see her. "Hi Sally, and to what do I owe the privilege of this totally unexpected visit? I thought you must have dropped off the face of the earth." Tommy said, ignoring Billy completely.

"I've been down in San Diego at Carl's. I had to come back up here to tend to a few things and Billy wanted to see your place, so I thought you wouldn't mind," she said.

"Oh, I see." The warm smile faded from his face. "Nice to see you again, Billy." He placed a little too much emphasis on Billy, there was an obvious strain in his voice. "Of course, you're welcome any time. May I show you around?" The words said Billy was welcome, but the eyes told another story.

"We'll just browse around for a while," Sally said. "Billy, why don't you look around for a few minutes while I talk to Tommy?"

"Sure. You really have an awfully nice place here Tommy." Billy said and he walked over toward what he thought must be a European race car. There were also several midget racers and at least one Indy 500 racer, commonly called 'big cars', that he could see. A couple of the midgets were very striking. One had a grille that appeared to be a hand fabricated replica of the 1939 La Salle just like in Carl's coupe and the one they planned to use in the Special. The other had a polished aluminum hood with swirl patterns covering it, commonly called engine turning or damascening.

Sally and Tommy talked in hushed tones. Whenever he looked over toward them Tommy still wore the stern look on his face and seemed a bit animated to Billy. Sally appeared calm and alternated between listening and speaking in what seemed to be a calm and deliberate manner.

Billy was curious about what was being discussed and he also felt a pang of jealousy. He was determined to keep that emotion under control. Despite his young age, he had the wisdom to understand that Sally did not belong to him. While it certainly seemed that she enjoyed his company and she gave every indication that their relationship was something very special, she was still free to do whatever she wanted. He sensed that only by allowing her total freedom could he ever hope to claim her heart. These were contradictory feelings that ran contrary to his instincts. It took a tremendous amount of self control to keep his emotions in check. He decided to totally focus on the spectacular machines parked in the space he now roamed.

Billy was engrossed in a stunning red single seat Alfa Romeo. He read the name in magazines a few times, but this was the first one he had seen in real life. The car had enormous wire spoke wheels held on by chromed knock off spinners. The hood was long and full of louvers, held down by leather straps. There were no fenders. Billy had no way of knowing he was looking at last year's works grand prix racecar. A very rare and special car, even in Italy, but the only such example in North America.

"It's a really pretty car isn't it?" Sally interrupted his thoughts. She slid against him and put her arm around his back and leaned her head on his chest.

"Yes it is." He could tell she was a little sad. "Did your talk with Tommy go well?" Billy asked.

"Of course not. His feelings are hurt. He's always thought he owned me. No matter how many times I've told him no, he's persisted. He says it's only a matter of time till I give in to him. I think seeing you here brought a touch of reality into his world, and he's not happy about that."

"Are things okay?"

"They will be. He'll get over it. He's really a nice guy at heart. He's just spent his whole life thinking he could have anything he wanted and one of the things he thinks he wants is me. I don't think I mean that much to him other than as another trophy. Something he can put on display. He's especially stung since I'm with 'that backwoods Texan for God's sake' is the way he put it. Now, don't get your feelings hurt, he was just upset and I'm sure he really didn't mean anything by it. He'll get over it." Sally assured Billy.

"Okay." Billy replied. Somehow the fun of looking at Tommy's cars had just evaporated. "Maybe we should leave."

They left the same way they came, using the service elevator. On the way out they passed two of the most beautiful cars Billy had ever seen. They were both coupes and very streamlined with oval windows and long graceful hoods full of louvers. They were nearly identical except one had its front wheels completely enclosed. It was the first car Billy ever saw with fender skirts on the front and rear wheels. The other coupes front wheels were exposed. They were magnificent chrome hoops laced to the center by wire spokes and secured at the center with knock off hubs, just like a real race car. Despite wanting to leave as quickly as possible, he paused to read the blue cloisonné emblem on the pointed grille shells. Talbot Lago was spelled out in chrome letters. He never heard of Talbot Lago before. Maybe he was a bit backwoods after all he thought.

Once they were in the car and driving through downtown LA, Sally's mood lifted noticeably. The time in Tommy's shop had been the first less than euphoric moment they spent together. The bond was growing stronger. Billy's because Sally had been so open and honest with him and Sally's because Billy maintained an even temper and hadn't exhibited any paranoia or melted down in a rage of jealousy. That was a good thing since she was certain Billy could squeeze Tommy like a bug if he wanted to. That thought made her smile, it also made her smile that she felt she could share her innermost thoughts with him and not be judged. As she found with most things involving Billy, this was yet another new experience for her.

Once again, Sally was driving. It only seemed logical since she knew the city so well and it was Billy's first visit. LA was certainly a vibrant place to be. Hustle and bustle was everywhere. Billy had no idea where they were going, but he just sat back and took in the sights. He was sure Sally had an objective even if it was just to drive around town to release the tension from the visit to Tommy's.

They were heading north he was pretty certain. Soon he could smell the ocean close by and the gulls were more numerous. Then they were driving along the ocean once more. This area was much more heavily populated than the drive north out of San Diego. They passed a large pier with a sign stating it was the Santa Monica Pier. It was a Friday afternoon and there were a few people on the beaches, but it was still too early in the day to be crowded.

Sally drove along the coast. There were brown mountains on their right. The further they drove, the more sparse it became, almost rural. Billy enjoyed the view, mountains and canyons on one side, ocean and beaches on the other. Along through here, there were a few beach houses, spread apart, almost isolated. They continued north, then Sally slowed and turned toward the beach. She pulled into a driveway for one of the houses. It was a low squat house with a flat roof almost hidden by the dunes. The side of the house facing the road was built onto the high sand bank that paralleled the highway. It appeared that the other side was above the beach supported by the stilts. Billy couldn't tell for sure. Sally turned off the car.

"Where are we?" Billy asked.

"This is Malibu. Isn't it beautiful?" she asked.

"Yes it is. Is this your house?"

"No, it's my brothers, but I have the key," she smiled; it was one of her dazzlers Billy thought. Every time she did it, it just melted his heart.

"Will he mind us going in?" Billy asked with concern.

"Of course not, if he minded, why would he have given me a key?" That seemed to make some sense to Billy, although he wasn't used to making himself at home in someone else's house, but Sally was giving him one of her looks. He had come to think of them as her "naughty" looks, a smile topped with a cocked eyebrow. He was powerless when confronted with that look.

"Come on," she said and led the way to the front door. Sure enough, she had the key and the large door swung inward effortlessly inviting them inside. Billy wasn't prepared for the view that awaited him. They entered into the main room of the house. The wall on the far side of the room facing the ocean was made up entirely of large glass panes. The view of the beach and ocean was spectacular. The floor of the room was gigantic square tiles of polished black marble, thin white veins flecked with gold wove their way through it tracing circuitous patterns. The wall to their left was light brown brick. The bricks were long and thin. The wall held a large fireplace with a built in wood rack. The rack was full of neatly cut and stacked wood. The wall to the right was also partially glass, but the area closest to them held the most modern looking kitchen Billy had ever seen separated from the main room by a bar. There were four bent bamboo barstools at the bar. The room was large and airy and held a pair of over-stuffed couches and assorted tables and chairs. Massive bare wood beams supporting the ceiling pointed toward the ocean, pulling your eye to the glass wall as if the view needed encouragement.

"Wow! This is beautiful," Billy exclaimed so overwhelmed he had no other words.

"Earle has good taste doesn't he?" Sally smiled.

"Does he ever!" Billy exclaimed. "I guess Earle is your brother? It must be great to live here."

"Oh, he doesn't live here. This is his hideaway. It's where he has been rendezvousing with some of the women in his life." She gave him another of those spectacular grins. "Make yourself at home; you want to bring our things in?" she asked.

Billy's mind boggled. How could anyone afford something as grand as this house with its only use as a clandestine rendezvous spot? "Won't your brother mind? What if he has a rendezvous planned?" Billy said with some concern.

"He's in New York City. We've got the place to ourselves. Luzia and I, Luzia is the housekeeper, have the only other keys. He gave one to me so I could use the place. Sometimes I just need to get away from everyone else you know? Of course, I think part of the reason was so I would keep it quiet. If Dad knew he had this place, then he'd want to use it."

"You mean your dad," he stopped abruptly in mid sentence realizing what he was about to say and stopping just in time. Still he couldn't help from blushing, embarrassed that he even had the thought.

"You were going to say, 'has other women in his life'? Yes, he does, a lot of them." Her smile faded.

"Does that bother you?" he asked.

"Of course it does. How could it not, knowing your daddy is carousing with every pretty girl in sight? It used to bother me a lot more, but what can I do about it? I think it drove my mother to her bottle of scotch too, but I finally realized that's just the way things are. After all, I was just a kid. I brought it up, with both of them, but it didn't do any good. I never have accepted it, but I have learned to live with it. That's why I need time away from them sometimes." Sally said with a hint of sadness in her voice.

Billy was amazed. His life and hers were so different; he might as well have come from another planet. Her family had money and power, but his had each other. There was no doubt in his mind that he came from the richer family. He turned and headed back to the car.

When he returned carrying their bags, Sally was in the kitchen. "Sandwich okay for you?" she asked.

"Sure," he set the bags down and went to the bar. She was just setting a pair of emerald green plates on the polished marble slab that formed the top surface of the bar. The sandwich looked delicious, crusty French bread, fresh lettuce and tomato, with thick sliced ham and cheddar cheese. Before he could get situated on one of the stools, she was pouring light golden wine into a pair of long stemmed glasses. Sally came around the bar and sat beside him.

Billy took a bite. It was as good as it looked. "How is this so fresh with your brother in New York?"

"Luzia does all the shopping. Her orders are to keep everything fresh so the place can be used at a moment's notice. She buys bread and produce twice a week I think."

"Wow" was the only thought that came to Billy's mind. They finished eating and Sally got up to take away the plates. "Where do you want me to put the bags?"

Sally picked up the wine bottle and both glasses and said "Follow me".

Sally led the way across the room to the corner formed by the glass and brick walls. There was a wide opening here that led into a short hallway. One side of the hall was glass and the other side was completely filled with drawers from floor to ceiling and by several narrow doors. They walked out of the hallway into the bedroom.

The bedroom was equally as spectacular as the living room had been, and nearly as large. The same brown brick used in the living room was on one wall of the bedroom. This wall held a duplicate of the fireplace in the living room, complete with its own built in, well stocked wood rack.

The biggest bed Billy had ever seen dominated the room. A dark multicolored velvet bedspread covered it, the low teak headboard almost obscured by a mound of matching and contrasting pillows. Each side of the headboard contained a built in nightstand flanked by matching doorways. The opposite wall was half glass just like the living room and held a small bar complete with its own pair of bamboo stools. Billy whistled.

"This place is really something. What does your brother do for a living?" he asked.

"He's my father's son, of course. Like I said, he has good taste and he built this place for impressing his little chickadee friends, remember."

"I'm not a chickadee, but I'm sure impressed," Billy said.

Sally laughed, "Oh, I don't know, you kind of look like a chickadee to me," and she gave him another of her naughty looks. She led the way through the closest of the two doorways. It was a very large bathroom with matching dressing areas on both sides. Billy was somewhat surprised to see clothes hanging in both dressing areas.

There was the largest black marble shower he had ever seen, it's sparkling glass walls framed in brass. On each side of the shower a matching black marble counter held identical sinks, backed by huge mirrors. On the wall opposite the counter was a built in marble tub. It was directly behind the wall holding the head of the bed and the tub was enormous. All the faucets and fittings were gold plated. Like the rest of the house, the styling was all very modern and except for the tubs and sinks, everything was streamlined and simple, deriving its richness from the materials and design, rather than from ornamentation.

"Put yours in there," Sally pointed to the dressing area close by, "and mine in that one." And she pointed to the one at the far end of the bathroom.

His area was full of expensive clothes and shoes. There was a platform that he guessed was built to hold an open suitcase. That's where he deposited his. The other dressing area didn't have nearly as many clothes, mostly robes and a few slacks and sweaters. Billy assumed that since the female visitors changed so frequently, these were backups for emergencies. He left Sally's suitcase on the shelf.

When he came out, Sally was waiting for him. "I'll show you the rest of the place." and led him back into the bedroom. She walked over to the glass wall and pushed a cleverly camouflaged lever he hadn't noticed and the entire glass panel became a door. He then realized that each of the glass panels making up the wall held identical levers. "Do all these panels open up?" he asked.

"Not only do they open, but watch this," she reached down and flipped another lever, then reached up and flipped another. Then she pushed the panel from the side and it slid smoothly along a track.

"The whole wall opens up?" Billy asked, a look of wonder on his face.

"Sure does. That's nifty don't you think?" she smiled.

"Oh yeah! Your brother thinks of everything doesn't he?"

Sally walked out onto what she referred to as a deck. To Billy's mind, decks were only on ships, but he could see the analogy. He would have called it a porch or veranda, but he thought 'deck' was a good word. The deck was built of sturdy wooden planks and stretched across the entire beach side of the house. A wooden banister surrounded the deck, and on the bedroom end, a wide stairway stretched down to the beach. Billy estimated the deck was 20 feet above the sand. The beach was wide here, maybe 50 yards to the water. There were a couple of other houses in view, but they were set some distance away. All of them were obviously expensive and all had some sort of deck and stairs down to the sand. The beach itself was deserted.

"Does anyone live in those houses?" There weren't any people in evidence on the beach. The nearest house was quite a distance away, but even from here it looked shut up and locked.

"There's probably a few people that live in them, but for the most part, they're only used on the weekends." Billy wondered how many people there might be here tomorrow, since today was Friday.

Several wood and cloth chairs were folded up and stored in compartments at each end of the deck.

"There's more firewood and chairs and things stored down under the deck. Stuff like you might use on the beach."

"This is the nicest house I've ever been in." Billy said.

That statement gave pause to Sally. She took things like this for granted. She never realized how much until that moment. She always thought her feet were well grounded, but that simple statement brought total focus to the life of privilege she had always enjoyed. It was a very sobering thought for her.

She looked at Billy, "Really?" she said.

"Oh, yeah," was the reply. "It's not a huge house," he said "but it's large for something a person would only use on weekends. And the materials used must have cost a fortune. This deck is teak isn't it?" Sally had no clue what it was, to her it was just wood.

"Is teak good?" she asked

"Teak is the best. They use it on ships and yachts because it doesn't rot. And look at the marble floors and counters. Yeah, this is the nicest house I've ever been in."

"I'm very glad I could share it with you then, because you are the very nicest person I've ever known in my life." Sally said and kissed him long and deep.

"I really enjoyed that, and I enjoy every minute I'm with you, but I'm really not that special you know." He said.

114

"And you thinking that way, is part of the reason that you are," and she kissed him again.

Sally retrieved the bottle of wine and glasses from where she had left them in the bedroom. They went to the living room and opened the glass panels and slid them all back so that the wall facing the Pacific was totally open. The sea breeze blew in through the huge opening.

Billy pulled one of the couches around and they lounged on it. He stretched out against one of the arms and a mound of pillows with Sally lounging against his side, her head on his chest. They spent the afternoon enjoying each other's company, the view, and the sound of crashing waves. Their conversation touched on all aspects of their lives. Innermost secrets were shared, each trusting the other completely. Both thought it the perfect afternoon. The sun was hot, but back in the shade of the room with the cool breeze it was perfect.

As the afternoon wore on, it was getting dark. The sunset had been spectacular. The setting sun seemed so close you could almost reach out and touch it. The day's heat deserted with the sun's disappearance.

The bottle of wine from lunch was long gone and another had followed it. It had been a dreamy relaxed afternoon. The strife earlier was completely forgotten. It was dark enough that they could barely make out the white of the surf as it broke along the beach. The lights of a fishing trawler twinkled several hundred yards off shore. The houses on both sides were simply gone, lost in the gloom, no lights showing.

"How about a swim," she asked.

"I still don't have a suit. Do you think your brother has one I can use?"

"We didn't need suits yesterday."

"This is not nearly as secluded as yesterday either, young lady."

"Do you seriously think that my brother and his guests wear suits when they visit?"

"Well....."

"Of course they don't! That's the whole point of this place! Come on!" she said standing up and starting to undress.

Even though he was a little leery, Billy really had no choice. Sally had already made the decision and he simply had to follow her lead. Before he even stood up, Sally was already to the stairs, her clothes scattered across the deck.

"Come on, slow poke!" She waited at the stairs laughing. They held hands down the stairs, their feet slapping against the smooth surface of the board steps. The sand, still warm from the days' sun a completely different feeling from the wood of the deck. They walked at first, but the closer they got to the surf, the more the urge built and they broke into a run charging into the sea just as a breaker hit the beach. Water broke over them and the world was suddenly black.   Then it was gone and they were in the starlight once more.

They swam out past the breakers and then tried to catch the waves as they formed and ride them into shore.   There was much splashing each other and laughter.   One playful prank after another was committed to roars of laughter.

Finally, they had enough fun in the ocean.   They walked out of the surf together and stood on the beach in a long embrace.   The couple turned and walked back toward the house.   They hadn't traveled more than 10 yards before they literally bumped into another couple strolling on the beach.   Billy and Sally were so intent on each other that they had not noticed the other's approach.   The other couple's attention was on the house noticing light inside the normally dark structure.

The couple was much older, old enough in fact to have been their grandparents.   "Oh shit!" were the first words out of Billy's mouth, he had a second to gain what composure he could muster.   "Please excuse us, we're terribly sorry!" he blurted out and seizing Sally's hand, dragged her around the old couple and breaking into a run toward the house.   Before they could get around them however, Sally saw the momentary shocked looks on the couple's faces had turned to smiles, then broad grins.   As they ran away, they heard the couple call out, first the man "Don't mention it, we rather enjoyed it!" and then the woman called "Yes we did enjoy it, anytime!" and then their words were drowned out by the surf.

As Billy and Sally ran to the house she said "Did you hear what they said?   And did you see the looks on their faces?   I think they did enjoy it!" she giggled.

"I'm sure the old man did." and he laughed.

"I think the old woman enjoyed it more!" they laughed harder.   When they had reached the stairs, the naked duo mounted them in a run, two steps at a time.

Once inside both headed toward the bathroom.   The shower was been designed with couples in mind. The water from multiple strategically placed heads felt like warm needles.   Nothing, it seemed, had been left to chance.   Getting the salt water off was great, but getting it off each other was even better.   The shower took longer than required.

Sally was wrapped in her big terry cloth robe, her hair still wet.   The light from the refrigerator softly lit her features.   "Bacon and eggs okay?"

"Sure, do we have any potatoes and onions? I'll make some of my mom's specialty."   Billy said.   He fixed home fried potatoes and onions while Sally cooked the rest.

While they were eating, Billy asked, "So is this what you do? You eat eggs and bacon after terrorizing little old couples?"

Sally elbowed him in the ribs hard enough that it knocked some of the wind out if him.   "Billy Pendleton! I have never done anything like that before in my life!" she paused for a second, "But

I'd do it again, just like the old lady said 'anytime'!" They both collapsed in laughter.

"That old man got an eye full and that's for sure," Billy said.

"That old lady got a bigger eye full!"

"What does that mean?" Billy asked with a grin.

"That you're a lot bigger than I am, silly!"

More laughter, their sides were hurting by this time.

Finally their laughter got under control. Billy noticed that the evening had gotten noticeably cooler. "I'll clean up this mess if you'll close up the wall." Sally said.

"Deal," Billy got up and started closing all the panels. Pushing them in place and then using the levers to latch them shut. He realized besides the striking appearance, the house had been designed to deal with the damp salt air. The marble and brick and even the gold plated fixtures were designed to be impervious to sea air. Once more he admired the thought and planning that went into its design. He was just finishing up when Sally called across the room "Would you start us a fire in the bedroom? I'll open another bottle of wine, okay?"

"Sure," and he headed into the bedroom. The only light they had were candles. It didn't seem right to turn on the electric lights in this house. Billy soon found that his host had thought of that too. In the built in wood storage area of the wall was a light switch. When he flipped it, soft light bathed the wood box and the fireplace. The light revealed a gas pipe in the bottom of the fireplace and its control valve on the wall between the fireplace and the wood box. The wood box also held a tin of long fireplace matches. The man really did think of everything! Billy mused.

In short order, Billy had a roaring fire going in the fireplace. Just as he was stepping back to admire his work, Sally appeared at his elbow, wine and glasses in hand. She sat the glasses on the nearest nightstand and poured them full. As they each took a glass Sally faced Billy in the soft light of the fire and said, "A toast," and paused. "To little old men," she said and held her glass up for him to toast. "To little old women," he added as their glasses clinked.

Later in bed, Billy reflected on the events of the day. The wine bottle was empty and the fire was a dull red bed of coals. Sally was curled against his side and already asleep. He reveled in her warmth. The bed was sensational. He had never slept in a bed large enough to accommodate his height, but this one did easily. He stroked Sally and she snuggled even more tightly against him. He thought even the coldest hardest rock he could imagine would be wonderful if Sally was with him, but right now he would luxuriate in her presence and this marvelous bed.

Billy awoke the next morning as Sally was crawling back into bed. Gray light filtered in the glass wall. Sally snuggled up next to him, kissing him on the cheek, "Good morning lover. Sorry I woke you." she whispered.

"Good morning sweetheart. Isn't this the most wonderful bed?" Billy was lying on his back, arms and legs stretched out completely. He was still amazed that even like this, there was room below his feet. His feet always hung off the end of the bed. Sally rolled partially onto him, her right leg over his. "What I find more remarkable is the bed's occupant." She kissed him once and then again. Billy had to agree, she was completely remarkable.

Later, they lay propped up on the pillows watching the surf roll in. "That coffee sure smells good." He said. He was about to get up to go get some, but Sally put her hand on his chest. "Stay here, I'll get it." She rolled across him and got out of bed on his side. She padded across the room and disappeared into the hall.

A moment later, she padded back into the room carrying two large mugs of steaming coffee. As she started across the room toward his side of the bed, Billy sat up and held his arms out wide. "Hold them like this," he said. She complied, a puzzled look on her face. "They were blocking the view," he said.

"Billy Pendleton!"

By the time they were through, the coffee was cool enough to drink. "Do you like music?" Sally asked.

"Sure, why?"

"I thought maybe you could take me dancing tonight. Would you mind?" she asked.

"Honey, I'll take you anywhere, but I think you should know, I'm a terrible dancer."

"You can't be that bad."

"Oh yes I can, but it's your feet. I would be delighted to take you anyplace your heart desires."

"Then dancing it is. I know a great place, I'll make a call and reserve us a table."

After they got dressed, Billy asked if they could visit the Offenhauser shop as Fred Offenhauser had been Harry Miller's shop foreman and might have knowledge of the Special's engine. He was anxious to find out all he could about the mysterious power plant.

"I don't really know Mr. Offenhauser, but I know where his shop is. I've met him a couple of times, and of course Carl and Tommy know him. If you want to drive over there, we can take our chances." Sally said.

"Yesterday, Ted said the shop had moved. Did you know that?" Billy asked.

"Yeah, but I'd forgotten. The only reason I know is that Mr. Offenhauser had a big party there when he opened the new place. It was on the Saturday after New Year's. Tommy was invited and asked me to go."

"Well, did you?"

"No, I turned him down. I didn't care anything about seeing the inside of an engine building shop." She smirked.

"You're going with me today. In fact, you brought it up."

"That's different. I'm going with you. You're interested in doing it, so I am too. Just like you going dancing tonight. Why are you doing that?" she asked.

118

"Because you want to."

"See what I mean? Tommy has never been able to get it in his head that I'm not interested in him romantically. I value his friendship, but that's it."

"Did you lead him on?" Billy was thinking of that day at Kearny Mesa when he met them both for the first time. He thought that Sally was Tommy's girlfriend and had said as much, only to have her put him in his place.

"Yes, I probably did, I'm sorry to say. Once upon a time I thought it was a game. Since I met you, all of that has changed. That's really why I got upset yesterday. I knew I hurt Tommy because I always let him think that someday it might happen. I never should have done that. It was childish of me and I'm really ashamed of it."

Sally leaned against him and he hugged her.

"We all do things we're ashamed of at times. You just have to put them behind you and resolve to do better in the future."

"Even you? You've done things you're ashamed of?"

"Sure."

"Like what? I don't believe it. You're Mister Goodie-two-shoes. Tell me something you've done!"

Billy realized too late that he painted himself into a box. He silently resolved to try and be smarter in the future.

"Come on, tell me! I just can't see you doing anything you're ashamed of."

"Okay, okay. My little brother, Jimmie, you know, we've talked about him."

She nodded that yes she knew who Jimmie was. Billy talked about him all the time

"You know I've told you what a daredevil he is. All the stunts he does on his bicycle."

She nodded some more. She remembered being amazed at the stories of Jimmie riding down the hill on the street where they lived, standing up on the seat with his arms straight out to the sides, or doing handstands on the handlebars.

"Well, Jimmie used to come running out the front door of the house, grab his bicycle and running full speed, he'd jump on the bike and pedaling as hard as he could, go up the street with his front wheel a foot in the air. It used to impress all the neighbor kids, and of course Jimmie loved that. He'd turn the front wheel back and forth just to emphasize the trick. So one day I thought it would be funny if something happened to his bike, sort of make his trick a little more spectacular, you know."

Sally was intently watching him. He had her full attention.

"So one day while Jimmie was in the house, I knew he'd be there for a while. Mom caught him and had him peeling potatoes. He always hated that and he wasn't any good at it either. But anyway, while he was in the house I loosened the bolt on the handlebars."

Sally gasped. "You didn't do that did you?"

119

"So anyway, when Jimmie got finished he was really anxious to get away from the house before she found anything else for him to do, so he came out running especially hard. He grabbed that bike and jumped on it right at the end of the driveway."

Sally was hanging on every word.

"He turned those handlebars to go up the street, and they turned, but the bike just went straight. He was already standing up, pumping for all he was worth on those pedals."

Sally's eyes were wide by this point.

"That old bike went right straight across the street and smashed right into the back of old man Dial's car. That bike just wedged right in between the rear fender and the bumper. It took three men and a bumper jack to get it unstuck afterwards."

"What else happened?" Sally's eyes were still wide. She couldn't believe this.

"Oh, it bent the frame and crumpled the front fender. The tire blew out when the wheel bent. Looked just like a pretzel."

"I don't mean the bike! What happened to Jimmie?!" she insisted.

"Oh, well he went flying over the handlebars. You should have seen the look on his face. It was like he couldn't believe this was happening. He didn't look scared at all."

"And then?"

"He landed right in the middle of the Dial's driveway. Hit right on his head. The dial's drive is gravel, you know. Some of the rocks, well they stuck right in his head. Looked kind of like an ice cream cone when they put those sprinkles on them you know?"

"Yes, I know! What happened to him!?!" she almost screamed.

"He broke his neck, of course. Oh yeah and it fractured his skull. I always thought his head was harder than that, but it sure broke it."

"You broke your brother's neck??"

"Yeah," This was getting harder for Billy. He wasn't sure he could keep himself under control much longer.

"What happened next?"

"Oh nuthin!"

"What do you mean 'nuthin', what happened to Jimmie?"

"Nuthin', Jimmie's fine."

"How can he be fine?" she asked impatiently.

"Cause I made it all up, and I'm really ashamed of it too." He barely got the last few words out he was laughing so hard. What made him lose it was the look of sudden comprehension on Sally's face. She suddenly realized she had been had. At that point Billy couldn't keep going any longer. He burst into laughter and Sally pounded him with fists and kicks. In the beginning the blows were hard enough to sting, but then they weakened as Sally started laughing herself.

"You're really going to pay for that one buster! Broke your brother's neck. And I fell for it!" she howled with laughter.

120

By this time Sally was laughing so hard she couldn't hit him anymore. She realized something new about her love. He wasn't going to allow her to get down on herself. As soon as she had, he immediately came up with this elaborate story to take her mind somewhere else. She grabbed him and hugged him close. "Let's go before I fall for something else you say." Still laughing, they went out the front door.

It was a beautiful day. The sky was bright blue and crystal clear. Smog was not a problem in those days. They cruised into LA with the top down. Traffic along the coast highway was heavier and the beaches were beginning to fill up some, as they did every Saturday.

The couple drove into an industrial part of town and pulled up in front of a large single story red brick building. A white sign with black lettering announced it as Offenhauser Engineering Company, 2001 West Gage Ave. Los Angeles, California.

"Must be the place." She said as she parked the car.

"Must be." They walked in the front door of the building. A bell tingled as they shut the door. There was an empty desk and a few drawings and pictures on the wall, there was nothing remarkable about the place. Nothing to let a visitor know that this establishment produced extraordinary racing engines that would eventually win 39 Indianapolis 500's.

Just as they were thinking maybe they should leave and come back sometime during the week, a short, pudgy, balding man walked around the corner carrying a pair of glasses in his hand. He wore a plaid short sleeved shirt and dark brown cotton trousers. His shoes were heavy leather and appeared oil soaked and well worn. The shirt's pocket held several pens and pencils and a steel machinists rule.

"May I help you folks?" The man said, then "Oh, hello, Miss Anthony isn't it?"

"Yes, it is Mr. Offenhauser. Thank you for remembering me." Sally said.

"A man doesn't soon forget a woman as pretty as you Miss Anthony." It was Sally's turn to blush. It was the first time Billy had seen her do that.

"Mr. Offenhauser you're much too kind, but please call me Sally and this is my friend, Billy Pendleton. Billy and Carl Mercer are building a car together."

"Pleased to make your acquaintance Mr. Pendleton," and he held out his hand.

"The pleasure is mine Mr. Offenhauser, please call me Billy."

"Carl is an old friend. I miss visiting with him since he moved to San Diego. Since we're all on a first name basis, please call me Fred. What kind of car are you building, and what brings you to my shop?"

"We're building a speedster to race on the dry lakes and maybe to drive occasionally on the street. We're sort of patterning it after Frank Lockhart's Black Hawk Special."

Fred was nodding his head. "That was the most beautiful car I've ever seen. Yes, I remember Frank and Carl were very good friends. Grew up together didn't they?"

"Why yes they did," Billy responded.

"What kind of engine are you using?" Fred wasted no time getting to the heart of the matter, Billy thought.

"It's one that Tommy Lee lent us. It's a 6 cylinder, half a V-12 Cadillac and I think your shop did some of the work. I wondered if you could tell me anything about it." Billy asked.

"Oh, yes, I remember that engine." Fred smiled an apologetic smile. "Harry took that job in when we were in the shop around the corner on Gramercy Place. I think it can rightfully be called a Miller. Most of the work was done when I still worked for Harry. To be honest, I don't think it was one of our better efforts."

"Is there something I should know about it? Is it defective?" Billy asked.

"No, no, I didn't mean that. It's just that it never made competitive power. If I remember correctly, Mr. Lee commissioned that project, not Tommy. I believe it was to power an Indy entry."

"Yes, that's what I've heard, but I didn't know Tommy's father started it."

"Yes, if I remember correctly he did. He brought us a number of projects over the years. He liked to tie them back to the dealership in some way. I believe that's why he wanted us to use a V-12 as the starting point. He was more interested in it looking like a Cadillac engine than he was in how much power it made. It would have been easier to start from scratch, much easier."

"But there aren't any major issues with the engine other than power output?" Billy asked cautiously.

"No, as I remember it, it was a very nicely turned out engine. Harry always insisted that everything look just so. The engine ran well and was smooth, it was probably better suited to a road car than a competition car. It should work well for your intended use. You know, we started on that project about the time Harry was selling out. We had new owners taking over and some of our most experienced employees left us. The new owners didn't understand the racing business and didn't really have the money to keep the shop open. It was all a mess. That engine got started and stopped so many times. I think I actually finished it and delivered it after I took over. I felt I owed the Lee's that much after all the business they've given us over the years. I just bought a new Cadillac from Tommy, by the way. He didn't mention the engine at all."

"I'm not surprised. I think he'd forgotten it existed until Carl asked him if we could use it."

"It's probably a much better choice for a speedster than that 318 Tommy had me build for his. Would you like to see the shop?"

"We'd love to if it's okay. I hate to interrupt you like this." Billy insisted.

"It's a welcome break. I've been working on the damn payroll all morning and I hate that!"

They all laughed as Fred opened the small gate in the waist high wall that separated the front door from the office area.

"Come on through and I'll show you around a bit. I'm sorry to say that we're not doing as much race work these days. Most of the shop is engaged in building airplane parts for Lockheed. We do still have a few engines in the shop though. It seems that the country is gearing up for a war, I sure hope we can avoid it." Fred led them down a short hallway. "That's my office in there." It was a small office with blueprints of engines on the walls and a paper-strewn desk.

"In here is the design and drafting department, Leo Goosen runs that." They looked through the open door at a large room filled with drawing tables, each covered with drawings and blue prints.

Fred walked to the end of the hall and opened the door into the shop area. Billy's first impression was how bright the work area was. It was a large open area with exposed rafters. The walls were lined with multi-pane windows. The morning sun streamed in reflecting off the white walls and ceiling. The space was filled with machine tools arranged in neat orderly rows. Shop lights were suspended above each machine. The far wall was lined with shelving from one side of the shop to the other. Closest to them were several steel topped benches. On the benches were what appeared to be two complete four cylinder engines and parts for several more.

"These are 97 inch midget engines. This one is the last one we'll do this year; it's going to Ted Halibrand. We're booked solid with aircraft work, so the racing business is suffering."

"You're kidding! I just met Ted yesterday, spent a couple of hours with him over at Frank Kurtis' shop." Billy said with excitement.

"Really? Ted's a nice guy and a good racer. He's building a new midget. Should be very nice, he's a talented craftsman."

"I noticed yesterday that he did great work. He showed me several things that will help me with mine. He doesn't say much does he?"

Fred chuckled. "No, he doesn't talk much, but being around Frank, he never gets a chance." Everyone laughed at that. "He's a knowledgeable guy, one of the best racers around."

They walked to the next table and Fred picked up a large aluminum disc covered in prominent fins. It was beautiful and looked more like a piece of sculpture than an engine part. "This is a supercharger we've built for Bud Winfield." He handed the supercharger to Billy. It was lighter than its size would indicate. It was simply magnificent, as much sculpture as automobile part. Billy had never seen better machine work, even at Consolidated.

123

"And these are several cranks and rods we're doing as replacement parts for racers." Fred continued, "We try to keep a good stock of semi-finished parts on hand. Once a customer places an order, we finish machining the parts to the customer's specs and ship in a day or two."

Billy whistled. "Do they supply those specifications to you or do you know them already?"

"Usually the customer supplies them. Of course, we have specs on every engine we've ever built, but you know racers. You never know what they're going to do to them, what modifications they've made along the way."

"Fred, what carburetors would you recommend I use on my engine?" Billy asked.

"There weren't any on it?" Fred asked.

"No there weren't."

"I wonder what happened to them? If I remember correctly, we used a pair of Winfield downdrafts when we ran the engine on the dynamometer, but you don't have to use Winfields. You could use almost anything really, like some Strombergs either 94's or 97's would work." Fred said thoughtfully.

"Okay, I'm sure we can come up with those."

Fred walked them around the shop showing them how they built the most successful racing engine in the world. He showed them the wooden patterns used to cast all the major parts, then how the castings were machined and finished and where the engines were assembled. They looked at the dynamometer where each engine was run on a test stand and its power output recorded. Billy found it incredible that he was standing in the shop where the engines for the past 15 Indianapolis 500 winners had been built, discussing his own project with the man that built them.

"Mr. Offenhauser, Fred, we've taken up enough of your time. Thank you for showing us your shop. It's more than I had ever imagined. And thanks for the information and tips on my engine. You've been an excellent host."

"It's been my pleasure. I always enjoy showing off the shop. I'm very proud of it and the work we do. It's been nice to meet you Billy, and it was a pleasure to see you again Sally. Please tell Carl and little Frank hello for me and give them my best."

"That we'll do. Thank you again."

Sally and Billy walked out through the office area the way they had come in. After they were outside Sally said, "What a nice man."

"Yes he is. He really was very cordial to us, wasn't he?"

They got in the Packard, Sally behind the wheel once again. "Where to?" she asked.

"Wherever you want to take me, I've seen everything I wanted to see related to the Special. I'm at your disposal."

"Really?" she gave him a rather wicked grin to go with the question.

Just the thought of what that grin meant was delicious to contemplate Billy thought.

"I know a great place for lunch, and this is a great day for it. Hungry?" Sally asked.

Billy wondered what she meant by that. "I could eat, that's for sure."

Sally drove back in the general direction of the beach house in Malibu. The top was down and the sun was getting pretty warm Billy thought. There wasn't a cloud in the sky.

The place Sally took him was perched high on a hillside overlooking the ocean. Billy was beginning to think that Sally liked ocean views. They sat outside on a covered wooden deck and had hamburgers and beer. The view was spectacular. In the shade with the ocean breeze, it was very pleasant.

"What is that island?" Billy asked.

"That's Catalina, or more correctly, Santa Catalina."

"It looks pretty. How far away is it?"

"I'm not sure, I think about 20 miles, maybe a little more."

"Is that where the broadcasts that start with 'from the beautiful Casino Ballroom overlooking Avalon Bay at Catalina Island' originate from?" Billy asked.

Sally was impressed and showed it. "Why yes it is! Do you listen to those radio programs?"

"I used to, back home in Texas. I built a crystal radio set and if reception was good at night I'd listen to the big bands. I haven't listened since I left home."

"You built your own radio?" The shock showed on Sally's face. There was much for her to learn about this man.

"Oh sure, it was a project when I was in the Scouts. Worked good too."

"Was it a big radio that the whole family could listen to?"

"No, no, it was just a small crystal set. It was mounted on a board about this big square." He used his hands to draw a square approximately a foot on each side.

"I wound my own tuning coil on a wood dowel. Used an old spoon for a tuner," he grinned remembering how proud he had been of the old radio.

"An old spoon?" Sally was plainly amazed, "and this thing played music?"

"Oh yeah, it worked great. Now it didn't have a big speaker, you had to listen on headphones. I got those at a salvage store, but they sounded good."

"I had no idea that a person could just build a radio out of boards and spoons."

"It wasn't a big deal and besides, it's all I could afford. I probably had fifty cents in it. That was a lot of money to me at the time."

Sally sat back in her chair and just looked at him. It was hard for her to comprehend that fifty cents was a lot of money to anyone, especially someone as handsome and smart as Billy. It made her think yet again how different their lives had been. She thought once more what a remarkable person Billy was and how lucky she was to be with him.

"Well mister, you're going to see the real thing tonight. Have you ever seen a big band in person?"

"Not a famous one. Some guys at school had a little band and they played for dances. You know just small things. Woody Herman was in Dallas once, but I didn't get to go. Who are we seeing tonight?"

"I'm not sure. I guess we'll just have to wait and see." Sally lied. She wanted it to be a surprise. She hadn't really thought about it till now, but she wanted to achieve maximum effect.

"We better be going. We've got to get back to the house and get dressed for tonight." Sally said.

Billy was relieved he had packed his sports coat and slacks 'just in case'. He was certain none of Sally's brother's clothes would even come close to fitting. He should have known 'just in case' always applied to Sally.

"How are we getting over there?" he asked as they got in the car to leave.

"There's a steamer, a couple of them as a matter of fact. They make several trips a day." Wow, a 20-mile steamer ride Billy thought! He had never been on a steamer before. He hoped he didn't get seasick!

They arrived back at the house and as they walked through the front door Billy thought how much he was going to miss this place. The stay had been so enjoyable, he couldn't imagine how it could have been better, even the old couple on the beach last night added something special. He would always remember it and he bet they would too and fondly from the sounds of their voices as he and Sally had run away.

They both headed for the bathroom. Sally started the shower. "Are you going to join me?" she asked coyly.

"Of course," Billy knew he was going to miss the showers. There was no way they would be able to continue them once they were back in San Diego. Better make the most of it while they could. He peeled off his clothes just in time to step in behind Sally and close the door. Yes, he was going to miss this shower. He never tired of looking at his companion either. Just then a water filled sponge hit him in the face.

"You better get busy mister! There'll be plenty of time later for looking if that's what you want to do. We've got to hurry now to make the steamer."

"Looking is exactly what I want to do, and you promise there'll be time later?"

"I promise!"

"I'll look forward to it" he said.

"Get busy!"

The Packard's tires crunched across the gravel parking lot. When Sally had said they would take a steamer, Billy just assumed it would be a drive on ferry and that they would take the Packard with them, but what awaited them was more like a passenger liner, in fact there were two of them! The ships were rakish and sleek, resplendent in white and nearly identical. Lettered on their bows were the names *Catalina* and *Avalon*. The parking lot was almost full already. They had to search for a parking spot and just finished putting up the top when the steamer's horn blasted across the lot like a shot and reverberated off the buildings across the street. "We better run, that's the signal they're about to leave!"

They ran toward the dock. When they cleared the last line of cars they could see that even though the deck crew had let go all the lines, the steamer was still taking on a few last minute arrivals like them. Their run slowed to a trot and even though they were the last on board, several other couples were just in front of them. As soon as they were on the deck, they heard the steamer's engines rev up and they could feel the deck tremble as they backed away from the dock. It arched backward and then reversed to head out of the harbor. Once they cleared the harbor entrance, Billy was surprised by the sudden acceleration as the steamer headed toward the island. It was funny to think of something as big as this being able to accelerate at a noticeable rate. Black smoke billowed out of the single smokestack. Up ahead Billy could see its twin churning a white wake and adding another column of smoke to the crystal blue sky. A dance band was playing from somewhere toward the stern. Sally smiled and pulled him along by the hand toward the music.

The ocean was relatively calm and the ride was smooth with very little rock. They stood at the rail and watched Los Angeles and the hills recede. For the first time Billy had a chance to look around. The ship carried mostly young couples, all of them dressed for a night out, many of them already dancing to the sounds of swing. The place is going to be full tonight he thought.

He also had time to admire Sally for a moment. They had been rushing so to make it on time that he didn't have time to let his eyes really linger. The only word that came to his mind was 'stunning'. This was the first time he ever saw her dressed to the nines and it was a sight to behold. She wore a blue strapless evening dress with a full skirt that ended at the knee. The dress made her eyes look even bluer, if that was possible. She wore a simple string of pearls tight around her throat; he heard people refer to such necklaces as 'chokers' for obvious reason and matching ear rings. She carried a white beaded bag that matched the pearls surprisingly well and she wore a white sweater draped over her bare shoulders. Sally had on red lipstick and stockings, of course. He carried a small bag that had her heels in it. She had on some nicely matching shoes, but they had much flatter heels than the strapless ones he carried. Billy noticed that many of the other men carried similar bags. Sally told him that there would be a lot of walking tonight. He guessed she was right since the Packard was back in LA.

The ride out was pleasant. The sun was setting and the sky was beautiful as usual. Catalina got closer and closer. Billy was amazed that the island was as large as it was. The steamers headed into the harbor.

The scene looked like one out of a fairy tale. The harbor was surrounded by an almost perfect crescent of sandy beach. The town was built on the steeply sloping hill sides that framed the beach. Brightly painted stucco walls with tile roofs, small wooden cottages, and what appeared to be a large adobe hacienda surrounded the small harbor. Above them all was a large white mansion. But dominating the entire scene was a large circular building looking for all the world like a huge ornate hatbox. It had a red tile roof and Moroccan style arches ringed its sides. This was the Grand Casino. It was brightly lit and Sally told him the point it stood on was known as Sugar Loaf Point. Billy couldn't see any resemblance to a sugar loaf, whatever that was, but it had a nice exotic sound to it. He was amazed that such a place was just a short boat ride away from the hustle and bustle of LA.

Two sleek speedboats raced out to meet them. The boats were gleaming mahogany and each carried a crew of two plus a pair of beautiful girls in swim suits who waved non-stop at the passengers.

The ship maneuvered into the pier with a revving of engines and tooting of horns. As soon as they were tied off, the gates were opened and the passengers disembarked walking in one long procession toward the Grand Casino.

It was a lovely evening. They were walking along a street aptly named Crescent Avenue as it paralleled the semi-circular beach. Tall palm trees lined the avenue with the beach on their right and quaint shops and restaurants on their left. The small harbor was filled with moored boats of every description and color from gaily painted rowboats to a couple yachts, and even a three masted schooner.

The architecture seemed to be a fairly even split between the Spanish influence of Southern California and the clapboards of Cape Cod. They decided to stop at an open-air bar for a beer before continuing on to the casino.

As they sat on stools made from lobster cages, Billy said, "This is really a beautiful place. How many people live on the island?"

"Not many, a few hundred I suppose," Sally answered.

I haven't seen any cars."

"There aren't any, or at least, there aren't very many. I think there are a few for emergency services and such, but for the most part, its walk, ride a bicycle, or ride a horse."

"How do they manage to enforce that?"

"The Wrigley's, you know the chewing gum family, they own the island or most of it anyway. They've done the developing and they want to keep it a slower simpler place. Everyone that comes here knows the rules. It's worked very well, I love it."

"So do I, I'm just amazed that we're only a few miles from LA and all the traffic and lights and all the noise. It's so peaceful here."

Sally slipped off her walking shoes and retrieved her 'heels' from the bag Billy was carrying. They were strapless with open toes and matched her dress. Billy thought they made her even more alluring than normal, an almost unsettling thought.

"Ready lover?" she said and took his arm as he stood. They made a very attractive couple as they walked the last block to the Casino through a wooden vine covered portico. Sally steered him to the 'Will Call' window where they picked up their tickets. Billy was shocked to see signboards posted advertising Glenn Miller and his orchestra as tonight's entertainment.

"Glenn Miller?" he looked at Sally, his eyes wide, "THE Glenn Miller?"

"Yes lover," she laughed.

"You didn't tell me Glenn Miller was playing tonight!"

"A girl must maintain her air of mystery to keep her place in a man's heart," she said with a very provocative look, "don't you know anything?"

Billy had no idea how to respond to this. "No, I guess not," was all he could manage.

It was a beautiful building. They mounted a series of long ramps to the second floor grand ballroom. The sight that awaited them was breathtaking. The room was enormous, actually 180 feet across, and circular. No columns supported the doomed ceiling nor marred the polished wood planking of the dance floor. The ceiling arched to a large central cupola surrounded by sparkling crystal chandeliers. The walls were adorned with art deco columns accented by the vertical beams of small spotlights. Tables ringed the outer periphery of the dance floor.

Sally handed their tickets to an usher who immediately took them out of line and escorted them across the floor to a table near the bandstand. There was a small pasteboard tent card on the table that read "Reserved for Miss Anthony and party". This caused Billy to chuckle.

"What's so funny lover?" she asked as they were seated.

"I think it's the first time I've been referred to as 'party'," he said.

"And maybe it won't be the last," she said as she gave his hand a squeeze and one of her patented smiles meant only for him.

Billy knew he was hopelessly in love with this woman. "How about if I go get us a beer before the band starts playing?" he asked.

"Sorry lover, they don't sell alcohol here. Mr. Wrigley doesn't approve you see, but you can get me a coke."

Billy walked across the room to the bar. There was a sign above it that proclaimed it as the 'Marine Bar'. It was really more soda fountain than bar he realized.

Billy ordered two cokes. As he waited, he couldn't help but overhear the conversation between a couple of guys also waiting at the bar.

"I tell you, we'll be at war by next summer."

"You're as full of shit as a Christmas turkey. We're not getting involved in any European war. The American people won't stand for it again. Look at how many Americans were killed in the last war, do you really think we'll do that all over again? If the damn Europeans can't get along, why is that our problem?"

"It will be, you ignoramus! Why do you think we're building so many airplanes?"

"Roosevelt said we're the 'Arsenal of Democracy' that's why! Hell we're building airplanes to supply England and Russia. We'll build them and let them fly 'em and they can fight Hitler all they want. I'll stay here and buck rivets while they dodge the bullets."

Billy turned to look at the guys having the conversation and realized he knew them, or at least he had met them at Kearney Mesa. They were part of Tommy's group. Before he had the opportunity to say anything, they looked around and he could see by their expressions they recognized him as well.

"Hey! How you doing?" The guy closest to Billy stuck out his hand. "I met you at Kearney Mesa didn't I?"

"You sure did. I'm Billy Pendleton." He replied.

"Yeah, I remember. Sally was showing you around, you lucky stiff!" He grinned. "I'm Jimmy Kellogg, this here's my dumb bunny buddy, Paul Neece. He thinks there's no way we'll get in another war."

"Hell no, we won't get in another war. We learned our lesson last time. Hell, Billy do you want to get in a war?" Paul asked.

"Well, no of course not," Billy was a little taken aback by that question. He'd not thought about that before.

"Dammit Paul, how the hell do you think any sane person would answer that question?" What ensued was another squabble between the two. Billy was already forming the opinion that these two argued all the time. He had seen people like that before, they argued constantly but were best friends even though their words might lead you to think otherwise.

Billy's cokes arrived. He paid for them and turned to leave. "Hey Billy, you here with someone?" Jimmy was eyeing the pair of cokes.

"Well, yes I am" Billy replied.

"A girl?" Jimmy asked.

"Yes"

"See there Paul, Billy just moved to California and he's already got a girl. You've lived here all your life and where's your girl?"

"Same place yours is wise ass!" Paul shot back.

"I could have been here with 20 girls Paul, but then who would have come with you?" Jimmy said with a very satisfied smirk. Billy had to bite his cheek to keep from laughing.

Paul replied with a glare, his brows so knotted they almost obscured his eyes. "Yeah, sure. There's not a woman in her right mind that would even give you the time of day. Can you believe this guy?" Paul appealed to Billy.

"I had three phone calls just today, women that wanted to come with me tonight." Jimmy smirked.

Billy cut into the argument. "I've gotta get back guys" and he turned and started back across the room. To his considerable consternation, Jimmy and Paul picked up their drinks and followed him across the dance floor arguing the whole way.

"Oh yeah, smart ass! What women called you today?"

"For your information Mr. Know-it-all, Judy the phone operator at work called me today." The "work" Jimmy referred to was Don Lee Cadillac where he worked in the parts department.

"Yeah sure! You don't even know her last name."

"Its Blankenship, moron!"

"Then why didn't you bring her?"

"Cause I'd already given my other ticket to you, that's why!" Jimmy's face was so red, Billy was sure he was about to slug Paul, even if Paul had a foot of height and sixty pounds on him.

"Well next time just keep your damn ticket. I don't want to be accused of depriving you of female companionship."

"Then I would have been feeling bad all night because you were sitting home alone while I was here listening to Glenn Miller and rubbing up against a very nice set of kazoombas all night."

"Why don't you just shut your mouth before I shut it for you? Permanently!" Paul hissed. He was beginning to turn red.

They arrived at Sally's table just about the time Billy was sure Paul was going to punch Jimmy in the nose.

"Sally!" Paul and Jimmy exclaimed simultaneously.

"Hi guys," Sally replied looking a little surprised. When she looked at Billy, all he could do is look back with his best, please forgive me expression.

"Gee Sally, it's great to see you! Billy said he was here with a girl, but he never told us it was you."

Billy thought, "you never gave me an opportunity to say anything and you still haven't." He was just about to turn this thought into words when the PA system crackled to life.

"Welcome ladies and gentlemen, and to our listening audience across the country and around the world. Tonight we have a very special treat for all of you. From the beautiful ballroom of the magnificent Grand Casino overlooking picturesque Avalon Bay on the island of Santa Catalina, we present Glenn Miller and his Orchestra, accompanied by Tex Beneke and the Modernaires!"

Applause erupted across the crowded ballroom as the lights dimmed and the band broke into 'In the Mood', Glenn Miller's signature song. Glenn Miller himself was on stage acknowledging the crowd's applause as he led his orchestra. Spotlights captured him in pools of light and roamed across other members of the band. The dance floor was quickly filling to everyone's favorite tune.

Billy seized his chance. He reached out and took Sally's hand and guided her onto the dance floor, his fear of dancing paling in comparison to listening to Jimmy and Paul bickering. As soon as they were a safe distance from the still arguing pair, he turned her to face him and moved to whisper in her ear. "I'm really sorry. They followed me to the table. I didn't invite them to join us!"

She smiled back, "I know lover. It'll be okay, they're harmless. Besides, it'll help me keep you on the dance floor."

In a flash all of Billy's self-doubts and concerns about not knowing how to dance returned. He concentrated on watching Sally and trying to do what she did. It seemed to him that she was a great dancer. All her movements seemed fluid and at ease while his were stiff and forced. One consolation was that when he took the time to listen, the music was great. He had never heard it with such clarity and definition. It was infinitely better than listening on the radio. Gradually he loosened up a bit, trying to move more in concert with the music. He would never be a good dancer, but eventually he would forget about being so self-conscious.

The next song was a slow one and while Billy liked 'swing', slow dancing with Sally was the best. He was acutely aware of how firm her body felt pressed against his as they swayed to the music. His senses were full of her. He wished the song would last forever, but of course, it didn't. They were going to have to go back to their table sooner or later. Maybe Jimmy and Paul would be gone he hoped. They worked their way through the crowd and as their table came into view, Billy's heart sank. They were still there and locked in heated discussion.

As soon as Jimmy and Paul noticed them approaching, they stopped arguing and were all smiles. Both guys' attention was locked on Sally ignoring Billy completely. "Sally, it really is nice to see you here, and totally unexpected." Jimmy said. Paul just grinned.

"It's nice to see you too, Jimmy, Paul. Did you guys come by yourselves?"

"Yeah, I had to give Paul here my spare ticket, otherwise he would have sat home alone all night." The smile on Paul's face suddenly became a scowl. Billy wondered if they ever came to blows. If they did, he didn't think Jimmy would last five seconds.

"Paul, it was very nice of you to come with Jimmy so he didn't have to come alone." Billy thought he was going to bust a gut laughing. Paul's scowl was now a big grin and it was Jimmy's turn to scowl. Billy admired how deftly Sally handled them so far. She constantly amazed him.

"So have you guys been to the lakes lately?" By lakes, she meant the dry lakes of the Mojave Desert east of LA. The dry lakebeds were the sites of speed trials for the car clubs in Los Angeles.

"Yeah, we went last weekend. Tommy got over Kearney Mesa and had Ernie working on tuning the speedster all week. They had the fenders and windshield stripped off of it, and it ran better, but still wasn't what Tommy hoped." Jimmy said.

"Did you know that Billy is building a car?" Sally asked. Both Jimmy and Paul shifted their attention to Billy. It was almost comical to watch, for all their bickering and arguing, they were very much alike.

"What are you building?" Paul asked, cutting off Jimmy and earning a dirty look in the process.

Billy tried his best to describe his project. He described it as a combination of Tommy's speedster, Danny Sakai's modified and Bill Worth's streamliner.

"Did you know that Bill's car is for sale?" Jimmy asked.

"No, I didn't! I would love to own it, but I wouldn't fit in it anyway," Billy said.

"Paul wouldn't either, but I'll drive it for you if you'll buy it," Jimmy said.

Billy couldn't phathom ever letting Jimmy drive anything he owned, let alone a high-powered race car. Besides, he thought, driving the car is the reward for building it. "Thanks Jimmy, but I want to try and learn to drive it myself," Billy said.

"Okay, but when you get it built, I'll be glad to give you a few pointers," Jimmy replied. "I think Stu Hilborn is going to buy Bill's car anyway. He wants to stuff a V-8 in it, but there ain't enough room in it for a V-8!" Jimmy exclaimed. "What kind of engine are you planning to use?"

Billy told him about the Miller modified LaSalle. "I remember that engine. I told Don it was never going to work as an Indy engine when he ordered it." Jimmy insisted.

"Oh yeah? Since when did Don Lee listen to his junior parts man? Hell Jimmy, you just started to work there when the V-12s came out. The only time he ever said a word to you was to tell you to shut your trap and get to work before he fired your sorry ass!" Paul said. Sally and Billy tried hard to suppress chuckles.

"Don used to ask me for advice all the time. He appreciated my years of experience more than some people I know!" Another major argument was forming.

Paul just grunted and rolled his eyes. Billy and Sally looked at each other, and then back at Paul. Almost on cue, they both lost control and erupted in laughter. After a few seconds hesitation, so did Paul. Jimmy looked offended for a few seconds, but then he joined in too. It was the icebreaker. Everyone seemed to relax and the rest of the evening went much more smoothly.

After the laughter all four of them began to talk. It was no longer as argumentative and Jimmy didn't dominate the conversation. The transformation was amazing to Billy, and he could see the friendship between these two regardless of how they talked to each other at times.

It wasn't long before the subject of war came up again. Even though he was employed building huge four engine bombers, Billy hadn't really taken the subject of the United States getting embroiled in a war seriously until that night. His father fought in France in the Great War. His uncle, whom he never knew, was killed in France. His little brother was named for him. Surely there was no way America would go to war, was there? He wondered.

Sally was growing more and more uncomfortable with the conversation. She was certain she had met the love of her life and to think that a war might come and take him away from her was a devastating thought. She couldn't bear to think about it anymore so she squeezed Billy's hand and got up. "Dance with me" was her simple request.

It was another slow song. She clung to Billy even tighter than before. "I don't want to talk about war anymore," she whispered in his ear. He could hear the emotion in her voice. He pulled back slightly to look at her face and was surprised to see tears in her eyes.

"What's wrong?" he asked.

She just shook her head and pulled tightly against him again. The next song was another slow one and they stayed on the dance floor. When it ended she led Billy over to the Marine Bar. She really wished they served something stronger, but they bought two cokes and headed outside to the balcony that ringed the building. They looked out on the harbor through arches that could have been on a maharaja's castle.

The night was beautiful. There weren't enough lights on the island to obscure the stars, and the heavens blazed. The bay was a sheet of glass, dotted with sailboats and motor launches.

"What upset you in there?" Billy asked with concern for her.

Sally turned and faced him. For several moments she said nothing, just searched his eyes. He knew this wasn't just a passing moment, a brief bout of anxiety. Sally was deeply shaken.

"For the first time in my life, I've found someone that truly cares about me because of me, nothing else. And I can't help being hopelessly in love with that person. I can see us together forever. That is the dream that's inside my head and in my heart." She confessed quietly.

He reached to pull her to him. She stopped him, "No let me finish," she insisted.

"I know you feel the same way about me. I know that. I can sense it, I can feel how kind and gentle you are. How you consider me before you consider yourself. Every gesture, every word tells me how you feel. I enjoy hearing you say it, but I don't need the words. What you do speaks louder than what you say. But war could destroy all of that. It could take you away from me and I just can't bear that thought."

134

The last few words were so garbled Billy could barely understand them. Sally started to sob and Billy pulled her to his chest. He didn't know what to do. He held her close and stroked her hair. "It was just talk. Nothing's going to happen. We'll never get in another war again." He tried to sound convincing, but feared he didn't sound that confidant. "I'll never leave you," he said.

"But you can't promise that! If war comes, you may have to go!" she sobbed.

He was at a loss. Her words hit too close to the truth, he couldn't think of any argument to refute them. Then he thought of one of his mother's sayings, something he himself found comforting. "Let's not borrow trouble. We can't predict what the future holds, but we can control right now. Let's not waste today worrying about tomorrow."

For a minute or two Sally continued to cry, eventually the sobs lessened in intensity and finally stopped. She stayed close against him, "You're right, your mother's right too. I'm wasting the time I have with you tonight. Right here, right now, I have exactly what I want. It couldn't be any better. Let's enjoy it. I promise to stay focused on today." She looked up at him and managed a smile. "Let's go see if that bar is still open."

"Okay!" Billy was glad she wasn't crying any more. They headed back inside to retrieve her things from the table. As soon as they entered the ballroom again and heard the music, she stopped dead in her tracks, "We can't leave, this is the first time you've ever heard Glenn Miller!"

Billy bent down close to her ear, "We *can* leave. I'd rather listen to you than Glenn Miller or anyone else in the world," and he softly bit her ear.

It was the perfect thing to say and do. Sally seemed to return to her old self almost instantly. The grin she flashed at him was one of the things he would remember the rest of his life. They made their way to the table, and to their amazement, Jimmy and Paul were nowhere to be seen. They retrieved Sally's sweater and bag and headed for the door.

As soon as they exited the Grand Casino, they knew the little bar was open. There was a steady stream of people going back and forth. Out for a fast drink and then back inside for more music and dancing. They were lucky to get a table outside and furthest away from the Casino, hence a bit quieter than the rest. They ordered two beers.

"I'm sorry about tonight, I don't know what came over me, I just felt the most intense sense of panic." Sally couldn't bring herself to even say the word 'war' at this point.

"And I thought I was the one that ruined the evening bringing Jimmy and Paul back to the table," Billy laughed.

"They're good guys. They just get carried away when they disagree. Of course, they seem to do that pretty often don't they?" They both laughed.

"They were arguing when I ran in to them at the bar, but it seems like they're really good friends." Billy observed.

"They are, they're almost inseparable. I don't think I've ever seen one without the other. And they love racing. They're always at the lakes."

"Are they always with Tommy?" Billy asked.

"Every time I've ever seen them they were."

The twin steamers, their white paint gleaming in the moonlight and deck lights aglow, were moored to either side of the dock. They could see the members of the bands each steamer carried, warming up in preparation for the trip back to the mainland.

They had another beer and watched all the activity. A few couples were already boarding. About a quarter till, they headed to the dock and boarded ahead of the crowd. They had their choice of seats and chose a pair at the rail on the upper deck. They had just seated themselves when the steamer's horn gave a mighty blast. They both jumped, startled by the sudden shriek.

"I should have been ready for that." Sally said. "They always toot the horn a couple of times before leaving to warn everyone."

"That was quite a toot!" They laughed. Looking back up Crescent Avenue, they could see crowds beginning to emerge from the Grand Casino and heading their way.

The steamers filled quickly, the last couples aboard were those that had stopped by the sidewalk bars to get one last beer. It was a pleasant night and the sea was calm. Even so the sea breeze was a little chilly and Sally huddled close against Billy's side. Not much was said on the ride home, speech was unnecessary, instead they reveled in each other's company as they watched the sea rush past, sounds of the band and the dancers on the floor below heard faintly in the background.

Once back in the harbor, they disembarked the steamer and cruised up the coast highway toward the beach house. Billy drove the Packard. There was still a lot of traffic on the road. It was Saturday night and the nightlife of Los Angeles rode on wheels. Lights and neon were everywhere trying to entice the passers-by to stop. Horns honked, gears ground, and brakes squealed. People yelled at each other out open car windows. Faces changed from darkened silhouettes to three dimensional figures full of color and life and then back again as they passed through pools of light. It was a dramatic change from the peace and tranquility of Catalina.

They pulled into the drive and walked arm in arm to the entrance. When Billy unlocked the door, he was amazed that it felt like home to him even though he had only spent the weekend there.

"Would you open a bottle of wine while I change?" Sally asked. Billy selected a bottle based solely on the beauty of the label and opened it. After getting out a pair of glasses, he lit a fire in the living room and turned off the lights. The fire's soft glow and crackle was much nicer than any artificial lighting and it allowed them to see the ocean through the glass wall. He just finished pouring the wine when Sally emerged from the hallway. She was wrapped in her terrycloth robe.

They lounged on the end of the couch, Sally leaning against Billy. The mood was somber. The view was of endless waves breaking on the beach, a study in black and white.

"If war comes, will you go?" Sally asked softly.

"I don't know. I suppose I would have to if it got bad enough. They've started up the draft you know."

"I don't want you to go. You work at Consolidated, isn't that important?"

"Yes it is, but I've only been there a short time. They could easily replace me. Sally, I won't go unless I have to. We don't even know that there will be a war. Remember, don't borrow trouble."

"Okay." Sally said, but she really didn't mean it. A deep-seated dread had settled inside of her. She would do her best to keep it hidden, but she couldn't make it go away. Not yet anyway.

After a while, Sally set her glass down still half full. She stood and took Billy's hand and led him to the bedroom. They embraced and there was a special urgency to their kisses that only comes after a couple has survived a crisis together. She began to tug at his belt. Their love making that night had a very special quality to it. A softness, almost reverence for each other, and finally they slept wrapped in each other's arms.

They awoke together, the room already light. Sally seemed to have put the concerns and somber mood of the previous night behind her. She smiled at Billy and said "Good morning, lover," followed by a kiss. "Last one up is a rotten egg!" She threw the covers back and jumped from bed running toward the hall.

"Hey! Aren't you forgetting something?" she turned to look back at him. He held her robe up a questioning look on his face.

"Yesterday you told me you wanted to look, so look!" and she disappeared into the hall.

Billy followed a minute or two later. Sally was in the kitchen and the smells of brewing coffee and frying bacon filled the room. As Billy crossed the living room, he stopped and picked up their glasses and the wine from last night. He walked over beside Sally and said "Wine for breakfast?"

"Why not?" she replied and rinsed out both glasses. Billy poured for both of them, and handed Sally hers. When breakfast was ready, she fixed plates for both of them and carried them to the bar. Billy helped by bringing the wine. She seated herself on a barstool and said "I can't eat it for you too!" Billy sat beside her and ate. It was a wonderful breakfast and so was the view, the best he had ever seen.

After they were finished, Sally took the plates to the sink and washed everything putting it away as she went. She then turned to face Billy. She walked up just in front of him and pulled the belt on his robe loose. "I get to look too, lover."

Later that morning, Billy finished loading their bags in the trunk of the Packard. He stood and looked around. Looking one way, he could see beach and ocean disappear in the distance. Looking the other, he could see the brown hills and mountains. This is a beautiful place to live he thought. He hoped they could visit again sometime. He had already formed an attachment for the place and had many pleasant memories to take with him when they left. Sally came out locking the door behind her. They got in the Packard with Billy behind the wheel and drove away.

Chapter 13

Carl was anxious to hear all about the trip and especially the visits to his old friends, Frank Kurtis and Fred Offenhauser. Billy told him every detail and then had to repeat it all again. He secretly thought Carl missed his friends in LA more than he let on. Even Babe was happy to see them return, and Billy didn't think it was just because he missed Sally's cooking.

Billy was anxious to get to work on the Special. He was surprised how much he missed working on it and in some strange way, just being near it. Carl made progress over the weekend and the basic frame was mostly welded together. It was time for the work to begin in earnest. Billy hoped it would be finished in time for the first event in the spring of '42.

Billy and Sally went out the back door walking across the lawn toward the old carriage house, turned race car shop. Carl immediately noticed the way they interacted had changed from just the week before. Although they both were intent on keeping their feelings toward each other private and as low key as possible, it was obvious to even the most casual observer that this was a special relationship. It was the small things that gave them away. The glances when they thought no one was looking, the casual touches that lingered just a fraction too long, the way they deferred to the others opinion in even the most casual conversation. Yes, Carl was certain there was a lot going on between those two. He was just as certain that he had done the right thing bringing them together. As random as everything seemed, not all had been left to chance. Carl made sure of that. The real objective of his actions had been Sally. He cared about Billy a great deal, and was truly concerned for his welfare, but he had been just as sure Billy could easily take care of himself. Sally, on the other hand, was a different matter all together. She was certainly a self-assured, confident, and smart young lady, but her exposure to someone like Billy was nonexistent. Billy had immediately impressed Carl with his sincerity and honesty, two traits that were sadly lacking in the circles Sally revolved in. Almost from the beginning, Carl had seen Billy as a worthy suitor. It was confirmed in his mind that day at Kearney Mesa. There was electricity between the two from the instant they met. He noticed it and so had Tommy. He knew Tommy had always been interested in Sally, at least since she blossomed into the lovely lady she now was. He even genuinely liked Tommy and there was no question Tommy could provide for her every need both now and in the future, as if she really needed that, but on the other hand, Carl could never picture Tommy being totally and completely in love with anyone beside himself. Even so, he knew Tommy would treat her well, but there would always be something lacking in any relationship involving Tommy. He had no such concerns about Billy. That had been his objective for years, to provide the very best he could for Sally and now he was quite pleased with himself. Things were going very well. *"Now,"* he thought, *"I better get out there and get busy on the Special, after all, it was one of the key pieces of the plan from the beginning."* He mused.

When Carl walked into the shop he was surprised to find them at work on the special's frame. He had really expected to interrupt a kiss, but instead Sally was at one end of the frame and Billy at the other with a tape measure stretched between them. Billy was saying, "It's called 'diamonding'. See, you measure from one corner to the opposite far end corner, then you do the same between the other two corners. If the measurement is the same, you can be pretty sure the frame is square." Billy said confidently.

"I see," Sally said. To Carl's familiar eye, she looked genuinely interested in the project. That was one of those things that just happened. He never would have bet on that. While she had always been around cars, it had been a circumstance of her birth and upbringing, not of her passion for the machines. Billy was a totally different proposition. Billy had the passion for the machine. He also had the passion for Sally, Carl was certain of that.

The pair pronounced the frame as square. "Did you expect me to weld it crooked?" Carl said, a look of mock outrage on his face and in his voice.

They both seemed to totally ignore his remark. "Carl, do you know where we might borrow a slip roller?" Billy asked. "I thought one might come in handy for making some of the body panels." A slip roller was a machine that used three long skinny rollers, similar to long rolling pins connected together to roll or curve a flat sheet of metal. The design of the Special was such that the belly pan hung below the frame rails. Billy thought a slip roller could easily bend the large radius required to make the side panels of the belly pan curve under the car and also to make the graceful curves he envisioned for the hood.

"No, I don't, but I'll ask around at work. Maybe someone knows of one. In the meantime, why don't we work on the nose? Do you have any more ideas about that?" Carl asked.

"Yeah, I do. I'd like to use a LaSalle grille, kind of like we discussed before. A '39 would be my preference if we can find a good used one. I don't want to pay for a new one."

"No, of course not. I'll handle finding a grille. Maybe I can get one tomorrow. I know the body shop foreman really well. He owes me several favors."

"Great! Tommy was nice enough to give us the use of the engine, I thought the least we could do was to be true to the original idea and call the car a LaSalle, even if most of the running gear is Ford." Billy said.

"Yeah, the LaSalle axles and hubs would be too big and heavy anyway. Besides that, the Ford stuff is easy to find and we already have the major pieces."

"You're using Ford parts to build the car?" Sally asked in surprise.

Billy explained to her about the gift of the '35 Ford pickup. He went on to tell her that most of the cars she saw at the time trials had Ford running gear, even Tommy's speedster. That shocked her a bit. She had always taken for granted that Tommy's car used Cadillac/LaSalle parts at the least or even more likely, specially designed and constructed components. It was almost startling to think that a car as stylish and expensive as Tommy's speedster was really a plain old Ford at heart. She asked why Ford parts were used.

Billy and Carl looked at each other for a moment. "I guess really because they're rugged and simple, but mainly because they're so available. The parts are everywhere and they're cheap. That part doesn't matter to someone like Tommy, but most guys building cars, like me, have to do it on the cheap. We can't afford to use expensive parts. If it wasn't for the gifts I've received, this project would look a lot different." Billy explained.

"Are the Ford parts safe?" Sally asked.

"Of course, look at how many Fords are on the road."

"Are the Ford brakes as good as, say, my Packard's?"

Billy and Carl looked at each other again. "Well......., maybe not quite as good as your Packard's, but"

Billy was instantly cut off by Sally's next remark. "Then let's use Packard brakes."

"They won't fit, at least not very easily. Then we'd have problems with everything else. I don't see how we could use them." Billy finished saying.

"I don't want you driving a car that has inferior brakes just because they're cheap." Sally was adamant.

Carl heard this tone in her voice before and he knew what it meant. "We can upgrade to Lincoln brakes. They're Bendix design, just like a Packard or Cadillac and they'll fit right on. No problems with the wheels or anything else."

Billy looked at Sally expectantly. "Okay," she said, "we use Lincoln brakes. Is that agreed?"

Billy nodded his approval. "Promise?" she asked.

"I promise. I'll scout some out this weekend. Maybe I can look for a grille at the same time." Billy suggested.

"I've got the grille covered. The body shop foreman owes me. Anything else you want, just say the word. He's got a lot of catching up to do." They all three chuckled.

They heard the muffled crash of a bicycle hitting the ground outside the shop door. Babe walked in, the cloth aviator's helmet Billy bought him perched askew on his head, the earflaps folded up and sticking out to each side like a pair of stubby wings. The chuckles turned into outright laughter at his grass-stained visage.

"What's so funny?" he asked.

Everyone just laughed more at his question. Babe was embarrassed with the embarrassment quickly turning to aggravation as the laughter continued. The look of annoyance soon faded to one of pleading. "Please?" he said. Sally gave in. "Pull your cap off and look at it," she said.

Babe jerked the aviator helmet off his head and looked. Dead center on the top was the remains of a huge moth. It had splattered onto the top of the helmet and stuck. Its wings were splayed out such that they looked sort of like a mouse's ears. When he had the cap on it looked like he had painted a set of ears sticking out the top. He remembered pedaling as hard and fast as he could down a nearby hill. Babe was pumping the pedals so hard with his head tucked down trying to coax the last bit of speed from his bike. He remembered something hitting his head. It was distinct enough he felt it, but it hadn't really hurt and he quickly forgot all about it. "I thought I hit a bird or something," he said. Everyone laughed that much harder. Babe looked a little perplexed.

"I guess it's good I had on my pilot hat," he said. This triggered a whole new wave of laughter as each person drew their own mental picture of Babe with giant moth wings sticking out of his brown hair. Then he really would have looked like he had mouse ears. Billy and Sally were laughing so hard tears were running down their cheeks. Babe finally gave in and joined the laughter.

After the laughter finally subsided, Carl asked, "How was the ball game today?"

"Great! I hit a home run!"

"That's wonderful, son. Are you turning into a power hitter?" Carl asked.

"Yep! Well, not really. Charlie misjudged the ball and charged in thinking it was going to drop in front of him and it sailed right over his head. I was already rounding third by the time he picked up the ball!" babe recounted.

"Wow, that's wonderful! You really are the Babe!" Sally said.

Babe basked in the attention. These three adults were all the family he knew. There were no aunts or uncles, no grandparents, just these people now standing in the shop and, of course there was baseball. Babe always thought of baseball as a member of his family. He was very happy that they were proud of his ability to play ball. This moment with the accolades ringing in his ears was one he would remember all his life. Every person carries memories of their childhood formed from totally unsuspected events. It's not always the big events we cherish, but many times it's the small ones that unexpectedly trigger emotion deep enough to forever etch the memory in our souls.

I sat quietly staring at a man truly lost in his memories, suddenly the silence was broken. "That was one of the happiest days of my life," Babe said. "I remember it like it was yesterday. Me standing there in grass stained jeans with the knees torn out and some old high top tennis shoes and wearing that cloth helmet. I knew beyond any shadow of a doubt that I was the king of the world. There were more joys ahead for me, but that moment was the best that ever was. I can see their faces now; I see them every night. Damn, I miss them!" There were tears in the old man's eyes. His voice was beginning to sound weary. It had gotten dark outside a while back. I looked at my watch. It was 3a.m.! I was shocked. We had been talking for over 15 hours!

"Babe, we both need some rest. I can't wait to hear the rest of the story, but I'm dragging, can we get a nap and resume in the morning?"

"Son, I've waited 50 years to tell this story, waiting till the morning to finish won't bother me a bit. You are beginning to look a little droopy eyed. You kids just can't take it like we used to," he grinned.

"I'm going to check into a motel nearby. I'll see you when I wake up. Babe, this means more to me that I'll ever be able to tell you. I never dreamed I would find out any level of detail about Uncle Billy beyond what I already knew. And to find out all this, his involvement in hotrods, all the people he knew, the things he did, it's just beyond description. Thank you so much for finding me."

"Son, this is an obligation I've carried for all these years. I owe those three people and I'm trying to pay my debt. I needed to pass the story on to someone that really cares. I never thought I would find such a person, but thank Great God Almighty, I finally did. Go get some sleep and come back when you're ready. I'm not going anywhere. Now get your ass out of here!"

I shook the old man's hand and left. The guard at the front desk looked a little startled when I walked out of the hall into the lobby, but he quickly recovered. I think I might have awoken him from a catnap. "I've been visiting Mr. Mercer" I said.

"Yeah, I know. Babe told me and everyone else in the place you were coming. You know Babe is usually pretty laid back unless the subject is baseball, but I've never seen him as excited as he's been lately. You some long lost relative or something?" he asked.

"Yeah, something like that. See you tomorrow night," I said and walked out the front door. You should have seen the look on his face.

I drove a couple of blocks down the street and woke up the night clerk at the Best Western. My mind was reeling with all I had been told. I checked in and walked into a generic motel room.

In my wildest fantasies I never could have imagined such an incredible story. How was it that all this had transpired and I had never been told anything about it? Had my dad known, had my grandmother? So many questions. Another was how did Babe know all this? True enough, he had lived through it, but how in the world did he know the intimate details of Billy and Sally's relationship? How could he possibly know what had transpired in the beach house in LA, or on a secluded beach? Had he made all this up? I was tremendously excited, but I was also at the point of exhaustion. I got in bed and my mind was still reeling with images and questions. After a while I finally faded out.

I woke up about nine the next morning, my mind a kaleidoscope of images from the day before. I couldn't wait to get back to Babe's but I wanted to be sure he was up and about before I showed up again. I showered, dressed and headed out for breakfast.

After I had eaten, I stopped and bought a spiral notebook and a couple of pens. I planned to take notes from now on. I headed back to Babe's.

Shirley greeted me with a cheery "good morning". As had been the case the day before, everyone I encountered seemed very happy, even delighted, to see me. It was still a bit unsettling. I walked down the hall and knocked on Babe's door. "Come in," he called in a surprisingly strong voice.

When I walked through the door he said, "What the hell took you so long?" I explained that I hadn't wanted to interrupt his rest and that I was concerned about him. "Hell son, that's what I'm worried about. When I go to sleep I don't know if I'll wake up in the morning or not. I need to pass this story on to you. No one else knows it but me. When I'm gone, it'll be up to you. 'Course you don't have the obligation to my family the way I do, but you'll be by God obligated to me! You make damn sure you pass this story on to someone else, someone who cares, you understand?"

"Yes sir, I understand" I said, feeling like a Marine Corps drill instructor had just dressed me down.

"Make damn sure you do. It's the least we can do." I saw another tear in his eye. "Those were the finest people I ever knew. They deserve to be remembered. What's that?" he asked indicating the spiral notebook I carried.

"I thought I needed to take notes so I bought this to write in," I said.

Just a hint of a smile crossed his face. "Damn good idea, you ready to get started?"

"Yes sir, I am, but I have a few questions I'd like to ask you first." I could tell this annoyed him a little bit, but I plunged ahead. "How do you know all this?" I asked.

"Goddamn it! I lived through it; I'm the only one left! Weren't you listening to me yesterday?"

"Yes sir, I was, but you were just a kid. How could you possibly know all the intimate details about Billy and Sally?" I had expended my biggest shot first. If he could answer that one, everything else should fall in place. I wanted to make sure he wasn't just suffering from the delusions of old age.

"Sit your ass down in that chair and start writing. When I get finished you'll understand. That's all you're going to get. Now shut the hell up and listen!"

I sat as instructed. My disappointment didn't last long as Babe jumped right back into the story. I was confident Babe would get to it. The story rolled on without hesitation. He never had to think about anything, there were no pauses, no thinking of what to say next. It was like he was simply recounting what happened yesterday.

"That was late summer of '41," he said. "We worked on that car every night, the four of us."

"You worked on it too?" I asked.

"You're damn right I worked on it!" I could tell I had irritated him again. I started to open my mouth to apologize, but he waved me off with his good hand. "I know what you're thinking, 'he was just a kid' and hell I was. I don't mean I built the damn thing, but I was in that shop every night with the rest of 'em. It was our family activity!" I resolved not to interrupt him again.

"They gave me small jobs, things I could handle. Sally and me, we got lots of the stuff that needed to be done, but didn't require Dad or Billy to do it. You know, we swept the floor, we sawed metal, we washed parts, we sanded things, that kind of stuff. Sometimes Sally would fix dinner and we would eat in the shop. I'd help her. I always enjoyed that. Sally was really special to me. She was the first woman I ever loved, and looking back, she was the mother I never had. Sally was the yardstick I used to measure all others by and they just couldn't compare. Only one ever did." He stared out the window for a minute or two. I just watched him, and waited on him to continue. All those years ago and there was still a tremendous amount of passion in this man. I realized how lucky I was that he was sharing it with me.

He cleared his throat and I wondered who the 'one' was, then he resumed. "Well, like I said, we each had our own jobs. I was lucky enough that I got to work with Sally on most of mine. Dad was the master mechanic. When it came to any of the mechanical points, everyone deferred to him. Hell, that's all he had ever done. It started when him and Frank were boys you know. You read any book you want to and it'll tell you Frank Lockhart was a true mechanical genius, well, I'm here to tell ya, my dad was right there with him. They were two peas in a pod, those two. Now Daddy couldn't drive a race car like Frank, never even wanted to, but he could damn sure work on one. Even Billy asked for his opinion on all the mechanical aspects of the car."

"Your uncle Billy, he was something. Once you got over his size, it was everything else about him that was extraordinary. He could do it all. Even though he didn't have Dad's years of experience, he had his same gift of mechanical ability. And he could make anything. But what really set him apart was that he could visualize how it all went together. He was like an artist. He knew exactly what the finished car should look like. He saw it in his mind. He could visualize what a part had to do and how to make it. He looked at the stuff we had and could tell what we could use and what we couldn't. What had to be modified and how, and what had to be built from scratch. He was the dreamer, the planner, the architect of the Special. All of us played a part, but it was Billy's vision that we built."

"I'll tell you something else about Billy. He was the first adult that really treated me as an equal. He was my older brother. He looked out for me, he included me in the things he did. Dad could see it; he saw it right from the start. Billy became part of our family, right from the first day. I think that's why I never resented his relationship with Sally. I was in love with her, but deep down inside I knew I was just a kid. I kind of saw Billy as myself all grown up. And the two of them, they always had time for me. You know how it is when you're a kid, you think you're an adult, but you really aren't, but they treated me like one most of the time. It was always fun for me."

"The Special took shape right before my eyes. In the beginning, I couldn't really understand what all the pieces did. It just looked like a pile of parts to me. I didn't have Billy's vision. He would try to explain it all and he was always very patient, but I just couldn't quite grasp it. Not only did I not have Billy's vision, but I didn't have his or my Dad's mechanical ability either. If my bicycle broke down, one of them fixed it for me. My talent, what talent I had that is, was for playing ball. But still I enjoyed that time we spent together in the shop. I wish it could have gone on forever."

He was getting warmed up now. There was a definite wistful look in his eye. As he resumed, once more he transported me back to that San Diego shop in 1941.

Babe watched Billy, fascinated. Billy was forming a piece of sheet metal by hammering it with a wooden mallet he made from the pieces of one of Babe's broken bats. He used the fat part of the bat known as the barrel, cut it off and reshaped it to resemble a teardrop. The teardrop had a hammer handle affixed to it. Billy had part of a tree stump he was using as his work surface. He had scooped a hollow in the top end of it. Lying in the hollow was a sand bag he made out of a piece of old blue jeans leg. He filled the leg full of sand from the beach and then rolled the open ends up and coarsely stitched them closed. The steel rested on top of the sand bag and Billy pounded it with his mallet.

Billy would hit the steel several licks with the mallet and then try fitting it to a form he made out of pieces of old lumber. Billy called the form a 'buck'. It didn't look anything like a deer to Babe and Billy could offer no explanation as to why it was called a buck, just that it was. He told Babe that the buck was actually a three dimensional pattern. He would hammer the metal and when he thought it was close, he would test fit it to the buck. He had a piece of chalk he was using to make marks on the metal to indicate high or low spots.

Once the piece was close to fitting, he would remove the sandbag from the stump and then hammer the metal directly on the wood of the stump. He called this 'plannishing'. He said this was smoothing the metal and his mallet blows were easier, but faster, a series of rapid but light taps. After he worked a piece to his satisfaction this way, he would finish it off by using a fender roller Carl borrowed from work. This was a pair of steel rollers mounted in a C shaped iron frame work. The body shop used them to smooth crumpled fenders and Billy used it for the same purpose, but in a different way. He clamped the roller in a vice and then rolled the piece of steel back and forth between the rollers much like running a piece of wet laundry through a washing machine ringer. The distance between the two rollers could be adjusted with a big screw. As Billy pulled the steel back and forth, the clamping force of the rollers wrung the lumps out of the steel just like a wringer wrung the water out of wet laundry. Babe thought the whole thing must be magic.

When the piece was finally shaped to Billy's liking, he used metal shears he called 'Dutchmans' to trim the edges. He then fit it to the other pieces and secured all of them to the buck with screws, he would weld the pieces together. As he welded, he would hand the torch to Babe to hold while he used a flat-faced hammer and a piece of steel he called a 'dolly' to hammer the still cherry red weld. He told Babe that when steel was welded, it actually shrunk along the seam where the heat fused the metal. What he was doing was hammering the weld, stretching it back to its original size and shape. He told Babe if he didn't do this, the steel would warp all out of shape. He used a few pieces of scrap to demonstrate what he was talking about. The differences were amazing. Babe was more convinced than ever that it was all magic. Who in their right mind would think that you could build a car using a broken baseball bat, the leg off an old worn out pair of jeans, a tree stump, and some sand as your tools? Babe mused.

As Babe watched, the nose of the car came to life. Carl had been true to his word and a '39 LaSalle grille, just like the one on the coupe was now screwed to the wooden buck. A picky owner had complained about a small piece of the chrome plating peeling off. It was barely visible and considering the price, (it was free), it was the perfect piece for the Special. Billy was overjoyed with it. With the grille secured to the buck, he was now fitting the metal to both the buck and the grille. At first, Babe wasn't exactly sure what Billy was doing, but after the first few pieces were welded in place he could see it! He could actually visualize what Billy was trying to describe to him.

Sally came in carrying a pitcher of tea and four glasses. Everyone was ready for a break. Carl was busy mounting the engine and transmission into the frame.

When work resumed, Sally stayed and watched with Babe, as Billy continued to form the nose. She was as fascinated as Babe was. The only difference was that she spent as much time watching the man as she did the work he was doing. While Babe was awe-struck with the work he was doing, Sally reserved her awe for the man himself.

147

After a while, Babe's eyelids began to get heavy. Sally noticed him doze off despite the pounding going on just a few feet away. "I think you should turn in for the night Babe. You've had a long day." Babe had gotten up early that morning as he and several of his buddies pedaled across town to play a group from another neighborhood. As usual Babe had been the star player. They played a double header and then rode back across town. Since he returned home, he was in the shop helping and watching. There was no doubt he was ready for bed. He kissed Sally goodnight, a ritual that had become his favorite part of the day, then given Billy and his dad quick hugs before trudging off to the house. Carl followed him in to make sure he made it.

As soon as Carl and Babe left, Sally could wait no longer and seized Billy in an embrace. "Save some of that energy for me, lover," she said. A long and passionate kiss followed.

"I'll try to save you a little bit," he said.

"We better break it up, Carl will be back any minute."

"Yeah, you're right" and they gave each other one more squeeze. What they didn't realize was that Carl had already returned. They were startled to hear him clear his throat.

Carl had to use all of his self-control to keep from smiling. "I didn't mean to interrupt, but I thought you should know I was here."

Billy was embarrassed and stammered a bit. Sally on the other hand, was the normal Sally. "Thanks Carl, we wouldn't want to embarrass you." Billy looked totally awe-struck.

"I'm glad you didn't, but I'll be happy to go back in the house if you'd like some privacy," Carl said.

"I don't think that'll be necessary, but if I change my mind, I'll let you know." Sally laughed. Carl joined in, Billy was too shocked to do anything but stand there and blush. He was amazed Carl and Sally talked so openly. That was something his upbringing had not prepared him for. After a moment's confusion, he decided the best thing to do was get back to shaping metal. He picked up his mallet and started hammering. It appeared he was concentrating on his work, but his brain was anywhere but on the piece of metal before him. He was worried what Carl would think. He already thought of Carl as family and he certainly didn't want to disappoint him in any way.

"I think I'll turn in for the night," Sally said with a yawn and a stretch. She walked over to Billy and gave him a kiss and then gave Carl a hug on her way out. "Goodnight," she said.

Billy continued hammering for several minutes after she left. Eventually he realized that the piece of steel he was hammering on bore no resemblance to the piece he started making originally. For the past several minutes he had been hammering with no thought to what he was doing. He put the mallet down. He decided he had to get this off his chest.

"Carl, about Sally and me," he began. Carl stopped what he was doing and gave Billy his undivided attention. He was silently chuckling at Billy's obvious unease.

"Yes?" Carl said. He had to work hard to conceal his amusement at Billy's obvious unease.

"Well, I thought you should know that Sally and I have strong feelings for each other."

"Oh really?" Carl said, feigning surprise.

"Yes sir, we do. I'll understand if you want me to move out." Billy said with resignation.

"Move out, why would I want you to move out?"

"I thought you might be disappointed in me. Maybe I had betrayed your trust."

"Son, nothing could be further from the truth. I could tell the first time you two laid eyes on each other at Kearney Mesa that the sparks were going to fly. And to tell you the truth, nothing could make me happier. I've never seen Sally so happy. Her wellbeing means more to me than you know and from the beginning I hoped you two would get together." Carl said truthfully.

Billy was stunned. He didn't know what to say. Carl handled that for him. "Let's call it a night. I can see that your mind isn't on that mangled piece of steel you've been banging on for the past hour," Carl said with a chuckle.

When Billy got in the house, he went to his room and picked up his robe and headed to the bathroom for a quick shower. Still in a state of confusion over all that had transpired, he went back to his room. He wasn't sure whether to go to Sally's room or not. She might already be asleep regardless of what she said earlier. The problem was solved when his door opened and Sally stepped in wearing her matching robe. She had that special smile reserved only for him on her face.

She looked at him for a minute and then dropped her robe. She wasn't wearing anything underneath. She stepped over to him and tugged the belt holding his robe closed. When it opened, she burrowed inside tight against him. "I bought this robe a little big with this in mind you know."

"I'm glad you did," followed by a kiss. "I told Carl about us," he said.

"You did?" Sally said a bit surprised.

"Yeah, I thought he should know."

"He already knew," she stated calmly.

"How do you know that?"

"Carl isn't stupid. He has eyes you know. And besides, I told him."

"You did what?!?" Billy exclaimed.

"I told him I had never met anyone like you. That there was something very special about you and that I wanted to see where all this might lead me."

"When did you tell him that?"

"Oh, the first day I was here, no maybe it was the second day." She giggled.

"What?! Why didn't you tell me?"

"Because I didn't know where it might wind up."

"Where has it taken you?"

"To your bed every night since. You know very well where it's taken me. You also know exactly how I feel about you, but just in case. I love you, totally and completely." Sally said, their eyes locked.

"I love you too, now and always." Billy replied, kissing her.

"Turn out the light."

Babe woke up early. He promised Charlie and the gang he would meet them at the ball diamond at 7am. The team they visited the day before was coming across town to play on their field today. Everyone agreed to meet early so they could practice and warm-up before the visitors arrived. Babe left his bedroom and headed downstairs to get a bowl of cereal before he left.

He was only a couple of steps down the stairs when the door to Billy's room opened and Sally stepped out into the hall. She was barefoot and wore her big white robe. Babe froze. She turned back and kissed Billy through the crack of the door, then shut it and turned to leave. That's when she saw him standing on the stairs, a stricken look on his face. She walked over to the bottom of the staircase and motioned him down.

When he got to the bottom step, she hugged him to her tightly. Although he still felt jealous, he reveled in the hug. The smell of her filled his nostrils, and he could feel the swells of her breasts pressed against him. It was total sensory overload. She kissed him on the forehead and whispered in his ear, "Good morning. Have fun today sweetheart and remember I love you," and then she was gone to her room.

Even though he knew in his heart that Sally and Billy were boyfriend – girlfriend, he still felt he owned a little bit of Sally's heart himself. He didn't understand what Sally's relationship with Billy meant, but he knew they were a couple now. There could be no other explanation for what he just witnessed. Babe didn't play quite as well as he had the day before. Everyone agreed that he didn't seem to have his head in the game that day.

That evening he waited until he was alone with his dad. "Daddy, are Billy and Sally boyfriend, girlfriend?"

"Well yes, son, I think they are."

"Are they in love?" Babe asked.

"Why all the questions?" Carl asked.

Babe proceeded to tell his dad about seeing Sally leave Billy's room that morning.

"What do you think?" Carl answered Babe's question with a question. He wanted Babe to draw his own conclusions.

"I think they are in love."

"What do you think that means?"

150

Babe paused on this one. Love meant love right? What was his dad asking him?

"It means they like each other." Babe said tentatively.

"Is that all you think it means, that they like each other?" Carl wouldn't be satisfied with easy answers, Babe knew how he could be sometimes. He screwed up his courage, he was going to have to let it all out.

"I think it must be more than just liking someone. I think it means they think about each other all the time. I've noticed the way they look at each other when they think no one is watching. It's like they know something no one else knows and kind of like there's no one else in the room." Babe continued.

"What else?" Carl was going to make sure it was all out in the open.

"That they want to spend all their time with each other. Maybe even get married?" Babe asked.

"Well, they might I suppose. Anything else?"

It was time for the big one; there just was no way to avoid it. "Do you think they're," Babe swallowed and then blurted it out, "sleeping together?" He wasn't completely sure what this meant. He was just at the stage where boys discuss such things but never in great detail. Almost always there's one boy who knows just a little more than the rest and invariably he tries to make everyone think he knows everything, and acts appalled that the others don't. Just how stupid could they be? After all, everyone knows what sleeping together means. The reality was none of them knew much, but it was the dawn of the awakening for them all. That was what Babe was thinking.

"Son, they might be. Do you think there's anything wrong with that?" Carl asked.   Like most fathers, this was the conversation that he dreaded would come one day and today was that day.

Babe thought long and hard before answering. He was sorry he ever mentioned this to his dad in the first place. He should have known better he thought. "No Dad, I don't think it's wrong, not if they love each other. You know; if they plan to get married and all."

Carl saw that Babe looked a little down. "What's wrong? You don't look very happy about any of this."

"Well, Dad, I don't want to lose Sally." Babe was close to tears.

"Son, you'll never lose Sally. She loves you and will love you forever, you know that don't you?" Carl wanted to assure him.

"But she loves Billy!" Babe blurted out.

"Yes son, I think she does, but it doesn't prevent her from loving you too. It's just a little different. Billy is that special man that she wants to build her life with. Have a family of her own with, but you, you have your very special place in her heart too. You always will have; to the ends of the earth."

His father always told him he would love him 'till the ends of the earth'. It was reassuring to hear his dad tell him that about Sally. After all, he couldn't say that Sally ignored him or treated him any differently since Billy came into their lives. On the contrary, Sally and Billy had both gone out of their way to include him in most of the things they did. As happens only with children, it was a simple, direct answer and he didn't look for any loopholes. It was like a weight was suddenly lifted. He felt much better. He grinned, "Thanks Dad! I knew Sally wouldn't forget about me!" He ran out the back door, the screen door flapping in his wake.

Carl stood in the kitchen and looked out the door as his son disappeared. He now had confirmation of what he suspected all along. He felt warm all over. He always worried about Sally. Not that she couldn't take care of herself, he knew she could. But still a parent worries about their kids even though they have great faith in their abilities and so Carl had worried about Sally. The world where she grew up in LA was not the one he would have chosen for her. He tried to make up for that as much as he could and since her adolescence, his house in San Diego had been her refuge. Things were working out very nicely. He should have known, after all, Sally came from good stock.

Chapter 14

Babe thought he could finally visualize what the Special was going to look like. Billy had been telling him all along, and he nodded his head like he understood, but in reality he did not. Now enough of the car was together to really begin to see what the final result would be.

School had started so he didn't have time to spend in the shop like he had in the summer. Now his dad saw to it that homework came first. He hated homework, but he knew better than not to do it. If his grades suffered so would his participation in baseball and he couldn't bear to think about that. The days were already getting shorter and that left very little time for baseball anyway. In his mind, the only good thing about this time of year was the pennant race leading up to that holiest of grails, the World Series.

Sally was still staying with them and he really enjoyed that. She had not returned to LA since her trip early in the summer, when Billy with with her. He assumed Sally would be staying with them from now on. No one had mentioned anything different. Babe thought it was curious that Sally never mentioned her parents. He heard his dad ask about Sally's mom a time or two, but other than that, nothing. He didn't always understand the things adults did anyway. Maybe she didn't like her parents, that might be it, he thought.

As all these thoughts ran through his head, he stood in the shop looking at the Special. He had just gotten home from school and was there by himself. His dad and Billy were still at work and Sally was gone. It was one of those rare days in San Diego when it was raining so all thoughts of baseball were gone.

The Special was sitting on its wheels and tires. Billy had finished the grille shell and it was mounted on the car. Babe thought it made the car look very 'pointy'. The engine was mounted in the frame. The firewall was in place behind the engine. The hood sides were in place between the firewall and the grille shell. The hood sides had large louvered panels in them. Billy had explained the louvers were needed to allow the air that came in through the grille to escape out of the car. The old seat Billy bought at the surplus store was mounted in the frame and brake and clutch pedals had been fabricated and installed. The steering was fixed in place and the steering wheel was in position, it's spokes bright and shiny. Heavy cord wrapped the rim of the wheel. Billy explained the cord gave a better grip on the wheel. Babe couldn't resist. He climbed into the seat and reached out for the steering wheel. Even sitting on the edge of the seat and stretching, his feet wouldn't reach the pedals. Billy's legs were just too long. As soon as his hands touched the wheel's rim, he could see himself hurtling across the dusty flat of the dry lakebed, his goggles down and crouched low out of the wind.

Sally walked in the door of the shop unnoticed by Babe. He was crouched down, both hands on the wheel, and seemed to be straining to get that last ounce of speed out of the Special even though he was sitting still. He was doing his best to imitate what he thought the engine would sound like as he sawed the wheel back and forth.

"You better get a muffler on that engine, mister!" Sally said over his shoulder. He jumped, startled by her voice, then blushed, embarrassed to be caught playing in the car.

"Have you given up baseball for racing?" she asked.

"Uhh, no!" he stammered as he started to scramble out of the car.

"You don't have to get out, no one minds if you play in the car," Sally said, but Babe's embarrassment was too much. He had to get out and pretend it never happened. "You certainly have the right name to be a racer." Sally was referring to his namesake, Frank Lockhart, one of the world's great drivers and a mechanical genius, not his nickname.

"Oh Sally stop, I know I have the name. Daddy told me he was the best ever, but I'd really rather play second base or short stop." Babe said.

"I know you would. I was just pulling your leg, and it really is okay for you to play in the car. No one minds, and besides you've worked on this project too. You deserve to get a little fun out of it."

The reference to his having contributed helped. It made him feel grown up, maybe everyone really did look at him as part of the team. His embarrassment began to fade. "When do you think we'll have it finished?" he asked as he caressed the steering wheel, his pride beginning to show. Sally noticed he used the word 'we' in reference to finishing the car.

"Your dad and Billy say we should have it finished by next summer. If things go really well we might be able to make the first meet next spring."

"That would be so swell! I can't wait to see it finished. Are we going to paint it and everything?" Babe asked.

"I think so."

"What color?" he inquired.

"Billy says black."

"That'll be pretty. I wonder if there's some way Billy can take me for a ride?"

"I don't know. Do you think you and Billy both can squeeze into that seat?" Sally asked.

Babe frowned. He didn't think Billy and anyone else, no matter how small, would fit. "I don't know. I don't think so."

"Me neither, but maybe you and I would fit. Maybe I could take you for a ride."

Babe was excited at the thought. "Do you think he would let you, really? I hope so, I hope so!"

"We'll see. We've got to get it finished first." Sally pointed out.

Now Babe could hardly wait to get to work on the Special, the sooner they got to work, the faster it would be finished. "I've got

154

to get in the house and get my homework finished so I can work on it tonight!" He was running toward the door before the last word left his mouth. Sally chuckled in amazement. That boy certainly had plenty of energy, if he was ever still, he was probably asleep.

She had been shopping for Billy and Carl today. They needed a welding rod and Billy needed a new pair of gloves. The man at the welding supply store had been very helpful. Although she was aware of it, she would never fully appreciate how special she was treated because of her appearance. Men, all men, were invariably nice to her. Many doors opened to her that were closed to others.

She paused to look at the Special herself. It was beginning to look like a car. She hadn't been able to see it in the beginning. All she saw was a pile of steel and some greasy parts and a very attractive motor. She trusted in Billy and his vision just as they all had. Now that trust was beginning to pay off. Of course, she trusted Billy completely. The mere thought of him was enough to excite her. She could barely wait for him to get home, and it was almost time. She wished she'd gone by to pick him up today, but she hadn't been sure if she would have time for all her errands.

She heard a car pull in the drive. Its engine had a deep throb, different than Carl's LaSalle, and besides it was too early for Carl. She wondered who it could be. She decided to investigate. As she looked out the door, she noticed it stopped raining.

When she returned from her errands, she pulled the Packard down the drive just past the house to allow Carl plenty of room to park the LaSalle. She couldn't see the front part of the drive until she was nearly to the corner of the house.

When she got to the corner she saw a big black Cadillac sedan in the drive. Just as she saw it, the door opened and Tommy got out. He saw her immediately and smiled and waved. "Oh Lord, what does he want?" was her first thought.

Tommy walked toward her. "I thought I might find you here," he said.

"And what brings you to San Diego?" she asked. Sally gave him a brief hug in welcome.

"Business. I still own the dealership here you know," he said. As they talked they walked slowly around to the front porch.

"We don't have any Cadillacs for sale here," she reminded him.

"I know Sally. I came by here to see you. Ever since our argument, I've felt terrible. I wanted to apologize, but I haven't seen you. I take it you've been here ever since?"

Tommy was standing on the broad porch, his back towards the street. Over his right shoulder, Sally could see Billy walking down the sidewalk on his way home from work. He wore his usual khakis, plaid shirt, and his crumpled felt fedora with the brim pinned up by his Consolidated badge. His lunchbox swung from his right hand. He was looking back at her. "Thank God he's home," she thought.

155

Tommy continued to talk, but she barely heard a word he said, her attention was on Billy coming up the walk. Tommy knew her attention was elsewhere and turned to look as Billy mounted the porch steps.

Sally reached for Billy, both arms around his neck pulling his head down. She kissed him longer and more passionately than was necessary or their norm. When they finally came up for air, she said "Hi, honey. Glad you're home." She pulled herself close against his side, one arm around his back, the other around his waist. Her intention was to leave no doubt in Tommy's mind at all where her affections lay. "Tommy was in town on business and decided to drop by."

It was Tommy's worst fear come to life. It had been her attention to Billy that caused the altercation at the dealership in LA. Tommy hoped that Billy had just been a passing fling. He could not understand for the life of him, how Sally could be involved with this guy. After all, he had no money, no society family, no rich and powerful friends, no social standing whatsoever. How would Sally ever be able to live without those things? The very fact that he had those thoughts indicated how little he understood Sally at all. As with everything else in his life, Sally was an object to conquer and possess. He had totally missed the fact she was her own person with her own wants and desires. Because of all this, it was a shock realizing that Billy was far more than a passing fling. Tommy was quick to recover. He kept his disappointment hidden, and reached for Billy's hand.

"Nice to see you again Billy. I hadn't seen Sally in some time and Carl said she was staying here. He also invited me by to check out the progress on 'the Special' as he calls it." Tommy said.

Before Billy could respond, Carl pulled into the drive behind Tommy's Cadillac. The door opened and Carl got out. "Well, look who's home" Tommy said.

"Hi Boss, I see you still know the way." Carl replied.

"I was just telling Billy and Sally that you invited me by to see the progress on the Special." Tommy said, shaking Carl's hand on the porch stops.

"You might as well stay for supper," Sally said. "I've got a pot of chili on the stove."

"Well, I..." Tommy didn't get to finish, Carl interrupted him to say "Certainly he's staying, aren't you Boss?"

"I suppose I can," Tommy replied.

They all went into the house. Sure enough, you could smell the chili simmering as soon as they entered.

Bottles of beer were opened all round and they headed out to the shop. Tommy had a very large operation that maintained and modified his own personal cars plus the maintenance facilities of his many dealerships. By comparison, construction of the Special was a small time operation. Yet taking all this into account, the Special was an impressive sight. The resources available to Billy and Carl were severely restricted and so far, the only labor had come from the family. Before he could even ask a question, Sally started to point out some of the finer and more innovative details of the car. Her involvement was even more impressive than the car. It was hard for Tommy to digest the fact that Sally was giving detailed explanations of the project with obvious pride. He had never known her to care much about cars.

For the longest time Tommy was speechless. This was beyond anything he expected. The Special itself was a very impressive car. There was no doubt in his mind that it would be fast. The fact that the entire household was involved in its construction was astounding. He became even more jealous that despite his riches, nothing in his life could compare with the project in Carl's backyard. It wasn't the Special, Tommy had any number of cars that were its equal, but he had nothing to rival the way these four people cared about each other.

"Tommy, I want to personally thank you, without your help none of this would be possible," Billy extended his hand and saw the momentary look of confusion on Tommy's face as he continued, "without the engine and the steering you loaned us, there's no way this would be the same project. It's your generosity that's got us to where we are." Billy said sincerely.

Tommy was totally taken aback. Nothing was going the way he expected. He was prepared to dislike Billy intensely, but here he was basking in his praise. The woman he always thought of only in the most feminine of ways was now proud of helping fabricate a racecar. Despite his misgivings, he could feel himself being sucked into the project.

"You know we've modeled much of this on your speedster." Billy was saying.

"Yeah, and Frank Kurtis gave Billy a lesson on metal forming when we were in LA." Sally added.

It was more than he could take. He had to reciprocate in some way. "Forget about the 'loan' of the engine and stuff. You've made far better use of it than I ever would, it's yours!" Tommy said.

"We couldn't accept that," Billy started and was almost immediately interrupted by Sally.

"Oh yes we can! Tommy you can be such a dear at times." she kissed him on the cheek.

As bittersweet as the kiss was, Tommy considered it more than ample payment for the goods. None of that stuff mattered to him anyway and it obviously was important to Billy and Carl. He wondered if Billy knew Sally could afford to buy him anything he might ever want? The more he thought about it, the more he realized Billy didn't know, but even if he did, he doubted that it would make any difference and he certainly couldn't see Billy ever asking for anything.

"It's yours and the matter's closed. When do we eat?" Tommy said and everyone laughed. They headed back toward the house. Being the last one out, Carl turned off the lights.

At the dinner table, one of the first things out of Babe's mouth was, "Come on, let's hurry and eat so we can go work on the Special."

Everyone is involved, this group of people has become a family, he thought. He was envious and not just of Billy and Sally's relationship, but of all of them.

"I think I better be on my way. I don't want to impede progress and Lord knows I'd be no help." Tommy said.

"No need to leave, you can spend the night here." Sally said.

"You don't have room for me."

"We can make room, can't we?" she looked first at Billy and then Carl. The implication was clear to Carl at least. She would spend the night in Billy's room, which she did anyway and Tommy could have hers.

Before Carl could say anything Tommy replied, "I have reservations at the Coronado, my normal suite. Actually I was rather looking forward to hearing the surf tonight and having room service for breakfast in the morning." He didn't mention that he thought tonight might be a good night to avail himself of the concierge's ability to secure 'services of a personal nature'. He idly wondered if any of the 'services' might be blue-eyed blondes?

Billy and Sally stood on the front porch and watched Tommy drive away. "Laid it on pretty thick didn't you?" Billy asked.

"Yes, I did. I wanted to be sure he got the message." She replied.

"I think he got it."

"Me too," she smiled and then kissed him long and hard. She wasn't satisfied until Billy's response was very obvious.

"I think you got that message too." She said as their lips parted.

"Indeed I did. We better head to the shop before we get in trouble."

"Spoil sport," she said before repeating the kiss.

They headed through the house to the shop where all the lights were on. Carl and Babe were already at work.

Billy was working on the pedal assemblies. Babe was his constant companion in the shop. He was fascinated at how Billy could just make things. The cockpit of the Special was going to be cramped. In a car as narrow as this one, there simply wasn't any excess room. This problem was compounded by Billy's desire to make things look as good as they functioned. Many decisions were made based on appearance; the pedals were one of those decisions.

Billy wanted to keep as much clutter out of the engine compartment as possible. He especially wanted the firewall to be clean. In order to do this, he decided to mount the master cylinder under the cowl inside the cockpit. The race car steering box also had to mount in this cramped area. The steering gear was a fairly large aluminum affair that stretched from one side of the cockpit to the other. It was basically a two inch diameter aluminum tube. Billy formed mounts for the pedals and the steering gear out of triangular shaped steel plates. He also made his own pedals out of quarter inch plate steel. The pedal mounts carried a split steel ring that clamped the steering gear in position. The part that really fascinated Babe was when Billy used pieces of music wire to fashion his own return springs for the pedals. Once finished, the design packed everything into a neat compact package.

Billy had been working on this part of the car for a couple of weeks. With Babe's help, or perhaps in spite of it, he was able to finish it up that night. Babe thought it strange that Billy and Sally both got tired and retired early that night. He simply filed it away in his file of strange things that adults do.

The house where they lived was in an old neighborhood of San Diego. All the houses stood on big lots covered by many large mature trees. The trees were one of the most attractive parts of the area. All the streets were green tunnels formed from the trees on both sides arching over the roadway. Huge oak trees surrounded the house. The trees had obviously been planted when the house was built as their placement was too regular to have been simply random.

Late one afternoon Babe was in the yard playing by himself. It was one of the rare days when he was alone; usually he was at a nearby park playing ball. This day he fancied himself Robin Hood just as he had seen Errol Flynn portray at the movie.

Babe climbed a sturdy oak beside the house to lie in wait to ambush the Sheriff of Nottingham. After finding a comfortable position he pulled a nearby acorn off a limb and he dropped it, "Bombs away!" he thought. He quickly decided that the first acorn would become his target and then began trying to hit it with others. It was getting dark and he had just managed to hit his target for the third time when he was startled by a light being turned on in the house. The light was in the window nearest the tree. He turned to look.

Sally had just gotten home from an afternoon spent grocery shopping. One of her favorite stops had been the farmer's market where she loved selecting ripe fruits and vegetables. Being so late in the year, Carl's backyard garden had already run its course. She loved fresh tomatoes and the market had a nice selection.

It was still warm in San Diego, even this late in the year. Today had been even warmer than normal. She felt all sticky and smelly after an afternoon shopping in the sun. After putting everything away, she headed to the bathroom for a quick shower before she started dinner. Billy and Carl were running an errand, but would be home soon.

Sally stepped into the bathroom, shut the door and turned on the light. She reached over and turned on the hot water. It always took a minute or two to warm up. Then she slipped out of her clothes. Getting rid of the sweat soaked garments made her feel better already. As she waited for the water to heat up, she studied her face in the mirror and ran both hands through her thick hair. She turned from side to side so she could see her profile in the mirror.

Babe thought his heart was going to jump out of his chest it was beating so hard. He was having difficulty breathing and nearly slipped and fell out of the tree, only a last second grab saved him. The light that had startled him came from the downstairs bathroom. The bathroom window was set high in the wall to ensure privacy, but had never been designed to take into account voyeurs in the trees. From Babe's perch in the tree, he had a perfect view into the bath.

Sally entered the room, closed the door and turned on the light that had startled him. As he watched she turned on the shower and immediately peeled off her clothes. Regardless of Sally's relationship with Billy, Babe still had a crush on her. It was only natural really; she was the only woman in his life except for his teachers. She had always paid special attention to him and was interested in the things he did. She took him with her while out shopping or running errands. And on top of all this, she was a beautiful older woman.

Babe had never been more intensely aware of her beauty than he was right now. She was only a few feet away from where he was perched and his view was perfect. Her body was as fine as any statue in the art books at the library. The pose she struck, her hands in her hair couldn't have been more revealing. Babe was frozen in the tree, his breathing labored. In the back of his mind he knew he should look away, but he couldn't. His heart continued to pound. He was afraid she would hear it and he would be found out. He tried in vain to regain control of himself. As he watched, she stepped toward the shower stall.

Sally stepped into the shower. The water felt so good. She didn't close the curtain leaving it open to improve the ventilation, it was so hot. She reached for the shampoo and lathered up. Her hair was so thick it wasn't easy to wash. Thank goodness it was cut fairly short. After several minutes spent lathering, she started to rinse. As she did so, she slowly turned in a circle so that the jets of water worked their way around her head.

When the shampoo was out of her hair, she started washing the rest of her body. After the afternoon spent in the hot sun, the shower was so refreshing. She lingered just an extra moment letting the water spray her back. Then she turned off the water and started to towel off.

Babe was so captivated by what he was seeing that he forgot where he was. He lost his balance and started to fall. In the split second it took for reality to snap back he grabbed for a branch, but it broke off in his hand. He hit the ground on his back with a resounding thud.

He saw sparks flash before his eyes. The shock of hitting the ground was solid and coursed through his entire body. After the sparks his eyesight compressed to a very narrow circle of twilight. It was almost dark outside anyway. The blow knocked the wind out of him. His mind couldn't comprehend what had happened for a moment. Slowly his ability to think and breathe returned. His first thought was that God had punished him for looking. He hurt so badly all over that he was sure he was paralyzed. He lay there on his back for the longest time, unable to move. He stared straight up wondering if anyone would find him or if he would die right here. The guilt he felt was almost as paralyzing as the fall. As it got darker and darker, his breathing returned to normal and he realized he could move his legs. Slowly movement returned and he was able to sit up. His head was getting clearer, but he still ached all over.

After what seemed an eternity he was able to stand on wobbly legs. He had to hold the trunk of the tree to keep from falling. Then the tremors came. A little shake at first then he was trembling almost uncontrollably all over, the tremors turning into sobs. He was consumed with guilt. Finally he was able to walk. The first hesitant steps turned into a run as he headed toward the house.

Billy was just starting out the front door to call him to dinner when Babe reached the steps. In the gloom, Billy didn't realize Babe was crying until he rushed past him and bounded up the stairs toward his room. Billy called after him, "Babe! What's the matter?" But his question was answered only with the sound of Babe's bedroom door slamming. Billy started to follow him upstairs, but thought better of it and returned to the kitchen where Carl and Sally were already seated at the table.

"Something's wrong with Babe," Billy said.

Both Carl and Sally instantly tensed. "What?" was Carl's immediate question.

"I don't know. I met him as he was coming up the porch steps. He was crying and he just ran right past me and up the stairs to his room."

"Was he hurt?" Sally asked.

"Not that I could tell. He certainly climbed the stairs like he was okay. He flew up them, but he never said a word to me, just sobbed." Billy said with concern.

Carl started getting up, but Sally was already out of her chair and headed toward the hall. "I'll go see about him. Carl, eat your dinner, if he's hurt or needs you, I'll come get you." Billy and Carl watched her leave.

"Carl, I really think he was okay. He wasn't bleeding and I couldn't tell that he was favoring anything."

We'll that's good." Carl seemed to relax a bit. "He's always run to Sally if she was here for hurts and things. She's the only woman he's ever been around. She'll take good care of him."

Babe was on his bed, his face buried in his pillow still crying. He heard a tap on his door but he ignored it. Another tap. "Go away!" he yelled.

The door opened slowly and Sally came in. She shut the door behind her and walked over and sat on the edge of the bed. She put her hand on Babe's back. She could feel his body tense at her touch. "What's the matter Babe?" she asked in a soft voice.

"Go away!" was the only response.

"Babe, honey, what's wrong?"

"Go away!"

"I'm not leaving until you tell me what's wrong." Sally insisted.

"I can't tell you! I can't tell anyone!"

"Why not? You can tell me; you can tell me anything." More sobs, "Sweetie, I love you, you can tell me anything, I promise."

"You can't love me! Go away!" Babe begged her to leave.

The 'you can't love me' statement puzzled Sally. What could that possibly mean?

"Babe did you get in trouble?" There was no response, just more sobs. "Honey did you do something wrong?" There was a very subtle change, just the slightest pause and then more sobbing.

"Babe honey, did you do something? You can tell me. It can be our secret, I promise."

The guilt Babe felt was overwhelming. He couldn't ever remember feeling so bad about anything. He was certain that God was punishing him. His mind swirled. Finally he simply couldn't take it anymore. Sally was rubbing his back and she kissed the back of his head repeatedly.

Babe was raised to be honest and to take responsibility for your own actions. The enormity of what he had done weighed on him. He had wronged one of the people he loved the most in all the world. He was dying of shame. Like a dam bursting he had to let it out and whatever happened to him, he deserved it.

"Babe, darling, you can tell me anything. I love you. Tell me, okay?"

The sobs slowed. He turned his head around, not where he was looking her in the eye, but where she could see the side of his face. It was very red and tears had wet his entire face.

"You'll never love me again," he said, his voice almost a whisper.

"Don't be silly hon, I'll love you forever," she assured him.

"No you won't. Not after you know what I did."

"I'll love you regardless of what you did. I promise."

Babe could stand it no longer. He had to come clean and own up to what he had done. "I saw you." He whispered, his voice riddled with shame.

"You saw me? What do you mean you saw me?"

He started to cry again. "Babe stop it and talk to me. I told you, you can tell me anything." Sally insisted.

"I saw you in the shower!" he buried his face in the pillow again and started to cry.

Sally was startled. He saw me in the shower? How did he do that? "Honey, honey, its okay. What do you mean you saw me in the shower?"

He turned his head back around at her continued urging. She continued stroking and petting his back. "I was in the tree beside the house."

She was beginning to understand. Maybe he did see her. "Why were you in the tree?"

"I was Robin Hood. Remember when Robin ambushed the Sheriff of Nottingham?" he asked still visualizing Errol Flynn as robin.

"Yes, I remember." Sally had taken Babe to see the Adventures of Robin Hood when it was showing at local theatres.

"I was Robin. Then you came in the bathroom and turned on the light. At first it scared me. I jumped and then I saw it was you in the bathroom."

Sally was thinking of everything she had done less than an hour ago in the bathroom. She refused to let herself get embarrassed or upset. Very calmly she asked, "and what happened then, hon?"

"You turned on the shower and took off your clothes."

It took some willpower, but she forged on. "And then what did you do?"

"I looked." He whispered.

"For how long?" she asked somewhat surprised.

"Until you finished."

"Finished what?"

"Until you finished your shower."

"Oh Lord!" she thought but didn't say. Thinking quickly about playing with her hair and leaving the curtain open and how she had lingered. "Oh Lord!" she thought again, "he did get an eyeful didn't he?!!"

"Honey, why didn't you look away? If I had been watching you, wouldn't you want me to look away?" she kept her voice steady and softly comforting. She didn't want to sound accusing.

"It's different."

"How is it different?"

"Sally, you're beautiful! You're the most beautiful woman in the whole world. Anyone would want to look at you! I'm ugly, no one wants to look at me!" He tried to explain.

She was momentarily taken aback by being called the most beautiful woman in the world. Wasn't he such a dear? How did he ever get the idea he was ugly?

"Honey, you're not ugly." Sally assured Babe.

"Yes I am. How would you know?"

"Babe I've seen you many times without your clothes. I used to change your diaper. How many times have I babysat with you? When you were little, we used to take baths together. You were too little to remember. You're not ugly, just the opposite, you're beautiful too." She said squeezing his arm tenderly.

Babe didn't remember being in the bath with Sally. How old had he been?

"We took baths together?"

"A few times we did."

"And that was okay?"

"Sure," she said.

A weight lifted off him. He grabbed Sally and hugged her as hard as he could. She still smelled all fresh and new from the shower. "I love you!"

"I love you too sweetie. Are you better now?"

"Yeah" then a momentary panic hit. "Are you going to tell Daddy? Are you going to tell Billy?"

"Of course not! I told you it was our secret."

"Promise?"

"I promise. Now why don't you come downstairs and eat dinner?"

"I'm too tired. I think I'll just stay here and sleep." Almost before he could get the words out, his eyes started to droop. All the tension had been released and he expended all the energy he had for the day. He was out like a light.

Sally undressed him and put him in bed. She pulled his covers up and kissed him just as any mother would. In the morning when he awoke, he would realize that Sally had put him to bed. He would wonder at it all. Maybe he really wasn't ugly after all. Maybe she meant what she said. They had taken baths together when he was little? It seemed he could very vaguely remember that. He tried to remember, yes there was a glimmer there. He felt so much better about yesterday. He no longer had the shame. Sally had made sure of that. She certainly was beautiful and she did care about him. A guy couldn't ask for more than that he thought. The memory of this event would stay with him the rest of his life. Regardless of what might happen in the future, he and Sally shared some special times of their own. Those times would always be very intimate memories in his mind; years later he hoped they were the same in hers.

Chapter 15

Halloween came and went. To everyone's surprise, Babe decided to dress as a race car driver rather than a baseball player. He told everyone that asked that he WAS a baseball player so how could he disguise himself as what he already was? So he wore the cloth pilot's helmet Billy ought him at the surplus store and found an old pair of goggles. Much to his disgust everyone thought he was dressed as a pilot. Still he managed to fill a paper shopping bag with goodies. In those days, trick or treating was a much safer pursuit.

Progress on the car was steady. The major systems such as fuel and brakes were almost finished. There was still much of the body yet to create, but Billy felt sure that if he really wanted to they could probably get the chassis to the point it could be driven sans body in a month or so.

They finished work for the night. Since it was a week night and Babe had school the next day, he turned in early. Carl saw to it that he got to spend a little time in the shop each night but made it clear from the beginning that school came first. Billy and Sally headed toward the house and as usual, Carl was the last one out, turning off the lights and locking the shop.

Billy and Sally went to their separate rooms. They usually did. After the rest of the house was quiet, one would go to the other's room. They didn't think it would be a problem, but they also didn't want to make a big production over it. In their minds being discreet was the proper way to handle it. After all, there was a youngster in the house.

Billy was turning down the bed when the door opened and Sally slipped in. As usual, she was wearing her white terry cloth robe and a smile. She closed the door quietly.

After they were settled in bed, Sally said, "Thanksgiving is coming up. Do you have any plans?"

"No, I hadn't given it much thought. There's no way I could go home to Texas. I'll only have a long weekend. What are you going to do?" He dreaded the possibility that she might go back to LA. He didn't want to spend the holidays without her.

"Well, I've been thinking," she said. "I want to spend Thanksgiving with Carl and Babe, but I thought we might leave after dinner here and drive up to LA. Maybe spend the weekend in the beach house. That is, if you're interested?"

"Are you kidding!? Of course, I'm interested!" Billy said enthusiastically.

She giggled and snuggled closer against his side. "I thought you might be."

"Will it be okay? I mean will your brother let us use it? Does he know about me?"

"No, he doesn't know about you, but I'm pretty sure I can get it. He's usually gone during the holidays. I'll call him and be sure, but I don't think there will be a problem," she replied.

They lay there for a few moments, each lost in their own thoughts, but happy to be in each other's company. "Do you think Carl and Babe will be upset if we leave them for the weekend?" Billy asked.

"I doubt it. They could probably use the break anyway. Believe it or not, I think Carl actually has a life that doesn't involve us."

Billy chuckled softly. "Yes, I guess he does. We spend so much time together I forget about that. Call your brother."

"Okay," she replied. "Goodnight lover."

"Goodnight nothing!" and she laughed.

Sally was sitting on the front porch when Billy got home from work the next day. She saw him get off the bus at the end of the next block and start walking down the sidewalk towards the house. She offered him the use of the Packard, had almost insisted that he use it to go back and forth to work, but he refused. He told her riding the bus worked just fine and it saved him the hassle of finding a parking place on the crowded lots surrounding the plant. Besides, he said, she needed the car to run errands during the day. As she watched him draw near, she marveled at the good fortune that had brought them together. In her eyes, Billy was perfect in every way. It was plain in everything he did or said that he loved her. He always put her welfare before his own. He never asked her for anything and had stubbornly refused anything she offered. She was sure that he had no idea how wealthy she really was. He never asked any questions about her family life. Carl told her that Billy never asked him any such questions either. Yes sir, she told herself, that man is the real deal, an honest man that truly loves me just for being me. And wasn't he good looking? Just watching him walk down the street made her tingle all over. She had to keep that under control, after all, Babe was in the house doing homework and Carl would be home soon. Still she allowed herself just a moment to let her mind roam free. How delicious it was.

He turned up the walk and as he mounted the porch steps he said, "Hello beautiful!"

She rose from her chair and greeted him with a lingering hug and kiss. "Hi lover, and you're much too kind."

"No ma'am. Not at all, not by half," and they kissed again. It was a ritual they repeated every afternoon.

He put his lunchbox down and they sat side by side on the porch swing holding hands. "How was your day?" she asked.

"It was good. I think I'm going to get to move into flight controls."

"Is that good?"

"Yeah, I think it'll be more interesting than bucking rivets all day. It's something I'd really like to do."

"Wonderful! Congratulations!" Sally said, hugging him.

"Thanks!" the duo shared another kiss to celebrate his new job assignment.

"I talked to Earle today."

"What did your brother have to say?"

"We can have the beach house. He's going to Florida. We can have it all through the holidays."

"Gee that's swell! We need to talk to Carl." And just as he said that, they could see the LaSalle coming down the street. As they watched, the black coupe slowed and turned into the drive, a smiling Carl behind the wheel. He shut off the engine, opened the door and stepped out.

"What are you two love birds brewing up?" He asked with a grin.

Billy blushed a bit and Sally replied. "We're making plans for Thanksgiving. Do you have any thoughts, oh, and by the way, we're glad to see you too!" Everyone chuckled.

"Nope, no plans at all, but I had hoped we could all be together for Thanksgiving dinner."

"Us too," Sally replied. "But we were thinking about going back to LA afterwards. Would you and Babe like to go with us?"

"Honey, you know I didn't leave anything in LA. Really, I'd rather stay here and besides, Babe won't want to miss a long weekend with his pals." Carl said.

"Okay, but you're more than welcome to go with us." Sally insisted.

"You two go ahead. You don't need us tagging along, we'd just be in the way," Carl smiled again.

"Then let's plan on dinner here. I'll go shopping and get a turkey and all the trimmings. We'll leave for LA on Friday morning. That sound alright to everyone?"

"Sounds good to me." Carl said.

"Me too." Billy chimed in.

"It's settled then. Speaking of dinner, I've got a meatloaf in the oven, anyone hungry?"

Both men answered by heading toward the door. Sally's meatloaf was a real treat.

Thanksgiving Day was a new experience for the Babe. He and his dad didn't really have a Thanksgiving tradition. More than once, they were invited to friends and co-workers houses for dinner. Several times Carl ordered turkey and dressing from a local restaurant. One time they went out to eat, and on one very forgettable occasion, Carl tried cooking turkey himself. Even Babe wondered how it was possible to burn the turkey to charcoal in one spot and leave it raw in another. While neither of them died of starvation, they also never experienced anything to rival week after week of Sally's cooking. It had become something they were accustomed to and didn't want to give up.

Finally the big day arrived. The smell of turkey baking mingled with dressing and pumpkin pie made Babe's mouth water. They were all in the kitchen; Sally cooking and all the men in happy anticipation.

"How did you ever learn to cook so well?" Billy asked. Sally's cooking rivaled his mother's and that was high praise indeed. This was the first Thanksgiving he spent away from his family; he couldn't help but think of them. He could see them all sitting down to their own turkey around the big round oak table in his mother's home.

"Dorothy taught me. She was our cook when I was a little girl. She was the most wonderful old white haired lady. She was as big around as she was tall. Dorothy was always laughing and happy. She had pink shiny cheeks, almost like two balloons and sparkling blue eyes, and oh, could she cook!"

"She doesn't cook for your family anymore?" Billy asked.

"No. She retired. She said she was just too old to do it every day. She went away to live with her daughter back east. We surely have missed her. Luzia cooks for us now and she's an excellent cook, but there was always something special about Dorothy." Sally said whistfully.

"I think she taught you everything she knew," Carl said.

"Hardly. I do okay, but I'm not in a league with Dorothy. She was always so sweet to me. Let me hang out in the kitchen and get in her way all the time. She taught me a lot."

"Is it ready yet? I'm ready to eat!" Babe added. Everyone laughed, after a few seconds hesitation, even the Babe joined in. He would remember it as the happiest Thanksgiving he ever experienced. He would always suspect that they all felt that way.

After the meal, the men sent Sally to the front porch to relax and enjoy a glass of wine while they handled the cleanup chores. After all, she had been cooking for almost two days straight; they felt she deserved a break.

Even though it was Thanksgiving Day, the weather in San Diego was still beautiful. Sally was enjoying the respite on the porch swing as she sipped her wine. She turned as the front screen door opened and the guys filed out, obviously whipped by the cleanup they had so gallantly insisted on doing. "Poor babies" she thought, "a few dishes were almost their undoing." They each carried a glass, even Babe to her surprise, and Billy carried the wine bottle.

Babe stuck his glass out. "I'll pour," Carl said and took the bottle from Billy. He poured Babe about a third of a glass. "That's it for you, young man."

"Aw, Dad!" For which he received a very stern look from Carl. "Oh, okay," he said.

Carl poured Billy a glass, topped off Sally's and then filled his own.

"A toast to the best cook in California," Carl said and they all touched glasses. Billy and the Babe added their affirmations to the toast.

"And to the handsomest and most gallant of companions," Sally said, and again the glasses clinked.

Billy sat beside Sally on the porch swing. Carl had a chair pulled up next to the swing and Babe sat on the top rail of the banister facing them.

They talked of small things as families often do. The wonderful meal they had just consumed was a major topic and Babe regaled them with tales of his recent prowess on the diamond. It was one of the first times that he felt included in the adult conversation almost as an equal. The few sips of wine he had been afforded underscored his thoughts of inclusion.

Glasses were almost empty. Carl poured more for Billy and Sally. Babe once again stuck his out. "Young man, I already told you no more."

"Aw, Dad! I'm okay, I can hardly feel anything."

"I said no more."

Babe had been leaning forward with his glass extended. He jerked backward and upright in a display of annoyance. When he did, his slightly precarious perch combined with his first taste of alcohol proved to be his undoing. He lost his balance and fell backwards off the banister, both legs pointed straight up in the air as he fell out of sight. His disappearance was immediately followed by the sound of limbs breaking.

All three of them leapt to their feet and peered over the banister. As they looked down, they were greeted by the most surprised look on the Babe's face as he lay on his back, his legs pointing straight up, his fall broken by a large bush in the flowerbed that stretched across the front of the porch. The breaking limbs of the bush had provided the sound effects and cushioned his fall.

As soon as they realized he wasn't hurt, they all three collapsed in laughter.

"So you don't feel a thing, huh?" Carl said and they all roared again.

Babe's senses were finally coming into sync with what had happened. This was the second time in recent memory that he had fallen immediately after doing something that he really shouldn't have been doing. Once again, he wondered if it was God's own punishment. He heard all the laughter from the porch and carefully began to extricate himself from the bush. He wasn't sure whether to be angry with the laughter or not and after a few seconds deliberation, decided to join in.

As he climbed the steps and headed in the front door, he said "I think that's enough for me."

Billy thought he was going to hyperventilate. The sight of Babe's legs straight up in the air and disappearing over the railing was just hilarious. And then when he walked back onto the porch carrying his empty glass, his hair all messed up and leaves and twigs stuck all over him, and said he had had enough, well that was simply more than Billy could handle. Carl and Sally must have felt the same way because they were laughing every bit as hard.

As some form of normalcy returned, Sally said, "I better go check on Babe and make sure his feelings aren't hurt," wiping the tears from her eyes.

Friday morning Billy finished putting their bags in the trunk of the Packard just as Sally and Carl came out onto the porch. Sally gave Carl a peck on the cheek and started down the steps toward the car. "You kids have fun!" Carl called as they backed out of the drive.

As usual, Billy was behind the wheel and also as usual, the sun was shining brightly on a beautiful day and the top was down. Billy learned his way around town quite well and needed no prompting as they made their way north to the coast highway.

Once on the highway Billy asked, "Any stops planned along the way?"

"I don't know, I didn't bring a suit."

"Neither did I."

"Then I'm sure a stop is in order," and they both chuckled, Sally snuggling close to Billy's side.

It was a glorious day to be driving this wonderful road, and it was made all the more enjoyable to be young and in love. Their thoughts focused mostly on each other with occasional breaks to enjoy the scenery and the weather.

Sunday morning as Billy locked the front door of the beach house, he was amazed at how much he hated leaving. In his two short stays he already thought of it as home, as his place. He knew that was a completely absurd idea, but still it persisted. He joined Sally in the Packard for their drive back to San Diego.

It had been a nice weekend spent in LA. He was able to visit Frank Kurtis again on Saturday. Frank's business was now almost completely switched over to defense contracts. Frank told him that none of the California race car shops were working on automobile related projects. All of them were making too much money as sub-contractors for the defense industry. Frank showed him a few more tricks on shaping and fabricating metal. It had been a good visit.

He also visited Bell Auto Parts and Karl Orr's speed shop. There were several parts he needed for the Special that he didn't really want to get from the junkyard. He picked up a fuel pressure pump and a few other odds and ends.

Billy assumed that Sally wanted to go out Saturday night, but was surprised when she suggested they stay at the house. They built a fire on the beach and cooked steaks over the coals. As luck would have it, they encountered the old couple walking on the beach after dark. Even though Billy and Sally were both fully clothed this time, the elderly couple recognized them immediately. After an awkward moment or two they introduced themselves and shared a bottle of wine and their fire with the couple whose name was Fulton. It was a great evening, the highlight of the trip really. The Fulton's lived on the beach and walked every night that 'the weather allowed' in Ken's words. They quickly pointed out that their walks shouldn't inhibit any of Billy and Sally's activities. This statement caused Billy to blush even though no one noticed in the darkness. He still remembered their first encounter when he and Sally had been skinny-dipping in the moonlight. Before the evening was over, they invited the Fulton's back to the house where they sampled another couple of bottles of wine. By the time they left, they were all laughing about their first meeting.

The drive home was uneventful. They would have been back in San Diego by early afternoon had they not stopped at what he was beginning to think of as 'their beach'. It was the same place they stopped on their first trip to LA. It really was a very secluded place. There was room to park only one car on the cliffs overlooking the beach, and no other access to the beach itself except the single trail. It was amazing, but somehow they both remembered to bring everything except their swim suits.

Chapter 16

The first Sunday morning of December dawned bright and clear. Billy was still dazzled by the wonderful weather in San Diego. Back home in Texas, the weather this time of year could be just as pleasant as this day was, but it was far more unpredictable. It was equally as common to have ice and snow, something unheard of here, or to have heat in the 90's.

After a family breakfast, they all adjourned to the shop except for Babe. He was getting in some more baseball on his weekend break. The shorter days and pressures of schoolwork had severely curtailed all such activity during the week.

The Special was coming along well. Even an outsider could walk in the shop and realize that a car was being built. After all, there was now a frame with fully sprung axles on each end supporting the wheels and a new set of Firestone tires. The steering gear was mounted along with the brake and clutch pedals. The beautiful engine was in place and attached to its transmission. All of this was crowned with Billy's greatest joy, the hand formed grille shell mounting the LaSalle grille. It still required some imagination to visualize the completed car, but that task was becoming easier by the day.

They were working on the exhaust system this weekend. They planned to build a tube header just like the Indy cars used. The job was made considerably easier by the fact that in the crate with the engine, they found a header 'flange'. This was the heavy steel plate that bolted to the cylinder head and supported each exhaust header pipe. All six pipes would curve smoothly into a long megaphone ending in a large straight pipe running down the side of the car.

Sally made a pattern for the 'megaphone'. This was a three-foot long tapered section of pipe where the six individual cylinder pipes terminated. It was 1 5/8 inches in diameter on the front end and three inches in diameter at the back. Once they had Sally's pattern, Billy and Carl cut the shape out of a sheet of steel. They used their hands to start curving the steel. Then they moved on to bending it around a piece of pipe. They finished up by using the big bench vise to do the final forming. In order to keep the vise from marring the surface of the megaphone, they removed the pipe jaws from the vice and wrapped the megaphone in a thick piece of leather. It took all morning to get the piece shaped. It was a slow process, sliding the megaphone through the jaws of the vice, stopping every few inches to tighten the jaws forcing the steel to bend in a curve. They hammered the edges and then moved down three or four inches and repeated the process. After many trips back and forth through the vice, they finally had the graceful tapered shape they were after. On the final pass through, they welded the seam together every inch or so. A few final taps and they were finished with the initial shaping.

Billy and Carl admired their handiwork. Sally looked it over and pronounced it a reasonable copy of her pattern. They placed it in its approximate location alongside the engine, but outside the hood. The majority of the exhaust would be exposed along the side of the car. Building the exhaust to this design did several things. It increased the torque of the engine. More torque allowed the car to accelerate quicker. This was important because the car would be driven on the street occasionally and also most of the dry lakes only allowed a mile or so to accelerate to top speed before the run was officially timed. Of course, the exposed exhaust also made the car look racy, and kept as much heat as possible out of the car. They all agreed this was a very desirable side benefit.

The next chore was to build the six individual pipes that carried the spent exhaust gas from each cylinder to the megaphone. They started with the front most pipe. This one would run straight out the side of the engine and end in a graceful 90 degree arc right into the front opening of the megaphone. Once the welding was done and dressed, it would look like one piece of steel. The other five pipes would all curve gracefully into the side of the megaphone. It was a design borrowed from the Miller race cars of the twenties and thirties and was still being used on many of the Indy cars of the day.

Bending each small diameter pipe was a tricky job. The pipe had to be bent 90 degrees in a small three inch radius bend, but without collapsing its sides. The only way they had to do this was to weld a cap on one end of each head pipe. Then they carefully filled the pipe with very dry sand. Finally they welded another cap on the other end. Taking the sand filled cylinder, they heated it with the torch until it was red hot and bent it around a six inch diameter pipe. They left a small hole in one end cap to allow any steam that might form while heating the pipe to escape. The last thing they wanted was to have the pipe explode.

They had just finished bending the second pipe when Carl looked up toward the shop door. Billy turned to see what he was looking at as did Sally.

Dave Fair, the next door neighbor, was standing in the doorway. While Billy didn't know him very well, he could tell something was wrong. He was very pale and had a strange vacant look on his face. All work in the shop stopped.

"What's wrong Dave? Is Lynda okay?" Carl asked. Dave's wife Lynda had been ill for several years and was mostly bed ridden. Dave took care of her and this accounted for Billy only seeing him on an infrequent basis.

Dave just stood there in the doorway with his vacant stare. Carl put down the cheater pipe he had been using to coax the bend into the header and walked toward the door, concerned about Dave. Obviously something had happened. Billy turned off the welding torch they were using. Sally set aside the pipe she had been fitting to the megaphone and started to the door.

All the people converging on him finally seemed to snap Dave back to reality.

"They just bombed us," he said.

173

"What? Who bombed us? What are you talking about Dave?" Carl asked.

"They bombed us. The Japanese, they bombed us at Pearl Harbor, it's on the radio." Dave was finally back to the present. His eyes met theirs and he could see the confusion on their faces.

"I heard you all working out here. I heard it on the radio. I was fixing Lynda lunch. I heard it. I didn't know what to do. I walked out on the back porch to have a cigarette. I don't like to smoke in the kitchen you know. Lynda always says she can tell when I've been smoking in the kitchen. I walked out on the porch and I heard you working out here. I didn't think you had a radio in the shop. The Japs, they bombed Pearl Harbor in Hawaii." He pronounced Hawaii as Hiwaya.

"Why did they bomb Hawaii?" Billy asked, still confused.

"That's our fleet anchorage in the Pacific," Carl answered. "How bad is it Dave?"

"I don't know. It's still on the radio. I heard you working and I came over here to tell you." The last sentence was delivered to a vacant shop. They had all pushed past him and were already going in the back door of the house on their way to the big Motorola console radio in the living room. Dave turned around and started back to his back porch where his cigarette still burned in the old saucer he used for an ashtray.

Sally, Carl and Billy all clustered around the big radio. The reports were sketchy at best. About all that was known for certain was that air elements of the Imperial Japanese Navy had attacked military bases in Hawaii including Pearl Harbor. No estimates of casualties or damage were yet available, but there were many reports of explosions, smoke and much gun fire. There were also reports of Japanese diplomats in Washington trying to negotiate at the same time their military had attacked. Already the shock, outrage and anger of America was being felt.

A threshold had been crossed. From this day forward, the lives of every human on earth would be indelibly changed. The world would never return to its pre December 7th state. The three people clustered around the radio would ultimately pay a high price for the breakdown of international relations.

Billy was the first to notice, probably because her fingertips were sinking into the flesh of his thigh. He turned to look at Sally and was shocked to see how pale and sick she looked. Carl was still staring at the front of the big Motorola as if it was going to show him pictures of what was going on 4,000 miles away.

"Honey, what's wrong? Are you okay?" Billy asked.

Sally looked at him, her eyes filling with tears. She didn't say a word. She stood up and left the room.

Billy was already standing when Carl said, "You better see to her."

Billy tapped on her door and went in without waiting on a response. Sally was on the bed, her face buried in a pillow, crying. He lay down beside her and as soon as he did, she turned and

174

seized him in a fierce embrace. Neither of them said anything for the longest time.

"I don't want to lose you." Sally said, "I can't lose you!"

"Darling, you won't. I'm right here and I'm not going anywhere."

Sally clutched him even harder. She was a surprisingly strong woman. Billy stroked her hair and kissed the top of her head, the only part of her he could actually see, so tightly was she pressed against him.

"It might not be your decision whether you have to leave." She warned.

Billy didn't say anything in reply.

"You know it too, don't you?" she said. Then, "Why did they have to do this? Why did they have to bomb us?" she started to cry again.

"Hon, come on, let's wait and see what happens. For all we know, maybe it's all a mistake. We don't know. My mother always told me to never borrow trouble." He continued to stroke her hair and hold her. She was still clenched tightly to him. Slowly the sobs stopped and she seemed to relax a bit.

"You know it's not a mistake," she said, her face still buried in his chest.

"But we don't know anything yet. Let's wait and see. We'll do what we have to do. That's all." She was still and quiet for a long time. He began to think she was asleep. He tried to remain as still as possible so as not to disturb her. If she was asleep, he certainly didn't want to wake her up.

But she wasn't asleep. Her mind was racing at the possibilities. She didn't know much at all about the armed forces or international relations. Really all she knew about Japan was what she read in National Geographic. She remembered images of paper houses, kimonos, and bamboo umbrellas. "Why would a country like that attack America? How could they?" she wondered silently.

Finally she stirred. For the first time since he entered the room, he saw her face. It always stunned him how beautiful it was. She scooted up so that she could kiss him, slowly and lightly at first, then more urgently. She pressed herself against him again. Her left arm was trapped under his body, but her right arm was free. It began to roam over his body; first on his chest, but then lower as the kisses became more urgent. She worked through his belt, then his fly. When it was open, she pulled her arm free and sat up on her knees.

As he watched she quickly undid her coveralls and shrugged her shoulders out of them. In a flash her bra was off and she stood on her knees and pulled the coveralls lower. Even though it was early December, the weather was still warm and all the windows were open, the blinds drawn.

"Hon, the windows. Someone might see," he said as the coveralls came off and were thrown to the floor.

175

"I don't care." She said. "I don't care if everyone sees!" She saw to it that Billy didn't care either.

Later they lay on the bed covered by the sheet. "What do we do next?" she asked.

"We keep working on the Special," was the reply.

"How can you think about a car at a time like this?"

"How can I not? Everything else is beyond my control. I don't know anything about wars or how to control them or what might happen to any of us, but I do know what we need to do to get the Special going. Besides if we concentrate on the Special, it should keep our minds occupied."

She realized this was one of the reasons she was so attracted to Billy in the beginning. He exhibited wisdom far beyond his years. He always seemed so calm no matter what happened. This was the second time she had fallen apart on him. Both times were over the same reason, impending war and the threat it posed to their relationship. She resolved to not let this happen again. She didn't fully understand what happened to her anyway. Normally, she was a very self-assured person and not easily rattled. The more she thought about it, the more she realized she never had this much to lose before. She had never been that close to her family. When she was younger, she and her mother were very close, but as the years passed and her mother's drinking got worse, they drifted apart. There was never the closeness to her father or her brother. They both had always seemed to withhold themselves, almost like she was a guest in their home and not a family member. They were cordial enough, but a girl expected her family to be more than cordial. Carl and Babe had fulfilled that role much better than her blood relatives ever had. She wondered about that again, and about her eyes.

Billy stirred and her thoughts were interrupted. "Let's get dressed before Carl comes looking for us," he said as he got out of bed and pulled on his clothes.

Sally rolled out of bed and walked around to Billy. She put her arms around his neck and drew his face to hers. "I'm sorry for going to pieces on you. I'll try not to do it again," and she kissed him very tenderly and long. As she did so, she could feel him respond. She took him by the hand and led him to the door. "Go on, get out of here or we'll be here all day! I'll be along as soon as I get dressed." She kissed him again then opened the door and pushed him out.

Billy walked back to the living room. Carl was still in front on the radio listening intently.

"Any more news?" Billy asked.

"Not really. They have some reports of extensive damage and columns of black smoke coming from the harbor and some of the military bases, but nothing official yet."

"I'm going back out to the shop." Billy said.

"How's Sally?" Carl asked with concern.

"She's better. She'll be out in a few minutes. This is the second time she's done this. The first time was when Jimmy Kellough and Paul Neece were arguing about us getting in the war in Europe."

"She's worried about you," Carl said.

"I know," and Billy left the room headed toward the back door.

A few minutes later, Sally walked in dressed in her coveralls. "Have they said anything else?" she asked.

Carl related the same thing he had told Billy.

"I'm sorry I fell apart," Sally said and hugged Carl. He was surprised at how tightly she hugged him. There was lots of emotion in it. "I'm just worried about what war might mean for all of us, but especially Billy." She said, the concern evident in her voice.

"I know dear, I'm worried about him too." They hugged another moment or two then, "Let's go check on him. He's out in the shop alone," and they headed out of the house.

When they walked in the shop, they found that Billy wasn't alone after all. Shortly after Billy returned to the shop, Babe rode up on his bicycle expecting to find everyone in the shop. He had already heard about Pearl Harbor and was full of questions. He and Billy had been talking ever since.

"Are we going to get bombed too?" Babe was asking as Carl and Sally walked through the door.

"I don't think so, Babe. It's a long way from Hawaii to San Diego. Even a Liberator would have a hard time making it all the way if it was carrying any bombs. And even if they did make it, they would be totally out of gas. I don't think we have anything to be worried about here." Billy said trying to sound confident.

"I agree with Billy. It's just too far." Carl said.

Many people in the United States were asking each other similar questions at that moment. Most people had heard of Hawaii, but they didn't know exactly where it was or how far away.

"How far is Hawaii from Japan?" Babe asked. It was a good question and caused Billy and Carl to look at each other.

"It's a long way, son." Carl replied.

"Then how were the Japs able to bomb it? Do they have a better airplane than the Liberator?"

"No one has a better airplane than the Liberator" Billy said, his pride showing a bit. After all he spent every working day of the last six months building them. His pride was somewhat justified. No other bomber in the world was the equal of the Liberator for range, speed, and bomb load.

"Son, the Japs probably flew off of an aircraft carrier. Remember when I took you to the Navy Base to see the Lexington and Saratoga that time?" Carl reminded Babe.

"I remember. It was fun. They sure were big." Babe's eyes got big when he was describing the carriers. "Are Jap aircraft carriers that big?"

"Yes, son, I suspect they are," Carl replied.

177

Like most Americans, Babe automatically thought that anything done by America was superior to the rest of the world. It came as a shock to him that anything Japan might have could be equal to or better than that of America. After all, Japan was full of Japs! They were little tiny people who wore glasses and funny wooden sandals. How could a tiny country like that bomb America? The events of the next few months would bring one shock after another and shake those convictions to their very core.

"Why didn't our Navy find them and stop them?" Babe asked.

"I don't know son. If someone snuck up behind you and hit you in the back, could you have stopped them if you didn't know they were there?" Carl asked.

"Why no, not if I didn't know they were there. How could I?"

"That's my point. I don't think the Navy knew they were there and that they were going to attack us."

"Well, they sure know they're there now. Why don't we send some battleships out to sink them?" Babe asked defiantly.

"I'm sure they're doing that very thing right now. Out fleet will be after them like a dog on a bone!" Carl said, but he couldn't have been more wrong. There wasn't a serviceable battleship left in the Pacific. The sneak attack on Pearl Harbor had seen to that. With the exception of a couple of aircraft carriers that had been at sea delivering fighters to Midway and Wake, the rest of the Pacific fleet was in shambles. It would be the threat of the missing carriers that would deter any further movement east by the Japanese. The days when the seas of the world were dominated by dreadnoughts were over, for the dreadnoughts now had something to dread, something to be in mortal fear of, the airplane.

"What do we do now?" Babe asked.

"We simply go on with our lives. You've got to go to school in the morning just like usual." Carl said reassuringly.

"Aw Dad! The Japs might be coming Dad! We've got to get ready for them. I don't want 'em sneaking up behind me!"

"You heard me. You better do your homework too." Carl warned.

"We get bombed and a guy can't even miss a day of school! Shucks!" Everyone chuckled a bit at that.

"What are we going to do with the car?" Babe asked next.

This time it was Billy that answered. "I think we need to keep working on it. For one thing it lets us focus on something we have some control over," his eyes strayed to Sally. Her face showed no trace of her earlier anxiety. "And for another, I want to finish it. I can't wait to see what it looks like and how fast it is. I was thinking though, that we might consider delaying some of the bodywork. We could finish it much quicker as a modified than as the streamliner we've planned."

"What's a modified?" Babe asked.

"A modified has no streamlining behind the driver's seat. Basically the body ends at the cockpit. They have a bob-tailed look. Do you remember Danny Sakai's car?"

Babe nodded that he did.

"Danny's car is a modified. By the way, I wonder what happened to Danny's car?" Billy asked.

Babe's face showed a puzzled look. "What do you mean, what happened to his car?" Babe asked.

"Danny was killed in a motorcycle crash back during the summer." Billy replied.

"I heard Willett has it," Carl said. He meant Willett Brown, Tommy's business manager and close friend.

"Is he going to race it?" Billy asked.

"I don't know, I doubt it. For one thing, I'm not sure he would fit in it very well. Danny built it just big enough for himself, and Danny wasn't very big."

"Well, anyway Babe, we could get the Special running much quicker if it was done like Danny's car. I thought we might consider that. Does anyone know when the next meet is?" By this Billy meant the next time trial, or race.

"No, not the exact dates, but there'll be one in the spring. We might have to go to the lakes though." Carl meant the dry lakes in the Mojave Desert east of Los Angeles. "I'll ask around at work. Some of the guys will know."

"Let's just continue on, I don't see anything else to do unless we just quit." Billy said.

"No! We're not going to quit," Sally said. It was her only contribution to the conversation. She was almost defiant. Billy thought she had never looked more beautiful.

"I think it's settled then. We continue and we'll try to make the first meet possible next year," Carl said. They all nodded agreement. "And I vote that we do our best to finish the body. We can forego the wheel pants for now, but let's get the boat tail done. Billy, I suggest since you're our expert on body work, that you spend all your time on that and leave the details to the rest of us." Carl suggested.

They all agreed and resumed the work they had been doing when Dave came to the door. Carl took the radio out of his bedroom and placed it in the shop so they could listen to the latest news as they worked. At first this was disturbing for Sally, but she eventually decided it was better to know than to wonder. After all, there was a chance this might not lead to her worst fears.

Sally's hopes were dealt a serious blow the next day when President Roosevelt addressed the country in a nationwide radio broadcast. He told them that a state of war existed between Japan and the United States and called on Congress to declare war, which they did in very short order. Before the day was out Hitler had declared war on the United States. The stage was set for the defining event of the 20th century. The event that would change all of their lives forever.

179

Chapter 17

"I was ten years old that Christmas," Babe said. "It was the worst Christmas of my life. Oh, I didn't know it yet, but there would be more to come that would be even worse, but that was the first year I ever remember worrying about things other than what do-dad was in the red box and did the green one have something terrible in it like clothes!"

We had talked all day. Scratch that, Babe talked all day and I listened. Still it was a remarkable story. I found myself hanging on every word, but I couldn't help but wonder how a ten-year-old kid knew so much. The detail was far beyond what I would expect anyone to know, much less a kid. I had to interrupt. "Babe, you were ten years old, right?"

"Damn it! I just told you that! Aren't you listening?" he shot back. He might be in a wheelchair, but his mind was sharp and so was his tongue. There was never any doubt as to who was in control.

"Well how is it that a ten-year-old knows so much detail? You've been telling me incredible detail. Take Billy and Sally for instance. Just how could you possibly know all the details, the intimate details of their relationship?" As soon as the words left my mouth, I knew it was a mistake. His face was blood red and getting redder. A vein stood out on his forehead. His eyes were even bluer. I prepared for the worst.

"Goddammit! Goddammit! Do you think I made all this shit up!?? You think I'm a goddamned liar?" The words were spit out like a machine gun spits bullets, each word every bit as lethal as a lead slug.

"No, no, I didn't mean that. I just meant that when I was ten I had no clue what adults did behind closed doors, that's all. I just wondered how you knew."

"Well I damn sure wasn't peeping in the keyhole if that's what you're wondering! I'll tell you how I know when I get to it. I've told you that already, now do you want to hear this story or not?"

"Of course, I do, and I never meant to imply anything, it's just that I wondered how you knew. Are you getting hungry?"

The look in his eyes changed when I asked if he was hungry. "What time is it?" he asked.

"One thirty" I said.

"Well hell! We've missed lunch! Hell the girls always come by and get me for lunch. I guess they thought since you were here they wouldn't disturb us. I wonder if they have anything left over."

"Let's go out and get something. You feel up to that?" I asked.

"Hell son, do you think I'm an invalid or something? Of course, I feel up to it. Do you mean you'll take me out to eat?"

"Of course, that's what I mean! Do you think I'm a goddamn liar?!!" I shot back at him. It did the trick. He started laughing, using his one good hand to slap his knee.

"You got me there didn't you? I guess I deserved that! I don't get to go out often. That worthless kid of mine never takes me. Shit head is too damn cheap! Afraid he might have to pay for it. Besides it's too damn much trouble to come by once a year and take his old man out to eat. Time's a wastin', let's go!"

Out the door we went, me pushing and Babe barking orders. I could imagine what it must have been like to be a rookie on one of Babe's teams when he was a manager. Sort of like Marine Corps boot camp.

I had parked around behind the building. Since I was in my Suburban and had my car hauler hitched to it, there wasn't room to park in the front lot.

As we rounded the corner of the building, my rig came into view. "That yours?" Babe asked.

"Yeah," I replied.

"Hot dang, that's a pretty thing. You feel like a man riding in that. Not like my idiot son who defines nice car as a mini-van with a TV screen!"

I chuckled. "Mine doesn't have TV" I assured him.

"Good!" was the reply.

I rolled him around to the passenger door.

"You're going to have to help me get in this thing. I can't do it anymore." You could tell it hurt him to admit it.

"No problem. There's been a time or two I needed a little help myself."

Once we were loaded, with Babe's chair stowed in the back, I headed out of the parking lot to the first major thoroughfare. "Where to," I asked.

"Son, anyplace you want to go. I can't tell you what a thrill this is for me." The smile on his face was all I needed to see. "I'm sorry for jumping your shit back there," he said.

"Don't worry about it. I didn't take any offense."

"I shouldn't have. I know it. You live alone for so long you forget how to deal with people."

"It wasn't a big deal." I tried to assure him.

We drove in silence for a few blocks. "I'll tell you how I know the things I do when we get to that part. Can you trust me till then?"

"Of course," I replied.

"I can understand why you might question what I'm telling you," he said.

"That's not it. I wasn't questioning, it's just that you seem to know so much detail. Far more detail than I ever knew when I was that age, that's all" I said.

"I know. I've carried this story around in my head for the last sixty years. When I was a young man, playing ball and all, I thought about it occasionally. You know, when you're on the road in some strange hotel room late at night. I'd think about it. An image would flash in my mind from that time and that would lead to another and another. It was really painful to think about them

181

in those days. It wasn't that long they had been gone. Now their memory seems as fresh, but I remember them with more of a smile than a tear. I guess because I know I'll be seeing them all again soon."

I didn't say anything.

"The older I got, the more I seemed to think about the story. Believe me, there's a lot you don't know yet. When I had my stroke, it took me quite a while to recover, mentally I mean. I was older than my dad was when he died, but it was a stroke that killed him. That's all I thought about, was I going to die, that and the fact that my baseball days were over. Who needs a manager in a wheelchair for Christ sake?" Besides they were over when my wife passed and I started drinking.

"After I finally got my head on straight again, I was already in the home. Hell, there wasn't anyone to take care of me. At least I was smart enough to realize I couldn't do it all myself. Anyway, once I recovered mentally and being in the home and all, I had a lot of time to think. The story started coming back to me more and more often, like it was trying to tell me something. Then finally it came to me, I was the only person on earth that knew the story. I needed to pass it on so that it wouldn't die. I owed at least that much to those people, to my family. But who would I pass it on to? All the people in the home were old folks, most of them older than I was. What good would that do? Pass it on to someone that would die the next week or month. Shit. Finally I got my idiot son out here. Just getting him to come out for the day was a miracle. Had to bribe him. Told him I had some stock that needed tending to. It was just like a shark sensing blood in the water, he thought there might be some cash in it for him, so hell he was here the next day. As soon as I started to talk his eyes glazed over and he didn't hear a word I said. I ran him off after the first 15 minutes. Made me so damn mad, I could have killed that worthless shithead. Didn't see him for six months after that. Geez."

We continued driving. I had totally forgotten that we were looking for lunch.

"Are you going to feed me or what?" he asked.

I snapped back to reality. "Oh sorry! Sure, do you have any preferences?"

"I'd love some Mexican food. I haven't had any in years. The kitchen at the home is full of 'em, Mexicans I mean, but they never fix any Mexican food. I guess the damn administrators think none of us old bastards can handle it."

"Mexican it is then," I said.

A few blocks down the street I saw a red, white and green sign. As I got closer, I could make out 'Rafael's El Rancho Santa Margarita'. "How about El Rancho Santa Margarita?" I asked.

"Sounds great to me. Wonderful old San Diego name too."

"Isn't that the ranch that became Camp Pendleton?"

"Sure is. Just like you. Was that named for one of your relatives or something?"

"Actually, it was, a pretty distant relation. No one I ever knew of personally."

We parked and went in. The place looked decent. Not too cheap and touristy, but not high brow either. A place we could be comfortable to continue our conversation in peace. No sooner had we taken our seats than a cute senorita showed up to take our order.

Babe turned on the charm. He had her giggling and blushing in no time. The compliments rolled out of his mouth in an endless stream. She lapped up each and every one. His blue eyes twinkled. It was easy to see this wasn't his first rodeo.

"Sonya, my dear, what a lovely name that is." He turned to look at me. "Doesn't it sound so lovely, so inviting?" as he turned back to her "Sonya," he drew the name out and he did make it sound sexy, "bring us a pitcher of top shelf margaritas, please. Did anyone ever tell you how lovely your eyes are?"

She giggled and briefly looked at the floor before engaging him again. "Senor, you are too kind."

"Not by half my dear, not by half. You have no idea how lovely you really are. Now run along muchacha and bring us our drinks." She left with a smile.

"You can really turn on the bullshit can't you?" I asked.

'It's called casting your bread upon the water, and besides, I don't get out much. Now where was I?" he asked.

"You were telling your son the story." I said.

"Oh shit, why did you have to remind me of that crap??"

"You asked."

"I know, just shut up and listen. I ran the asshole off. Hell, he wasn't no more interested than the man in the moon anyway. I love the turd, but he's pretty much worthless. All he got from either of his parents was his mother's looks. A faraway look came over him just then. "You should have seen his mother. She was a real looker. You could walk into any place with her on your arm and people would turn to look, just like they did when Sally walked into a room. She was the perfect companion for all those years. I just can't tell you..." His voice trailed off and he stared out the window. I was completely forgotten. He was in another place entirely, remembering his own story I suppose.

Luckily at that point Sonya interrupted his reminisce with our pitcher of margaritas.

"You do like margaritas don't you?" he asked as she poured my glass full.

"Love 'em." I replied.

"I knew you would. I could tell by looking," he said. He took a sip from the salt rimmed glass. "Heaven." He pronounced and seemed to relax more than he had since I met him.

"You know really, my son's not so bad. I love him. I don't always understand him, but I love him. He has no passion. About the only thing I can tell he cares about is the green folding stuff, but I guess lots of folks are that way." He took another sip. "His mom, now there's another story for another day, she had passion, let's get back to where I was."

"After his mother died and I gave up on him, I didn't know who I could tell the story to. I thought and thought, but I couldn't come up with anyone. I thought about writing it all down, but hell, I don't know how to write a story. Besides that, my damn arm and hand are worthless. Trying to sign a check looks like a two year old did it."

"So I decided I would tell myself the story. I did this over and over to be sure that when someone did come along, I would be ready. I wanted to be sure I remembered everything since I didn't have a copy."

"Copy?" I asked.

"Oh shit! I told you just be patient, I'll get there." About that time Sonya appeared with our food. It was different than the Tex-Mex I was used to, but good never the less. I could tell Babe loved it.

"This is Heaven for me," he said again. "I can't remember the last time I had such a meal. Fill my glass again will you? I have a little trouble with that pitcher."

I did as he requested. "We'll head back as soon as I finish this and tell lovely Sonya bye." I sat back to enjoy the spectacle.

Once we were safely back in the parking lot of the home, Babe turned to me and said, "Thanks for that. It was wonderful and the most fun I've had since I don't know when. Is it all right if we sit out here and talk? I get so tired of that room. Even as nice as everyone is, it's still like a prison at times."

"Sure, we can sit out here. Would you rather go somewhere else?"

"No, that would be too much trouble, here's alright."

"Babe look, it's no trouble. We can go anyplace you want. The beach?"

"Oh no. It's too crowded. We'd just get sand all over everything anyway."

"Point Loma?" I asked and I could tell immediately I had hit pay dirt. Even though he continued to say the parking lot was fine, it was obvious Point Loma was a place he would like to go. Without another word, I got out and unhitched the trailer. I put the tongue lock on it and away we went.

I parked in the lot immediately below the visitor center. It had a wonderful view of the bay and San Diego. As we sat there, we were treated as a carrier battle group deployed to sea passing through the channel immediately below us. It was quite a sight. In the distance we could see Coronado and the bay bridge connecting it to the mainland.

"This is where we came the first day Sally visited us with Billy here. I remember that cloth pilot hat he bought me at the surplus store. I was wearing that and playing like I was an airplane. I ran all over that hillside below us here. Hard to believe I was that young now." His eyes got a little misty as he remembered those days. I wondered if it was from missing the people or missing his youth. I didn't have long to wonder.

"I really miss those folks. They were my family. Billy included, he was as much family as my Dad and Sally were."

My ears perked up at the Sally part. Was Sally family? I started to ask and thought better of it. I decided to just be patient and let him tell me in his own way.

"Like I was telling you, I told myself the story. I worked on it just the way you would work on a speech or presentation you had to deliver before a big crowd. I have worked on this for years getting ready to tell someone the story. You're that someone. I had faith someone that was interested would come along, I had to have faith, what else could I do? So you're the person. You think I'm being nice telling you this story, but I'm not. I'm taking that obligation off my back and putting it on yours."

I laughed. "I wouldn't laugh if I were you," he said. There was no smile on his face this time. "I'm not trying to be cute. Hell, I'm not even trying to be nice. I do like you, you seem like a nice enough guy and that only makes it harder. This is a burden I've been carrying for all these years. She comes to me in my dreams you know?"

"What are you talking about? Who comes to you in your dreams?" I asked. This was beginning to sound a little flaky to me. What the hell was Babe talking about? Was the whole thing a load of bullshit? Was it all the product of a senile mind? He didn't seem senile, but what was he talking about?

"Sally, of course. She comes to me. She just stands there and looks at me. Never says a word, but I know what she wants, she wants me to pass the story on. Pass it on to you."

"Pass on what?" I asked.

"Just shut up and listen," was the reply I got. "I told you, I've been practicing this for years, but she's been after me for a long time. I need to tell it the way I've rehearsed it. If I get off the script I might forget something, maybe something important." This last was almost pleading. That seemed decidedly out of character for the Babe. I had this much invested; I might as well see it through. I wondered if this whole thing about the visits from Sally and all was related to the pitcher of margaritas we had just consumed.

"Okay, go on." I said.

He rewarded me with what can only be described as a grateful smile. He seemed to gather himself up and as he talked we were once more on our way back to 1941.

"Like I was telling you, it was a pretty grim Christmas. We had just been forced into World War II. The Japanese were running wild in the Pacific. Places I had never heard of before were being overrun, Wake Island, the Philippines, Bataan, Corregidor. The news stories were filtering out of Pearl Harbor. Even though we weren't getting the kind of news coverage we have today, still it was easy to tell the Japs had kicked our ass big time. We were down for the count. None of the news was good. Already we were hearing rumors about friends of friends being killed or missing. It was terrible. It was such a shock, a blow to our pride. Most Americans were used to thinking how powerful a country we were, and along comes little Japan and they just mopped the floor with us. People didn't like that. Already there were lines at the recruitment offices, guys enlisting left and right. There were a few folks that had already taped the windows in their houses and started stacking sandbags around the walls. They looked like fortresses right there in the neighborhood. There were rifle carrying guards and barbed wire on the beaches. It was all so crazy. So there wasn't much Christmas cheer to be had."

They were all sitting around the Christmas tree in the living room. In the center of the floor in front of the tree was a small mountain of ripped up wrapping paper, bows, ribbon, and cardboard boxes.

"So son, did you get everything you wanted? Was Santa good to you?" Carl asked.

There was a mound of baseball equipment on the floor in front of Babe, a new glove, a bat and several balls. He had a new wool Yankees cap perched on his head.

"Not really." was his reply.

All of them were a little surprised, Carl especially. Babe never had been one to ask for a lot, but Carl did his best to get all the things he did ask for.

"What did he miss?" Carl asked meaning what did Santa leave out.

"I want this war to be over!" Babe said.

"I know son, we all do." Carl replied.

Sally squeezed Billy's hand. She was sitting beside him appropriately enough on the love seat. Even though she tried hard to hide it, Billy could tell she tensed at any mention of the war.

"And how about you ma'am? Did you get everything you wanted?" Billy asked.

"I did indeed," she replied, a large grin appearing quickly to cover the anxiety. "I love my bracelet, it's beautiful. I'll never take it off." She said proudly showing it off.

Billy had gotten her a simple gold bracelet with very small diamonds and sapphires mounted around it. He worked with a downtown jeweler to be sure the sapphires were of a shade called Boston Blue that came close to matching her eyes. Even though he knew it was cheap compared to what she was used to, it was a major purchase for him and had been on lay away for several months as he paid it out. It was the best he could do and that thought made him proud. Sally understood that too, and that fact made the bracelet all the more dear to her. Even as she looked at him, her fingers were tracing its outline.

"And you sir, how do you like yours?" she asked.

Sally bought Billy a beautiful gold Bulova watch. It was a long rectangular shape and the case and crystal curved to match the curve of his wrist. The strap was dark brown alligator. On the back of the case was engraved, "Yours forever, Sally, 12-25-41." Billy had never seen a finer watch. "It's beautiful. It's the prettiest watch I've ever seen. I especially like the inscription." Billy said proudly.

"What inscription? Let me see. What does it say?" came from Babe instantly.

"Now son, that's private. If they want you to see it, they'll show it to you." Carl cautioned.

"But Dad!" Babe started to protest, but was cut short by a rather stern look from Carl.

"Let's get this mess cleaned up." Carl said, putting an end to that entire discussion. "We've still got Christmas dinner to fix and eat. Hop to."

"Aw Dad!"

"Don't aw Dad me, get busy."

And as sons do everywhere, Babe started picking up. He wasn't happy about it, but he had a very healthy respect for his father's direct orders.

As they picked up all the debris from the morning, Carl paused to admire his gifts from Sally and Billy. Billy had given him a pair of Ray-Ban sunglasses, the kind with the large dark lenses and thin gold wire frames. The kind pilots wear. Carl always admired them, but would never splurge on himself enough to buy any. And then there was Sally's gift. A truly magnificent fountain pen and matching mechanical pencil in deep black enamel with gold trim, his initials engraved on the solid gold clasps.

"You kids went way overboard on my presents," he said. He cut their protests short by saying, "you shouldn't be spending your money on an old man like me." But they could both tell by the way he admired his gifts that they had fulfilled secret desires he never would have addressed himself.

"Let's go cook!" Sally said in an especially cheery voice as she led the way to the kitchen. All the men followed, their arms full of boxes and crumpled wrapping paper.

The three adults cooked Christmas dinner together. Babe was off comparing gifts with his buddies. He had strict orders to be home in time to eat with the family.

After dinner, they sat on the front porch as the day faded. One of the great things about living in San Diego was it was nice and warm even on Christmas Day.

"How's the family?" Carl asked. Billy had received a large package wrapped in brown paper and tied with twine yesterday. Carl noticed the return address was Fort Worth, Texas.

Sally looked closely at Billy, but didn't say anything.

"They're doing well. They sent me a sweater for Christmas. My little brother, Jimmie, sent a letter telling me he was dropping

187

out of school to join the Marines." Sally never took her eyes off Billy's face.

"How old is Jimmie?" Carl asked.

"Seventeen." was the one word reply.

Carl didn't say anything in response; instead he just stared out toward the street as did Billy. Sally continued to watch Billy's face. She shot an occasional glance at Carl, but most of her effort was trying to read what was going on in Billy's brain.

Everyone sat in silence for several minutes. "None of the war news has been good has it?" Carl asked.

"No it hasn't. It sounds like we've lost most of the Pacific already. I wonder if Hawaii is next?" Billy said.

"If Hawaii goes, we're next." Carl said.

No one said anything for several minutes. It was already dark.

"Well, I think I'll shower and turn in early." Sally said with just the hint of Christmas cheer in her voice. She got up and hugged Carl's neck. "Thanks for the perfume Uncle Carl." she said and kissed his cheek.

"You're welcome hon, good night," he replied.

Then it was Billy's turn. He got a kiss on the lips and a whispered 'drop by later' in his ear and then she was gone.

After the screen door closed and the sound of her footsteps faded away, Carl said, "What do you intend to do about her?"

"I'd marry her today and settle down to raise a family if it weren't for this war," Billy replied.

"Why don't you do it anyway? Your job at Consolidated exempts you from the draft doesn't it?"

"For now it does, but we're being told that will probably change soon. They're already hiring women to take our place. They're learning quickly too, they won't need me much longer." Billy warned.

Nothing more was said for several minutes.

"Carl, the other thing is how can I sit here and do nothing while the rest of the country marches off to war. My little brother is leaving for God's sake. I have to do my part don't I?"

"That's a question only you can answer, son. It seems to me that you are already contributing to the war effort at Consolidated. But, I can understand your doubt. Are you planning to enlist right away?" Carl asked with concern, fully understanding what that meant for him, for Babe, and most of all for Sally.

There were a few minutes of silence and then, "No, not for a while. I need to give Sally some time. Also, I think I need to stay on at Consolidated until the new people get fully trained. Lots of guys are thinking about enlisting and if we all did it at the same time, production would stop right when they're trying to increase it."

"What do you want to do about the Special?" Carl asked.

"I want to finish it, or at least get it running so we can race it once! Do you think there'll be any more meets?" Billy wondered out loud.

"I'm sure there will be some. At least as long as there are guys around to race and gas for the cars." Carl said reassuringly.

"I hadn't thought about gasoline. You think it'll be in short supply?"

"I wouldn't be surprised. The U-boat attacks are terrible already and bound to get worse now that Germany entered the war too."

"Yeah, I guess so. Kind of bleak for Christmas isn't it?" Billy said solemnly.

"Yes, son, it is."

"I think I'll go get cheered up." Billy stood up to go inside.

"I need to turn in too. I think you've got a good idea. We've got to get busy on the Special. I'll ask around about any meets that are planned, out at the Mesa or on one of the lakes."

"See you in the morning." Billy went inside and went straight to his room. Only seconds later he heard the front door close, then Carl's footsteps climbing the stairs to his bedroom.

A few minutes later Billy opened his door. The house was dark and quiet. He walked down the hall to Sally's room and knocked quietly on her door. After a moment's hesitation, the door opened a crack, a slice of Sally's face peered out the opening. As soon as she was sure it was Billy the door opened.

Billy stepped inside. The room was lit only by a candle, its flame glittering on the night stand. As soon as he was inside and the door shut, he turned and saw Sally. The sight caused his heart to skip a beat. She had a huge grin on her face, her eyes sparkled in the candle light. Besides the grin, all she wore was a large white ribbon around her waist and an enormous white bow over one hip. In one hand she had two long stemmed glasses crossed at the stem and in the other an open bottle of wine. Her arms were spread wide as she embraced him. "Merry Christmas," she said just before their lips met.

"You must be my final present?" Billy asked.

"I am indeed," she said.

Billy was certain it was his best present ever.

Chapter 18

The view was extraordinary. The deep blue of the sea merged with the bright blue of the sky. Sunlight reflected off the wave tops and flew under him in a blur. It was like riding on Aladdin's own flying carpet he thought. It was just like a flying carpet except for a few glaring differences. The first difference was that everything in this blue world vibrated and shook to the overpowering din that would have deafened him had it not been for the helmet he wore with its tight fitting earphones. The other difference was the twin handles of the .50 caliber machine gun he grasped.

Billy was in the nose of a Navy B-24 bomber as it skimmed just over the wave tops at almost 200 knots, its four huge Pratt & Whitney R-1830 engines straining to get the last possible ounce of speed over the sea. They were so low that Billy felt like he could reach out and touch the water. He mentally jerked his concentration back to the task at hand. This was no time to get mesmerized by the spectacle going on around him, this was deadly business and he guessed that was the final difference between being in the nose of a Liberator at war and taking a ride on Aladdin's carpet. There was no magic at work here, only the cold hard laws of physics. Seventy two enormous pistons slammed up and down in their bores of hell as they drove the four huge props clawing through the air like massive windmills. Every piece of the enormous airplane vibrated and resonated to the collective beat of the massive engines and props. Billy could even feel his internal organs vibrating in harmony.

Billy's earphones hissed and crackled. "Target in sight. Beginning bombing run. Nose and top gunners engage when in range. Waist and tail engage on egress."

"Nose, aye aye, sir," was Billy's reply followed by the same from the top turret gunner.

Billy thought he could see a smudge of dark gray on the horizon. He lined it up in his sight ring. With each second the smudge took on detail until he could see that it was a submarine on the surface. White foam boiled around its bow and along its sides.

He aligned his sight ring on the conning tower and pressed the firing lever with his thumbs. His gun began to buck and jerk and added its own staccato to the din around him to the point that it drowned out all other sounds. A ball of fire blossomed at the gun's muzzle and hot smoking brass flew out the gun's breach to ricochet off the Plexiglas of the nose and bounce onto the floor under his feet. The air around him was filled with the stench of burned cordite. He saw the orange of his tracers reach out for the submarine and the sea around it erupted in geysers of spray kicked up by the heavy armor-piercing slugs of the '50'.

Billy strained to keep his sight ring centered on the sub as it got closer and closer depressing his gun to stay on target until finally it flashed below his feet and he released the firing lever.

Only then did he become aware of the noise coming through his headphones. As the Liberator flashed over the sub, the waist and tail gunners had taken up the fight. "Tail engaged," followed by "left waist engaged," as the big bomber banked away to the left and the sound of multiple 50's resounded through the airframe and over the intercom.

Billy braced against the wrenching turn and checked his gun to be sure it was feeding properly and prepared to re-engage. The bank increased as the pilot tightened his turn to line up on the stern of the fleeing sub and make another pass. If they could get around quick enough to make a stern pass before the sub completely submerged this would be the coup de gras. The stern pass provided the best target to the bomber. The bombing run would be parallel with the long axis of the target greatly increasing the chance of a hit.

Billy was already lining up his sight ring when his earphones crackled once more, "Gunners do not, repeat DO NOT engage. This pass will be bombs only." The disappointment was immense. Billy's 'blood had been up' and he was looking to make the kill. "Aye sir," was his reply, the disappointment plain even over the intercom.

His earphones rattled again, "Take it easy nose. It's just too dangerous from this angle. You'll have to wait for the real thing."

The sub drew closer and closer. The view from the stern was much better and this time there were no screening geysers from the heavy machine guns slugs to obscure the view. Billy felt the jolt as the bombs released. "Bombs away," crackled in his ears as the big plane began to bank away and climb.

As the target flashed underneath, Billy could see that it wasn't a sub at all, simply a collection of telephone poles all bundled together with a wooden structure on top to resemble a conning tower. The whole thing was being towed through the water by a long cable attached to a Navy tugboat. As they flashed over the tug, a pair of sailors in blue dungarees and white caps waved. Billy waved back.

The roar of the big four-engined bomber was deafening as it passed over the tug, scarcely a hundred feet above the water. It passed so close overhead Mike was certain he could see the color of the nose gunner's eyes as the crewman waved at him. Just as he thought after every strafing run by one of the big Liberators, he was very glad they were shooting at the target he towed 500 yards behind instead of at his tug. The firepower of the bomber was devastating. Mike was certain that the ten heavy machine guns could easily sink any submarine by themselves even without the bomb bay full of depth charges they all carried.

Mike Arredondo was 'captain' of the U.S. Navy tug Half Moon Bay even though his rank was only Petty Officer 2nd class. The 'Hambone', as everyone had taken to calling it, was a snub-nosed 42 foot wooden hulled tug. Until six months ago, it had been an aging privately owned boat that barely scratched out a living for her owner/captain working odd jobs that came her way in and around San Diego harbor. The Navy took possession of her in return for a fair cash payment to her owner. He was only too happy to sell the rundown tug. After all, he was over sixty years old and his tug was too small and under-powered to get the really good paying jobs. The war and the Navy's interest in his boat had been a windfall for him. He took the money and bought a small frame house in the hills and a nearly new '40 Ford Fordor. Despite the war, life was good for the ex-owner.

In return for their generous payment, the Navy got a 30-year-old leaky tug built of western oak and cedar planking. She mounted a 300 horsepower diesel engine that kept her bilges well lubricated with a mixture of cheap lube oil and diesel fuel. As desperate as the Navy was for tug boats, they still took the time to make her ship shape before pressing her into service towing targets to train Naval aviators in the art of gunnery and bombing.

Mike saw her for the first time five months ago. He was a Florida boy from Fort Walton Beach, a sleepy coastal town in the panhandle. He grew up hanging around the docks and fishing boats of his hometown. For as long as he could remember, all he wanted in life was to stand in the wheelhouse of his own boat. One of the boat captains had taken Mike under his wing and taught him the finer points of seamanship as it applied to fishing boats. He learned how to maneuver in tight spaces and how to read the water and sky. While he loved everything to do with piloting the boat and the sea, he never cared for the fishing that paid the bills. As soon as he was of age, he joined the Navy. That was seven years ago, and finally five months ago, his dream was realized.

The Navy was quick to realize his skills in small boat handling, first in whaleboats and then progressing through the inventory to tugs. There he found his true love, but until the war and the Hambone came along, he never had his own 'command'.

That changed when orders were cut giving him USN Half Moon Bay. The name had been abbreviated to HMB which naturally led everyone to call the boat 'Hambone'. The name seemed to fit.

The first time he saw her, it was love at first sight. It was good that Mike was chosen as her skipper because everyone else that had seen her referred to her as a derelict scow or worse, and most thought she should be scrapped immediately. Mike had only seen the beauty underneath, not the peeling paint and rust.

When he first saw her, she wore the original paint applied by her builders. Her hull was mostly black with a white wheelhouse and a red ring around her stack. The large winch gear on her after deck was a solid mass of rust. Rust stains streaked the paint under every metal fitting. Her deck planking was a filthy grey, spotted with a mass of stains.

Mike was given two months to whip her into shape. Unfortunately, the only resources he had were his crew of two able bodied seamen, both of whom only shaved once a week and neither could legally buy a beer north of the border. Nevertheless, they eagerly attacked the job of refurbishing what they already considered 'their boat'. After all, there was a war on and they both had visions of the USN Half Moon Bay steaming into harm's way and saving San Diego from the treacherous Japanese.

Hambone now wore a fresh coat of Navy gray with a glossy black stripe around her hull and funnel. The wheelhouse was the same shade of gray with her windows neatly trimmed in the same glossy black. Her name was stenciled in white block letters on the black boards on either side of the wheelhouse.

Mike was even able to use his contacts to get the engine replaced with a brand new Gray Marine diesel. He proudly thought the Hambone was the equal of any tug in the Navy and he was secretly sure she was better than the rest. He still reveled in her freshly stained and oiled deck planks, neat caulking filling all the seams. He could feel the power of her new engine through his feet and legs as he swung the wheel over and headed back to port. He was confident that the Hambone had been chosen to tow targets for the advanced training of Liberator crews because she was the fastest tug on the West Coast.

One thing was for sure, the Navy trained their aircrews well. This afternoon certainly underscored that thought. The gunners on the big Liberator had demolished the conning tower on the target he towed. Called the 'Admiral Donitz' by the crew and named for the admiral commanding the Nazi submarine service, the target had been hastily constructed out of wood to resemble a German U-boat. It was a good thing that the depth bombs they dropped had only been concrete filled casings because as closely as they had bracketed the Donitz, they surely would have blown her into toothpicks. As it was, he was going to have to get the carpenters to work half the night building a new 'conning tower'.

Mike's reverie was suddenly broken by the thunder of radial engines as the Liberator roared overhead once more, this time even closer than before. Mike reflexively ducked his head even though he was inside the wheelhouse. The plane passed close to port and as it started to climb away, the pilot rocked his wings back and forth in salute. Mike almost felt sorry for any enemy sub unlucky enough to find itself caught on the surface by that crew. Almost.

Billy's earphones crackled once more. "Excellent surface attack all." Billy's crew was training as a unit and they had two instructors on board to evaluate their performance on what amounted to their graduation day. They had been together for two months now, flying almost every day since picking up their new Liberator, designated PB4Y-1 by the Navy, at the San Diego factory. That was a fun day for Billy getting to see a few of the guys he worked with at Consolidated. They all assured him that they had triple checked his aircraft and that it was a good one. Their assurances were confirmed over the past two months.

Billy was looking forward to the next month. Ever since enlisting back in August his training had been non-stop, first at

Navy Pier in Chicago, then Florida and for the past two months back here in San Diego. That had been a stroke of luck really. The Navy was looking for crews to man their newly acquired Liberator bombers. There was an urgent need to combat the German U-boats that roamed across the Atlantic seemingly at will, sinking Allied ships in droves.

All manner of tactics were being tried to reduce the U-boat threat and protect the all important convoys. The Liberator had been chosen for this duty because it had the longest range, highest top speed, and carried the largest payload of all the aircraft in the inventory. It was also heavily armed and was a formidable opponent. It was easily more than a match for any U-boat. Unknown to Billy and his crew, plans were already being made to base them out of southern England where they could interdict real U-boats as they traversed the Bay of Biscay from their sub pens on the French coast.

The crew's training was all but over at this point. They were given a month's leave prior to their deployment overseas. All but Billy had already made travel plans to their homes, leaving as soon as tomorrow. Billy was looking forward to spending time with Sally. Also this coming week he was finally going to get to run the Special! He could hardly wait, first to spend every minute possible with Sally and then for them both to see how the Special would perform.

He was thankful once again for how Sally had handled his enlistment. As things turned out, eventually he would have been drafted anyway. Before he left Consolidated many jobs were already being filled by women who seemed to do the job every bit as well and in some cases better than the men they replaced. By enlisting he was able to choose his service. Once the Navy recruiter found out about his experience at Consolidated it was a pretty simple matter to get him assigned to Liberators as a machinist mate. Since then it had all been a blur shuttling from place to place to complete his training. Now here he was in the nose of a Liberator, a still warm Browning machine gun in front of him.

Several hours later, Billy was on board the base bus headed toward the main gate. His plan was to ride it downtown and transfer to a civilian bus to get home to Carl's. As they approached the front gate, he was surprised and happy to see Sally's Packard convertible sitting just outside the main gate. He asked the driver to stop the bus.

Before the bus was even stopped Sally was out of the car and waving, a huge grin on her face. As Billy grabbed his sea bag and worked his way off the bus, the cat calls and wolf whistles had already started, accompanied with, "Way to go sailor!", "Get a load of that dish!", and similar remarks.

Sally rushed into his arms as the bus pulled away with twenty pairs of envious eyes staring at them. Even the shore patrol guarding the gates was all grins. All the gawkers wondered how this sailor had gotten so lucky, as did Billy.

Sally smothered him in kisses and her body seemed to melt and form itself to his. "I missed you," was all she said between kisses.

"I missed you too," he managed to get in. Having Sally against him was the most wonderful sensation he had ever experienced. After another long wet kiss, he said, "Let's get out of here." Another car passed honking with laughing sailors yelling out the window, "Kiss her once for me!" Billy felt obliged to do so before throwing his sea bag in the trunk of the Packard.

Sally was nestled against his side as they drove away. It had been two weeks since they had seen each other. Billy was dressed in his blues. Sally loved the way he looked in the dark blue wool. She thought it made him look even taller. The other thing she liked was the way the pants buttoned up each side instead of the middle. She found that very convenient, especially while he was driving. Her fingers started working the buttons closest to her. "I missed you," she hissed in his ear.

"I can tell," he chuckled.

"Is everything still on for this weekend?" he asked several minutes later.

"Carl already has the Special hooked up to the LaSalle. I've got all our things packed. All we have to do is load it in the car. I think Babe is already sitting in the car waiting on us. They're both almost as excited as I am to see you. You need to change clothes anyway, how about if I help you out of your uniform on the way home to save time?"

Billy laughed, "I think we might both be embarrassed if I got out of the car nude."

"Speak for yourself big boy," she said.

"Are we taking one car or two?" he asked.

"I thought we would take two. That gives me more time alone with you!"

"Sounds good to me," he chuckled as she made him squirm again.

When they turned the corner onto Carl's street, sure enough, he could see the front of the LaSalle parked nose out in the drive. When he turned into the drive, he was greeted with a yelp as Babe came running out the front door and down the steps, the screen door banging shut behind him. "Billyeeeeeeeeeeee!" he screamed at the top of his lungs. Babe stood in the yard and jumped up and down until Billy could get out of the car before leaping into his arms almost knocking Billy down. Carl followed out the front door taking time to shut the screen and chuckling at the scene before him.

"Welcome home, son," Carl said as Billy finally let Babe back down to the ground.

"I'm glad to be home Carl. It looks like you've got the Special all ready to go." Billy noted.

"I tried. I hope it's up to your standards," Carl said.

195

"I'm sure it is." Billy said with Babe's arms still wrapped around his waist on one side and Sally draped on the other. They all moved slowly around the LaSalle to see the Special.

The grin on Billy's face just got wider. The Special had turned out to be all he had envisioned and so much more. It was a large car, but still slim and muscular at the same time. The tall thin LaSalle grille dominated the front view, a mirror image of the tow car's but much more streamlined. The hand crafted grille shell only 18 inches wide in contrast to the broad front of the coupe. The chrome header protruded through the left hood side and ran down the side of the car to the graceful boat tail. They decided to forego the wheel pants because of time constraints and scarcity of materials. When they did so, they decided to shorten the boat tail to keep everything in proportion.

"You got the blisters finished!" Billy said, looking at the streamlined bulges that covered where the radius rods entered the sides of the belly pan and where the end of the steering gear protruded from the right side of the cowl. Each blister was attached with a neat row of evenly spaced screws.

"It looks even better than my dreams." Billy said trying hard to take it all in.

"He's worked on it every spare minute, Sally too!" Babe explained.

"I can tell." Billy said.

"You got the shocks finished too," Billy said, squatting down by the front wheel to examine them.

"Actually you had already done most of the work," Carl said. They were multi-arm friction shocks that Billy designed and built before leaving for the Navy. Their polished finish gleamed at each corner of the slim racer.

"And look at that paint and the interior!" Billy ran his hand along the top of the hood and felt the soft leather lining the cockpit rim. The car was a gleaming gloss black contrasting with the natural finish leather on the seat and on the cockpit rim. "How did you do all this?" Billy could hardly believe his eyes.

"I called in a few favors," Carl said, a satisfied smile on his face.

"More than a few I bet! This thing looks like a professional racecar! I bet we could enter it in the 500 mile race!" Billy exclaimed.

Carl chuckled. "Oh, we could enter it all right, but I don't think we have enough motor to be competitive, but I think Frank would be proud," meaning Frank Lockhart his childhood friend.

"It's beautiful," Billy said again.

Sally was still hugging one arm and Babe was hugging his waist, big grins on their faces. "I helped too!" Babe said proudly, "and Sally worked on it every day!"

Billy hugged them both. He kissed Sally on the lips and Babe on the head. He wanted to say something to let them know how he felt, but he couldn't find the words. Instead he just hugged them more tightly and kissed them again.

"Okay, everyone, let's get in gear and get everything loaded up. We've got a long drive ahead of us and it's almost dark already" Carl told them.

"I don't even know where we're going," Billy said.

"We're going to race the Special!" Babe blurted.

"I know Babe, but I don't know where," Billy replied.

"We're going to El Mirage dry lake. The last official meet was in July. The SCTA has shut down operations for the duration, but Tommy is taking his own timing equipment. Some of the LA guys will be there and Tommy is taking several of his cars," Carl said.

"What's SCTA and what does duration mean?" Babe asked, a puzzled look on his face.

"SCTA stands for Southern California Timing Association. That's a group of car clubs that sponsors the races on the dry lakes. They have the timing equipment to measure how fast the cars are and they organize the races. Duration means until the end of the war. So many members of the SCTA are now in the military that they have to shut down their events until after the war is over." Carl told him.

Billy and Sally headed in the house to get their things. A few minutes later, they came back out, Billy now wearing a pair of khaki pants and a plaid shirt instead of his uniform. As Billy carried their bags to the Packard, Sally called, "Is everyone finished in the house?"

Carl and Babe were checking the lights on the Special. They looked up and told Sally they were finished in the house. Sally locked the door and then went down the steps to the Packard.

"We'll follow you," Billy called as he started the convertible and backed out of the drive.

Carl started the LaSalle coupe and slowly pulled out of the drive, the Special towed behind it by a tow bar made from an old Ford wishbone.

"How long till we get there?" Babe asked before they were even in the street.

"It'll take us most of the night, son." Carl told him.

"Aw, Dad, that's too long!"

Babe was asleep before they left the San Diego city limits.

Chapter 19

Babe awoke to the roar of an unmuffled exhaust just outside his window. He was wrapped in a thick wool blanket and had been asleep in the front seat of the LaSalle.

The view that greeted him was eerie. The flat gray expanse of the lakebed stretched away for miles. Dawn was breaking over jagged mountains in the distance. While the sun had not made its appearance over the rim yet, it was still light enough to see short distances. In his field of view, a number of cars were parked haphazardly pointing in all directions. Some were obviously race cars as they were stripped of fenders, windshields, lights and everything else that added weight or wind resistance. Several young men in jackets, their collars pulled up against the morning chill, milled about the cars. Some had their heads under hoods or were attending to other mechanical issues while others just stood around and watched with their hands in their pockets or wrapped around steaming cups of coffee. Several camp fires glowed dull red, their night time flames now reduced to coals. Trash, blankets, tools, and car parts littered the ground in jumbled confusion. Everything was already covered in a blanket of fine gray dust.

The dry lakes of the high desert made nearly ideal places to test the top speed of their modified cars. The lakebeds provided long flat surfaces free of obstructions and traffic. They were formed by winter rains having nowhere to drain except the low spot which became the lake. Actually during the rainy season it was simply a very large puddle sometimes miles across and only inches deep. The desert winds worked the water back and forth depositing the silt it carried into a flat smooth surface. After the rainy season, the desert sun dried the water and baked the silt into a firm hardpan of dried mud. It was very flat and until disturbed, free of holes or ruts. The cars used the wide-open expanse to accelerate for a mile or more before being timed for top speed. The only problem with the lake bed was that after a few runs the tires of the accelerating racers threw up the top layer of silt into enormous rooster tails of dust that coated every person and thing for miles. They also broke through the relatively hard top surface churning it up into ruts and washboard. When the surface became too rough, they simply moved the racecourse over a few yards to an undisturbed area.

As Babe sat up in the seat and his field of view increased, he could see there were still bodies wrapped in blankets and quilts lying on the ground around the nearly spent campfires. Even as he watched, several of the bodies began to stir and people started to sit up.

Babe was in the coupe alone. He opened the door and stepped out. It was colder than he expected. He could see his breath and he kept the blanket wrapped around him and even with his jacket on under it, he was still cold.

The trunk of the LaSalle was open with his dad's toolbox open on the trunk floor. The Special was parked directly behind the LaSalle and the tow bar had already been removed. His dad and Billy were attending to last minute mechanical checks in preparation for starting the engine.

Billy looked up. "You look cold, Babe."

Babe just nodded.

"Sally has some donuts and milk in the car," Billy said.

Babe was already headed toward the Packard before the words were out of Billy's mouth. Carl just shook his head and turned back to the engine.

As Babe opened the driver's door of the Packard, the smell of fresh donuts and coffee flooded over him. He wasn't sure anything had ever smelled as good.

"Good morning, baby," Sally said. Had it been later in the day and had he been warm and more awake, he would have been offended at anyone, even Sally, calling him 'baby', but as it was he just scooted over next to her and snuggled against her side. Sally too was wrapped in a blanket and her warmth and the aromas were very pleasant.

"How about a donut?" Sally asked as she reached for a white box setting on the open glove box door. A thermos cup of coffee also sat on the door.

Babe munched on a donut and drank the bottle of milk Sally handed him. "Where did the donuts come from?" he asked.

"We got them the last time we stopped for gas, don't you remember?"

Babe just shook his head. "I don't remember anything," he said. Sally laughed.

Just then the Special started with a roar. It's six-cylinder engine having a unique sound compared to the rest of the car's fours and eights. Sally got out to watch, while Babe decided to stay in the car and have another donut.

It was the first time Billy heard the engine run. Although the engine had been in the car for some time, Carl had finished the wiring and plumbing necessary to make it run after Billy left for the Navy. Even after he reported to San Diego, the training regimen was so intense that he had very little time to work on the car.

The engine sounded very healthy, much different than the other cars. Its distinctive exhaust note echoed across the flat of the lakebed. Heads turned in their direction, everyone looking for the source of the new sound. Next to Tommy Lee's Offenhauser powered special and his fleet of European racecars, nothing else on the lakes had such an exotic sound.

As if on cue, Sally saw Tommy walk around the front of the LaSalle, several members of his normal entourage in his wake. "I see they finally got it finished," he said, "And good morning to you Miss Anthony, or is it Mrs. Pendleton?" he asked.

Sally felt herself flush and as she opened her mouth to rip into Tommy, he realized that he had hit a nerve and cut her off. "I'm sorry, I'm sorry! It was a joke, and I apologize, it was a very bad one. Will you forgive me? I really didn't mean for it to come out that way." He said contritely.

Somewhat mollified, Sally relaxed a little. "Okay Tommy Lee, I'll give you that one, but let's not get off on the wrong foot. I want to have a pleasant weekend." She warned.

"Me too, Sally. I promise and I really am sorry."

Billy and Carl heard none of this conversation, the noise of the Special's engine drowned out all other sounds and their attention was on adjusting carburetors and timing and checking for leaks. Billy gave the throttle one final blip and then cut the ignition. Silence suddenly returned to the lake bed.

"It sounds really good, maybe I should have kept that engine and put it in my special." Tommy said with a grin. The startled look on Billy's and especially Carl's face told him that once more he had overstepped his bounds. "I'm sorry, it must be my morning to put my foot in my mouth," and he glanced at Sally.

Billy saw this and looked askance at Sally. She silently mouthed "later", and added, "Yes, it does sound marvelous doesn't it?"

"Yes it does. I think that's the first time I've ever heard that engine run," Tommy added.

"We'll see how it stacks up against that Offenhauser of yours, then we'll know how good it sounds." Carl said.

"This car is gorgeous." Tommy said as he walked all the way around it. "The workmanship is as nice as any I've seen." He continued to walk around it, stopping several times to look at details.

"Thanks, but I think Carl and Sally deserve the credit," Billy said.

"Don't be ridiculous, you've always been the driving force behind this car." Carl insisted.

The sun had risen above the mountains and was burning off the chill. Everyone was up and milling about by now. Most were working on cars, but a few were still just watching.

"We'll have the clocks set up soon. When you're ready you can get in line at the timing stand. By the way, I brought steaks for tonight. We'll have a cookout this evening; I hope all of you will be my guests."

"Thanks, Tommy, we'd love to join you." Billy said quickly. He had some concern that Sally might say something to the contrary, so he hadn't given her the opportunity. He felt gratitude toward Tommy for all the help he had given them and even for the opportunity to run the car.

"Good luck, I'll see you in line." Tommy turned and walked back to his own cars.

After Tommy left, Billy walked over to Sally and put his arms around her. "Are you okay? Did he say something to you?" he asked.

"It was nothing, just a lame joke. I don't think he meant anything by it. I think Tommy was trying to be as good as Tommy can be." She replied.

Billy decided to let the issue drop. Carl was already engrossed in last minute checks again. This time using a lug wrench to be sure all the lugs were good and tight. He looked up to see Billy looking at him. "I've seen too many cars lose wheels because someone forgot to tighten the lug nuts."

"Good idea," Billy replied. Billy got the tire gauge and went around the car behind Carl checking tire pressures. He used the pump they had brought along to make adjustments.

They wiped their hands and went to the passenger side of the Packard to have another donut and refill their coffee cups. Babe was beginning to shake the sleep off and was more his normal self. It had warmed up some, but it would remain cool all day. Cool enough that they were all glad to have their jackets on.

Some of the racecars were starting up and then driving to get in line for their timed runs. There was a chaos of blipped throttles and spinning tires. Dust was thrown everywhere, men cursed and yelled. The noise made speech almost impossible.

"Let's go." Carl said tapping Billy on the arm. With that Billy opened the Packard's trunk to get his helmet, goggles and gloves. Sally stayed close by his side being sure he got everything okay. Carl and Babe went to get the Special started.

Sally watched Billy pull on the cloth helmet and goggles. She gave him a stern look, "Be careful okay?" she asked.

"I will be. The first couple of runs I just plan to take it easy and make sure everything works. I'm not going to take any chances." Billy replied.

"See that you don't, okay? Remember, I love you."

"I won't. I love you too." A kiss and they walked over to the car.

Billy climbed in. The cockpit fit like a glove. It should have, Billy designed it to fit. It made the car a bit longer, but a long wheelbase was good for a top speed racecar. The length served to make the car more stable. The shift lever in the center of the cockpit protruded between his legs and angled over his right thigh, it took a little getting used to, but he thought it would work just fine. The stick also made it a little difficult getting in and out, but that was just the way single seat cars were. He blipped the throttle a few times as Carl closed the hood, buckled the leather straps that kept it secure and stood away from the car. Billy slipped the Special in gear and eased out on the clutch. For the very first time, the Special moved under its own power.

Billy drove the short distance to the growing line of cars waiting to make their run through the timing traps. The car felt good, its exhaust note clean and crisp out the long side pipe and burbled over his left shoulder. Billy pulled to the end of the line and stopped. He blipped the throttle and killed the engine. Several cars ahead of him Tommy sat in his Frank Kurtis built special with the big Offenhauser engine. Its dark blue paint glistened and sparkled in the morning sun. Billy took pride that his car was every bit as graceful and easily the equal of Tommy's professionally built beauty.

Babe, Sally and Carl walked up on either side of the car to wait with Billy. Carl opened the left side hood and made one final check. Everyone looked up as Tommy fired up his booming engine and roared off down the course. The speedster threw up a huge rooster tail of fine gray dust as it accelerated down the course. The dust was the same consistency as talcum powder and soon coated every surface and found its way into everything. Babe had at least worn the cloth flying helmet and goggles that Billy bought him. Other than what he tasted, the dust didn't bother him too much with his goggles down and he wondered if anyone thought he was one of the race car drivers. He hoped so. The line moved and they all pitched in and pushed the car forward.

Soon there was only one car ahead of Billy. As soon as it was flagged away, Billy started the Special's engine. It took at least two to three minutes for a car to make its run and clear the course and Billy planned to run his engine that long to be sure it was warm before he made his run. Carl made yet another last minute check, finally closing the hood and securing it by buckling the twin leather straps. Billy found himself anxious to get away. Thankfully there was a light breeze that blew the worst of the dust away so that the course became visible shortly after the last car left.

Then it was his turn. He pulled up to the starter. His goggles were already down. The starter stood between the cars and the timing stand which was on the upwind side of the course. Three men sat at the old wooden table that was the nerve center for the meet. The timing equipment was designed and developed by Otto Crocker. He originally built the clocks to time boats, but found that the car racers were an even bigger market. Tommy had contracted with Otto to time all of his events. One of the men sitting at the table was Otto himself with his beat up felt hat pulled down tightly and his leather jacket on. He was the official timer. The equipment he designed electrically timed the cars through a precisely measured distance at the end of the course. The amount of time it took the car to pass between the two sensors called the timing 'traps' could be precisely measured and mathematically converted into miles per hour.

Two other men sat at the table. One was Otto's assistant timer, who checked every time. All steps to time a car were checked by both men then results compared. Times were not official until both men agreed. The third man was the telephone operator. A battery-powered telephone was set up to communicate with the far end of the course. The telephone operator also had a set of binoculars so that he could visually track the cars and see the far end of the course. The crew at the far end had a set of colored flags to signal with visually in addition to the telephone.

The starter made eye contact with Billy and indicated he should get ready. The starter then checked one last time with the telephone operator. The operator nodded that the course was clear. The starter turned back to Billy and made eye contact. Billy felt his pulse increase. His concentration on the starter was complete. The starter pointed at Billy. Billy nodded he was ready and the starter waved him off with a green flag.

Billy eased out the clutch. He wanted to be careful not to spin the tires, easy to do on the packed dirt of the lakebed. If he spun the tires it would cover the starting line personnel with even more dust, a sure way to alienate all the officials, not to mention Carl, Babe and Sally.

He was away! The car accelerated briskly even taking it easy. He shifted into second, this was a little awkward as he wasn't used to shifting with the lever between his knees yet. It was easy to follow the course just by staying in the ruts the previous cars had made. There were also wooden stakes driven in the ground every 50 yards or so on the upwind side with red cloth fluttering from them.

He revved to 5000 RPM and shifted into high gear. The car continued to accelerate briskly, and then he put his foot all the way to the floor. The exhaust had sounded very crisp, but suddenly changed to an angry shriek and the rear tires broke traction with the lake bed. The car started to fishtail although it was easily controllable because of the long wheelbase and the well thought out suspension. Billy was thankful they had devoted so much time to designing a strong solid car with good springs and heavy-duty friction shock absorbers copied from an Alfa Romeo Grand Prix car owned by Tommy. Billy let up slightly on the throttle and then got back into it, but more gradually this time. The engine note rose again but he was able to maintain traction this time. The car tracked like it was on rails. Billy crouched low in the cockpit just barely able to peer over its edge. The stakes were a blur.

He saw the timing trap approaching in a rush. This marked the end of the course. He flashed through them. He saw a man standing on the upwind side of the course waving a checkered flag. He was through the course. He lifted off the accelerator, careful to ease off slowly to maintain control. At high speed the worst thing you could do was make abrupt changes, even if it was lifting off the gas.

The car slowed. He couldn't believe it was all over so soon. He had completed his first run! But it was so quick! He could remember every instant of the run, his concentration was so complete, unlike anything else he had ever experienced. He would always remember that first run. How different the daylight inside the cockpit had been. The amazing clarity his vision acquired. He would never be able to explain it to anyone, but time seemed to slow to a stop, he had time to notice a scratch on the steering wheel and the tiny 'Made in USA' on the instruments. He turned off the course and felt himself relax a bit from the adrenaline rush he had been on during the run. As he headed back down the return road toward the gaggle of cars that was the pits, time returned to normal, and that special quality daylight he experienced during the run was gone.

Billy wound through the maze of parked cars and pulled up behind Carl's LaSalle coupe. While driving through the pits he couldn't help but notice the admiring looks and the thumbs up. As he parked he was almost swamped by Babe, Sally and Carl. They were all smiles and clapping him on the back sending up small clouds of dust, and congratulating him on a great run before he could even climb out of the cockpit.

They made him ask what he had turned. "127.57 miles per hour," Babe said, and then added "I got your time from Mr. Crocker myself." Babe beamed.

"That's a really great run, son," Carl said, obviously he was very pleased. A crowd was starting to form already. "That's the fastest time of the day so far. That's faster than most of these cars have ever gone." Before Billy could ask him any more questions, Carl was swamped with admirers asking question after question about the car. He already had the hood up and was explaining something to a group of several young men. Several more were examining virtually every part of the Special. Babe was jumping in pointing out details, obviously proud to be part of the team.

Sally grabbed Billy by the arm and dragged him away from the throng to the Packard. Billy noticed that Sally got as many admiring glances as the Special. He couldn't blame them. Had the roles been reversed, he was sure he would have looked too.

Sally opened the passenger door and pushed him inside, then got in beside him and slammed the door. It was amazing how much calmer it was inside the car. "I haven't had any time alone with you all day," she said as she smothered him in kisses.

"Did you know you beat Tommy's time by five miles per hour?" she asked. Billy shook his head. "Of course not, how could you have known? Were you really careful? How could you have gone so fast if you were being careful?"

"Honey, I was careful. I had to lift part way through the run because I lost traction."

"Oh Lord!" Sally interrupted.

"Really, it wasn't anything. I lifted and the car straightened right up. It's so stable Babe could drive it."

Sally relaxed a bit. "Still, you take it easy. I don't want you spending time in the hospital or worse."

He assured her that he would be very careful. "What do you have planned for the rest of your leave?"

"Well, I thought we could spend a few days with Carl and Babe. Then I was hoping we could spend some time at the beach house. Do you think we can get it?" Billy asked.

"I was hoping that's what you wanted! I've already made arrangements. It's ours for as long as we want it."

"It's okay with your brother?"

"He's out of town so much these days. Besides, he has several hideouts and the beach house isn't as much fun in the winter. He would much rather spend his time at San Simeon with the Chief or at one of his mountain hideaways."

Billy just shook his head. It was hard for him to comprehend a life style so lavish. In his experience a man was lucky to own one house for his family, let alone multiple clandestine hideaways to share with mistresses. Oh well, he knew how lucky he was to have access to the beach house and he planned to make the most of it.

"I better get back out there and see if Carl needs any help, sweetheart." Billy said.

Billy made four more runs that day. The last run was his fastest, 141.37 MPH. It stood as the fastest run of the day. Tommy's special couldn't hope to match this speed and was second fastest at 127.49 MPH. Billy found that the Special was more than he had ever dared to hope for. When he and Carl discussed the idea of building a car the first time, he hoped they could top 100 MPH with a Ford based car. The Special used a lot of Ford parts simply because they were easily available, cheap, adaptable and better suited to a racecar size vehicle than larger LaSalle/Cadillac components. But it was the specially constructed and modified parts that really set the Special apart from the other cars competing on the lakes. Carl's previous racing experience and his access to specialists had been crucial. Studying successful contemporary racecars had also shaped the car into what it was. Billy felt certain that they had only scratched the surface. Carl had already secured a Mercedes Benz supercharger that he was just itching to adapt to the Special's engine. He was certain with its addition they could add at least 15 MPH. Maybe after the war they could try that out Billy thought.

All the runs were over for the day. The pits were mostly quiet. Many of the racers were putting street equipment back on their cars or hooking up tow bars in preparation for the long trip home. A lucky few were spending the night on the lake and would get to make a few runs on Sunday. These were Tommy's closest friends and most of them were in his employ.

As darkness descended on the lakebed a large fire was built. Tommy had a huge iron grille that was placed over the coals. A sack full of potatoes was buried in the coals and beers were opened all around. Tommy himself started cooking steaks. Billy thought it showed the contradiction that was Tommy Lee.

Tommy was a child of privilege. Born with not silver, but a golden spoon in his mouth. He was the only child of the sole Cadillac distributor for the state of California. Every Cadillac or LaSalle sold in the state was sold through a Lee dealership. Also his father, Don, owned a radio network and even started the first regularly scheduled television broadcasts in the country. Tommy had grown up in a virtual paradise. The beautiful weather and scenery of California combined with all the money anyone could ever want. When his father passed away in 1934, the entire empire passed to Tommy. Oh, his stepmother fought for the fortune, but after all, Tommy was his father's only natural born child and he had control of the majority of the money. A further complication was that most of Tommy's friends were really employees or were dependent on him in some manner. Tommy wasn't stupid; this thought was always in the back of his mind. He was never certain if people were his friends because they really cared about him as a person or simply cared about what he could do for them. One of the few people that didn't fall in this category was Sally. Her father had been one of his father's best friends and biggest competitors as the California Packard distributor. Neither money, nor power could influence Sally. Tommy at heart wanted to be just one of the guys, but with his money and obligations there was no way this could ever be.

Tonight Tommy was in a good mood. It had been a good day racing cars. The only car faster than his had one of his motors in it after all. The other thing was, he had secretly smuggled the latest Mercedes Grand Prix car into the country. Virtually no one knew about this and he decided to keep it secret since the country was now at war with Germany. Still it made him feel good to know he owned the fastest racecar in the world. In a private celebration that only he knew about, he had thrown on the feed tonight. Tommy was personally cooking the steaks and handing out the beer. And even if he couldn't have Sally, he did have a stunning raven-haired beauty molded to his side that seemed completely incapable of keeping her tongue out of his ear. It was going to be an interesting night indeed.

The steak was delicious, one of the best Billy ever had. It was getting cool again and the group was huddling closer to the fire. The beer was flowing freely and everyone seemed to be having a very good time, especially Tommy. The conversations were getting louder and more boisterous. Billy and Sally took this opportunity to sneak away from the group. They found Carl back at his car, Babe was already asleep in the back seat wrapped in blankets.

"We're going to drive out on the lake. We'll see you in the morning." Billy said.

"Be sure you get off the lake bed itself," Carl said, "some of those fools get enough beer in them and they might make some high speed night runs across the lake. Okay?"

"We'll be sure. Thanks for all you've done."

"Get out of here. See you tomorrow."

Sally and Billy quietly left the clump of cars. Billy drove slowly and with the lights off. Once they were well away from the group, he used the windshield-mounted spotlight to find a protected parking spot off the lake. There were large brush covered mounds that hid them from view. As cold as the night was; neither seemed to notice.

Chapter 20

They didn't arrive back home in San Diego until the wee hours of Monday morning. They only took time to push the Special into the shop then they all headed to bed.

Billy and Sally were filthy. The fine dust from the lakes was in every pore. They decided they had to shower before they could possibly get in bed. To make it as quick as possible, they showered together. There was little chance anyone would notice. Babe had been a zombie coming into the house. Besides they both were certain Carl knew everything anyway. They left the bathroom wrapped in their fluffy white robes and collapsed into bed. The clean sheets and a real bed felt wonderful after two days spent in the car.

Sally awoke to a knock on her door. Bright sunlight was streaming in the windows. It took a minute for her to come fully awake and realize that the noise she was hearing was actually knocking on the door. She jumped out of bed and pulled on her robe. Billy was beginning to stir, but wasn't fully awake yet. He had done all the driving on the trip while she was able to nap.

Sally opened the door a crack. Carl stood in the hall. "I'm cooking breakfast. It'll be ready in five minutes. I brought coffee for you and Billy." He handed her two steaming white mugs of black coffee. "I thought you might need a wake up." He chuckled and headed back to the kitchen.

She shut the door with her foot and turned to set the mugs of coffee on the night stand. As she stooped to set the mugs down, Billy's arm reached out of the covers and his hand found its way inside her robe.

"Well, good morning lover," she said. "Nice of you to join me this morning."

She sat down on Billy's side of the bed, his hand still inside her robe. "We don't have time for this, babe. That was Carl at the door and breakfast is ready. Maybe after?"

"Oh if you insist!" he said and rolled out of bed as she stood. There was one longing kiss and then they dressed and headed to the kitchen. The aroma of bacon and coffee was almost overwhelming.

As they were cleaning up after breakfast, Carl asked, "So what are your plans?"

"I think we'll spend a couple of days here. I want to get the Special cleaned up, and spend a little time with you and Babe. Then I think we're going up to the beach house for a while" Billy replied.

"Great! I know Babe wants to spend some time with you. Let's go take a look at the Special."

They spent all day stripping parts off and washing the racer. A thin layer of gray dust covered every surface and had found its way into every opening. As they worked, Carl and Billy discussed future improvements for the car. Carl thought the supercharger would add at least 15 MPH. Billy wasn't so sure, at least not with the car remaining in its current configuration.

"I don't think more power is going to do us any good unless we change the gearing. It seemed to me that I had plenty of power for the gearing we have. I think the limiting factor wasn't power, but the fact that the engine was at maximum RPM already. In fact, I had to be easy on the throttle. It would easily spin the tires, even in high gear."

"I can find us some taller gearing. We've got a 4:11 in there now, and I'm sure I can find a 3:54. We can also add taller wheels," Carl added.

"Once we do that, I think the wheel pants would help too. What do you think?"

"That sounds good." Billy said.

"That's the way I'll go. I'll find a gear, but I want to do some work adapting that supercharger."

"How can we drive that thing?" Billy wondered.

"I was thinking about driving it with a belt of some type. Mercedes used a gear drive, but we don't have that provision on our engine. There just isn't any way to do that without a total redesign and spending a lot of money."

"I'm sure you'll come up with something. This thing is swell as it is. A blower on it would really be fun." Billy said. "Sorry I won't be around to help you work that out. It ought to be fun and I hate to leave all the work to you."

"I think you're going to have your hands full. Where do you go next?"

"I've got 30 days leave. I plan to spend most of it with Sally at the beach. I have orders to report to the East Coast. We'll pick up our new ship there. I'm going to stop in Fort Worth and spend a few days with my folks. I doubt that I'll get to see Jimmie. He's still somewhere in the States I think, but I'm sure they're going to ship out sometime soon."

"So you're pretty sure you'll be fighting Germany, not Japan?" Carl asked.

"Yeah, I think so. Since we're picking up our new ship on the east coast, I'm sure we'll be involved in the Battle of the Atlantic. Those German U-Boats have been raising hell with our convoys for months. We've got to stop that some way and the Liberator is well suited for the work."

"How can an airplane fight a submarine?"

"They can't stay underwater forever, they have to come up to charge their battery. If we catch them on the surface, they're dead meat."

"Can we change the subject, please?" Sally begged.

"Oh sure, sorry, hon," Billy said.

They soon finished attending to all the details on the car. They played with it a little driving it around the neighborhood, its open exhaust booming and bellowing. Carl and Sally both drove it around to experience the sensations of it. It was, by far, the most responsive, high performance car either of them had ever driven. Considering its performance compared to Tommy's thoroughbred stable of cars, it was one of the most high performance cars in the country. Sure it fell short in some areas because it was built out of mostly discarded passenger car parts and everything else was fabricated in a backyard workshop without benefit of a trained engineer. Still the sum of its parts was considerable. And it was fun.

Billy watched Sally come down the street. Her blonde hair was blowing in the wind and a bright colored scarf fluttered from her neck. Even a block away, he could see the grin on her face. The exhaust was a snarl as she at first accelerated, then let off to slow and turn into the drive. She was gone for nearly half an hour. She slowed almost to a stop to make the turn in, the Special sat very low and she didn't want to scrape the bodywork on the gutter. Once in the drive, she stopped and blipped the throttle once to clear the plugs before switching off the ignition. She did so while looking at Billy with an enormous grin.

"This thing is fun! Let's build me one!" she said.

"Okay, we'll put that on the 'To Do List'. Do you want to start on it tomorrow instead of going to the beach?"

Billy was rewarded with eye-darts for this comment. The grin was gone from Sally's face. "Billy Pendleton, you are on very shaky ground!"

Billy grinned his most disarming grin. "It was just a joke! I would rather go to the beach myself!"

A smile grew on Sally's face. "It is fun to drive though isn't it?"

"It sure is. It accelerates hard doesn't it?"

"I'll say. The next time we take it to the lakes, can I drive it?"

"Of course, how do you think Tommy will take you beating him?"

"Oh my God!" a stricken look on her face.

Carl had just walked up. Sally was still sitting in the car. "What's wrong?" he asked.

"Sally wants to drive the next time we go to the lakes, which I think is a great idea. I just asked her how she thought Tommy would take her beating him?"

Carl laughed. "I don't think he would take it well at all. But seriously, I doubt that will happen."

"Why not? We beat him like a drum this weekend. How can he get that much faster?"

"In one word? Money. Money is never an issue for Tommy. If he wants something, he just buys it. It's just like you. In your case, if you want something, you just build it. Tommy buys it. Two different talents and situations." Carl said.

"What would he buy?" Billy asked.

Oh, anything. Don't you think that Maserati that won the 500 mile race this year is faster than the Special?"

"Oh it is, without a doubt. That thing is damn fast. Do you think he could buy it?"

"Yeah he can buy it. But he won't because he already bought something faster." Carl said.

"What? He already has something faster? What could be faster than that Maserati?" Billy asked impatiently.

"The Mercedes Grand Prix car that beat the Maserati in Europe." Carl replied.

Now it was Billy's turn to have a stricken look on his face. He turned and looked at Sally, then back at Carl. "He has one of those? How did he get that? We're at war with Germany."

"He smuggled it out of Germany somehow. I'm not supposed to know any of this and neither are you."

"Why didn't he have it at the lakes last weekend?" Billy asked.

"Because he doesn't want anyone to know he has it. I doubt you see it until after this war is over. But he'll drag it out then. I don't know if he'll race it on the lakes. He'll probably take it to Indianapolis and have a real pro drive it. It should easily win the 500 mile race."

"That's for sure. Wow, a Mercedes Grand Prix car. I read that those cars have over 650 horse power." Billy just shook his head. He never even considered that a private individual could own such a vehicle.

"Well, then beating Tommy on the lakes won't be a concern."

"Damn! I was already thinking how good that would feel!" Sally said.

They all laughed.

"Carl, do you want to drive the car again before we put it back in the shop?" Billy asked.

"No, I can drive it anytime. I drive it around a little to test it out from time to time anyway. It's fun isn't it?"

"Oh yeah," Sally replied, "I wish my Packard was this much fun!"

"If we could double the horsepower and halve the weight, it would be," Billy chuckled.

With that, Sally started the engine, blipped the throttle a couple of times and then burned rubber down the driveway to the shop. Billy and Carl looked at each other and then laughed and turned to follow.

Chapter 21

Billy was always amazed at how at home he felt at the beach house. It wasn't his home and he had only spent a handful of days there, but still he felt at ease the instant he walked in. He sincerely hoped after the war somehow he and Sally could buy it and truly make it their home.

There were fresh flowers in all the vases and the refrigerator was well stocked. Several cases of wine and one of champagne were in the pantry. He was sure that Sally's brother must have taken extra pains to be sure everything was well stocked for their stay.

They arrived in the late afternoon, after spending as much time as possible with Babe before they left. Babe made them all smile. He was as pure as a person could be. He liked what he liked which was baseball and all of them. Past that, he liked the Special and going to the lakes, but beyond that he was at best lukewarm on everything else.

It was winter and even here in California, the weather was cooler than the last time they had been here. It wasn't cold like other parts of the country, you didn't need to wear heavy jackets and such, but a sweater felt good in the evening.

Sally cooked shrimp for supper. The Packard was in the garage and they had no plans to leave the house for several days at least. Everything they needed was in the house. The duo shared a bottle of wine with supper and Billy built a fire in the fireplace. They finished their last glass on the couch in front of the fire.

"How about a walk on the beach?" Sally suggested.

"Yeah, that sounds like fun," Billy replied. They pulled on heavy sweaters and headed out the back onto the deck and down the stairs to the beach. They walked out to the surf arm in arm. The night was dark, the wind was brisk off the water, and low clouds scudded across the sky partially obscuring the stars. There was no moon. They walked with the surf on their left and the breakers barely visible in the dark.

The pair walked in silence arms interlocked, each lost in their own thoughts. They reveled in each other's presence and the warmth of each other's body, grateful for the sweaters they wore. The surf drowned out all other sound.

They walked maybe a quarter of a mile when another couple materialized out of the dark right in front of them.

"Hello," a cheery voice called. Before they could respond, "Billy is that you?"

"Mr. Fulton?" Billy replied.

Then they were face to face. "It's Ken, I don't know a Mr. Fulton." Ken said with a laugh.

They greeted each other warmly with hugs all around. Ken and Melba Fulton were the couple they had literally run into on the beach on their first visit. They were wearing considerably less clothing on that encounter to say the least.

"How have you been, Melba?" Sally asked.

"I've been fine Sally, and you?" Melba responded.

They exchanged normal pleasantries back and forth for a couple of minutes.

"Would you two like to walk with us for a while? It would give us a chance to get caught up. We're actually on our way back to our house. I think we might have something to drink there. Want to join us for a nightcap?" Melba suggested.

"Well sure, thanks for the invitation, is that all right with you, dear?" Sally asked.

"Sure," and off they all went. As they walked through the night the Fulton's pumped them for what had transpired since the last time they saw each other. They wanted to hear all about the Special. Ken was openly amazed that they built a car in their backyard shop that ran over 140 MPH. The subject of Billy's enlistment came up. They asked question after question about the Navy. Both were saddened to hear he was on leave preparatory to shipping overseas. They told Billy and Sally that the only excitement they experienced was after December 7 when everyone was certain a Japanese fleet would appear over the horizon with an invasion force. Even now, there were armed guards patrolling the beach, something that Sally and Billy didn't know.

By this time they arrived at the Fulton's home. The rear of the house faced the beach and was arranged in a similar manner to theirs. There was a ground-level entrance that their house lacked. In fact, the Fulton's house was larger in all regards than Sally's brother's. The beach side entrance was fronted by a flagstone patio covered with a wooden deck that also served as a balcony for the second floor. Off to the right was a wooden structure Billy couldn't identify in the dark.

They entered the house through French doors into a wood paneled library. The walls were lined with built-in bookcases filled to overflowing with books. There were ship models scattered about along with other nautical paraphernalia. Several over-stuffed leather chairs and a matching leather couch filed the room. A painting of a clipper ship in full sail hung over the rock fireplace.

Ken walked over to some louvered doors and opened them to reveal a very well stocked bar. "Brandy okay for everyone?" he asked.

In short order, all of them held large snifters of the amber fire. They left the doors open when they came in. Ken led the way back to the patio. Over to one side was a large rock fireplace. Wood was neatly stacked in the firebox. Ken turned a knob and then lit a match that ignited a fire immediately.

"Do you have natural gas in that fireplace?" Billy asked with an amazed look on his face.

"Sure do" Ken replied.

Soon the fire was roaring. Their faces lit by the red flicker, they were warmed on the outside by the fire and warmed on the inside by the brandy. It was a cozy world there on the patio under the over-hanging deck.

As Billy looked around the patio he asked, "What's that?" pointing at the structure he noticed on the way in.

"Oh, that's our hot tub," Ken replied proudly, leading the group over to it.

"Ken's very proud of this," Melba added.

"What's a hot tub?" Billy asked.

Ken reached down and untied a rope and then pulled back the canvas cover to reveal what appeared to be a huge wooden barrel cut in half and full of water. There was a wooden step built all around the structure.

"Put your hand in there," Ken said.

Billy and Sally did as he asked.

"Oh" Sally said, "It's warm!"

"Sure is, 98 to 100 degrees," Ken said proudly.

"Do you bathe in this?" Billy asked somewhat confused.

"No, you sit in it and drink wine" Ken said.

Sally looked at Melba who nodded her head, a big smile on her face. "When you're as old as we are, it feels really wonderful in the evening with all the aches and pains we have."

"We were up in Sonoma visiting some friends at their vineyard. They had their barrel maker build them one based on an idea they got from a hot spring they had visited in Yosemite. They used a wood fire to heat theirs. I liked the fire burning beside the tub, but it took hours for theirs to get warm enough to sit in. We sat in theirs every night while visiting them. There's nothing like it on a cool evening with friends and a bottle or two of vino."

"What do you sit on?" Sally asked.

"Oh, there's benches built around the sides. Before we left Sonoma, I made arrangements for their barrel maker to build us one to my design. Ours is larger than theirs. I also incorporated a gas heater into mine. It works exactly like a hot water heater only larger. During the winter months I keep it at a constant 98-100 degrees," Ken said. "You want to try it out?"

"What do you wear in that thing?" Billy asked.

"Well, we don't wear anything do we honey?" Ken said. Melba shook her head, a mischievous grin on her face. "You have to be with friends of course. If you want to try it out, Melba and I can go inside and you're welcome to stay as long as you like."

"Well, we're friends, don't you want to join us?" Sally asked, looking first to Billy who nodded, then to Melba and Ken.

"I thought you'd never ask!" Ken said. If you want, you can go ahead and get in while I go get us some wine and glasses."

"Okay," was the only response.

Ken and Melba headed back in the house. Billy and Sally were alone beside the tub. "You sure about this?" Billy asked.

"Of course I am. Why wouldn't I be?" she replied.

"Well, there's no way we're not going to show some things sitting in that thing naked."

"Of course we will. Does that bother you Mr. Modesty?" she asked pulling off her sweater.

"Not on your life ma'am," Billy said as he undid his belt and stepped out of his pants.

They were in the tub, the water up to their necks and facing the ocean when the Fulton's came back. They were in robes and Ken carried a bottle of wine and four glasses. He sat these on a shelf that ringed the rim of the tub. Then he and Melba dropped their robes and climbed into the tub. Billy and Sally kept their gaze discreetly averted toward the surf.

Once in, Ken poured a glass of wine and handed it to Sally. "Thank you sir," she said. Then he poured for Melba, then Billy and finely serving himself last, ever the good host.

Sally thought the sensations of the hot water, the coolness of the evening, and the warmth inside from the alcohol were very relaxing. Ever since falling head over heels in love with Billy, she worried about the war and the possible impact on him. Tonight she resolved to let herself go, to relax completely and live only in the moment. The future was too uncertain and the possibilities simply too staggering for her to deal with. She let herself go and pushed all thoughts of the future out of her mind.

Sally sat on the bench beside Billy leaning against him. Only a year ago he had just been a kid back home in Texas. Now here he sat in a tub of hot water with the most beautiful woman he had ever seen, sharing a bottle of wine with a couple old enough to be his grandparents on a California beach listening to the surf roll; and all of them nude. The changes in his life this year were dramatic beyond belief. All this and not to mention that he was now Machinist Mate in the U.S. Navy and on his way to a world war. And then there was the past weekend with the Special. Sally was nestled against his side and as always he was intensely aware of her presence. He felt her body relax and the sensation was as if her body was warm liquid and molded itself to his even more completely.

Ken wanted to hear all about the Special and the weekend racing it on the dry lakes. To Billy's surprise, he was very knowledgeable about automobiles. It turned out that Ken had known Harry Miller when Miller first started in business. He followed racing for years and made the trip to Indianapolis on several occasions as Miller's personal guest. Sally talked about the Special every bit as much as Billy and it was obvious she was just as proud of it as he was. She talked on and on about how much fun it was to drive. Billy could already see another racer being built just for Sally. That would be a fun project. He wondered what they could use for an engine. His thoughts were brought suddenly back to the present as he felt Sally's free hand exploring under the water.

Ken was saying, "And you two built this car in the backyard from scratch?"

"We surely did, but Carl helped, in fact, Carl was a major part of it, wasn't he honey?" Sally replied.

Billy had to concentrate on the conversation; Sally's hand was a major distraction. "We never could have done it without Carl. His expertise in everything is incredible. Also, his contacts helped so much. He knows everyone. He grew up with Frank Lockhart, they were best friends. Carl was involved with Frank's early racing. I've heard him talk about hanging around Harry Miller's shop back in the twenties. Maybe you met him there?"

"I'm sure that I did. I remember Lockhart. Now there was a real talent. There's never been another like him, before or since. It almost seemed that he knew he only had a short time to make his mark. He had an intensity like I've never seen before. Besides being the best driver in the world, he was a mechanical genius too. He always had a rocky relationship with Harry because of that. Two geniuses that close together and you know there will be sparks and there were. Harry recognized his mechanical ability and Harry was jealous of it, but he admired it too. Harry hated for anyone to modify one of his designs, but Frank couldn't help it. He had an intuitive sense of what worked and what didn't and he got the most out of Harry's cars. It was such a remarkable time. And those board tracks, they were so fast. You know we had one of the best here in Los Angeles."

"Oh, I loved to go to the races there." Melba chimed in. "Those cars were just a blur going around that track. It was so exciting!"

The conversation paused at this point. Each of the participants lost in their own thoughts. Finally the pause was broken when Ken announced, "I think we're out of wine."

"You old fool, why didn't you bring two bottles?" Melba chided.

"I just didn't think. We usually just drink one, but we never have company either. If I can get these old bones moving, I'll go get us another bottle," and he began to stir in preparation to getting up.

"No, don't get up. I'll go get it if you'll just tell me where it is." Sally said.

"You are an angel, my dear. If you go through the door on the far side of the library there is a wine rack mounted on the wall of the hall. The shelf about chest high has several bottles missing. Just get a bottle off of that row."

"Okay." Sally said, and stood up in the waist deep water. As Sally climbed out of the tub, Ken said, "You can use my robe if you want, Sally."

"Oh, I don't think I need one," she said and padded off into the library. She was gone for just a few seconds and came back outside carrying a bottle of wine. She walked back to the side of the tub and Ken reached for the bottle. "Do you have the cork puller out here?" she asked.

"Oh no! The cork puller is in the hall, in the center drawer on the opposite side of the hall from the wine rack. I'm sorry my dear, I should have thought about that."

215

"No problem. I'll be back." She went back in the library. A few moments later she reappeared, this time with an open bottle.

She walked back to the edge of the tub. "Ken, you want to take this while I get back in?"

"Of course, my dear. I must say you are a lovely sight."

"Why thank you sir." She said and as she climbed over the side and stepped into the water, "It was a little cooler than I thought; I'm covered in goose bumps."

"You certainly are," Ken chimed in.

Melba elbowed Ken in the side, "You're enjoying this way too much you old fool!"

"Umph!" he said as her elbow bit into his ribs, but the smile never left his face. "I certainly am! Sally, next to my Melba, you are the most beautiful woman I've ever seen."

"I was never that pretty!" Melba interrupted.

"You most certainly were." Ken turned back to Billy and Sally. Sally was still standing. She reached for Billy's and her own wine glasses and held them out for Ken to pour.

"You were every bit as pretty as Sally is. Seeing Sally does take me back. Do you remember when we went to Yosemite that time?"

As he poured, Ken launched off into another story. "Melba and I went to Yosemite years ago when we were young and before we had a family." He paused as he was pouring the wine, after all, he <u>was</u> enjoying the view. "We went with our friends from Sonoma. We were all young. We didn't have cars in those days, least ways that you could trust on a trip, and of course there weren't any paved roads. We rode the train to a friend's ranch house where we took horses into the mountains. We camped for a couple of weeks in the wilderness. It was the most beautiful unspoiled country you've ever seen. Never saw another human being the entire two weeks." He finally finished pouring and Sally sat back down.

"It's about time!" Melba said and elbowed him again.

"Umph! It was worth it. Really takes me back. That's where the original idea of this tub took shape. The Yosemite is full of hot springs and there was one close by our campsite. At first we took turns going to the spring to bathe, but it wasn't long before we were all in the spring together in the evenings after dark. Remember, you used to enjoy going for wine and you really enjoyed pouring for everyone before you sat down. Umph!" he said again as Melba's elbow once more found its mark.

"You better stop babbling old man."

"You did though, didn't you?"

"Well........."

"You did, now admit it. And Sally, she was every bit as beautiful as you are. Standing there in that spring in the moonlight, she looked like a Greek statue, a Venus de Milo. Until tonight I had never seen anything as beautiful. Thank you so much for sharing your beauty with us and thank you too, Billy."

The evening seemed to go on and on. All thoughts of the war and an uncertain future were gone. Ken regaled them with story after story of the old days. Melba put in her two cents worth from time to time in an attempt to keep Ken honest, but it was obvious that he enjoyed the telling.

Sally made another trip to retrieve more wine. This time taking a cue from Ken's story, she did the pouring. They all enjoyed it, even Melba as the story Ken had told was true. It was like a flashback and she enjoyed it. He had also been correct that she was a beauty in her own right, and even though she was almost three times Sally's age, Melba was still an attractive woman, her figure a good one even for a woman half her age. When the third bottle was empty, Melba stood up and went for the wine. This brought satisfied smiles from everyone and Melba was delighted to find some of that old excitement returned, even more so when she decided to make the trip sans robe. Ken was certain that she was as lovely as ever.

It was a very late night. Much wine was consumed. Somehow, Sally and Billy made it back to their house. The next morning was not that pleasant for any of them. Vino always extracts its revenge. But despite all this, strong bonds had been established that would last years into the future.

The rest of their stay at the beach house followed the same pattern. For this window of time, they had no obligations except to each other. Lazy days were spent in long conversations, reading, walking on the beach, or sunning on the deck. They sometimes spent afternoons preparing elaborate dinners, which they shared over lit candles. Some evenings they cooked on the beach, sometimes alone and sometimes with the Fultons. On several other occasions they repeated their evening in the hot tub where long stories and deep conversations were held.

It was an idyllic time, one that neither of them would ever forget. In the months and years to come they would both look back on this time and lose themselves in the memories.

All too soon, it was over. It was time to pack up and head back to San Diego. Billy's leave was almost over. He planned to stop in Fort Worth on his journey to the East Coast. He hadn't been home since coming to California and he wanted to spend some time with his parents. Who knew when he would get to see them again.

Billy hated to leave. This was his favorite place and where he hoped to spend the rest of his life with Sally. He took one final look at the marble and the glass walls with the ocean view and then he closed and locked the door.

Chapter 22

"That's it, sir. Right at the bottom of the hill on the left," Billy said.

The black sedan pulled to the curb in front of the white clapboard house. Billy got out of the passenger door and pulled his sea bag out of the back seat. "Thanks for the ride sir," he said through the window to the driver.

"Don't mention it, son, I'm proud to have one of our brave servicemen as a passenger, goodbye and good luck," and the man drove away. When Billy arrived at the train station he walked out to the bus stop to catch a bus home. He was wearing his dress blues and almost as soon as he set his sea bag down, the man in the black sedan pulled up to the curb and offered him a ride. Billy asked which direction he was going. The man told him it didn't matter; it was the least he could do to help the war effort and a fellow Texan. Such things were common during the war.

Billy hefted the sea bag onto his shoulder and walked up the narrow concrete driveway. There was a heavy knee high concrete retaining wall down the left side of the drive extending past the house and ending at the rock single car garage. Billy walked up the steps from the drive onto a broad wood porch surrounded by a banister. The single front door had three small rectangular glass windows in its upper third. The center pane held a vertical cloth banner, white with a red border and two blue stars arranged one above the other in its middle. This banner represented the fact that this family had two sons serving their country in the military.

Billy turned the knob and entered. As he walked in the door into the living room, a head appeared across the house in the door to the kitchen. It was a dark haired woman beginning to gray and wearing wire rimmed glasses. As soon as she saw Billy she dropped the rolling pin and it clattered to the floor.

The woman that now ran across the house waving her hands and screaming was a tall sturdy woman in her late forties, dressed in a simple print short sleeved dress with a flour covered apron around her waist. She ran into Billy's arms smothering him in kisses laughing and crying "Billy! Billy! Billy!" over and over. Her hands were also covered in flour and every place she touched him she left a print on his dark blue uniform.

"Hello Mom!" he said, swinging her around as if she were a doll. Even to the casual observer, the resemblance between mother and son was remarkable. It was a time of joy in the woman's life equaled only by the return of her other son Jimmie, Billy's little brother.

When Billy walked in, his mother, Essie Anna, was cooking supper in anticipation of her husband returning home. She had been rolling biscuits. After almost an hour's interruption, kissing Billy, asking question after question and stroking his arms and hands just to prove to herself that he really was home, she returned to her kitchen with the flour stained Billy in tow.

A short time later, Billy heard a car in the drive and looked out the back door of the screened-in porch to see a new Studebaker sedan pull to a stop in front of the garage. The sedan had a roof rack on it and several long boards were carefully tied to the rack.

He looked at his mom. "Go on, go surprise your father."

Billy walked out into the backyard just as a man got out of the driver's side and walked around the back of the car. The man was average height and wore paint stained white overalls, a white shirt and a white cloth cap. As soon as he saw Billy, his eyes lit up and a broad grin creased his weathered face. All that he said was "Son!" as they embraced, then "Welcome home, son," his voice breaking from the emotion.

As they finally pulled apart, Billy noticed his father wiping tears from his eyes. The sight brought home to him how much he really missed his family even with all that transpired in his life over the last year.

"Here Dad, let me help you with that." Billy helped untie the long boards secured to the roof of the car. They were his father's 'running boards' a sort of scaffold his father used in his work as a house painter and paper hanger. His father Bill, was a master at his craft and it showed in the care he exercised with his tools and equipment.

"Son, judging from your uniform, I think you should have worn your whites instead of those blues," Bill said with a chuckle.

Billy had to laugh as he looked at himself while carrying the running boards into the garage. There were white handprints all over his blues.

His father, took time to make sure all of his brushes were properly cared for. His finishing brushes were each suspended in their own can of turpentine so that the bristles hung suspended in the amber liquid, the bristles perfectly formed.

Once all the tools were stowed, Bill pulled the Studebaker into the garage and closed the white painted wooden doors. He paused and lit a Camel from the pack in his shirt pocket offering one to Billy who readily accepted. They stood in the backyard enjoying their smokes.

Parked under the huge elm tree in the center of the yard was a 1932 Ford Model B roadster. It was dark green with black fenders. It belonged to Billy before he left for California. When he left, he sold it to his younger brother Jimmie. Now that Jimmie was in the Marines, the car sat with one tire flat and another quite low.

Billy's gaze fell on the roadster. He still admired the lines of the one year only model. "Have you heard from Jimmie?"

"He shipped out a couple of months ago." His father replied. "Don't know where, he couldn't say, but it had to be the Pacific. He left from California. Jimmie stopped by here on his way west. Spent several weeks with us."

"Was he doing all right?"

"You know your brother. Confidence has never been one of his problems. He's a Corporal you know. A squad leader. Machine gunner."

"That doesn't sound all that safe does it?"

"Son, there aren't any safe jobs in a war. It sounds just as safe as flying around the ocean in an airplane looking for trouble."

"Yeah Dad, I guess you're right. Have you heard anything about Jimmy Carey or Red?" Jimmy Carey and Red Manus were two of Billy's friends from high school.

"No son, I haven't heard anything. While you're here you ought to visit with their folks. If you can get those tires fixed, you ought to take the roadster. I think it will still start."

They finished their cigarettes, flicking the butts into the yard. "Mom ought to have supper about ready," Billy said and they headed in the house, Billy taking one last look at the roadster.

The days flew by. His mother's cooking was every bit as good as he remembered it to be. In fact he was sure he added a couple of pounds by the way his clothes fit.

He did get the old Ford running without too much trouble. One tire had to be patched and he rolled it to a nearby service station on Hemphill Street to get it fixed. It was a station he frequented before the war and everyone knew him. They told him to bring the roadster there for gas, they would give him all he needed. This solved one problem since gasoline was now rationed and his father needed all he could get to keep his business running.

Once the roadster was going, he visited with as many folks as possible. He was lucky enough to see a few friends home on leave, but most were away in the armed forces somewhere.

Cruising around town in the Ford brought back a flood of memories. The roadster wasn't a new Packard and it certainly wasn't equal to the Special, but it ran well. His brother had improved it after Billy left for California, rebuilding the engine with bored out cylinders and higher compression. The Model B was equipped with a 4-cylinder engine that in many ways was the equal of the more glamorous V-8. Billy remembered one night when he and Jimmie pushed the roadster over 85 mph coming down Chalk Hill on the outskirts of Dallas. It was well known that a motorcycle cop always sat at the bottom of the long downhill and wrote speeding tickets to the unwary, especially kids. On that memorable night, Jimmie and Billy decided to see if that motor cop could catch them. Sure enough, as they flashed down the hill, there sat the cop. It was still crystal clear in Billy's mind. As they roared past, the cop was already jumping on the kick start lever to fire up the Harley. They caught him totally unaware. As he concentrated on keeping the flying Ford on the road, Billy chanced a quick glance in the rearview mirror, Jimmie yelling like a banshee in the seat beside him and slapping the door as if whipping the Ford ever faster. The motorcycle was after them, red lights flashing, but the Ford had too much of a head start. The lights behind them got smaller and smaller. Several miles down the road they turned off

Highway 80 and found their way home in the wee hours of the morning on a spider web of back roads.

That memory brought a smile to his face. He thought back about all the times he and Jimmie had great adventures together. His brother was a daredevil if there ever was one. No foe was too big, or stunt too dangerous for Jimmie. He sure did miss him and really regretted that he didn't get to see him one more time before he shipped out.

He missed Sally terribly. He had grown so accustomed to her presence; it was as if they had always been together. Their farewell had been a gut wrenching experience. For days before he left, Sally would just burst into tears and sob uncontrollably. During these episodes, it was impossible to console her. He assured her countless times that he would be fine, but still she sobbed as if she had a portent of impending doom.

They discussed marriage, but at this point, gone no further. Billy was concerned that if something should happen to him, he wanted Sally to go on with her life and find someone else to be happy with. He saw now that as noble as that sounded, married or not, the emotional attachment was the same. In their hearts they would be forever committed to each other.

As for her part, Sally told him that if something did happen, she wanted the insurance and any other benefits to go to his parents. After all, she certainly didn't need the money and red tape being what it was; she didn't want them to do anything that might endanger that arrangement.

Now he wasn't as sure. He missed her terribly. He had written her every night. It was impossible to make long distance calls anymore. All the long lines were in use by the government. His mother noticed the letter writing of course, and he finally confided that yes he did have a girl, but had dropped it at that, finding it too hard to discuss. Worse yet, he had no idea when he might see her again. He was under orders to report to Baltimore in preparation for shipping out to who knew where. One thing was for sure, he wasn't the only guy in this predicament, virtually the entire country was in the same shape. He made a vow to himself that if he ever saw her again, he would do everything in his power to make her his wife. It was the best he could do under the circumstances.

His time in Fort Worth came to a rapid close; his leave exhausted. His folks took him downtown to the Union Pacific train station to see him off. It was a teary farewell for everyone, his mom especially. Although she kept it to herself, she had a feeling of dread about Billy leaving. This made saying goodbye all that much harder for her. She cried for days after he left.

Chapter 23

Sally thought about Billy constantly since he left. If asked, she would have a hard time explaining why Billy captivated her so completely. In his own way he was a striking looking man. He towered over virtually everyone. He was easy to find in any crowd. He had thick jet black hair and green eyes, but even so she had known many men that would have been considered more handsome.

He wasn't the richest or most powerful man; in fact he was far from either. He had no money at all, no famous powerful family and little in the way of prospects, but she would trust him with everything she had. Without a doubt he was the most sincere man she had ever known. He fell in love with her the first time they met out at Kearney Mesa, she was sure of it. He hadn't known one thing about her; in fact, he thought she was Tommy's girlfriend. Yet every time he looked at her, every word he said made her even more certain of the way he felt.

Since their first meeting, her feelings had only gotten stronger. She never felt so complete, so happy in her life. And now he was gone. Off to only God knew where to fight in this damned war. And he hadn't left to fill some non-combat support role, but rather as a crewmember on a combat aircraft. Could it be any worse? She didn't see how.

Sally got a letter every day while Billy was in Texas. That helped somewhat. She didn't even know where he was going and neither did he. He had orders to report to Bombing Patrol Squadron 105, whatever that meant. She had to find out where he was going and how she could get closer to him. How could she do that? Surely, with everyone she knew she could manage that couldn't she? Just then, a loud roar followed by the screech of burning rubber interrupted her thoughts.

She looked out across the front porch just in time to see Babe ride into the driveway on his bicycle. The fender braces were all lined with playing cards held on by clothespins and flapping on the wheel spokes creating the din that interrupted her thoughts. As he flashed into the drive, he slammed on the coaster brake locking the rear wheel and coming to a stop in a J hook slide. He was wearing the cloth pilot's helmet and goggles that Billy bought him, the goggles down over his eyes, a huge grin on his face.

"Hi Sally!" he yelled.

"Is that your motorcycle?" she asked.

"Naw! It's the Special! Can't you see that?!"

"Oh, I'm sorry, something must have gotten in my eyes," she replied and realized she wasn't the only one missing Billy. It was another assurance of his character that Billy had written to Babe also. Not just a note in her letters, but long letters written directly to and addressed to Babe alone. Every time he received a letter, Babe's eyes lit up and he would go off to some quiet place to read them. She noticed that he read them over and over, and then put them in a special box in his desk drawer reserved only for

Billy's letters. She also noticed that many of the baseball pictures that adorned the walls of his room had been replaced with pictures of B-24 Liberators and even a snapshot of Billy and Sally.

"Where have you been?" she asked.

"Me and the boys played a little ball, then we rode down to the Navy base and watched the Liberators land and take off."

"Were there many?"

"Oh yeah, there's lots of them. They're training just like Billy did. Did you know the newest Liberators have nose turrets on them now?"

"I didn't know that," she replied.

"Well they sure do! I wonder how Billy likes that. He's a nose gunner you know?" he said as if he were the expert on all things Billy.

"I heard that somewhere," she said, a faraway look in her eyes.

"That's an important job, being nose gunner you know. He protects the airplane in the front. I think it's the most important job there is. I wonder if Billy can fit in those new turrets."

"I'm sure he'll find a way," she said.

"Of course he will. He could rebuild that whole Liberator all by himself if he had to you know," the pride obvious in his voice.

"I know honey, I know." By this time Babe parked his bike on the sidewalk and took a seat beside Sally on the front porch. She put her arm around him and pulled him close in an enormous hug. Babe loved this. Nothing in the world smelled as sweet as Sally or felt as good as his face being mashed into her chest. It made him tingle all over. He stayed in that position as long as he could.

After a while, "Your dad will be home soon," she said.

"I know."

"I better get up and start supper."

Reluctantly, Babe sat up and Sally stood and left for the kitchen. As she went in the screen door she looked back, "You could come help you know."

His eyes brightened again. "Okay!" and he followed her at his usual run.

Babe was certain that there was not a more beautiful woman in the world than Sally. The relationship they shared was a complicated one. In many ways he thought of her almost as his mother. He knew who his real mother had been, he even had pictures of her, but he never knew her. The only woman he could ever remember in his life was Sally. At other times, she was his big sister, but always one he adored. He confided his innermost thoughts and dreams to her like other boys did to their mothers. And then there was the crush he had on her. At the moment the crush was the most prominent feeling, the hug on the front porch seeing to that. At his age, he didn't really understand what he was feeling, but the feeling was there none the less. Visions of the afternoon he fell out of the tree kept appearing in his mind,

223

especially after one of *those* hugs. He was only too happy to help her in the kitchen or anywhere else, really.

She had him peel potatoes in the kitchen. Babe didn't like to peel potatoes, but in his frame of mind, anything to be near Sally was okay by him. He loved the way she smelled; it was a light delicate scent. He thought it was like spring, but with something special and indefinable mixed in. He kept sneaking peeks at her legs too. She wore khaki shorts that ended at mid thigh and leather sandals from Mexico. And she wore a white sleeveless blouse that buttoned up the front. It was thin enough that he could see the outline of her bra through it and he glimpsed a peek when the cloth occasionally gapped between the buttons. Yes sir, he could peel potatoes all day if that's what she wanted.

His reverie was shattered as he heard his father's LaSalle pull into the drive. In a flash he was out the back door, the screen slamming behind him. Even before Carl could kill the engine and get out, Babe was hanging on the door, his grinning face in the driver's window.

"Hi Pop!" he said.

"Hello son. You scratch the paint on that door and you'll be mowing yards for the next six months to pay for it," Carl said with a chuckle.

"Aw Dad! I wouldn't do that!"

Carl got out of the car and mounted the back steps, Babe in his wake. The screen door slammed again behind Babe. Carl and Sally both turned and stared at him.

"What?!" he said.

"I see you plan to mow yards for the next six months to buy a new screen door?" Carl said.

"Aw Dad!" Everyone laughed, but the point had been made.

Carl and Sally were doing the dishes after supper. "Have you heard from Billy?" Carl already knew the answer, but it was a good way to initiate conversation.

"Got a letter today," she said with a smile.

"How's he doing, and what's he doing?"

"He's fine. He should be on his way to the East Coast by now. He was visiting with his folks in Texas for a few days, but he should be gone now."

"Does he know where he's going yet?"

"If he does, he can't say."

"Loose lips, sink ships." Carl replied.

"Yes, but I really want to know where he is. I need to work on that."

"What do you have up your sleeve, young lady?"

She gave Carl a furtive look. "I know a few people you know."

"Oh, you do? And you think you know someone that knows where Billy is headed?"

"Well, maybe not Billy personally, but I think someone will know where his unit is going," she said.

"The next time you write him, I'd like to stick a note in. Will that be okay?"

"Of course, but you better get busy on your note, because my letter is half finished already."

"Must be nice to have all day to write letters." Even before it was out of his mouth, Carl could see the color begin to rise in Sally's face.

"Listen mister! How would you like this skillet bounced off your head? And besides cooking, you can start doing your own washing and cleaning too!"

"Sorry, sorry! It was just a joke! I know you're busy here all day. I really don't know how Babe and I ever got along without you!" Carl pleaded.

"Well...okay, I guess," Sally replied. "You might have to before long you know."

Now it was Carl's turn to be on the spot. "What do you mean? I didn't make you that mad did I? I didn't mean to. It really was just a joke. A terrible one, but you know me. Talking isn't my strong suit."

Sally didn't say anything for a few minutes as she finished up the last of the dishes.

Now Carl was really starting to get worried. He never meant to hurt her feelings. Damn it all, he just wasn't used to living with a woman in the house. You never knew when the most innocent word was going to set them off.

"Sally, I truly didn't mean to hurt your feelings. I was just joking with you. I apologize."

"Oh, don't be silly! I know, that's not what I'm talking about," she replied.

"Well then what are you talking about?"

All she would ever say was "We'll see."

Carl went to bed that night with one thought on his mind. Women were definitely the hardest creatures to understand that he had ever encountered. After turning and tossing for what seemed like hours, he finally drifted off into a fitful sleep.

Chapter 24

There are three basic types of people in the world. There are those that wonder what happened, there are those that watch what happens, and finally there are those that make things happen. Sally definitely belonged to the final group, and she had absolutely no intention of watching the love of her life go off to war while she sat at home wondering what happened.

After touching base with Carl, she loaded a few things in the Packard and headed up the coast highway to Los Angeles. It was the same route that she and Billy always used and it was filled with memories of him. Even though many of the thoughts brought tears and intense sadness because he was away, they also made her even more determined than ever to do something positive about the situation.

She spent most of the time since Billy left working on ideas. She thought that with her contacts, she might have been able to keep Billy from being assigned overseas and almost certainly could have prevented his assignment to a combat unit. She considered trying to do just that, but she knew in her heart that Billy would never agree to it. She also considered going behind his back to do it, but even as desperately as she loved him, she couldn't force herself to betray someone she loved. She knew Billy wanted 'to do his part' and wouldn't rest until he did. That very attitude was part of what she loved about him and she was smart enough not to want to change the things she loved.

That left her with only one other alternative that she could see. She had to find out exactly where he was and then find a way to get there. She was determined to make the most of each day as it came. Certainly, she thought, in this world there are no guarantees.

She had some ideas and some people to see. It was spring of 1943 and as far as Americans were concerned, the war was almost 18 months old at this point. She was sure that would help her. In the first months of the war there was so much chaos and such a frantic sense of urgency, she thought it would have been harder to get time with the influential people she needed to see. Even so, it wasn't going to be easy, but she had a plan and even if it took a while to accomplish, she was on her way.

She made herself relax and she did her best to enjoy the drive and to keep all the negative thoughts out of her mind. Maybe she could see the Fultons while she was in LA. In fact, the more she thought about it the better that idea sounded. The thought of it brought just a hint of a smile. Maybe the trip wouldn't be so bad after all.

Rather than stop by her family's home, she decided to continue on up the coast to the Fulton's. She wasn't sure exactly why, but something seemed to pull her in that direction. They were close friends, but not family, and they were old enough to have the judgment to help her work through her plan. At least she hoped it would work out that way.

It was a beautiful day and the drive had to be one of the best in the country. She had the top down as she cruised along the curvy asphalt. The ocean off to the left was bright blue and from time to time, she could clearly hear the surf. Traffic was light. Most people couldn't afford to drive that much. Gasoline rationing was having a dramatic effect. While she supported the war effort and conservation of resources, she felt she was on a mission in the best interest of national security. And besides, she had access to all the rationing coupons she could use. That was one of the perks of having a father, and a suitor that together controlled the luxury car market for the entire state of California.

She drove straight on through the sprawl of LA. It was a relief as she finally passed through it and was once more headed north on the coast highway.

This was the same route that she and Billy took to the beach house, but this time rather than going there, she stopped at the Fulton's place. It was the first time that she entered their house from the front. Although she and Billy visited several times, they always came in from the beach. She pulled the Packard into the drive and killed the engine. She hoped they were home as she really felt like she needed their guidance, and council. As self-assured as she was, she wanted to be sure that what she planned would win the approval of people she respected.

It was a sturdy white stucco house, built in the style popular in the teens and twenties. It was one of the first houses built along this stretch of beach. In later years the whole area would be one house jammed against the next, but that had yet to happen. There was only open beach to either side. The house was considerably older and far more traditional in style and construction than her brother's house, but just as she felt instantly at ease with the inhabitants, so the house made her feel at home. She announced her presence with the heavy cast iron knocker in the center of an intricately crafted oak door.

She finally decided that there must not be anyone home and turned to leave, disappointment beginning to well up inside her. Just then, the door opened and Melba was standing there. "Sally! What a surprise! Come in dear, come in."

Sally's mood instantly brightened as she saw Melba and entered the house.

"What brings you here? Is Billy with you? Oh dear, nothing has happened has it?" Melba didn't give Sally time to answer one question before she asked the next.

"No, no, nothing has happened. Billy has already left," Sally assured her. "I just needed someone to talk to and I couldn't think of anyone better than you and Ken. I hope I'm not imposing."

"Oh, don't be silly my dear. We're honored, don't you think any more about that." Melba took her by the hand and led her into the large living room. While the style and furnishings were much more traditional than her brother's house, it was arranged similarly. A wall of windows giving a breathtaking view of the beach dominated the room. There was a large brass telescope on a heavy wooden tripod sitting in front of one of the windows.

Melba raised her voice, "Ken! Ken! Sally is here to visit!" Then in a more normal tone, "May I get you something to drink? I just finished brewing a pot of coffee."

"Coffee would be fine, thanks." Sally responded. Melba left the room and a couple of minutes later re-entered carrying a tray with three mugs of steaming black liquid. The aroma was wonderful.

"Where's Ken?" she asked.

Sally indicated she didn't know.

Melba yelled for him again. After setting the coffee down on the table in front of Sally, she left the room muttering, "Where is that man?"

Just then Ken came in the room. "Sally! What brings you here?"

"Hi Ken." Sally replied, "I really came to ask your advice on a few things."

Melba had returned as well. "My dear, giving advice is one of the few joys of old age. We would be delighted to give all you want," Ken said, "but first let's try some of Melba's wonderful coffee."

As they sipped the steaming liquid, Sally told them of her plan. If there was any way humanly possible, she wanted to find Billy and place herself as close to him as possible.

Over the rim of his cup, Ken's eyes belied the ancient body that housed them. They were clear, alert, and very intelligent. They stayed fixed on Sally as she related her plan and occasionally flicked over to meet Melba's for a second or two.

Finally when Sally finished without interruption, Ken said. "What if Billy is stationed somewhere that civilians aren't allowed?"

"If that's the case, I'll make the best of it, but I think that's unlikely, don't you?"

"I agree, but the possibility does exist." Ken continued to sip his coffee. It was obvious he was considering the possibilities. His eyes now went from Sally to Melba, then after a while his gaze shifted to the wall of windows and the Pacific Ocean beyond.

To Sally's surprise, it was Melba that spoke first. "What about Sonny?" she said, mostly to Ken.

"I was thinking the same thing," Ken replied, his eyes now on Melba's.

"Who is Sonny?" Sally asked.

After a pause, Melba replied, "He's my baby sister's oldest boy."

"Does he have anything to do with the Navy?" Sally asked.

Ken replied, "I think so, he's an Admiral."

They looked at each other for a moment or two and then they all smiled. Sally thought that her instincts had been spot on. When she left San Diego, she planned to go to her father's office and ask his help, but changed her mind on the drive. She was happy she had, certain now that the Fulton's made far better co-conspirators.

"Can you get in contact with him?" Sally asked.

"I think so; I'll go call him now." Melba replied.

"All the long distance circuits are being used by the government. I tried to call Billy in Texas but couldn't," Sally warned.

"Oh, that shouldn't be a problem. It's a local call."

Sally's smile turned into a wide grin. Yes, it had been a wonderful idea to come here after all.

Chapter 25

On the train ride east, Billy's thoughts were mostly of Sally. He was formulating a plan of his own should he ever see her again. He also had thoughts about what the future might hold. The visit with his parents had been a good one and reminded him how much they loved each other. He wished he could have seen Jimmie, but that just hadn't worked out. Now since he was headed east and Jimmie was in the Pacific, it didn't look like he would be seeing him any time soon. Sandwiched in between all these thoughts he daydreamed about the Special.

The train was filled with military, all of them headed east. The majority were Army personnel, probably two thirds in Billy's estimation. The other third was Navy personnel with just a handful of Marines. All the Marines were assigned to shipboard duty with the Atlantic fleet, or training units on the east coast. There were no Marine combat units in the Atlantic theater.

The clickity-clack of the rails made it easy to drift off into frequent naps, but all the activity on the train kept waking him up. As with any place where young men were packed together, there was a tremendous amount of energy to expend.

All the cars were filled with cigarette smoke. There were more than a few bottles and hip flasks that were clandestinely being passed around. This made for a volatile situation. There were several card and crap games in progress at any given time. Not everyone was interested in this nonsense and after the first few hours, the train seemed to shake itself out where the calmer, more laid back passengers, like Billy, gravitated together and the more energetic congregated around the games of chance.

It was a relief to Billy to be in a quieter car. Most of the guys on the train were traveling as units, or at least there were people on the train they knew. Billy knew no one. He was reporting to a new unit in Baltimore. The unit was VB-105. The VB stood for Naval Bombing squadron. He knew the squadron just returned to the states from Bristol Field, Argentia, Newfoundland where they had been operating PBY-5 Catalinas. The squadron was now transitioning from the amphibious Catalina to the land based Liberator. Despite the bureaucracy and red tape of the Navy, they made the only sensible decision and assigned Billy to a Liberator squadron where his intimate knowledge of the aircraft could be put to best use.

He hated being away from the people he loved. After all, he now thought of himself as having two families, one in Texas and the other in California. No one could replace his mom, dad and brother, but still Carl and Babe were very much a part of his life. And then there was Sally. He came to the realization that Sally was the one. There was no doubt she was the love of his life, pure and simple.

The kaleidoscope that was America flashed past the window of his car. He hoped he would have time to visit all parts of the country after the war. Seeing the country was one of the reasons he had went to California in the first place. As with most Americans, he never had a thought that America might lose the war or that his freedoms would ever be impinged.

As the light began to fade, Billy and his seatmate, a sailor from Oklahoma on his way to Norfolk, headed to the dining car for dinner. So far the food had been very good. They were served in the dining car exactly as train passengers were served before the war. Another thing that impressed Billy was that as they continued their trip east, other trains pulled off onto sidings as they passed. It was obvious they had priority over all other trains.

Besides the military personnel on board, there was a small group of civilians. This group was the object of much discussion and conjecture among the sailors and soldiers.

The civilians had sequestered themselves at one end of Billy's car and as Billy and his buddy were headed down the aisle toward the dining car, the civilians did the same. Up until this time, Billy had not paid much attention to them. As the group stood to leave, Billy noted that there were four all together, three men and a woman. Billy felt sorry for the woman being on this train. Even though she was not as stunning as Sally by any means, she was still an attractive woman. Billy guessed her to be in her mid to late twenties. She had dark blond hair and green eyes. As she stood, every eye in the car followed her. The looks turned to cat calls and whistles as they passed into the next car which was far more rowdy. Just as Billy thought things might get out of control, one of the lady's companions put a stop to it all just by looking at the offenders.

The man that accomplished this feat was tall and relatively slender. He was dressed well in a tailored double-breasted suit in navy. The man had black hair combed straight back. Billy couldn't get a good look at his face. He wondered what the man could have possibly done to quiet the rowdies with just a look.

The lady's other companions weren't as intimidating, at least on the surface. The larger of the two was every bit as tall as the thinner man, but much heavier, almost flabby. He seemed jovial, his dark hair heavily streaked with gray and a red beard of all things. He too wore an expensive wool suit.

The third companion was younger and more average looking. He had red hair and brown eyes and wore a plaid sports coat over tan slacks.

Even though the group was dressed as civilians, they moved with precision and seemed to have a more acute awareness of their surroundings than normal people do. Even the smiling fat man's eyes never stopped surveying the car. Billy's instincts told him these people were something beyond the norm as certainly they were, or they wouldn't be on this train.

After they arrived in the dining car, Billy, his buddy and two other sailors were seated at a table set for four. Complete with white starched tablecloths and napkins. Black stewards in white jackets and black pants served dinner with reserved grace. Candles

J E PENDLETON

glowed on each table as the world outside the windows had turned dark and still the train roared through the night.

Dinner was excellent, roast beef, carrots and potatoes, followed by chocolate cake. They finished their coffee and as they were about to leave the group of civilians stood and started back toward their car. As they passed by, Billy got a better look at the thin man. The man had a long thin face and a chin that brought to mind the word chiseled. He wasn't handsome, there was a cruel look to him. He had piercing black eyes that Billy could only describe as cold.

The sailors at Billy's table rose and followed the civilians out. As the groups entered the rowdy car, it was even more raucous than it had been before. Billy was sure that more drinking had taken place and sure enough the smell of alcohol reeked.

As the civilians were passing the area where the worst of the catcalls had come earlier, they fired up once more. Just as the thin man was turning to stare his icy stare, a khaki clad arm reached out and the attached hand planted itself on the lady's hip.

The thin man moved as a blur. Billy had never seen anyone move so fast. Somehow a dark bladed stiletto with a gleaming edge appeared in his hand and its point pressed into the neck of the soldier just above the jugular vein. It was pressed into the neck just far enough that a drop of blood had already appeared and ran down the man's neck to his collar. Several of the soldier's friends started to rise from their seats. They never made it. A blue steel automatic pistol unlike any Billy had ever seen appeared in the fat man's hand. His eyes still twinkled and the smile never left his face. "Sit gentlemen, please," he said in an accent Billy couldn't identify. The soldiers sat back down, eyes wide. Then Billy realized that similar pistols were in the red headed kid's hand and the woman's. The thin man whispered something in the soldier's ear. The man withdrew his arm and Billy didn't think he even breathed. He was white as a sheet. There was no sound in the car. As quickly as it started, it was over. The civilians continued down the aisle, all weapons disappeared.

Billy's group stood and watched them leave. Billy's buddy bent over and asked the soldier what the thin man said. For a minute it seemed that the man couldn't say anything. The man looked up, his eyes still wide, all color drained from his face making the drop of blood stand out all that much more. Finally he said, "You have one second to decide." They all looked at each other. Then without another word, they continued their journey back to their car. As they walked into the car, the civilians were already seated together and from all outward appearances, you couldn't tell that anything ever happened.

Once Billy and his group were back in their seats at the other end of the car, the first question out of his buddy's mouth was "Who are those people?"

Billy just shook his head. He had no idea. One of the other sailors asked, "Where did that knife come from? Did you see that thing? It made the hair on my neck stand up. Those things scare the hell out of me!"

"What about the guns? They don't scare you?"

"Not as much as a knife, especially one like that one. Knives like that are only meant to kill people. That thing was so sharp he couldn't even touch that guy without drawing blood."

One of the other guys said, "I saw it, it came out of his sleeve."

"How about the guns? Where did they come from and what kind were they? I've never seen anything like them."

"I saw the kid, and his gun came out of his jacket. A shoulder holster I think. And those guns were Walther PPK's."

"What are those? How did you know what they are?"

"Those are German pistols. They're the favorite of the German brass."

"How'd you know that?"

"My father's a gunsmith."

The four sailors looked at each other then they all sat back. Each lost in thought. Their questions would never be answered. How could they be? Certainly no one was going to walk up and ask the civilians who they were and what they were doing on the train. Nothing else was said and before long Billy dozed off, his stomach full, lulled by the clickity-clack.

Billy woke with a start. Morning sunshine was streaming in the windows. As he looked around his companions were also stirring. Then he realized the train was stopped. He looked out the window. All he could see was a plowed field planted with something he couldn't identify. He stood to stretch. As he looked down the aisle, he instantly noticed the civilians were gone.

"Hey guys, the civies are gone," he said.

The other three immediately turned to look. Billy's buddy walked down the aisle and started talking with the soldiers at the end of the car. In a moment he returned.

"Where'd they go?" One of the others asked.

"No one knows. Those guys didn't even know about the knife fight last night. No one saw them leave. I guess they left sometime during the night.

"I wonder who they were?"

The train lurched and they were rolling again, quickly gaining speed.

Chapter 26

The doorbell rang and Sally answered the door. There was a tall, rather distinguished looking man in his early forties at the door. He was dressed in a well-tailored sports jacket that accentuated his athletic frame and nicely contrasting slacks. He had black wavy hair and blue eyes that registered an instant of surprise when Sally opened the door. A Lopsided grin slowly grew across the craggy face. "Hello," he said, "I'm Sonny Cunningham," extending his hand.

Sally took his hand in a firm handshake. "I'm Sally, and I'm very pleased to meet you. Please come in Admiral."

As he came in the door he said, "Sally, it's my pleasure, and please call me Sonny. Everyone else in the family does, and besides 'Admiral' sounds a little too formal for an evening with a woman as beautiful as you."

Sally momentarily flushed, "You flatter me sir, I think Admiral fits you well, but if you insist, it'll be Sonny."

"I insist," he replied.

"Well then Sonny, may I get you a drink?"

"If I'm not mistaken, Uncle Ken keeps some single malt scotch hidden out somewhere, if you know where, I'll have one of those on the rocks please."

They walked into the living room. Sally went to the drink cart to fix drinks as Ken came into the room.

"Sonny! Glad to see you could make it!" Ken walked across the living room extending his hand.

"Uncle Ken, how could I have possibly refused an invitation for dinner and my Aunt Melba's cooking? Then I get here and Sally greets me at the door and is pouring me some of your famous scotch. I'm beginning to feel a little bit like the fatted calf."

"Oh, don't be ridiculous, we're just happy to see you. How is work going?"

"Hectic, as you can imagine." Sonny said.

"Sally, could you make me one of those also?" Ken asked.

"My pleasure sir," Sally replied.

Sonny proceeded to tell Ken how things were going in the war effort, careful to keep things on a positive note and not reveal any classified information. "You know, we really whipped 'em at Midway last year, kicked their arrogant little asses good and proper. Since then we've been the ones on the offensive and they're the ones back on their heels. Oh, Sally, please forgive my language."

"No apologies necessary, that's one of the first good things I've heard in months," Sally replied.

"Come, let's go to the kitchen and see if Melba needs any help and you can tell us all about it." They all trailed off to the kitchen, drinks in hand. Sally carried a pair of martinis, one for Melba and the other for herself.

After a wonderful dinner of pot roast with all the trimmings, they adjourned to the deck for coffee. After several sips, Ken said, "Let's try out the hot tub. What do you say, Sonny?"

"Well, I didn't bring a suit, I'm afraid."

"That's okay, I've got a new one that's never been worn. You can borrow that. How about it?"

Sonny looked at Sally who just grinned over the rim of her cup. "Okay, but you have to promise not to get me drunk like last time."

Ken and Melba were already in the tub, wineglasses in hand. Sonny came out of the house and eased into the hot water. "That feels gooooood. Where's Sally?"

Just then Sally came out in her white cotton robe. "Here I am, sorry to keep everyone waiting," and she shrugged out of the robe. As she stepped into the tub, Sonny couldn't help but admire her. She wore a plain black swimsuit, modest as it was, the result was still stunning. She rewarded his admiring glance with a dazzling smile.

"Okay," he said. "Enough is enough. Whatever it is you people want from me, you can have it. When I'm finished telling you everything I know, please call the Shore Patrol and have me arrested!" Everyone laughed.

"Admiral, whatever could you possibly mean?" Sally said in her best Scarlet O'Hara accent.

"You know very well what I mean. Let's hear it. What do you need, a battleship or maybe just a destroyer?"

Ken and Melba were laughing. Melba said, "Oh Sonny, don't be ridiculous, we just need one little favor, that's all. You will remember all the dinners I've fixed for you over the years however."

"Yes Ma'am, every one. Now what can I do for you fine folks?"

After Sally's explanation, Sonny grinned. "Oh is that all? I'll make a few inquiries and call you tomorrow, now let's finish off that bottle of wine."

Sally was relieved. This had been the part of her plan where she had the least influence. Thank God for the Fultons. Once she knew where Billy was stationed, and hopefully that would be tomorrow, she could get on with it.

Late the next afternoon, the phone rang and Melba answered. "Sally! It's Sonny on the line!"

Sally quickly joined from an extension in the study.

"I found out where your friend is going." Sonny said. "He and the rest of his squadron, VB-105 are en route to Kindley Field, Bermuda."

"Sonny, are you saying he's stationed in Bermuda?" Sally asked scarcely believing her ears.

"Yes Sally, that's correct. He is stationed in Bermuda, or soon will be."

"That's wonderful! I never dreamed he would be stationed there. There aren't any Nazis close to Bermuda are there?"

"Sally, don't get too excited. Remember he is a Liberator crewman and as such flies combat missions on a regular basis. His aircraft has one mission, to find and destroy the enemy. In the

235

case of VB-105, that enemy is mostly Nazi submarines. They fly very long missions over empty ocean in all kinds of weather. They are always subject to mechanical failure and accident. Then on the rare occasion when they might find a U-boat, a deadly battle ensues. Some of those U-boats carry heavy anti-aircraft armament. Please keep all that in mind."

Sally's feeling of elation deflated somewhat as she let Sonny's words sink in. The initial thought of Billy being stationed in beautiful Bermuda was just too good to be true. "But Admiral, isn't Bermuda relatively safe?" Sally asked.

Sonny drew a long breath and hesitated for a moment. Sally instantly sensed there was more to the story. "Sonny, what is it you aren't telling me?"

"Sally, you can't share this with anyone, do I have your solemn word on that? Any leaks could put your friend in danger, do you understand?" Sonny warned ominously.

"Yes, I do. Believe me, I wouldn't do anything to endanger him or anyone else," she replied.

"Sally VB-105 is in Bermuda just to train. You're right, Bermuda is a relatively safe place. Still there are U-boats in that part of the Atlantic. They're training, but at the same time, they're also flying combat patrols. They'll only be there a few months."

An icy hand gripped Sally's heart. She held her breath for a few seconds until she just couldn't any longer. "Then where do they go?"

"There's only one place to go. They're going to form up with a new unit being called Fleet Air Wing 7. Sally we have to stop the U-boats. They're playing havoc with our convoys to supply England. We've been losing almost a ship a day to U-boats. Your friend and his shipmates are going to stop that. They will carry the fight to the U-boats and make the hunter the hunted."

"Sonny, where will he be?"

"The only place he can be Sally. All the U-boats are based along the coast of France. Their only two routes to open ocean are through the English Channel or across the Bay of Biscay. He'll be on the southern coast of England, Sally, at a small hamlet called Dunkeswell."

Chapter 27

At first it was just a smudge on the horizon; a single dot of color in a world of blue. The first time Billy saw it he was filled with excitement and curiosity. Different emotions filled him on this day. They were flying their final mission from Kindley Field. They had been in Bermuda since June. It was now August. Their time in Bermuda had been enjoyable. It was easy living really, except for the missions, which were grueling 12 hour flights, spent searching empty sea hour after boring hour.

During those hours and days of grinding boredom, regardless of the importance of the mission, no one could remain totally focused. Everyone's mind roamed, you could only remain alert for so long. No one in the squadron sighted a single U-boat in their entire time in Bermuda. They had flown missions every other day since their arrival. The crews trained on their new aircraft, but beyond that it had been an agony of boredom.

He liked their new ship. It was the latest right off the assembly line back in San Diego. The Navy knew it as the PB4Y-1. It was the same aircraft flown by the Army Air Forces, but with a few significant changes to tailor it for its mission of hunting U-boats. The most obvious change was the paint scheme. The squadron ships were all painted a dirty white with the top surfaces painted dark blue. When Billy first saw the white paint job, he thought someone had lost their mind. White was too visible. They'd be sitting ducks to a Nazi deck gunner, but after watching his squadron mates land and take off in the past months, his mind completely changed. Against the bright blue sky, even the huge Liberator was almost invisible. And when seen from above, the dark blue on the upper surface blended very well with the blue of the ocean.

Another important change to the PB4Y was that the ball turret was removed from the vulnerable belly of the plane and replaced with a radar dome. The radar was used to detect surfaced U-boats and was top secret. At the very low altitudes they flew most of the time, a turret on the bottom side or belly of the aircraft wasn't of much use anyway.

The final modification affected Billy personally. The glassed in nose or, bow as the Navy insisted on calling it, was replaced with an electrically controlled ERCO turret. Billy had mixed feelings about the turret. There was no doubt that it gave the bomber more firepower. In the old style nose, there were three 50 caliber machine guns, but they were each fixed into separate sockets, one facing to each side and one straight ahead. That meant that no more than one of them could be brought to bear on any given target. Another problem was that to track a target across the front of the aircraft meant moving from one gun to another. While this was technically possible, as a practical matter, the speed at which most aerial combat occurred made it impossible. The new turret replaced the old arrangement with a pair of guns, one on either side of his seat, they moved back and forth, called traversing, and up and down, electrically. Both guns were sighted in to hit the same point, effectively doubling firepower and allowing him to engage and track targets anywhere in the front hemisphere of the aircraft. All these were good things. The bad thing was that the turret was a Plexiglas ball that he had to enter to control. The turret had to be aligned with the aircraft's centerline in order for him to enter, or more importantly, to leave the dome. As the turret moved side to side, the hatch moved also sealing him in the turret. All the bow gunners secretly feared battle damage trapping them in their turret as their aircraft went down. The other concern with the turret was that it was very cramped. His six foot six inch frame was hard to fold into the cramped space. One good thing was that none of the crew wore parachutes. At the low altitude where they flew, typically 500 feet or less, sometimes much lower, a parachute didn't have time to open anyway. The added bulk of a parachute would have made it impossible for him to fit in the confined space.

In many ways he was going to miss Bermuda. The weather here was ideal for flight operations. The days were mostly sunny and warm, allowing them the luxury of flying in dungarees and only a light jacket. The scenery was beautiful; lush greenery and bright white and pastel cottages and buildings.

It was an idyllic setting. The people were friendly and spoke English with a heavy British accent. The island had been opened up to them. Beautiful beaches to roam at will. For the first time in his life, Billy had been sailing. The base had a number of small sailboats available for the men to use. Billy's co-pilot was an avid sailor and talked Billy into going with him the first time. To Billy's surprise, he enjoyed himself immensely. Since then, every chance they had, they checked out a boat and went sailing. The co-pilot was an officer, Lieutenant John Goodrich, but away from the rest of the crew, they had a laid back, cordial friendship. John was a couple of years older than Billy, but they found they enjoyed the same things. John introduced Billy to sailing and Billy told him about building the Special. John couldn't hear enough about the car.

Aircrews were closer and had a more informal relationship than the rest of the Navy. The crew was just ten men, all of them totally dependent on each other once they were in the air. Their missions were long and tedious. All that time together made for a closer bonding of the men. They played golf together, they fished together, they sailed, rode bicycles and they hunted U-boats together. Now it was time to load up and leave this place for England. They would take a few days to pack up their things and to check the ship over with a fine toothed comb, then at the end of the week whey would fly back to Norfolk. There they would re-equip in preparation for the flight to England.

There was another thing that was eating at Billy. He had written Sally nearly every day since he had left California. And in the beginning, he received quite a few letters from her as well. But as time went on, it seemed her letters slacked off a bit. And another thing that worried him was that her letters seemed to have no connection to his. She hardly ever answered a question anymore. She almost never made reference to anything he had written. He was still confident that they would forever be devoted to each other, but still he had no explanation for it. Surely she wasn't losing interest in him already was she? Billy heard stories all the time of guys getting "Dear John" letters from their girls back home. He was certain Sally would never send him one, yet he had no explanation for her vagueness.

They were getting close to the island now, wheels down in preparation for landing. Maybe he could get in one last sail with John before they left, he hoped so. He would be sure he had all his gear squared away as quickly as possible just in case John could break away. In the meantime he wanted to write Sally another letter. Writing her was his favorite activity of all. His thoughts were totally focused on her and with telling her of his daily activities and adventures. He did his best to keep it upbeat and lighthearted. So far his slice of this war had not been action filled. Still flying combat missions in a four-engine bomber, loaded to the brim with explosives and high-test gasoline over open ocean, hundreds of miles from land could never be considered safe.

Just then the surf line flashed under the nose and they were over land. Lt. North, the pilot and aircraft commander was already lining up on the runway. Billy's mind shifted quickly back to his duties and he exited his turret for the safer confines of the main fuselage. Tomorrow he would take off from this same field one last time on the first leg of his journey to England.

Chapter 28

Sally stood on the bridge of the HMS Queen Mary and took in the breathtaking sight of the great ocean liner slicing through the North Atlantic at high speed. The great ship had been pressed into service as a troop transport and was found to be ideally suited to the task. She could carry over 10,000 troops in relative comfort and her speed made her almost immune to U-boats.

The captain was saying in his proper English accent, "our speed is presently 30 knots. When combined with our random zigzag course, no U-boat in Jerry's Navy can target us." The captain stated this as pure fact and Sally and the others were impressed with his confidence. He was resplendent in his immaculate white uniform. The brim of his cap was covered in gold braid. Sally had heard some Americans refer to it as 'scrambled eggs'.

The captain was obviously enjoying the opportunity to show off his luxury liner, the holder of numerous trans-Atlantic speed records and the crown jewel of the Cunard Line. He also was enjoying the attention of his audience. He was surrounded by some of the most beautiful women in the world; each of them hanging on his every word.

The bridge was the control center of one of the largest, most complex machines in the world. The view out the windows that completely lined the sides and front of the bridge was stunning; the sharp bow of the ship pointing the way to the horizon.

The exterior of the ship had been repainted in a drab camouflage, all the brightwork and white paint covered or removed. But here on the bridge no such actions and been necessary. The instruments were all surrounded with polished brass and the decks gleamed. The watch crew was all turned out in their best uniforms and even though they went about their jobs with typical British bearing and competency, the sailors couldn't help but sneak peeks at the cluster of beauties surrounding their captain. Some of the beauties peeked back and even an occasional wink and smile were exchanged.

All this, while not escaping her notice, did not include Sally. She certainly received more than her fair share of peeks, but she simply wasn't interested. She was here for one reason and one reason only. Her plan was to station herself as close to Billy as possible and she was on her way to do just that.

The plan had come together quite nicely. Having been raised in Los Angeles as a member of a very wealthy and influential family, it was inevitable that she knew many members of the entertainment industry. Her father knew virtually all of them, counting most as his customers, and some as close friends. His forays into radio and early experiments with television cemented these relationships.

Sally exploited those contacts to become part of the USO. That was easy really. The USO was always looking for beautiful women. Their purpose was to entertain the troops and they discovered the age-old solution. Young men were always most interested in young women. It really didn't matter if the young women could sing or dance, or had any other talent. Just being there was enough.

The 'men' were boys really. Their average age was just nineteen. For most of them, it was their first time away from home and family. They had a duty to perform, and they were intent on getting that done so that they could get on with their lives. They believed in their country and they believed in their duty to overcome the enemy, but most of all they believed in each other. Whenever and wherever the USO appeared, it allowed them to escape their awesome responsibility for a brief time and revert back to simply being young men.

Sally joined the USO effort to get a ticket to England. The first thing she did was try to buy a ticket to England as a private citizen. She quickly found this to be impossible. So then she decided to try the USO. This proved surprisingly easy, no doubt made much easier by her network of contacts, but even more so by her striking appearance. She was exactly what the USO wanted.

She was exceptionally beautiful. Anytime she walked into a room, it was certain that all eyes would be on her. She was willing to devote all of her time to the cause. She was several years older than the average soldier, sailor or Marine at 24. Still young enough to be at the height of her allure and beauty, but old enough to have the maturity necessary to give just enough of herself without giving too much. She had to be something to all of them. And finally, as icing on the cake, not only did she refuse to accept any salary, she also insisted on paying for many things herself.

Sally found the experience to be very fulfilling. She saw a tiny bit of Billy in each of them. It warmed her heart to know she was able to do something to brighten their day. She instantly became a sort of big sister to them with one major difference. It was a rare soldier indeed that came into contact with Sally that didn't develop an instant crush. She discovered she had a real talent for just listening. She would give occasional advice or encouragement, but usually just listening was what was required. She never knew how many of the boys she met flashed back to their few minutes together and took great courage from her words. Many of them worried about how they would perform in battle, would they do their duty or would they be cowards. She quietly assured each of them that they would do what was necessary when the time came and they did. Many of them heard her words and when they were the most terrified, found the courage to face their fears because of the confidence she had given them. Others were concerned about the girl they left at home that maybe hadn't written as often as they hoped or maybe had written one letter too many dashing cherished hopes and dreams of a future after the war. Invariably Sally gave them encouragement and a renewed sense of worth and self-esteem. None left without a personal compliment, the color of their hair, their smile, the look in their eyes. If a woman as beautiful as this thinks I'm attractive, they thought, then surely any other woman will too. Many of them fought through their fears, no matter what form they took, simply because they felt Sally expected them to and they didn't want to let her down. Sometimes something as simple as that made all the difference. More than a few would remember meeting the 'most beautiful lady' the rest of their lives, some lucky ones into their eighties and beyond.

Now she found herself on the bridge of the Queen Mary racing across the Atlantic to England. The great ship was crammed to overflowing with soldiers, on their way to their dates with destiny. Each of them carried some concern about the threat of a sudden U-boat attack. To some it was nothing more than that, just a concern much like the concern of encountering a sudden storm but most were confident that 'nothing bad' could happen to them. To others, it was more than a concern; it was a constantly gnawing fear. It brought home to Sally what an important job Billy and others like him were doing. They patrolled these waters constantly searching for the enemy. Always on the lookout for a U-boat surfacing to charge its battery or the white feather of a periscope searching for prey. Sally felt completely secure that they would all reach England safe and sound. She didn't know at the time that this was more because of the Queen Mary's speed than because of patrolling aircraft. The war was still almost a year away from Allied aircraft winning control of the sea from their underwater rivals.

She turned her attention back to the captain. He was explaining how they steered a zigzag course to make it nearly impossible for a submarine to get in a position to carry through an attack. He also mentioned air patrols and that mention made Sally's day.

Chapter 29

It was cold in the nose of the airplane. The Navy called it the bow, just like on a ship, but Billy never called it anything except the nose. That's what they called it at Consolidated where he helped build them. In his official duties it was the bow, but in his heart it would always be the nose.

Billy huddled inside his jacket. It was made from a heavy khaki colored canvas and had thin insulation, but it wasn't enough to keep out the cold. It was more than enough when flying out of Kindley Field, Bermuda, but it certainly wasn't adequate here. They had just left Reykjavik, Iceland and were on the final leg of their flight deploying to England.

Billy was in the main fuselage just aft of his turret. The turret was cramped and even colder than it was here. He had a wool blanket wrapped around his shoulders over his jacket and a knit watch standers cap pulled low over his ears and wore gloves. There was no way he could have used the blanket inside the turret.

There was no reason to be at battle stations here. They were far from the reach of any enemy planes. They were flying at 2500 feet. From here, looking out Billy could see the solid overcast of dark gray clouds 500 feet overhead, stretch all the way to the horizon where it met the white capped sea, a slightly different shade of gray. It was like looking out of a fish bowl into a world of gray. There was almost no contrast between the sea and sky.

They were flying on the wing, slightly above and behind another Liberator piloted by the VB-105 squadron commander, Lieutenant Commander Francis E. Nuessle. The men of the squadron all liked their commander. They had confidence in him for two reasons; he always led from the front just as he was doing now, and he had already proven himself in combat.

Commander Nuessle, called Frankie by his friends, was an old PBY Catalina pilot. While stationed in Bermuda in 1942 he commanded the seaplane tender U.S.S. Gannet. In June of that year, he sailed his ship in search of a torpedoed merchantman, the Westmoreland. While searching for survivors at night, the Gannet herself was torpedoed. She sank within five minutes. Commander Nuessle supervised the abandon ship drill and got all 60 of the crewmen off the sinking ship and into life rafts before the stricken ship went under. He then ordered all the rafts be lashed together and he took care of the wounded as best they could. They were rescued the next day and many of the crew credited Commander Nuessle's cool head with saving their lives. Five months later he assumed command of VB-105 and now they were deploying to England in search of his old foe.

Billy's gaze returned to the confines of the fuselage. He was sharing the cramped space with Ensign Victor D'Harlingue the navigator/ bombardier. Vic, as Billy called him during the much more informal atmosphere of flight operations, was crouched over his small table plotting their course. It was important that he kept current on where they were, even though Commander Nuessle's plane was leading, in the event the two aircraft became separated Vic's calculations would be all that stood between a bitterly cold dunking in the Atlantic and an uneventful flight on to England.

Billy pulled a letter from Carl from an inside pocket and began to read. It was at least the tenth time he had read it, but still he savored every word trying to imagine himself back in San Diego.

Dear Billy,   August 2, 1943

Hope this finds you in good health and good spirits. All is well here. We received your last letter yesterday. Sorry to hear you are leaving Bermuda. I guess it's true that all good things come to an end.

The Babe is doing well. He has been playing some organized ball in an Optimist Club league and his coach, an ex AAA ball player, tells me he has real talent. Hell, we always knew that didn't we? He's scraping by in school. I have to stay on him all the time to do his homework. He's been writing you a letter for over two weeks. It beats me how anyone who can swing a bat like he does, can be so intimidated by a pencil. I guess it's a good thing he can play ball because his education isn't going to get him anywhere.

I saw Tommy last week and he asked about you. He said to sink one for him. To be such a smart man he really doesn't have a clue at times does he? Still he's a good boss and a good friend, really.

I've been looking at the Special. I think I will start making it street drivable as we discussed if you don't have any objections. I have been talking to a couple of the body shop guys and we have come up with a set of headlights that look like they were made for it. Billy, I mean these things fit that grille shell you made so perfect you can't even see daylight through the gap. They're 1937 Studebaker and the shape of them really fits the car. They have that perfect tear drop shape you like so much. Found some DeSoto tail lights that match the headlights pretty good. I'll have to make some stands for them. I wish you were here to do that. You really have a knack for shaping that metal. Get all this done and then I can show Tommy that he isn't the only one that can drive his speedster on the street!

Take care of yourself. Don't take any unnecessary chances. You already know that but I thought I'd tell you anyway. Write and tell me what you think.

Your friend,

Carl

Billy had a smile on his face as he finished the letter yet again. That Babe, he was something else! He wasn't stupid, he just didn't care about school. He was almost as big a scamp as Jimmie was. Now that would be a pair wouldn't it? Put those two together and world watch out. Of course, Jimmie was a lot older than the Babe. Well maybe someday after this mess was over he could get them together.

So Carl was going ahead with their plan to make the Special a street driven car. He always visualized it that way, but they simply didn't have the time to do it. They were lucky to get it running at all and to be able to take it to El Mirage when Tommy had his timing gear there. He couldn't wait to get back. He knew there was a lot more speed left in the Special. He was certain he and Carl could get it out.

Carl had not mentioned Sally. Surely, that was simply because he knew Sally wrote all the time, but still something wasn't quite right. Billy could feel it. He hoped she wasn't sick or something. Surely, Carl would have told him if there was a problem. Oh, Sally wrote often enough, but there was something cold about her letters. They seemed strangely out of touch. Well, regardless, he was happy she wrote. His thoughts never strayed far from her. He was anxious to get to England and get this mess over with so he could get back in her arms.

"Bill... Bill?... Bill!" Vic said, finally shaking his shoulder.

Billy looked up startled from his reverie, his eyes wide.

"Hey Bill, that must be some letter. Is it from Sally?" Vic asked. Everyone in the crew knew about Sally. Billy was one of those people that seemed to instantly be everyone's friend. Although he had the same opportunities as the rest of the crew with women, Billy always held back and found something else to do. At first, some of them thought he was married, but eventually they all discovered the truth about Sally. When they did there wasn't one among them that wouldn't trade places with him in a heartbeat. In fact, once they finally persuaded him to show them a picture of Sally, half the crew, and probably more, fell instantly in love with her.

"No Vic, this one's from Carl. Sorry, I was sort of in a trance there for a minute. What's up?" Billy said instantly throwing off his blanket and looking outside ready to climb into his turret.

"Everything's okay, I just have some fresh joe ready, you want a cup?"

"Boy do I! I've got a chill down to my bones. Maybe it'll warm me up."

"Me too!" Vic chuckled. He had a blanket draped around his shoulders also. "These tropic weight jackets don't cut it way up here do they?"

"They sure don't!" Billy said.

"Yeah, BUAER must not understand that it's cold enough to freeze the balls off a brass monkey in Iceland even if it is August!"

"Ain't it the truth. We on course?"

BUAER stood for the U.S. Navy Bureau of Aeronautics. It was standard procedure to blame anything that went wrong on BUAER.

"Yeah, I think we're right on the beam. We should be making landfall over Ireland in a couple of hours, then to St. Eval an hour or so later." Vic said.

"I sure hope it's warmer there." Billy said.

"Me too, but I don't think it will be."

"Really?"

"No, I'm sorry, but I don't think it will be. I don't think England is ever very warm. It's sure as hell never close to as warm as Texas or San Diego."

"You're just full of good news aren't you?" Billy said.

They both laughed and Vic handed him a steaming mug of black liquid. One thing the Navy always had in good supply was coffee.

Billy wrapped both hands around the mug to warm them and took a sip. It was almost hot enough to scald his tongue, just what he needed to warm up a little.

"This is great! Thanks, it sure hits the spot." He returned to his seated position with the blanket draped around him.

Both men had to yell to be heard over the roar of the four engines and the wind passing over and through the airplane. Its designers never considered crew comfort as a design criteria. It was cold, loud, and uncomfortable. Liberator crews constantly cussed the airplane but all of them loved and defended it at the same time. It had a reputation for toughness and the ability to get its crew home even after sustaining heavy battle damage. To its crew, those qualities meant more than anything else. For now, both men settled back to enjoy their coffee; each of them pulling their blankets just a bit tighter around them. They looked out over the gray of the ocean to where it met the gray of the sky and wondered what lay ahead.

Chapter 30

The last of the four propellers wound down. The absence of engine noise and vibration was dramatic after almost ten solid hours of a universe filled with it. Instead of the engine's roar the sounds that now filled the fuselage were those of the crew deplaning and the creaks and pops of hot metal cooling.

The B-24 Liberator is a large four engine bomber. The airplane is divided in half by its huge bomb bay. To move between the front of the airplane and the rear, crew members had to crawl through a tunnel across the bomb bay. The crew of the front half of the airplane entered and exited through a hatch in the nose gear wheel well.

Billy was the first one out of the plane as he had the least duties to perform once the aircraft landed. He was soon followed by the top gunner Harry Counts, also the crew chief and senior enlisted man on the crew. Together they made sure the wheels were properly chocked and the aircraft was properly secured on the ground.

It was great to be out of the airplane after all those hours, but after the warm sunny days in Bermuda, this was a real let down. Gray wet clouds scudded across the sky driven by a brisk wind. It wasn't really raining, but Billy soon discovered that just a few minutes outside in what was close to a mist and a guy would be damp to the bone. To make things worse, if he stepped off the tarmac he was standing ankle deep in mud.

The crew from the back of the plane came around the main landing gear and under the high wing to join him. Just then the rest of the crew including Lt. Raymond North, the aircraft commander and pilot and Lt. John Goodrich, the co-pilot and his sailing friend from Bermuda emerged from the front hatch. There weren't any smiling faces. It was obvious everyone missed Bermuda.

The aircraft was parked on a round pad well away from anything else. They followed a jeep with a 'Follow Me' sign across its rear window to the desolate spot. Billy hd just glimpsed the top of the jeep as it went out of sight behind a shallow rise. In that same direction he could see the top of the tower and some hangers. They were some distance away; it would be a long walk in this mud.

In the opposite direction from the buildings they could see Commander Nuessle's plane parked in a manner similar to their own. There were other Liberators in sight. All of them with canvas covers over their engines.

The whole crew looked around searching for some form of life out here and finding none. Everyone looked a bit bewildered, even Lt. North. Every time they had landed anywhere, at their home airfield or in transit, ground crew and some type of ground transport always met them on the tarmac. Being stranded like this was a first.

"Ain't this a fine kettle of fish?" Lee Merritt said. "I guess they've just gone off and forgot us. They expect us to hoof it all the way in carryin' all our gear and everything?" Merritt was always the first person to speak. In fact he talked almost constantly. "I say let's fire up R, and go pay them ole' boys a visit. What you say?" All the airplanes in the squadron were identified by letters, theirs was R.

"Belay that. Okay men, stay here, try to stay dry and make yourselves comfortable while I go see the commander," Lt. North said and then headed off at a trot, toward the squadron commander's aircraft a quarter of a mile away.

"I still say we ought," Merritt was cut off in mid-sentence by Lt. Goodrich. "Merritt, you heard the Lieutenant, now put a sock in it. Let's get as comfortable as we can while we wait for someone to pick us up."

There were a few grumbles, mostly from Merritt, but everyone did as they were ordered.

Billy made himself as comfortable as possible with his sea bag against the huge tire of the main landing gear. Several others followed his lead and they all sat down to await transport. At least they were relatively dry under the airplane.

Except for the wind, it was quiet here. There were rolling hills in all directions and all of them covered in green. As they had seen from the air, the entire countryside was arrayed in irregular squares and rectangles defined by hedgerows. Other than an occasional bird, they saw no movement anywhere.

"I thought this was a war zone?" It was Merritt again. "Pretty damn quiet war if you ask me."

"Nobody asked you Merritt, now shut the hell up," said Harry Counts.

"Aye, aye," was the response.

Harry Counts was an Aircraft Machinist Mate 1st Class. He was the ranking enlisted rating in the crew and as such was crew chief of the airplane. He was responsible for all the maintenance on the aircraft, all its systems, and the enlisted crewmen. As if this weren't enough, Harry Counts was the squadron boxing champion for the last four years running. When he talked, everyone listened, even Merritt. Harry could back up what he said in more ways than one.

All was quiet again for a few minutes, then, "I still say," it was Merritt again. A steely glare from Counts shut him up in mid-sentence.

"Merritt, if you say one more damn word I'm gonna kick your ass all the way to them buildings over there, have I made myself clear?"

"Aye," was the one word response.

This time there were a few chuckles from some of the others. After all Merritt was definitely asking for whatever he got at this point. Everyone knew that Merritt couldn't keep his mouth shut for any length of time, so they were looking forward to watching Harry kick his ass.

The tension was broken when Malounek said, "Here comes the Lieutenant."

They all turned to see Lt. North come jogging back.

"You men stay here, the commander and I will walk over to operations and get someone to come pick you up."

"Aye Aye, Sir," Lt. Goodrich said and saluted. Lt. North jogged off to catch up with Commander Nuessle, already walking in the direction of the tower.

Billy snuggled tighter against his sea bag and pulled his blue watch standers cap lower over his eyes. He was soon asleep as were most of the rest of the crew.

He dreamed of Sally. They were cruising along the coast in the Packard towing the Special on their way to the beach house. It was a beautiful sunny day. The top was down and they both wore sunglasses and were laughing. There was a horn honking somewhere. Billy couldn't figure out where it was coming from. Then someone kicked him in the foot.

Billy woke with a start. Everyone was standing up. Lt. North came driving up in a trunk honking his horn. As they were all piling in the back Billy saw another truck stopping at the commander's plane.

"Did they forget us Lieutenant?" Merritt asked and Harry instantly turned beet red. It looked like his eyeballs were going to pop out of his head. It was a good thing that Merritt wasn't within reach of Harry. Billy had no doubt that Harry would thump him like a ripe watermelon if he could get to him.

"Would you believe it's their tea time?" Lt. North said.

"What's tea time?" asked Merritt.

"It's their coffee break you idiot!" Harry seethed.

"Gee Harry do they get to drink coffee in the middle of a war?" Just as Harry was coiling to jump across the truck and strangle Merritt, Walter Brown, the radar operator laid a hand on Harry's shoulder.

"Harry, they might court marshal a guy for killing a defenseless ignoramus like him."

"Ignoramus? Hell, he's a genuine gross ignoramus. That's 144 times worse than your regular everyday ignoramus." Pawlye said and the whole bunch dissolved in laughter, even Harry after a short pause. The only one not laughing was Merritt. He looked around with a blank look on his face trying to figure out what had happened. The dumber Merrit looked, the more everyone laughed as they bounced across the grass to the nearest taxi-way.

Just then a brace of Spitfires roared across the field throttles firewalled, and with all eyes on them they pulled into a climbing turn, the lead airplane going into a victory roll.

Merritt had the last word after all. "Well I'll be damned, maybe it is a war zone."

Chapter 31

They parked the trucks at the operations building and the officers all went inside to secure temporary quarters for everyone. The men stayed in the trucks and took in the scene around them. They were at an airfield called St. Eval in Cornwall in southern England.

There was some activity at this place after all. As they watched, the two Spitfires they had seen flash across the field taxied up. Both airplanes were met by mechanics that chocked the wheels and then jumped up on the low wing to help the pilots out of the cramped cockpits. As graceful as the Spitfire looked in the air, it looked spindly and awkward on its narrow tracked landing gear.

The lead Spitfire had seven swastikas painted along the cockpit rail. The other had three. Both airplanes had black streaks along the leading edge of their wings where the muzzle blasts of their machine guns had burned the paint.

They watched the pilots climb out. Both were dressed in heavy sheepskin jackets and flying helmets. They wore heavy boots also lined in sheepskin. As they watched, both pilots and mechanics examined the rudder of the lead airplane. It was obvious, even from the truck that the rudder had several holes in it. Billy looked over both airplanes, several small patches were scattered over the fuselages and wings.

"Man, I sure would like to have one of them coats!" Merritt said. "I might could get warm in one of those." Everyone, even Harry, murmured their agreement. Actually, both bomber crews were a bit in awe of the two fighters and their pilots. After all, this was their first glimpse of someone that had actually been in combat, and from the looks of things, only minutes before they landed.

The spell broke when the group around the tail of the Spitfire dissolved. The senior pilot laughed and clapped the other one on the back. As they turned to walk into the operations building, they seemed to be aware of the men in the two trucks for the first time. As they walked into the building, they both smiled and waved, then they were gone.

"Man if I was flying one of those I'd," once more Merritt was cut off by Harry, even he had been awed by the up close look at the fighters and for the first time since landing addressed Merritt by his first name and without venom in his voice.

"Lee, if you'd been flying one of them Spitfires, some Jerry would be painting a little American flag on his cockpit rail and you'd be feeding the fish at the bottom of the English Channel." Both trucks dissolved in laughter and Merritt started to stammer how a great pilot like him could never lose to any Jerry.

Just then commander Nuessle and Lt. North appeared at the operations building entrance. They were accompanied by a British sergeant. All three of them smiled at the two truckloads of laughing men, but their facial expressions showed they had no idea what was going on.

"What's so funny Lieutenant?" Commander Nuessle asked.

"Just a short commentary on Merritt's abilities as a fighter pilot, sir." Lt. Goodrich replied.

"I didn't realize Merritt had any abilities as a fighter pilot?" Commander Nuessle said.

"Neither did we, sir, they only exist in his warped imagination, sir." Counts replied and both trucks erupted in laughter once again. Some of the men were laughing so hard they had tears in their eyes. It was as much a release of the tension from the long flight across the Atlantic as it was a response to Merritt's comments.

The officers stood there bewildered for a few minutes while everyone else continued to laugh. As the uproar began to subside, Commander Nuessle and Lt. North climbed into the cabs of the trucks, the British sergeant joining the commander. The engines started, gears clashed, and with a jerk that sent everyone grabbing for balance they lurched away through a maze of huts and outbuildings.

The streets, if you could call them that, were muddy rutted paths between rows of buildings. Most of the personnel they saw were British, but they did see a couple of American sailors walking down one of the streets, their dungaree pantlegs covered with mud. The sailors waved as they drove past.

The trucks stopped at a long low building crudely constructed out of rough sawn lumber and covered in black tar paper. It wasn't what anyone expected. England had conjured up images of quaint, but sturdy rock cottages with thick thatched roofs, not tar paper shacks. There were disappointed groans all around. The officers got out and told everyone to bring their gear inside.

Inside was even worse. There were rough sawn planks for a floor and the walls were exposed framing. It had obviously been hastily constructed. The lighting was a string of bare bulbs hanging from their wires down the middle of the hut. The only heat was a small peat-burning stove located near the door.

As the men came in, their smiles turned to frowns and scowls. It was almost like entering a damp cold cave. There were a few small windows but that was the only attempt to brighten the place up. The bunks were nothing more than a wooden frame that supported a latticework of rope and a straw mattress.

"It sure as hell ain't Bermuda," someone growled.

Commander Nuessle quickly recovered from his initial shock at the primitive conditions. "Men, gather up," he said.

The men gathered as he requested, but the grumbling continued.

"Men, this is Sergeant Brightly, he will be our liaison while we are at St. Eval. We will only be here a short time. We're waiting for the Air Corps to vacate the base at Dunkeswell where we'll be permanently stationed. While we're here, we'll be getting some additional training in aircraft identification, German fighter tactics, and aerial gunnery. I know these quarters aren't what any of us expected, but let's make the most of it while we're here. I'll be certain that we get moved to Dunkeswell as quickly as possible." What he didn't know was that in the beginning, Dunkeswell wouldn't be any better.

"Let's take the rest of today and tomorrow to get settled in. We'll begin our training day after tomorrow. The officers and I are quartered down the road a few miles. We're going to leave you with Sgt. Brightly for now, but we'll be back in the morning. Thank you all for your outstanding performance on the flight over," and with that the officers left.

Sergeant Brightly gave everyone a quick briefing on where everything was located on the base. There wasn't much to tell so it didn't take long.

"Breakfast at 0600 in the mess hall," he said and turned to leave.

"What's for breakfast, Sarge?" someone called.

Brightly turned back and with a forced smile said, "Boiled potatoes, of course," and left.

That was VB-105's introduction to England.

252

Once all of the VB-105 squadron aircraft arrived at St. Eval, intensive training for the coming mission began.

Up to this point in the war, none of the wing aircraft had had to contend with German fighters. They called the training 'fighter affiliation'. The Germans were employing several types of long range fighters in what would become Fleet Air Wing 7's area of operations, the English Channel, and especially the Bay of Biscay. Fleet Air Wing (FAW) 7 was the wing to which Billy's squadron, VB-105, was assigned.

U.S. Navy aircraft were assuming a major portion of the U-boat suppression mission, taking over from Army Air Corps B-24s that had been operating out of Dunkeswell for the past several months.

The mission was a simple one. The Wing's aircraft would fly solitary patrols over the Bay of Biscay searching for surfaced German submarines, commonly called U-boats. If one was found, it would be immediately attacked using depth charges, acoustically homing torpedoes, and machine guns.

At this point in the war, all German submarines were based on the French coast; the boats themselves were housed in huge steel reinforced concrete bunkers called 'pens'. The U-boat pens had enormously thick roofs that were bomb proof making the U-boats invulnerable while at their home base. Since 1939 the U-boats had extracted a terrible toll on the convoys that so far had kept England alive. In order for the U-boats to reach their hunting grounds in the Atlantic, they had to traverse the Bay of Biscay around the southern tip of England, or head north through the English Channel to the North Sea.

FAW 7's job was to patrol the Bay of Biscay route and even more important than attacking the few surfaced U-boats found, the constant pressure served to keep them submerged. The World War II era submarine was essentially a surface warship that could submerge for short periods of time while stalking and attacking its quarry. When submerged, the submarine operated on power supplied by large lead acid batteries very similar to an automobile battery only larger. When on battery power the sub's speed was cut to only two to three knots per hour. When free to operate on the surface using its powerful diesel engines the sub could make as much as 18 knots while also charging its batteries. By keeping the U-boats submerged, the time required to cross the bay was extended six to eight times. This decreased the time the submarine had to operate in its prime hunting area. It was also felt that spending so much time submerged under constant threat of attack took a heavy toll on the combat readiness of the sub's crews.

As pressure on the U-boats mounted and more and more of them were lost to the patrolling aircraft, the Germans did not sit idly by. Instead they deployed long-range fighter aircraft to escort U-boats in and out of their bases and to interdict the allied aircraft blockading their ports. The battleground was the Bay of Biscay.

The training while at St. Eval was intense. All aircrews were drilled on identification and recognition of enemy fighter aircraft. They would face primarily twin engine fighters, as the single engine types lacked the range to be truly effective over most of the Wing's patrol area.

Although the American crews didn't think much of their living quarters or the English food that consisted mostly of boiled potatoes, boiled cabbage, boiled carrots, occasionally boiled meat and weak tea, they paid close attention to what they had to say about the Germans. After all, the British had been fighting them for four years already.

The fighter types arrayed against the Americans consisted of Messerschmitt Me-110 (Bf-110), Me210, Me-410 and Junkers JU-88. Of these, the most prevalent and arguably the most dangerous was the JU-88 C6. The Americans discovered that this type carried a crew of three. It was also heavily armed with four fixed machine guns and up to three automatic cannons in the nose all firing forward. In addition, for defensive armament, it carried a pair of machine guns firing rearward from the aft cockpit plus another rearward firing machine gun in the belly of the plane. It had a range of over 1100 miles and its twin BMW engines could push it over 310 MPH. Not as fast as the best single engine fighters, but still over 30 MPH faster than the best a B-24 could manage. To make matters worse, the JU-88's usually operated in groups of six to twelve planes. Most of the time the German JU-88's would attack B-24's with at least a six to one advantage.

Besides the extensive lectures on fighter types, and the tactics they employed, many training flights were scheduled and a heavy emphasis was placed on aerial gunnery.

While all this time was called training, the deadly seriousness of their mission was driven home to all of them when one of their own failed to return from a training flight.

Billy was sitting on his bunk writing a letter to Sally. The door to the hut opened and closed, but Billy paid no attention. It was a rare break from training because their aircraft was grounded with an engine problem. While the ground crew worked on fixing the issue, the crew had some free time.

Billy finally realized that someone had come in the door and was now standing beside him. Billy looked up to find Walt Pawlyk next to his bunk with a completely blank look on his face as pale as a sheet.

Walt Pawlyk was a big strapping Polock from Philadelphia. He was the rear or stern gunner and had the bunk next to Billy's. They hung around together and since they were the two lowest ranking crew members, they pulled much of the same duty.

"What's wrong Walt? You look like you've seen a ghost," Billy said.

Walt didn't reply. Billy looked up again. "What's the matter Walt?"

Finally Walt responded, "Lt. Brown's plane is missing," he said.

Billy dropped his pen. "What? What do you mean his plane is missing?"

"Don just told me that 'O' crashed in the ocean at a place called Bude Bay." Don was Don Sweeney the bow gunner on 'P'. Letters identified all the squadron aircraft. Each aircraft had its own letter painted on each side of the fuselage. Billy and Walt's aircraft was 'R' for Ruth.

"What happened to them? Why'd they go down? Did anyone get out?" Billy asked, without pausing for a reply.

"I don't know." Walt said as he sat down on his bunk, the blank look still on his face.

"How did you find out? Are you sure?"

"Brightly told Lt. North. He said they got a radio message from a spotter on the coast. Claimed he saw them crash into the water. No survivors."

"Were they shot down? Did they have a mechanical problem?"

"I don't know Billy. From what I heard, no one does."

Billy sat in stunned silence, so did Walt. The reality of what they were doing started to creep in. They had always known it was dangerous, but this was too close to home. They saw those guys every day. They ate boiled potatoes with them in the mess hall. They played baseball with them. They went on liberty with them and now they were all gone, just like that, Billy thought. This morning they were here and now they were gone.

It took a long time before Billy could finish the letter. He tried not to let it affect him, but nothing would ever be the same again. As much as he tried to hide it, Sally would pick up on it immediately. She wouldn't know why, but there was a definite change in tone. He debated about telling her about it, but decided against it. No use in her getting upset he thought. As much as he tried, he would never be able to hide his feelings from her.

They never knew what happened to Lt. Brown's aircraft. There were no radio transmissions and no fighter activity reported in the area. There were many explanations, but few that met all the criteria. The popular theories were that it was pilot error or that the aircraft had experienced a catastrophic failure while operating at low altitude. Of course, there were a vocal few certain that German fighters had shot them down or that they were the victim of friendly fire. There was even a story floating around that 'O' had been the target of a Nazi secret weapon. No one would ever know for sure.

As the fall progressed, their time at St. Eval was almost over. Their sister squadron, VB-103, had already moved on to Dunkeswell. The Air Corps was pulling out as quickly as possible. As soon as they left, VB-105, Billy's squadron, would be moving in and assuming anti-submarine patrols over the Bay. Everyone was anxious to move on. There was nothing at St. Eval that endeared it to anyone.

As much as the British military tried to be good hosts, there was still friction. Many of the English soldiers were resentful of the American's money and most of all, their attitude. In their eyes, the Americans came to their country and immediately took over, seeing everything as belonging to them including all the young women. They were grateful for the American's help, but wished they would act more as guests instead of owners.

Chapter 33

Dunkeswell looked like a page out of National Geographic magazine. It was the prototypical English village complete with stone cottages with thatched roofs surrounded by stone fences and hedgerows. Even this time of year there was still an amazing amount of green. There weren't streets like Billy was used to back home in Texas or San Diego, but instead there were lanes not much larger than a path. The word that came to mind was quaint.

Of course, National Geographic pictures were usually taken on bright sunshiny days. Those were in decidedly short supply at Dunkeswell. It seemed that there was nearly constant drizzle if not a downpour. The wind would whip the drizzle into almost a solid wall of water. There was simply no way to stay dry. The ground was perpetual mud. It was so bad that it quickly earned the base the nickname of Mudville Heights.

What made matters even worse was that the living conditions were even more deplorable than at St. Eval. It was true culture shock for the officers. At St. Eval while the enlisted men were quartered in the hastily constructed huts, the officers were housed eight miles down the road at the Trevelque Hotel. They lived in comparative luxury that even included daily maid service. That was the tradition of their British hosts. In the British military, officers lived a life of luxury while the enlisted ranks barely existed.

At Dunkeswell, a totally American base, it was an entirely different matter. All personnel were quartered in damp and drafty Nissen huts. There weren't enough huts, so conditions were very crowded. There was next to no heat. The conditions made it nearly impossible to get dry and comfortable. Officers and enlisted alike shared the same conditions.

To compound matters, there was an extreme shortage of the simple things in life. The plumbing was extremely primitive. There was a shortage of water even though tons of it fell from the sky every day. Showers became a treat. There was no toilet paper. Instead there was something that the men referred to as laminated wood on rolls stamped as Government Property. It, like everything else furnished by the British, was substandard in American minds.

The only saving grace was that this was a U.S. Navy base and they didn't have to contend with the British military. The Navy cooks produced food far superior in both quality and quantity to any they had experienced at St. Eval and it was much more to the liking of the American palate.

They still were inadequately equipped for the weather. Few of the crews had warm flying clothes. Even so, they began to fly missions over the bay almost immediately.

Something else, which began almost immediately, was confrontation with enemy fighters. On their fourth day at Dunkeswell, while on patrol one of the squadron aircraft was attacked by six German JU-88s. As they had been instructed in their training, the Liberator crew escaped into a cloudbank, but it was a sobering experience for everyone.

The crews were flying missions every other day. The missions usually lasted twelve hours or more, virtually all of it spent flying over open ocean at low altitude. They quickly learned to love bad weather as German fighters rarely operated in marginal weather conditions, and in the marginal visibility, their radar gave them a good chance to surprise a surfaced U-boat.

Two days after their first encounter with German fighters and only their sixth day flying operational patrols, the squadron lost two more aircraft and crews. Lt. Evert's aircraft failed to return from a patrol over the Bay of Biscay. No radio signals were ever received, but all assumed German fighters had taken their toll. Another Liberator crashed on takeoff, killing all on board. After arriving in England only three weeks earlier with fifteen aircraft, the squadron was already down to twelve with thirty crewmen killed.

It was late evening. Billy and his crew had just returned from patrol. Everyone was dead tired. They stopped by the mess hall where they gorged on meatloaf and mashed potatoes washed down with fresh milk.

They returned to their hut where Billy collapsed on his bunk after changing into some clean dungarees. He had new letters from Sally and Carl. It was a good day. He devoured Sally's letter. It was great to get a letter from her, she was always upbeat and he could see her beautiful face and feel her presence as he read. As great as it was, there was still something that bothered him just a bit. Try as he might, he still couldn't put his finger on it, but something wasn't quite right. It was almost like she was writing in a vacuum, like she had never received his letters at all. He wondered if there was some problem with the mail. After all, she was still living with Carl and the Babe in San Diego and they certainly wrote like they had been getting his mail. It was curious. He moved on to Carl's letter.

Carl had more details on the Special. Other than details on Babe's activities, his letters mostly concerned the Special. Billy loved that. The Special served as his escape. He could immerse himself in details of the car. The engineering details, improvements he wanted to make, how one change might affect other aspects of the car. He visualized each detail of the Special and how he could change things to enhance its performance and comfort.

Carl was working on making the car street legal. He was adding all the things necessary for street operation. Things like headlights and taillights. Billy and Carl discussed these items over and over. They both wanted to put the car on the street, but they wanted the parts added to look like they belonged there, not added as some afterthought.

The headlights were a case in point. Since his first thought of the Special, he was committed to making it as streamlined as possible. He had two reasons for this. The easier the car passed through the air, the faster it could go with the same amount of power. The other reason was that a streamlined car just looked better to his eye and he subscribed to the old adage that if it looked good, it probably was.

He was so lost in his day dream that he never heard the car drive up and stop on the street outside. A short time later there was a knock on the door to the hut.

Walt was lying on the bunk beside Billy's reading a Dick Tracy comic book for the hundredth time. He jumped to his feet at the sound of the knock. He couldn't remember anyone ever knocking on the door before. Billy was so lost in his letter, he hardly noticed Walt getting up. Several of the other guys looked up as Walt went to the door.

Harry watched Walt open the door. He heard a murmur from outside, but from his vantage point he couldn't tell that Walt said a word. Instead Walt turned and looked at Billy with that same blank look on his face that he had the day Lt. Brown was lost. Walt turned back to the door, then back to stare at Billy again. The third time he did that it was more than Harry could take.

"What's wrong Walt?" he said and started to get up and head toward the door.

Billy finally looked up toward Walt.

When Walt saw Billy look up he said, "It's her."

Billy looked puzzled, "What?" he asked.

"It's her," was the reply.

Billy put down the letter and stood up. "What are you talking about?" Walt just stared at him then turned back to the door.

Billy walked over and looked over Walt's shoulder out the door. He wasn't prepared for what he saw. He would forever think that his heart stopped at that exact moment and when it finally started again, it was like the trip hammer of all trip hammers going off in his chest.

The person standing in the door was Sally.

Chapter 34

Billy was certain he had lost his mind, the vision before him certainly looked like Sally. As soon as his body would respond to commands, he flew past Walt sending him spinning almost to the floor and causing such a commotion that everyone else in the hut rushed to the door. One of the guys had been playing with a yo-yo that went skittering across the floor, tripping a late arrival and adding to the pandemonium.

As Billy cleared the door, Sally leapt into his arms. They hugged each other so tight they almost stopped each other's breathing, or so it seemed. Then came the kisses and the tears.

Billy lifted Sally's feet off the ground and swung her around laughing, kissing and crying all at the same time. He could smell her, the faint sweetness of her perfume; he could feel her warmth and the firm swell of her breasts against his chest, the flare of her hips. He reveled in every inch of her and she in him. It was the most joyous moment of his life. At this instant nothing else in the world existed for them, only each other.

"How did you get here?" he asked, totally at a loss.

She smothered him with more kisses. "Does it matter?"

"No." Questions and answers were replaced with "I love you."

Behind them, the doorway was filled with the faces of the crew. They had all seen pictures of Sally and more than a few harbored secret crushes. All would agree that even the best picture didn't come close to doing her justice. There were smiles, laughs and more than a few slack jaws and wide eyes from the crew. Walt just kept mumbling "It's her" over and over, the blank look still on his face. He was pushed aside and nearly fell once more by others wanting a better look.

Billy still couldn't believe it. Until two minutes ago, he wondered if he would ever see Sally again. Now she was in his arms, or was it just a dream? If it was, it was the most realistic one he'd ever had. Nothing had ever felt as good as Sally's body pressing against his.

As lost as he was in Sally's sudden appearance and in all the hugs and kisses, he finally realized that his whole crew and several passersby were having great sport watching them.

"Is that your car?" he asked Sally indicating a Ford sedan parked in the street.

"Yes," was the reply sandwiched between another barrage of kisses.

"Let's go," he said, pulling Sally to the car door. They got in as if they were one person, neither of them wanting to lose contact with the other. Billy slid behind the wheel. As they drove away sliding in the mud of the street, a group of sailors overflowed out of the hut and watched them until they turned out of sight.

"How did you get here? I want to be sure I'm not dreaming."

"I came over with the USO show."

"How did you do that?"

"Baby, I grew up in LA, remember? My family is rich. We know all the right people, all the society types in California, which means we know all the show business people. All it took was a few phone calls." She was beaming, very proud of herself and thrilled to be with her love once more.

"How did you know where to find me?" he asked clearly baffled.

Sally chuckled. "The Fultons."

"Ken and Melba? How could they know where I was?"

"Well, my dear, it turns out they have a nephew, Sonny Cunningham is his name. Would you believe Sonny is an Admiral? All it took was an invitation to dinner, a little vino, an hour in the hot tub and I knew all about Fleet Air Wing 7." Sally was still plastered against his side.

"You got an admiral in the hot tub?"

"Oh yeah, we had suits on, of course."

"Of course," Billy replied. "You didn't bat those blue eyes at him did you?"

"Why no! You don't think I would do something like that do you? And to an admiral?" she said, her voice full of mock indignation. They both laughed.

Billy drove out past the supply dump. Here the road ended at a hedgerow in a clump of trees. It was about as private a place as there was on the base. While Sally could leave anytime she wanted, the enlisted personnel were restricted to the base without a pass. The Shore Patrol was responsible for base security, but they rarely came by this area. There simply was nothing here of importance to protect. They spent most of their time guarding the aircraft and armaments. Billy and Sally were especially grateful that this part of the base held nothing of interest as their focus was totally on each other.

Chapter 35

It was dark as Billy started the car. Even though he had spent the last hour inside it, this was his first conscious thought about it. "Where'd you get the Ford?"

"I bought it last week in London. I wanted a Packard, but there weren't any to be had. This will work out fine. I don't think we'll be driving that much anyway.

"How long can you stay?"

"I'm here till you leave." Sally replied.

"How can you do that, hon? Aren't you with a USO show?"

"I was. We toured bases around England and the rest of the show left for the States yesterday. I stayed behind. I thought we could go home together."

"I'm ready. Unfortunately, I think Uncle Sam has other ideas. Where are you going to stay?"

"For right now, I've taken a room in the village with a Mrs. Driver. I only just met her today. She's so sweet. She said there might be a cottage available I could rent. Can you spend the night with me?"

Billy looked troubled. "I don't know. Usually we can't get off base at night without a pass. We fly every other day and I flew today, so I'm off tomorrow. Let's drive back to the hut and I'll ask Harry what he thinks."

"Who's Harry?"

"Harry Counts, Aircraft Machinist Mate 1st Class Harold Counts. He's the crew chief for our airplane. He's the ranking enlisted man on the crew. He'll know what to do."

He stopped the car outside the hut. The car slid in the mud even though they were going quite slow.

"Is it always so muddy here?" Sally asked.

Billy laughed. "Yeah, it is, it hasn't dried out since we've been here. Mud's always ankle deep, in fact we call the place 'Mudville Heights'," they both laughed.

"From what I've seen so far, I think the name is appropriate." Sally said, "and besides all that, it's cold here too!"

"I've been cold since I got here. Fly all day in a tropic weight jacket and then come home to a cold hut."

"Why don't you wear your leather jacket?" Sally asked.

"What leather jacket?"

"The ones all you flyboys look so dashing in, of course."

"Honey, we don't have any leather jackets. You just sit tight while I go visit with Harry for a couple minutes." Billy left Sally in the car with the heater running. So far as he knew inside the Ford was the warmest, driest place on the base.

Sally couldn't believe Billy didn't have a warm jacket for flying. How could that be? Didn't the Navy understand it was cold and damp here all the time? She was outraged. How could the Navy expect people to risk their lives without proper equipment? She wondered what she could do about that. It was already dark and she was glad Billy left the heater running.

A band of yellow light fell across the car as the door to the hut opened and Billy came out followed by what could only be described as a fire plug of a man made all the more evident when compared to the long and lanky Billy. After all, Billy made everyone look short.

As the two men got in the car, Billy said, "Sally, this is Harry Counts, he's going with us to see the skipper."

"Hello Harry, nice to meet you."

"It's my pleasure Miss Anthony."

Sally thought two things, despite his looks, Harry was a very polite man and she was surprised he knew her last name.

"Call me Sally, please, and by the way Harry, how did you know my last name?"

"Yes Ma'am, whatever you say ma'am, me and the boys, well we know all about you."

Sally sat back and looked at Billy with arched eyebrows. "Oh you do, do you? And how do you know that?"

Billy blushed although no one could tell in the dark. "It's not what you think, hon. Some of the guys saw your picture and wanted to know about you. Really, it's almost like you're a part of the crew. The guys are always asking about you."

"That's a fact ma'am. In fact, I think a few of the guys might even have a crush on you, ma'am, but Billy, he never shares anything of a personal nature so to speak." Harry didn't add that he was one of those that had a secret crush. She was even lovelier in person than in any of the pictures. Now Harry was afraid he said too much and might even have gotten Billy in trouble. "What I meant to say ma'am, was that Billy, well he, well uh, he ain't never shared anything voluntary like. We, uh, I mean the boys, they have to beg him. Why, it's like you're everyone's sister or somethin'."

"Harry, could we change the subject?" Billy asked.

"Now don't be getting on Harry. I think it's sweet." It was Sally's turn to blush. At that moment she felt unworthy. She couldn't believe it. Here was an entire airplane crew that every other day, as regular as clockwork, flew out into harm's way and they were begging for scraps of news about her? Why? Other than Harry five minutes ago, she had never met any of them. She never considered anything like this. The only person she thought would even know she was in England was Billy. Now it seemed she had an entire fan club she never knew about. Her heart swelled with gratitude towards these brave men. She made herself a promise that whatever she could do to make their lives better, she would. She looked out the side window so that Billy and Harry couldn't see the tears in her eyes.

They drew up to another set of huts, very much like the one the crew shared. "Honey, why don't you stay in the car while Harry and I visit with the skipper?" Sally nodded her assent, not trusting herself to say anything afraid her voice would betray the emotional upheaval going on inside her.

Billy once more left the car running so that the heater worked. They were gone maybe ten minutes when the door to the hut opened and Billy and Harry came out accompanied by three other men. Several others took quick peeks out the door then shut it.

The group walked around to Sally's side of the car and leaned against the door. Sally rolled down the window. Billy made introductions all around. The men were Lieutenants Ray North and John Goodrich, the pilots of Billy's plane and Ensign Vic D'Harlingue, the navigator. These three plus Billy and Harry were the 'front half' crew of Billy's Liberator, separated from the other five men by the massive bomb bay. Harry being the crew chief also manned the top turret just behind the flight deck when at battle stations.

As nose gunner, Billy was part of this group. The nose gunner also assisted the crew chief with keeping the aircraft flying and all the systems operating properly when not at battle stations manning the guns in the nose turret. Billy was chosen for this role despite his size which was a major detriment in the cramped confines of the turret, but this was more than offset by his depth of knowledge of the Liberator from his time at Consolidated. Coupling this knowledge with his innate mechanical ability and he was a natural. He also consistently made the best scores at aerial gunnery. Not a bad thing considering that current German fighter tactics favored head-on attacks. Many Liberators currently in service were still without nose turrets, leaving them more vulnerable to this type of attack.

"Miss Anthony, I insisted that Billy introduce me. We all thought he'd been trying to fool us about your existence. It was even money with the crew that he just carried around some movie starlet's picture." Lieutenant North said with a chuckle poking fun at Billy.

"Don't listen to Ray, Sally. He's as jealous of Billy as the rest of us are. Not only are you the most beautiful woman I've ever met, but you came all the way to England in the middle of a war just to be with him. I'm more jealous of him than ever. Never the less, we're all delighted that you're here." John Goodrich said with a big grin.

It was obvious to Sally that this was a close knit group and that despite their differences in rank all liked and respected each other. She felt honored to be in their presence, and immediately she began to feel a part of this family of men.

The visit only lasted a couple of minutes. Harry got back in the car with Billy and they drove back to the crew hut where Harry got out, still calling Sally 'ma'am'. She realized he had never addressed her by anything other than Miss Anthony or ma'am. What an incongruous man she thought. He looked like he could chew up an anvil and spit out nails, yet he had been polite to a fault with her, almost embarrassed to be in her presence.

After Harry left and they were alone again, Billy explained what happened. "The skipper gave me a 24 hour pass. We're good till tomorrow evening. He said we would talk about things when I get back."

"What did he mean by that?" Sally asked.

"Well, I think he wants to know how long you're going to be in England? And then if you intend to stay at Dunkeswell all that time."

"Darling, I intend to stay here as long as you do. That's my plan. Pretty simple isn't it?"

"It sounds good to me except for one thing."

"Oh?"

"Sally, England isn't all that safe. The Luftwaffe could attack this base anytime. The village is so close it could be dangerous."

"Not as dangerous as flying over the ocean looking to pick a fight with any Germans that come along." Sally challenged.

Billy couldn't think of an effective argument, so he didn't say anything. He certainly wasn't going to spoil this night by arguing over the fact that she was here. Even though he knew there was some danger, he was thrilled beyond words to be with her.

"Oh, there is one more thing you need to know." Sally said.

"What's that, hon?"

"Mrs. Driver is a little straight laced. I decided to make things simple; I told her you were my husband."

Chapter 36

Much to Billy's surprise the skipper, Lt. North, told him that he could stay off base with Sally as long as he was on time for all his assignments. That was even better than he could have expected. Sally of course, was thrilled beyond words. She was already beginning to think of the crew as 'family'.

They were in a big feather bed in Mrs. Driver's spare bedroom. It was their second night together since Sally arrived. Billy was more comfortable than he had been since arriving in England.

"This bed is really something. It's so warm!" he said.

"Speaking of warm, why don't you have one of those heavy leather flying jackets?"

"Beats me. We're the only Naval Air unit in Europe. The skipper thinks it's a bureaucratic snafu. He thinks they simply didn't think we would need cold weather gear until the winter. Then you couple that with the normal shortages and red tape and it all adds up to no jackets."

"So how do you stay warm?"

"For the most part we don't. We've been taking blankets and we wrap up in those as much as we can. That helps. Of course, I can't really use one inside the turret."

"Why not?"

"It's just too cramped, I'm afraid it would jam something and that's the last thing I need. At best a jam would lock me in the turret; at worst it could prevent me from firing my guns when we need them the most."

"It could lock you in the turret? What does that mean?"

"You can only get in and out of the turret when it is pointed straight ahead. Once the turret turns to one side or the other, the edge of the turret covers the entrance. It's like a ball sitting in a cup. There's a small hole in the ball and that's where I get in. If the ball moves, the hole moves with it, then I can't get out."

As Sally was digesting this information, the realization sank in. What happened if the turret was damaged?

"What happens if you get locked in the turret and you need to bail out or the airplane has to ditch in the ocean?"

Billy was silent. Sally waited. "Well?" she said.

Billy shrugged his shoulders and Sally burst into tears, burying her face in his shoulder. Billy tried his best to console her.

"Sally, don't worry, nothing like that's going to happen. I haven't heard of that happening even once to anyone."

It seemed to have no effect. After a while she quit sobbing and clung to him, and then she reached over and turned off the lamp. She held him all night.

Early the next morning Billy left for the base. She insisted that he take the car. After he had left, she joined Mrs. Driver for a cup of tea and a muffin.

"Mrs. Driver, I need to buy some warm flying jackets. Do you have any idea where I might find them?"

"How many do you need?" Mrs. Driver asked, somewhat surprised at the question.

"I need ten, no make that eleven," after all she needed one for herself.

"Oh dear, so many?"

"Yes, I'm afraid so."

"Let's go visit Mr. Faulkenwell. He knows about such things. After all, his son was a pilot."

"Was?"

"Oh dear. Yes, he was, he was shot down over three years ago when Jerry was attacking us every day."

Sally was silent and stared out the small window toward the airbase where the tip of a Liberator tail was just visible over the trees.

Mr. Faulkenwell was a very nice man who lived alone just down the lane from Mrs. Driver's cottage. Sally thought he showed no sign of his loss. That was remarkable. She explained what she needed and why.

"You need them straightaway then," he said.

"Yes sir, as soon as I can get them."

"There's a man in Exeter that makes flying coats for the RAF. I don't know if he makes any in the Yank pattern, but we can go see."

"There's no need for you to go. I can find my way I'm sure."

"Oh, I never doubted you could find your way. You seem a very competent young woman. But I know the man. We may have to twist his arm to get the coats as soon as you want them."

"I would certainly be grateful for your help. I will pay for your time."

"Don't be silly young lady. After all, your husband and his crew are here to help us fight the Hun are they not?"

"Yes they are."

"Then anything I can do to help is well worth it. Tried to enlist you know, but even Winston doesn't want anyone as old as me."

"You're not old!"

"My dear, Martha never warned me you were such a flirt." He said. They all chuckled, and then they were off to Exeter in Mr. Falkenwell's old Bentley Saloon.

The building was a large stone barn set on the edge of a pasture. As they parked the car, Sally saw there was an enormous wooden water wheel extending from the side of the building and into a mill race. It turned slowly with a rhythmic beat and splash.

They walked in the open double doors on the end of the building. There was a flatbed truck parked outside along with a small sedan and a large cluster of bicycles.

Sally wasn't prepared for the sight that greeted them. The smell of leather totally overwhelmed them. The chatter of heavy sewing machines was incessant. All the machines were driven by a series of wide belts affixed to shafts and pulleys suspended from

267

the exposed rafters of the roof. Several women sat at the machines and stitched continuously on great piles of brown shearling. There were a couple of boys pulling carts of shearling hides and completed coats in between the aisles of machines. A large loft that at one time stored hay, but now held more hides than Sally had ever seen, all banded together in waist high bales and the bales stacked three high.

Mr. Faulkenwell introduced Sally to the owner of the business, a Mr. Wilkerson. After a brief exchange of pleasantries, Mr. Wilkerson got down to business. Somehow Sally knew that he rarely wasted a minute or a motion.

"So what can I do for you Mrs. Pendleton?"

"I need some flying jackets, Mr. Wilkerson."

"How many?"

"Eleven."

"And when might you need them?"

"Today," Sally replied.

There was a momentary pause. Obviously Mr. Wilkerson was not prepared for such a request.

"Today? Really, Mrs. Pendleton, you can't be serious can you?"

"Mr. Wilkerson, when could you deliver them if not today?" she asked.

"Oh, I should say I could deliver them by next spring."

There was another brief pause.

"Mr. Wilkerson, my husband," Sally continued the charade she started with Mrs. Driver since she saw little reason not to, "and his crew are here in England to help defend you and all other Englishmen against that Nazi madman, Adolph Hitler. They have been shipped here from Bermuda with only tropical weight clothing. Every day they fly 12-hour patrols over the Bay of Biscay and they are reduced to wrapping themselves in blankets to stay warm. My husband can't get in his turret wrapped up in a blanket." Tears began to well in her eyes. "They have no idea when they might be properly equipped, but until then they freeze everyday so that you might stay here and run what appears to be a very prosperous business. Yes, Mr. Wilkerson, I need the coats today."

Mr. Wilkerson and Mr. Faulkenwell were both somewhat taken aback. Neither of them had any experience dealing with such a forceful, plainspoken woman.

"Mrs. Pendleton, I only make Irvin style jackets. That is the style worn by the RAF. I doubt that they would be acceptable to American forces."

Sally was prepared for this as Mr. Faulkenwell already told her that Mr. Wilkerson only made coats for the RAF. She had been in England long enough and visited enough military bases to have seen many examples of both types.

"Mr. Wilkerson, if you would simply leave the waist belt off and replace it with a small attached belt and buckle on each side of the waist, I'm sure they will be more than sufficient."

"Mrs. Pendleton, my hides are a different color than the Americans use," Mr. Wilkerson protested.

"Mr. Wilkerson, these brave men are freezing every day. They are going in harm's way for you. I'm sure that the color of their jacket doesn't mean very much if it keeps them warm."

He knew he was defeated. He couldn't think of a single rational argument to refute any of the things she said.

"Do you have sizes?" he said in complete submission.

"I do."

"Then let's get to it, shall we?"

Chapter 37

Billy and the rest of the crew collapsed on their bunks after their de-briefing session. Some de-brief Billy thought; took off in a seriously overloaded aircraft filled with high explosives and aviation gasoline, flew twelve hours over the ocean, saw absolutely zero, and then landed still filled with said high explosives. Froze our asses off the whole time. End of story.

On one hand, he was frustrated with their mission so far, but on the other, he was thrilled with the prospect of seeing Sally again. John, that was Mr. Goodrich, his co-pilot, had taken Billy aside and told him that the skipper decided to let Billy stay off base as much as possible. They would work out something for emergency situations.

Billy thanked him over and over. He really hadn't expected any consideration like that. John told him that the effort Sally went to just to be with him had impressed everyone, even Commander Nuessle. Billy was stunned to hear that the squadron commander knew about his situation. Still he was thankful for their decision. He knew he was lucky to be in such an outfit.

Even as he was thinking these thoughts, he heard a car pull up and stop on the street outside the hut. He couldn't keep the grin off his face. As he got up and headed toward the door, every eye in the hut was on him.

He opened the door and stepped outside. Sure enough it was Sally in the Ford sedan. She opened the door and got out before he could walk the three steps to her door. This confused him momentarily. He expected her to stay in the car while he collected his things for the night.

"I have some good news," he said, the confusion still apparent on his face. Even more so now that Sally walked around to the trunk, or boot as they called it here in England.

"Oh? What would that be darling?" she said just before embracing him for a long and very satisfying kiss.

"The skipper says I can stay off base as much as possible as long as you're here."

"Wonderful!" That led to another long embrace.

"I've got some good news too." Sally said.

"What's that?"

Sally reached down and opened the trunk lid. It rose on its springs revealing the pile of shearling jackets. The new leather smell was almost overpowering.

Billy's eyes were almost the size of saucers. "Where did you get these!??!" he asked as he ran his hands over the smooth leather and fluffy pile.

"Try this one on," and she pulled the top one from the pile. It fit him perfectly.

"Wow! This thing fits great!" Billy was not used to trying on clothes that fit. All his life he had been too tall for anything 'off the rack' to fit. "This thing is like putting on a heat wave!"

Sally was beaming. "I know the color is wrong."

"Who cares! It's warm! I love it." Then he looked at her with a hopeful look on his face. "Are these," he indicated the rest of the jackets, "for the rest of the guys?"

"They sure are." Sally was obviously pleased with herself.

"How did you do this? Did you steal them?" he laughed.

"I'm not sure Merry Old England is ready for an American girl like me."

"I know they aren't, but I sure am!" and Billy grabbed her and lifted her completely off the ground swinging her around. "Come on, we're going to introduce you to the rest of the crew," as he dragged her to the door of the hut.

Billy opened the door and stuck his head in to make sure everyone was still dressed. Normally they were, it was too cold not to be. Most everyone looked up when the door opened. Billy had his new jacket on. Eyes were already going wide. "Hey everyone! I have someone I want you to meet." He pulled Sally inside, "This is Sally Anthony, my girl from California."

Those not already standing jumped to their feet. They would have been thrilled to meet anyone from home, but to meet a young woman as beautiful as Sally was a treat no matter where she was from.

Billy introduced her to each enlisted member of the crew. The officers were all in their own hut, of course. Billy's jacket was getting almost as many envious looks as Sally. Several of the crew asked where he got it. As soon as all the introductions were made, Billy asked everyone to come outside. He led the way around to the trunk of the Ford.

Once everyone was around the back of the car, he reached down and opened the trunk lid.

"Look at that will you!"

"Man oh man! Jackets!"

"Son of a bitch!"

"Whoopee!"

"These are presents from Sally guys!"

Then there were a chorus of thank you's followed by hugs and laughter and guys trying on jackets. It was like Christmas for the whole crew. Meeting Sally and getting new jackets, something everyone wanted and truly needed, it was definitely Christmas even though it was only October.

Sally had the officer's jackets in a separate bundle. She also had her own which she now put on to the applause and wolf whistles of the crew. There was so much commotion that other hut doors were opening and more than a few onlookers were beginning to congregate.

Every member of the crew personally thanked Sally and was rewarded with a hug. It was time to move on. Everyone was a little self-conscious of the attention they were getting from the other crews.

271

Billy and Sally got in the Ford and drove off. Several members of the crew were still in the street showing off their new jackets to the crowd.

"You're going to the officer's hut, right?"

"Sure thing, baby. You've really made some guys happy. How did you manage to do this, really?"

Sally gave him a brief history on how she got the jackets.

"You really are something. Poor Mr. Wilkerson never had a chance did he?'

"Nope," as she snuggled close.

They were at the officer's hut. Billy stopped the car. They got out and knocked on the door. John Goodrich opened the door. Billy had the package of jackets in his arm.

"Good evening sir. Sally has a present for you, the skipper and Mr. D'Harlingue," and he handed the package to John. By then the skipper and Vic were at the door. It was a repeat of the celebration from a few minutes earlier.

The officers thanked Sally profusely. "I hope the color will be okay," she said. The jackets were a reddish brown and the pile was a similar color. American B-3 jackets were a dark chocolate brown with a cream color shearling.

"Miss Anthony, the color is fine. I really don't know how to thank you. The Wing commander has been trying to get jackets for everyone ever since we got here. I think he's ready to personally hijack a supply truck if he has to," he laughed. "Believe me, no one will complain about the color."

They had a short visit; all of them wearing their new jackets. After more thanks and brief hugs, they drove off to Mrs. Driver's. For most of the crew, it was the most enjoyable night they had spent in England.

They were busy doing the preflight check of the airplane. The entire crew was outfitted in their new jackets, their pride in them obvious. Everyone was taking special care not to get the jackets dirty or mar them in any way.

Billy was checking the nose landing gear. The hatch where he entered the airplane was in the nose gear wheel well, so it only made sense that he inspect the gear. He finished and squatted back out of the wheel well. He was surprised to find the rest of the crew clustered around the nose waiting on him. As soon as he stood up, the skipper stepped forward.

"Billy, the crew has asked me to act as their spokesman. We're all very appreciative of what Sally has done. It's amazing that a single lady thousands of miles from home was able to accomplish in one day what the Department of the Navy has been unable to do in two months. The men wish to express their gratitude by naming our aircraft in her honor. With your permission and hers of course, we'd like to name the ship *California Girl*."

Billy was momentarily stunned. Then he broke out in a huge grin, "I think she would be honored, guys." Handshakes and slaps on the back were exchanged all around. "And one more thing, the guys would like to paint a picture of Sally on the nose. Again, if Sally and you approve" Lt. North said.

"Billy, we'll hire a real artist to do it, we've already taken up a collection from everyone to pay for it," Harry said.

"I'll ask her tonight guys. I'm sure she'll approve."

"Okay, men, let's get aboard and get on patrol." Across the field, other Liberators were firing up their engines. The ground crew was already pushing the engines through, a task made necessary by the radial design of the engines. They had to make sure that the oil in the cylinders was dissipated; otherwise it was possible to hydraulic lock an engine with disastrous results.

Soon they were in the airplane and queued up waiting their turn to begin the takeoff run. The takeoff was part of the flight they all dreaded. There was significant risk during this time. The aircraft was loaded to the max with weapons and fuel. They were carrying 8800 pounds of high explosives and 2700 gallons of high-octane aviation gasoline. They were a gigantic rolling bomb rushing headlong down the runway, all four Pratt and Whitney R-1830 engines with throttles firewalled. Despite their power, the engines strained to the limit to accelerate the 60,000 pounds of aircraft to flying speed. To make matters worse, right in the middle of the takeoff run there was a significant dip where the two runways crossed. Everyone on board held their collective breaths while encountering the dip. Liberators had a reputation for the landing gear, especially the nose wheel, being weak. It wasn't unheard of for the nose gear, especially, to collapse. VB-105 had already lost one aircraft and crew to the combination of weak nose gear, overload, and dip. Finally the newly named California Girl lumbered into the air almost to the end of the runway, and cleared the hedgerow marking the edge of the field with only feet to spare.

Everyone on board breathed a sigh of relief. The tension of takeoff was many times the most stressful part of the mission. Other than flying into a gaggle of German fighters, it was the most dreaded event of the day.

Lt. North throttled back slightly and began the climb to altitude. Normally they traversed land at three to five thousand feet. Once they were over water and had reached their patrol sector, they flew low, rarely over 200 feet. They did this for several reasons, but the primary one was to increase the possibility of surprising a U-boat on the surface. The submarine would get no advance warning of their presence. By the time they could be heard, they would already be in sight of their prey. While it was true that flying higher would have given them a larger visual search area, they carried search radar that could detect anomalies on the surface at longer range.

Once over water, the gunners became more alert. The threat from enemy fighters was a very real one. German JU-88's had been known to operate everywhere in their operational area once they were over water. The Liberators search radar only

273

worked for surface contacts, it was useless against aerial targets. This left them with their only warning of enemy fighters as the old Mark I human eyeball. Everyone was equipped with binoculars to enhance the ability of their Mark I's. As soon as they were over water, they had seven pairs in constant action searching for threats and targets.

Boredom and keeping their aircraft in the air were as big a risk as enemy activity. The Liberator could be a cantankerous airplane. Besides the landing gear, it had other issues such as the famous Davis wing, named for its inventor. Although it generated great amounts of lift, under the extreme load conditions they flew under, it twisted and increased drag to the point their cruise speed could be reduced by 15% or more. The airplane was very heavy on the controls sometimes requiring the combined strength of both pilot and co-pilot to complete a maneuver. To make matters worse, the airplane was also unstable. When heavily loaded, as they almost always were, the wingtips twisted reducing aileron effectiveness. Add to all this the further complication that they had to constantly transfer fuel from one tank to another to satisfy the thirst of the four engines. It wasn't uncommon for an engine to starve for fuel and cease running even when plenty of gasoline was on board.

It was a dreary day. The ceiling was low and once more the whole world was shades of gray. The dirty gray of the cloud cover and the blue gray of the ocean merged so that they almost seemed one. The sea was covered in frothy white caps. Intermittently they ran through patches of mist. It was cold. The entire crew reveled in their new shearling flight jackets. Everyone that had seen them was envious. They were the talk of the base.

For three hours they maintained their solitary patrol, flying very low over the rough sea. All hands maintained vigilance for enemy fighters, but they had already learned that the much-feared Junkers were seldom seen in such bad weather conditions.

Then the intercom crackled in everyone's headset. "Skipper, I've got a surface contact to port, range 3000 yards." It was Aircraft Radio Mate 1st Class Walt Brown, the crew's radar operator. The Sperry search radar was a dome mounted on the aircraft's belly that replaced the ball gun turret carried on Air Corps Liberators. They were able to store the radar totally inside the aircraft fuselage during takeoff and landings and then lower it via an electric winch once airborne.

Even though no squadron aircraft had yet sighted a submarine, occasional surface contacts were made. Mostly these were fishing boats, some from England and Ireland, and sometimes from Spain, Portugal or France.

"Battle stations surface, prepare for surface attack!" Lt. North announced over the intercom. This was immediately followed by a change in engine RPM as Lt. North advanced the throttles to full military power and the big aircraft accelerated noticeably and banked to port toward the reported contact.

Billy and the other gunners were already at their posts, but now they were fully alert and their guns were slewed around in the direction of the reported contact.

The airplane rumbled as the bomb bay doors rolled up into the sides of the fuselage, a feature unique to the Liberator. Most bombers had doors that opened similar to a clamshell, but the Liberators doors slid up onto the sides of the fuselage. This feature eliminated the aerodynamic drag of open bomb bay doors that slowed other bombers speed by as much as 30 knots when open. A bomber in the attack; that is in the act of delivering its weapons on target needs all the speed possible, so this design feature was a big one in the Liberator's favor.

Vic, Ensign Victor D'Harlingue, slid into the bombardier's position in the nose below Billy's turret. It would be his job to aim and release their depth charges and torpedoes should that prove necessary.

The airplane continued to accelerate. All eyes were searching the ocean in front of them. Billy, inside the nose turret, had the best view in the airplane, but visibility wasn't that good through the light mist. It hid the U-boats from visual detection, but it couldn't hide them from the radar.

In only a matter of seconds from the initial radar contact, there it was. Even though Billy was very alert and looking for the contact, he was startled when it appeared.

It was a German U-boat and they were virtually on top of it before it was visible. It was gray and almost the same color as the surrounding ocean. Only the conning tower was visible, the decks were already covered with white foam as the boat tried desperately to submerge.

"Open fire!" blared over the intercom. Billy's thumbs were already pushing the firing buttons down as hard as he could, as if pushing harder would make the guns fire faster. Orange balls of fire erupted from either side of the turret as both machine guns began their deadly work. Like colossal jackhammers of fire a steady stream of tracers arrowed toward the U-boat.

Billy was surprised to see no one visible on the boat. The back half of the conning tower bristled with antiaircraft guns. Luckily the boat decided to run rather than fight. Billy was certain that even if they'd been throwing rocks, they could have hit the Liberator as it passed overhead they were so low. Billy watched his tracers impact the conning tower, some of them bouncing away in bright orange showers of sparks. Even with the hammering of his guns, he felt the airplane lurch as depth bombs were released. Instinctively he knew they had missed. Vic had also been startled by the sub's sudden appearance and had released too late.

The submarine disappeared from Billy's view as they flashed overhead. He released the firing buttons, the reduction in noise and vibration was incredible. He could hear the guns in the aft end of the fuselage having their turn. The waist guns only had a fleeting glimpse, but the stern or tail gunner had the longest look.

275

Pawlyk kept firing until his tracers fell short of the disappearing boat.

"Walt! What's the BDA?" Lt. North yelled over the intercom as he banked the airplane hard to port to come around for another pass. BDA meant Bomb Damage Assessment, in other words did they hit the sub?

"Both fell long, skipper!" Pawlyk yelled. "He's submerging!"

The airplane came around again. On the first pass they had also released a smoke bomb designed to float on the surface and mark the spot of the original attack with smoke. This was done so the airplane could quickly relocate the approximate position of the submarine if it was no longer visible.

Once Lt. North had the plane turned for another pass, the ocean was empty. Their smoke bomb was there, but all signs of the U-boat were gone.

"Vic! We're going to drop a Zombie on his last known track." The Zombie was officially known as the Mark 24 Aerial Mine. This was a top secret collaboration of General Electric, Howard and Bell Laboratories and was actually an aerial torpedo. It was designed to be dropped from an aircraft and once in the water it could detect the cavitation noise of a submarine's propellers. Once it detected the noise, it would start its own engine and home on the sound. Since its first operational use in March of '43, it had already accounted for several U-boats being sunk.

They all knew it was a long shot. As soon as the submarine was submerged, it could have turned in any direction. Of course, even with the smoke, finding the exact spot where the sub had been was pretty much luck.

Billy's adrenaline was up. He strained to catch sight of the U-boat as the Liberator completed its turn. As the wings leveled up, there was the smoke, but no sign of the sub. He quickly scanned in all directions, but there was no sign of it. Still he was tensed with his thumbs hovering over the firing buttons.

"Vic! Drop on my mark!" the skipper's voice cracked over the intercom. Then once more, "Three!...Two!...One!...Drop! Drop! Drop!" The airplane lurched as the almost 700 pound weapon was released.

"Weapon released!" Vic responded.

"Splash!" Pawlyk called from the stern. He was the only crewmember that could see the weapon actually enter the water.

The Zombie had a range of 4000 yards or about two and a quarter miles. It had a top speed of 12 knots, far faster than any submerged submarine, and it packed an explosive punch of 92 pounds of Torpex.

Even though they were the enemy, Billy couldn't help but feel a flash of compassion for the German crew. There they were in their steel tube under the freezing water of the North Atlantic and every one of them could hear the Zombie pinging and searching for them. This was the mission of FAW 7 Liberators, to strike fear in the hearts of all U-boat crews.

Lt. North flew a wide circle over the now sputtering smoke bomb. After several minutes it was obvious that the Zombie had not found its quarry. No underwater explosions were observed. They continued to orbit in ever widening circles hoping against hope that their prey would surface once more. After a half hour search of the area, they resumed their normal patrol, which proved uneventful. It was a letdown for the crew, Vic especially, who held himself totally responsible for not sinking the U-boat. If he had only released the depth charges a split second earlier.

As if sensing the crew's mood, Lt. North's voice crackled over the intercom once more, "Crew, congratulations on a textbook attack on an enemy submarine. I am proud of each one of you. You are the first FAW 7 crew to actually sight and press home an attack on an enemy U-boat which you damaged significantly with gunfire. You performed your duties in a manner consistent with the highest traditions of the Naval Service. You have my, and Lt. Goodrich's thanks for a job well done. Let's stay alert and look sharp. We all know how quickly things happen now."

The lieutenant was right. Things did happen quickly. The entire attack, from the time Walt saw the first blip on the radar until they dropped the Zombie as a last act of desperation had not lasted over two minutes. Now they were back to the boredom and drudgery of patrolling.

After returning to base that evening, their normal five minute de-brief had taken two hours. It seemed that every officer in the Wing wanted to hear their story. Billy was certain he had gone over every detail of the combat at least thirty times. As far as he could tell, nothing they did had been any different than any other patrol. They had just gotten lucky this time, that's all.

As they stowed their gear after the de-brief, Billy thought about the events of the day. All the officers treated them as something special simply because they had been the first crew to see a U-boat. Since deploying to England, the wing lost seven Liberators and crews. In Billy's mind, this meant the score was the German's 7 and the Navy 0. He hoped the numbers would change.

That night, lying in bed with Sally, he recounted the events of the day one last time. Sally didn't say a word, she just listened. Billy could feel her body tense against his own. He wondered if even telling her was a good idea, but otherwise how could he have explained the long de-brief. Besides, by tomorrow, everyone on base would know the story.

As he lay there, he tried to think of some way, something to say to put her more at ease. Then it dawned on him, the jackets! He had totally forgotten about them!

"Honey, everyone loved the jackets."

"They did? Did they keep you warm?"

"Sure did. Every single member of the crew made a point of telling me how wonderful they are and how lucky they think I am to be with you. In fact, they are so impressed with you and what you've done for them, that they want to name our ship for you. That is, if you approve."

"Of course, I approve, but I didn't really do anything. They want to name your airplane Sally?"

Billy chuckled, "Well, not exactly. I think they decided on *California Girl*, if it's okay with you."

"How did they come up with *California Girl*?"

"That's what they call you. They've always joked with me about having a California girl. I think you should take that as a compliment. They all think California is full of beautiful women."

"I do take it as a compliment, and California *is* full of beautiful women. You can tell them for me that I would be honored if they named their airplane *California Girl*. I can't believe that they would even consider it, but I'm thrilled they did."

"I'll tell them. Oh, and there's one more thing."

"What's that, babe?"

"They'd like you to pose for the nose. They want to paint your picture on the nose of the airplane. Would you mind? Actually, I think all you would have to do is pose for a photo. One of the guys knows a guy in the Air Corps. They've got a real artist that paints all their ships. He'd work from a photo."

Sally thought a minute. "Of course, I'll pose. It would be an honor. What do I wear for this picture?"

Now it was Billy's turn to be surprised. "Why I don't know what they want, but you're not posing nude." He insisted.

"Why not? I don't mind. It's for your crew."

"The why not is that I don't want them all ogling you any more than they already do."

"Honey, it's no big deal. If it would keep you safe, I'd pose for every airplane in England."

"I know you would, but no, I don't want you nude on the side of the airplane. How about a nice conservative swim suit, that'll be bad enough."

"Whatever you say, dear."

Billy lay there silent for a few minutes. "On the other hand, if you wanted to pose for me now, just the two of us, that's an entirely different matter."

Without a moment's hesitation, Sally took him up on his suggestion. Her display left no doubt in Billy's mind that painted on the nose of a Liberator, the result would have been erotically stunning, just as his night turned out to be.

Chapter 38

Carl really missed Billy and Sally. He regarded Billy as a son and best friend. It surprised him how quickly they became close. Carl never made friends so quickly. Of course, Sally was Sally. He always thought of her as his daughter and always would. He wished this mess was over and they, and all those like them, could just come home.

Billy talked about his little brother Jimmie several times. Carl knew he was a Marine assigned to the 3rd Marine Division. Carl read in the paper how the 3rd Division had invaded Bougainville in the Solomon Islands. Until he read about it in the paper, Carl never even knew that an island named Bougainville existed. According to the paper, the fighting had been heavy and bloody. Carl wondered how a tiny speck of land in the middle of an ocean he had never heard of could be worth the lives of all those young men.

Babe was still at home and Carl prayed that surely this war would be over before he was old enough to serve. Babe was different than he was. Babe lived for baseball. He was never fascinated with how things work like Carl and Billy were. Even though Babe spent time in the shop with them while they worked on the Special, there was never a doubt that baseball was number one with him. He only spent time in the shop when he couldn't play ball.

There was no doubt that Babe was a gifted ball player. Carl had always played pitch with him in the yard, but that was the extent of his expertise in baseball. He was never able to instruct Babe in the fundamentals of the game. Instead, Babe seemed to know how to do things instinctively.

Carl took some time off from work, accompanied by Sally and Billy to watch Babe play a few games. They were all amazed watching him. He was a natural switch hitter. Carl was at a loss as to how he learned to bat from both sides of the plate. When he asked Babe how he learned to bat that way, Babe just gave him a blank stare. It wasn't something he learned he said, it was something he just knew.

Something else that amazed them all was that Babe could play any position. Part of this had to be that he was simply better than anyone else on the field. All the other kids knew it too and they all deferred to Babe when on the diamond.

Carl hoped that baseball would work out for Babe because he certainly didn't devote much effort to school. The issue was not his intelligence; because there was no doubt he was smart, but Carl was convinced he spent all his time daydreaming about baseball. Babe proved that old adage that you could take a horse to water, but you couldn't make him drink.

Carl returned his attention to the Special. There wasn't a time he looked at it that it didn't stir him. Part of it was that they had all worked on it together. All the people in his life that really mattered had been involved in its creation. The other thing was that it really turned out better than he imagined. In large measure that was because of Billy's vision. While Carl was confident he could build almost anything, especially automotive, he didn't have the vision to see the finished product before any part of it was created the way Billy could.

That was something else that Carl marveled at. Billy had talent far beyond the norm. As far as Carl was concerned, Billy was in the same league as Frank Kurtis and Harry Miller. He had visualized the Special and sketched it out on a piece of Babe's notebook paper when they first discussed the project. Even though numerous changes took place in its construction, caused mainly because of parts that had come their way, overall the car that sat before him now was amazingly close to that original sketch.

Carl had been around top echelon racecars most of his life. His best friend had been Frank Lockhart who history would remember as one of the greatest drivers and racecar designers that ever lived. Even though there was no similarity in their appearance, Billy being a foot taller than Frank, in many other ways they were similar. Not in personality, but in ability. They both had the ability to visualize the end result of a project. They both possessed innate mechanical design ability even though neither had any formal training, and they both had the ability to create their visions with their own two hands.

The car sitting in front of him was testament to that. Its lines were more than pleasing. Carl was certain that it was more beautiful than any car racing in America at that time. He also thought it was as streamlined as the best of them.

Billy designed the car to accommodate his size. Part of the reason for this was that Billy had always intended to drive the car on the street. No accommodation had been made for the car to seat more than one person, so he would have room to comfortably drive the car but still keep the overall size small. They built the car only 30 inches wide. This width was decided on because of existing SCTA rules that called for all modified cars to be at least that wide. That width also worked well for Billy's size.

Carl was now working on adding the equipment necessary to make the car street legal. He was particularly proud of his choice for headlights. They were from a '37 Studebaker. They were perfect teardrop shapes that fit well with other parts of the car such as the blisters over the steering gear and the 'blisters' where the front radius rods entered the belly pan. The other thing was the headlights fit the grille shell that Billy had built perfectly. Carl thought that he would have to build new or at least modify the headlight mounts, but he didn't have to do anything except drill holes and bolt them on.

Carl also discovered that '37 DeSoto Airflow taillights were a perfect match for the headlights. He wasn't as lucky here. The lights were perfect, but he was going to have to build mounts. He wished Billy was there to do that. He had no doubt that he could mount them where they would be sturdy and would never fail, but he didn't have the aesthetic eye that Billy did. He would give it his best try.

Another thing he wanted to do was to fabricate a top. He and Billy discussed this many times and at least in this case, he had some sketches Billy did of his ideas. He was going to try to match Billy's ideas as much as possible. To accomplish this he was going to build a three dimensional model out of wood to fit all the pieces to. He hoped by doing this first, the part would come closer to what Billy had designed.

A major surprise to Carl had been the engine's performance. It performed much closer to a street engine, albeit a very powerful one, rather than a high strung racing engine. There was no doubt in his mind why the engine was never used by Tommy's father to race at Indianapolis. It simply did not make enough power to be competitive. It was almost a miracle that the engine even existed. The design wasn't a good one. Tommy's dad was far more interested in making a tie to the new Cadillac power plants than in building the best racing engine in existence. That Harry Miller had even been involved was incredible. For all his shortcomings, Miller was one of the great engine designers of all time. He never would have built such an engine on his own. Of course, Miller sold his business a very short time after work on the engine began. So in reality, the project passed from group to group until Fred Offenhauser finally finished it up just to get it out of the shop. Still, it made for a nice street engine and there was no doubt that it was as beautiful as any engine he had ever seen. He marveled that Tommy had given it to them free gratis.

Tommy was an entirely different subject. If ever there was an enigma, it was Tommy. He could be a good and generous boss one minute and an ogre the next. He had been a good friend to Carl over the years and Carl returned his friendship, but still there were times when Tommy acted like the only relationship was that of employer and employee. It was almost impossible to predict how Tommy would react to anything. Carl came to grips with this fact years before by learning to never count on Tommy for anything.

There was no doubt in Carl's mind that Tommy was a very lonely man. For all his money and all his houses and success in the business world, he was that unhappy in his private life. He sincerely wanted to fit in, but he never would.

The other issue with Tommy was Sally. Carl was convinced that Tommy was in love with her. It was easy to see why. Her father, Carl always had trouble with that term, was Earle Anthony the Packard distributor for California. Earle was Don Lee's biggest competitor, but also his closest friend. Anthony's wealth matched that of Lee's. For this reason, they had lots of things in common, the same social life, the same friends, even a history as family friends. Carl was certain that because of his money, everyone that came into Tommy's life was looked at with a certain amount of suspicion. Sally didn't fall into this group. She was born into his life. Tommy was friends with her brother all his life. Sally never treated Tommy special in any way. Most of the people Tommy came into contact with treated him with deference, but not Sally. Never once did she try to curry favor. Added to all this, you simply couldn't overlook the physical presence of Sally. She was one of the most beautiful women he had ever seen, and her personality simply sparkled. Yes, it was no wonder Tommy was in love with her, even if she was half his age. The problem for Tommy was that Billy came along. Not that Carl thought for one minute Sally had ever been interested in Tommy romantically. She was much too down to earth for that. No, Tommy was just going to have to learn to live with that.

Since Sally left for England, Tommy had changed. He still had any number of girlfriends, but Carl was certain it was Sally that truly interested him. Partly, Carl was sure, because he couldn't have her. Thinking about it, Sally might have been the very first thing in Tommy's life that he couldn't have. Every single time Carl saw Tommy, he asked how Sally was doing. Carl told him that Sally joined the USO and was now in England, but Tommy still wanted any and every shred of news about her that he could get. Yes, there was no doubt in Carl's mind as to Tommy's interests.

Carl had to admit that Tommy stayed busy. The business consumed a lot of his time. He had Willet to run the business, but still Tommy visited each location at least once a month. He also continued with his speed events on the dry lakes. This was not to mention his radio stations and his dabbles in television. Carl thought if he ever got the time, he really should build a receiver, he knew Tommy would like that, after all his television station broadcast an hour every day but Sunday. Maybe someday, Tommy would broadcast a speed trial, now that would really be something.

SCTA and all the other car clubs that sponsored the speed runs suspended their events for the duration of the war. Two main reasons accounted for this. The first was that a large percentage of the participants were young men that were now serving in the armed services and scattered around the globe. The other was that gasoline and rubber rationing was in effect. Even if any participants were available, they barely had enough gasoline to drive to work, let alone trek to the desert dry lakes to race. They also couldn't buy tires.

Tommy, on the other hand, had no such restrictions. He was a rich and powerful man with rich and powerful friends and associates. He could get all the gasoline and tires he needed, partly because of his business of selling and servicing all the Cadillac automobiles sold in California, and because his friends served on all the rationing boards. It was their responsibility to administer all activities involving rationing.

Tommy realized that having a dry lakes meet wasn't any fun by himself, so he made available gas rationing coupons to all the people he invited to participate. In fact, Tommy kept a large fish bowl full of gas rationing coupons in the shop so that all his friends and associates could help themselves to whatever they needed.

Tommy owned his own timing equipment and hired qualified people, usually its inventor, to run it during the meets. Thus, all the times were certified just as they were when the SCTA sponsored meets. And finally, if someone was in dire need of tires, Tommy could handle that need as well.

Carl attended a couple of Tommy's meets. The one with Billy and Sally when they ran the Special, and one since then when he and Babe took the LaSalle coupe to Rosamond Dry Lake just as spectators. Tommy's meets were smaller and much less attended than the pre-war events had been. There were very few spectators because of the rationing issues. There were fewer participants just because so many were in the service. Still Tommy's events were fun. It was more like a company picnic than a competitive event. He would pay his employees overtime to drive many of the cars in his personal collection to the lake for the weekend. This always accounted for five to ten cars, all of them European exotics such as Delahayes, Alfa Romeos, Bugattis and Mercedes. Many were ex-factory Grand Prix race cars. He usually brought his Frank Kurtis built, Offenhauser powered speedster along. He was always accompanied by at least one drop dead gorgeous Hollywood starlet, sometimes several, but this last event had been a little different, at least as far as female companions was concerned.

All the Don Lee Cadillac employees that had the desire to do so came and participated. Tommy brought five cars himself, and he enlisted any interested employee to drive one of the cars out to the lakes. Tommy drove the speedster himself.

The normal pre-war lakes racers were all invited; at least the ones still in California were anyway. A few had defense jobs that exempted them from military service and a few were too old for military service. Several of these folks joined the group and when all was said and done, there were over forty cars in attendance.

Carl considered bringing the Special, but he didn't want to drive it and didn't think it was right for anyone else to do so. He would wait until Billy and Sally returned and one or both of them could do the driving.

It was a typical summer day on the high desert. They arrived early on Saturday morning, the sun already up and burning the night chill away. In short order it was hot and getting hotter as the sun climbed in the sky. A stiff breeze kept most of the dust kicked up by the cars away, but still everything was soon coated with a fine layer of silt from the dry lakebed.

Shortly after their arrival, Babe found a buddy to play pitch with. After he left, Carl walked over to Tommy's pit area. As Carl walked around one of his boss's favorite V-16 sedans, Tommy saw him and instantly stopped what he was doing to greet him.

"Hello Carl! It's good to see you, glad you could come. Did you bring Babe? How is he?"

They exchanged the normal pleasantries. Then Tommy said, "Did you bring the Special?"

"No I didn't. Sorry."

"I'm disappointed; we've got the speedster running quite well. I wanted to see if we were up to snuff yet. Have you heard anything from Sally?"

"Who's Sally?" asked a beautiful brunette that had just walked up to stand close to Tommy's side, taking his arm as she did so.

"My dear, Sally is Carl's niece, Carl may I present Ellen Stockton, Ellen this is Carl Mercer. Carl is the shop foreman at the San Diego store. I've known him for many years. Carl, Ellen is our new assistant at the LA store. She comes to us very highly recommended."

Carl could see her recommendations all right, they were straining the buttons on the front of her blouse and one recommendation was pushed tightly against Tommy's left arm.

"Pleased to meet you Ellen."

"Ellen rode up with me in the speedster. She was very anxious to see the dry lakes for the first time."

I bet she was, Carl thought, I wonder what else she was anxious to see. "So Miss Stockton, what do you think so far?"

"I just love it here, and Tommy has been so kind and thoughtful to show me everything! It's so exciting here, but please, call me Ellen."

Carl had known her for all of two minutes and he was certain that this young woman was only interested in what knowing Tommy, and knowing him quite well from the look of it, could do for her personally.

"Tommy's always been a thoughtful and exciting guy." Carl said, thinking I bet that's not the half of it.

Carl changed his focus from the nubile Ellen Stockton to the original question.

"Sally's doing fine. Apparently England is agreeing with her."

"When is she coming back? She's been over there quite a while. I didn't know USO shows stayed overseas that long." Tommy said.

"Oh, you didn't know? She's not with the USO anymore. She's with Billy at some little place on the southern coast called Dunkeswell."

Carl saw a pained look flash across Tommy's face. His whole body must have tensed because even Ellen looked up at his face to see what was wrong.

"No, I didn't know. Well, it seems that she takes doing her part for the war effort seriously doesn't she?"

"Yes, she does. I'll tell her you asked about her. If you'd like I can give you her address."

"That would be nice. Thank you." Tommy replied and then started asking questions about the Special to change the subject.

They walked over to the speedster to look at the latest modifications. Carl noted that Ellen stayed firmly attached to Tommy's arm, her recommendation pressed firmly against him.

It was a good day overall. The small number of cars making timed runs allowed for an even more laid back relaxed atmosphere than usual. The small number of racers didn't tear up the lake surface as badly as a larger meet would have.

The day passed quickly. Carl visited with several people he saw only on an infrequent basis. It was obvious that the level of workmanship was getting better all the time. The speeds steadily increased from meet to meet. Carl didn't think any of them measured up to the Special and even if he was biased, which he was, he was right, but still there were things to be learned from many of the competitors.

The day wore down, the sun set very quickly as it seemed to do only in the high desert. As the sun disappeared over the horizon, it took all warmth with it. He was glad for the leather jacket he brought along. Babe showed up with his jacket buttoned up to his throat and his wool cap pulled down around his ears. They were both hungry and as at all of Tommy's meets, they headed to the bonfire in Tommy's pits.

They were in the middle of the Mojave Desert. Once the sun went down, there wasn't a light visible in any direction. The only light on the lakebed came from several campfires, Tommy's being the largest. That in itself was a feat as all the wood had to be brought in.

One of the things that genuinely seemed to please Tommy was personally cooking steaks for his circle of friends and associates while at the lakes. He had a large grill made from heavy steel rods that stood over the fire on sturdy legs. He used a custom designed and hand crafted implement he called simply 'the hook' to tend to the steaks while they were on the fire. The hook was a steel rod almost three feet long. On one end there was a wooden handle with Tommy's initials inlaid in silver. On the other, business end, was a cleverly designed hook. With this device, Tommy could arrange steaks on the red hot grille and flip them over with just a flick of the wrist. He was very adept at this and never let anyone else help. There were mounds of potatoes buried in the coals of the fire.

Carl and the Babe made their way to the fire. Its warmth was welcome in the cold of the desert night. This was one of the things they both looked forward to at the lakes. Tommy was always the perfect host during these events and made it a point to have a personal conversation with each person as he prepared their steak.

"So Babe, what did you think about the Series this year?" Tommy asked. He was talking about the World Series; of course, they had just finished up a couple of weeks before, the Yankees winning in five games over the Cardinals.

"Mr. Lee," Babe started but was interrupted immediately by Tommy.

"Please call me Tommy."

"Yes sir, Tommy," Babe said with a grin. He suddenly felt older and more a part of the adults all around him. And Tommy

285

asked him about a topic that Babe knew as well as anyone and considerably better than most.

"It turned out just the way I thought it would. The Yankees are just too good. They should have won last year when the Redbirds embarrassed them; they didn't forget that this year." The year before, 1942, the underdog Cardinals embarrassed the mighty Yankees by defeating them soundly in the World Series, sweeping all four games. The Yankees had appeared in eight World Series since 1926 winning them all until the upstart Redbirds upset them.

"They certainly didn't forget, I'll give you that, but the Bombers didn't have their stars this year. The Clipper (meaning Joe DiMaggio), Rizzuto, and Ruffing are all in the service," Tommy said.

"That's true, but they still have the best pitcher in baseball." Babe replied, referring to Spud Chandler, a twenty game winner in 1943. "And don't forget Charlie Keller and Joe Gordon, they can really swing the lumber."

"But the 'Birds have Musial. He had a great year. What did he hit?"

".357," Babe answered.

"That's phenomenal," Tommy said.

"It gave him the batting title sure enough, but the Bombers still have too much fire power for the Redbirds. Good pitching always wins out over good hitting; you can take that to the bank."

Carl listened to his son speak. When the subject was baseball, Babe could hold his own with anyone. He couldn't help smiling with pride as Babe went on and on with his analysis of the series. He noticed that more than a few of the people ringing the fire were listening intently to what his son said, including Ellen, and to his surprise, she seemed more interested in Babe than Tommy for the moment.

"The 'Birds have good pitching too, don't you think?" Tommy asked.

"Yes sir, they do. In fact Pollet, Lanier and Cooper have the best ERA's in the National League. The problem was, only Cooper delivered in the series and it's remarkable he did, what with his father and all." Babe said. He was referring to the fact that the Cardinals star pitcher, Mort Cooper's father had died the day before game two. Mort pitched that game and his brother Walker, also on the Cardinal team, supplied three hits and a sacrifice bunt. Despite the two brothers' inspired play, the Yankees wound up on top 4-3.

"I guess you're right," Tommy conceded, "but I was certainly pulling for the 'Birds."

"I think a lot of people were, but last year was a fluke. No one can beat the Bombers two years in a row."

"You sure know your baseball, son," Tommy said, "and I know steaks and yours is done."

Babe extended his plate and Tommy deftly plopped the sizzling inch-thick strip right in the middle of it. "Help yourself to a potato; be careful not to burn your fingers. There's milk and Coca Cola in the cooler over there."

After Babe walked away to get his drink, Tommy turned to Carl. "He really knows his baseball doesn't he?"

"Sure does, in fact I don't believe he thinks of much else."

"The next time I'm in town, I'd like to see him play if you don't mind. I've got some friends that are major league scouts, maybe I could put in a good word."

"Me too!" Ellen chimed in as she watched Babe help himself to a bottle of milk.

"That would be wonderful Tommy. Of course you can come see him play, you too Ellen. He would love it. He looks up to you. Thank you for taking the time to talk with him like you did. I know he really likes it."

"Don't be silly. I talk to him like that because he knows more about baseball than anyone else in this group, including me. It was my pleasure." Tommy had Carl's steak on the hook now. Carl extended his plate and was rewarded with his own steak, even a bit larger than Babe's.

"You know where everything is. There's also beer in the green cooler. If you want something a little stouter,"

Carl cut that statement off. "Beer will be fine Tommy, thanks."

Ellen was close by throughout the evening, bringing more steaks as Tommy had room on the grill and making sure his drink glass was never empty. She wore a pair of men's Levi's and cowboy boots and had on Tommy's brown leather jacket over a white turtleneck sweater. Carl had to admit she was beautiful. Somehow she seemed smarter and more genuine than his first impression, but he also admitted that her intentions toward Tommy were rather obvious. She had been careful to keep Tommy in sight ever since he met her that morning. He wondered what would become of all this as he took his steak and joined Babe to enjoy their meal.

Babe was perched atop a stack of wheels and tires busily forking bits of steak and potato into his mouth. Carl sat down beside him on a box of spare parts.

"Steak good?" he asked.

"Sure is!" Babe said between mouthfuls, "Mr. Lee sure knows his baseball."

Carl chuckled. "That's funny; he said the exact same thing about you."

"He sure did, and you do know baseball. My father was a baseball fanatic and you sound just like him!" Ellen said with a dazzling smile. She drifted over to stand by Babe, her approach completely unnoticed by the Babe and Carl.

"Thanks!" Babe blushed, a big grin on his face.

"We're going to come watch you play next time we're in town, you know." Ellen replied.

"Geez that would be swell!" Babe said.

This pleased Babe greatly and it showed. He continued eating his steak as if he were on a mission. In short order the last bite disappeared along with the final gulp of milk. Carl could see his eyelids beginning to droop.

"Why don't you turn in?" Carl suggested.

Babe yawned and said, "I think I will Pop, see you in the morning." He then left his perch on the stack of tires and headed toward the coupe, but not before getting a big hug from Ellen; his first from any woman besides Sally.

"Your pillow's in the trunk, and be sure you cover up with the blanket. It gets cold out here, remember?" Carl called to him as he slumped away.

His only answer was a half-hearted wave from Babe's arm. The kid was wiped out, that was for sure. Every time Carl was him that day, Babe was in motion playing pitch or flys and skinners with a couple of other kids his age. A full stomach was the last straw. He was finished for the night. Much to his surprise, Ellen escorted Babe to the car and made sure he was tucked in and snug, just the way Sally always did.

Less than five minutes later Ellen returned, "You have a wonderful son there, Mr. Mercer."

"Thanks," Carl said as he retrieved another beer and headed back to the campfire. Maybe he'd have to revise his first opinion of Ellen completely he thought. Tommy was still at the grill, a drink in his hand, the grill now empty; all the steaks had been cooked. The once roaring fire had been allowed to die down while the steaks were cooked and was now a large mound of dull red coals. It still radiated a fair amount of heat, but not nearly as much light as before.

"The steaks were great Tommy, thanks. Babe and I really enjoyed them." Carl said as he walked up. Tommy had been staring into the fire and looked up as Carl spoke.

"You're welcome, Carl. I'm really glad you could join us this weekend. I always enjoy your company. And by the way, I was serious about the Babe. I want to see him play and if there's any way I can help, I want to do that too."

"Thanks again, Tommy. The next time you're in town we'll do that." Carl thought that Tommy was being uncharacteristically sincere about wanting to help Babe. He wondered why. Tommy was a little tipsy, but he didn't seem drunk. Could it be he had a genuine interest in Babe?

Just as Carl was opening his mouth to speak, Ellen appeared out of the gloom. She gave Carl a dazzling grin; her white teeth seemed to sparkle in the dim light. She really is beautiful, I can certainly see why Tommy's interested in her, he thought.

"Hello Carl," she said slightly slurring her words. "I thought Tommy might be cold after all that cooking, are you boss?" This last was directed at Tommy.

"I'm fine my dear," he replied.

"You look cold," she said. Then turning towards Carl, "doesn't he look cold to you?"

Carl just grinned; he wasn't sure how to answer that question, although it wouldn't have surprised him if Tommy was cold. Ellen still had on his jacket. Then for the first time he realized that the turtleneck she was wearing earlier was gone. If there was anything on under the jacket he couldn't tell it, and it was unzipped far enough to tell. For an instant Carl felt a slight twinge of jealousy and was instantly ashamed.

"Come on boss, it's time we turned in," then turning back to face Carl, "besides Carl looks tired too. Are you tired Carl?" She reached up and brushed Carl's cheek with her fingertips.

Without waiting for an answer, she took the drink glass from Tommy's hand and gave it to Carl. He numbly took it, his cheek still on fire from her touch.

Then taking Tommy by the arm, she proceeded to guide him toward the big Cadillac V-16 sedan. She flashed Carl with another of those dazzling grins and said, "Goodnight Carl."

Tommy gave Carl a lopsided smile and he too said goodnight.

Carl stood there in stunned silence and watched Ellen lead Tommy to the car. The dome light came on momentarily as they got in the back door, then the light went out.

Carl still stood there, Tommy's drink in his hand. He had never seen anyone exercise such total control over Tommy before, except for Sally. He didn't know what to think. He looked at the glass, then thought what the hell and took a sip, single malt scotch. He tossed the rest down and then headed to the coupe.

Chapter 39

Billy stood looking at his airplane. The artist was every bit as good as Walt had promised. Emblazoned on the fuselage side was a nearly full size painting of Sally in a conservative black swimsuit. She stood on tip toes and stretched, her back arched. She was superimposed over a yellow-orange disk that Billy thought must represent the sun, and around the periphery of the disk the words *'California Girl'* were neatly lettered in red. This is risqué enough he thought. After all, she is my girl, and I'm sharing enough of her with the crew already.

As he was standing there admiring the vision, he was startled by a voice beside him. "She really is lovely, Billy."

It was John Goodrich, the co-pilot. Since leaving Bermuda, they didn't have many occasions to continue their friendship outside the bounds of military custom.

"Thanks, John," Billy replied.

"I think you're a very lucky guy. To have a girl that looks like that is one thing, but to have her follow you halfway around the world and in the middle of a world war, well, I'm speechless to say the least."

"She is something special," Billy didn't know what else to say.

"That she is, getting us those jackets. That's the talk of the base you know. The commodore has been trying to do that since we got here and he hasn't succeeded yet. Sally is here one day and the whole crew is wearing them."

"Just remember that the commodore is trying to get jackets for the whole wing, not just one crew. Of course, Commodore or no Commodore, he doesn't have the powers of persuasion Sally does."

John chuckled, "I bet not."

They stood there for another moment staring up at the side of the airplane.

"It looks just like her," John said.

"Yeah, that Air Corps guy did a great job. I was just wondering when all this is over if I could cut the picture off and take it home with me."

"I bet you can. We'll be sure to do that when this mess is over."

Their conversation was interrupted by the remainder of the crew, minus Lt. North, showing up in the back of a dark blue Navy truck.

As Walt Pawlyk jumped out dressed for flying and carrying his parachute, he whistled. "I told you Franklin was good! That looks just like her, don't it?"

The whole crew gathered round and all agreed. As they were admiring the artwork a staff car pulled up and Lt. North got out.

"Wow! That looks great. Alright men, we've got a mission to fly, let's get on with it and get 'the Girl' in the air so we can earn our keep."

The crew dispersed, all going about their duties in preparation for flight. As Billy started to duck into the entry hatch, he reached up and patted Sally's picture for luck. Unwittingly, he had started what would become a crew tradition. Everyone, including Lieutenants North and Goodrich, got in the habit of patting Sally as they boarded the aircraft before each flight.

The engines fired up, each of the big radials belching clouds of dirty blue smoke as they initially fired, then cleaning up to run smoothly. Lt. North advanced the throttles and the propellers blurred as they bit the air and the huge bomber bobbed and lumbered its way out onto the taxiway. Shortly thereafter VB-105 R, newly named *California Girl*, broke ground on her solitary mission patrolling off the southern coast of England.

Sally, herself, had not seen the artwork yet. The photography session went well and actually quicker than expected. The only swimsuit she had with her was a fairly modest black one piece, after all, how much use would one have for a swimsuit in England. It was the same one she wore at the Fulton's when Admiral Cunningham was coerced, actually. The thought of that brought a brief smile to her face. Looking back on it, she was certain he would have told her what she needed to know without the elaborate preparation, still she had enjoyed the cat and mouse game. She smiled thinking there probably weren't many people that thought of Admiral Sonny Cunningham as a mouse.

She was on her way to look at a cottage Mrs. Driver told her was now available. The old woman who lived there had moved out and into an apartment in nearby Exeter because of the noise of the Liberators taking off. The cottage was just off the main runway and on full military power, the four big radial engines of a heavily loaded Liberator literally made the little structure shake. Still it was the only private residence available in the tiny hamlet, and Sally was intent on getting a place where she and Billy could enjoy some privacy.

She pulled up in front of a small stone cottage. It looked similar to most others in the hamlet. There was a waist high fence built around the yard, it too was constructed of the local rock. The cottage was small and had a thick thatched roof. There were chimneys on each end of the structure. Sally knocked on the door just to be sure, but when no one answered, she turned the iron knob and pushed the small oaken door open. Billy will definitely have to duck to get in this door she thought.

The room that was revealed was small and dark. There were two windows, one on either side of the door, but they had their heavy wooden shutters drawn and latched. She opened the shutters then went back to her exploration.

That was much better, the windows let in enough light so she could see. The room was flanked on the right by a fireplace built into the wall. The mantle was made of the same stone the walls were made of. The interior walls were all whitewashed and fairly recently from what she could tell. There were a few pieces of old furniture in the room, a leather sofa and chair and a wooden dining table and four chairs.

Two doors opened off the main room. Sally went through the first to find a tiny kitchen containing a small cast iron coal burning cook stove. There was a bin in the corner filled with a mound of the black lumps. Besides the stove there was a small wooden cupboard on the wooden wall. Sally realized that this part of the cottage had been added on at a later date. It was constructed of wooden planks instead of the stone used throughout the rest of the house. There was also a small porcelain sink with a cast iron water pump.

Then Sally went to the last room of the house. This was the bedroom, and for the first time since arriving, she smiled. The bedroom was dominated by two things. A large bed, the top of which was so far off the floor she feared she may need a stool to climb in, and another large rock fireplace, the twin to the one in the main room. She could picture herself and Billy in the big old bed on a dark night, the room lit by the glow of the fire. The thought made her smile again, a tingle in the pit of her stomach.

Just then, the cottage began to rumble. It seemed that the bed started to walk around the floor. For a fleeting instant she wondered if it was an earthquake like the ones she was familiar with back home. Then the rumble changed to a deafening roar that moved across the house. She ran to the front door just in time to see a Liberator, wheels up and crabbing into the prevailing wind, flash over the house. It was low enough she almost thought she could touch it. Then the big airplane banked to the right and as it did so, she could see what had to be her picture painted on its nose as it turned away to the south.

That was Billy taking off! She was certain that had to be an omen and a good one at that. She was going to rent the cottage. They would find a way to deal with the noise. Besides, it was the only one available! She was going to start work on it right now so that when Billy got back from his mission, she could bring him here, to their home.

It had been another long and boring flight. There was a lot of tension because of the weather. It had been bright and sunny, unrestricted visibility, not a cloud in the sky. A perfect day for Jerry to be flying his fighters.

The men of the Wing had quickly learned to respect and fear the Junkers JU-88's they most often encountered. The JU-88's had already accounted for the downing of several Liberators. In these conditions, the only recourse if they encountered them was to fight it out. There was no place to run. Their standing orders were to avoid enemy fighters if at all possible and if attacked to try to hide in the clouds and to fly due west. The idea being that by flying west, it took the Junkers further from their base so that perhaps they would break off any attack for fear of running out of fuel and being unable to make it back to France. The American and German crews both knew that if the Germans had to ditch at sea, there was little hope they would be rescued by their own side. The best they could hope for was for the British or Americans to find them and take them prisoner.

The only noteworthy event on the flight was when several small black dots were seen passing from north to south across the eastern horizon. The aircraft were too far away to identify them as anything but dots, but Lt. North had immediately turned west and accelerated to their best possible speed.

They would never know if the aircraft were enemy or not. As far as they could tell, they had not given chase. After 15 minutes of flying due west, everyone relaxed somewhat and normal patrol activity resumed. Nothing else was sighted for the remainder of the flight.

The sun was getting low when they returned to Dunkeswell. Their landing was uneventful even though the bomb bay still carried enough high explosives to leave a huge crater in the ground and totally disintegrate them, their aircraft, and everything around them for at least a hundred yards. They were always apprehensive about landing, but it wasn't as bad as taking off.

After landing, they taxied and parked the big airplane. Several members of the ground crew were there to service the aircraft. A stake bed Navy truck appeared to transport them to the de-briefing. The only item of interest to the de-briefers was the aircraft sighting. Since there really wasn't much to discuss they were only there for five minutes.

After de-brief, they dropped their flight gear in the locker room. They all retained their sheepskin jackets, but left items such as their Mae West life preservers and parachutes in their lockers. Once finished, they headed out the door together. They were headed to the mess hall because all they had eaten while flying was a cold sandwich. As the group came out the door, Billy immediately saw Sally's car in the parking lot. He peeled away from the group and headed toward the Ford. The rest of the guys waved, but continued on to chow.

Billy trotted up to the driver's door. Sally greeted him with a big grin, the collar of her sheepskin jacket framed her face and for the ten thousandth time, Billy's heart skipped a beat at her beauty. She didn't slide over to let him drive as she usually did.

"Hi honey," he said, a bit of a question in his voice.

"Get in good lookin', I'm driving today."

Billy went around and got in. She backed out and headed toward the gate. They passed through with just a wave, the SPs were used to them by this point. Billy was surprised when instead of proceeding straight down the lane to the village, she turned left on a gravel path. He looked askance at her, but she just smiled and continued down the lane, eyes to the front.

Billy was totally confused. They had never come this way before. Sally hadn't said a word since they went through the gate.

J E PENDLETON

He guessed they were skirting the base and were getting close to the end of the runway. He contained himself as long as possible and just as he was opening his mouth to ask what the hell was going on, Sally turned through an opening in the hedgerow to the left.

There was a small rock cottage inside a rock fence. Behind the cottage a dense row of trees hid the end of the runway from view. Sally pulled up to the gate and stopped, killing the car.

"What's this?" he asked.

"It's our new house," she replied, scarcely able to contain the grin threatening to break out on her face.

Billy just looked at her, his face blank.

"Our what?"

"It's our house. I rented it. What do you think? It really doesn't matter because it's the only one available."

Billy was speechless. Sally opened her door and got out, Billy did the same. When they got to the door, Sally opened it and stepped aside.

Billy ducked his head and went in. The door was too low for him to get in otherwise. Sally had spent the whole day cleaning and getting the place ready for him. A fresh bouquet of flowers was in a clear glass vase in the middle of the table. A small fire was burning in the fireplace. The few personal items Sally brought with her to England were in the room.

"What do you think?" she asked, her face a wall to wall grin.

There was one thing about this woman he thought. If I live to be a thousand, she'll still surprise me.

"I love it. And you, my dear, are an absolute wonder!" He swept her off her feet and into his arms swinging her around, her feet not touching the floor. She was laughing the whole time. She loved it when he did that, it almost made her feel like a little girl again.

"Put me down you oaf!" she shouted, mock indignation in her voice. He started to set her down, just before her feet touched the floor again she shouted, "Not here, in there!" and pointed to the bedroom door.

He carried her through the door, stooping to do so. He threw her onto the bed. She almost disappeared in the fluffy featherbed. He jumped in right behind her. It was wonderful, the smell of fresh sheets almost overwhelmed him. The bed was like lying on a cloud.

"Now what do you think?" she asked as she unzipped the jacket revealing nothing underneath.

He didn't say anything, he was speechless as he watched while she slipped out of the jacket and sent it sailing over the side of the bed.

"I think this will do quite nicely" he replied, as he descended on her, covering her in kisses to her delighted giggles.

Chapter 40

The weather in the south of England grew steadily worse. As November wore on, more and more flight operations were cancelled because of weather unfit even for the Liberators of FAW 7 to fly in.

The crews of all the grounded planes found nothing about their inactivity to complain about. It was boring being confined to their huts, but it was often just as boring flying patrols, however, when flying patrols there was always the possibility of sudden death, from enemy fighters, mechanical failure, personnel error or just plain bad luck.

The last cause, luck, was the topic of heated discussion among the men. Most felt that luck played a vital role in whether they lived or died. Others argued that there was no such thing as luck. Many others violently objected and things could get ugly if anyone or anything obstructed the observance of pre-flight rituals.

Billy's crew for instance, had taken to patting Sally's butt, the nose painting of her that is, before each mission. At first, this bothered Billy a little. After all, Sally was his girl and she was here in England. To him that seemed to make things more awkward, but then again it was his crew, his buddies, their lives depended on each other. He finally came to the realization that if patting a picture of Sally brought them back, then what could be wrong with it. After agonizing consideration he finally told Sally about the ritual. He didn't think it was right to keep it from her. He wasn't sure what kind of reaction to expect, but he certainly hadn't expected what he got. She was actually happy about it. It was like she was a part of the crew. Anyway she could help was more than okay with her. He'd just have to get used to everyone patting her on the bottom, that's all there was to it.

Their missions were cancelled for several days because of the bad weather. It was cold and there was lots of snow. Even the Liberators looked cold sitting on their hardstands, a circular patch of concrete where the big bombers were parked, each on their own snow covered circle. Their engines were covered with tarps and the snow was up to the axles on the main landing gear. The weather was unusual for this part of England and there weren't adequate snowplows to keep the runways clear or the heavy equipment necessary to de-ice the aircraft.

The crews played in the snow. The number of snowballs thrown was staggering. Sally and Billy visited the base and as soon as they opened the doors on the Ford, they were pelted with the white missiles. Bedlam ensued, people running in all directions, stooping to grab more ammunition, throwers finding their targets and being rewarded with explosions of white powder, gasps, screams, curses, but above all, laughter and giggles.

Sally was everyone's chosen target except Billy's. She would have been his had he not felt compelled to defend her. It was a good thing she was wearing her shearling jacket and she had a navy blue with white polka dot silk scarf wrapped around her head, still some snow found its way inside her jacket and even through her heavy gray sweater. She being from California and Billy from Texas, neither of them had much experience with snow, but they enjoyed themselves tremendously. Being completely out numbered they finally succumbed to their assailants. They were laughing so hard they all had tears running down their cheeks which quickly froze in place.

After everyone had somewhat caught their breath and the laugher had died down a bit, Harry said, "You guys coming to the Aero Club tonight to help decorate?"

He was asking about decorating for the upcoming Christmas party. The Aero Club was the enlisted men's club on base. It featured a bar, bartenders, and most weekends a live band, usually made up of Wing personnel, but occasionally a civilian band or USO production.

Billy looked at Sally. Her face was flushed from the cold, contrasted against the white background and the blue of her scarf, her eyes were even more electric blue than normal and they were already the bluest he'd ever seen. He guessed he got lost when their eyes met because he momentarily forgot there was anyone else around except for her. Then suddenly Harry interrupted his reverie.

"Aw, come on guys! You've got to come. We never get to see Sally!"

This was joined by a chorus of "Yeahs!"

They smiled at each other. Billy knew there was no way to say no at this point. He was certain that in Sally's mind, the crew was already part of her 'family'. If they wanted her to do something, then she'd do it if it were humanly possible. Besides, it would probably be fun.

Sally could tell from the look in Billy's eyes what he was thinking. She would forever think that part of the reason she loved him so was because of the way they communicated with only a look. From the first time she saw him, she knew what he was thinking simply by looking at those green eyes.

"We'll be there. What time?" she asked.

Another chorus of "Hoorays!" and "Oh boys!" broke out.

"We're going to start gathering right after chow," Harry said, this meant about 6:30.

"Okay, we'll be there....." Billy's words were cut short as a snowball hit his forehead and exploded. His watch standers cap went from dark blue wool to white snow instantly. Snow was packed on his left eyelid and slid down his nose. He never said another word, just stooped over to grab a handful of the powdery white snow. The fight was on again everyone laughing and giggling. It was the most they had laughed since arriving in England.

Billy and Sally walked into the Quonset hut that was called the Aero Club. The club was the center of all social activity on base. It was early evening, but already the club was full. It was still a couple of weeks before Christmas, but everyone was already in the Christmas mood. It helped that the flying schedule was curtailed due to inclement weather so no losses had been incurred for several weeks.

The crowd was more than just the enlisted and NCOs. Several officers were scattered about. There were also quite a few females present. Some were American nurses that were dating base personnel, and some were eligible age young ladies from the surrounding countryside. Everyone was having a great time if the noise and activity was any indication.

The stated purpose of the evening was to make and put up Christmas decorations, but it was also to have a good time and maybe to have more than a few drinks. After all, it was the Aero Club, and the Aero Club did have a bar, and that bar was open.

As soon as they came in the door shaking the loose snow off their shoes, Harry spotted them.

"Glad you two could make it!" he said, shaking Billy's hand and then getting a hug from Sally. Sally's hugs were always in great demand and highly coveted by the entire crew. Billy came to accept this. He knew beyond any doubt that Sally's heart belonged to him; he could certainly afford to share a hug with his closest friends in the world.

"The gang's over here. We've got the chore to make and hang the garland. Maybe Sally's got an eye for design, because I know you don't Billy."

"Harry, what did I ever do to you?" Billy chuckled.

"It's obvious just looking at you two that Sally is the one with a sense of style, while you, Mr. Pendleton, have no imagination at all."

By this time Sally was laughing out loud. Billy was standing with his mouth open and his arms out to the sides.

The point of all this, besides poking fun at Billy, was that Billy was dressed just like every other enlisted man in the club. That is in Navy issue blue dungarees and his shearling flight jacket. Sally on the other hand was wearing khaki wool slacks, a white blouse and a red sweater, all topped by her flight jacket. One of Billy's white silk scarves hung from her neck; the bright blue USN showing on each end.

Harry led them across the room to a long wooden table made by stacking long planks on a pair of saw horses. The rest of the crew was there, less the officers. There were also three local girls that had been dating members of the crew.

Introductions were exchanged all around. It was obvious that there was more drinking and joking going on than serious work on the garland. Several people were busy cutting strips of red and green paper. Others were busy making rings out of the strips and gluing alternating colors together to form a red and green paper chain. Still others were just as busy gluing signs to unsuspecting people's backs and making red and green crowns while the more tipsy in attendance roared with laughter. This only served to egg on the jokesters.

Their plan was to stretch a wire around the periphery of the room and hang the chain from the wire. They had scrounged the wire from the radio shop. Sally was immediately enlisted to make the chain with the other girls while Billy was dragged off to help string the wire. He was seen as a natural for this duty as all the work had to be done from a ladder and Billy's height and reach were an asset. A couple of other crew members made it their responsibility to be sure that everyone, male and female alike, were provided with a constant supply of beer.

Pawlyk had more than his share of the English Ale. He was totally engrossed with some project no one could figure out. He tried to keep his work hidden from everyone. Finally he snuck up behind his date and reaching around her revealed his top secret handiwork, a red paper bra he was doing his best to install on her rather ample bosom. His efforts earned him a startled look followed by a resounding slap across his face. The sharp crack of the slap was followed by a string of profanity delivered in a very English accent. All eyes in the club turned to see Pawlyk with a completely dumbfounded look on his face and both hands holding cones of red paper with green stars on the ends over his girl's boobs. A bright red whelp spreading across one cheek, both hands still firmly planted on her breasts.

"Get your bloody mitts off my knockers you sodding pervert!" she shrieked, followed with what Harry would later describe as 'the perfect uppercut' that sent him sprawling backward over a chair to land flat on his back.

The room was in stunned silence. Pawlyk lay on the floor, his eyes as big as saucers, his mouth open in surprise, his girl at his feet with fists clinched in defiance on each hip as she glared down at him. When she saw the look on his face, the glare faded to a look of concern, then tears.

"Oh Pawly! Have you hurt yourself?!" she cried as she dropped to her knees to smother the still bewildered Pawlyk in kisses. The room erupted in guffaws of laughter.

"Next time pick on someone your own size!"

"Made it a little too tight did you Pawlyk?!"

"Let me fit it for you honey!"

"He had cold hands that's what!"

Pawlyk finally struggled to his feet. As he did so, his girl planted a very wet kiss on his lips to a chorus of cheers around the room.

As the room returned to normal, Sally was busy using a brush and a pot of white glue joining the links together. She didn't notice the man walk up beside her.

"Sally! What in the world are you doing here?" the man asked.

Sally looked up and was surprised to see an old acquaintance, Joe Kennedy, dressed in the green wool uniform of a Naval aviator, gold wings on his chest.

"Hello Joe," she said; not being particularly fond of him.

"Hello? Is that all I get?" he said, holding his arms out for a hug. When Sally didn't immediately react, he took matters into his own hands and pulled her toward him. She did not return the hug. Joe Kennedy was Lt. Joseph P. Kennedy Jr., the oldest son of Ambassador to England, Joseph P. Kennedy Sr. of Boston, Massachusetts, and older brother to the future President of the United States, John F. Kennedy.

Sally met Joe Jr. several times, the first on a visit to the East Coast with her family as a teenager. Joe Jr. had been quite taken with the long legged blonde beauty from California and made his feelings painfully obvious to Sally. He was a son of privilege and used to getting his way in all things, especially with young women that met his fancy, most of whom were only too happy to succumb to his roguish good looks, Boston accent, and last but not least, wealth. Sally was an entirely different matter. She steadfastly refused each and every advance.

Joe Jr. took every rebuff as a sign she wanted him all the more, and was simply playing hard to get. Having never been spurned and unable to conceive of the possibility, Joe persisted just as he was doing now.

"I knew you had a crush on me! You followed me all the way here!" and he leaned over to kiss her.

"Joe please!" she said and pushed him away.

The grin never left his face. She was one of the prettiest women he ever saw and certainly was the most beautiful in this God-forsaken mud hole. Pushing him away simply made him want her all the more.

"May I get you a drink?" he said deciding to turn on the Irish charm he possessed in spades.

"No thank you. I have one already," she replied.

"Seriously Sally, what are you doing here?" he persisted.

"I'm making a garland out of this paper, of course."

"I didn't mean that! What are you doing here in England?"

Sally sat down the glue brush she had held up till now and turned to face him. "Joe, I'm here because I want to be here, and I'm not sure it's any of your business why."

Part of what attracted Joe to her so much was because she didn't fawn on him like most other young women. He didn't understand this and was certain at some point that she would. It was simply up to him to play the game and find the right button to push. He considered it great sport.

"And you want to be here to be in close proximity to me, right?"

"Hardly!" she resumed gluing strips of paper together, the festive mood now broken by his presence.

"Are you with someone?"

"Why yes I am, actually. Do you see that tall dark haired man on the ladder across the room?" she indicated the direction with her chin.

Joe turned to look. "My God, you can't be serious?" he said, a look of disbelief on his face. "An enlisted man? You really can't be serious!"

"Oh, but I am. Joe, that's one of your problems. You define a person's worth by their wealth and social status. I don't. Now would you please leave before you ruin my entire evening?"

Joe was taken aback. Sally had always been hard to get, but this was beyond his comprehension. She followed an enlisted man all the way here? Could this possibly be true?

The grin had fled his face, replaced now with a touch of concern, "Who is that young man?" he asked.

"His name is William Wade Pendleton, his friends, which I'm sure doesn't include you, call him Billy."

Joe continued, unabashed, "that's his name, but who is he?"

"He's the nose gunner on *California Girl.* That's who he is. He's from Texas where his father paints houses and hangs paper for a living. Honest work, something that you know nothing about!" Sally was warming to the task now. She would never forget a night in the backseat of a Cadillac driven by Joe's brother Jack. It was as close to hand to hand combat as she had ever experienced. She managed to maintain her virginity, but only by the slimmest of margins, her dress in tatters and her fingernails bloody. The thing that infuriated her most was Joe's attitude. Even when he was scratched and punched, he carried on as if having a rollicking good time. Every time she saw him, he tried to resume where he left off. She had to give him an A+ for persistence. It suddenly occurred to her that perhaps his conduct was well inside what he considered normal and proper. That was a staggering thought.

"A Texan? Indeed! And oh, Sally, by the way, you're absolutely right, I've never performed an honest day's work in my life. I really never considered that I'm any worse off as a result. Of course, I am a Naval aviator and I do fly patrols every other day, just like your William. Does that count?"

"Look Joe, I never expected to see you again, let alone here. I didn't come here tonight to debate Joe Kennedy's worth. I would appreciate you leaving me alone. Totally. Is that clear?"

"Bill, that officer from 110 has been talking to Sally for a long time. You noticed?"

Harry was assisting Billy string the garland to a wire running the length of the building. Billy was up on a step ladder and had a very clear view over everyone's head to where Sally stood talking to the officer in his green wool. Billy could see the gold aviator's wings marking the man as a pilot. He could also see the squadron insignia of a flying fox inside a red ring on the man's shoulder indicating squadron VB-110.

"He's a guest in here," Harry said, meaning that this was an enlisted men's facility and all officers except those on official business, were only allowed entrance if they were invited. It also meant that they could be asked to leave at any time. "He has no business talking to Sally!"

"We can toss his ass out if we want to. You want me to go do that?"

Billy looked down from his perch on the ladder, a string of paper garland in his hands.

"Sally can take care of herself, Harry."

Harry didn't look convinced.

"Really Harry, Sally can take care of herself."

"I know, but it still pisses me off! I oughta go over there and thump his melon!"

Billy could tell Harry was getting angrier the longer the conversation lasted. He decided the only way to prevent a problem was to go see what was going on. He climbed down off the ladder.

As he started to walk toward Sally, Harry was right beside him. "Let's kick that son-of-a-bitch out the door!" he hissed.

Billy stopped and turned to face Harry. "You stay here Harry. We don't even know why he's talking to her."

"He's up to no good. I can see it on the bastard's face." Harry was pissed, that was certain.

"Just the same, you stay here. If I need you, I'll look over here, okay?"

"You got it buddy! You look over here and I'll nail that son-of-a-bitch before he knows what hit him."

"Just stay here and let me handle it."

"Okay, shipmate, but you need me, you just glance over here and I'll knock that sucker into next week!"

Billy resumed walking to where Sally and the officer were talking.

"I said, is that CLEAR?" Sally repeated.

Joe wasn't quite sure what was going on. It was very unusual for him not to be totally sure of himself. As he looked Sally in the eye, and they were certainly lovely eyes, the bluest he had ever seen, he was still baffled. He had never encountered a woman that didn't want him. Oh, some put up more of a fight than others, but they all gave in eventually. After all, he was Joe Kennedy, son of the millionaire Ambassador to England and he did plan to be President of the U.S. someday. What woman wouldn't want him? So far he had only gotten a taste of Sally, and he liked it. His gaze wandered away from Sally's eyes to her bosom. He could still remember that night. He had held one of those lovely breasts in his hand, but only for a second before Sally punched him in the nose. She certainly had a lot of spunk, but that would only make it better once she gave in.

"I'm waiting," she said, annoyance dripping from every pore.

"For what? Me?" and he flashed that Irish grin that always worked in the past.

"Yes, I'm waiting on you to answer me and to get your eyes off my chest! I want you to leave me alone. Period! Get it? Now get lost!"

He could see in her eyes that now wasn't the time for further discussion. He would try again when the mood was better. She was simply too tempting a treat to ignore. Especially here in this part of rural England.

"As you request, my dear. Until we meet again." He inclined his head and walked away.

"What was that all about?" Billy asked as he walked up.

"Nothing!" Sally said through clenched teeth.

For the first time Billy began to think that perhaps Harry was right. Maybe he did need to go after that green suited SOB. He turned to look at him making his way through the crowd.

Sally sensed Billy's tension. She realized he might do something they would all regret.

"Really, it was nothing." She said in the most relaxed voice she could muster. "He's an old acquaintance. Actually, his father and mine are friends. He's always tried to get something started between us. I just had to tell him the way things are, that's all. It's not easy letting someone down easy you know." Sally added the last little part as a small white lie hoping she could defuse Billy before he really became angry. Actually, she had never seen his temper flare. She wondered what it was like. From the color that leapt into his face in a flash, she guessed it was considerable.

"Really darling, it was nothing." She took Billy's arm and hugged him making sure she pushed her breast into it.

"He won't be back. He understands I'm taken."

Billy didn't say a word, he just watched until the officer left the building.

"Sally, you want me to cold cock that son-of-a-bitch? Excuse my language, please." Harry said as he walked up.

"Harry, I don't need your help." Billy said. One look at Billy's face told Harry that was true. Harry would give a month's pay to watch Billy kick that candy-assed officer's tail, and kick it there was no doubt.

"No Harry, everything's fine, but would you get us all a fresh beer please?" Sally asked.

"Yes ma'am, I'd be glad to, but if you need that SOB's head thumped, you just let me know. Three beers, coming right up," and Harry left in the direction of the bar.

"Bill, look at me," she said.

Billy turned and looked her in the eye. After a minute she grinned and he couldn't help but do the same. The tension broke just as Harry returned with three mugs of amber ale. The evening was going to be fun after all.

Chapter 41

Christmas of 1943 came and went without much fanfare. There was the official Christmas party for all enlisted men at the Aero Club. This was the event that everyone worked so hard decorating the club for. It was a fun event accompanied by a Christmas feast with all the trimmings.

Sally had not seen Joe Kennedy again after their confrontation a week earlier. He did not come to the party. She wondered if that was because he had the decency not to come or if he was specifically told his presence was not wanted. She thought a great deal about why he acted the way he did. She never given him any indication that she was interested in him romantically or otherwise, yet he acted almost as if she belonged to him. Thinking about it, he and Tommy Lee acted a great deal alike in that regard. One thing about Tommy was that he at least kept his hands to himself and he certainly never ripped her clothes off as Joe had. Thinking back on that event, at least Joe came to his senses after she socked him in the nose. There were a few panicky seconds there when she was certain she was going to be raped in the back seat of the Cadillac. The more she thought about it, the more certain she became that Joe saw nothing wrong with his actions. He was simply acting as he thought he was entitled. In fact, that was the way he acted all the time, as if he was the lord of the manor and everyone else was there simply to meet his needs. That assumption fit and it certainly explained much of his behavior.

Billy on the other hand, was Joe's total opposite. From the very first moment, he always treated her with respect and as an equal. There was more to it than that of course, but that was the initial thing that attracted her to him. He also was kind in everything he did. He seemed to consider other people and their feelings and needs. That was something she never experienced in her life up to that point from anyone except Carl. Certainly her father and his circle of friends never acted that way. They were more like Joe.

She worried about Billy. Since the Wing deployed to England in September, they had already lost ten aircraft and crews. That was a hundred crewmen lost in twelve weeks of operation. She didn't know what she would do if Billy didn't come back. She made herself think about other things.

She got Billy a pair of flying boots for Christmas. The Navy finally supplied the Wing with proper clothing for the conditions, but she had already ordered the shearling boots to be custom made. He loved them as she knew he would. It thrilled her so to make him happy.

He got her a small gold locket in the shape of a heart. It was engraved with both their initials. It flipped open to reveal a small photo of Billy. She loved it and swore she would never be without it again. She wore it around her neck on a thin gold chain. It rested just above her heart.

The weather finally improved. That was bad for all of them. Normal flight operations had resumed with crews flying approximately every other day. Billy was off today. He had taken the car and driven to Exeter to pick up something for Mrs. Driver or "Granny" as all the men called her. She was really a sweet lady and lived up to her nickname by being a grandmother to everyone. It was thanks to her that Sally was able to rent the cottage. She and Billy visited with Granny on Christmas, as had a surprising number of the crews. All of them left a special present with her, much of it food that civilians couldn't get. Sally knew Granny. She wouldn't use any of it for herself, she would instead, divide it out among the people of the village.

All in all, it was a good Christmas with only one reminder of the war. On Christmas Eve a pair of squadron VB-110 planes sighted and attacked a German convoy. It was late in the day and they had barely been able to press home an attack as darkness fell.

The next day, Christmas, another pair of Liberators, this time from VB-103 were able to make contact with the enemy convoy and press home an attack. Both aircraft were damaged, but managed to return to base with no injuries. The word had quickly spread that the convoys were mostly German destroyers escorting a pair of blockade-runners. The convoy was heavily armed and the flak had been intense.

Yesterday, December 27th, another pair of wing Liberators had shadowed another convoy across the bay. Their reports were that British surface ships joined the battle and several German ships were sunk. Sally was thankful Billy's crew had missed out on this action.

She heard tires crunching on gravel. Billy must be home! She rushed to the door to great him. She opened the door and sure enough, there was Billy walking up the gravel walk, a small bouquet of flowers in his hand. It was Christmas, where did he find flowers this time of year? That was so typical of him.

Sally was just about to embrace Billy in a combination hug of welcome home and thanks for the flowers when a loud siren started up from just behind the tree line. It was so loud and sudden that it startled her. Billy's grin instantly disappeared. He grabbed her in an embrace.

"That's the return to base siren," he said. "I've got to get my gear and get to the base. Will you drive me?"

She nodded her head while fighting back tears. She had never heard the siren before and that made it all the more ominous. She didn't want Billy to see her crying. He pushed past her to gather his gear. Sally went to the Ford and started turning it around as Billy came out wearing his flight jacket, new boots and carrying his ditty bag. He jumped in the passenger door and off they went. The cottage adjoined one boundary of the base, but to get to the gate was almost a mile long drive. Even as they drove through the gate, the SP's frantically waving them on, they could see Liberator's starting engines and beginning to taxi. Sally drove directly to the briefing shack.

She crunched to a halt in the gravel just outside the door. Several trucks were parked outside, their engines idling, drivers ready to deliver crews to their aircraft. A pair of carbine armed guards flanked the door. The letters 'SP stenciled in black block letters on their white helmets.

"Gotta go honey, I love you with all my heart," Billy said as he leaned over and kissed her. Then he was out of the car and walking in the shack past the guards, his bag in his hand.

It happened so quickly, Sally didn't know what else to do, she backed out, turned around and headed back to the cottage. On her way to the gate, she saw a pair of ground crewmen she met several times. They were assigned to VB-105, Billy's squadron. She pulled over to the edge of the road beside them and rolled down her window.

A pair of grins greeted her.

"Hey Sally! Where you goin'?" said the man she knew only as Charlie.

"Back to the cottage, Charlie. I just brought Billy in to the briefing hut. What's going on?"

Charlie glanced around to see if anyone was near. "It's that German convoy again. They're sending out as many crews as they can to try and stop them."

Sally's heart sank, her worst fear coming true. "Thanks Charlie," she said and drove off. She drove out through the gate and back to the cottage.

Almost as soon as she entered the house, the first Liberator roared overhead shaking everything inside the tiny dwelling. Even before the roar of its engines could fade, it was followed by another, and then another, and finally one more. It was horrible being in the house when they roared overhead. Their motors began to fade into the distance.

Sally went to the cupboard to retrieve the bottle of whiskey they kept there for special occasions. She needed something to calm her nerves. Just as she began to pour herself a drink another Liberator thundered off the runway startling her and causing her to drop the bottle. It shattered into a thousand pieces; the din of the take-off completely masking the sound of the breaking glass.

Sally ran out the open door into the small yard and watched the bomber disappear over the trees. In seconds another roared past. Then a third, as she watched this one she could see a likeness of herself on the side of the fuselage. It was Billy!

She watched it disappear over the trees. Soon after, it was followed by three more. There was then another short lull. In the distance she saw the six Liberators that had just taken off get into formation. They passed by the field at a distance and headed to the east. As she was watching, more Liberators took off at short intervals. The whole world seemed to vibrate in sync with their bellowing exhaust and the thumping beat of their propellers. She wasn't positive, but she thought she counted fifteen in all. Finally silence returned; the last of the big airplanes passing over the far horizon.

For the longest time she simply stood in the yard of the cottage, her arms tightly hugging herself and watching, hoping it was all a mistake and the bombers would return to base. She never knew for sure how long she stood there. Finally she noticed a burning sensation in her ankles. When she looked down she was surprised to see several red lines from her ankles down to her shoes. One ankle had a small sliver of glass still sticking in the skin. She was bleeding from fragments of the exploding bottle. Sally couldn't bear to be alone another minute. She didn't even take time to remove the sliver of glass or close the cottage door. She got in the Ford and drove off to Granny Driver's leaving the cottage in a shower of gravel thrown up by her fishtailing tires.

Billy had never taken part in anything like this before. The base had assembled a strike force of 15 Liberators and dispatched them all on their deadly mission. There were six planes from VB-105 led by Lt. Comdr. Don Gay. Their mission was to intercept and if possible destroy the German convoy.

The Germans attempted to get two blockade-runners across the Bay of Biscay. The first blockade runner was a ship named *Osorno.* The Germans sent a battle fleet of six destroyers and two torpedo boats out to escort the *Osorno* across the bay. The previous day, although damaged, she had managed to beach herself near Bordeaux. The battle raged for two days across the Bay of Biscay.

Once the *Osorno* made it across, the Germans sent her sister, the *Alsterufer* across. The Allies saw the crossing of the *Osorno* as defeat and were more determined than ever to prevent the *Alsterufer* from repeating the performance. All the stops had been pulled out and the day before a Liberator assigned to Czech Squadron No. 311 spotted the solitary *Alsterufer* and attacked with a fulisade of aerial rockets. The rockets had found their mark and the ill-fated *Alsterufer* slipped beneath the waves of the bay.

The Germans were unaware that their prize had been sunk and determined to repeat the success of the *Osorno*, they dispatched the entire 8th Destroyer Flotilla consisting of six destroyers and the 4th Torpedo Boat Flotilla consisting of four heavily armed motor torpedo boats to escort *Alsterufer* to port. This was the first time in the war that such a show of strength had been undertaken. In a matching response, the Allies devoted all available air assets into the battle. Fleet Air Wing 7 was the largest part of this force. It was a match of strength against strength.

Even though all fifteen Liberators took off within minutes of each other, each squadron group formed up individually and was making their intercept independently. The idea being that even if the three groups should make contact with the German fleet at the same time, they could coordinate their attack better on site than they could develop a *set piece* battle plan before take-off.

All the bombers carried ten 350 pound bombs fitted with contact fuses, meaning that the bomb would explode on contact with a hard object. This was the first time Billy's airplane carried contact bombs instead of their normal armament of depth charges. The difference being that this time they were hunting surface ships instead of submarines.

In their briefing they were given the approximate location of the convoy. Other FAW 7 aircraft had been in contact with it off and on for the past two days. The cargo carried by the blockade-runner was now at the bottom of the sea, but the German warships were out in the open for the first time. They were the targets of this mission.

When they took off, all aircraft were at maximum gross weight. Besides their full bomb load, they also carried spare ammunition for their eight heavy machine guns. Everyone knew the German ships were heavily armed with anti-aircraft weapons.

The six VB-105 aircraft formed a defensive formation, called a 'box' in case enemy fighters were encountered for their long flight into the Bay. The idea of the 'box' was that each aircraft's guns were assigned an area of the sky that not only protected itself but also one or more of the other aircraft as well. The areas overlapped so that several pairs of heavy machine guns would engage an enemy fighter at the same time. This way each aircraft protected all the others. It was a very formidable formation.

All the crewmen on the Liberator were equipped with Bausch & Lomb binoculars. The binoculars were their primary instrument for locating targets. A major part of the gunner's job was searching air and sea for enemy planes and ships. Billy was in his turret, his guns armed, and his binoculars up and searching.

Lt. Master's aircraft radioed "Tallyho! Enemy in sight!" Pulse rates throughout the flight soared. Dry throats tried to swallow. Loading handles on machine guns were checked to make sure all was ready.

The intercom crackled in Billy's ears, it was Lt. North's voice, "Gunners, keep an eye out for fighters! I have the enemy ships in sight, but we don't want a Junkers jumping our ass while we're all watching the ships. Everyone got that?" He was rewarded by a series of clicks as each gunner clicked their microphone talk button to signify they received and understood the message. While all of them scanned the heavens looking for enemy planes, they couldn't help but steal a glance toward the enemy ships.

It was an impressive sight. The ships were spread across a wide area of the sea. The German ships were in their own version of the 'box'. The ships spread out where their fires could support each other and so that they were not lumped together in a line where they would be easy targets.

As the flight of Liberators drew closer, the trailing ships of the formation sprouted bright orange muzzle flashes. Tracers arced through the sky and dirty black puffs of smoke erupted in front of the flight. They were still out of range, but the Germans wanted to be sure they knew they were in for a fight. The flight banked away from the flak, but kept the ships in sight.

The intercom crackled to life once more. "Everyone listen up. The flight is going to split up. Lt. Comdr. Gay will lead one element against the port line of ships and we'll lead the starboard element. We'll make our run at 800 feet. Vic pickle one bomb per target."

"Understood, one bomb per ship, aye aye, sir!!" Vic responded. 'Pickle' was the term they used for dropping a bomb. Its origins were lost over time, but apparently some flyer at some time, thought his bomb release button looked or felt like a pickle. The term stuck.

"Gunners, give those Nazi bastards hell!"

A chorus of "Aye aye sirs," rewarded him!

The aircraft banked to the right or starboard side. Billy could just glimpse the other three aircraft split away to the left, or port side. From his position in the nose, he couldn't see the aircraft following their lead. They formed up for the attack.

"Okay everyone, here we go. Gunners concentrate your fire on the enemy guns. Vic, make those bombs count!"

The airplane surged ahead as Lt. North firewalled the throttles. He also put the airplane in a shallow dive; they accelerated to their best speed, the ships growing larger ahead.

All of a sudden there were bright muzzle flashes from the trailing ship, a destroyer. Shells exploded directly ahead of them, a bright red flash and then a patch of dirty black smoke. The concussions rocked the airplane. The destroyer turned hard to port. As it did so, more guns were brought to bear and several streams of orange tracers arced toward them. The ship had the advantage of longer ranged weapons; Billy had to hold his fire for another few seconds.

Now! He pressed his firing buttons and was rewarded with bright balls of fire at the ends of his muzzles. He concentrated his fire on a gun tub housing a twin Bofors 40MM automatic cannon. He could see the crew of the Bofors frantically loading shells. His tracers found their mark and there were flashes and sparks in and around the gun tub. He saw several tracers ricochet off the steel ring of the tub and one German sailor was hurled over the edge and off the side of the ship. The Bofors stopped firing; its barrels no longer tracked the aircraft. Just as they flashed over the ship, he felt a lurch as one bomb was pickled away. He released his firing buttons and the pounding roar of his twin guns stopped. The smell of cordite was strong inside the turret.

The Germans were smart. When the bombers began their run on the starboard string of ships, just as they came in range, every other ship in the line turned hard in the opposite directions. This did two things. It presented the side of the ship to the onrushing aircraft. As the ship's guns were arrayed fore and aft, more of them were brought to bear on the attackers. It also confused the attack as streams of ships went in both directions. Those that were out of the immediate path of the aircraft still were within range so that their fire helped protect their comrades under direct attack. Also the attackers were momentarily confused as to which ships to follow. This served to throw off the bombardiers aim for a split second, which was enough to cause a miss, and it worked, all bombs dropped by the Liberators missed.

In a matter of seconds they were past the column of ships. Billy realized he was trembling. He could still hear and feel the tail gunner firing at the retreating line of ships. The aircraft flew on straight and level.

"Good job everyone! We will come about and make our next pass bow on. Pawlyk! Were any aircraft hit?"

"None I saw skipper!" Pawlyk the tail gunner yelled.

"Did we score any hits?"

"All the bombs missed. A couple of the ships, a destroyer and an E-boat (the slang for a motor torpedo boat) are trailing light smoke. I think our gun fire raised some hell with them alright!"

Billy couldn't get the picture of that German sailor flying off the side of the destroyer out of his mind. He was certain he had personally killed at least one enemy sailor and probably many more. His tracers certainly put that one Bofors position out of service. He also raked the decks of two additional ships with fire. He felt the aircraft bank as they came about for another pass.

The guy had a wide-eyed look of surprise on his face. Billy was certain of it. 800 feet was close. In an airplane flying overhead, you almost felt like you could reach out and touch someone. His twin 50 caliber Brownings had certainly done that. In the distance, he could see the gray hulls of the ships, the white bone of their bow wakes in their teeth. All the ships seemed to be going in different directions. As they got closer, he could tell that as confused as the ship formation looked, there was deadly intent behind it. No two ships were lined up in such a way that they could attack them on the same pass, but the ships were close enough together for mutual fire support and overlapping fields of fire. These guys sure knew their business. The thought of it sent a chill down Billy's spine. He checked both guns, they were ready. The engines accelerated to maximum power once more and the skipper lowered the nose aiming their trajectory to intercept what appeared to be the largest of the destroyers.

The destroyer skipper realized their intention and once they were committed, he turned into them. Neither vessel turned instantly so all the maneuvering basically ended in a draw. The Liberator intercepted the destroyer at roughly a 45-degree angle bow on.

The destroyer erupted in bright orange muzzle flashes as her gunners engaged the warplane. Billy and Harry both responded with steady streams of tracers from their turrets.

The 50 caliber Browning heavy machine gun is a devastating weapon against all but the most heavily armored targets. It fires a projectile one half inch in diameter and weighing almost a quarter pound at over 3000 feet per second, 600 rounds per minute. Each turret, Billy's in the nose, and Harry's on top had a pair of the big guns. Sitting in the turret, a Browning on either side was like sitting between two of the devil's own jackhammers. The sound and fury were tremendous and this was on the 'friendly' end. At the target, the huge slugs were arriving over twelve per second, each with more than 10,000 pounds of energy, enough force to easily cut completely through an automobile including right through the engine block.

As the Liberator bore down on its prey, Billy was startled as a cannon shell exploded very close to the front of the airplane. He heard the shrapnel rattle across the fuselage like a handful of gravel on a tin roof.

Billy concentrated his fire on the bridge of the onrushing destroyer. Once more they were close enough to see the damage his guns were making. He saw glass exploding as his slugs ripped through the windows of the bridge. Sparks flew and he saw pieces of the ship fly away as the rounds impacted. He sensed that Harry must have focused on the same target as it seemed the rounds impacted much too quickly to have only come from his pair of guns.

The intercom was nothing but yells and screams as each gunner fought back at the gray monster of the destroyer. Flak burst all around them and the air was full of tracers going both directions. The sea around the destroyer was full of white geysers from machine gun slugs impacting the water, and then they were past. All the guns fell silent except for Pawlyk in the rear that continued to fire until his rounds fell short. Then even though the four mighty engines roared and wind whistled past and through the fuselage, relative silence cloaked the ship. The intercom had fallen silent.

There was a crackle and hiss on the intercom again. "Is everyone okay? Check in!" Lt. North sounded as if he had just run a marathon.

Everyone checked in, there were no injuries. "What hit us? Check for battle damage." Billy surveyed his turret, all looked well. He really couldn't see much else of the plane unless he left the turret, something he couldn't do while at battle stations. Vic shared the forward compartment with him and crawled out of the bombardier's position directly under Billy's turret to check for battle damage.

The crew checked in one by one. There were a couple of small shrapnel holes in the aft fuselage, but that was all that could be found. All engines seemed to be running properly and they weren't loosing fuel at a measurable rate.

The other two aircraft had formed up on their port wing. They checked in with Lt. North and reported no problems. The other formation of three reported the same. So far they had dropped over half their bomb load and had nothing to show for it except a couple of near misses. Amazingly enough, both forces survived the huge exchange of ordnance with all ships and aircraft still operational.

They climbed to about 3000 feet and flew a racetrack shaped pattern around the German Convoy. Billy assumed that Lt. Comdr. Gay and all the aircraft commanders were discussing their options. Billy could see weather building up to the north. It was getting late in the day. In Billy's opinion, there wasn't time for more than one more attack. He searched the horizon for black dots that would be enemy fighters coming up in defense of the flotilla. Actually he was surprised that none had joined the battle so far.

"Listen up everyone," it was Lt. North once more. "We're going to make one more attack. It'll be getting dark soon and we have some weather building up. We're changing tactics this time. We'll attack in line astern (meaning the bombers would come at their target in single file", with enough interval between us that after the Jerries commit to their maneuvers, maybe planes later in line can pick them off. We'll be leading the port line." Everyone groaned. This meant they would be the first airplane in the attack and thus most likely to draw the biggest volume of massed fire. After their attack, the follow on planes would only have to deal with individual ships. Sort of like a cue ball busting a rack of billiard balls. Once the cue hit, individual balls went in all directions.

The engines accelerated and the nose dipped, they were going in once more. This time rather than trying to maneuver with the lead ship, they instead focused on the trailing vessel. Once it committed, they had more time to maneuver themselves.

Billy watched bright red tennis balls float up to meet them. The tennis balls were mixed in with the black smoke of the larger caliber flak. The balls were tracers from the 40MM Bofors, the Black puffs were 88MM cannons set with proximity fuses. Proximity fuses caused the artillery shell to explode at a preset height sending clouds of lethal shrapnel in all directions. Then there were the bright pink flashes of machine gun tracers. Every gun in the German fleet was firing and they all aimed at them. It wouldn't have surprised Billy if the ship captains weren't on their bridges firing their pistols at them as well.

As they passed the lead ship, Billy and Harry each gave it a burst. This time they didn't pass directly over the ship as their target was the last in line. They made for it. Unfortunately it was an E-boat, something they didn't discover until it was too late. The E-boats were heavily armed, not as much as a destroyer, but they were smaller, faster, and more maneuverable. They did their best to stay on the small craft, Billy and Harry firing burst after burst in its direction. Finally, as they over flew the craft Billy felt the plane lurch as the remaining bombs were released. The aircraft continued away from the flotilla, Pawlyk firing as long as he was in range.

All aircraft formed up. Apparently none had suffered severe damage. Billy thought it was a miracle that they all survived. With all the steel that had been flying through the air around them, he couldn't understand how they could possibly have escaped unhurt, yet here they were on their way home. He climbed out of the turret, brass shell casings were everywhere, some of them still smoking, he had to be careful not to have one roll out from under him like stepping on a bunch of roller bearings.

The aircraft split up and made their individual ways home. This was because it was generally thought safer for the airplanes to fly alone rather than in formation. Flying in formation, especially after everyone was exhausted from the battle, was too dangerous, the chance of one airplane straying into another's path was high.

They didn't make it back to Dunkeswell until almost dark. Even though all the aircraft had survived the battle, not all were as lucky returning to base. The weather had worsened all the way home. Visibility was severely limited when they reached England and one of the squadron VB-110 Liberators flew into a hill near Dartmoor killing the entire crew. On this day, the green hills of home had proven a more formidable enemy that an entire fleet of enemy warships.

And so it was throughout the war. All the survivors will tell you that those that perished and those that survived were determined as much by luck or some other unfathomable force as anything anyone could understand.

Chapter 42

Sally heard the rumble of engines and at first thought it might be far away thunder. When they persisted, she ran out the front door of Granny Driver's house into the yard. She saw a Liberator with gear down on its final approach to the base. Even though it was almost dark and the clouds were low, she saw another in the distance. She didn't even take time to say goodbye, she just ran to the Ford and as soon as the engine caught, she was racing toward the base, the Ford's Flathead V-8 engine screaming in protest.

She was sitting in the visitor's parking lot when she saw the California Girl roll down the runway. It was as if a huge weight had been lifted from her shoulders. She could actually breathe again. Then the sobs began, great streams of tears coursed her face. She slumped over in the seat, suddenly aware of how tense she had been. She laid back in the seat, dried her tears, and a smile flitted across her face as she instantly drifted off.

Sally awoke from Billy tapping on the glass of the driver's window. She opened the door and sprang into his arms. The smell of him, even reeking of cordite, and the feel of him was all she ever wanted. If she had died that instant, she would have died a happy woman.

That evening after they were at home and in bed Billy recounted the day's events.

"I killed a man today. Probably several men, but at least one I'm certain. I saw the look on his face. He was surprised," he said.

She held him for the longest while. He didn't say any more after that. She assured him he had only done his duty, and that he was protecting England and America by doing so. Still she could tell that he wasn't the same. Something in him changed. After a while she too became silent and just held him.

They stayed like that for what seemed like hours. In each other's arms, the only light and sound came from the fireplace where a small mound of coal burned.

"Let's get married," Billy said all of a sudden. Then he paused for a moment, and then said, "I mean, will you marry me Sally? I love you with all my heart and I want to be with you forever, will you marry me?"

Sally was startled. They had discussed marriage before, but for several reasons had postponed it. One reason was that it was against regulations for spouses to be 'in theater'. As a civilian the Navy had no real jurisdiction over Sally, but if she were married to a sailor then all sorts of rules and regulations applied to her. She was afraid she would find herself on the next ship home. "I thought it was against regulations?" she said.

"Sally, I don't give a <u>damn</u> about regulations. This has nothing to do with the Navy, the War Department, or even the United States of America, this only has to do with you, me, and God. Will you marry me?" he asked again.

"Oh yes, my dear! I'll marry you! Nothing in this world could make me any happier." She laughed and cried and they hugged and kissed for a long time.

"How can we get all the approvals to get married? I thought you needed the wing Commander's permission. Won't they send me home, will they?" Sally was really worried about that.

"Sally, I don't mean go through normal channels. Surely we can find a minister that will marry us just because we love each other. Couldn't Granny help us find someone?" It seemed that Granny Driver was the authority on everything British to all the Americans on the base.

"Oh dear!" Sally said, a shocked look on her face.

"What's wrong?"

"I forgot to tell her goodbye. I was at her house all day. I just couldn't stand to be here alone all day worried sick I might never see you again. I went to her house for company. When I heard the engines returning, I ran out of the house and jumped in the car. I never even said goodbye."

"I'm sure she understands."

"Yes, she will, of course. She's so sweet."

Then a few seconds later, "Why now?"

"What do you mean?"

"We've talked about marriage before. Why did you decide now was the time?" she asked.

"That guy's face today, darling. My bullet hit him full in the chest and he just flew right over the side of the ship. I could see his face so clearly. He looked so surprised, nothing else, just surprised. I've been thinking about that ever since. I think that's the common reaction in wartime especially. Everyone thinks the bad shit only happens to the other guy. It could never possibly happen to me. That's what everyone thinks, but it can honey. It could happen to me tomorrow or it could happen to you. The Germans could decide to bomb the base and they could hit you by mistake or a Liberator might crash into this place on take-off."

"Well of course, anything could happen, but,"

Billy cut her off, "That's the point. Anything could happen, just like it happened to that poor guy today. He wasn't any different than me. He was just doing his duty, and he was trying his best to shoot us down, to kill us. Not because Adolph told him to, but simply to keep us from killing him and his shipmates, that's all. When he woke up this morning, he expected to be in his bunk tonight safe and sound. Instead, he's at the bottom of the Bay of Biscay somewhere. And that could happen to me."

"Oh Billy, don't say things like that!"

"No, baby, I mean it. Who knows what will happen tomorrow? None of us knows. If something should happen, I want to have professed my love for you before Almighty God. I don't know if that makes any difference to anyone, but it will to me, and I hope to you, and that's enough for me."

Sally kissed him. It might have been one of the best kisses ever.

When it was finally over, "Oh dear!" she said again.

"What is it now?" he asked.

"I told Granny when we first met that we were already married. That's why she let us stay in her house and helped me find this cottage. Now I have to ask for her help to find someone to really marry us and to do it without any of the proper authorizations. Oh dear!"

"Baby, somehow I don't think that it's important to God that we have a signed piece of paper saying that the duly appointed representative of the U.S. Navy grants his permission for us to marry. And besides all that, don't you think Mrs. Driver will be anxious to resolve the issue of us 'living in sin'?"

It turned out that Billy was right. Granny Driver was more than happy to help. When Sally had broached the subject with her, apologizing for ever having told her that she and Billy were already married, Mrs. Driver had poo pooed the entire affair.

"My dear, I never thought you were. On the other hand, I never doubted for an instant how in love you were," she said.

"The other problem we have is that we don't have an authorization from the Navy to get married. They won't grant any to the enlisted men, at least not now. But, even if they did, as soon as the ceremony was over, they'd ship me back to the States. Spouses aren't allowed in war zones you know."

"Don't you worry your pretty head about that for one minute. I know a minister who will be glad to help. I even think he will share Billy's thought that marriage in God's eyes doesn't require a piece of paper granting permission. I could talk to him today, provided of course, that I had a lovely young woman with an automobile that wouldn't mind driving me."

They both laughed and plans were made. Right after lunch they would visit the Reverend. Sally wondered why she had ever worried about talking to Granny. The woman seemed to know everything, everybody and most of all, she had an intuitive grasp of the way people thought and acted.

The drive across the English countryside was pleasant. Even though there was a war on and it was hard to escape signs of that, still much of their trip brought them down narrow tree lined lanes through picturesque open fields where cows grazed as they had for hundreds of years.

The visit with the minister went even better than the drive. After being apprised of the situation, he was only too happy to help.

"Miss Anthony, I can assure you that marriage as described in the Holy Scriptures does not require any approval from the secular world. I will also assure you that, under the circumstances, I would be happy to perform such a ceremony. I will caution you however, that even though you will be married in the eyes of God and the eyes of the Church, you will not be in secular terms."

"I understand, Reverend."

315

"It's settled then!" and he grasped her hands in an embrace. "When would you like to schedule the ceremony? And how many people will be attending?"

That was a question she really hadn't considered until that moment. After a moment's reflection she thought it best that the ceremony was kept as private as possible, especially where Navy personnel were involved. She didn't think anything would come of it; and she didn't want to put anyone in a position where they had to lie or disavow knowledge of the union.

"As small a number as possible. Perhaps Mrs. Driver would like to attend?"

"I would be honored my dear, and may I suggest that Mr. Faulkenwell be included? I think he would be very pleased," Granny Driver said.

"Of course, he can come. I think that should just about do it, Reverend," Sally said, and she had the sudden thought, *I wonder if Granny Driver and Mr. Faulkenwell have their own relationship going on?* She mused.

It was decided that the ceremony would take place one week hence and that the only witnesses in attendance would be one Mrs. Driver accompanied by one Mr. Faulkenwell, both of Dunkeswell hamlet.

Chapter 43

Babe flew down the tree-lined street crouched low over the handlebars. Parked cars whizzed by on either side of him. He was pedaling so fast he couldn't pedal any faster.

He imagined himself the pilot of a Liberator making a bombing run on a Nazi U-boat. Messerschmitt fighters were being swatted from the air like so many pesky mosquitoes by his dead-eye gunners. Just as his front wheel dipped into the gutter of his driveway, he released his load of depth bombs obliterating the goose-stepping SS Captain and his henchmen. He steered around the LaSalle coupe and came to a halt at the front door of the converted carriage house shop in a J-hook sliding stop. As he dropped the bike to the ground, he could still smell the burned rubber from his rear tire. He ran through the open shop door.

After the bright sunlight of outdoors it was almost like entering a cave. Exposed bare light bulbs under white enamel reflectors lit the workspace, but could never rival Mother Nature's light source.

"Hello son," his father said, hunched over the Special.

"Hi Dad!" Babe responded.

As Babe's eyes adjusted, he could see his dad was bent over the long hood and, what was he doing?!

"What are you doing to the Special?!!!" Babe cried not believing his eyes.

His dad had been working on the Special ever since Billy and Sally left for Europe. Babe had grown very accustomed to its gleaming presence in the shop. His father spent a lot of time adding headlights and taillights, but also all the other details to make it a car that could be driven on the street in relative comfort and style. To contribute to the style, many of the exterior components had been chromed or polished. To the Babe, it was the most beautiful car he ever saw; prettier even than Mr. Lee's speedster. Now what was his father doing? He had ruined the car!

His father stood up, a razor sharp putty knife gleamed in his hand. Much of the Special's paint lay in black paper thin curls on the floor

"What are you doing?!" Babe demanded once more.

A smile crept across his father's face, "I'm scraping the paint off, of course."

"Why?!" the outrage evident in Babe's voice.

"It'll be okay Babe, just calm down, son. The paint job was just a quickie that one of the apprentices at work did for me. He used some bad paint or didn't prepare the surface properly because some of it had already bubbled up. I'm scraping it all off so we can repaint it properly. I'll get someone that really knows what they're doing to do it."

Babe was still dubious. He couldn't get the look of suspicion off his face. He wondered if his father had taken complete leave of his senses. Carl could see Babe thought he was crazy. "Come here son, let me show you."

Babe walked, rather reluctantly, over to where his father was pointing at the tail of the speedster. He was careful not to get too close to the knife his father still held, he was afraid he might wind up looking like the poor Special did, his outer layer scraped off and lying in ribbons on the floor.

As he looked his father pointed to a spot on the tail and sure enough, the paint was bubbled up. "See, the paint didn't stick here. Like I said, I don't know if it was because he didn't prepare the surface properly, or because the paint's bad."

Babe reached out rather tentatively and pushed on the softball sized bulge. Sure enough, it was a bubble where the paint had lost its adhesion to the body.

"Here," his father said and handed the knife to Babe. "Be careful, it's very sharp."

He showed Babe how to hold it and keep its blade flat on the surface of the car without digging the corners into the metal. The bubble sliced off with virtually no effort.

"The bubbles are easy. What takes work is where the paint stuck like it's supposed to." His dad retrieved the knife and began scraping on the tail. When done properly, the paint came off in long ribbons of wrinkled black paint and fell to the floor.

"What about where the paint won't come off?" Babe asked.

"I'll scrape it as best I can and if I can't get it off with the scraper, I'll have to sand it off."

"Are you going to fire the guy that did this?" Babe asked.

His dad chuckled. "No son, I'm not going to fire anyone. This was probably the first car he ever painted and he used some old paint that had been around the shop for years. I knew it wasn't a great job, I just hoped it would last longer than this. But now's a good time to fix it, don't you think, with Billy gone and all?"

"Yeah, it is, I guess. I really miss Billy and Sally."

"I know you do son." Carl hugged Babe close to him. "I miss them too. Maybe they'll be home soon and the damn war will be over."

"I hope so."

Just then they heard a car pull into the drive. There was no mistaking the sound. They both knew who it was without looking. Its deep rumble announced that Tommy had come for a visit in his speedster.

Babe looked at his dad and grinned. He enjoyed Tommy's visits. Tommy always talked to him as an equal, not as a kid. He liked that.

"It's Mr. Lee," he said and ran for the door. Carl followed, wiping his hands on a rag he carried dangling from his hip pocket for that very purpose.

As Carl walked into the bright daylight he had to momentarily squint, his eyes more accustomed to the relative darkness of the shop. Babe had already run the length of the drive way to greet their visitor, no visitors, Carl corrected himself. It

318

seemed that Tommy had a female companion. Just then Tommy saw him and waved. Carl continued down the drive.

"Hello Tommy, welcome," he said extending his hand.

"Hello Carl, hope you don't mind us just dropping by. We were taking a Sunday drive and were in the area and hoped you and the Babe would join us for dinner. You remember Ellen Stockton, of course." Tommy said.

"Of course, I don't know how any male could ever forget her. Welcome, Miss Stockton." Carl replied. She was even more stunning than he remembered her. Very young and beautiful with dark brown hair almost black, very thick and luxurious, shoulder length. Blue eyes against a peaches and cream complexion, she was a vision to behold. It surprised him to notice that this had not escaped Babe's notice if the look of enchantment on his face meant anything. Somewhat in confusion over his son's open admiration, he realized that maybe now baseball wasn't the only thing that ever entered his mind. That was a very unsettling thought.

"Please call me Ellen, and do excuse us for dropping by totally out of the blue."

"It's okay, you can stop by anytime!" Babe said with a dreamy look on his face.

Carl was still shocked. He'd never seen Babe act like this before. He had to admit that he could understand any man taking a second look, but damnitall, Babe wasn't a man just yet! She certainly was an eyeful. Her breasts were straining the cloth of the white button front blouse she wore, and it looked like she was melted and then poured into the mid calf length jeans she wore. The pants were form fitting and since there were no discernible panty lines Carl couldn't help but wonder what she had on under them. His mind raced back to the evening on the lakes when he was certain she had nothing on under Tommy's jacket. He blushed at the thought.

Tommy was talking and Carl finally realized that he had missed the first part of the conversation. Obviously, Ellen had a similar effect on both father and son. "We were just out enjoying the day on the coast highway. I think before I even realized it, we were already in San Diego. It's close to dinner time and I thought you and Babe might like to join us."

"Well certainly, we didn't have any plans."

"Oh boy, yippee!" Babe blurted.

"Where did you have in mind?" Carl asked while putting a hand on Babe's shoulder to try and control his obvious enthusiasm.

"I was thinking of that Italian place on the water. You know, Sally's favorite."

Carl saw Ellen's eyes spark instantly at the mention of Sally, her whole demeanor changing from relaxed to tense.

"Oh honey, I'm really not in the mood for Italian. Could we go somewhere else?" Ellen asked taking Tommy's arm and as she did so pressing her breast firmly into his forearm.

"Of course, my dear. We can go anyplace you like. Any suggestions, Carl?" Tommy asked.

On a hunch, Carl responded with "I know a new Mexican place right on the beach down by Coronado. I think I'm the only one in the family that's ever been there. Want to try it?" He watched for Ellen's reaction. When he mentioned that he was the only one 'in the family' to have ever been there, she visibly relaxed a bit.

"That would be perfect. Is it okay with you, honey?" Carl didn't miss that Tommy was now 'honey'.

"Sounds great!" Tommy replied. "Let's go."

"Give us a few minutes to clean up."

"Aw Dad!" Babe whined.

"In the house young man!" Carl commanded. They all chuckled as Babe trudged toward the door.

The dinner was excellent just as Carl said it would be. The restaurant was built right on the beach. After they finished eating, they moved out to a wide covered veranda for an after dinner drink. As Tommy and Carl enjoyed their drinks, Ellen and Babe went out to walk on the beach. In no time they were running and laughing, an impromptu session of tag ensued.

Carl could hear the laughter even above the sound of the surf. Babe and Ellen were chasing each other all over, even into the water several times. He couldn't help but smile. He looked over and saw that Tommy was obviously enjoying the spectacle himself, a wide grin on his face.

Tommy noticed Carl looking at him. "She's really something isn't she?"

"Yes sir, she is, I must admit." Carl replied. He was being honest and had to admit that maybe he had judged Ellen too hastily. While there was still no doubt in his mind that she was 'after' Tommy, he was beginning to think that she had nothing but honorable intentions in mind. The very thought made his smile turn into a grin.

"What?" Tommy asked.

Carl turned to look at him. "Boss, I don't know what to say. I've seen you with I don't know how many beautiful women. Other than Sally, I've never seen you look so happy. And I must say that Ellen is starting to impress me with more than her beauty. Is there something going on here?"

Tommy didn't say anything for a few minutes. Carl noticed that when he mentioned Sally's name, the expression on Tommy's face froze for an instant.

Tommy turned to face him. "I'm not sure how to answer that question. She is different than all the others, no doubt about that, and it goes deeper than her appearance, which is extraordinary, wouldn't you agree?"

Carl nodded his agreement.

"She's not Sally. Carl, you know I've always been crazy about Sally, but that was never going to be what I wanted it to be, even before Billy came along. It's finally dawned on me, with Sally's help that you simply can't make someone love you, no matter how badly you want it, no matter how hard you try. It simply doesn't work."

Tommy took another sip of his drink. Both men watching the game a while longer without any further discussion. After a few minutes Tommy spoke again.

"Carl, I just don't know. She's not Sally and that's for sure. Sally will be in my heart forever, but maybe I've got room for someone else in there too, ya know?"

"Yes, I think I do." Carl was simply amazed. He never suspected Tommy could fall in love with anyone except Sally. Secretly he had always thought the only reason Tommy thought he loved Sally was because he knew beyond a doubt that Sally wouldn't have him. He was certain that Tommy would never really 'love' anyone. Maybe he was wrong, maybe Tommy was changing with age, time would tell.

Babe and Ellen ran up to the banister that surrounded the veranda, both of them laughing and out of breath. Ellen's hair was disheveled and she was beginning to perspire. There was sand stuck to her face and on her legs. Tommy thought it made her even more attractive.

"Told you I could beat you!" Babe shouted at her, laughing.

"Only because you had a head start!" Ellen shot back and laughed with him. Then she gave him a big hug he obviously enjoyed as he made no effort at all to pull away from her, quite the contrary Carl noticed. He would have to keep a closer eye on the boy he decided. He wasn't sure he liked this new development. In his mind, Babe had always been the perfect boy. He'd never really considered him becoming anything else. Now, it looked like he wouldn't have a choice.

"Looks like you two had fun," Tommy said.

"Yeah, we did," Ellen said and gave Babe another hug.

"I think it's about time we call it an evening, don't you Babe?" Carl said.

"Aw shucks Dad! I was just starting to have some fun."

"Well, I think we better get going. After all, tomorrow's a school day."

"Well, okay," he drug this out, then, "But I want to ride with Tommy and Ellen!"

"You better ride with me..."

Tommy cut him off, "Carl it's okay, he can ride with us."

"But it's out of your way."

"That doesn't matter. We're just out to enjoy the day and evening anyway."

Carl looked a little dubious, but eventually gave in. Babe was overjoyed. He took off as hard as he could run making a beeline for the sleek blue speedster in the parking lot.

The speedster was not built with more than two people in mind. It had a single seat that was narrow even by the standards of the day. Besides the narrow seat, there was a long chrome plated shifter protruding from the floor that definitely encroached on any room for a passenger in the middle of the seat. It was a good thing that he was several years away from being grown. As it was, he had to squeeze in between Tommy and Ellen. He didn't mind this, of course. He was excited for a number of reasons to be riding with them. For one thing, he was getting a ride in the speedster. He had seen the car many times, but had never ridden in it. It was custom built for Tommy by one of his employees, Frank Kurtis, who went on to become a legend in the racing car world. A famous Offenhauser racing engine, the largest one ever produced at 318 cubic inches, powered the car. The car's exterior was as sleek and sexy as any car of the time, with four brightly chromed exhaust pipes running down its right side. It was an open car, and Babe never liked a roof over his head. And then there was Ellen, who was sharing her seating space with him. This had to be as good as it got for a twelve-year-old.

Shortly after they started home, the cumulative effects of the food he ate and the energy he expended on the beach got the better of him. The excitement of being so close to Ellen gave way to comfort. Before long his head was drooping and as soon as Ellen noticed this she put her arm around his shoulders and drew him even closer. The exhaust emitted a burbling bark and the wind blew his hair. As he drifted off to sleep his head rested on Ellen's breast and his arm lay on her thigh. Indeed it was twelve-year-old heaven.

Chapter 44

The wedding ceremony took only ten minutes. Sally would always remember it as perfect. The chapel was a wonderful setting, old, substantial, reserved and beautiful without ostentation. The reverend spoke in a clear direct manner. His wife played the organ. Granny Driver and Mr. Faulkenwell had been their witnesses. There was no marriage license. In Sally's mind, and Billy's too, the ceremony was between them and God. They saw no need to involve any governmental agency, especially the U.S. Navy.

The weather in England that winter was terrible. Flight operations were once again curtailed. Because of the weather forecast with no break in the snow, one storm following another, Billy had been granted a 96-hour pass away from the base. They decided to use the time as their honeymoon. Again on Granny's suggestion, they found a small inn nearby with beautiful views of the sea. The roads were terrible and even though it was only a few miles, it had been a difficult journey.

They spent their time at the inn lost in each other, thoughts of the war pushed aside. It was their last opportunity to totally forget their surroundings. They took walks in the snow, went on sleigh rides, had snowball fights, and even built a snow man.

All too soon, their time was over and they had to return to the base. The weather was still awful. Flight operations wouldn't be resumed for another week.

There was little for the flight crews to do while their aircraft were grounded because of weather. The big bombers were parked dispersed around the field each on its own circular hardstand. The engines were covered with canvas as were gun barrels and other delicate equipment. A few training sessions were held, but most of the crews had been flying for several months and knew their duties very well by this point.

Free time was spent as any group of young men will do. All manner of sleds were built out of any material not already performing a military function. A nearby hill provided the venue and a simple afternoon sledding down the hill soon turned into a full-fledged competition, complete with hastily written rules, protests and a grand prize of a one gallon tin of pineapple chunks.

Sally participated as a member of VB-105 crew R's team. She had long ago been accepted as one of the guys. The more observant members of the crew noticed a subtle change in her. Although not considered high strung, especially for a woman of her beauty, she was more relaxed than before. On one occasion when her left glove was off, Harry was quick to notice a gold band on her finger. He kept his observation to himself.

The next day, while in the classroom going over the latest information on German fighter tactics, he noticed a matching band on Billy's finger. Once more, he kept the observation to himself. If Billy and Sally were indeed married, and had chosen not to broadcast the news, then he would be respectful of their decision. Secretly he hoped it was so. He was well aware of the Navy regulations, but in this case especially, he couldn't see that it was any of the Navy's business.

The run of bad weather finally broke and normal flight operations resumed. Everyone was relieved to be operating off of dry runways instead of the sheet ice of just a week ago.

The biggest news on base was Commander Neuselle moving on and being replaced by Lt. Cmdr. Gay as commander of squadron VB-105. Gay was respected and liked by the men. They would all miss Neuselle, but all agreed that Gay, having been with them from the beginning, was a fine replacement.

The other big news was that replacement crews were scheduled to start arriving in February so that the original crews could be rotated out. They were in need of this as most were in continuous operation since September. Other than the occasional weather shutdown, patrols had been ongoing with crews flying 12-13 hour patrols every other day.

When Sally heard this, for the first time since Billy enlisted, she saw a reason for hope. The crews were scheduled to be rotated out at the rate of four per month. She was keeping her fingers crossed.

By the beginning of February flight operations were back to normal. The drudgery of the long patrols returned.

No U-boats had been sighted for some time. That all changed when aircraft of VB-103 and VB-110 sighted and attacked a U-boat at the end of January. The aircraft were escorting an American convoy as it approached the southern coast of England. The attack resulted in sinking of the U-boat, but not before Red Dean, the tail gunner on one of the aircraft noticed something very unusual about the boat. It had appeared to be equipped with two periscopes. This was a topic of much discussion and eventually it was determined that this was the first appearance of a device called a *schnorkel* by the Germans. This device allowed the submarine to run submerged just below the surface while still running its diesel engine and charging its battery.

The very next day a VB-110 sighted another fully surfaced U-boat and attacked it. While several depth charges were dropped there were no conclusive results.

As the weather improved, activity picked up on both sides. The Liberators flew more patrols and to counter that threat, the Germans put up more fighter patrols. The Liberators were having a telling effect on the effectiveness of the submarine fleet.

On the 17th of February the Wing lost another aircraft to German fighters. *Worry Bird* of VB-103 was attacked by two JU-88s while on patrol. In a combat that only lasted three minutes one fighter was shot down and so was the Liberator, which successfully ditched in the Bay of Biscay about 50 miles off the French coast. Three crewmen were lost, but the rest were rescued after spending a night in the water.

The ditching was the talk of all the aircrews on base. It was certainly bad luck that the Junkers were active again, but it was good luck that most of the crew survived. This event and the announcement of the upcoming rotations back to the States served to give everyone a lift in spirit.

It was a mixed blessing really. There was an end in sight, but the Hun was once again on the prowl. It was no secret that there would soon be an invasion of the continent. Everywhere one looked there was a buildup of men and materials. The Germans were as aware of this as anyone and they were stepping up their efforts to interdict delivery of the goods needed to make the invasion a success.

Billy was up at 4 a.m. He sat on the edge of the bed and pulled on his shearling lined boots. He was flying today and had to be in the briefing room by 5 a.m. Sally was up too. She was going to drive Billy to the base so that she could keep the car. She and Granny Driver were going to Exeter for the day.

Sally had coffee brewing and the smell was wonderful. Somehow the Navy always had the best coffee. Billy walked into the room in search of the source of the wonderful smell. Sally was already pouring him a steaming mug. One small lamp lit the room and mixed with the smell of fresh brewed coffee there was also the smell of coal burning in the fireplace.

Besides his flying boots, Billy had on the long woolen underwear called 'long handles' by the Navy. Over this he had on a thick wool uniform, his shearling jacket was draped over the back of a chair by the door.

"Smells great, honey," he took a sip of the black coffee, "ummm, tastes even better." Then he paused, put down the cup and pulled her to him for a long good morning kiss. "That tastes great too."

"Then let's try another," she replied followed by an even longer embrace.

Finally breaking apart he said, "We better stop that or I'll be late."

"I noticed," Sally replied and they both laughed.

"Let's go then, before you notice something else!" and out the front door they went.

It was still dark and cold. The stars looked like millions of ice sparkles across the black sky. From the looks of it, it was going to be a clear day, Billy groaned inside, but never said a word about it to Sally. It was Junkers weather for sure.

Sally made their way down the narrow lane to the base road, her nearly blacked out headlights casting a dim glow. They passed through the front gate where a lone SP huddled against the morning cold; their appearance at this hour a common sight to the guards on duty.

Sally drove through the narrow streets of the base to the ready room, so called because it was used for the preflight briefings of the crews, making them 'ready' for take-off. She pulled into the small parking area and left the motor running. This was as far as she could go with him.

"'Bye darling, thanks for the ride. I love you," he said as he leaned over and they kissed again, long and full of passion.

"I love you too, Mr. Pendleton, you be careful up there today!"

"I will Mrs. Pendleton, you be careful yourself." He opened the door and got out, but leaned back in, "I love you," he said again looking deep in her eyes.

"And I love you," she said returning his gaze. He closed the door and walked to the ready room door. Just before he disappeared inside, he turned and waved goodbye. Sally waved back, not knowing it would be the last time she would ever see him.

Sally put the Ford in gear and drove away, back to the cottage. She could never go back to sleep after Billy left, so she stirred the fire and added a few more lumps. Then she got out the clothes she was going to wear and started an iron heating.

She was reading the last issue of Stars & Stripes, dawn breaking outside when the Liberator roared overhead. She ran out in the yard to watch it disappear over the row of trees, its exhaust shooting orange and purple flame.

She returned to the house to get dressed. Sally promised Granny to be at her house early for breakfast. The men of the base always saw to it that she was well supplied with bacon, eggs and coffee. The meat and coffee were especially hard to come by for the civilians of the area.

The two women had a great day together. Exeter was small, but still considerably larger than Dunkeswell. They spent the day in one shop and then another. They had lunch at one of the small cafes in town finishing their meal with a glass of wine.

Granny Driver was the very proud owner of a new hat she planned to wear for the first time on Easter Sunday. Sally had bought herself and Billy hand knitted sweaters from Ireland. The wool was as fine as any she had ever seen.

On the drive home, they laughed and laughed as Granny told one funny story after another about some of the more colorful 'characters' of the village.

Sally dropped her at her house and then proceeded on to the cottage. She drove down the narrow lane and as she rounded the curve by the cottage, her heart froze as she saw a jeep parked outside the yard. Then she saw Joe Kennedy sitting on the rock wall beside the gate and the ice turned to fire as her anger grew. When would that son-of-a-bitch get the message!

She slammed on the brakes and threw the door open, ready for a fight. As she walked around the back of the car, her blue eyes blazing, Joe met her halfway.

"I thought I told you to leave me alone!" her voice crackling with anger.

Joe seemed completely unfazed by her angry tirade. She had been so mad that she hadn't heard a word he said. It was the look in his eyes that finally snapped the spell and her anger broke as she finally heard the words.

"...I was in the Operations shack when I heard. I rushed right over here; I thought you should know right away."

"Know what right away? What was it you heard?" the tears were already beginning to well up in her eyes. "Joe, goddamnit! What did you hear?" This time she screamed.

Joe stood up to it and kept the solemn look and the carefully spoken words. "Sally, I'm sorry, but Billy's plane is missing in action."

"What do you mean 'missing in action'? Can't the goddamn Navy keep up with a goddamned airplane that's as big as a house?!" she screamed. "How in the hell can they lose an airplane? Joe, what in the hell are you telling me?" In her heart she already knew, had known as soon as she rounded the bend and saw the jeep, but she had to hear the words, until she did, everything was still okay, there was still hope.

"Sally, I was in the operations shack, I heard the radio call come in. It was Billy's plane. They were attacked by German fighters. Then there was a 'Mayday' call and then nothing else."

The icy dagger pierced her heart and all the way to her feet. She felt cold and hollow inside. In a small voice, she asked, "What does 'Mayday' mean?"

"It means they're in trouble. It means that the airplane is going in, into the water. It means they were shot down."

"That doesn't mean they were killed! I know it doesn't! That crew last week, they went in too, but they're all safe and sound!" This was a fierce defense as if she were debating the issue in a school competition.

"Sally, I know it doesn't mean they were killed. It just means they were attacked and now they're missing, we don't know yet." Joe said, as evenly as possible.

"Why aren't you out there?" The anger was returning now. "You're a pilot aren't you? Why aren't you out there looking for them?"

"Sally, they're mounting a search. All aircraft in the area were directed over to look for them. They're sending out flying boats. Surface ships are being diverted. Everything that can be done is being done."

She looked deep into his eyes, looking for the lie, the trick that would make this all go away. It wasn't there. For once in his life, at least as far as Sally could discern, Joe was telling the truth.

It was more than she could bear. Her brain simply ceased to function and what happened next she would never know. The world got out of focus and her field of view shrank. The very last sight she saw was Joe's face strangely several feet above her.

Sally awoke to find herself in her bed. When her eyes finally opened, it took a second for her to process the fact that she was in bed by herself. Where was Billy? She rose up to look around the room. When she did so, she saw Granny Driver dozing in the rocker beside the bed. What was she doing there?

Then it all came crashing back to her. Billy was missing in action! What a horrible thing for three such simple words. She went cold inside all over again. Her heart was an ice cube. How could she go on without Billy? He had only been in her life for such a short time. She was his wife!

Granny Driver had been dozing, she was awakened by a sob from the bed. She looked over at Sally and saw that she was finally awake. It was almost two days since Billy was declared missing.

When she fainted, Joe Kennedy scooped her up and when she didn't immediately regain consciousness, he put her in the jeep and rushed her over to Granny's. He knew intuitively that Sally needed a female to take care of her instead of the doctor on base.

Granny took her in, placing her in her own bed and sent Joe to fetch the doctor from Exeter.

Now Sally had finally decided to rejoin the living. That was exactly the way Granny thought of it.

After what seemed like an eternity of sobbing, Sally was finally able to talk a little, actually it sounded more like a croak than speech.

Granny was able to relate to her the latest information. There were no more messages from Billy's airplane. Only the two Joe told her about, that they were being attacked by fighters, and later a mayday and their location. Another Liberator was flying patrol in the adjacent search area. Upon hearing the mayday, the other plane immediately left their assigned area and headed to the radioed location at maximum speed. When they arrived, less than 30 minutes later, they found two oil slicks and a pair of dinghies, one of the type carried by Liberators and one of the type carried by the Junkers JU-88, the most prevalent type of German fighter encountered by the Wing. Other search aircraft in the area found nothing more.

Still without evidence to the contrary, there was the barest glimmer of hope that maybe the crew had survived. It was only a spark, but Sally clung to it like a drowning swimmer will cling to anything that floats.

It was two more days before Sally was able to get out of bed. Granny was a godsend, caring for her every need, being the mother she needed beyond all else. Billy had been her world, in reality her only world ever. Forever she would know that her life had not started until she met him. Now he was gone. It would take years for her to come to grips with this horrible thought. Once she was able to think a little more clearly, the first thing she did was to wire the news to Carl.

Chapter 45

Babe rode his bike, a red and white Columbia with springer front fork, down the tree lined street and the closer he got to his house, the more convinced he became that something was wrong. From at least a block away, he could see his dad sitting on the front porch. There were two things wrong with this. His dad hardly ever sat on the porch alone, and he was slouched in the chair. Babe could never remember seeing his dad sit like that before. Babe had just finished a ballgame and was riding home, his glove slung over one side of the handlebar and his favorite bat laid across the handgrips.

He rode up in the driveway and there was no doubt something was very wrong. His dad never even looked up as he turned into the yard. Babe's apprehension made him more sedate than usual. Rather than drop his bike on the grass and run up the steps reaching the front door before the wheels ceased being a blur, this time he came to a safe silent stop, dismounted and put down his kickstand. He looked up at his father, who still sat with his head slumped to his chest, never looking up.

As Babe mounted the steps to the porch he asked, "Dad, what's wrong?" Fear of the unknown was beginning to take root; he never saw his father act like this. He still didn't respond.

Babe walked over and gingerly put his arm around his dad's shoulders. "Dad, what's the matter?" he asked again.

His touch finally made his dad stir. Carl turned to look at him. Babe was really scared now. Tears began to well up, he had no idea what could cause his father to act like this. "Dad?"

"Son, it's Billy. Son, he's missing in action."

Billy? Missing? What did that mean?

"What does that mean, Dad? Missing in action?" Babe asked.

"It means that Billy's airplane was attacked by fighters over the Bay of Biscay and no one knows what happened. They never returned to base." Carl said.

Babe started to cry, "He was shot down?"

"Yes, son, I think he was."

"Is he dead, Dad? Is he dead?" Babe was sobbing now.

"I don't know Babe. No one knows. There's a chance that they might have landed in the water and a boat picked them up. I just don't know."

"I hate the Germans! I hate them! I hate them!" Babe cried, tears streaming down his cheeks, he buried his face in his father's shoulder.

"It's the war, Babe. Don't hate the Germans. Some of them yes, but most of them are just doing their duty just like Billy"

Carl took Babe into his lap even though Babe was getting a bit big for that. He was still only twelve and still a boy.

They sat on the front porch for some time, neither saying much. Finally, Babe's sobs subsided somewhat.

"How did you find out, Dad?" Babe asked.

"I got a telegram from Sally."

"Is she okay?"

"I don't know son. I guess she's as okay as she can be. She is really in love with Billy you know."

"I know she is. You can see it in her eyes when she looks at him."

"Yes, you can."

"Can I see the telegram?"

Carl let him read it.

"What does 'Mayday' mean?" Babe asked.

"It's a distress call. It probably means that their airplane was too damaged to fly. They were radioing for help."

"Where's the Bay of Biscay?"

"It's off the coast of France and south of England. It's a part of the ocean."

"Why do they have dumb old wars anyway?"

"I don't know, son." Babe was crying again. He didn't notice that there were tears rolling down his father's cheeks too.

"How long will they look for him?"

"Till there's no hope, son. They'll look for him till there's no hope."

They sat on the porch until it started to get dark. Then Carl and Babe put his bicycle in the workshop. While they were doing that, Babe saw the Special sitting there. Carl had stripped it of most of its paint and it was partially disassembled. His dad was planning on making it sparkle. The engine and transmission were out. His dad told him he was going to polish all the aluminum so that it all was so shiny you could see your face in it. Those had been happy thoughts. His dad laughed when Babe made funny faces and asked if you'd be able to see that in the reflections. Now Babe saw the Special sitting there shorn of its beauty, and even the Special looked like it was crying. The curls of black paint lay on the floor looking for all the world like black tears shed by a now shorn car. The paint crunched under their feet as they turned out the lights, locked the door, and went into the house.

About a week later, they received a letter from Sally. She gave them all the information she had, which wasn't much more than she shared in the telegram. Billy had flown a routine mission on February 26. About 10:45 in the morning a radio message was received reporting that they were under attack by enemy aircraft. A short time later a Mayday message was received. Another Liberator that was close by was dispatched to the area. All they found were a couple of oil slicks, Carl had to explain what an oil slick was, and a pair of rubber dinghies, one German and one American. No more had been found. What happened was a mystery.

Sally told them she planned to stay in England for a while. She was still hopeful that Billy would turn up. Maybe a ship or fishing boat picked them up. In any event, she was more likely to hear something in England than in California.

The weeks wore on and no word came. It was springtime and baseball was in the air, but Babe didn't play. He couldn't get his mind off Billy. He was also worried about his father. He had never seen him so morose. He went to work every day as he always did, but there was no emotion in it. He just went through the motions. He hadn't gone back in the shop since they received the telegram.

Babe was so worried about his father that one day after school, he rode his bicycle downtown to the dealership. He was careful to avoid the shop where his father's office was located. Instead, he went inside and asked for the manager. He had met the man a couple of times when he went to work with his dad on rainy Saturday mornings.

Babe told the manager that he was worried and asked him to let Mr. Lee know. It was all he could think of to do. After all, he was only twelve and other than Billy and Sally, he had no other family that he was aware of. Mr. Lee was the only person he could think of to turn to.

After riding home that afternoon, he wrote a letter to Sally. He wanted to let her know how concerned he was about his dad. He didn't want to burden her with something else, but he didn't know what else to do. He found one of Sally's letters and got the address off of it. He rode his bike to a mailbox several blocks away to mail the letter. Babe didn't want his dad to know he had written to Sally expressing his concerns.

The next day as he rode home from school, he saw Tommy's car in the driveway. He was happy that Tommy had come, but he hoped his dad didn't know why.

As he rolled into the driveway behind Tommy's car, his heart skipped a beat. Ellen was sitting on the porch and as soon as she saw him ride up, she was up and coming down the front porch steps, a big grin on her lovely face. Tommy and his dad were nowhere to be seen.

He was excited to see Ellen. They had formed a relationship right from the start. There was something special between them and they both knew it. As Ellen got closer, even though she wore a big grin, he could tell from her eyes that something was wrong.

"What's wrong?" he asked, not waiting for her to speak, she was still several steps away.

When she didn't immediately respond and the grin on her face became more forced, he felt the icy fingers close on his heart once again. Tears were welling in his eyes.

"What's wrong!" he yelled.

Ellen was beside him now, her arms were around him and she pulled him to her chest. Just seconds before this would have excited him beyond his own understanding, but now he was scared. He didn't know what was wrong, but he knew something was.

"Oh Babe, everything will be okay, you'll see," she said. "It's your father."

331

"Where is he?" Babe was sobbing now; his tears were wetting the front of Ellen's shirt. "What's wrong with him?"

"He's in the hospital. We're not sure what's wrong, Babe honey. He collapsed at work. Tommy rode to the hospital with him in the ambulance and I came here to wait on you."

"I want to see him!" Babe cried.

"Sure honey, I'll take you. Let's put up your things and then we'll go, okay?"

Babe let her lead him into the house. They tossed his books on the couch. Ellen took him to the bathroom and washed his face and combed his hair. Then they got in the car and rode to the hospital.

They walked into the waiting room and the first person Babe saw was Tommy, a grave look on his face. As soon as Tommy saw them, he replaced the frown with a grin every bit as artificial as the one Ellen greeted him with.

"Hi ya sport!" Tommy said and gave Babe a hug.

"Where's Dad? I want to see him."

"Okay. I can take you to his room. We can only stay a few minutes. They want him to rest as much as possible."

"What's wrong with him?"

"The doctors think he had a stroke."

"What does 'stroke' mean? Will he be okay?" Babe voice was trembling. He was fearful of the answers he might receive.

"Stroke means that a blood vessel in the brain ruptured." Tommy told him.

"I don't understand; is he going to be okay?"

"Babe, it means that the blood flow to part of his brain got interrupted. We hope he'll be okay, but we don't know yet. Well have to wait and see."

This was one of the things that Babe always liked about Tommy. Tommy talked to him as an equal.

Through all of this, Ellen held him close, he could feel her warmth, her softness, and he could feel her breathe. Now Tommy held his hand and Ellen stayed right with him and they went down the hall to see his dad.

Carl was in a hospital bed. Babe was startled to see how white and old he looked. The immediate thought Babe had was that if you touched him too hard, your hand would go right through him. His eyes were closed and he didn't open them. His breathing sounded shallow and labored. As far as Babe could tell, he didn't know they were there. Babe began to cry again and he clutched his father's hand. There was no response.

Tommy and Ellen tried to console Babe, but he knew nothing he saw was good. As he stood there crying holding his father's hand, a nurse came. She looked at Carl and listened with her stethoscope, then hurried out of the room.

A minute later a doctor entered the room with the nurse. He listened to Carl's chest and held his wrist.

"I'm afraid I need to ask you people to leave for a little while. We're going to have to put Mr. Mercer on oxygen and we'll need a few minutes to get that all set up."

"Is he going to be okay, Doctor?" Babe asked, tears streaming down his face.

"We'll do everything we can for him son, you have my word on that. Now's let's get the oxygen in here. That's the very best thing we can do right now."

They left the room just as another nurse and an orderly came down the hall wheeling a gleaming chrome cart that carried a large green cylinder. Babe looked back just in time to see them turn into his dad's room.

"He'll be okay Babe. They're going to do everything for him they can, okay?"

"I know" Babe sobbed.

"It's going to take them a while, let's go get something to eat." Tommy said.

"NO! I don't want to leave him!"

"Babe, honey, there isn't anything we can do right now. Let's go get something to eat and then we'll come back and check on him, okay?"

Babe thought if Ellen thought it was okay and if Tommy thought it was all right, it must be the right thing to do. He didn't want to leave his dad, but they were right, there wasn't anything they could do for him sitting in the waiting room.

After dinner, they went back to the hospital. They very quietly entered his dad's room. Now there was a canvas tent affair that had been erected around his dad's head and shoulders. There were clear windows so that they could see Carl inside. His breathing was better, Babe could tell that right away. There was also a little color back in his face. The green cylinder, it was just like the cylinders of his dad's welder Babe realized, was connected to the tent. A nurse sat in a straight back chair and smiled at him when he looked her way.

The nurse got up and came over to them. She said in a very quiet voice, "He's doing better, but he needs to rest. Could you come back tomorrow?"

"Has he said anything?" Babe asked.

"No dear, he hasn't woken up yet."

Babe touched his dad's hand again and said, "Daddy, we'll be back in the morning. Sleep good and get well. I love you." He gave the hand a quick squeeze and they left the room.

As they walked down the hall, Tommy looked across at Ellen and saw a tear in her eye.

"Why don't you two go back to the house? I'll stay here tonight just in case they need me. Is that okay with you Babe?" Tommy asked.

Babe nodded his head. He was still sniffling, but his dad did look better. Ellen kissed Tommy and said, "We'll see you in the morning."

On the ride home, Babe lay on the seat, his head in Ellen's lap. It was important to him not to break physical contact with her. She made him feel more relaxed.

Once they were home, Ellen told him to take his bath and get ready for bed. Babe didn't want to. They finally compromised with using the downstairs bath and leaving the door open. Ellen was in Sally's room just across the hall.

After his bath, Babe came out in his jockey shorts, the way he always slept. The door to Ellen's room was ajar. Babe knocked lightly on the door and peeked in.

"Come on in, honey," Ellen called.

She was sitting at the dressing table in front of the mirror brushing her hair. She hadn't expected to be spending the night in Babe's house, and hadn't packed accordingly. Consequently, she was in her nightgown. A short, thin affair of pink silk suspended by a pair of spaghetti straps.

"It's okay, you can come over here and sit with me" she said and patted the bench beside her.

He walked over there hesitantly. The only light in the room was a small lamp on the dressing table and an even smaller one on a table beside the bed. He was a little self-conscious. The only girl that had ever seen him in his underwear was Sally. He sat down on the bench.

Babe looked in the mirror, Ellen was smiling at him. He smiled back and started to blush as he realized what he looked like. His gaze shifted back to Ellen, oh boy was she beautiful. This caused him to blush even more.

As he watched her brush, he couldn't help but notice how her breasts pushed against the silk of her gown. Even before he realized what was happening, he felt himself stir. He quickly put his hands in his lap and blushed beet red.

Ellen saw what was happening and put down the brush. She hugged him close. She smelled wonderful and she was much softer and warmer than she had ever felt before.

"It's okay, darling, really it is." She kissed him on the top of his head. "You don't understand yet, but it's really quite a compliment."

She held him for several more minutes until he finally stopped blushing so badly. He never did move his hands. He couldn't believe what happened. How embarrassing!

"Let's go to bed, okay?"

He nodded, not really trusting himself to say anything. He was undecided what to do. He wanted to stay here with Ellen, but he was so embarrassed by what happened to himself. He couldn't understand how Ellen could still be talking to him, much less hugging him. Maybe she hadn't noticed. But if she didn't, why had she said it was okay and a compliment?

"Come on, you can stay here with me if you want."

He nodded again. She led him to the bed. He jumped in quickly, pulling the covers up to hide his embarrassment. Ellen just smiled and walked around to the other side. Peering over the edge of the covers, he couldn't keep his eyes off her jiggles. As she bent to get in the bed, he peeped down her front. He didn't think she noticed.

"You can turn out the lamp now, honey," she said.

What a dope! He turned over and quickly turned out the lamp. He felt her arms around him and then the warmth of her body against his back.

"Relax dear, everything will be okay. Go to sleep now."

He was stiff as a board, as tense as could be. He wasn't sure if it was his dad or if it was Ellen or what.

She snuggled close to him. Her warmth and softness were at once exciting and soothing. He didn't think he could ever fall asleep, but before he had another thought he was fast asleep. All the day's tension released.

The next morning he awoke to brilliant sunshine streaming in the windows. It took him a minute to realize where he was and why. The thought of his dad in the hospital crashed down on him. He remembered Ellen holding him last night, he was alone now. Where was she? Then he realized he heard the shower running across the hall.

Babe got up and padded out into the hall in his bare feet. The door to the bathroom was ajar and the shower was running. He was still standing in the hall rubbing the sleep from his eyes when the shower stopped. He realized he really needed to use the bathroom. He could go upstairs, but the thought of climbing the stairs was more than he thought he could manage. He was already at the limit of his endurance.

"Can I come in and use the bathroom?" he called through the open door.

"Sure Babe, come on in." Ellen called back.

He barely made it to the toilet. The relief was wonderful. As he finished and flushed, Ellen asked "are you decent, honey?"

"Yes," was all he could manage.

The shower curtain slid back to reveal Ellen wrapped in a towel, another wrapped around her head. She stepped out of the stall.

"Good morning, sweetheart," she said and gave him a hug. He loved the way she smelled fresh from the shower, and the way she felt, soft and warm and something else he didn't know how to define, but one thing for sure, he liked it. When he was wrapped in her arms, he felt safe, he didn't worry about his dad so much, the pressure wasn't as crushing.

"You get dressed and I'll finish getting ready and start breakfast. Sound okay with you?" she asked.

He nodded his agreement. She gave him a kiss on top of the head and left the room. He watched her out the door and then he went upstairs to his room to get dressed.

After breakfast, Ellen drove them to the hospital. The closer they got, the more apprehensive he became. At home, especially

335

with Ellen's arms around him, he could almost relax, but now all the tension and worry returned.

When they walked into the waiting room, the only person there was Tommy. He looked terrible, his eyes were bloodshot and he had a cup of coffee in his hands. He smiled as they walked in. Ellen embraced him and gave him a long kiss. Babe was immediately jealous. "You look like hell, honey," she said. "How is he?"

"No change really, he's still in an oxygen tent. The doctor says we'll just have to wait and see."

"I want to see him," Babe said.

"Sure, let's go." Tommy led the way.

When they walked in the room, Babe's attention was totally fixed on his dad. He went right to the bed and held his dad's hand. There was no response. He looked at his dad through the clear windows of the oxygen tent, but there was no movement. Babe thought his father looked almost like he was made of wax. His head didn't move, the eyelids never even flickered. Babe started to cry once more. He was really scared now. The thought that his dad would never hold him, or pitch him a ball or even look at him was just too much. He broke down into sobs.

Ellen led him out of the room hugging him close.

"It'll be alright, honey. Don't worry; I'll stay with you, okay?"

He nodded and clung to her. She was his island, his safe port in this storm. The longer she held him, the less he cried.

Tommy walked into the room just behind them.

"Honey, you really do look like hell. Did you get any sleep at all?"

"I dozed a little bit. Those chairs aren't very comfortable."

"Go home and get some rest. Babe and I will stay, won't we?" She looked down at him.

He nodded his agreement, never releasing his grip as he clutched to her.

Tommy looked at her, a questioning look on his face.

"Go on, we'll be fine."

Tommy left. Babe and Ellen spent the day at the hospital. They went in and visited his dad several times during the day. They also got to talk to the doctor. He told them there was no way to know what the outcome might be, but that full recoveries were rare and that they should be prepared for whatever might happen. Babe cried some more. The doctor took time to sit down with him and explain what happened. He also explained what the outcome might be. Most of it was bad, but at least he understood what was happening.

During the day they took several walks outside the hospital. On one of their walks, they visited a nearby park. It was deserted during the day on a school day. They went to the swings and swung together. It was soon a contest on who could swing the highest. They were laughing and talking the whole time, each challenging the other to try and match their best. Each time Ellen swung forward, her skirt blew back exposing her thighs. She didn't seem to notice, but Babe sure did.

After they finally tired of swinging they just sat on the swings and talked. They talked about a lot of things. What were their favorite desserts, their favorite colors, who was going to be in the World Series. As Babe felt more and more comfortable, he opened up more, eventually confiding that he was scared about what would become of him if things didn't go well with his father. Ellen told him not to worry, that she would stay with him as long as necessary.

Then it hit him. He needed to contact Sally. As soon as he brought up Sally's name, he could tell that Ellen didn't like it. He didn't understand this, who wouldn't like Sally? Still that feeling wouldn't go away, he was certain that he was right and Ellen didn't like her.

"Is there some way we can get word to Sally? Like a telegram? Can we send her one to let her know?"

"We can do that if that's what you want to do, but I'll take care of you."

Babe tried to think, he was sure that Ellen never even met Sally, why would she not like her? It was a mystery. He decided to drop the subject for the moment, he was certain that adults were awfully strange.

"Where were you born?" he asked.

"Los Angeles," she replied.

"Oh yeah, me too. What hospital?"

The pair were born in the same hospital. Before long she was her old self again. He resolved not to bring up Sally again unless he absolutely had to.

There was no change in Carl's condition that day, or the next. They continued their rotation with Ellen and Babe at the hospital all day and Tommy there at night. Tommy needed to return to LA for a couple of days to handle some business issues. They discussed all of them going, but Babe didn't want to leave his dad. Ellen said she would stay with him, and so Tommy left, promising to be back by Sunday.

This suited Babe to a T. Having Ellen totally to himself was just what he wanted. Ellen was spoiling him rotten and he was enjoying every minute of it. He was worried about his dad and Ellen was the only thing that took his mind off of it.

Before Tommy left, Babe caught him while Ellen was in another part of the house.

"Mr. Lee," he began.

"Babe, please call me Tommy, okay?"

"Dad told me to always call you Mr. Lee."

"I think your dad will understand that I really feel more comfortable with Tommy, is that okay with you?"

"Sure Tommy, if that's what you want. Would you send Sally a telegram and let her know Dad's in the hospital?"

337

"Of course I will. I don't know why I didn't think of that. Do you have her address?"

Babe pulled a scrap of paper out of his pocket; it had her address scrawled on it.

"Don't let Ellen see that," Babe cautioned.

"Oh? And why shouldn't Ellen see it?"

"I don't think she likes Sally."

"What makes you say that?"

"I just don't think she does," Babe said.

"Okay, I'll take your word for it. I don't think she likes her either, but I don't have any idea why. I'll send a telegram today."

"Thanks Tommy," Babe said.

The rest of the week, Babe and Ellen spent every day at the hospital. There was no change in his dad's condition. They took their walks and visited the park several more times. They went shopping at a small shop near the hospital. Ellen hadn't brought enough clothes to stay indefinitely. And finally Ellen insisted that they visit Babe's school to talk to his teacher. They left with an armload of makeup work. Babe wasn't happy about that, but when Ellen explained that if he didn't do the work, he would wind up repeating the sixth grade, he decided it was the lesser of two evils. He certainly didn't want to repeat a grade!

Carl passed away that Saturday night without ever regaining consciousness. The doctor later confided to Tommy that he thought Carl was nothing but a vegetable when they brought him in.

On Sunday Tommy sent Sally another telegram. In it he asked her to come home. He thought Babe needed her. He wondered if he needed her too.

Chapter 46

Sally had been staying with Granny Driver ever since Billy went missing. It had been a very trying time for her. She decided that she really didn't want to go on living without him. After making that decision several other thoughts ran through her mind. Although he was listed as MIA, if no word was heard of him, he would eventually be listed as KIA, or Killed in Action, but even if he were, the possibility still existed that he was alive and a prisoner of the Germans.

She was convinced it was a long shot that Billy was still alive, but she wouldn't ignore the possibility.

The other possibility she couldn't ignore was the fact that she might be pregnant. That thought had sustained her through the darkest days immediately after Billy failed to return. That possibility had now proven incorrect. She wasn't pregnant. She plunged yet deeper into depression. The thoughts of joining Billy once again filled her head despite Granny Driver's best efforts to cheer her up.

Joe Kennedy did his best to keep her spirits up too. Contrary to his earlier behavior, he had been nothing but a perfect gentleman ever since he brought her the horrible news about Billy. He made it his normal routine to visit Sally and Granny several times a week. He always came bearing gifts of rationed foodstuffs and the latest news from the Wing. He spent considerable energy trying to cheer up Sally.

Sally had to admit that maybe she was wrong about Joe. He always acted as if the only thing that mattered were his own needs, as if the entire world revolved around him. He had now done a complete 180. His focus seemed totally on her and her needs.

Between Joe's visits and Granny's constant urging, Sally managed to survive when she was certain she could not. She was sitting on the front porch with Granny when a white haired man rode up on a bicycle, a Western Union cap perched on his head at a jaunty angle.

Sally's heart jumped. Her only thought was that it must be some word about Billy. The man walked up and after she identified herself as Sally Anthony, presented her with the telegram.

Sally opened it with trembling fingers. She wasn't prepared for the message it contained. Carl was dead. How could that be? He wasn't that old. What was he, maybe 43, 44? No more than 45 certainly. Was he her father? She had always wondered, but now she would never know. Tommy sent the telegram and the last sentence hit her like a thunderclap. It read, "Please come home, Babe needs you."

My God! Babe! Who was going to take care of Babe? She wondered. There wasn't anyone except her. She had to get home as quickly as possible. Babe needed her. How could she do that? If she went by ship it might take a month. She needed to be home sooner than that!

"Granny, how can I get home to California as quickly as possible?"

Granny looked up from reading the telegram.

"Why my dear, why don't you ask Joe? I'm sure he'll be here shortly."

What a wonderful idea. Maybe Joe could help; if not maybe she could pull some strings through the USO or family friends, or even the American Embassy.

Sure enough, Joe showed up less than an hour later. He wasn't expecting what he found. Sally was more energized than he had seen her since that night at the Aero Club. Once he found out she wanted his help getting back to the States as quickly as possible, he couldn't help but be disappointed, but he did his best to hide his true feelings.

He decided the best thing was to do all he could to comply with her wishes. After all, the last thing he wanted was to wind up in the doghouse again. He decided that he was going to change her opinion of him and he had already made a good start. If he continued who knew where it might lead?

The quickest way he knew to get back to the states was to fly in a Liberator returning at the end of a tour of duty. There was one leaving this week he thought. Of course, carrying a civilian passenger on a war plane, especially a female passenger, broke every rule in the book, but the only rules that really applied to Joe were his own.

"Would you fly in a Liberator?"

"Of course!"

"It wouldn't be very comfortable, and I think we might have to sneak you on. Would you do that?"

"Joe, I'll do whatever I need to do to get home quickly, Babe needs me."

"I'll see what I can do. You might get a few things together, and be ready to leave on very short notice. You'll only be able to take a small bag with you; actually you should take a sea bag, just like the rest of the crew. Everything else you'll have to ship back."

"I can be ready to leave in 15 minutes, sooner if I have to!"

"Okay!" Joe laughed. "I'll be back in touch, probably tomorrow."

Sally, with Granny in tow, headed to the cottage to start packing. She used Billy's sea bag. She no longer had time to grieve, she could do that later. That's what Billy and Carl both would want her to do, she was sure of it.

Joe came through. There was a VB-105 Liberator, that was Billy's squadron, leaving for the States tomorrow. Once Joe explained the situation, the entire crew was falling all over themselves to help. Everything would be handled "back Channel" meaning the only people knowing anything about it were the crew and Joe. Even better news was that the aircraft was going all the way to San Diego. It would take several days and would be very uncomfortable, but there was no doubt it was the quickest way home. No aircraft in the world was faster over long distances than the Liberator.

Joe showed up in a Navy car to take her to the base. Before getting in the car with Joe, Sally gave Granny the keys to the Ford telling her it was hers. It was the first automobile she ever owned. They promised to stay in touch and to immediately wire any news about Billy.

Joe drove her up to a Liberator, its engines already idling. The last of the crew was busy loading a stack of sea bags in the fuselage door.

Joe introduced Sally to the crew and they threw her bag on board. She was dressed in her shearling flight jacket and boots and a pair of Navy issue shearling pants that Joe had come up with somewhere. The plane was ready to go, Sally thanked Joe for all he had done and was the last one to board. Just as she turned to head to the door Joe called out, "Sally!"

She turned to see what was wrong and Joe grabbed her in his arms and kissed her full on the lips. There was no mistaking the passion in the kiss. She was totally taken by surprise. Before she had time to react, he turned her around and almost pushed her into the airplane.

The door closed and immediately the airplane started to move. What the hell was that all about? Maybe she was wrong about Joe once more. She looked out the tiny window to see him still standing on the hardstand. When he saw her face in the window, he waved with a lopsided grin on his face. It's too bad for Joe she thought. Her heart belonged to Billy and always would. Somehow, she was sure Joe would never accept that. It was the last time she ever saw him. She did get several letters, but five months later Joe would be killed at the controls of a specially modified B-24 that was packed full of explosives turning it into a flying bomb. The idea was that once the aircraft was in the air, the pilot would bail out and the airplane would be flown by remote control until it crashed into its target. The airplane exploded in mid-air before Joe could parachute to safety. Their plan was to crash the explosives laden aircraft into the submarine pens on the French coast.

Sally settled down for the long flight home. Shortly after take-off she saw the cottage she had shared with Billy, her husband for such a short time. Her eyes filled with tears. The crew made her a very comfortable place to rest by arranging a stack of sea bags just so. As she lay back, her thoughts refocused on Carl and Babe. She willed herself to sleep.

The flight home wasn't direct. The Liberator didn't have the range to fly the Atlantic non-stop without adding additional fuel tanks. There was no need for this. They stopped to refuel in Scotland, Iceland, Nova Scotia and then Maine.

At each stop, the crew made sure she had the best facilities possible. She doubted that she would have been treated better if she were an admiral.

Once they made it to Maine, they had a scheduled layover to have the big bomber serviced and checked from stem to stern. This gave the crew a chance to get some rest and enjoy some decent food. Once again, the crew snuck her into their quarters and even stood guard while she showered. She was completely convinced that Naval Aviators were the best guys in the world. Sally was treated like a queen the whole trip.

The next day it was off to Omaha. It was great to be flying over the United States of America! They were home! Even though the flight was still fraught with peril, somehow it didn't seem so dangerous now that they were flying over U.S. soil.

They did another layover in Omaha. Several of the crew got off here as it was closer to their homes and they were all on 30 day liberties.

The next morning they took off for the final leg of the flight to San Diego. The aircraft was going to receive the latest updates at the Consolidated plant.

Looking out the small window in the side of the fuselage it brought tears to her eyes when they flew over Point Loma. Then Coronado was in view and they were on final approach.

There was a squeal from the tires as the main gear touched down followed by the normal rumble as they were now rolling across the bumpy tarmac instead of flying. They were home in San Diego! It was nearly a full year since Sally left. It was home, but now without Billy and Carl it would never be the same.

Oh Billy! Nothing will ever be the same now. She struggled with her thoughts and resolved to focus on Babe. He needed her and was the only family that really counted. She was as convinced as ever that Babe was really her brother. She would never think of him in any other way.

She hitched a ride to the main gate where there were always taxis waiting. Once the driver saw she was a woman with a large sea bag, he came running to take it from her. Sally gave him the address and they were soon driving through the streets of San Diego.

Before she knew it they were driving down the street just a block away from the house. Her eyes began to mist up once more, but she willed herself not to cry. She would miss her men forever, but she had to concentrate on the future.

The taxi stopped in front of the house. There was a new Cadillac convertible in the driveway. Who did that belong to she thought? Could it be Tommy? It was a weekday and she really expected to find Babe in school. Why would Tommy be here if Babe was in school?

She paid the driver who insisted on carrying her sea bag to the front door. He was curious to know what a woman was doing with a sea bag and dressed in U.S. Navy dungarees, but he didn't say anything. After all, it was none of his business and he had already received a very nice tip. He dropped the sea bag at the front

342

door, touched the bill of his cap, "Ma'am," he said and walked back to his taxi.

The front door was open. Sally started to open the screen and go in, but decided to ring the bell instead since she had no idea who was there. She pushed the button.

She heard a female voice call, "Coming" and a few seconds later a very attractive dark haired young woman appeared at the door.

Sally had no idea who this person was.

"Hello, I'm . . ."

"I know who you are. I suppose you want to come in." The last was more of a statement than question. The woman opened the screen door but made no effort to help with the sea bag.

There was no mistaking the chill in the air. It was obvious that the woman was not welcoming her home. Sally wrestled the sea bag in the door, then she turned to look at the other woman. She had a hard time keeping the irritation out of her voice.

"You may know who I am, but I have no idea who you are."

"I'm Ellen Stockton," the woman said. She volunteered no more.

"Well Ellen, let me put my things away and freshen up a little, then we can get to know each other a bit." Sally started down the hall toward her room.

"That's my room; you'll need to stay at the other end of the hall."

It took all of Sally's restraint to keep from slapping the shit out of this bitch. Still she bit her tongue and turned toward what had been Billy's room. She hoped she could stay in there without completely coming apart. She decided she could for a day or so until she gave this Ellen bitch the heave ho out the front door.

She opened the door and memories flooded over her. It was almost a physical presence. The times she spent in this room with Billy. The nights they shared here together. It still smelled like him. When she opened the closet, some of his clothes still hung there. She couldn't keep it in any longer, the tears would no longer be denied.

She lay on the bed, the same one she had shared with Billy so many times. She fought for control. She had to get herself together. Babe would be home from school soon and she didn't want him to see her any way but happy to see him and to be home. She also needed to get things straight with that bitch Ellen, she thought of her no other way than bitch.

She heard the screen door slam. That had to be Babe! She took a few more seconds to get fully composed then opened the door and walked out into the hall. No one was in sight but she heard voices from the kitchen. She walked to the sound.

As she turned the corner that led to the kitchen, she saw Babe hugging the bitch. Worse yet, the bitch was hugging Babe and it was obvious there was a connection between them. Sally felt the sudden sting of jealousy.

"Hello stranger," Sally said.

As soon as he heard her voice, Babe turned into instant motion. He nearly knocked her down running to her. "Sally!" he screamed over and over, jumping up and down as he hugged her in a death grip.

Sally forgot all about the bitch as she and Babe celebrated their reunion. They were laughing and crying at the same time. Both tried to talk at the same time and finally they just hugged each other as tightly as possible, reveling in each other's presence. Sally didn't know how long they stood there in the hall hugging but it was a long time. Finally, they were able to loosen their grip and talk.

"It's great to be home, you've grown a foot since I left," she said.

"You're home, you're home, you're home!" Babe said.

More hugs and kisses. Babe finally got himself under control a bit.

"Sally have you met Ellen?" Babe asked.

Yeah, I've met the bitch, Sally thought, but instead of saying that, she said, "We've met," while giving Ellen a hateful look that she was happy to see returned.

If Babe noticed any of this, he didn't show it.

"Ellen's been staying with me since Dad," and at that point his voice broke.

"Oh Babe, I'm so sorry," Sally said.

She noticed that Ellen had taken a step toward them when Babe got choked up. Maybe the bitch cared something about him, but it was hard for Sally to attribute any charitable thoughts to the bitch.

Sally couldn't contain her curiosity any longer. "Where did you meet Ellen, Babe?"

"I'm Tommy's friend," Ellen said defiantly.

"Oh, I see," Sally said.

"What is that supposed to mean?" Ellen shot back.

"It's not supposed to mean anything. Look let's call a cease fire for the moment, okay?"

The only response Sally got from Ellen was a smoldering look. *What was it with the bitch anyway? I haven't said half a dozen words to her* Sally thought. Then it hit her. Ellen was jealous of Sally's return. She had to get that straightened out before they killed each other. Tommy would never be more than a very good friend. There would never be room in her heart for anyone except Billy.

Babe picked up on the hostility. He released his grip on Sally and stepped back to look at both of them. He didn't say anything, but after a moment he returned to Sally's side and gave her a hug. Then he went to Ellen and did the same.

Without saying a word, Babe had weighed in on the subject. They were both important to him. Had he been forced to make a decision, Sally would have won out, of course. She was part of his

344

life forever, no one could replace her. On the other hand, Ellen was, well she was Ellen. They had been inseparable since his dad went to the hospital. She mothered him, she had been his friend, and she had been his playmate. She consoled him through the loss of his dad and Billy. She fixed his meals and she went to watch him play ball where she was his biggest fan. They slept in the same bed every night where he fell asleep in her arms knowing that he would be okay. Ellen was part of his life, that's just the way it was. He wondered how he could get both of them to feel as good about each other as he felt about them. He never got the chance.

The telephone rang. Ellen pushed past them with a frosty "Excuse me," and answered the phone.

She said hello and nothing else, listening intently. Sally and Babe were both looking at her and saw the color drain from her face and the knuckles on her hand go white as she gripped the receiver hard enough to almost leave an imprint of her hand.

Then, "Where is he?" and she listened for a short time, "I'll be there as quickly as I can get there." She slammed down the phone and without a word raced down the hall to what she had called "her" room.

Babe and Sally looked at each other and then followed her down the hall. The door to her room was open. When they looked in, Ellen already had her bag open on the bed and was throwing her clothes in it as quickly as possible.

Sally looked down at Babe and saw the stricken look on his face.

"Where are you going Ellen?" his voice wavering.

"Oh honey!" she said and rushed over to him. "Tommy's been in a car wreck. He's hurt badly and is in the hospital."

"My God!" Sally gasped then covered her mouth with her hand. Is every man I know going to die at the same time she thought?

Her gasp only made Ellen all the more certain that Sally was a dangerous rival for Tommy's affection.

"You *will* stay here with Babe won't you while I go take care of Tommy?"

It took every ounce of self control Sally had to keep from slapping her. "Yes, of course I will, after all I *did* travel half way around the world to take care of him."

Babe hugged Sally then went to Ellen as she was closing her suitcase and hugged her. "I don't want you to leave," he said, his voice still wavering.

Ellen turned her full attention to Babe. "I know, honey, but I have to. Tommy needs me and Sally is here now. You'll be fine and I'll be back just as soon as I can, okay?" she was holding his face between her hands. She kissed him on his lips then on each eye. She put her arm around him and hugging him close she retrieved her suitcase and started for the front door. Sally followed them out.

In the drive, Ellen opened the trunk of the Cadillac and threw in her suitcase. Then she opened the door and got behind the wheel starting the engine.

She kissed Babe once more through the open window and put the car in reverse.

"I promise I'll be back as soon as I can, okay honey?"

Babe nodded, his eyes full of tears.

As she started backing out of the drive Sally stopped her. "Do you know where my car is?" she asked.

Ellen gave her another frosty look and pointed down the drive. "In there," she said pointing to the shop. She backed into the street and left with a chirp of rubber and the engine roaring.

Sally hugged Babe to her. There was no doubt that Babe had a special relationship with the bitch. He was obviously upset with her leaving. There was no need to make things worse. "Don't worry, sweetie. She'll be back as soon as she can."

"I know," he said, no enthusiasm in his voice.

"Come on; let's see if we can get my car out."

They walked back to the shop. There was a padlock on the door. This surprised Sally, there had never been a lock there before.

Babe seemed to perk up.

"I'll go get the key," he said and ran for the back door. The screen slammed once more and Babe was sprinting across the yard, key in hand. He put in it the lock and was pushing the door open, almost in one fluid movement.

The door opened to reveal the black 1939 LaSalle coupe that had been Carl's pride and joy. She looked past it and in the space that had been occupied by the Special, sat her Packard convertible.

Her heart was gripped in panic.

"Where's the Special?" she gasped.

"Tommy moved it," Babe said.

"Moved it where?" Sally demanded.

"He moved it out to the farm."

"What farm."

"Dad's farm."

"I don't know what you're talking about."

"Yeah, that property that Dad bought out in the country. I think its 20 acres or something like that. You know, it's just outside town."

"Do you know where it is?"

"Sure."

"Then let's go out there this weekend, okay?"

"Sure!"

"Let's see if we can get my car out."

Both cars started easily. Babe told her that a mechanic from the dealership came over once a week and started the cars and made sure they were in tiptop shape. Every other week he got both cars out and drove them around a while. When he did this he also washed both cars then dried them and parked them back inside the shop.

"That's a good idea, I think we'll drive the Packard one week and the LaSalle the next. That way we keep them both running. What do you think?"

Babe felt important. She was asking his opinion about the best way to maintain the cars. He was now the man of the house!

"I think that's a swell idea. Could we drive the Packard first?" he asked.

"Sure!" It had been a long time since she had driven it. She found she was as anxious to drive it again as Babe was to ride in it. Sitting in it brought back a flood of memories, but almost everything she did brought back memories of Billy. She was simply going to have to learn to deal with them.

With the Packard sitting in the drive she turned to Babe.

"I need to take a quick shower and get out of these clothes," she was still in the dungarees from the flight, "and then I'll make dinner. How does that sound?"

"I think it sounds great. I'm going to miss Ellen, but I'm really, really glad you're home Sally. I love you."

"I love you too."

They walked into the house together.

Sally came out of the bathroom in her white terry cloth robe fresh from her shower. She was still drying her hair with a towel.

Babe really took notice. He paid attention to the way Ellen looked fresh out of the shower wrapped in a towel. He had always thought Ellen looked especially beautiful while her face was still flushed from the heat of the shower. Contrasted by her dark hair, blue eyes and almost translucent skin, she was a sight to behold.

Now he had the opportunity to compare Ellen to Sally. Ellen was an exceptional beauty, he was certain that was true, but Sally was nothing short of stunning. He wondered why he never noticed that before. He had visited the memory of the way she looked in the shower many, many times, but seeing her now, she was more beautiful even than his memories.

A few minutes later, Sally came into the kitchen in shorts and a sleeveless blouse. After Ellen left, she had quickly reclaimed her room.

Babe sat at the table and watched, mesmerized as she started to cook dinner.

Suddenly she turned to face him.

"And just what is it you're doing young man?"

Panic coursed through his body. My God, how could she tell what I was thinking? How could she know I was daydreaming about her without the shorts and blouse? How could she have caught me? Does it show on my face?

"Well. . . I was . . . um," he was blushing bright red.

"Get yourself over here and help young man. You don't get to sit and watch, you're old enough to help out."

Sweet relief! Maybe she didn't really know after all!

His mind was soon occupied with trying to peel potatoes. Sally made it look so easy. The potatoes he peeled, he found that half the potato wound up in the trash attached to the peel. This was hard work!

After dinner, they sat on the front porch and caught up a little. They sat side by side in the porch swing. Babe leaned against Sally, neither of them wanted to separate, each needing support from the other.

It was a very pleasant evening. Babe didn't want it to end.

"You need to go take your bath," Sally said.

"I don't need a bath," he replied.

Sally pulled back to look at him.

"You most certainly do need a bath."

"I didn't even play any ball," he protested.

"You need a bath every day period, whether you played ball or not. Is that clear?"

"Ohhh…. All right," he said thoroughly disgusted.

He got up, his head hanging and went inside the house.

Sally chuckled, then sat back and relaxed. She was bone tired from the long flight home, the tension. Even though she slept as much as possible, it was at best dozing for minutes at a time, never really comfortable. The overnight stops helped, but she was still beat.

This was where she needed to be. She could feel it. Somehow she felt closer to both Billy and Carl here. This was a place they had both loved. Tears welled in her eyes.

She sat there a few more minutes and then went inside. The bathroom door was still shut. She went into her room and changed to a night gown then put her robe over it. Sally sat down at the dressing table and started to brush her hair.

She heard the bathroom door open followed by a soft knock on the door frame of her room. She turned to see Babe standing at her door in a pair of jockey shorts.

"Can I sleep with you?" he asked in a quiet voice.

What is this about she thought?

He could see the question on her face even though she hadn't said a word.

"I've been sleeping with Ellen. She hugs me and it helps me sleep," his face looked pleading.

She thought a few seconds. *What could it hurt?* Somehow she didn't like the thought of him sleeping with Ellen. Was it jealousy she was feeling? Could that possibly be? She was suddenly glad she had a gown on under the robe. She and Billy had always slept nude and if it were a bit warmer, that's probably the way she would have slept. Even so, the gown wasn't all that modest.

"Oh Babe, I don't know, all I have is a gown," Babe cut her off before she could finish.

"That's what Ellen always wore."

"Oh it is, is it?"

"Yeah, I didn't mind," he said.

What does that have to do with it, she thought?

"Please, I get scared by myself."

"Well, okay I guess."

He ran to her and gave her a big kiss and hug, and then he jumped in the bed.

She brushed her hair a few more times then got up and took off the robe.

Babe peeked over the edge of the covers as she walked around the end of the bed to her side. As beautiful as Ellen was, he was sure Sally was prettier, and her jiggles were just as good!

The gown Sally had on was very similar to the one Ellen wore, except Sally's was white where Ellen's was pink. Babe liked the white better. It hid even less than the pink!

"You can turn out the lamp now," Sally said bending to get in bed.

"Okay!" Babe turned over to the lamp but not before getting one last peek.

Sally was a little surprised when Babe scooted up against her.

"Ellen always hugged me till I went to sleep."

She did, did she?

"Would you hug me?"

Sally put her arms around him a bit reluctantly.

"I like your gown, it's just like Ellen's."

Oh it is, she thought.

"Go to sleep sweetheart."

Five minutes later, he complied.

Chapter 47

The next day Sally got Babe off to school. This sleeping in the same bed was something she was going to have to work on. Babe was too close to puberty and she noticed he was much too interested in watching her. Whether he liked it or not this was going to change.

She needed to find some news about Tommy. She had no confidence at all that Ellen would call to let her know. Ellen hadn't even bothered to let them know which hospital he was in.

She would call her father, he would know. Funny, she still thought of Earle Anthony using that word while she was almost certain Carl had been her real father. That was a mystery she wondered if she would ever solve. The only person that knew for sure was her mother, and she spent so many years deep in the bottle, Sally doubted she would ever get the truth out of her. Then again, maybe alcohol would bring the truth to the surface. It was something she needed to explore. Still calling Earle was the quickest way to get the truth about Tommy's condition. She wasn't looking forward to the call, but it was something she needed to do.

Oh Billy! The thoughts of him and the tremendous pressure of the loss were with her all the time. It was almost impossible to do anything. All she wanted to do was sit around and cry and think about Billy. There was nothing she could do to bring him back. Maybe he was a prisoner of war somewhere! It was hope, only the thinnest sliver, but still it was hope.

"Mr. Anthony's office, may I help you?" a female voice said.

"Loren, its Sally, is Dad in?"

"Why yes Miss Sally he is. It's good to hear your voice, we've missed you. I'll ring you right through." Loren was Loren Brandt her dad's secretary. She was a very attractive blond about forty, single and totally devoted to Earle. Sally always suspected that she was more than a secretary, but in Loren's defense she had never been anything but professional and competent dealing with Sally. She also seemed to exhibit a personal interest. Regardless of what she was, Sally liked her and was sure the feeling was mutual.

There was a short buzz on the line, then a male voice answered, "Sally! Where the devil are you?"

"Hi Dad, I'm in San Diego at Carl's. I'm taking care of Babe."

"Who is Babe?"

Of course her dad wouldn't know who Babe was. Billy had given Frank that nickname, but only a couple of years ago. There was no chance Frank had even crossed her dad's mind in that time; especially since she had been away from home practically the entire time.

"I'm sorry Dad. Babe is Frank Mercer's nickname. You know how much he loves baseball and all."

"Why yes, of course." She could tell her dad had no idea but was simply faking it. "How are you, darling? Is everything alright?"

"Dad, I'm fine, but I'm not sure that everything is alright. I heard Tommy was in a car wreck, I'm trying to find out the details."

"How did you hear about that?" her dad asked.

"When I got here yesterday, a friend of Tommy's named Ellen something was here taking care of Babe. Right after I arrived, she got a phone call about the wreck. She left immediately. I just want to know how he's doing; he's always been a good friend."

"Indeed he has. So you met Ellen Stockton did you? What did you think?"

"Yes I met her." Sally had to concentrate to keep from calling her a bitch. "She's a very pretty girl, but I don't think we got along very well."

She heard her dad chuckle over the phone. "Yes, she's a gorgeous woman, but I'm sure she saw you as competition for Tommy. I believe she's already staked out Tommy as her own."

"It's ridiculous for her to think that!" Sally shot back, a little more forcefully than she intended.

"You can put the fangs away, my dear. I know you don't harbor any romantic interest in Tommy, but as far as Ellen is concerned, what he thinks about you is far more important. And on that front, I don't think she has nearly as much reason to be confident."

"Oh Dad!"

"Don't 'Oh Dad' me. You know I'm right. Tommy has always carried a torch for you. Lord, knows why, you've slammed the door on him so many times."

"I would rather not dredge up ancient history or discuss my romantic interests if it's all the same to you."

"Where have you been for the past months?" her dad asked, shifting gears to another subject.

"Dad, I called to find out about Tommy."

There was a pause and then her dad answered. "Very well, as you already know, Tommy was in a serious automobile accident yesterday. You know how he is; he was driving one of those European death traps of his. Had he been in a decent automobile like a Packard or even one of his Cadillacs, he would probably be fine. As it is, he's in the hospital in critical condition. The other car ran a red light and struck him in the driver's door. The impact nearly tore his car in half. It took four men to pull him out of the wreckage. His pelvis and lower spine are crushed."

Sally gasped. "Have you talked to anyone today? What is the prognosis?"

"I talked to the physician in charge just an hour ago. It's Peter Hump from the club. He's the finest surgeon in the state. He says Tommy will probably walk again, but he says complete recovery is still in doubt. That's barring complications of course."

"Oh dear."

"Yes, it isn't the best news, but it isn't the worst either. Peter is cautiously optimistic, but Tommy has a long road ahead of him."

"How long will he be in the hospital?"

"I think it's too soon to know for sure, but I should think a month or so, at least. I'm sure when he goes home he'll still need 24 hour a day care."

"I'm sure Ellen will see to that." Sally said.

Her dad chuckled. "I'm sure she will, at least until she loses interest. You know Tommy, he isn't going to be the easiest person to be around. She may decide the grass is greener elsewhere."

"I don't know, she seemed pretty devoted."

"We'll see won't we? Loren has the hospital room telephone number."

"Thanks Dad, that's what I needed to know. How's Mom?"

"As she always is. You ought to get by to see her. She'd like that you know."

Sally couldn't generate any enthusiasm about visiting her mother. The woman had been a drunk as far back as Sally could remember. Their visits were never pleasant.

"Dad, I want to visit Tommy, but I think I'll wait a couple of weeks. When I come to town I'll visit Mom, okay?"

"I think that would be very nice of you my dear. Actually, I wouldn't mind seeing you myself. You could stop by to see me too you know."

Sally was shocked. Her dad never showed any interest in her. What was up with this?

"I'll stop by Dad, I promise."

"Thank you. Do you need anything? How about the car? I think I've got a new one stashed."

Automobiles were in short supply with the war on. There had been no civilian production for two years. But knowing her dad, he had several 'stashed'. All Packards that came into the state came through his distributorship and then went to dealerships he either owned or controlled. His clientele wasn't used to waiting for anything. Since he counted most of them as personal friends, Sally was certain that he kept enough cars put back to keep them happy for the duration.

"The car is fine Dad."

"Are you sure? I have a new Darrin I think you would like."

A 'Darrin' was a custom bodied Packard. Darrin was a coach builder, meaning a company that built custom bodies for automobiles. Packard Darrins were very desirable cars for the affluent, status symbols for the movie people of Hollywood.

"I'll look at it when I drop by if it'll make you happy, okay?"

"I'll look forward to seeing you. Take care of yourself."

"You too, Dad."

The phone went dead. The conversation didn't end with 'I love you', it never did. On the other hand, it was one of the more pleasant conversations she'd had with her dad in many years. They had never bonded, not really, not the way most daughters did with their fathers. Of course, she had suspicions that Earle wasn't her father. Maybe that was true, but maybe it was the simple fact she felt that way. Oh well, the only person that knew for sure was her mom, and it was doubtful she would ever tell or even that she remembered after spending the past twenty years at the bottom of a bottle of scotch.

Oh Billy! What has become of you? Are you ever going to come back to me? The logical part of her brain told her it was unlikely. Every day that went by with no word to the contrary made it even less likely that he was coming back. That was the logical part of her that said that. The emotional side of her couldn't accept the fact he was gone. She would never accept that.

One thing was for sure, she had to learn to deal with the uncertainty. It almost paralyzed her at times. She couldn't afford for that to happen any longer. It was one thing to cry all day when she was staying with Granny Driver, but she couldn't do that now. Babe needed her. He didn't have anyone else and when it came down to it, she didn't either.

Sally went out to the shop. The Special was gone. All the tools were still there. She looked around. The headlights that they had decided to put on the Special were still sitting on the workbench. There was something all over the floor. It crunched when she walked on it. She stooped down to examine it and found that it was curls of dried black paint. From the Special? She would have to ask Babe about that. Why would the Special's paint be on the floor of the shop?

She looked around. All the tools seemed to be there along with a few other parts that Carl was planning to put on the Special to make it legal to drive on the street. That was something they all wanted to do.

As she looked around the shop, memories came flooding back to her. Memories of Billy, how he looked when he was intent on building a part for the Special. How he looked when they had discussed some design feature. How his arms felt around her, how his lips tasted.

Enough! She couldn't deal with this! She left the shop and went back to the house. Sally needed to clean. The laundry needed to be done. She would stay busy so her mind wouldn't wander. She threw herself into the chores associated with maintaining a household.

Three hours later she admitted defeat. The house looked better, but she was only kidding herself if she thought hard work would keep her mind off Billy. Everything she touched, everything she saw brought back a memory.

She had to learn to deal with this. When Babe was home, he kept her occupied, but when he was gone and she was left alone with her thoughts, they simply overwhelmed her.

That afternoon, she sat down at the kitchen table with several sheets of paper and a pen and she began to write.

The initial idea was to write a letter to Billy. As she started she wrote how terrible she felt and how she cried all the time, how much she missed him every minute of every day.

She stopped writing and went back and read what she had just written. Disgusted with herself and the pity party she was hosting, she crumpled the paper up and threw it in the trash. That certainly didn't work the way she planned!

They needed some things; there was virtually no food in the house. Ellen must not have been too high on grocery shopping. It surprised Sally to find that she was thinking of her as Ellen instead of as 'that bitch'.

Sally stopped in the drug store to get a few things. As she was walking down one of the aisles a small display caught her eye. The display was for journals, small hardbound notebooks. A neatly hand lettered sign said, 'Record your innermost thoughts of those you love'. She paused in the aisle and read the sign then reread it. Then she picked up one of the books and continued with her other shopping.

Late that evening she finally got Babe in bed. It had been an ordeal to get him back to sleeping alone. They had finally come to a compromise. Instead of his own room upstairs, he was now in what had been Billy's room at the opposite end of the hall on the first floor. He didn't like it, but she stood firm, convinced that the longer this went on, the harder it would be to break the habit.

She tiptoed down the hall and peeked in the open door. Babe was fast asleep, sprawled across the bed. She smiled to herself. Part of his argument was that he would never be able to sleep by himself. Hopefully things were getting back to normal as far as Babe was concerned, or as normal as they could be.

She walked back to her room and picked up the journal, turning it over and over in her hands, fanning through the blank pages. Thoughts of Billy crowded her mind. She picked up her pen and returned to the kitchen.

Sally sat down at the table, the open journal before her. At first she didn't look at it. She stared out the back door toward the shop, but her vision had nothing to do with the view before her. Instead, the vision in her mind was the race at Kearney Mesa three years before. As she transported herself back to that time, a smile began to spread across her face. When the smile was a large grin, she picked up the pen and began to write. The words came faster than she could write them.

The first time I ever saw you, she wrote, *Carl was introducing you to Tommy. There was something about you that caught my interest before I even knew your name. It wasn't the way you looked or how tall you were. I noticed those things, but it was what I saw in your eyes that immediately caught my imagination. I had never experienced that before. It was an eerie feeling. I know this sounds strange, but it was almost like warm oil was poured over my entire body. You hadn't seen me yet. I was behind Tommy's Cadillac and I just watched you. It was obvious that you and Carl liked each other. I wonder if you know how unusual that is. Carl has never made friends easily and for him to truly like someone is almost unheard of. Carl has always been a part of my life and I couldn't imagine how he could have come to like someone as much as he did you without me knowing about it. You shook Tommy's hand and the three of you chitchatted and I watched you. I made sure I wasn't noticed. I needed a little time to determine what was going on inside me. It was such a new and unique experience. I waited as long as I could. When I was certain that you and Carl were about to walk off, I decided I had to make my appearance. I was terrified that everyone would know what was going on in my mind, so I decided at the last instant to play up my relationship with Tommy for more than it was. It was a smokescreen, something I could hide behind. So what do I do? I walk over and put my arm around Tommy and kiss him way more passionately than I had intended. Did you notice how his eyes went wide? I had never kissed him like that before. That miscue on my part has caused a lot of problems with Tommy. He has always thought that he was in love with me. I've never been sure he knows what love is, but he thinks he does. That one kiss was like throwing gasoline on a bonfire. It was your reaction that interested me. I'll never forget the look on your face the first time you saw me. I could tell that your reaction to me was similar to mine to you. Looking back on it, the die was cast that first instant. Do you remember walking around with me, looking at cars and meeting people? I really couldn't have cared less about that; I was totally focused on you. Could you tell? I tried to hide what I was thinking but I don't know how successful I was. The fact was, you could have dragged me off behind the bushes right that second and had your way with me and I would have gone willingly, happily. Of course, part of the reason I felt that way was that I knew you wouldn't do it. Isn't it funny how our minds work? I wanted to be in your arms in the throes of passionate love making and I was sure you felt the same way and the fact that you didn't rip my clothes off right then just made me want you all the more. Instead, we just walked around making small talk to avoid the real issue. At one point, you called me Tommy's girl, which made me angry. You thought I was mad at you, but it was my actions earlier that upset me. I was angry with myself. That day was one of the most memorable of my life. It took all my self-control to keep my hands off you. When it came time to leave, I couldn't resist any longer, I had to kiss you. I had to do it to satisfy myself and I needed to taste you to make sure you were real, not just a dream I was having. Then I had to give you something to think about until the next time I saw you. That was the most important thing, to be sure you knew that you were something very special to me, to leave you with a little bit of mystery. I remember when I got in the car and we drove off, looking back out the window, you were looking at me. I knew right then that you were as hooked as I was. Did you think about me in the next*

*two weeks? I know you did because you told me you did, but how
much? What kind of thoughts did you have? I hope your thoughts
were as interesting as mine. I wondered what our children were
going to look like with your black hair and green eyes and my blond
hair and blue eyes. No doubt they are going to be tall. I'm already
as tall, or taller than all the men I know, except you, and you tower
above everyone. Those next two weeks were a real test of my self-
discipline. It was all I could do to keep from jumping in the car and
driving down to Uncle Carl's the minute I got back. And I almost did
it just to see the look on your face, well...maybe there was more to it
than that. Still I had to clean up a few loose ends and I didn't want
it to look like I was shamelessly throwing myself at you, even though
I was, totally. So I forced myself to wait two weeks. Every hour was
agony, my dear. Each day a prison sentence, but I knew you were
waiting there at the end of it. Just like you are now. I know you are
waiting for me somewhere. Until we meet once more, I will write to
you every day. I will write every thought I've ever had about you
since that first day, everything we've ever done together and my
thoughts while we were doing them. Until tomorrow my love. I will
go to sleep tonight thinking of you and wake up tomorrow still
thinking of you.*

Sally laid her pen down, the smile still on her face. She felt
better, sad of course, but still better. It was the next best thing to
talking to Billy. She found that a little bit of the tension had finally
released.

She decided that she would do this every single day. She
would write every thought she ever had about Billy. She would
describe every event in as much detail as possible. Her journals
were going to be only for her and Billy. Much as their wedding had
been, she saw no need for anyone else to ever see them. Because of
this she saw no need to restrain her description of the events. She
hoped to relive those events in her mind and one day to share them
all once more with Billy.

Sally closed the journal, collected her pen and went to her
room. It was time for bed. She was happy Babe was in his own
bed. She loved him, but she didn't think it was healthy for him to
sleep with her. He was becoming much too aware of girls.

With no Babe, there was no need for the gown. She would
sleep as she had with Billy, in the nude and hopefully he would
come to her in her dreams.

Chapter 48

They left the house early Sunday morning, a picnic lunch in the back seat of the Packard, on their way to 'the farm'. Sally had to see where the Special was. It made her uneasy for it to be stored at such a remote location.

It was a beautiful summer day for a drive. They had the top down. The pair drove down the tree-lined streets of San Diego toward the country. The city was a much busier place than before the war. There had always been a substantial military presence here, but it had quadrupled since Pearl Harbor. The bomber plant was also at peak capacity and employed thousands and thousands building Liberators. There wasn't a room to be had anywhere in town.

The farm was located to the east of town toward the mountains. Once they left the city proper, the drive was much more enjoyable with very few cars on the road.

Babe hadn't wanted to get up this morning. He still didn't look like he was happy to be along for the ride, but since she had never been to 'the farm', she needed Babe along as a guide.

"What's wrong?" she asked.

"Nothing." Was the one word reply, a sure sign that something was.

"C'mon, something's wrong, what is it?"

"I told you nothing was wrong."

"You're pouting and you know it. Out with it."

There was silence. Babe sat huddled against the opposite door, swelled up like an old toad frog. One thing was for sure, the Babe was upset over something, all his protests aside.

"Babe we can't ever work it out if you won't tell me what the problem is."

"Okay!" then more silence.

"Okay are you going to tell me? Or okay and you can go to hell?" Sally asked.

"I don't like sleeping alone."

"Alright. Thank you for the answer. Why don't you like sleeping alone?"

"I just don't okay?"

"There's a reason you don't, what is it?"

"I'm not as relaxed, that's why. I don't think about things so much if I'm not alone."

"Why don't you think as much?"

"I don't know, I just don't, that's all," he said.

"There must be a reason."

Was she never going to let this rest? Wasn't it bad enough that she had sent him to his own room? Now she was going to pick at him and pick at him until he said whatever it was that she wanted to hear.

"I like the way it feels with you against me, or Ellen, okay!" he almost shouted the answer.

"And what is it you like about the way we feel?"

"I don't know," he said, really tiring of this conversation, but Sally wouldn't leave it alone.

"Yes you do. Now tell me what you like about the way we feel."

Babe was really getting angry. He felt like he was kicked out of bed for no good reason. Probably because it was something that Ellen started and because Sally didn't like Ellen he was paying the price. It wasn't fair!

"Okay! Dammit!"

"Watch your mouth!" Sally warned.

"I like the way you feel. It's soft and warm and it makes me relax."

Do Ellen and I feel the same?"

"Yeah, I mean no, well sort of."

Sally resisted the urge to chuckle. This was much too serious a conversation for Babe to think she took it lightly, which she certainly did not.

"Do we feel the same?"

Babe was really confused now. He didn't know how to respond. One thing was for sure, if he didn't Sally would continue to pick at him till he did. He decided to tell the truth since he was too confused to lie.

"No you don't feel the same!"

"What's the difference?"

"Aw Sally!"

"Hey, I didn't say it, you did. Now what's the difference?"

"Okay! Ellen feels softer, more gooshy than you do! Are you satisfied?" he was really getting irritated.

"Gooshy?"

"Yes, gooshy."

"How do I feel?"

"I'm tired of this," was his response.

"I don't care. Answer the question."

"You're firmer, but not as large," as soon as he said it he realized what he had said and blushed beet red.

"I see. What else?"

No response.

"I said what else."

"I already told you."

"Tell me what else you feel."

"I told you already," he wasn't comfortable with where this conversation had gone. All along he'd thought this was his own little secret. Sally acted like she knew exactly what was going on in his mind.

"No you didn't. You only told me what you thought you could get away with to get me to stop asking questions. Now what else?"

He didn't reply.

"Okay, so you're not comfortable are you? You wish I'd quit asking don't you?"

"Yes!"

"Well I won't. What do our nipples feel like Babe?"

Oh my God! She didn't really ask that did she? Women don't talk about such things do they? How could he possibly answer that question?

"Do you like the way they feel? Pushing against your back? It sure seemed like you liked it. You certainly did your best to rub up against them. So what do you say? Did you like that?" she turned to look at him.

He was almost drawn up into a ball.

"I'm waiting."

He couldn't answer. There was no way he could make his mouth form a reply. Finally he nodded his head. He was certain he would die from embarrassment.

"Thank you for your honesty. That wasn't pleasant was it?"

He shook his head still not trusting himself to speak.

"You see Babe," Sally continued in a normal conversational tone. How could she talk about something like this so calmly he wondered?

"You see, you noticed these things, and it's all right that you did. You're becoming a man Babe, and men notice these things. Children don't. And since men notice these things it's best that men and women don't sleep together. You see, I noticed that you noticed. You had an erection didn't you?"

He didn't know what 'erection' meant. He turned to look at her, a puzzled look on his face.

She smiled a warm smile at him. "Honey that means you got hard. Down there, you know what I mean. You did, didn't you?"

The shame was almost unbearable. How could she talk about this stuff?

"Ellen said it was a compliment!" he blurted out and wished he hadn't as soon as his mouth closed. Now I've gotten Ellen in trouble he thought.

"Ellen's correct, honey, but that should really be reserved for people that are married. Just like men and women sleeping together."

"You and Billy weren't married!" He saw Sally turn pale. If he had a gun, he thought he'd shoot himself that very moment. He was considering opening the car door and jumping out, maybe that would kill him. How had he said such a heartless thing? It just came out! He wished he'd been born without a mouth!

"I'm sorry, Sally. I never meant to say that!" he was starting to cry.

Sally was looking straight ahead. Her knuckles were white as she gripped the steering wheel. The car slowed and then pulled off the road.

Good, he thought. She's going to kill me and get this over with. Instead she stopped the car calmly and turned off the engine. Then she turned to face him.

For several moments, the only sound was the ticking of the hot engine and the birds in the nearby trees.

Finally she said, "What I am about to tell you is a secret. It's between you and me and that's all. It will hurt me very deeply if you ever tell another soul. Can I trust you?"

He nodded his head.

"Billy and I were married."

The shock was evident on his face.

"We were married in England."

He didn't know what to say. It was as if he had been struck by lightning. One thing was certain, he had a damn big mouth that he had absolutely no control over, but he was proud Sally would share her secret with him. He was also ashamed at his actions that made it necessary. Tears welled up in his eyes. He couldn't help it. He started to cry.

Sally hugged him to her. She was crying too. They sat on the side of the road for several minutes hugging and crying.

"I'm sorry for all the things I said," Babe said. "I didn't understand, I mean I don't, oh, I don't know what I mean!"

"It's alright, I know you didn't."

It was one of those moments in which everything changes. Their relationship would never be the same again. The boy had taken his first step into manhood. Intuitively he understood that Sally trusted him with what very well could have been her most cherished secret. The fact that she trusted him enough to do so was a life-altering event for him. He would never again question her motives or her advice.

Several minutes later, Sally started the car and they continued their drive. The sky was bluer and the grass greener on the second part of their journey. He laughed a lot more. When he looked at Sally, it was with greater respect, almost awe. From that day forward, Babe felt that Sally treated him as an adult, an equal. Many more secrets would be shared between them, and Babe would always think of it as The Day.

They turned off the main highway onto a gravel road. The road had a fence down each side, the fence rows lined with trees. Soon, they came to a gate.

"This is it!" Babe cried.

Sally had an uncertain look on her face. "Are you sure Babe?" she asked.

"Yeah, this is it."

Babe jumped out and opened the gate so Sally could drive through. Twin tracks led over the crest of a hill. Babe jumped back in the car, leaving the gate open.

"How did your dad get this place? I don't ever remember him saying anything about it."

"I think one of the men he worked with owed him some money and couldn't pay Dad back. Dad got this place instead of the money. Drive over this rise, you'll see the shed on the other side."

As Sally drove over the rise, sure enough, there was a frame building at the end of the twin tracks. In Sally's mind, it was more a barn than a shed. Still, it was fairly small, about the size of the shop back in town. Sally pulled the Packard up to the front and killed the engine.

There was a double door on the front of the building. Sally didn't see any windows. An iron bar that dropped into a bracket on the opposing door secured it. There was no lock.

Babe pushed the bar up and pulled on the door. The interior of the building was dark. The floor was dirt. There was a collection of what looked like old farm equipment and a few pieces of old furniture strewn about inside. The Special sat right inside.

Sally gasped when she saw the condition of the car, "What happened to the paint?"

"Dad had to scrape it off."

"What on earth for?"

"It was all bubbling up. Dad said the person that painted it was an 'apprentice' and he either didn't know what he was doing or used some bad paint or something. Dad was going to repaint it." The last sentence barely got out. Babe's voice was getting thick with emotion.

Sally was walking around the car. There was no exhaust header sticking out of the left hood side. She undid the leather straps and opened the left hood. The engine bay was empty.

"Where's the engine?" she asked, a look of horror on her face.

"I don't know. Dad pulled it out, I'm not sure why. Is it here somewhere?" They both looked all over the shed. It wasn't there.

"Do you think someone stole it?" Babe asked.

"I don't know honey. There sure isn't any sign of a lock on this place is there? But if someone stole it, why didn't they take the Special too?"

"Maybe Tommy took it back. That's where Billy and Dad got it to begin with wasn't it?"

"Well, that's certainly a possibility. I don't like the car being here, but I guess it is dry and it gives us a place to park both cars at home. There isn't much we can do about the motor until I talk to Tommy. I thought I would wait a while before I visit him. Do you want to come with me when I go?"

"Sure!" Babe said with obvious enthusiasm. Sally suspected it had more to do with seeing Ellen than with Tommy.

"Maybe we can go in a week or two. I want to give him enough time to heal a little before we go visit."

"Okay with me, and I'd like to see Ellen too."

Suspicion confirmed, Sally thought, but didn't say anything.

"I know you and Ellen didn't hit it off, but she's really nice."

"I'm sure she is." Sally replied.

Chapter 49

Sally heard the postman putting mail in the slot. She left the dishes, dried her hands and went to retrieve it.

There was a letter from Granny Driver. It always made her heart jump to receive a letter from Granny. There was still hope in her heart that Billy would be found.

She carried the mail back to the kitchen before opening it. She sat down at the table; her fingers trembled ever so slightly as she tore the air mail envelope open.

Dearest Sally,

I trust this finds you and the Babe well and in good spirits. I think of you often and miss your company terribly.

I fear that I am the bearer of bad news. On Saturday last, that very nice Mr. Kennedy was lost. A Liberator took off and not long afterward we heard a loud explosion. From what is known, his airplane exploded in mid air. It is all very hush hush, but apparently there was some sort of mechanical malfunction.

It is such a shame that this terrible war has claimed so many of our very best and our hope for the future. I cry many nights thinking of your Billy and Mr. Faulkenwell's son. I have never had the pleasure to know finer young men than they. Now I have to add Mr. Kennedy to my list.

Sally put the letter aside, her eyes so full of tears she couldn't continue. So the damn war claimed Joe Kennedy. She wasn't even sure how she felt about that. Certainly it was a tragedy he was gone. He was so helpful after Billy was lost and she might still be in England waiting to get home if it hadn't been for him. On the other hand, she always felt like he only saw her as a particularly desirable toy.

At least the war news was good. The invasion of Europe had been accomplished and the Allies were racing across France. She prayed every day that the war would soon be over. This goddamn war! She hoped it was worth the terrible cost!

Sally sat lost in her thoughts for some time. When the trance finally broke, she went to her room and unlocked her cedar chest. She took out her journal and returned to the kitchen table where she began to write. It was the only activity she found that allowed her mind to rest once she was in one of the downhill spirals. As therapeutic as the writing was, Sally was always careful to do it only when she was alone. The journals were her communication with Billy, she had no intention of sharing them with anyone and that included the Babe. To that end, she always kept them locked in her cedar chest.

After writing, she felt better. Sally decided it was time to arrange a visit with Tommy. She knew he was doing better because she checked with her dad again. Certainly Tommy was out of danger. The doctor was very confident he would walk again, but was still hesitant to predict a complete recovery. She didn't like the sound of that, but she knew that everything that could be done was being done.

When Babe got home, she let him know she planned to leave in the morning. He was very excited, especially when she told him they would probably be staying several days.

"Will we get to see Ellen?" he asked.

"I'm sure we will." What was it with Ellen? He couldn't have known her that long.

"Can we take the Packard?"

"Of course. In fact my Dad wants me to look at a new one he has put back. He wants me to trade cars," she said.

A stricken look passed over Babe's face. "Is it a convertible?" he asked as if he were afraid of the answer.

"I don't know hon, but my Dad knows I like them best. We'll just have to wait and see."

"We have to have a convertible," he said. It was a statement, there was no question.

"Oh? And why is that mister?" Sally asked, a bit amused by his assertion.

"Because I like them best, that's why."

"Yes sir. I'll be certain to let my Dad know that; I'm sure he is unaware of that requirement and will do everything in his power to accommodate your every desire." Sally said, just the hint of a chuckle in her voice.

Babe wasn't sure if she was making fun of him or not. He decided to let the issue drop. But it just had to be a convertible! They already had one closed car!

The drive up the coast the next day was wonderful as far as the Babe was concerned. The weather was perfect. Sally put the top down and the Packard purred up the road, swooping around one curve and then the next.

Sally's thoughts were quite different. It was a glorious day to be driving up the coast highway, but it seemed that every turn brought back more memories of this same route taken with Billy. Each time she passed one of the turn-offs that led to a secluded stretch of beach; her mind was filled with visions of Billy and the times they shared. At first she tried to put these memories out of her mind, but eventually discovered that was impossible. Instead she embraced them. She reveled in the memories. Why hide from the best period in your life she thought? Why not relive those experiences as much as possible?

As Sally drove she also thought about where they were going to stay. She thought that the beach house would be too filled with memories, but now the beach house might be the perfect place. Besides, she would like to see the Fultons. She had written them, of course, but still a visit would be fun. She also wanted them to meet the Babe. She certainly talked their ear off about him and it was time they met. Those decisions worked out in her mind, she settled back to enjoy what was left of the drive.

They drove straight to the hospital. After inquiring at the front desk, they headed to Tommy's room, stopping first to buy flowers in the hospital gift shop.

Neither of them was quite prepared for the sight that awaited them in Tommy's room. When they knocked softly on the door, there was a faint 'Come in'.

Tommy looked terrible. He was in a cast that stretched from his chest down over his hips and totally encompassed one leg. The leg was suspended by a block and pulley arrangement. Tommy's face was almost as white and chalky as the cast was. He didn't stir as they entered the room.

Ellen was sitting in a chair in the corner of the room. She stood as they entered. There were dark circles under her eyes and her normally radiant black ball of hair had lost some of its luster. It was obvious she had spent several days in that chair without a break. A half-eaten sandwich lay on a napkin on the small table beside the chair. A disorderly stack of magazines and a couple of newspapers lay on the floor. Her blue eyes still contained ice when they looked at Sally, but melted completely when she saw Babe.

"Ellen!" he cried and ran into her outstretched arms. Sally was a bit shocked to see that he and Ellen were the same height. She would have sworn that first day that he was almost a head shorter. Had he grown that much in such a short time? Almost as if Ellen could read her thoughts, she said, "Look how much you've grown!" She continued to hug him, from the looks of things he didn't mind.

"I didn't notice so much until I saw him with you, but he has grown like a weed hasn't he?" Sally said.

Ellen looked up at her, only the slightest trace of annoyance in her eyes now, "yes he has. He's almost a man now isn't he?" pride obvious in her voice.

Sally realized with a start that she was right. Babe was almost a man. It wouldn't be long at the rate he was growing.

Sally looked over at Tommy. He looked awful. He still hadn't moved. His eyes were closed and his mouth hung open, his head lolling to the side.

After a minute Ellen noticed her looking at him. "He's doing better. The doctors have him on painkillers and it keeps him knocked out most of the time. He's in a lot of pain as you can imagine."

"What all is wrong with him?" Sally asked. "Dad said his pelvis is broken and so is his leg. Is that right?"

"Crushed is more like it; especially his thigh. They thought for a while that they might have to amputate his leg." It was the first time Ellen spoke to her without venom in her voice.

Ellen walked over to the bed, one arm still around Babe. "Wake up Tommy, see who's here," she said patting on his hand.

"Don't disturb him," Sally said.

"He would never forgive me if I let him sleep through your visit. He hasn't had that many visitors you know, and he always asks about you." Ellen replied, the ice between them truly beginning to melt.

"Wake up hon, you have visitors, its Sally and Babe."

Tommy's eyelids flickered, then rolled up like window shades. When his eyes opened he looked confused, Ellen was still holding his hand. He looked far older than Sally had ever seen him.

His eyes slowly focused and a little color returned to his face. "Sally," he said in a near whisper, then "and Babe," his head turning ever so slightly. He made an effort at smiling. Ellen continued to hold his hand.

Sally had walked in with every intention of asking Tommy where the engine for the Special was. Considering his condition, she decided not to bring up the subject at all. She doubted he could answer the question anyway. After a couple of minutes of small talk, she could see Tommy was exhausted and he drifted off again. A nurse came in and checked his vitals and then gave him an injection. While the nurse was there, they stepped out into the hall.

"He looks terrible," Sally said, "he's so weak."

"He's better than he was," Ellen replied.

"Babe, here's some money, would you go down to the cafeteria and get us each a Coke and some snacks? Ellen, is there anything you need?"

"Yeah, I'm starving, Babe honey, could you get me a cheeseburger?"

Babe beamed, "Sure. I'll be right back," and he started off down the hall.

Ellen watched him walk away. "He really has grown."

"I know, I was shocked to see him beside you, he's almost as tall as you are." Sally replied. "You care about him a great deal don't you?"

Ellen's eyes had never left him as he disappeared at the elevators. "Yes, I do. I miss him even more than I thought I would."

"Well he certainly misses you too. And one more thing, I care about Tommy, he's been a friend all my life, but I'm not interested in him romantically, okay?"

Ellen turned to look at her. "I know. It was never you caring about him that concerned me; it was him caring about you. You have an amazing effect on men, all men, even Babe."

"And you don't?" Sally asked.

"Not the way you do."

"I'm not so sure of that. It looks just the opposite from where I sit. Let's bury the hatchet, and not in each other's backs. It looks to me like we've got two men that need taking care of. It will work much better if we cooperate don't you think?" Sally said.

Ellen continued to look at her. "Your boyfriend, the one in England, what about him?"

She saw tears well up in Sally's eyes.

"He's missing in action," Sally managed to get out in a whisper.

"Oh dear Lord, I'm so sorry, I didn't know." Ellen said as she hugged Sally. "Is there anything I can do?"

I'm going to have to quit thinking of her as 'that bitch' I guess, Sally thought. "There is one thing you can do." Sally said still in Ellen's embrace.

"Just name it, honey."

"Take my car and Babe and go get cleaned up and get some rest. I'll stay here with Tommy tonight."

"Oh, I couldn't do that."

"And why not?" Sally said pulling away.

"That's too much to ask."

"You didn't ask, I offered. Besides, I thought we agreed to bury the hatchet?"

"Well, you agreed, I didn't say anything" Ellen replied.

"But you did hug me."

"And I will again," Ellen hugged her once more. "Thanks for the offer, I could use a shower and a good night's sleep."

Just then Babe walked up, holding a cardboard tray containing three paper cups, several candy bars, a bag of peanuts, and a white sack with the top neatly folded over.

"Take your drinks and leave me the rest" Sally said.

Babe stood there, a look of confusion on his face.

"Go on, take your drink," Sally repeated.

"Babe honey, you and I are taking the car and I'm going home to get some rest and clean up a bit. Sally's going to sit with Tommy tonight." Ellen said.

As she took the tray of food, Sally handed Ellen the keys to the car.

"Thanks for doing this Sally," Ellen said, "really."

"Get out of here. See you tomorrow." Sally said as she walked back into Tommy's room.

Home turned out to be a small, neat apartment in a white stucco building with a red tile roof.

When they walked in the front door, Ellen pitched the keys on a small table by the door.

"Babe, make yourself at home. The radio's right over there. I'm going to get cleaned up and then I'll fix us something to eat. Okay?"

"Sure," was the one word reply.

Ellen went into the bedroom. Babe went over to the radio and turned it on. He played with the turner till he found a baseball game. Then he looked around the room. There were a few pictures in frames on the sideboard. He heard the shower running.

Babe walked over to look at the pictures. There were a couple of what he assumed was Ellen as a little girl; a couple of others that must be her parents. He glanced around the room. The door to the bedroom was open a crack. He didn't seem able to resist. The harder he tried, the more he couldn't resist. He went over and peeked in the door.

The angle of sight offered by the cracked door only gave him a view of one wall of the room. There was a dressing table on that wall with a stool and a large round mirror mounted above it. The mirror reflected a pretty good view of much of the rest of the room. Ellen's clothes lay in a heap on the floor.

He sucked in his breath and his heart rate soared. There was Ellen's bare backside as she walked into the bathroom and stepped into the shower closing the curtain behind her.

For the next few minutes he wrestled with his conscience. He knew when the water went off Ellen would have to exit the shower. Should he look or shouldn't he look? In the end, when the water went off, he peeked through the crack.

He thought his heart was going to explode. He was actually trembling. It seemed forever since the water had turned off and still the shower curtain hadn't moved. What was taking so long? Finally, the curtain slipped back and Ellen stepped out, wrapped in a towel! She took another towel off a rack and began drying her hair with it. His heart sank. It was like he deflated. He was disappointed but relieved at the same time. Babe glanced around the room and when he looked back, Ellen walked to the pile of dirty clothes which she picked up and walked out of sight of the mirror. Then she came back into view when she walked to the dressing table and began to brush her hair.

He was just about to move to another part of the room when Ellen's eyes flicked across the mirror and seemed to stare right at him! He blushed. He wondered if she could see him looking at her. Her eyes flicked back to concentrate on her hair again. Surely she hadn't been able to see him. If she had, she showed no sign of it, continuing to brush her hair. He relaxed again.

The muscles in his legs tensed as he was about to stand when a flash of movement caught his eye. Ellen stood up from her seat on the stool and as he watched, she dropped the towel. His eyes bugged and his heart rate raced once more, he couldn't believe what he was seeing. As he watched, she seemed to be examining her body in the mirror, taking a moment to powder herself with a large puff. Then she turned around facing him and picked up her hand mirror so she could see her back. She turned slightly this way then that carefully examining herself using the two mirrors. Babe was on the verge of hyperventilating. He was having a difficult job standing up, his pulse rate soared and his heart felt like a runaway trip hammer beating against the side of his chest. Just then she finished, her eyes once more flashed to seemingly meet his and then she put down the mirror, turned and walked out of his view.

He was still trying to get his breathing under control when the bedroom door opened and Ellen walked out. She wore a bathrobe open down the front over plaid pajamas.

"I see you found a ball game on the radio?"

He nodded, he didn't trust himself to say anything just now. He was still blushing, if she noticed she didn't say anything.

"How about some bacon and eggs? I'm starving," she said and walked into the small kitchen. She stuck her head back out the door. "Want to come help?

He was barely able to make his legs work. He was certain that when he walked in she would confront him about his peeking. He walked into the small space.

"There are some potatoes in the bin there under the sink and a peeler in the drawer. If you'll peel a couple, I'll add hash browns to the menu," she said, her voice bright and cheery.

They finished eating and did the dishes. She never said a word about it. Maybe she hadn't seen him. After all, it was darker in the living room than in the bedroom. He finally started to relax.

"Time to turn in for me. I haven't slept much in the past couple of weeks," she said and started toward the bedroom.

"What about me?" blurted out of his mouth. "Can I come too?"

The answer was delayed, Ellen paused looking at him intently, there was almost a smile of indulgence on her face. After what seemed forever she said, "Okay, come on." Then she turned and went in the bedroom.

He got in bed after the lights went out and started to scoot over to Ellen's side. An arm blocked his path and a voice came out of the dark. "Turn over mister." He did and faced the other way. Ellen's arm dropped over his waist. He started to scoot against her and the arm stiffened, making it clear this was the best it was going to get. Eventually he fell asleep.

That was the last time Babe saw Ellen for several years. Tommy left the hospital and went home to his secluded house on Kings Road in the Hollywood hills. Ellen went with him. He would live in severe pain the rest of his life and become addicted to pain pills after the accident. Eventually the relationship with Ellen unraveled, there was no romance in Tommy after the accident. She was nothing more than a housekeeper and nurse by that time. Tommy withdrew into himself, his only communication with her was to harangue her for some imagined slight or yell for another pill. At the end of her endurance, Ellen moved out and never heard from Tommy again.

Chapter 50

Babe and the Fultons struck it off famously from the minute they laid eyes on each other. In the years following the war, Sally took Babe to the beach house in Malibu several times a year. It was close enough to drive and Babe loved playing on the beach. Each time they visited, they spent a lot of time with the Fultons who had come to think of Sally as their own daughter.

Ken and Babe shared a passion for baseball. They could sit for hours and talk about the intricacies of the game. Ken had spent time with several young men obsessed with baseball over the years, but never had he met one with such a deep understanding of the game. This intrigued Ken enough that he decided to visit San Diego so he could see Babe play ball in person.

On his first visit, to say Ken was astounded with Babe's ability would be a gross understatement. Sitting in the bleachers five minutes into the first game he had ever seen Babe play, Ken turned to Sally and said, "Sally he's a man among boys on the field! I don't believe I've ever seen such a young talent."

Sally just grinned, beamed really, "I told you so," she said, her pride in Babe obvious.

By the end of that first game, Ken had already made his decision. Unbeknownst to either Sally or Babe, he was going to invite an old friend who just happened to be a major league scout, to come see Babe play.

After watching one game, Ken's friend was as enthusiastic as Ken had been. After the game, Ken's friend, Wirt Williams, was anxious to talk to Babe and Sally.

After the introductions and usual pleasantries were exchanged, Ken said, "Babe, Mr. Williams is a major league scout. I believe he was impressed with how you play ball."

"I certainly was, young man." Babe's heart soared. A major league scout! And he likes the way I play! Babe was so thrilled, he missed much of what the man said.

".....And Miss Anthony, with your permission, I'd like to have a coach work out with Babe from time to time. Maybe tidy up his swing a little bit and find out what his true ability is; would that be alright with you, and of course, you too Babe?"

Babe was so excited he nearly wet himself. A major league coach! Working out with a big leaguer!

Sally just looked at him and smiled. "Of course, it's alright with me, and from the looks of him, Babe thinks it's alright too."

"You bet I do!" Babe blurted.

Babe was walking on a cloud. Nothing could be better than this he thought. The coach showed up a couple of days later and the five of them, Mr. Fulton, Mr. Williams, the coach whose name was Skeets Malone, and Sally all trooped off to the park for the first work out.

Ken, Wirt and Sally sat on a bench and watched the workout. Skeets started out by simply playing some catch with Babe. The speed of the throws started to escalate until it became a game of 'burn out', the throws hitting the gloves with resounding cracks and stinging palms. Just when the balls were flying as fast as either could muster, Skeets made a throw that skipped the ball across the grass to Babe's right. Babe had to dig out to reach it, he made a leap to snag the ball which he fired back hitting Skeets right in the glove. The next throw was to his left; he made that stop too and followed it up with another perfect throw.

Skeets switched to a fungo bat, sending grounder after grounder at Babe who snagged them all. After a while, they saw Skeets go over and talk to Babe, his arm around Babe's shoulders. Babe was obviously listening intently, his head nodding as he listened.

Across the park a group of boys had arrived and were beginning a pickup game. A shrill whistle echoed across the park. When Babe looked in their direction, several of the boys were waving for him to come join them. Obviously, Skeets told him to go as he broke into a trot and loped across the park to the game.

Skeets walked over to the bench, a smile growing on his face.

"What do you think?" Wirt asked.

Skeets was massaging his left hand. "I switched to the fungo because he was hurting me with the pepper." Skeets smile turned to a sheepish grin.

Wirt laughed. "Hurt you did he? Maybe you should have brought your catcher's mitt."

"Don't worry, I will next time."

"You think he's got something then if there's going to be a next time." It was a statement, not a question.

"You wouldn't have called me if he didn't have something now would you?"

"I suppose not," Wirt agreed.

"Gentlemen, if I may, would you please tell me in English what you think and where we go from here." Sally said.

"Yes ma'am, of course." Skeets answered.

"I think Babe is a perfect nickname for him. He's a very talented ball player, especially for his age. How old is he?"

"Fourteen," she replied.

Skeets whistled and shook his head. "He's exceptional for his age, maybe the best I've ever seen. I have to add that I haven't seen him swing a bat yet."

"He's got a good swing," Wirt added.

"We'll see. I'm going to take my car around the park and watch that game they've got going. I hope he doesn't notice me. I'd like to watch him in as relaxed a setting as possible. But, to answer your question; what's next is that I plan to work with him the next couple of days and then I'll be back every month or two to work with him. We'll see what he can do."

Despite all he said, Skeets thought much more. Babe was the best, by far, he had ever seen at his age. The thing that impressed Skeets the most was his understanding of the game; the strategy of how a game should be played and where each player should be and how they should play their position.

When Skeets drove around the park and watched the sandlot game, he was amazed to watch Babe function as the manager for both teams; giving instruction to everyone on the field. He watched Babe bat. He really was good, he hit home runs at every at bat, but that was because there was only one decent pitcher on the field and that was Babe.

Skeets was excited. He had about four years to work with Babe. If he was right, and he had over forty years experience with the game, Babe would be one of the best ever and Skeets Malone would be one of the reasons why.

Chapter 51

Babe was sixteen the spring of 1947. He had been working on his baseball skills with Skeets Malone as his mentor for two years. Skeets showed him countless tricks of the trade, things that took normal players years to develop if they ever did.

Skeets had Babe playing in the Pony League. Babe was way better than his competition, but Skeets said it was important to play real games not just sandlot play.

Babe enjoyed it. They actually had real uniforms supplied by their team sponsor, Sunrise Bakery. The uniforms were off white with orange numbers trimmed in yellow. The bakery owner's wife picked them out because she said they looked like sunrise colors. Babe thought he would have picked something different, but he did like the uniforms. He liked running out onto the field at the start of the game when the home plate umpire called 'Play Ball'. He also loved the fact that they had real umpires calling all the games. No more arguing over who was safe or if a pitch was a ball or a strike.

The level of play was sufficiently high that the games always attracted a good crowd. The fields they played on were well kept and were equipped with bleachers behind chain link fences that made up the backstop and the dugouts. It wasn't unusual to have a couple of hundred people in the stands, sometimes more.

Sally was always in the stands if Babe was playing. She was his biggest fan, but she wasn't the only one. There were always a number of Babe fans scattered throughout the crowd. After all, he was the star player.

Skeets was always there too. Invariably he sat with Sally. They had become good friends. Although Babe hadn't seemed to notice, Skeets had confided in Sally, that now he was simply a fan like everyone else in the stands. He had exhausted his ability to teach Babe anything else. Whatever Babe learned from this point on was on his own, he had exceeded Skeets' knowledge. Also in the stands were Ken and Melba Fulton. They too were sitting with Sally and Skeets. They were getting on in years and they didn't come as often as they used to, but still they tried to make several trips a year to San Diego. They were part of the family now. The five of them spent all the holidays together.

Babe was warming up on the field with the rest of the players. He was pitching today. Skeets was convinced pitcher was his natural position, 'for as long as your arm holds out' Skeets had told him. He was near the side of the field where Sally and the rest were sitting. Babe would glance their way often and flash a grin. He was in his element and glad to have such a supporting group.

He still missed his Dad and Billy. He and Sally both had maintained hope that Billy would be found in a prisoner of war camp when the war ended, but it wasn't to be. Billy had not come back and he never would, leaving gaping holes in both their hearts. There wasn't a day that went by that he wasn't thought about, that he didn't come up in conversation, that a tear wasn't shed. Babe still found Sally crying from time to time. It made his heart ache all the more, but he didn't know what to do about it. Sometimes he cried too.

It was almost time for the game to start. Babe glanced over at his personal cheering section and noticed a commotion. A man was making his way through the stands to where Sally and the rest were sitting. The man was frail and seemed in constant danger of falling, but he made his way seemingly oblivious to everyone and everything around him. There was something familiar about the man. Then it hit him. It was Tommy!

Babe had not seen Tommy since that day in the hospital after his accident. That was what, about two, no three years ago he thought. He looked around for Ellen. In fact, his concentration was so broken that a ball went whistling right past him to bounce out into the outfield. He didn't see her. Wasn't she with Tommy? He thought they were still together, whatever that meant. He asked Sally about her on several occasions, but really hadn't gotten very good answers. Even though the two women had put on a good show about burying the hatchet, he was sure there was still friction between them. Even when Sally was in a really good mood, mention of Ellen was sure to sour things quickly. Babe never did understand that.

He continued to search the stands and one thing was certain, there was no Ellen with Tommy. His heart sank. He missed Ellen terribly and even worse was the fact he couldn't even speak her name without fear of upsetting Sally. Babe noticed that Tommy looked far older and much more frail than Babe remembered him. Even from here, it looked like his face wore a pained expression.

Tommy sat down beside Sally. Skeets had been there, but when Tommy arrived, he simply turned and started to sit, taking for granted that everyone would move out of his way, which they did, but only just. This caused a ripple effect down the entire bench and earned Tommy more than one dirty look. No one said anything, although a couple of people had started to but they could see, Tommy was obviously not a well man. The skin on his face was drawn and pale. More than one had the word cadaver come to mind when they looked at him. He seemed almost transparent.

Sally nearly gasped when she saw him. He sat beside her, "Hello Sally," he said as he sat down. He glanced at her briefly, the barest hint of a smile on his face and then it was gone.

"Tommy! It's wonderful to see you! How are you feeling?" Sally asked trying hard to sound cheerful and upbeat despite his ghostly appearance. When she hugged him she was startled by how thin he felt.

"I'm getting by," he said, his concentration now on the players on the field. Babe waved at him and Tommy waved back.

"He's really grown hasn't he?" Tommy asked.

"He sure has. He's six feet tall already."

"What is he, sixteen or seventeen now?"

373

"He's sixteen, he'll be seventeen in October," Sally replied.

Tommy didn't reply, instead he pulled a small aluminum tube from his pocket and unscrewed the cap dumping a pair of pills into his palm, which he quickly swallowed. He tried to screw the cap back on, but his hands were trembling too much to get it started. Sally took it and screwed the lid back on. Tommy stashed the tube back in his pocket, but never let go of Sally's hand. He sat now with his legs apart, his hands on his knees, the right one still clutching Sally's. His eyes never left the field, his expression never changed. In fact the only movement Sally could detect was an occasional tremor in his hand and his eyes following play on the field.

"Tommy, are you all right?" she asked, concerned.

After a moment's pause, "Yes, of course I am, why do you ask?"

Sally didn't know exactly how to answer that, but finally she said, "Well, the pills and all. You don't act like you feel well."

"I'm fine. The pills just help take the edge off. He's really talented isn't he? That fast ball of his has some pop to it doesn't it? Any scouts from the majors shown an interest in him yet?"

"Yes, in fact that man you're sitting beside is a big league coach that's been working with him for the past two years." Sally replied.

"Is that so? That's good then, I was going to make a few calls, but it seems like everything is already handled."

They watched the game for a few more minutes. "Where's Ellen?" Sally asked.

"Ellen?" he asked.

"Yes, Ellen, you remember the pretty black haired girl?"

"Oh yeah," his concentration was back on the game, almost as an afterthought, "she left some time ago. I don't know where she is." His eyes, nor his concentration ever left the field.

Sally let him watch. One thing that still bothered her was the missing engine for the Special. She never had found out what happened to it. She didn't know exactly what she would do with it if she had it. Maybe she could get the Special running again.

"Tommy, whatever happened to the engine for the Special?" she asked.

"What are you talking about?" his eyes didn't leave the field though he still clutched her left hand on his knee.

"You know, that engine that you loaned Carl and Billy for the Special."

For the first time he half turned so that he could look at her.

"I told Carl he could have it. Why?"

"When you had it moved to the farm, the Special that is, after Carl died, it's been missing ever since. I wondered if you knew what happened to it?"

Tommy looked puzzled. It was the most emotion he had shown since his arrival.

"I had it moved to the farm to give room to store your car and Carl's behind the house," he said.

"Yeah, both cars were in the shop building when I got home from England. The Special.."

Tommy interrupted her, "by 'Special', do you mean the speedster? It's at the farm, stored in that shed."

"I know it is, but the engine isn't there."

"The engine's missing?"

"Yes, dear, that's what I'm asking about. Do you know where the engine is?"

She could finally see some understanding come to Tommy's face. She had finally gotten through to him. She wondered if it was those pills he was taking.

"No, Sally, I have no idea. I didn't know the engine was gone. Was it in the car when they moved it?"

"No, it wasn't. Carl had pulled it out. He was going to do something with it. I don't know what exactly, but it's gone."

"I'll do some checking Sally. It wasn't stolen out of the shed was it?"

"I don't think so. Babe and I went out there the week after I got back. The week after your accident," Sally felt his hand tense when she mentioned his accident, "and it wasn't there. In fact, it doesn't look like it ever made the trip."

"I'll find out and let you know."

"Okay, thanks."

Tommy pulled the aluminum tube out once more and unscrewed the cap shaking out another couple of small pills.

"You're not taking too many of those are you? What are they?"

Tommy looked defensive. "The doctor prescribes them for me. Well, I better be going. Goodbye Sally, tell Babe hello for me. He looks really good. If either of you need anything, call me, okay?"

And then he was making his way out of the bleachers the same way he had come, as if there wasn't another person there. Strangely detached from what he was doing.

Sally watched him as he walked very stiff-legged with a pronounced limp around behind the bleachers to the parking lot. A new Cadillac sedan was parked there with a driver that opened the rear door for Tommy and then ran around the car to drive it away.

"Who was that?" Skeets asked.

"That was Tommy Lee," she said.

"Is he high on something?"

"Yes, I think he is."

After the game, Babe ran up. "Where's Tommy?" he asked.

"He left, honey." Sally replied.

"He left? But I didn't even get to say hi to him!" Babe protested.

"I know hon, I don't think he was feeling very well."

"From what I could see he didn't look good." Babe said with a serious look on his face. Then his mood lightened and he asked in a far more cheery voice, "Where was Ellen?"

Sally looked at him a moment before she answered. "I don't know where Ellen is and neither did Tommy."

She saw the confused look on his face. "Really hon, I don't know. Tommy said she left some time ago and he doesn't know where she is."

"Oh," the disappointment was evident. Then, "he doesn't even know where she went?"

"No honey, he said he had no idea. I didn't push it past that."

"Okay," Babe said again the disappointment obvious.

Just then Skeets and the Fultons walked up. The Fultons congratulated him on such a fine pitching performance and Skeets asked how his arm felt. He answered the questions and carried on small talk, but Sally could tell his mind was somewhere else.

It's been two years since he's seen her and he was only a child then, still is, and he's still smitten with her. What kind of magic spell had that bitch worked on him? Sally mused.

Chapter 52

Sally carefully loaded her bags into the trunk of the Packard. Thoughts of Billy doing the same thing exploded into her mind. For some reason lately, she had been consumed with the notion that any minute he was going to come walking down the sidewalk or through the front door. The thoughts were so real she couldn't get them out of her head. Intellectually, she knew it wasn't going to happen. It had been over five years since Billy went missing with the rest of the crew of *California Girl*. The war had been over for more than four years. For months after Germany surrendered she hoped against hope he would turn up, but it hadn't happened. The truth was, he wasn't coming back, ever. Still she couldn't shake that feeling. In all the years since he'd been gone, she never felt like this.

Sally closed the trunk lid and couldn't help but look down the street toward the bus stop. How many times had she seen him walking toward her on the sidewalk, swinging his lunch box in one hand, that grin of his getting bigger the closer he got?

No one was there. There wasn't anyone on the sidewalk. She sighed. *Oh Billy!* she thought, *why did it have to be you? Why aren't you here in my arms right now? Why aren't there little Billys and Sallys running around in the yard and making us crazy trying to keep up with them?*

She couldn't help a tear that broke loose and ran down her cheek. Sally took another deep breath. She walked around to get in the driver's side of the Packard, and then, on a whim, she put the top down. She hadn't had it down in a very long time. But today she was going to be driving north to LA and she was taking the coast highway. The same route she and Billy took so many times together.

It was a beautiful drive with the blue Pacific on one side, gorgeous scenery on the other, hills and bluffs, cliffs and beach.

The Packard purred along, its smoothness belied its years. Still there was no denying that it was showing its age. Her father had offered a replacement. Was he really her father she thought for the thousandth time, every time she looked in the mirror she saw Carl's electric blue eyes staring back at her, the same eyes Babe carried. She knew the answer, but she didn't know. Her father, or at least the man she had always called father, tried to give her a new model every time she talked to him. She just hadn't been able to bring herself to do it. She couldn't give up the car she shared with Billy, the same one he drove up this very same highway so many times. There was that feeling again, like Billy was waiting for her just around the next bend in the road. She was actually beginning to look for him; a feeling of happy anticipation began to invade her thoughts. What was going on? *Billy! Where are you,* she thought?

Sally was on her way to Sacramento to see Babe play ball. He was in the Pirates farm system playing AAA Ball and considered a very hot and promising big league prospect. She had been to several of his games and had never seen him happier.

When he reached driving age, she gave him Carl's LaSalle. Technically she supposed, it was his all along, but in her mind, she had given it to him. He drove it his last year in high school and then off to Sacramento to play ball professionally. As far as she knew, he was still driving it, but she didn't think that would last much longer. Babe was quite the eligible young bachelor, a point that had been driven home with some authority on her last visit. As she waited for him outside the stadium after the game, she couldn't help but notice the group of young girls clustered around the players' entrance. She assumed they were players' girlfriends and possibly even some young wives. She was astounded when Babe strolled out, his canvas bag in one hand, that he was literally mobbed by the girls. It took him at least 15 minutes to sign all the autographs and work his way through the throng getting kiss after kiss and hug after hug. She also couldn't forget all the hateful and jealous looks she got as he got in the car with her, giving her a peck on the cheek as they drove away. Babe certainly had a bevy of young admirers. She wouldn't be surprised to see him driving a new Cadillac convertible when she got there. If Tommy knew he was in the market for one, she was certain Tommy would simply give it to him.

Sally was going to stop and see Tommy on her way. He had never been the same since his accident. The pain never left him. Because of that he took way too many pills and the combination of pills and the pain together changed Tommy forever. She missed the old Tommy. He had never been a happy go lucky sort, but now he was almost a zombie, prone to attacks of severe depression. She hoped he was better or at least having one of his better days. She intended to ask him about the Special's engine one last time. Maybe he found it, if he even remembered to look that is.

Every turn in the road brought back a fresh memory of Billy. That was the turn out where they stopped and watched a sailboat far out to sea. That was the spot where they walked down to the beach for a picnic, another spot where Billy changed a flat tire.

Oh Billy! I miss you so! She thought for the ten thousandth time.

Sally had already driven past Camp Pendleton. Every time she saw that name it brought back more memories. That was really one of the reasons she was going to watch Babe play. She hoped it would get her mind on something else.

She drove through one of the small seaside towns that straddled the coast highway. There was a small café where she and Billy had stopped once for lunch. The place looked just the same as it did the day they had stopped. For reasons she would never know, she pulled over and parked at the curb in front of the café. Neatly lettered on the plate glass window in gold, trimmed in red were the words, 'Fresh Seafood, Steaks, Homemade Pie, Coffee 5¢.

She remembered the sign from when they stopped before. Nothing had changed. Even the coffee was still a nickel, most places were now a dime.

She opened the door, got out, and walked in through twin heavy screen doors. The door's push bars were blue and white enameled signs that read 'Blue Mountain Roast Coffee Served here'.

It was a small place. On the right there was a counter with half a dozen swivel stools. There were several small tables, each with four wooden chairs. None of the furniture matched, but it was all neat and clean. Several ceiling fans turned slowly overhead. On the counter by the doors stood a large black cast iron cash register, flanked by two glass jars, one holding mints and the other holding colorful jawbreakers. There was no one inside. A bell, attached to the doors, rang as she entered announcing her presence. A male voice called out, "Sit wherever you like, I'll be right with you."

Sally sat at one of the counter stools. The wall behind the counter was bead board, its ancient white paint flaking and turned a burnished ivory. A narrow shelf ran its length and held several glass covers over the most beautiful pies she had ever seen. *The meringue on them must be six inches thick!* she thought. She remembered Billy had tried the chocolate, proclaiming it the best he had ever eaten, next to his mother's, of course.

Over the pies there hung a collection of photographs in simple black frames. These were a new addition since her last visit with Billy. So far as she could tell, they were the only things different. Sally was surprised to see several pictures of B-24 Liberators, both in the air and on the ground. One of the pictures showed a crew picture, the officers standing and the enlisted men squatting in front, their Liberator in the background. Another picture showed a couple of young men in B-3 shearling flying jackets posing with the nose of the big bomber that had 'Dago's Dinger' painted on it under a picture of a very voluptuous young lady covered only by a strategically placed elbow and baseball bat.

Once more, memories flooded back. She could see Billy and his crew hamming it up for the camera; showing off her picture on the nose of the *California Girl* or playing baseball using the airplane as a backstop. She could also see their faces after they returned from a mission. The sunken eyes, the cold stares, the silence. In the center of the wall was a picture frame that held no picture. Instead there was a rectangular banner, white with a red border and a gold star in the center.

Sally saw movement through the window to the kitchen and then an old man came through the kitchen door. He was several inches shorter than Sally, red faced, thin white hair showing under a paper hat, and a white apron around his ample waist. He was drying his hands on a towel. "May I help you, Miss?" he asked. He walked with a noticeable limp.

"I'll have a slice of that gorgeous chocolate pie and a cup of coffee, please."

"Coming right up," the man replied, already on his way to the coffee urn and a stack of white porcelain mugs.

Within a minute, there was a steaming mug of coffee and an enormous slice of chocolate pie on the counter in front of Sally. She took a bite. It tasted even better than it looked. "This is delicious!"

"Thank you ma'am," the man replied, his pleasure at the compliment obvious.

Sally took another bite. After swallowing she said, "I couldn't help but notice your pictures."

The grin froze on the man's face for just an instant, then he seemed to recover. "Yes, that's my son's plane and crew."

"I saw the gold star," Sally said with a look of concern on her face.

His smile faded a bit. "We lost him the summer of '44."

"I'm sorry. My husband flew Liberators too." She realized with a start that it was the first time since leaving England that she referred to Billy as her husband to anyone except Babe, and then only the one time.

"He did? Where was he stationed?"

"England."

"So was my son Danny. He was in the 8th Air Force. What unit was your husband in?"

"Fleet Air Wing 7. He was stationed at a small base named Dunkeswell in the very south of England."

"Fleet Air Wing?" the man said, a puzzled look on his face, "was that part of the Navy? I didn't know the Navy flew any Liberators."

"They patrolled for submarines and blockade runners. He was lost in February of '44."

By this time, they were each a little lost in their own thoughts and their eyes began to tear.

Then with a big grin, "Is that your Packard at the curb?"

"Why yes, it is."

"That's a beautiful car. You know, I think the automakers lost something after the war. They just don't seem to have the quality of the ones built earlier, you know? They don't have the styling either. Everything looks like a box on wheels now. Not graceful and full of curves like yours."

"I think so too. My husband and I drove that car together and I just can't make myself part with it. We used to drive this road often. We even stopped in here for lunch a time or two. My husband loved your pie. It was a lot busier then as I recall."

"Yeah, everyone's in too much of a hurry to stop anymore. The cars, they flash by here doing 60 or better. Lord help you if you should step in front of one of them. They all stop down the road where you can eat in your car. Drive-in, that's what they call it, only serves sandwiches and hamburgers." He looked a bit wistful. "Oh well, times change don't they? I still get pretty good business from the locals at meal times. The rest of the time it's just me."

Sally took her last bite of pie. "I better be on my way. How much do I owe you?" she asked as she stood to leave.

"All Liberator crews eat free here."

Sally looked at him for a long minute, then extended her hand. "I'm Sally Pendleton," she said. It was the first time she had ever introduced herself that way.

"I'm Dan Delvicio," he said shaking her hand. "You come back anytime, Sally, it's been a pleasure meeting you. I mean it now, anytime you drive this road you stop, I'll be here."

"Thanks, Dan, I will," and she walked out the door. As she was getting in the car, a red sedan flashed past startling her. Its slipstream almost blew the door out of her hand. A bit rattled by the conversation and the passing car, she started the Packard and pulled away from the curb just as another car whizzed past.

So far, she thought as she drove away, this trip has done the exact opposite of getting her mind off Billy. On the contrary, it brought him into even more focus. It would be better once she got to Sacramento and could see Babe. He always had a way of taking up all of her attention.

Sally drove up the coast highway toward LA. Her plans were to visit with Tommy and drop in on the Fultons. They had declined her invitation to accompany her to Sacramento and because of this, she was concerned about them. She didn't know exactly how old they were, but she thought they were close to eighty. Travel wasn't easy for them any longer.

Joe paused for just an instant as he opened the driver's door of the brand new '49 Chevrolet ton and a half stake bed truck. Neatly lettered on the door in a pale shade of yellow that contrasted nicely against the dark green of the door were the words 'Joe Flores Landscaping' and below this in slightly smaller font was 'Los Angeles' and a phone number.

He was Joe Flores, well Jose Flores actually, but he thought the Anglican version of his name brought him more business. Most Latinos in the LA area couldn't afford to hire a landscaper, and especially one successful enough to be driving a brand new truck with their name painted on the door, he thought rather smugly.

Joe was born in the United States, the son of migrant workers. His mother and father came across the border illegally to pick fruit. In those days no one thought much about it. All the fruit pickers lived in Mexico in the off season, those that didn't find other work that is. His parents had done that for several years before Joe came along. By virtue of his birth on American soil, Joe was legally a U. S. citizen. After Joe was born his parents never again returned to Mexico in the winter when all the fruit had been picked. They were afraid they might jeopardize their son's citizenship in some way and that was much too important to take chances with. Instead, they had left the orchards and moved into the sprawl of Los Angeles. His father found work at countless odd jobs and his mother began making tamales in the kitchen of their one room rented shack to help make ends meet.

Joe's mother, Sonya, was a good cook. Her tamales were well liked and soon the demand was greater than she could handle in the tiny kitchen area of the shack. They moved out of the shack and into a garage apartment that had a separate bedroom, kitchen and its own bathroom with hot and cold running water, the first they ever had. They never returned to the fields and orchards that brought them there in the beginning.

It wasn't long before the demand for Sonya's tamales once more exceeded her capacity to produce them in the small kitchen of the apartment. She and Jose Sr. sat down at the kitchen table and discussed their options. They decided to take the small nest egg they managed to scratch out and open a store that sold Sonya's tamales. Jose would find the place, rent it and make whatever repairs were necessary. Once it was ready, he would move the operation in and do whatever he could, working side by side with Sonya to make it a success.

He was able to find a small store front building on the edge of the barrio not far from their rented apartment. The storefront had a small office area in back that Jose was able to convert into a tiny apartment for the family. They moved in on Thanksgiving Day of 1935, the year that Joe started school. By Christmas they had already added four small tables and a selection of odd chairs to the front where people of the barrio could enjoy Sonya's tamales with an ice-cold bottle of beer or orange soda.

As soon as Jose Jr., he always called himself Joe, was old enough, he was put to work in what they all now thought of as the family business. Joe swept and mopped the floors, bussed tables, washed dishes and carried ice. He worked hard, but his parents made sure the work never interfered with school. Although most of their customers only spoke Spanish, Joe's parents insisted that when the family was alone, only English be spoken. They impressed on Joe that the way to get ahead in America was to be American, an American that worked hard for sure, but an American, and Americans spoke English. They were proud of their heritage, but they were also anxious to start a new one in their adopted country.

As Sonya's Tamales flourished, so did the family. Three sisters came along and finally a little brother. The girls were a blessing for the business. They grew up in the kitchen and eventually what started out as a tiny tamale factory grew into a Mexican restaurant that in addition had a bakery, a tortilla factory and the original tamale business all attached.

Joe was the first Flores to ever graduate from high school. He only stood five feet five inches tall, but he was thick and everything there was muscle. His parents naturally assumed that Joe would continue in the family business, but he wasted no time telling them he wanted to run his own.

Another family meeting was convened around the kitchen table and it was decided that the Flores family could manage to keep everything going while Joe began his own venture.

Starting with a Model A Ford pickup purchased for the princely sum of $25, and a collection of second hand yard equipment, Joe worked 12 and 14 hour days, seven days a week to get started.

Post war Los Angeles was the perfect place for a new business to start up. California in general, but the Los Angeles area especially was booming. Many of the servicemen that passed through there during the war had been impressed with the year round climate, the beaches, the mountains and the opportunity. The area was one of the major aircraft production centers during the war and now those businesses and spin-offs from them were busily converting to the production of civilian goods. Houses were being built on every scrap of vacant land, or so it seemed, and demands for lawns, trees, flowers and all types of landscaping was at an all time high. Joe Flores Landscaping came along at exactly the right time. The Model A was almost immediately augmented by a newer but still well used Ford and then a Navy surplus GMC. And only last month the new Chevy stake bed had joined the fleet, its dark green and black paint glistening and the pale yellow logo painted proudly on both doors.

Joe was justly proud of what he and his family had accomplished as he drove down Sunset Blvd. The bed of the truck was filled with a collection of Bartlett Pear trees, their roots tied up in balls of burlap and hemp rope, along with twenty flats of assorted flowers all bound for a new housing addition. The developer discovered that he could get premium prices for his homes if they had landscaped yards. Joe now had five crews working seven days a week and he still couldn't keep up. He was in a hurry to get the Bartlett Pears delivered because he had to rush back to the nursery to pick up another load going to the other side of town. The new Chevy's engine had no trouble keeping up with traffic and then some. If he really pushed it, maybe he would have time to swing by the restaurant for a cold one and some of Mama's home cooking.

Sally pulled the Packard into Tommy's driveway. The house had a closed up look to it that she couldn't really put her finger on. No cars were in evidence. The blinds were drawn over the windows. She got out and went to the door. She gave the cast iron knocker three heavy raps. The sound seemed to echo through the house. After waiting at least thirty seconds, she repeated the procedure listening carefully for movement inside the house. There wasn't any. After waiting more than long enough for someone to come to the door she gave up.

Sally couldn't understand no answer at the door. She had been to Tommy's house many times and someone had always come to the door. Usually it was the housekeeper and occasionally the cook, but there was always someone there. She decided to walk around back.

As she walked around the corner of the large house, she was hailed by a male voice, "May I help you, Miss?" Momentarily confused, Sally couldn't determine the source of the voice. No one was in sight.

"Up here, Miss," the voice said again. This time Sally looked up and was surprised to see a man on the roof of the four-car garage.

I'm sorry, I couldn't tell where you were," Sally flashed a dazzling smile, "I'm looking for Tommy." She realized the man had tools and was apparently patching a broken shingle on the roof.

"Yes ma'am, Mr. Lee is out at the castle," the man replied.

Now Sally was really confused, "The castle?" she said.

"Yes ma'am, the castle, Shea Castle, Mr. Lee bought it you know, and he's living out there now."

Sally simply stared at the man on the roof. This was totally unexpected. *Shea Castle? What the hell was Shea Castle?* She wondered.

Sensing her confusion the man said, "Do you know Shea Castle, ma'am?"

Recovering from her stunned state, Sally said, "Why no, I have no idea what you're talking about."

"It's that castle that crazy Irishman built out in the desert near Elizabeth Lake."

"Oh! I know where that is. It's built out of solid rock isn't it?"

"Yes ma'am, that's the one."

"And Tommy lives there now?"

"Yes ma'am, he does."

"Thank you!" Sally said as she turned to leave.

"My pleasure ma'am."

Sally walked back to the Packard. What on earth is Tommy doing out in the desert in a castle of all things? Truth be told, Tommy had always been sort of a loaner no matter how hard he tried not to be. She wondered if he had truly turned into a hermit. She got in, started the Packard, reversed, turning around on the broad gravel drive and pulled out on King's Road heading back down the hill the way she came. She decided she would go on to the Fulton's tonight and stop by 'the castle' on her way out of town tomorrow.

She had just gotten this worked out in her mind and was traversing the sharp turns of the steep downhill road when she was suddenly overcome with that eerie feeling that Billy was around the next bend. She knew that was impossible, but she couldn't shake the feeling. The anticipation grew with every turn of the winding track.

She came around the last turn and there he was! That grin on his face she knew so well. Her heart nearly stopped then it pounded like a sledgehammer. *Oh Billy! Where have you been?*

Tears were streaming down her cheeks. Billy was still there grinning and waving. She gunned the Packard across the intersection; she couldn't get to Billy quickly enough. She never even noticed the red light.

It's amazing in times of great stress and danger that sometimes the human brain goes into sort of an overdrive where it processes images and events at a vastly accelerated rate. People that have experienced this have the feeling that time has slowed down and they see things with a clarity that doesn't exist in everyday life. Joe Flores experienced one of those events.

One minute he was thinking about everything he needed to get done that day and the next instant a cream colored Packard convertible flashed into the intersection directly in front of him. As the flood of adrenaline coursed through his body it was like everything was happening in slow motion. He was almost in the intersection when the Packard appeared. As he slammed on the brakes and hit the horn with way too much force, he saw that a beautiful blond haired woman was driving the Packard. His brain realized that the woman had tears streaming down her face, but she seemed to be laughing at the same time. His horn was blaring, he'd paid extra to have a pair of chrome trumpet style horns mounted on the roof of the cab. They were so loud he wondered why the glass didn't break. On top of this, all six of his wheels were locked up and sliding, clouds of burning rubber smoke were boiling up and he was yelling, "NO!" at the top of his lungs. The beautiful woman never seemed to notice, her gaze was fixed across the street and she never even glanced in his direction even as his truck smashed directly into the driver's door of the Packard. Just as the hood of the truck exploded upward obscuring his view he hit the steering column and then the windshield, the trees in the bed collapsed the cab from the rear. Then everything turned black.

Chapter 53

Tommy hated Friday the 13th just as he hated black cats crossing his path and green racecars. He was, after all, a superstitious man. If he had been fully in command of all his faculties, and of course he hadn't been since his wreck, he never would have allowed his dentist visit to be scheduled on that unluckiest of all days. Not only that, but besides visiting the dentist which would almost certainly result in some sort of painful experience, he was going to have to fly into LA. Tommy didn't like to fly on Friday the 13th. He came within an inch of telling his nurse, Jeanne Shiffler, to reschedule. He was mostly drunk on a combination of booze and pills when she made the appointment, just to piss him off he was sure. It would serve her right if he cancelled the appointment; after all, she needed to remember who the boss was. But then Bob, that was Bob Hanley his pilot, had already gone out to preflight and warm up the Mallard. Tommy thought, what the hell, and took another handful of pills and washed it down with a long pull straight from the neck of a bottle of Glenlivet.

The pills and booze didn't work as well as they once had. It had been years since his wreck, but his leg and hip still hurt like hell. He thought it would get better, but it never did. Then he thought he might get used to it, but that didn't happen either. Now his goddamn back was hurting almost as much as the goddamned leg. And it seemed like the more pills he took, the less they helped.

Nothing else was going worth a damn either. Those shitheads at Cadillac had royally screwed up his business, the ungrateful bastards. When his dad started the business, every Cadillac sold in California came through his hands and he sold a ton of them; enough to make Cadillac the premier luxury car in the world. Now the greedy bastards wanted more of the profits for themselves and broke his stranglehold on Golden State Cadillac distribution. Oh, he still had several dealerships, but he didn't have all of them like he did before the war, the bastards.

Then there was the television and radio business. That had all been his too, but now every Tom, Dick and Harry with a few bucks in their pocket thought they could open their own station. It seemed none of them cared about him anymore. The damned shitheads, who the hell was it that started television anyway? It was Thomas Stewart Lee damn it! He had been broadcasting regularly scheduled programming eight years before those dumbasses in New York managed to make a broadcast. Now those same assholes contrived how to cut him out of that too. Life just wasn't fair.

The thing that hurt him the most though, was that Sally was gone; Sally and all the rest of his friends. There wasn't anyone he cared about around anymore. How the hell could Sally be gone? He cried over her every day and every night since her accident and that was how long ago, six months? He couldn't keep track of time anymore. Damn it, why the hell weren't cars safer anyway? Hell the reason he was all screwed up now was that some asshole had T-boned him right in the driver's side door. If he'd been in a V-16 Cadillac sedan, one of the biggest, heaviest cars in the world he still would have been a virtual cripple. Sally had been in her Packard convertible, not as heavy as the Cadillac, but still a substantial car by any standard, and it killed her, oh God! How could beautiful Sally be dead?! There just wasn't any car that could stand up to a goddamned stake bed truck, fully loaded with trees of all goddamned things, running ninety to nothing hitting you square in the goddamned door. That was the sad truth of it. Maybe he would talk to the guys in the shop and see if they could come up with something to make cars safer. Beautiful sweet Sally was gone because some idiot driving a goddamned truck wasn't paying attention. It should have been him in that Packard, if it were then he would be out of his misery and sweet Sally would still be alive. Without her, life just wasn't worth living, especially if your damned leg felt like some asshole was driving a chisel through it with the devil's own sledgehammer.

Carl was gone too. Carl had been his best friend. He still missed him too. And Ellen, you know he might have had a chance with Ellen if it hadn't been for his accident. She stuck by him through the long stay in the hospital, but she said she just couldn't take watching him destroy himself with the pills and the booze. At first he tried to cut back, but the pain was too much for him. She finally came to him and told him to make a choice, either the pills or her. He wanted her. She was nice to him and she really seemed to care about him. She didn't ever ask for anything either, not one dime. But after he spent two weeks out of it on the pills, she told him to choose. He tried to choose her, he really did, but he just couldn't keep away from the pills. She found out, of course, and when she did, she didn't say a word, she just left. She had been so beautiful, almost as beautiful as Sally, but now they were both gone.

It seemed like everything in life that gave him pleasure was gone. Well, he still had his cars, but hell most of the time he hurt too damn bad to drive them. He'd tried hard to win Indy for the past several years, even going so far as to buy that Grand Prix Mercedes, the absolute best that maniac Hitler's Germany could produce, and that fell on its face too. To keep the cranky son-of-a-bitch running he guessed he would need to buy the whole goddamned country.

To hell with it; he thought as he popped another handful of pills, he'd go to that damned sadist that called himself a dentist. Maybe his mouth would take his mind off his leg and back. Then he had one cheery thought. Maybe the damned airplane would crash on their way into LA and it would all be over. Now that was the first good thought all day!

Almost to his surprise, the flight in went without a hitch. Considering the date, in his present state of mind, Tommy would have given even money they wouldn't make it. With this in mind, he sat in the rear seat by himself and put Jeanne up front with Bob. Normally he sat up front himself, but he just wasn't interested today. Instead he sat in back and dozed. With luck they would have crashed while he was asleep and he never would have known the difference.

After landing at the Glendale airport, they taxied to his hangar where he kept a Cadillac limousine. Bob parked the plane and they all climbed out. Getting in and out of the plane caused Tommy a great deal of pain. By the time he was seated in the backseat of the car, he broke out in a cold sweat.

The drive in to the Pellisier Building on Wilshire Blvd. went without a hitch. Once more Bob and Jeanne sat in front and Tommy sat in back and brooded. His mood darkened.

When they pulled up to the building, Tommy told Bob and Jeanne to wait in the car. "I'll only be a few minutes, no need for either of you to come in." Tommy said.

They both thought it was the first thing he said in days that was halfway civil. They were both only too happy to stay in the car, much preferring each other's company to Tommy's.

Tommy walked in the building with a noticeable limp. When he got on the elevator he told the operator the twelfth floor even though his dentist's office was on the eleventh. He walked out of the elevator and hobbled down to the end of the hall to a door marked "Roof Access". He opened the door and walked out onto the roof. He walked over to the fire escape stairs.

As he looked out over Los Angeles he took a cigarette from his pocket and lit up. He could see his shop on Santa Monica Blvd. from here. He had quite a collection of automobiles in that building he thought with some pride. That damn Mercedes W163 Grand Prix car was even parked in there. There was no doubt that building held more exotic European and American automobiles than existed in the rest of the country.

Tommy took a few minutes to think over each car and the memories he associated with it. That Mercedes was one example. He had it flown all the way from Europe. He remembered unloading it out of the airplane. Duke Nalon drove it at Indy and qualified second fastest, and then went on to lead most of the race. Then it burned a piston and that was that.

His speedster was in that building as well. He remembered when Frank Kurtis finished it, that it was the envy of every car enthusiast in California. He remembered taking Sally for a ride in it. She was his first passenger. He could still remember how pretty she was, the sun flashing off her hair as they rode down the coast highway, the Pacific Ocean on one side and the mountains on the other. It was one of his best days. He was determined this would be a good day too. He stubbed out his cigarette, thought about Sally and stepped off the roof.

Chapter 54

Babe was in the house in San Diego alone when the phone rang. When he answered he was surprised that it was the manager of the San Diego Cadillac dealership. He said he had just gotten a call from a friend in LA that said Tommy killed himself by jumping off a building. He promised to call back with funeral arrangements when he knew them. Babe got a beer and walked out on the front porch.

All the adults in his life were just about gone. It was only six months since Sally was killed. Life certainly wasn't fair. He never even knew his mom. Then Billy was killed, his dad never recovered from that, then Sally, now Tommy. Tommy hadn't been in his life all that much, especially these last few years, but still he knew Tommy thought about him. There were always cards at Christmas and on his birthdays, and they were always accompanied by a nice gift.

He saw Tommy at Sally's funeral. Tommy was really torn up. He sobbed through almost all of the service. Afterwards at the graveside, Tommy sought him out to tell him how sorry he was. It was difficult to listen to Tommy, his voice nearly failing him on several occasions, tears filling his eyes. Babe realized that Tommy loved Sally every bit as much as he himself had. Tommy insisted that Babe join him for dinner and spend the night. While at Tommy's house, Tommy had noticed he was driving the LaSalle coupe that had belonged to Carl.

"I didn't realize you were still driving Carl's car" Tommy said.

"Yeah, still am. I'm saving up to buy a new car. Maybe someday."

Tommy looked at him a moment then put his hand on the grille of the LaSalle. "I remember the day your dad bought this car, he was so proud of it."

"Yeah, he was."

"I've always liked it. I thought LaSalle had the best styling in the country. Harley Earle designed it; he got his start working for my dad you know. I'd like to add this car to my collection." Tommy said.

"Oh, I don't know if I could part with it." Babe replied.

"It's in perfect shape then, I'm sure it will last forever." Tommy said just the hint of a smile on his face as he eyed a scraped fender.

"No, it's not in all that great a shape, but someday I'll fix everything."

"Tell you what I'll do, Babe. You give me the coupe and I'll have my guys make it just like new again. When it's done, any time you want to you can drive it. I'll store it with my others and take good care of it. The only reason I'm interested in it is because it belonged to my best friend."

The last sentence really touched Babe. Tommy's voice cracked trying to get it out.

"I don't have enough saved up to buy something else just yet, but when I do, it's yours." Babe said.

"I'm sorry Babe, I didn't make myself clear. You give me the coupe and you can take your pick of any new Cadillac. You know that new overhead valve V-8 is really something, not to mention Harley's new styling. He was inspired by the P-38 Lightning you know. I took him for a ride in mine and scared the shit out of him." Tommy said and even chuckled. He almost seemed like the Tommy of old.

"Gee Tommy, I don't know what to say."

"Just say 'It's a deal' and don't worry about it." Tommy said, then added, "Babe, it's really what I want to do. You need a new car and I want this one to look just like it did when it was your Dad's."

"It's a deal then." Babe said.

Tommy shook his hand and said, "We'll go pick one out tomorrow morning. Now let's go inside and see if I can interest you in a drink and dinner. I haven't had anyone to talk baseball with in forever."

They went in the house and had a very pleasant evening, considering they had just buried the most significant person in both their lives. They were always able to discuss baseball at a level most people couldn't comprehend. For that night and the next day, looking back on it, Babe thought, Tommy enjoyed himself.

The next morning they rode downtown to the dealership in the back of one of Tommy's limousines. Once there, Tommy got the general manager and told him to give Babe whatever he wanted. The manager, whose name was Peters, took one look at Babe and said, "I've got just the car for you."

He and Babe walked into the back of the dealership and there it sat. It was a cream colored 1949 Cadillac convertible. It had a red leather interior and a black top. It had the polished stainless steel Cadillac sombrero hubcaps and white wall tires. Babe fell instantly in love. It was the most beautiful car he ever saw, next to the Special. Its chrome gleamed in the light from the windows.

"This one has the new 331 cubic inch overhead valve V-8 and a hydromatic transmission. It'll run a hole in the wind. Not to mention, you get in this thing and put the top down and go cruising and you'll pick up every piece of pussy in LA, guaranteed!"

It was obvious Mr. Peters knew how to sell cars. Babe already pictured himself doing just that. He drove it off the lot and all the way back to San Diego. There was no doubt the women liked it. It was everything Mr. Peters had promised.

Babe thought all this as he sat on his porch sipping his beer, looking at the Cadillac sitting in the driveway. Well, he might as well get a few things packed. He was going to be attending another funeral. He was really getting tired of that. The only people left in his life were Skeets and the Fultons and they were getting up there in years. He resolved to do his best to get by the

Fulton's while he was in LA. Maybe a visit with them would be just what the doctor ordered to cheer him up. He couldn't wait for spring training to start next month.

Babe was shocked by how many people attended Tommy's funeral. Where were all these people when Tommy was alive and needed friends? It turned into a social event with clusters of people all dressed in black chatting merrily to each other, seeing and being seen at what was really a gathering of the rich and powerful and the wannabes and hangers-on. It almost made him sick to see.

He drove from the chapel to the graveside services alone, the convertible just another Cadillac in a long stream of Cadillac's all with their headlights on making up the procession behind the hearse.

Once at the graveside, he stood on the fringe. He didn't care who he saw or who saw him. He was there strictly to pay his respects to an old family friend who had done so many things not just for the Babe, but for all of them. Already the vultures were gathering to feed on the dead man's estate. Who was going to get what seemed to be the preferred topic of conversation interspersed with snippets of 'was he pushed or did he jump' and 'wasn't it a shame he was so addicted to his pain pills and booze'. As soon as the brief sermon was over, Babe wasted no time heading back to the Cadillac.

As he walked back down the long line of cars, he idly thought about his dad's LaSalle coupe. He wondered if Tommy had lived up to the promise to make it new again. Actually, he didn't think enough time had elapsed to do it, but on the other hand, Tommy did have an army of mechanics and body men and the most complete parts inventory outside of Detroit to do it. In any event, Babe doubted he'd ever see the coupe again with Tommy gone.

Babe walked up to the Cadillac and opened the door to get in. A female voice came from behind him catching him by surprise. "Aren't you even going to say hi?" the voice asked.

Babe whipped his head around, the voice sounded familiar. He hadn't even realized anyone was near the car. He saw a woman dressed in a black suit stand from the marble bench where she had been sitting under a tree directly behind him. She wore a black hat and veil and clutched a small black purse in both hands in front of her.

Babe was confused. He didn't know what to say.

"Well?" the woman said and started to walk toward him, careful to keep her heels from sinking in the soft earth.

A smile was trying to form on Babe's face. It was obvious the woman knew him and he was a bit embarrassed and confused that he didn't recognize her. That damn veil she was wearing completely hid her face.

The woman walked up to Babe and stopped, looking up at him, then she reached up and took off the hat.

Shock and surprise registered on Babe's face almost instantly replaced by glee.

"Ellen!" he yelled and wrapping both arms around her he lifted her completely off the ground and swung her around causing one shoe to come off and she her dropped her purse and her hat flew off.

They were both laughing as he turned round and round, Ellen in his arms.

"I guess that will serve as hello," Ellen laughed.

"Where have you been? What are you doing?"

"Put me down, people are beginning to stare!" she laughed.

"Let them, I don't care, do you?"

"No, but I can't breathe either!"

"Oh, okay!" and he put her down, but kept his arms around her as if he was afraid she might disappear at any second. Then he kissed her, a chaste kiss for sure, but he just couldn't contain his joy. He never expected to see her again.

Ellen was laughing right along with Babe. Although both of them had missed the other terribly, they were still equally surprised at how happy they were to be in each other's presence.

After Babe tried to ask ten questions at once, Ellen laughingly responded with a happy look of confusion and 'where do I begin?' Babe opened the door and said, "Get in; you've got to come to lunch with me, okay?"

Ellen hesitated, "Well..." she started to say.

"Oh come on! You know you want to!"

"Okay!" Ellen said happily and got in; sliding over so Babe could get in.

As Babe started the car, a look of panic flashed across his face.

"Do you have a car here?" he blurted.

"No, I rode with Loren Brandt, an old friend from the dealership."

"Great!" The panic stricken look replaced by a big grin, then the panic returned, "Will she be looking for you?"

"Not for long I'm sure. I told her I was going to talk to another old friend."

"Wonderful! Let's go!" and he put the Cadillac in gear and pulled away from the curb.

"There she is now!" Ellen said as they passed another woman dressed in black walking down the line of parked cars. The women waved at each other. "She won't be looking for me now will she?" Ellen turned back toward Babe, a big smile on her face. "Just look at you! What a fine looking man you've become! And this car! I bet you can't beat the girls off with a stick."

Babe blushed.

"Can you?" Ellen asked, her grin growing, obviously enjoying Babe's discomfort. Babe blushed even more, his ears felt like they were on fire.

"Aw Ellen! I don't want to talk about girls; I want to talk about you!"

"And I want to talk about you, and I'll wager that talk includes girls and lots of them," she laughed.

Babe loved the sound of her laugh. He could smell her perfume, and he swore he could feel heat from her body all the way across the seat. Coupled with the sound of her voice and her laughter, his body responded which just caused him to blush more. Her presence was overpowering. She was even more beautiful than he remembered.

Babe asked for and got a recommendation on a good place to eat lunch, a place where they could have the privacy to carry on a conversation and 'catch up'.

The 'place' turned out to be an Italian restaurant that had been in business in the same location and run by the same family since the 20's. Along the back wall of the dining room were a series of booths, each with its own enclosing wall to separate it from its neighbors. The place was dark and cozy. The only light came from the windows across the room and the candle set in a wax covered Chianti bottle on the table. It was perfect in his mind. The waiter suggested a wine, which Babe readily accepted. After he poured for them and taken their order, he withdrew, leaving them alone.

"So tell me where you've been, we'd lost track of you. I didn't think I'd ever see you again." Babe said.

"I'd much rather hear about you. I haven't had any news for years," she replied.

"You know, you really look terrific, you're even more beautiful now than I remember."

Now it was Ellen's turn to blush. She even averted her eyes. His gaze was simply too intense. She wasn't used to it. It was a long time since she had been so openly admired. After she left Tommy, she shunned all advances. There were no other men in her life.

"Very well then, I'll start. The last time I saw you was right after Tommy's accident," she said.

"Oh, I remember very well!"

She turned bright red at the thought. The memory flooded back to her. She wasn't sure why she let him peek like that, but there was no denying the fact she had, or the fact she enjoyed it. She pushed that thought out of her mind, it made her too uncomfortable. She briefly wondered why. She hoped he didn't realize she knew he was spying on her and she let him.

"I stayed with Tommy for maybe six months after the accident, until he could at least get out of bed by himself. He got hooked on his pain pills and scotch. He ate the pills like candy and washed them down with the booze. Tommy had at least three doctors writing him prescriptions for those damned pills, maybe more. Needless to say, he had an unlimited supply."

"You know, I really liked Tommy before the accident. I know he didn't act like this toward everyone, but to me he was always thoughtful and kind. He seemed genuinely concerned with what I thought about a great many things. I enjoyed being around him. After the accident all that changed. The joy and happiness all left him. He would brood for days at a time and then explode over the most trivial thing. I knew it was the drugs and the booze, but he just wouldn't stop. Lord knows I tried to get him to. Finally, I decided to play my ultimate trump card; I told him it was the pills or me. He glared at me for a minute or two then reached over, opened his pill bottle, and took out a whole handful and swallowed them, looking at me the whole time. I was devastated. I felt like he had just wiped his feet on me. I turned around and walked out. I haven't seen him since, until today."

Even now, tears welled up in her eyes. Babe wasn't sure what to do. He wanted to jump over the table and take her in his arms but instead he said, "That must have been terrible."

"I didn't think I had a job anymore. I hadn't been at the dealership since the accident. I had still gotten my paycheck, but I spent all my time at the hospital or later at Tommy's house. I did what I could to help the nurses and I ran errands and that sort of thing. He was completely helpless you know? I was just trying to help, but he couldn't see that, so I left. It was all I could do. I thought my leaving might shock him enough to get himself straightened out, but it didn't. I just couldn't watch him destroy himself anymore."

They stared at each other in silence for a few minutes and then the waiter appeared with their food. The interruption changed the mood. After the food arrived, Ellen seemed to cheer up.

"So I've told you some, now it's your turn young man. What have you been doing?"

"I'm playing in the Pacific Coast League," he said.

Ellen dropped her fork and looked at him, shock and surprise on her face. "Are you really?" she asked.

"Sure am," he answered grinning from ear to ear.

"What position are you playing?" she asked, obviously impressed.

"I'm pitching. I'm in the Pirates farm system." He said.

"Babe, that's wonderful!" The look on her face made him warm all over. It was amazing, he'd never felt anything like it before. Babe filled her in on baseball and how he hoped to be called up to the major league which he called simply 'the bigs' sometime this coming season. He could tell she was genuinely surprised, but pleased and proud. That made him feel better than he'd ever felt before. As the conversation continued and the wine bottle emptied, he marveled at how much her approval meant to him.

She leaned against the back of the booth and stared intently at him, holding her wineglass in front of her with both hands. She was looking at him intently as if studying him, her eyes were deep pools of blue and she smiled.

"What?" he laughed.

"Oh, you," she said almost as if a trance had been broken.

"What do you mean, me?" he asked.

"I just meant that Sally really did a good job with you."

A puzzled look appeared to flash across his face and his smile momentarily froze. "I mean that she raised you well. Look at yourself, you're what, nineteen?"

"Twenty," he replied, "almost twenty-one." In her presence he was a little defensive about his age.

"Okay, twenty one," she said. He loved the way her eyes sparkled. "And look at how you came in here and ordered lunch complete with wine as if there was nothing to it. You're very well spoken, your manners are above reproach, I just think Sally did a great job, and I know she had to be tremendously proud of you."

"Thank you, I'm sure Sally would have been very pleased to hear you say that. I miss her terribly."

"I'm sure you do." Ellen said, the look on her face changing slightly. The wine was gone, all the dishes had been cleared away. Ellen looked around. "I think we should leave now, they may need this booth for someone else, and I need to get home."

Once they were in the car and Ellen had given him directions, he realized it was already late afternoon. They must have spent at least a couple of hours in the restaurant.

He pulled the Cadillac to the curb in front of the single story apartments. It wasn't the same place he visited when Tommy was in the hospital, he knew that for sure. He visited her old apartment looking for her a couple of years before. The new tenant, an old gray haired lady had never known Ellen.

He turned to her as he turned off the ignition. "Let me take you to dinner later," he said.

"Oh Babe, I don't know," she began.

"Look, I've enjoyed myself more today than I have since I don't know when, what do you say?"

She looked at him for what seemed an almost uncomfortable amount of time and then said, "Alright, I suppose, what can it hurt?"

She was rewarded with a huge grin as he jumped out and ran around the front of the car to open her door. He walked her to the step in front of her door, it had a brass number 7 screwed to its center.

"What time should I pick you up?" he asked.

"Where are you staying?" she asked.

A stricken look flashed across his face. "I, uh, planned to stay with the Fultons." He had totally forgotten that he was in LA.

"They're way out in Malibu aren't they?"

"Uh, yeah, they are," then his face brightened, "no problem! I'll just get a motel close by somewhere."

She looked at him a minute. "Don't be silly, you can stay here. Get your things."

"Are you sure?" he asked, afraid she might change her mind.

"You can sleep on the couch; it's one of those that makes a bed."

Babe was certain as he ran back to the car for his bag that his feet never touched the ground. Then he was standing in her living room. He remembered some of the things from before, especially the pictures.

"Make yourself at home while I change. This black suit isn't the most comfortable thing I own." Ellen said as she walked down the hall to her bedroom.

"Sounds like a good idea, I think I'll change too."

Once he heard her door close, he took off the suit and slipped into a pair of wash softened chinos and a knit polo shirt. He felt much more at ease out of the suit. He heard a rustle behind him and turned to see Ellen in a pair of slacks and a sweater.

"Feel better?" he asked.

"Yeah!"

"Me too."

"We were discussing current events, where did the Cadillac come from?"

Babe told her the story, which led to another, then another. Babe discovered that after Ellen left Tommy, she moved to this apartment. She told him she wanted a fresh start. She took a job with an interior decorator. Ellen wanted to be completely away from Tommy. She knew he could find her if he really wanted to, but since she left there had been no contact with him. That was more than five years ago.

For his part, Babe told her all about Skeets and how he was scouted and every other aspect of his life he could think about, including the fact that in the off season he still lived in the house in San Diego.

"You're still living in that big old house?" she asked, amazed.

"Yep, sure am."

"All by yourself?"

"Yeah, I'm a big boy now, or haven't you noticed?"

"I noticed," she said meeting his eyes briefly, but quickly changing the subject.

They left the apartment in the Cadillac, the top down, and drove along the beach. Babe decided he would drive until he saw a likely looking place to eat, and then stop.

As he drove, he couldn't keep his eyes off her. Several times as he stole a quick glance, she locked eyes with him. She didn't smile. He wondered if he made her angry. She seemed to simply be tolerating him; at least that's what he feared. One thing was for sure, the things that worked on the girls he normally spent time with wouldn't work on Ellen. He hoped that was good.

He found a place and parked the car. They continued to catch up over dinner. Ellen asked several questions, all of them good ones, about baseball and the Pacific League. Babe discovered that he was relaxed with her and apprehensive at the same time.

He enjoyed her company and she was even more beautiful than he remembered, if that were possible, still she seemed distant some way. He couldn't quite figure that out. Almost as if she was afraid of him.

After dinner they drove back to her apartment. They had just walked into the living room when their eyes met once more. This time she didn't break contact.

"This isn't going to work," she said simply.

"Why won't this work?" he asked, his heart doing a flip flop.

"Well, for one thing, I'm old enough to be your mother."

"No you aren't, you're eight years older than me, that would have made you a very young mother."

"You'll get tired of me and then dump me on the side of the road for some chickadee your own age." There was the barest bit of a waiver to her voice.

"You are so wrong," he said and he saw that tears were welling in her eyes. He didn't say another word, instead he pulled her to him and kissed her, softly at first, but then more hungrily and demanding. They pressed together, his need now readily apparent as she pressed herself against him. All thoughts of restraint were lost as the hunger consumed them. She had tried, but in the end she wanted him every bit as much as he wanted her.

Later as they lay in her bed temporarily sated, she turned to him again. "Babe that was a mistake, I understand it was my fault. You're not obligated to anything. Okay?"

He met her gaze but didn't say a word, simply looked into her eyes. She was beginning to wonder what he was thinking when he finally broke his silence. "Please don't ever say anything like that to me ever again. Promise me." It was a command, not a request.

She wasn't sure what to think. She searched his eyes once more.

"I've been in love with you since that day on the beach, you remember?" She nodded. She didn't trust herself to speak.

"You've felt the same way, haven't you?" he asked.

She flushed, the shame swept over her. "God forgive me," she thought "I have been in love with you for so long. That's why it was so easy to leave Tommy." She turned away from him without saying a word, unwilling to admit any more of her feelings.

Babe wouldn't be denied. He put a hand on her shoulder and turned her back to face him. He locked eyes with her; he wouldn't let her turn away. "You have, haven't you?" he asked again.

It was no use denying it any longer. She had carried it for so long keeping it hidden. How could she deny him any longer?

"Yes," was all she said.

He just looked at her for a long minute and she feared maybe he had been playing with her after all, but then his face split in a big grin. "I love you," he said for the second time.

This time she replied, "And I love you my darling."

397

The next morning Babe awoke. He was lying on his back and when his eyes opened, he blinked and then his eyes surveyed what he could see of the room without moving his body. Memories of the night flooded back. It was incredible, it had been more than that, but he couldn't think of the words. As the images flashed through his mind, a grin came to his face. He turned his head slightly to see if she was still there, he didn't want to disturb her.

Babe was almost startled to see a pair of beautiful blue eyes staring intently at him over the top of a crumpled pillow. He laughed. "What were you doing? Watching me?"

The eyes nodded. The rest of her face was still hidden behind the pillow.

"Were you afraid I'd run away?"

The eyes nodded again. This time he grabbed the pillow and yanked it away sending it flying over the edge of the bed. He was rewarded with her laughing face.

"I'm still here!" he shouted, then proved it beyond any doubt.

Later he lay there once more staring at the ceiling. This time Ellen's head was using his chest for a pillow, hers having been thrown across the room.

"I just have one question for you," he said.

"Oh, just one?" she chuckled, the fingers of her left hand tracing patterns on his chest.

"Yep, just one." She waited, but he said no more.

"Well?" she said.

"Oh!" he exclaimed as if he had been in a reverie, "you mean you'll answer the question?"

"Anything for you."

"Okay. Remember when Sally and I came to visit Tommy in the hospital?"

"Yes...."

"And remember I spent the night at your apartment?"

"Yes...."

"Did you let me peek?" he blurted out.

Her fingers kept tracing patterns on his stomach now.

"You peeked?"

"Uh, yeah, I did," he said.

"And what did you see?"

"Well, pretty much everything," he replied.

"You did?" she exclaimed in mock shock.

By this time her fingers were tracing patterns below his navel.

"Yeah," he said with some effort.

Now her fingers were tracing patterns where they could no longer be ignored.

"What do you think?" she asked with a husky chuckle.

It took all of his concentration to answer this time. "Yeah, I think you let me."

"I let you? Is that all?" she said as her fingers now clutched him.

It really was impossible for him to think at this point.

"Uh, you mean, you set that up?"

This time she didn't respond, she just pushed the sheet aside and kissed him. He groaned with delight.

"Can I have another peek?" he croaked.

She flipped over onto her back kicking the sheet off into the floor. "I thought you'd never ask," she laughed.

Chapter 55

Ellen packed her things and drove back to San Diego with him. They drove down the coast highway with the top down. It was as beautiful and held as much excitement for them as it had for Billy and Sally. Unknowingly they even stopped once at the very same place their predecessors had stopped. The beach had lost none of its allure.

There was no family to invite to the ceremony. A few minutes in front of the justice of the peace and it was done. The answer to both of their prayers had come so quickly, so easily. Rather than question their good fortune, they had simply gone with it. Every day spent together seemingly better than the day before.

After several weeks in the house, Ellen only naturally, wanted to make it her own. They were staying in Babe's old room, one of the smallest in the house. Ellen was somewhat appalled to find that Babe had done nothing to any of the other rooms. He simply closed the door on Sally's room and left it. His father's room still held many of his father's things.

"Why didn't you clean these rooms out?"

"I don't know," he said with a nervous chuckle, "laziness?"

"Well then, I'm going to start cleaning, okay?"

"Help yourself."

Ellen accompanied Babe to spring training that year. They got a cheap motel room close by. It had a kitchenette. Ellen turned out to be a surprisingly good cook. She went to every practice too. There was no doubt she was his biggest fan.

That season they took a small apartment in Sacramento. Ellen traveled to as many games as possible, missing only a handful. Babe had a great year. He was the happiest he'd ever been and he played that way. His coach told him he was almost certain to be called up to 'the bigs' the next year since he managed to add a vicious sinker to his fastball and curve.

Ellen was just beginning to show with their first child when they returned to San Diego that fall. Babe wasn't the only happy one. Life with Babe was all she thought it would be and then some.

They got the house squared away pretty well. They had moved into the master bedroom and were converting Babe's old room into a nursery. Once the nursery was finished, the only room remaining was Sally's.

Ellen knew Sally's room would be a challenge. Sally was the closest thing Babe ever had to a mother and she hadn't been gone all that long. She resolved to do as much of the work herself as she could manage, coming up with any number of chores and odd jobs for Babe to keep him occupied elsewhere.

Ellen surveyed the room. All of Sally's things were still there. There were pictures of Carl and Babe on her dresser, and of course, one of Billy. Ellen thought those pictures would work nicely in the living room. Maybe that lamp would work in there as well she thought.

Really this was her favorite room in the house. She would have insisted that she and Babe take it as their own except for two things. Their upstairs room sometimes got a better breeze on hot and sticky nights, and more importantly, Babe's old room was right next door and made an ideal nursery. Still she could see why Sally liked this room so well. She loved all the windows and Sally had certainly decorated it well, her taste in furniture was excellent. Take that huge cedar chest at the foot of the bed as an example. It was gorgeous.

Ellen walked over and felt its surface. It seemed to glow; the wood had that much character. She thought she might have Babe carry it upstairs once she got it emptied.

After finding the key in a dresser drawer, she opened the lid. Inside she found linens for the bed neatly ironed and folded and a couple of quilts in beautiful patterns. As she removed the quilts, she was surprised to find several identical cloth covered books all bound together with a pink ribbon tied in a pretty bow.

Puzzled, she took the stack and sat on the edge of the bed, the books in her lap. She untied the ribbon, set the stack beside her and opened the top book. It was filled, page after page with Sally's neat clear hand. What was this? A diary? A journal? Curiosity overwhelmed her and she began to read.

Ellen looked up as she finished reading the first book to notice the light outside was fading. She heard Babe calling her and quickly put the stack of journals back in the cedar chest.

"There you are! I've been looking all over for you. I thought you'd left me." Babe said with a chuckle as he came through the door.

"Never would I leave you, darling," she said and patted the bed beside her for him to sit.

"What have you been doing?"

"Oh, just trying to decide what to do with this room," she replied. He sat down beside her and put his arm around her. She leaned against him.

"Do you remember that first night I spent in this house?" Ellen asked.

"I sure do. It was in this room while Sally was in England. "My Dad had just passed away." Babe said, the emotion clear in his voice.

Ellen kissed him on the cheek and snuggled closer to his side. She took his free hand and held it in her lap. For several minutes, neither of them said a word, each lost in their own thoughts. Babe was thinking about his father. Ellen was thinking about what she had just read.

After a few minutes, Ellen kissed him again.

"Do you remember that first night?" she asked again.

"Of course I do Baby, how could I forget the first night I ever slept with you?"

"Do you remember your reaction when you saw me in my gown?"

401

"Oh yeah," he chuckled, "I was so embarrassed."

She turned to look him in the eye. "Do you think you could manage that again?"

Silently, he pulled his hand back from her lap pulling hers with his until it was in his own lap.

"Oh," she said, then she reached over and turned off the lamp.

Over the course of the next few weeks, whenever she could do so clandestinely, Ellen read the books. She came to think of them as Sally's journals. She didn't mention them to Babe until she had read them all.

Babe was sitting on the front porch reading the newspaper. The screen door opened and Ellen came out. She had a small stack of slim books in one arm and in the other hand a couple of long necked beers, their icy brown surface glistened in sweat. She sat down beside Babe and handed him one of the beers.

"Wow! And to what do I owe all this?"

"Take a drink," she said.

"Yes ma'am, my pleasure." Babe took a long pull from the bottle.

When he finished, she sat the journals in his lap.

"What are these?"

"I think you should read them," she replied.

"But, what are they?" he asked again.

"Just read! Start with the top one," was all she said, and then she took a drink from her bottle, got up and went back in the house.

Half an hour later, the screen opened again. It was Ellen with another pair of beers in her hand. She sat down beside Babe once more and handed him one.

"So what do you think?" she said.

"I don't know what to think. I almost feel like a peeping Tom," he replied.

"I understand. I almost didn't give them to you but I thought the good outweighed the bad. They really did love each other didn't they?" By 'they' she meant Billy and Sally.

"Yeah, they did. I'm still, I don't know, uncomfortable I guess, reading them."

She patted his leg and stood up.

"I'm going to leave you to your reading. I'll bring you another beer after a while?"

"Okay," was his only reply and Ellen went back inside.

Later that evening across the dinner table he asked, "What did you think about the journals?"

Ellen looked at him for a moment before replying then said, "I thought it was the most beautiful love story I've ever read. I feel ashamed of myself, I was always jealous of Sally and I had no reason to be. The other thing is, just like you, I felt like a peeping Tom."

"Why do you think she wrote all that stuff?"

"I think it's just what she said it was in the first book. When Billy went missing, I think she nearly lost her mind." Ellen said.

"Yeah, she must have," Babe responded.

"Eventually, she started writing to him like he was still alive and someday would return. I think recounting all that helped get her through the grief."

I can't believe she wrote every little detail, all the thoughts she had, everything. It's almost embarrassing to read."

"I know dear, but I think that's what got her through those times. It was how she dealt with her loneliness. Remember, she never wrote those journals for anyone to read, they were just for her and maybe for Billy if a miracle might happen and he came back when the war was over. She kept that hope alive, you know, I think all the way till the accident there was still a little glimmer of hope that he might be found alive, maybe behind the Iron Curtain."

They ate in silence for a few moments, each lost with their own thoughts.

"What do you think we should do with them, the journals I mean?" Babe asked.

"I've been thinking about that," she said. "I'd hate to have someone find them and read them. Someone that never even knew Sally or Billy."

"Yeah, me too. What if a kid found them?"

"What if our kid found them?" She rolled her eyes as she said it.

"A safe deposit box maybe?" he suggested.

"I thought about that too, but then I thought why? Why save them? Who would you save them for? Who would you want to read them?"

"You've had longer to think about this than I have. I haven't even finished reading them yet," he said.

"I know. Why don't you finish them and then we'll discuss it."

"No tell me what you're thinking."

She looked him in the eye like she had the first time he'd told her he loved her, like she was trying to read his mind through his eyes.

"When was the last time you talked to the Fultons?" she asked.

"What's that got to do with anything?"

She glared at him. "Okay, okay, it's been several months," he answered

"How long?"

"I don't know, before we got married I guess."

"Well, what I was thinking was that we could go visit them. Maybe they could show us the beach house where Sally and Billy spent so much time. I sensed that was the place where they were the happiest. Maybe we could go to that place on the beach and in the evening, we could build a fire, open a bottle of wine, and then," she looked deep in his eyes once more, "burn the books. Their ashes would be on the spot they cherished above all others."

He looked back, this time it was Ellen that felt him probing her mind with his eyes. She never got over the vibrant shade of blue they were. At times they were icy, but now they were almost electric in their intensity.

"Let me finish them. I'll call the Fultons, I need to talk to them anyway."

And so that is what they did. Babe and Ellen went to visit the Fultons. They were both old and feeble. Melba would die only a few months later and Ken only a week after she passed. They no longer went for their nightly walks on the beach, but they described the house which was only half a mile away.

That evening Babe and Ellen took a blanket, wine and glasses, and the journals down the beach. As they walked in the growing gloom, Babe gathered what drift wood he could find, much of it surprisingly dry.

They found the house without problem. It was dark. They walked up to it just to be sure. Somehow it made them both get goose bumps to be where much of Sally's narrative had taken place.

They walked back onto the beach and lit a fire and spread their blanket. Babe opened the wine and poured. When both their glasses were full he held his up and said, "To Billy and Sally." His eyes were full of tears.

Ellen touched her glass to his and they drank.

"May they rest together always," she said and once more they touched glasses.

Solemnly they placed each book in the now roaring fire. The night was dark and the breakers crashing on the beach and the crackling of the fire were the only sounds.

After all the wine was gone, Ellen looked at Babe. "Did you remember to bring a suit?" she asked.

"Why no, I don't think I did," he replied.

"Me either," she said as she stood and stepped out of her dress. There was nothing underneath it.

"You going to join me?" she asked, as the fire light reflected in her eyes.

"Certainly my dear." He said as he slipped out of his shorts and shirt.

They held hands as they ran laughing into the surf.

Chapter 56

"Well son, that's the story," the old man I had met as Frank, but now knew as Babe said. The sparkle that had been in his eyes and the fire that seemed to live inside him had finally ebbed away as the story came to a close. I looked at him for a moment or two.

"Tell me the rest," I said.

"I already told you all of it, don't your ears work?"

I was happy to see some of the feistiness return. "What I meant was, tell me about the rest of your life." I said.

"That ain't got nothin' to do with Billy."

"But I'm interested," I argued.

He looked at me a while, then the barest hint of a smile seemed to cross his face. "Yeah," he said, "I guess we are kind of family, ain't we?"

I nodded my assent.

"Ellen and I were together for forty wonderful years. Every single day I was with her I thanked God. She was the most wonderful wife a man could ever have. She was funny; she always took care of me. She was gorgeous and every night was an adventure. Yeah, she was really something."

His eyes got a faraway look and he didn't say anything for a while. I guess he was reliving some of their time together. Then a shadow seemed to pass over him and tears welled up in his eyes.

"She got cancer you know. Breast cancer. That was back in '88, they didn't know as much about it then as they do now. She fought it, Lord did she fight it, but it was just too much for her. Cancer is just the most despicable, evil goddamned thing. Eats people up from the inside out. Some day they'll be able to cure it, but not back then. She wasted away to nearly nothing and then she died." Tears ran down his cheeks and he looked away. He finally took a Kleenex from the end table and dried his face.

After a while, he turned back to me.

"We just had the one boy. He was 39 when she died. He's a good boy. He's never amounted to much, can't really hold a job you know, but still he's a good boy. Comes to visit me sometimes, especially when he needs something," and he laughed. "Especially when that something he needs is long, green and you can fold it to fit in your wallet."

The twinkle was back in his eyes; noticing that made me feel better somehow.

"Did you stay in San Diego the whole time?" I asked.

He nodded, "Or somewhere close for the most part," he replied. "Those early days I was still playing ball and we moved around some, you know."

"Tell me about the baseball career."

"Not that much to tell," and he laughed again. "I was pretty good you know. The year after we got married I made it to 'the bigs' for part of a season. I was a real hot shot you know." He got that far away look on his face again.

"Yeah, I went back to Dago that fall bound and determined to work on my arm till I became the second coming of Sy Young. Skeets tried to tell me, but hell he was an old man and I was a big leaguer now. I wouldn't listen" He paused.

"Shit, he was right. I should have listened to him 'cause I pitched my arm out, tore up my damned shoulder. They cut on the goddamned thing but it didn't do no damned good. I was done, my playing days were over. I came home and moped around the house for most of a year. I was a real son-of-a-bitch to be around I tell you. That is 'till Ellen had enough of me! That woman finally had enough and she landed on my chest with both feet and the fur started to fly. She told me to stop the damned pity party and get on with life. Not every jack ass that comes down the pike gets to be a big league pitcher don't you know." He looked at me and grinned.

"Besides all that, she told me there'd be no more pussy for me until I got my shit straight. Hell, I started feeling better right away. It's funny how just changing the way you look at a thing can change your whole life," he winked at me.

"I was a different guy from that minute on. I loved my wife way too much to be cut off from the 'jade gate' as the Chinese call it," and he laughed.

"She was really something, she really was," he paused. "By the next day, I had a job interview as a pitching coach. I spent the next thirty years in baseball coaching various positions, hell I was even the manager of an AAA team. Then Ellen got sick," the shadow returned.

"After she died, well I kind of went off the deep end for a while; tried to drink myself through it. Hell the boy, shit he was off on his own life so to speak, and I just sat around and felt sorry for myself and drank. There wasn't any Ellen around to kick my ass into shape that time."

"I just became a goddamned drunk, there's no other way to describe it. Then one day I woke up in the hospital. I had no idea what happened. It seems I'd gone on a real bender, several days, shit, maybe several weeks, who knows?" he said with a grin.

"It seems I was trying to drive myself from one bar to the next when I drove straight into a huge oak tree. The tree won. Totaled the damned car, a nearly new Caddy by God. Put my ass in the hospital. All it did to the tree was knock a little chunk of bark off," he laughed again.

"I guess it was a blessing in disguise, 'cause while I was in the hospital I had the stroke. If I'd been anywhere else, I'd probably have died. They were able to save me, at first I wondered why. I thought they should have just let me die."

He teared up briefly, and then started up again. "Ellen came to me in a dream I guess. She kicked my ass again good and proper. Told me I needed to be there for our boy. I needed to be there for the grandbabies. She ripped me a new one I'll tell you for sure, but it was the last thing she said to me that really got to me," he didn't say any more. I kept waiting, but he didn't do anything but look at me. Finally I asked.

"What did she say?"

He smiled, and then he said, "She told me I had to pass Billy and Sally's story on to you."

Epilogue

Babe's life became full again. He worked in the front office of various teams and also scouted for several others.

His son married and the grandbabies came. One of them a blond haired beauty with those brilliant blue eyes. Babe told me she looked so much like Sally that his heart skips a beat every time he sees her. The other granddaughter reminds him of Ellen. It's not so much the looks as the way she acts and her voice. He says that voice gets him every time.

We retrieved what was left of the Special. It was as bad as he told me. But, the story and the "family" I gained was of far more value to me than any artifact.

Once back in Texas, I began a re-creation of the long lost car. As I worked on the car, the story of its creation just wouldn't leave me alone. Those thoughts were constantly clamoring for attention in my mind. Strange things happened that I still can't explain, I can only recite them for the reader to draw his or her own conclusions.

Serendipity has intervened several times during the project. Missing parts have materialized when needed almost by magic. Case in point, I needed a grille for a 1939 LaSalle, a very rare and highly sought after part in these modern days. I decided to check EBay and found an almost pristine example with less than an hour to run on the auction. Although I bid a modest sum mine was the winning bid. I even received an email from a man in Australia who had been watching the same part. He needed the grille for a long term restoration project and somehow missed the end of the auction. He tried to buy the grille from me.

Another case in point; I received an e-mail totally out of the blue from a man named Terry Cowan. Terry was the founder and head honcho of a web based organization named Metalshapers. He heard of my project and offered his shop, all his tools, and his knowledge of metal shaping to help me start the project. I told him the only real piece I had was the grille and he said that's all we needed. That newly acquired piece became the focal point of the first weekend at Terry's.

Serendipity raised its head again as just when we needed an English wheel, one appeared. A friend of a friend worked for a company that bought an English wheel for a contract they were trying to win. They didn't get the contract, but they had the wheel. They loaned it to us indefinitely. Their wheel was used to build most of the Special.

And so the construction of the car has gone. When something was needed, it has appeared. In many ways it has been an eerie experience.

Then there was the issue of the history of the car, which really was the history of a group of people. It was the story Babe entrusted to me. I found that virtually every waking moment was consumed with thoughts of building the car or the story of how the original had come to be. Babe also left me with the obligation to retell the story. How could I do that?

The idea of a book began to form. I could write a book detailing the history of the special and the people involved! The only problem was, I'd never done anything like that before. All I had was an old man's story. Was it true? How should I proceed?

I bought a spiral bound tablet and started to write. As I got into the story, I started to research as many of the facts as possible. Old newspaper clippings, old books, magazines, the internet were all used. Many events could be verified, and many could not. I decided to write the book as a novel. I have tried to recount the story as factually as I know it, but where exact facts were not known or were 'fuzzy', I've used my best estimate of what happened, always guided by Babe's tale, of course.

During the course of writing this book and doing the research, I have learned a great deal about my uncle that I never knew. I have learned facts that were unknown to my family. The greatest mystery surrounded Billy's disappearance. The date was known, February 26, 1944. Two radio transmissions were received, one stating they were being attacked and the other shortly thereafter, a Mayday. Both of these are related in the book, but that is all we've known for over 60 years. I discovered a pair of books I never knew existed while researching that shed more light on this fatal event. Billy's aircraft was attacked by a pair of long range German fighters. These were Junkers JU-88 aircraft operating from their base in France. The attack took place about 60 miles south of the southern tip of Ireland. In the ensuing combat my uncle's aircraft and one of the German fighters were both shot down. The Liberator carried a crew of ten and the Junkers a crew of three. All were lost.

It was at this time that another eerie event occurred. In April, 2005, the same week I wrote about Billy's disappearance, a strange discovery took place in the ocean south of Ireland. A fishing trawler pulled up its nets only to find the nearly pristine landing gear of an airplane tangled inside. Upon their return to port experts examined the over nine-foot-long artifact and using serial numbers engraved on the part traced it to Billy's aircraft! When I received news of the find, I was sitting at my desk where I had just written about Billy's disappearance only a week or so before. At virtually the same time I was writing his final flight, the trawler found the huge part of his airplane! I sat at my desk and cried. I grieved for him in a way I never had before. In the course of recreating his car and writing the book about him, he became so much more a real person to me.

Now the story is written. My wife Nancy has typed the manuscript. The entire book was written in longhand. The text filled five large spiral bound notebooks. Nancy transcribed it all making real words out of my scratching and correcting spelling mistakes that border on the hilarious. She helped me edit and has

2

prodded me along many times when I needed prodding. She is without any doubt, *my Sally.*

Now I have fulfilled my obligation and passed the story along. It is my hope that this book and the Special have the same effect on you. It's not so much the car, it's the people and the hopes and dreams that built it. It's Billy and Sally, it's Carl and the Babe and all the others. You can do your part by keeping their memory alive, I hope you will.

Jim Pendleton
July 2005

jependleton.com

J. E. Pendleton is an independently published author who simply wanted to share a story. Those who write and choose to self-publish or use an indie press are responsible for marketing their work as well. The best tools for success for any author are the readers.

If you have enjoyed reading my book, I would very much appreciate you taking a few minutes to write a review and post that review on amazon.com. The opinion of readers can help prospective readers make a purchasing decision.

The author, J.E. (Jim) would enjoy hearing from you and would like to know what your interests may be. You may drop him a line at the locations listed below, or simply visit his website to stay current on future projects.

jim@jependleton.com

Twitter: @jependleton

jependleton.com

J. E. (Jim) Pendleton was born and raised in Fort Worth, Texas. He has been interested in automobiles and history for most of his life. He spent several years as an SCCA road racer and a lifetime involved with hotrods. It wasn't until after he retired from a long career in the telecommunications industry that Jim decided to pursue another of his dreams and write his first book.

His first novel, The Special, was born from his love of family, hotrods and history. These are topics that are sure to be the center of future works. He is currently working on a series of novels where a young China Marine watches regional conflict explode into what becomes World War II. Jim has long considered World War II the single most important historical event of the twentieth century. His father fought in the Pacific and his uncle, Billy Pendleton is the main character in The Special and was lost in the Battle of the Atlantic.

Made in the USA
San Bernardino, CA
25 February 2014